osig

BENT ROAD

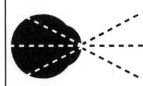This Large Print Book carries the
Seal of Approval of N.A.V.H.

BENT ROAD

LORI ROY

THORNDIKE PRESS
A part of Gale, Cengage Learning

Detroit • New York • San Francisco • New Haven, Conn • Waterville, Maine • London

GALE
CENGAGE Learning™

LIBRARY OF CONGRESS CATALOGING-IN-PUBLICATION DATA

Roy, Lori.
   Bent Road / by Lori Roy.
      p. cm. — (Thorndike Press large print reviewers' choice)
   ISBN-13: 978-1-4104-3955-0 (hardcover)
   ISBN-10: 1-4104-3955-0 (hardcover)
   1. Country life—Kansas—Fiction. 2. Farm life—Kansas—Fiction. 3. Rural
families—Fiction. 4. Girls—Crimes against—Fiction. 5. Large type books.
I. Title.
PS3618.O89265B46 2011b
813'.6—dc22   2011014374

Published in 2011 by arrangement with Dutton, a member of Penguin
Group (USA) Inc.

Printed in the United States of America
1 2 3 4 5 6 7 15 14 13 12 11

To Bill, Andrew, and Savanna

CHAPTER 1

Celia squeezes the steering wheel and squints into the darkness. Her tires bounce across the dirt road and kick up gravel that rains down like hail. Sweat gathers where the flat underbelly of her chin meets her neck. She leans forward but can't see Arthur's truck. There is a shuffling in the backseat. If they were still living in Detroit, maybe driving to St. Alban's for Sunday mass, she would check on Evie and Daniel. But not now. For three days she has driven, slept one night in a motel, all five of the family in one room, another in her own car, and now that the trip is nearly over, Arthur is gone.

"Are we there yet, Mama?" Evie says, her small voice drifting out of the backseat.

Celia presses on the brake. The car rattles beneath her hands. She tightens her grip, clenches her teeth, holds her arms firm.

"No, baby," she whispers. "Soon."

"Can you see Daddy and Elaine?" Evie says.

"Not now, honey. Try to sleep. I'll wake you kids when we get to Grandma's."

Outside Celia's window, quiet fields glow under the moonlight and roll off into the darkness. She knows to call them fields, not pastures. She knows the wheat will have been harvested by now and the fields left bare. On their last night in Detroit, Arthur had lain next to her in bed and whispered about their new life in Kansas. "Fields are best laid flat," he had said, tracing a line down Celia's neck. "Wheat will rot in a low spot, scatter if it's too high." Then he pulled the satin ribbon tied in a delicate bow at her neckline. "Pastures, those are for grazing. Most any land will do for a good pasture."

Celia shivers, not sure if it's because of the memory of his warm breath on the tip of her earlobe or the words that, like her new life, are finally seeping in. In Kansas, Arthur will be the son; she, just the wife.

As the car climbs another hill, the front tires slip and spin in the dry dirt. The back end rides low, packed full of her mother's antique linens and bone china, the things she wouldn't let Arthur strap to his truck. She blinks, tries to look beyond the yellow cone that her headlights spray across the road. She's sure she will see Arthur parked up ahead, waiting for her to catch up. The clouds shift and the night grows brighter. It's a good sign.

From the backseat, Evie fluffs her favorite pillow, the one that Celia's mother embroidered with lavender lilacs. Celia inhales her mother's perfume and blinks away the thought of her grave and Father's, both left untouched now that Celia is gone. Taking another deep breath, she lets her hands and arms relax. Her knuckles burn as she loosens her grip. She rolls her head from side to side. Driving uphill is easier.

Broken glass, sparkling green and brown shards scattered across Willingham Avenue on a Sunday morning in the spring of 1965, had been the first sign of the move to come. "This is trouble," Arthur said, dumping the glass into a trash barrel with a tip of his metal dustpan. "Just kids," Celia said. But soon after the glass, the phone calls began. Negro boys, whose words tilted a different way, calling for Elaine. They used ma'am and sir, but still Arthur said he knew a Negro's voice. A colored man had no place in the life of one of Arthur Scott's daughters. Of this, he was damned sure, and after twenty years away, those phone calls must

9

have scared Arthur more than the thought of moving back to Kansas.

Not once, in all their time together, has Arthur taken Celia back to his hometown, never even considered a visit. Here, on Bent Road, he lost his oldest sister, Eve, when he was a teenager. She died, killed in a fashion that Arthur has never been willing to share. He'll look at Evie sometimes, their youngest daughter, usually when the morning light catches her blue eyes or when her hair is freshly washed and combed, and he'll smile and say she is the spitting image of his sister. Nothing more, rarely even uses her name — Eve. But now, the closer he gets to home, the faster he drives, as if he is suddenly regretting all those years away.

Under the full moon, Daniel leans forward, hanging his arms over the front seat. Dad's truck is definitely gone. Ever since sunset, Mama has clenched the steering wheel with both hands, leaned forward with a straight back and struggled to keep Dad's taillights in sight. But the road ahead has been dark for the last several minutes.

At the top of the hill, Daniel lifts his hind end off his seat and stretches to get the best view. That could be a set of taillights disappearing over the next rise. Mama must see them, too, because she presses on the gas. Once they've crested the hill, the wind grabs the station wagon, rocking it from side to side. Daniel lays a hand on Mama's shoulder. Since he's not old enough to drive, it's the best he can do. Before they left Detroit, Dad said he hoped Kansas would make a man of Daniel since Detroit damn sure didn't. A hand on Mama's shoulder is part of being a man.

"Mama, look there," he whispers, sitting back so that he can see out the window on the other side of Evie. For a moment, he sounds like Dad, but then his voice breaks and he is a boy again.

"Is it your father?" Mama leans right and then left, straining to see what lies ahead.

"No," Daniel says. "Out in the field. Something is out there."

Mama locks her elbows. "I can't look right now. What is it?"

"I see it," Evie says. "Two of them. Three maybe. What are they?"

"There," Daniels says. "Coming toward us. They're getting closer."

Outside the passenger side window, two shadows race toward the car — round, clumsy shadows that bounce and skip over the rolling field. Behind them comes a third. The shadows grow, jumping higher as they near the road. The wind picks up the third and tosses it ahead of the second. They're several times the size of watermelons and gaining speed as they draw closer.

"What do you see, Daniel?" Mama asks.

"Don't know, Mama. I don't know."

Nearing another shallow valley, Mama eases up on the brakes.

There they are again. As the car begins another climb, the front end riding higher than the back, the shadows return, running along the side of the road, gaining on the car as the hill slows it down. The shadows skip into the moonlight and turn into round bunches of bristle, rolling, tumbling.

"Tumbleweeds," Evie shouts, rolling down her window. "They're tumbleweeds." The wind rushes into the car, drowning out the last of her voice.

"Daniel, do you see your father?" Mama tries to shout but there's not much left of her voice. It barely carries over the noise of the wind. She leans forward, like she's willing the car up the hill, willing Dad's truck to reappear. "Close that window," she says.

The rush of air slows as Evie cranks her window shut. On her small, chubby hands, tiny dimples pucker over each knuckle. Outside the car, the tumbleweeds are trailing them, gaining on them. It's almost as if they're hunting them. Up ahead, near the top of the hill, the road curves.

"Daniel, look. Can you see him?"

"No, Mama. No."

A tight swirl of dust, rising like smoke in the yellow light, marks the road ahead. Mama drives into the cloud that is probably dirt kicked up by Dad's truck. The road bends hard to the right and disappears beyond the top of the hill. Mama jams her palms against the steering wheel, leans into the door. The wind slams into the long, broad side of the station wagon.

"Hold tight," she shouts.

Daniel thinks it's another tumbleweed at first, coming at them from the other side. A large dark shadow darting across the road in front of the car. But those are arms, heavy and thick, and a rounded back. Two legs take long, clumsy steps.

"Mama," Daniel shouts. "Look out."

Mama yanks on the steering wheel, pulling it hard to the right. The car slides toward the dark ditch and stops, throwing Daniel and Evie forward. Outside the front window, the running shadow stumbles, rolls down into the ditch, disappears. The round weeds spin and bounce toward them, tumble over one another and fall into a bristly pile, snagged up by a barbed-wire fence strung between limestone posts.

Slowly unwrapping her fingers from the steering wheel, Mama shifts the car into park. Beneath them, the engine still rattles. Headlights throw cloudy light into the field. The dust settles. Mama exhales one loud breath. Leaning over Evie, Daniel presses his hands to the side window. The road drops off into a deep ditch and rises up again into the bare field that stretches out before them. At the bottom of the dark valley they have just driven out of, a pond reflects the full moon. The shadow is gone.

Evie shoves Daniel aside and takes his place at the window. "Mama, look at all the tumbleweeds," she says. "Look how many. They're all stuck together."

"Did we hit him?" Daniel says. "Did we hit that man?"

Evie looks back at him. "There's no man, silly," she says, starting to roll down her window so she can stick her head out. "Those are tumbleweeds."

"No, don't." Daniel slaps her hand away. "Didn't you see him?"

This isn't at all what Evie thought Kansas would look like. Mama said it would be flat and covered with yellow wheat. She tosses her arms over the front seat and stands on the floorboard for a better look. At the top of the hill, a fence follows the gentle curve of the road like a giant lazy tail draped across the field. The tumbleweeds, hundreds of them, thousands maybe, snagged up by the barbed wire, look like a monster's arching spine.

"It's not a man. It's a monster," she says, pointing straight ahead. "See? That's its back and tail." Maybe this is why Daddy never wanted to visit Kansas.

"Mama," Daniel says. "You saw him, too, didn't you?"

"You two sit," Mama says. She exhales, wipes a hand over her face and down the front of her dress, not even bothering with a handkerchief. Mama never did that in Detroit. She would have told Evie it was bad manners. "I didn't hit anything, Daniel. Just took the curve too fast. Everything is fine now. I'm sorry I frightened you, but you shouldn't shout out like that. Not when I'm driving."

"But I think we did hit him. The man in the road. I saw him fall."

Evie shakes her head. "No, it's tumbleweeds."

Resting on the steering wheel, Mama stares out the front window. "I'm sure it was just a deer or a coyote maybe," she says

15

and with her elbow pushes down the lock and motions with her head for Evie to do the same. She turns and smiles. "We'll ask your father. Whatever it was, it's gone now."

"Yeah, Daniel," Evie says. "There's no man. Just tumbleweeds." She throws her arms over the front seat again and rests her chin there. "Look, Mama."

Near the bottom of the hill, Daddy's truck sits where the road turns into a long drive. It is weighted down by all of their furniture, wrapped with a tarp and tied off with Daddy's sisal rope. The truck's cab lights up when the driver's side door opens. Daddy steps out, and waddling into the glow of the headlights is Grandma Reesa. Evie has never met Grandma Reesa. Neither has Daniel, because Daddy always said that come hell or high water, he'd never set foot in Kansas again. That was before the Negro boys called Elaine on the telephone.

Mama drops her head one last time and breathes in through her nose and out through her mouth. Keeping both hands on the steering wheel, she lets her head hang between her arms. She looks like she's saying a prayer.

"Guess we made it," Evie says.

This is the road, Bent Road, where Daddy grew up.

"Yes," Mama says. "Looks like we're home."

CHAPTER 2

Daniel opens his eyes and there, peeking through the bedroom door, is Mama. Smiling, she presses one finger to her lips, draws her hands together, holds them to her cheek and tilts her head as if to say, "Go back to sleep." The door closes and Mama whispers with Elaine on the other side. She is probably telling Elaine that things will be fine. Since the day Dad sat at the head of the dinner table and announced that the family was moving to Kansas, Elaine has pouted and Mama has told her things would be fine, just fine.

Waiting until Mama's voice fades down the hallway, Daniel sits up and shades his eyes with one hand. At the foot of the bed, a statue of the Virgin Mary, wearing a brown shawl over a simple blue gown, stands on a small end table. Her arms reach out, as if toward Daniel, but both hands are missing. The paint has chipped away from her wrists, uncovering the red clay she is molded from. The Virgin Mary is bleeding. On the table near her feet lie her missing hands.

"Hey," Evie says from her spot next to Daniel where she had been sleeping. "We're here, aren't we?" She first smiles at the Virgin Mary but frowns when she notices the missing hands. "This is Grandma Reesa's house."

"Guess so," Daniel says, pushing his hair from his eyes.

Evie pops to her knees and crawls to the head of the bed. "Come see," she says, leaning so the fan propped in the window doesn't hit her. "It's Kansas. All the way, as far as I can see." She starts jumping, the box springs creaking every time she lands.

"Hush already," Daniel says, not sure why he cares except that the bleeding statue makes him think Grandma Reesa likes a quiet house.

"There's cows, Danny," she says. "Four of them."

Daniel crawls across the bed until he can see out the second-story window. When he's kneeling next to Evie, who is standing, they're almost the same size. She lifts onto her tiptoes and smiles down on Daniel. He rolls his eyes at her but doesn't say anything. Evie's being small stopped seeming funny

19

when she was six. Now, at nine years old, she is lucky to be mistaken for a kindergartner. Even though Mama says Evie will grow plenty tall in her own time, Daniel knows she is hoping that people will be smaller in Kansas, that she will be the right size.

Besides seeing four cows, Daniel gets his first glimpse of Kansas in the daylight. He cocks his head, trying to decide if the buildings outside are crooked or if Grandma Reesa's house tilts. He wonders what Mama will have to say about Grandma's crooked house. Before they left Detroit, Mama smiled every time Dad mentioned Kansas, but it wasn't the smile she gave when she was really happy. When she smiled about Kansas, Mama never showed her teeth and she always nodded her head along with the smile, probably thinking the nod would do the trick if the smile didn't.

Beyond the garage and shed, brown fields outlined by barbed-wire fences stretch to the horizon. Dad says most of the old fence posts are made from hedge tree branches and a few from limestone. He says there will be plenty of fence post driving in Daniel's future, plenty for sure. That'll make a man of him. Squinting out the window, Daniel counts the posts that carry the fence up and over the curve in Bent Road where the tumbleweeds were snagged up. The man he saw last night must have run through Grandma Reesa's pasture and hopped the fence at the hill's highest point. No sign of him now. Dad said it was probably a deer, but Daniel is sure it was a man — a large man in a big hurry. Dad promised to check the ditches to make sure the man wasn't lying there dead. Daniel drops his eyes back to Grandma's driveway where the four cows raise their heads and together walk toward the fence. He hears it before he sees it, a truck driving up Grandma Reesa's gravel drive.

"Hey," Evie says, popping off the bed, her bare feet skipping across the wooden floor. "Look at this."

"Yeah, what is it?" Daniel says, still watching through the window.

A red truck pulls around the side of the house and parks in front of the sagging garage.

"They're dresses," Evie says. "Look how many."

Across the room, Evie holds a blue dress up by its hanger, rotating it so she sees both sides. The dress flutters as the fan sweeps across the room, the tips of its hem dragging on the wooden floor. Frowning, Evie pulls at the frayed ends of a piece of blue trim left unstitched at the collar.

"Stop that," Daniel says. "You're getting it dirty. Those are Grandma Reesa's."

Evie frowns at the bleeding Virgin Mary. "No they aren't. Grandma Reesa is too big for these dresses."

"Well, they belong to somebody."

"Whoever wore these was small like me," Evie says, holding up a second dress. "Not big like Grandma Reesa."

"Just put them back and close that door," Daniel says as a second truck that is towing a trailer pulls into the drive. "I think Uncle Ray and Aunt Ruth are here. We'd better get downstairs."

Letting the hug fade, Celia slowly pulls away, feeling that Ruth's slender arms might never let go. While Arthur is tall and broad enough to fill any doorway, his older sister is petite, almost breakable, and her skin is cool, as if she doesn't have the strength to warm herself on a hot August afternoon. On the other side of the car, Ruth's husband, Ray, shakes Arthur's hand. Reesa stands behind them, watching, nodding.

"Damn good to see you," Ray says, taking off his hat and slapping it against his thigh. Underneath, his dark hair is matted and sweat sparkles on his forehead. Even from several feet away, he smells of bourbon.

After shaking Arthur's hand, Ray replaces his hat and bends down to look through the truck's cab. His cloudy gray eye, the left one, which Celia only remembers when she sees him up close again, wanders off to the side while the eye that is clear and brown stares at Celia. He winks the bad eye.

"Well, if you damn sure aren't still the prettiest thing I ever seen," he says, scratching his two-day-old beard. "The good Lord's done well by you, Arthur."

Ray's good eye inches down Celia's body and settles at her waist. He had looked at her the same way on her wedding day, like her taking one man meant she would take any man.

Celia wrinkles her nose at his sour smell. "So good to see you, Ruth," she says, reaching for the pie that Ruth holds out to her.

"It's strawberry." Ruth straightens the pleats on her tan calico dress. "We had a late season this year. Thought they'd never ripen."

Celia cups the chilled pie plate. "You always did bake up the nicest desserts."

Celia says this even though her own wedding was the last and only time she saw Ruth. Almost twenty years ago. They were barely more than kids; Ruth a new bride

23

herself. The years have worn heavy on her, stooped her shoulders, yellowed her skin, and peppered her brown hair with gray, though she still wears it in the same tightly knit bun that she did all those years ago.

"Arthur said you had an accident on your way in," Ruth says, still pressing her pleats. "You and the children are all right?"

Celia rubs her neck with one hand and rolls her head from side to side. "Shook us up a little. Frightened the children, but we're fine."

Once they finally settled into bed the night before, Arthur had said they probably saw a deer. Or maybe not. Never could tell. "But that spot at the top of Bent Road is a tricky one," he had said. "Better take it slow next time." Celia had rolled over, putting her back to him, and said that perhaps next time he would be inclined to slow himself down. When she woke this morning, she had a sore neck, an ache in her lower back and made Arthur promise to check the front of her car for damage. He found nothing but still couldn't say for sure what they had seen out there.

"Good God damn," Ray shouts to the driver of a second truck towing a trailer into the drive. "I don't pay you to drive like a fool, boy."

A young man steps out of the other truck. His light brown hair hangs below his collar and covers the tips of his ears. He wears a sleeveless chambray shirt, the frayed shirt-tail left untucked. Ruth tells Celia that his name is Jonathon Howard. He's a local boy who has come to help Ray, though he's not so much a boy anymore.

"You don't pay me at all, Ray," Jonathon says. "Quit all that fuss you're making." He nods at Celia and Arthur, tugs on the raw edge of his Silver Belly hat and walks toward his trailer.

At the back porch, the screened door squeals open and slams shut. Elaine walks across the drive, blotting her cheeks with a tissue. Though she is small like Celia — narrow shoulders, a slender waist, hips that flare ever so slightly beneath her skirt — she has Arthur's brown hair and eyes.

"Elaine," Celia says. "Come say hello to Aunt Ruth."

Tucking the tissue into her apron and smoothing back her hair that hangs in dark waves down her back, Elaine steps around the truck's open door and leans inside to hug Ruth. "So nice to meet you, Aunt Ruth," she says, and standing straight, she looks down the drive toward the young man with the frayed chambray shirt. As if trying to get a better view of him, she leans away from the truck and stumbles over Celia. "Sorry," she says.

"Quite all right." Celia smiles and glances between Elaine and the young man.

"Celia," Ray shouts through the truck's open cab. Seeing Elaine, he studies her for a moment, tips his hat and stands. "Get those kids out here. Good God damn, I brought this thing for them."

"Ray brought the children a cow," Ruth says. "You go on and see it. I'll check on lunch and send the children out."

Celia steps aside to let Ruth pass. Across the drive, Reesa and Arthur follow Ray toward the trailer. Celia watches Ray, fearing that he'll take another look at Elaine, but he doesn't. As the three pass a small shed, which sets across the drive, Arthur stops and studies it, perhaps considering how to best fix the sagging roof or straighten the crooked walls. Reesa stops alongside him, stepping into his shadow. A thick patch of cordgrass grows around the small building and nearly swallows it up. The two of them stand silently for a moment, and then Reesa pats him on the back and, with both hands, gently pulls him away and they continue toward the trailer.

Celia knew there would be secrets between

Arthur and his mother, a history that they share and that Celia has had no part in. Surely, Reesa knows what kept Arthur away all these years, and as they pass by, neither of them looking at Celia, it is clear that the past is already flaring up.

When everyone is clustered around the new cow and Ray gives a loud shout of laughter, Ruth walks toward the back door. She smells them before she sees them — a patch of devil's claw growing between the garage and the back porch. The pink flowers, thriving in dry sandy soil, give off a nasty smell that is strong this year, stronger every year since Father died. He was dead and buried before Mother called to tell Arthur. "No need to trouble him so far away," she had said. "It's his own father," Ruth said. "Let him make peace with his own father."

Mother had turned away, the black cotton dress she wore to the church service only lightly creased. "A funeral is no place for making peace," she had said. "That time is dead and buried for both of them."

The flowers, whose feathery centers are sprinkled with red and purple freckles, have grown thicker this year and richer in color. The plant's broad, heart-shaped leaves give off the bitter smell and pods hang like okra from the hairy stems. Eventually, the woody husks will split open and curl like claws that will grab onto passing animals who will spread the seeds.

As a new bride, Ruth had picked the plump green pods, sliced them and sautéed them in buttery onions and garlic. They'll bring a strong woman twins, her mother's mother once said. Ruth cooked up these pods because, had Eve lived, she would have done the same. In the weeks and months following Eve's death, everything Ruth did was because Eve would have done the same. Ruth began to visit Ray every week since Eve no longer could. When his laundry piled up in the hamper, she washed it and hung it to dry on the line. She swept his floors, scrubbed his bathroom tile and left casseroles in his icebox. Because Ray was a young man who needed a wife and because it was the thing Eve would have done, Ruth married him and began to wish for a baby. But soon enough her marriage aged a few years, and Ray realized that Ruth would never be the woman he had intended to marry. She would never be Eve. So she stopped cooking the pods and never looked back when she passed a patch of devil's claw.

Inside the kitchen, Ruth puts the pie into the refrigerator and lifts the lid on the cast-iron skillet where several pieces of Mother's fried chicken sizzle and pop. A rich, salty smell fills the house. She turns down the flame, checks the timer on the sweet bread and slides a pot of chicken broth onto the stove. In the open window, the curtains hang motionless. Outside, everyone is still gathered around the cow that Ray bought cheap at the sale barn because no one wants an apple-assed cow. Patting the animal on its hind end and saying something that Ruth can't hear, Ray throws back his head and laughs. Ruth steps away from the window and turns when footsteps cross the living room and stop at the kitchen's threshold.

"Are you Aunt Ruth?"

Ruth dries her hands on a dish towel. "I am," she says. "And you are Eve?"

"Evie."

Evie has long, fuzzy braids and a heavy fringe of white bangs that fall across her forehead and catch in her eyelashes. Her skin is like pink satin.

"Evie," Ruth says, trying out the name. "And you're Daniel?"

Daniel is only a few months shy of Arthur's height, and eventually, after some good Kansas cooking, he'll be as broad, too. However, unlike his father, Daniel is blond with pale blue eyes that shine against his tanned skin.

"I'm so glad you've moved to Kansas." Ruth pats her face with the dish towel that smells of soap and bleach.

"We're happy to be here, ma'am," Daniel says, staring at his feet.

"Please, call me Aunt Ruth."

"Whose room is that upstairs?" Evie asks, tapping the floor with the toe of one black shoe. "The one we slept in?"

Ruth swallows before she can answer. "I'm not sure which room you were in, sweet pea." She slips, forgets that Evie is not her sister, calls her sweet pea. A sugary, delicate bloom like Eve.

Evie looks at her brother and then at the ground. "The one with the statue and the dresses."

"That's Eve's room," Ruth says. Her chin quivers. She clears her throat. "My sister, Eve."

"Eve," Evie says. "Like me."

Ruth smiles. "Yes, very much like you."

"She's small, too, isn't she? I can tell from the dresses. Small like me, and you, too. Not like Grandma Reesa."

Ruth laughs aloud. The first in so long. "She was perfect like you. The exact right size."

"I like her dresses," Evie says, standing

where the living room meets the kitchen. "Will she come for dinner, too?"

"No, I'm afraid not."

The chicken broth has grown from a slow simmer to a rolling boil. From outside, Ray gives off another burst of laughter. Ruth steps aside and waves Evie and Daniel toward the kitchen window.

"Come," she says. "See what Uncle Ray has brought for you."

While Daniel hangs back, not seeming to care about the shouts and laughter coming from outside, Evie joins Ruth at the window and hoists herself up onto the counter for a better view.

"A cow," she says, her pink cheeks plumping up with a smile. "Uncle Ray has brought us a cow. And he's a cowboy, Dan." She slides off the counter and turns toward her brother. "He's wearing a hat and boots, too. He's a real cowboy."

Ruth brushes aside the fringe of bangs that fall across Evie's brow. "You two should go on out and get a closer look."

"Yes, ma'am," Daniel says, taking Evie's hand.

Evie stops before disappearing into the back hallway. "I'm glad we're here, Aunt Ruth," she says. "I'm going to like Kansas very much."

31

"And we're happy to have you."

The hinges on the back door whine as they open and close. Pressing the dish towel to her face, Ruth returns to the kitchen window and breathes in the lemon-scented soap until she knows she won't cry. She is a child again, nine years old, seeing her own sister, Eve. She was the oldest, perfect in almost every way. Evie is so like her, has her light blue eyes and shimmering blond hair. They could be twins, Eve and Evie, separated by many years but twins just the same.

Outside the kitchen window, Evie skips across the drive, kicking up small clouds of dust. Nearing the cow, she slows and walks to Ray's side. She raises one hand to her forehead, shielding her eyes from the sun, and looks up at him. Ray steps back and lifts the brim of his hat as if taking a closer look. All these years, Arthur has lived with this painful reminder. Now Ruth and Ray will do the same.

CHAPTER 3

Evie sits next to Daddy in the cab of his truck, her stomach stuffed full from her first Kansas meal. Daniel slouches in the seat next to her, a dish of Grandma's leftover fried chicken resting on his knees. After everyone finished eating lunch, Grandma asked them to take the food to the Buchers because Mrs. Bucher just had a new baby. Uncle Ray said the Buchers are one lucky family because their baby was born a blue baby and nearly died. Evie asked Daddy what a blue baby was, and he said the Bucher baby was pink as any other.

Cradling a loaf of sweet bread, Evie leans against Daddy so he'll shield her from the hot dry wind blowing through the truck. "Tell me about Aunt Eve," she says.

Keeping one hand on the steering wheel, Daddy wipes the other over his eyes and down his face. "She always wore her hair in braids when she was a girl. Same as you."

Daddy looks down at Evie. "Looked a good damn bit like you."

Over lunch, Grandma Reesa said that in her house Evie is to be called Eve. Mama frowned and asked Daddy what he thought about that. Instead of giving Mama an answer, Daddy patted his stomach and said Grandma's fried chicken was the best in the Midwest. Mama frowned about that, too. But Evie won't mind being called Eve. It makes her believe that in Kansas she'll grow like a weed and one day soon, she'll be big enough to wear Aunt Eve's dresses.

Evie giggles to hear Daddy curse. "She doesn't live here anymore?"

Daddy shakes his head, stops and shakes it again. His white teeth shine against his dark skin. "No, Evie, not anymore."

Driving through the dust kicked up by Jonathon's truck, they near the tumbleweed-lined fence. Jonathon is towing their cow to the new house. Mama had thought Elaine should get to name the cow because she is the oldest, but Uncle Ray said he figured it was a job for the youngest in the family, so Evie picked Mama's middle name — Olivia. This made Uncle Ray smile. He tugged on one of Evie's braids and then winked his milky eye at Mama, patted the new cow on the rump and said that Olivia was a damn fine name. Mama frowned about that, too, but it was too late because Olivia was already Olivia.

Daddy slows at the top of the hill and the truck drifts toward the side of the road until it feels that the wheels might slip off into the ditch. Evie looks for the monster they saw the night before. Daniel leans forward, too, but he's probably looking for the man he thinks Mama hit. In the daylight, Evie doesn't see a monster, only a fence that Daddy says will cave in if someone doesn't pull off those weeds soon. She doesn't see a strange man, either. Once over the highest point, a truck driving the other direction appears. The other truck swerves toward the tumbleweed fence, slows and stops. Daddy stops, too.

A dark hand hangs out of the driver's side window of the other truck. "Damn good to see you, Arthur." A man wearing a round straw hat leans out his open window.

"Afternoon, Orville." Daddy nods and lifts one finger. "Good to be back."

The man glances in his rearview mirror. "Been a long damn time."

Daddy nods. "These here are two of my kids," he says, tipping his head in Evie and Daniel's direction.

Evie leans forward and waves at the man.

Daniel lifts a hand.

"Pleasure," the man says. Mama would have said he had a strong nose. Thick creases fan out from the corners of his eyes and his skin is as dark as any Negro except he isn't a Negro.

Daddy and the man talk for a few minutes about the long drive from Detroit, the price of wheat and when the next good rain will fall. Then with another tip of his round straw hat, the man says, "Glad you remembered this stretch of road. Can be a good bit tricky. You all take care." And slapping the side of his truck, the man pulls away.

As Daddy eases onto road, Evie looks back toward the tumbleweed monster. In the other truck, a young girl stares out the rear window, one hand and her nose pressed to the glass. She must have been scrunched down in the seat because Evie didn't see her before. She is about Evie's age and has long blond hair that hangs over her shoulders. The girl lifts her hand from the glass and waves. Evie waves back and watches until the truck disappears down Bent Road, and the girl is gone.

Daniel climbs out of the truck, glances at the Buchers' house and then at the group of boys near the barn — the Bucher brothers — and wishes he had a hat to pull on like Dad's. So far, not one person in Kansas has blond hair except Evie and Mama.

"Go on over and say hello," Dad says, taking the dish of chicken from Daniel. "You've been so worried about friends. Well, there's a whole mess of them."

Tugging at the tan pants Mama made him wear because he was meeting new people, Daniel walks toward five boys who are huddled together, digging a hole in the ground with their bare hands. The youngest is probably seven; the oldest, fifteen or sixteen. All are barefooted and dirty up to their ankles. One boy close to Daniel's age sits off by himself, leaning against the barn.

"Hey," the tallest brother says. "You one of the Scotts?"

Daniel nods. "Yeah. Daniel."

The boys drift together and stand with their arms crossed over their chests. They all have straight dark hair that hangs over their ears and wear jeans cut off at the knee instead of tan pants with a crease ironed into each leg.

"Moving into the old Murray place?" one of them says.

A smaller boy steps forward, tossing back his head to get the hair out of his eyes. "Yeah, it's the Murray place," he says before

Daniel can answer. "Saw them hauling off Mrs. Murray's stuff."

"She died in that house, you know," another of the younger boys says. With his elbow, he nudges the brother next to him. "About six years ago. They found her dead, slumped over the radiator. Cooked up real good."

The oldest-looking boy shoves his brother. "Shut up. She was just old."

Daniel jams his hands in his pockets and steps into the shade so his hair won't sparkle. Behind him, the boy leaning against the barn pulls the fuzzy seeds off a giant foxtail, holds them between two fingers and blows them away.

"Sure she was old, but that ain't what killed her," the same younger boy says. "It was one of them crazy guys from Clark City. You know about Clark City, right?"

"Never heard of it," Daniel says as he digs a hole in the ground with the toe of his left shoe, wearing off the shine Mama made him buff on before they left the house.

"That's where they lock up crazy folks," the tallest boy says. He leans against a tree and gestures with his head off to the left. "It's a town about twenty miles southwest of here. Happens a few times a year. One of them gets out and heads this way. Should probably lock up your house. But mostly they're just looking for food. Mostly."

Behind Daniel, the screened door opens and slams shut with a bang. Evie steps onto the porch.

"One just escaped," one of the smaller boys says, nudging the same brother again. "Seen it in yesterday's paper. Say his name is Jack Mayer. Has a taste for boys. Don't know the difference between his wife and kid's hind end."

The tallest brother kicks a cloud of dust at the smaller boy. "No paper said nothing about hind ends."

"No," the boy says. "But it did say Jack Mayer couldn't be found because his skin is black as night. Said he's as good as invisible when the sun sets."

Walking up behind Daniel and standing next to him, Evie flips her braids over her shoulders, crosses her arms and stares up at the new boys. Back near the barn, the boy sitting by himself uses both hands to push off the ground and walks toward them.

"Anyone see that fellow around here?" Daniel asks. "Any of you see him?"

"Got one," shouts a different boy as he walks out of a shed a few yards beyond the barn. This one, who is five, maybe six years old, has a kitten cupped in his hands. He walks over to the hole that the boys were digging when Daniel first walked up.

"You got to watch this," one of the brothers says, ignoring Daniel's question.

The boy who was sitting near the barn has almost reached them. Up close, his head seems too large for his body, as if his neck can't quite hold it up, and both legs bow to the right. He has the same dark hair but his is cut high off his forehead.

"Come on," the crippled boy says. "These guys are stupid."

The youngest boy is still fussing with the hole and the kitten, patting down the dirt like he is planting a tomato. An older brother walks toward the hole with a weed whip.

Following the boy across the drive, Daniel tucks Evie under one arm and presses her face into his side, holding tight so she can't squirm away. The boy walks with an awkward rhythm — step, step, pause, step, step, pause — as if he has to think about each set of steps before he takes them. Reaching Dad's truck, the crippled boy throws open the passenger side door and Daniel shoves Evie inside.

Up on the porch, Dad walks out of the house, followed by a large man who must be Mr. Bucher, although he seems too big to have a son as small and broken as this boy. The two men shake hands and Dad walks down the steps, his hat tucked under his arm.

"Thanks," Daniel says to the boy and climbs in after Evie. "See you around?"

The boy nods and limps toward the house. "Lock your windows," he says. "Doors, too. Just in case."

From over near the barn, someone calls out, "Fore."

Ray must feel it, too, Ruth thinks as they pull away from Arthur's new house. Jonathon has taken Mother home and Arthur and his family are settled in their new house. They have full stomachs, freshly made beds, and fans are perched in every bedroom window. She worried that when Arthur came home, he would look at her like all of the others in town. She worried that he, like everyone else, had always wondered if Ruth married the man who killed her own sister. Ruth swallows, blinks away the feeling that she's betraying Eve, thinking ill of the dead. But Arthur didn't look at her like the rest of them. He looked at her like they were young again, before anything bad happened. Before Eve died. He looked at her like he still loved her.

Rolling down her window, Ruth inhales the smell of cut feed and freshly plowed sod. Nearing the top of the hill that separates her and Ray's house from Arthur's new home, the landscape even seems prettier. The gently rolling hills, the dark fields, the brome-lined ditches. Ray must see it, too. He seemed happier today. He stopped with one glass of whiskey at Mother's. His eyes never drooped. His speech never slurred. At Arthur's new house, just half a mile from Ruth and Ray's home, Ray had worked hard, unpacking and piecing together the bed frames, hauling boxes in from the truck, unwrapping dishes and silverware. And as they began the short ride home, he drove with his hat pushed high on his head and one arm draped around Ruth's shoulders. He had seemed content with Ruth, as happy as he had been in their earliest days together. Never as happy as he had been with Eve. But almost happy.

Once they are over the top of the hill, Ruth sees their house down below. As new and different as the landscape looks and the air smells, their house is the same. By the time they reach the bottom of the hill, the happiness is gone. It's a subtle change, like a shifting shadow. Arthur is home again and he still loves Ruth, but no one else is coming with him. He is a reminder of happier times but also of all that has been lost. And Evie, too. Ruth had wondered if Ray would notice the resemblance. When Evie first walked out of Mother's house, skipping across the gravel drive, cheeks flushed with heat, braids swinging behind, bangs brushing her forehead, Ray had blinked and cleared his throat into a closed fist as he looked down on her. Then the memory was gone, or Ruth thought it was. Now, as she and Ray sit in front of their house, the truck idling beneath them, she realizes they have not come home to the same place they have lived for twenty years. They have come home to a worse place, a lonelier place, and Ruth is more afraid of Ray than ever.

CHAPTER 4

Walking down St. Anthony's stone steps for the first time, Celia pins her pillbox hat to her head with one white-gloved hand. In Detroit, all of the ladies wore gloves to church. Here, the women have bare hands and dirty nails. Midway down the stairs that widen as they near street level, Celia stops, the other parishioners filtering around her, and plucks a few cockleburs from the hem of her blue cotton skirt. She frowns at the brown oval smudges that stain each fingertip of her white Sunday gloves. Perhaps the reason none of the women wear them. Having lost Arthur in the crowd that filed out of the church following the end of service, she lets the flow of the other churchgoers lead her. All around, people talk in whispers even though church is over.

"Didn't you hear?" one woman asks another.

"Such terrible news," says a third. "Simply

terrible."

Tugging off her stained gloves one finger at a time, Celia scans the crowd until she finds Ruth standing near the bottom of the stairs where everyone seems to be gathering. Her perfectly formed oval face wrapped in a blue and yellow print scarf is tilted up, smiling.

While fending off houseflies with her church bulletin, Celia had spent her first Kansas sermon looking from one hometown parishioner to the next, noticing, as they shifted about on the pews and swatted at flies, that they all had the same overgrown ears and fleshy noses. There were a few, probably in-laws like herself, and the priest, Father Flannery, who hadn't inherited the trait. And as she studied them, she felt them studying her. Her navy blue skirt was too proper with its sharp pleats and tailored waistband. The other women wore skirts that ballooned over their large hips. They wore floral scarves, not gossamer trimmed hats. Theirs were white cotton blouses, wrinkled and nearly gray. Hers was a silk print, hand washed and dried flat on a towel. By the end of the service, Celia even looked at Arthur, crossing and uncrossing her legs so she could turn unnoticed to study the size and shape of his ears and nose, but he looked like an outsider, and Ruth, too, with her delicate brow and graceful neck. Reesa, however, could have birthed the entire congregation.

"Good morning," Ruth says, clasping her hands together and stepping back when Celia reaches the bottom stair. Her eyelashes cast a feathery shadow on her cheeks and the silver and gray in her hair shimmers in the sunlight. "Lovely service."

"Yes," Celia says. "A little warm though," and she shields her eyes. No sign of Arthur, though she does spot Reesa standing with the three women who were whispering about the terrible news. She is shaking her head as the women talk. Feeling that she has spent the better part of her short time in Kansas swatting bugs, swallowing dust and searching for Arthur, Celia drops her hand and stops looking.

Ruth smiles with closed lips. "There he is," she says, pointing up at Arthur, who is standing at the top of the stairs among a group of men wearing short-sleeve dress shirts and thick black belts.

Celia nods and gives a small wave when Arthur motions in her direction as if to point out his wife to his old friends. Elaine stands nearby at Jonathon's side, both of them talking with the other young men who must, like Jonathon, work in the oil fields. Weeks of moaning and complaining and already Elaine is at home. Ray, who is also standing with Jonathon, seems to return Celia's wave, which was meant for Elaine, but because of the way his left eye drifts off to the side, she's not quite sure where he's looking. She frowns anyway and after the group of men, all of whom have large ears and noses, turns away, she asks, "Is this where everyone meets?"

"Yes," Ruth says. "The sheriff will talk from up there." She motions toward the church's double doors at the top of the stone staircase. "Except if it's wintertime. Then we all gather in the church basement."

"Does he come every Sunday?"

"No. Only when he has business, news to tell."

Celia pulls the gold pins from her pillbox hat, drops them into her change pouch and tucks the hat under one arm. "News of what?"

Ruth lowers her head and glances over her shoulder in a way that Celia has come to recognize as common.

"A girl," she says. "A local girl's gone missing."

Behind them, a car pulls up to the curb and parks. The congregation quiets as a

47

small, narrow-shouldered man steps out of a black and white police car. He wears a dark blue uniform and a beige tie that has pulled loose at the knot and hangs crooked around his open collar. Passing them by, he tips his hat, seemingly at Ruth, and shakes a few hands as he makes his way to the top of the stairs, where he waits silently, hands on hips. The churchgoers gathering on the sidewalk push Celia and Ruth to the back.

"Some of you folks will already be knowing this," the sheriff says, clearing his throat into a closed fist. The six-pointed silver star pinned to his shirt sparkles in the sunlight. "But I'll tell you all now. Little Julianne Robison has turned up missing." He pauses again. "Her folks called us in last evening. Now, chances are the child has just wandered off. Lost her way in the fields or maybe down by the river. Out playing is all she was doing."

Shielding her eyes with one hand and holding her hair with the other, Celia steps away from the crowd so she can see Daniel and Evie. They both stand where last she saw them — in the steeple's shadow this side of the whitewashed fence that wraps around the church's small cemetery. Evie is bent down near the fence, picking the downy-like seeds from a dandelion. Daniel, standing with both hands shoved in his front pockets, watches the sheriff.

"I'll need for any of you kids to talk with me if you've seen our Julianne of late," the sheriff says. "Some of us men have already been out looking but I'd like the rest of you gentlemen to join us in a search. We'll start our looking in town and work our way out. Orville and Mary say the girl's prone to going off alone. A hungry stomach'll probably bring her home, but the more of you can help, the quicker we'll all get home to Sunday supper."

Taking a step backward because the shade from the steeple keeps falling away from him, Daniel sees the crippled boy leaning on the bumper of a truck parked across the street, rubbing his thighs with the palm of each hand. Waiting until the boy glances his way, Daniel gives a wave. The boy waves back, pushes himself off the bumper and walks across the street. Step, step, pause. Step, step, pause, until he reaches the tip of the shade where Daniel stands.

"Hey," the boy says, crossing his arms and leaning against the white wooden fence that separates them from the cemetery.

"Hey."

"Name's Ian."

"I'm Daniel. This is Evie."

Evie blows a tuft of dandelion feathers at Ian.

"What do you think?" Ian asks, nodding at the sheriff still standing near the church doors.

"Didn't know her."

"She's younger." He dips his head toward Evie. "More about her age."

"Sounds like she'll be home by dinner," Daniel says, watching all the Bucher brothers meet up at the truck Ian had been leaning against. Like the red ants in Mama's kitchen, they keep coming, one after another.

"Like hell," Ian says, shuffling closer. "I know what happened. I know exactly what happened." He pauses and looks around like he's afraid someone might hear. "After Jack Mayer escaped from Clark City, he snatched her right up. That's what happened."

Daniel crosses his arms over his chest. "Think I might have seen that Jack Mayer," he says. "The night we got here. Pretty sure I saw him."

"At your place?" Ian says, shifting his weight from his short leg to his long one. "You catch him stealing food?"

Daniel shakes his head. "Back that way. On the drive in. Saw him running across the road. Car might have hit him. Can't be sure. He must have been black as midnight because I could barely see him. Just like you said."

"It was a tumbleweed," Evie says, peeling apart a dandelion stem and draping the thin pieces across her bare knee.

Daniel nudges her with his foot. "Wasn't a tumbleweed."

"Over on Bent Road?" Ian asks. "Where the road takes a hard turn? That where you saw him?"

Daniel nods.

"Could have happened. That's the only spot that still has water this time of year. Everything else has dried up. That's where a fellow'd have to head." Ian looks up at Daniel and smiles. "Yeah, could have happened just that way."

"Sure, I guess."

All night, Daniel had lain awake, imagining the whites of Jack Mayer's eyes shining outside his bedroom window, which he had locked and checked twice. Probably chains hung from both wrists and he did all his traveling at night because his coal-black skin hid him in the darkness. Jack Mayer is a big man, that's for sure. Even in the dark, at the top of Bent Road, Daniel could judge the man's size. Hearing a rattle inside Ian's chest, Daniel takes a step backward.

"Yep, snatched her up," Ian says. "Probably right out of her own front yard. 'Course, that means you didn't hit him with your car. Would have been dead if you did. Couldn't swipe Julianne Robison if he was dead."

Evie brushes the rounded, fuzzy tip of another dandelion against her cheek and looks up at Ian, her pinched eyebrows making a crease above her nose.

"Maybe," Daniel says, glancing down at Evie. "Or maybe she just wandered off."

"Nobody wanders off for a whole night." Ian gives a wave to the group of brothers across the street. "Hey," he says. "I got to go. We're going searching for her. Me and my brothers. Be out all day." He takes a few steps, his left foot swinging out because it's too long. Then he stops and looks back at Daniel. "You know," he says, "your house is the first place those crazies come across when they escape. After the old Brewster place, that is. Just be sure you make a lot of noise when you get home. Bang around for a while. It'll scare them off if they're inside."

"Sure thing," Daniel says, crossing his arms over his chest and thinking he'll let Dad go inside first. "We'll do."

■ ■ ■ ■

After the sheriff finishes his announcement, the crowd breaks up and Celia drifts back toward Ruth, all the while keeping Evie and Daniel in sight. From the top of the church steps, the sheriff points and gestures to the group of men who have gathered with him, his black pistol slapping against his thigh. Every so often, he pats the gun and scans the crowd as if one of these fine Christians is hiding Julianne Robison in an attic or under a porch. After all of the men have gone their separate ways, apparently following the direction of the sheriff, Arthur walks down the stairs toward Celia. With arms crossed and feet spread wide, the sheriff watches Arthur take the stairs two at a time and hand Celia his car keys and tie. The sheriff is listening and nodding to the men standing around him but he is watching Arthur.

"Why don't you and the kids go on home?" Arthur says. "I'll be along later. And take Ruth. No sense Mother driving her."

When Arthur leans in to kiss Celia's cheek, she grabs his upper arm and draws him to her. "Arthur, I don't like this," she says, still watching the sheriff. "I'd rather have you home." She glances at Evie and Daniel and whispers, "This will scare the children."

"Nothing to worry about," Arthur says, laying one hand over Celia's. "We'll have her home in no time." He kisses Celia's cheek, peels open her fingers and gives her a wave as he walks away.

Still standing at the top of the stairs, the sheriff watches Arthur until he climbs into Jonathon's truck. This seems to put him at ease because he lets both arms drop and walks toward his patrol car. As he passes by, he tips his hat in Celia's direction. She exhales, only then realizing that she had been holding her breath.

"Guess it's just us," she says and waves at Daniel and Evie, motioning for them to come along.

"Poor Mary must be sick with worry," Ruth says.

"How did you know?" Celia glances at Ruth across the top of the car. She pauses while the children run toward them. Daniel outpaces Evie, who struggles to keep up in black leather shoes that are too big and slip off her heels with every stride. A few car lengths ahead, where he stands at his truck waiting to follow the sheriff and the other men, Ray watches Evie, too. He removes his hat, wipes his forehead with a kerchief and when Evie finally reaches the car, her face red and her upper lip damp with perspiration, he slips into his truck. Once Daniel and Evie have crawled into the backseat, and while Elaine is too far away to hear, Celia says, "You already knew about the little girl, didn't you?"

Ruth makes a small motion as if she is going to look over her shoulder but stops herself. "A person hears things."

"Do you think it was that man everyone is on the lookout for?" Celia asks. "The one Daniel thinks we saw the other night?"

Ruth shakes her head. "Those fellows from Clark City are harmless. Never caused any trouble before."

At the end of the block, where the street changes from concrete to dirt, Ray's truck kicks up dust and then disappears. Celia opens her door and Elaine slips into the backseat alongside Evie and Daniel.

"They share a pew with us," Ruth says once both women are inside the car. She unrolls her window after Celia starts the engine. "Orville and Mary Robison sit on the other end of our pew. Them with only one child. Me and Ray without any. We fit fine."

Heading south out of town, Celia holds

the steering wheel with two hands, her shoulders and forearms still sore from driving so much a few days earlier. "Do you know them well?" she says.

"As well as anyone, I suppose. And no better than most. We were friends, closer friends, when we were young. A long time ago."

"We saw that girl, Mama," Evie says, leaning forward and draping her arms over the front seat. "We saw her on the way to Ian's house." She turns toward Daniel. "In the truck. You remember?"

Daniel shrugs.

"Is that right, Daniel?" Celia asks, keeping her eyes on the road. "Did you see her?"

"Don't know. I wasn't looking."

"I saw her. I know I did," Evie says. "Will I go missing, too?"

"No, Evie," Celia says, not turning around because she's afraid of losing her grip on the steering wheel. "Julianne will be home by dinner. The sheriff said so. No one is going missing. No one."

Ruth smiles at Celia's children sitting shoulder to shoulder across the backseat and rests her smile the longest on Evie so she'll believe what her mama told her — that bad things don't happen to nice girls.

Except Ruth knows that's not true. Sheriff Bigler must know it, too. He was full of hope up on those steps, shielding his eyes and looking at the Robisons' house three doors down from the church as if Julianne might walk right up the sidewalk at any moment. But early this morning when he knocked on Ruth's back door, he wasn't so hopeful. Standing on her porch, his hat in hand, he must have known that if a hungry stomach was all it took to bring Julianne Robison home, she would have already eaten Mary Robison's Saturday night roast and potatoes and been tucked in good and tight. Instead, at 7:00 on Sunday morning when the sheriff came knocking, Julianne Robison had been missing for well over twelve hours and a hungry stomach hadn't done a thing to help her.

"It's Floyd," he had said when Ruth pulled open the curtain on the back door. "Floyd Bigler. Sorry for the early hour."

Ruth tugged at her terrycloth belt and smoothed back her hair. "Ray's sleeping," she said, steaming the windowpane as she talked through the glass. Dark clouds in the east dampened the rising sun so Ruth flipped on the porch light. Floyd stepped back, the glare making him squint and bow his head.

"Yes, ma'am, I know it's early. A quick word is all. Just a few questions."

Over the backdrop of a percolating coffeepot, with Floyd sitting at her kitchen table, Ruth learned that Julianne Robison hadn't come home to supper the day before. Mary Robison had walked the neighborhood searching for her, calling out the way mothers do when the kids wander too far. She was mad as a grizzly when she first called Floyd, but after he drove the town for two hours and darkness settled in, she wasn't so mad. Just plain scared. A group of fellows from town were already looking for her, had been all night, and Floyd had been to see most folks living in the outlying areas, asking them to search their barns, abandoned wells, cellars, any place a young girl might get herself stuck. He'd been checking in with all the folks. Good old-fashioned questions. Maybe someone had seen the girl out walking one of the back roads or catching a ride. Ruth told him that she and Ray had spent Saturday helping her brother and his family settle in. Arthur was gone a good many years but he's back now. Thank goodness. They all met at Mother's, ate a heavy lunch and unloaded the truck at the new house. Ruth baked a strawberry pie — not so nice with brown sugar on top — and they unpacked boxes until late afternoon. Didn't see a thing out of the ordinary. Not a thing.

"I'm real sorry to hear this," Ruth said, hoping that Floyd would forget about his cup of coffee. "Real sorry indeed."

When Floyd took another sip, Ruth pressed both hands into the pockets of her robe. In her right one were the two stones she had pulled from Ray's pants pocket that morning. Both stones were smooth and together fit in the palm of her hand. Waiting for what Floyd would say next, Ruth rolled the stones between her fingers and rubbed her thumb over their smooth edges. Outside, the breeze that kicked up with the early-morning clouds had died out and the air was still. Maybe it wouldn't rain after all.

"I'll keep a good eye out. Any more questions? Is that all?"

"I suspect it is. For now, I'd say yes. Please ask Ray to have a look around the place. You, too, if you have a mind to."

Watching behind Floyd, waiting for the bedroom door to open, Ruth wiped her top lip with a dish towel. She has known Julianne Robison since she was a bundle wrapped in a pink fleece blanket. "There's still time for you," Mary had said as she handed Julianne to Ruth on the first Sunday the Robisons brought their new baby to

59

church. Mary Robison was Ruth's age, even a few years older, and Orville Robison was a good bit older than Ray. Still, the Robisons had been blessed with a little girl. Now, the sweet baby that had smelled of talc and vanilla was gone.

"Will you come again?" Ruth said. "Ask any more questions?"

Floyd twisted his lips up the same way he did when they were kids figuring multiplication facts in Mrs. Franklin's class. "Might be more. Can't tell. I'll come along if there are."

Ruth leaned against the kitchen counter, shifting a little to the right so she could see the knob on the bedroom door. "I'm real sorry," she said. "Mary must be beside herself from worry. You tell her I'll bring her a casserole. A real nice one."

Taking his hat from the table and tucking it under his arm, Floyd stood and pushed in his chair. "Sorry to bother you so early, Ruth. I'll see myself out."

Ruth tightened her robe. "No bother."

"One more quick question." Floyd slapped his beige hat against his left thigh a few times. "You say you were busy at your brother's all afternoon."

Ruth nodded, swallowed and continued to watch the bedroom door.

"And you folks came home around five o'clock?"

Again, Ruth nodded.

"Didn't stay for supper?"

"Arthur's family had such a long day and Mother made a late lunch. Didn't bother with eating again. Left them alone to a quiet evening."

"So, you and Ray were home here all night?"

Behind Floyd, the bedroom door opened.

Floyd turned. "Morning, Ray," he said. "Hope I didn't wake you."

Ray ran one hand through his dark hair, pushing it off his face. "First thing home, ate some of Ruth's meat loaf," he said. Both eyes, even the gray overcast one, settled directly on Floyd. "Leftover pie for dessert."

"She does make a fine pie," Floyd said and at the same time studied Ruth as if waiting for her to confirm Ray's story.

Ruth cleared her throat and nodded again. "Pie wasn't so nice. Strawberries were tart."

Lowering her eyes to avoid Floyd's stare, Ruth tried to remember the last time she had seen little Julianne. Church, probably. Most likely, last Sunday. Julianne, with silky blond hair that hung to her waist, always wore a pink dress to services. She'd wear it until she outgrew it or until the weather

61

turned too cold.

"Guess you heard, then," Floyd said because it seemed that Ray had listened to their conversation. "You know the girl? Know what she looks like?"

"Sure do," Ray said, nodding once.

"Good enough." Floyd pulled on his hat. "If you don't mind, give things a good going over. I suspect someone'll show up with her at church this morning. Probably found her out wandering, gave her a bed to sleep in and a warm breakfast. But in case that doesn't happen, Father's going to cut the service short and I'll be gathering up some more fellows. Continue the search. Suppose you can give a hand if it comes to that?"

"Will do," Ray had said. "Won't leave a stone unturned."

Ruth smiles one last time at Evie, who is chewing on her lower lip as if she is still worried about disappearing like Julianne, and then lifting her face into the hot, dry wind that blows through her open car window, Ruth tightens the knot on her scarf so it won't slip from under her chin. It's been a long time since she's bothered with one, but she doesn't want Arthur and Celia to see her bruises. All through church, she wore the scarf. Most of the other ladies slip theirs off once inside and tie them on again as services end. Ruth's scarf, however, draped over her head and tied under her chin, covers the red spot on her lower jaw where Ray struck her with the back of his hand when Floyd left the house that morning. Without the hangover that Ruth could smell on Ray even after his shower, he might have ignored Floyd's visit. But wherever Ray had been the night before, which was not at home eating strawberry pie, he had drunk plenty.

"I think you're right, Celia," Ruth says, smiling back at Evie again. "Julianne will be home by supper."

But two months later, Julianne Robison is still not home.

CHAPTER 5

Standing at her own kitchen sink, Celia pushes aside the yellow gingham curtains and white sheers and takes in her first icy breath since moving to Kansas two months earlier. Outside the window, the waxy leaves of a silver maple filter quiet rain. The leaves flutter in the gentle breeze, their silvery white undersides sparkling beneath the gray sky. Even on the hottest August days, the tree had cast a cool, heavy shadow over the kitchen but the sprinkling of golden leaves among the green reminds Celia that soon the tree will be bare. Leaning on the counter, rinsing a colander of white beans that have soaked through the night, Celia misses her Detroit kitchen window. She misses the sound of Al Templeton pull starting his lawn mower, Sarah Jenkins beating her kitchen rugs with a broom handle, the garbage truck hissing in the back alley.

Feeling heavy footsteps coming toward

her, Celia lifts her head. She straightens, wrings out her washcloth and hangs it over the faucet. The footsteps slow and stop directly behind her. She closes her eyes. Arthur leans against her, wrapping his arms around her waist.

"Good morning," he whispers.

His coarse voice, the voice she normally only hears when he lies on the pillow next to her, makes her smile.

"Coffee?" he asks. His breath is warm on her left ear.

Celia draws one hand across his rough cheek and nods toward the pot that is still steaming. "You need a shave," she says, her smile fading when she looks back outside and sees the golden leaves.

Arthur pushes aside her loose hair and rubs his rough chin and jaw against her neck. "No razors on Saturday."

In Detroit, Arthur ran a lathe, carving metal into ball bearings and shafts that were shipped to the automotive factories where they ended up in alternators and generators. The red and blue patch that Celia sewed on the front of each work shirt read MACHINIST. Spinning metal for ten hours a day made Arthur's forearms strong and hard and he came home most nights smelling of motor oil and rubbing the back of his neck. Now, in Kansas, thanks to Gene Bucher, he drives a backhoe and a grader for the county and he comes home at night rubbing his lower back, sometimes hurting so badly from the vibration of the heavy equipment that his legs flare out at the knee and he walks with a rounded back. Grading the dry roads that ride like a washboard gives him the worst ache, and on those nights, Celia rubs Evie's old baby oil between her palms to warm it and kneads it into his back and shoulders.

"Will you work today? What with the rain." Celia stretches and relaxes into Arthur's hold. He seems bigger here in Kansas and thicker through the chest.

"Later," Arthur whispers. "I'll drive around, check the outlying roads." He leans closer, moving his hands over her stomach. "Better not take the car out until the ground drains. Don't want to gut the driveway." Pressing against her, he gathers two handfuls of her skirt and gently pulls until the hem lifts up over her knees. "The kids still sleeping?"

Celia tries to reach for a mug in the cupboard overhead, but Arthur keeps his hold on her.

"All except Elaine. She's gone off fishing with Jonathon."

Arthur rubs his jaw against her cheek.

"Ruth's coming today," Celia says, nodding toward the white beans she has rinsed and set aside. "She'll be helping me with those ham and beans you were wanting."

In Detroit, Celia had shopped daily at Ambrozy's Deli where Mr. Ambrozy made the best kielbasa in the city. He added beef and veal to the finest cuts of pork and cooked it up with garlic and a touch of marjoram, his secret ingredient. Every Friday, she made Hunter's Stew with Mr. Ambrozy's kielbasa and sweet sauerkraut, and Arthur always liked her cooking just fine. But on the first morning in September, he had said that a good old-fashioned plate of ham and beans sure would be nice. Not knowing how to prepare such a thing, Celia had asked for Ruth's help.

Arthur mumbles something about Ruth always running late. Then he drops Celia's skirt and presses against the entire length of her body.

"Now stop that," she says, smiling and trying to turn into his embrace, but he places his hands on the counter, trapping her so she can't move. "Ruth will have food for the Robisons, too. Will probably want you to run it over straightaway."

"What is that?" Arthur says, his tone suddenly clear and strong. His voice comes from over the top of Celia's head instead of near her left ear. "What the hell is that?"

Studying the three sets of muddy footprints on her kitchen floor, Ruth takes a bottle of ammonia from under the sink and sets it on the counter so she won't forget to clean them when the men leave. Next, she checks the timer she set for her banana bread. It'll be ready in seven minutes and she hopes the men will be gone by then.

"Sorry to barge in like this," Floyd says, pushing the creamer across the table to the other two men.

Ruth pours three cups of coffee.

"Mostly these two fellows are going to ask the same questions I have."

One of the men, the larger of the two and the one who doesn't bother to take off his hat, pulls out a small pad of paper. He taps a pencil on the edge of the kitchen table and tips his head to one side, giving Ruth a sideways glance. "Won't take long, ma'am," he says.

The other man, who is no bigger than Floyd, nods down at the floor. "Sorry about this mess." Then he pours cream in his coffee and after checking the sole of each shoe, he glances up at Ruth and smiles with closed lips.

"More questions?" Ruth asks, standing at the kitchen sink where she can watch out the window for Ray's truck. Floyd must have waited until Ray left for the day because not five minutes after he pulled away, Floyd drove up with these two men in his car.

"These fellows are from Wichita. Work for the Kansas Bureau of Investigation. They've been down here helping us search for Julianne seeing as how we haven't gotten so far."

"That's good," Ruth says. "That's very good."

"Where's your husband off to this morning?" the larger man says. He knows Ray is gone without asking.

"Smells mighty good," the smaller man says, nodding at the stove where two loaves of banana bread are baking.

"The Stockland Café," Ruth says, answering the larger man's question. "Always has breakfast there on Saturday mornings. And then to the farm."

Their own land is too small to make a living from, so Ray has leased the Hathaway place since Mr. Hathaway died fifteen years earlier. It's a twelve-mile drive toward town and usually, almost always, keeps Ray away until dusk.

The larger man studies his pad of paper. "That's the Hathaway place you're talking about?"

"Yes," Ruth says, glancing out the window before letting her eyes settle on the center of the kitchen table. "Goes there every day."

The larger man asks most of the questions. They are the same ones Floyd asked on his three other trips to the house. A few days after Floyd's first visit, he came back with a black notebook and a ballpoint pen and said he hadn't taken notes the first time, would Ruth and Ray mind going over the questions again. He said that most folks in town were getting the same visit. The third time he came, he asked how many acres Ray figured he had between the two farms and did he know of any place that might put a young girl in trouble. A fellow who lived over near Stockton found a soft spot on his land that must have been an old shaft or a dug-out foundation. Nothing in there but the fellow never would have found it if he hadn't looked. Floyd offered to help Ray check over his land and the Hathaways' since Mrs. Hathaway couldn't be expected to do it. "Can look plenty good on my own," Ray had said, so Floyd tipped his hat and didn't come back again until today.

"Sure I can't clean up for you, ma'am?" the smaller man says, waving a hand toward the muddy footprints.

He's the kinder of the two and seems to believe Ruth when she tells her story about strawberry pie and a quiet evening at home. The larger man doesn't believe so easily. He shakes his head when he scribbles in his book like he knows what he's writing isn't true. Floyd has surely told them about the past, about how Ray only married Ruth because Eve died. The men from Wichita, especially the larger one, look at Ruth like most of the people in town do, like anything bad she has to bear is her own doing so she shouldn't complain.

The whole town, Floyd included, has always thought that Ray was the one who killed Eve because no other killer was ever found. Father told everyone a crazy man did it. Broke in the house, took his daughter, slaughtered her on a dirt floor. But the town never believed it. They have always figured that Ruth married the man who killed her sister. But Ray didn't kill Eve. He loved her and no good will come from digging up the past. No good will come from speaking ill of the dead.

But these men sitting in Ruth's kitchen don't know how much Ray loved Eve. All three of them suspect Ray did something to little Julianne Robison because, even though she was just a child, she looked so much like Eve. Blond hair, blue eyes, pink satin skin. And Ray is a troublemaker, always has been because he drinks too much and Floyd is constantly throwing him out of Williamson's bar.

Despite the twenty-five years that separate the lives of Julianne and Eve, Floyd and these two men think their looking alike means something, and Ruth will let them keep thinking that because then they will keep a close eye on Ray. If these men believe the past has something to do with what happened to Julianne Robison and that Julianne's disappearance will turn out to be Palco's first murder in twenty-five years, they won't believe Ruth's lie and they'll keep digging. If Ray is the one who took Julianne Robison, they'll figure it out as long as they keep looking. Because Ruth's too afraid to tell Floyd the truth about that Saturday night, this is the best she can do.

With Arthur still trapping her against the counter, Celia looks through the maple's branches, makes a small humming sound and says, "I don't see anything."

Arthur stands straight, his sudden movement causing Celia to stumble.

"The paddock," he says. "The God damned paddock is empty."

Celia looks again, this time leaning over the sink. The gate near the barn hangs open.

"I've told that boy to mind the latch," Arthur says as he grabs his hat from the top of the refrigerator. "Dan. Get out here."

"Arthur, please," Celia says, following him toward the porch.

Ever since Julianne Robison went missing and stayed missing, Celia feels a rush of fear every time she or Arthur gets angry with the children. It's the fear that anger will be the thing they are left with should one of them go missing, too. It's silly, she knows, but even eight weeks later, even as the town seems to be forgetting, even as the search has ended for Julianne Robison, the fear is a reflex.

"Maybe she's gone around the back of the barn," Celia says. "You don't know she got out. Please don't overreact."

"Well, that's not the point, is it?"

While Celia tries to rein in her anger and frustration since Julianne disappeared, Arthur has unleashed his. His temper explodes without warning as if he thinks Julianne must have been careless, irresponsible, and that these two things led to her disappearance. He won't have the same happen to his children.

"Dan," Arthur shouts again. "Get out here."

Pulling on a shirt, Daniel stumbles from his room. "What?" he says, blinking and forcing his eyes open. "What is it?"

"You latch Olivia's gate last night?" Arthur says, pulling on his second boot.

"Sir?"

"The gate. You latch it?"

"Yes, sir."

Giving his boot a final tug, Arthur stands straight. "You sure about that?"

"I'll check, sir."

"He'll check," Celia says, reaching for Arthur's hand. "Let him check."

Arthur yanks away. "I'll give you your answer, son. You didn't latch it. Now get your shoes on and see to it that cow hasn't gotten out."

Daniel walks into his room, his shoulders rounded, his arms hanging at his sides, while Arthur stands in the threshold leading onto the back porch. He crosses his arms, leans against the doorjamb and stares at Celia.

"Don't be too hard on him," she says. "He's still learning."

Standing straight so that his shoulders fill

the doorway, Arthur says, "He's had plenty of time for learning."

"Please be patient. It's only been a couple months."

Arthur yanks on his hat. "Two months is long enough. That boy doesn't give one damn thought to what he's doing around here, and it's high time that changes."

At the end of the driveway, Ruth stands behind the cover of an evergreen. Cradling the two loaves of banana bread and a chicken and broccoli casserole, she leans forward, checking right and left and right again. Floyd and the men from Wichita left without finishing their coffee, and if Ruth hurries, she can get to Arthur's house before anyone worries. From inside the tree, she straightens and listens. It is definitely a truck she hears, driving east to west. She takes two steps back, knowing just where to stand so that the tree's branches will wrap around her, hide her.

Yes, it's a truck, not a car. The wide tires, the heavy cab, the tailgate. She listens, holding her breath as she waits for the change in pitch of a truck slowing to turn. A tailgate rattles, metal slapping against metal. Just like Ray's. Large tires kick up muddy gravel, almost close enough to spray it across

Ruth's face if she weren't hidden inside the tree. She slowly exhales, listening but not hearing the change in pitch. The truck drives by, never slowing to turn. It's blue with a white cab. Out-of-state tags. Nebraska. Not Ray.

Stepping out of the tree, a branch pulls the hood from Ruth's head. The banana bread that she stirred up the night before and baked while Floyd and the men from Wichita drank their coffee is warm in her arms. Outside the evergreen, the rain has slowed to a mist and the road to Arthur's house is empty except for the deep scars carved into it by the blue and white truck. Balancing the casserole dish and bread loaves on one hip, Ruth pulls the braid that hangs down her back from under her coat and lets it fall between her shoulder blades.

She goes to Arthur's now every Saturday morning, each time taking food for Orville and Mary Robison. Most weekends she only manages a small batch of cookies or half dozen sweet rolls. Never too much. Ray might notice. She leaves the food with Celia, who always promises to take it straight to the Robisons and then they drink coffee and sometimes eat cookies or maybe a sweet roll if Ruth made extra. After a few weeks of these trips, Ruth has started to put on a little weight, filling out like she was when she was younger. Her hip bones are cushioned now and her shoulders softened. Even her hair is stronger and thicker since Arthur's family moved home. This past week, as they sipped coffee in Celia's kitchen, Celia had brushed Ruth's hair, carefully so as not to tear the ends, and wove it into a thick braid that she tied off with one of Evie's pink hair bands. "The apple cider vinegar is working," Celia said as she brushed out Ruth's hair. Thinking Ray might notice her new braid, Ruth had practiced and was ready to show him how she could braid her own hair, but she had no explanation for the pink band. Standing on the edge of the road, she smiles and tosses her head from side to side, the braid swinging softly across her back.

Arthur's home is a half mile away. At the top of the hill that separates their two houses, Ruth slows. This is where she stops every Saturday morning and scans the tightly knit rows of winter wheat sprouts that etch the fields, hoping for a glimpse of Julianne Robison. Tattered yellow ribbons tied to a dozen fence posts along the road by the high school kids in the early days following Julianne's disappearance remind Ruth how long the child has been gone. Too long. But still Ruth watches for her from the top of the hill.

There are other reminders besides the yellow ribbons. The flyers with Julianne's black and white picture, wrinkled and faded, that still cling to the telephone poles along Main Street. The car wash that the Boy Scouts held a month ago. They gave the money to Mary and Orville. Mary said she would tuck it away for a rainy day. The abandoned well that James Williamson reported last Sunday. Floyd Bigler and a half dozen of the town's men gathered around the hole while their women gathered at the church just in case. But the men found nothing and backfilled the hole with crushed rock and cement.

Careful to avoid the soft ruts carved by the truck that drove past, Ruth walks to the edge of the road and fingers one of the yellow ribbons. On her next trip to Arthur's house, she'll bring along some yellow fabric scraps and tie them over the tattered plastic ribbons. She scans both sides of the road, counting the ribbons so she'll know how many to cut. And then she hears it. Yelling, shouting. It sounds like Arthur. She walks to the center of the road and from there she sees them.

Arthur is running down the hill, away from Ruth. He is waving and shouting at

Daniel, who is running along the other side of the road, trailed by Evie. Between them, Olivia the cow weaves left and right, first toward Arthur and then toward Daniel. Near the bottom of the hill, where gravity seems to get the better of him, Arthur tries to slow down but slips in the mud instead. He stumbles, arms shooting up into the air, both feet flying out from under him, and lands on his hind end. Daniel stops, coming up a few steps short of his father, and leans over, resting both hands on his knees. This gives Evie time to catch up. Arthur holds up one hand as if to quiet them and pushes himself off the ground. He shakes the dirt from his boots and stands straight, his muddy hands hanging at his sides.

As the commotion settles down, Olivia stops a few feet in front of them. She drops her head and nuzzles something on the ground. Everyone seems to be resting until Arthur suddenly breaks into a sprint, slipping and stumbling for several strides before finding his footing. Olivia startles, jerks her head, throws her hind legs into the air, kicking up mud and gravel, and begins to run. Daniel and Evie duck, both holding their hands over their faces and run after their father. Ruth hugs her bread and laughs. She laughs, without making any sound. She laughs until tears pool in the corner of each eye. She laughs until she hears another truck.

Up ahead, Jonathon drives around the curve in the road. Daniel stops running, leans forward and props himself up by bracing his hands on his knees. Jonathon parks his truck at an angle, blocking the road. Through the windshield, Daniel sees Elaine sitting in the center of the front seat, nearly in Jonathon's lap. Since the afternoon Jonathon loaded Olivia in his trailer and followed Uncle Ray to Grandma Reesa's, he has been at their house almost every day. He comes straight from work and stays for dinner, always talking about the house he is building from scraps and spare parts. He's been around so much that he has become Dad's extra set of hands. Before they moved from Detroit, Dad said that the farm would turn Daniel into a man, that it would roughen up his hands and put hair on his chest. Instead, Dad found Jonathon, who is already a man, and Daniel is still Mama's extra set of hands.

Elaine is smiling as Jonathon slowly and quietly opens his door and slides out of the truck. She follows, both of them stifling their laughter so they don't startle Olivia, who has stopped in the center of the road. The truck has confused her or maybe she is plain tired out.

"Give you a hand, Arthur?" Jonathon says, tugging on his gray hat.

"We've got her from this side," Dad says and motions Daniel to close the gap between them and the cow.

"I'd say this old gal has had about enough." Jonathon bends to look into Olivia's face. He takes two steps forward, reaches out with one hand and grabs her neck strap. "Yep, good and tired."

"How many times is that, Dan?" Elaine says, standing next to Jonathon and hooking a finger onto one of his belt loops. "Three?"

"Why'd you get so made up to go fishing?" Daniel says as Dad walks over to take the lead from Jonathon.

"Get over here, Dan," Dad says, giving Elaine a second look. She is wearing a lavender dress and her brown hair hangs in soft waves the way it does when she sleeps in rag curlers. "You two catch anything?"

"Daddy, don't be silly," Elaine says. "Who fishes in the rain?"

"Daddy fishes in the rain all the time," Evie says, smiling up at Jonathon. He tugs one of her braids.

"Caught a lot of fine fish in the rain," Dad says, holding onto Olivia and studying Elaine. Olivia snorts and tosses her head. Dad jerks her lead. "Hold up there, girl."

Daniel thinks maybe Dad will forget to ground him since Elaine is too dressed up for fishing.

"We went to my mother's for breakfast, sir," Jonathon says, patting Olivia's jowl. "She enjoys the company."

"Good enough," Dad says. "Daniel, get this animal home."

"Yes, sir," Daniel says, wrapping both hands around the leather lead.

"Are you coming to Grandma's for lunch tomorrow?" Evie asks Jonathon. She twirls a braid around her finger, the same braid Jonathon tugged. "She makes fried chicken. Daddy says it's the best ever."

"Imagine so, squirt," Jonathon says, giving Evie a pat on the head and turning on one heel to leave.

"Don't forget to latch the gate, Dan," Elaine says, laughing and still hanging onto Jonathon's belt loop as they walk back to the truck.

While Dad directs Jonathon so his truck won't get stuck in one of the muddy ditches, Evie waves goodbye and Daniel pulls Olivia until her head turns toward home. Thinking he'll check for mail because Mama says his old friends are sure to write any day now, Daniel stops at the mailbox, tugs open the small door and looks inside. Empty. Not a single letter since they moved. Already, every Detroit friend has forgotten him. He shakes his head, gives Olivia's lead another yank to get her moving and looks up. There, at the top of the hill, he sees them.

"Hey, Dad," he says, squinting up the road. "Isn't that Aunt Ruth up there?"

At the top of the hill that separates Aunt Ruth and Uncle Ray's house from their house, Uncle Ray has parked his truck and is standing next to the passenger side door, which is open. At first, Daniel thinks Uncle Ray has come to help catch Olivia, too — that Dad has called out the whole county to run her down. But then he sees Aunt Ruth standing at the side of the road. Her shoulders are hunched forward as if she is carrying something and she looks no bigger than Evie from so far away. Uncle Ray motions for Aunt Ruth to get into the truck but instead she stares down the road where Daniel stands with Olivia. Daniel looks over at his cow. Her chestnut coat is slick and shiny, her breath comes in short, heavy snorts. She hangs her head, then looks up at Daniel with her brown eyes and bats her thick, black lashes.

When Daniel looks back, Aunt Ruth is gone. The truck door is closed. And Uncle Ray is walking back to the driver's side. He pauses as he passes in front of the truck, waves down at Daniel and his family and slips inside the cab. Evie jumps up and down, waves her hands over her head. Dad watches as the truck rolls backward down the far side of the hill. He is looking for something, though Daniel isn't sure what.

CHAPTER 6

Breathing in the cool morning air that ruffles her kitchen curtains and still smells of rain, Ruth crosses her legs, Indian style as Evie would say, and rearranges her skirt so it lies around her on the floor like a halo. Pieces of broken glass scatter as she settles into position. On the stove, a small saucepan sets inside a larger one that is filled with two inches of boiling water — a homemade double boiler. A cheesecloth draped over both traps the heavy, rising steam. On the counter, where it will stay cool, waits a small brown bottle.

From her spot on the floor, Ruth glances at the clock sitting on the stove and dips a teaspoon into a box of baking soda, levels it by dragging it under the box top and drops it into a small glass dish. Using a tight whipping motion, she stirs it into the water already in the bowl and, thinking the paste isn't thick enough yet, she adds another scoop of soda. She taps her spoon on the side of the glass bowl. Still not thick enough. As she adds a third spoonful, a truck pulls around the side of the house and parks near the garage. A door slams followed by footsteps that climb the outside stairs. Ruth pulls her knees to her chest, cups the small bowl in one hand and stirs the baking soda paste with the other.

The screened door rattles in its frame.

"Ruth. Ruth. You in there?"

Ruth lets her legs fall down into a crisscross position again and uses the back of her spoon to mash the paste against the side of the bowl.

"Ruth, it's Arthur. You home? I saw you out there on the road. You and Ray. Olivia got out again. Did you see? Damn cow. Everything okay in there?"

The screen creaks as it opens. Arthur knocks on the wooden door loud enough that Ruth feels it through the floorboards. She closes her eyes, actually only her left eye, and holds her breath, bracing herself. But the vibration beneath her is not enough to stir up the pain. She'll feel it tomorrow.

"Thought you might have something to eat in there," Arthur says, shaking the locked doorknob. "Eggs are cold at my house. You in there?"

Ruth sets aside the glass bowl and, supporting herself with one hand, she stretches toward a silver frame that lies barely within reach. She hooks the frame with one finger, pulls it toward her and sits straight again. Because the glass is broken, she slips off the cardboard backing, removes the picture and sets it on the floor next to her. A spot of blood drips off the palm that braced her when she reached for the frame. The blood lands on the center of the picture just below Eve's right eye. First one drop and then another. Eve was fifteen when the picture was taken, maybe sixteen. A few years before she died. Ruth pulls a small shard of glass from her palm and presses her hand against her skirt to stop the bleeding.

"Ruth, hey, Ruth." Arthur knocks again. "Celia says to come on over for coffee. She's got those white beans ready to go. Thought you'd like a ride."

Heavy footsteps cross the porch, pause and walk back. The door rattles in its frame as Arthur tries it again.

"You in there?"

Once the bleeding has stopped, Ruth dips a corner of her skirt into the baking soda paste and begins to polish the silver frame. She starts at the top, scrubbing in tiny circles, a white haze marking her path. The frame had been a wedding present. She polishes it every month, sometimes with baking soda, sometimes with toothpaste. The tarnish is quick to gather in the scalloped edges. Cheap silver, Ray always says.

Having finished the top, Ruth adjusts her grip, folding her hand over the jagged edges of glass clinging to the frame. The pointed shards prick her fingers. She changes position, shifting her weight from side to side, her back beginning to ache where he kicked her. Something cuts into her hip. Another piece of glass, she thinks. All around her, glass lays shattered. Crescent-shaped pieces of wine-glasses never used, cleared out of the china hutch with one swipe of Ray's right hand. The frame had been an accident. It bounced across the wooden floor and came to rest at Ray's feet. From inside the silver frame, Eve's shattered face, her eyes bright, smiled up at him from under the brim of her best Sunday hat.

He had stood for a moment, staring at the photo, his clenched fists at his side and without bothering to look at her, he called Ruth a whore, a God damned whore with no business sneaking off like she did. A God damned whore wearing a pink band in her hair who had no business feeding the folks who thought he stole their girl. He had seen those Wichita men down at Izzy's café. Thought he'd have himself a decent God damned breakfast for once but then he sees those men with Floyd. Those God damned Wichita men tipped their hats at him, told him what a pleasant wife he had and what good coffee Ruth brewed up for them. Whole damn town is talking about it now. Everyone talking about how much that girl looked like Eve, talking about it like it means something. Ruth couldn't lie when Ray asked if they'd been to talk to her but promised him that she only told those men the truth — that Ray'd been home all night, eating meat loaf and strawberry pie. The truth is all. Ray had stood for a long time, his good eye staring at Ruth before he kicked the silver frame across the floor into the kitchen. As Ruth crawled after it, glass crackling under her knees, he lifted the same boot and kicked her in the back and again in the left side of the head. When Ruth woke, he was gone.

A door slams and Arthur's truck fires up. Gravel crunches beneath his tires as he slowly backs up and starts down the driveway. The truck stops when it passes the front of the house, idles there for a moment, and the sound of the engine fades as he drives away.

CHAPTER 7

Celia stands at Reesa's stove, a place she finds herself now every Sunday after church services, with a teaspoon in hand and a checkered apron tied at her waist. Using her forearm to brush the hair from her eyes, she inhales the steam rising off a pot of simmering chicken broth, turns her head and coughs. The others sit behind her at the kitchen table. They are watching her, waiting for her, crossing and uncrossing their legs. The vinyl seat covers squeak as they shift positions. Someone drums his fingers on the table. Someone else sighs. Someone's stomach growls.

"Once it boils, you can start dropping dumplings," Reesa says. "Be sure that dough is plenty thick this time. Add more flour if it calls you to."

"And use small spoonfuls," Elaine says. "Jonathon and Dad like the small noodles. Right, Dad?"

Arthur doesn't answer. He knows better, Celia thinks, tapping her teaspoon on the side of the pot. The drumming fingers stop.

"Next time," Reesa says, "set the burner on high and we won't be holding up lunch until that broth boils. Lord a mercy. Father Flannery will be preaching next Sunday's mass before those noodles are done."

Celia digs a spoon into the thick batter and flashes a toothy grin at her mother-in-law whose large body spills over the chair. Scooping up a wad of dough the size of a chicken egg, she holds it over the pot, not really intending to drop it in, but wanting to enjoy the feeling of ruining Sunday lunch before dropping in a proper sized dumpling — one the size of a nickel. But as she holds the dough over the simmering broth, she hears a loud pop that startles her and the dumpling wad falls. Hot broth slashes her arms and face. She jumps back.

"Ray'll have to get that fixed one of these days," Arthur says at the sound of Ray's truck backfiring a second time. He stands, glances out the kitchen widow and walks toward the back door.

Jonathon scoots back from the table and pulls out Elaine's chair for her. "Let's give it a look," he says.

As the three of them walk from the

kitchen, leaving Celia and Reesa alone, Celia turns her back on the stove, the chicken broth bubbling up behind her, and leans over the sink so she can see out the window. Ray hasn't moved from behind the steering wheel and the engine is choking and sputtering. In the passenger seat, Ruth sits with her head lowered. Celia crosses her arms and smiles, thinking she'll have to tease Arthur for all his worrying. All through church, he had fidgeted, shifting in his seat, crossing and uncrossing his legs as he watched the doors and scanned the pews. Ruth never misses a Sunday. Never, he whispered as the congregation began its first hymn. Perhaps she's under the weather or Ray overslept. Arthur only nodded and hung his arm over the back of the pew so he could watch the heavy wooden doors at the rear of the church.

"Mind that chicken doesn't burn," Reesa says, nodding toward the chicken frying in a cast-iron skillet and then she pushes back from the table, the legs of her chair grinding across the linoleum floor. "I'll go see to helping Ruth with her dessert. And get those dumplings going. We'll be all day waiting if you don't get started."

When Reesa has left the kitchen and Celia is alone, she looks back outside. Ruth's head is still lowered as if she's looking down at folded hands and Ray is beating on the steering wheel, seemingly because the truck's engine won't stop running. He is still ranting when Arthur walks up to the truck, followed by Elaine, Jonathon and Reesa. Celia steps back from the sink, pokes at the one giant dumpling that has floated to the top of the broth and, as the rolling bubbles grow into a heavy boil, she thinks she'll serve this one to Reesa. Reaching for the second burner, where the fried chicken sizzles and pops, Celia smiles as she turns up the heat.

Daniel, startled by a loud pop, ducks and presses against the wall, the wooden slats rough and wet against his back. Inside the small shed, it's dark and the air smells like Grandma Reesa's basement — moldy and stale. He tries to breathe through his mouth, thinking the air won't feel so heavy if he does.

For six weeks, Ian has asked Daniel to look inside the shed at Grandma Reesa's place. Ian's oldest brothers thought for sure Julianne Robison was rotting away inside, but Daniel said that was stupid because Grandma Reesa would have smelled her. Ian said to check anyway because his brothers were smart and a fellow could never be sure until he saw it with his own eyes.

Daniel readjusts his feet, careful not to break through one of the floorboards that creak every time he moves. Hearing another pop, he recognizes the sound as Uncle Ray's truck and, squinting with one eye, he looks through a small hole where part of a plank has rotted away. Dad walks out of the house, smiling, almost laughing. He turns to say something to Jonathon. Elaine laughs, latches onto Jonathon's side and dips her head into his shoulder. The back door swings open again and Grandma Reesa walks out, rocking from side to side with each step. Daniel thinks of Ian, how he walks with a staggered stride, too, but for a different reason. Tomorrow at school, Daniel will tell Ian that Julianne Robison is definitely not rotting in the shed.

As Grandma Reesa nears the truck where the others are standing and watching Uncle Ray curse the engine that won't stop rattling, she turns toward the shed and stops, her feet spread wide to support her weight, her hands on her hips. Daniel drops down and presses his head between his knees. He sits motionless, waiting, listening.

Every Sunday after church services, Daniel changes into his work clothes when they get to Grandma Reesa's so he can cut her lawn. Sometimes, Dad gives him other chores to do, too — clean the gutters, spray down the screens, tighten the banisters — but at least until the first hard frost, he mows every Sunday. And every week, as Dad pulls the reel mower from the garage, he says, "Don't bother around the shed. That's for later." But later has never come. "I could take a weed whip to it," Daniel said one Sunday, remembering Ian's brothers and the kitten in the hole. He was glad when Dad shook his head and said, "Not today, son." Since they moved to Kansas, Dad and Jonathon have used a truck and cables to straighten Grandma's garage and have hammered in new support beams on the porch. They have replaced her rotted windowpanes and reshingled her chimney but Dad hasn't lifted a single hammer or nail to fix the sagging shed that is no more than six feet by eight with a flat roof and lone door. Daniel asked Aunt Ruth once why Dad wouldn't let anyone near the shed. "Mind your father," she had said. "Some things are meant to rest in peace."

Afraid to look through the rotted plank again, Daniel hugs his knees to his chest and wraps himself into a tight ball. Large cobwebs hanging from the corners of the shed sparkle in the slivers of light that shine through the loosely woven wooden roof. Daniel muffles a cough by pressing his mouth to his forearm. Sitting in the dark and wondering if Grandma Reesa saw him, Daniel remembers the crazy men from Clark City and scans the empty shed for a set of eyes that might be watching him. It's definitely time to get out.

Lifting up on his knees so he can peek through the hole again, Daniel sees that Dad has stopped a few feet in front of Uncle Ray's truck. He isn't laughing anymore. He is staring straight ahead at Aunt Ruth, who has stepped out of the truck and is standing near the front bumper, her arms hanging at her sides. The hem of her blue calico dress flutters in the breeze. Dad stands with a straight back, his feet planted wide. His hat sits low on his forehead. After Dad is done staring at Aunt Ruth, he turns toward Uncle Ray.

Evie climbs onto the bed when she hears a loud pop outside. Holding up the hem of the blue silky dress that slips off her shoulders and bags at the neckline, she tiptoes across the white bedspread so she doesn't make the springs squeak. Daniel will be angry if he knows she's tried on the dresses.

He'll probably tell Mama, and Daddy will take a switch to her hind end. That's what Grandma Reesa did when Daddy was a boy. On their second visit to Grandma Reesa's house, Daddy had taken Evie out back and showed her a weeping willow tree. It had long, lazy branches that hung to the ground. "That old tree sure gave up her share of switches," Daddy had said, rubbing his hind end and laughing.

Evie stops in the middle of the bed, one foot in front of the other, her hands spread wide for balance. Hearing no one in the hallway outside the bedroom, she takes another step toward the window. Another loud pop comes from down below, but this time she smiles because she knows it's only Uncle Ray's truck backfiring. The handkerchief hem of the dress brushes against her toes. She wiggles them, gathers up the skirt again and leans against the headboard where she can see outside.

After Daddy and the others have walked out the door toward Uncle Ray's truck, Evie goes back to imagining that she is Aunt Eve. She pushes away from the window, presses her shoulders back and lifts her chin so that she'll feel taller — as tall as Aunt Eve. No one ever told Aunt Eve she was too small to be a third grader or called her names. Aunt

Eve always had friends to sit with in the cafeteria and never sat alone on the steps outside her classroom, watching the swings hang empty or beating the dust from Miss Olson's erasers. No one ever told Aunt Eve that she was going to disappear like Julianne Robison. Aunt Eve is beautiful and perfect and has the finest dresses. She was never, ever the smallest.

Wrapping her arms around her waist, Evie hugs the soft dress and smells Aunt Eve's perfume — sweet and light, like the bouquets of wildflowers that Aunt Ruth brings every Saturday morning. Evie closes her eyes and slowly twirls around, the bedsprings squeaking under foot. She spreads her arms wide, spinning faster and faster, lifting her knees to her chest so she won't trip on the hem and finally dropping down onto the center of the mattress with a loud crash.

She sits in the middle of the bed, not moving, not breathing, wondering if she has made the bed collapse. The headboard is still standing. She leans over the side. The bed is still standing, too. Then she hears the sound again. It's coming from outside. She crawls back to the window and lifts up high enough to see out. Daddy, now standing at the front of Uncle Ray's truck with Jonathon right behind him, is waving one hand toward Aunt Ruth and pointing at Uncle Ray with the other. As Jonathon reaches out for Daddy, Daddy bangs his fist on the truck's hood. The same crash that Evie heard. Daddy shakes off Jonathon and holds up one hand to stop Grandma Reesa, who has started walking toward him. Uncle Ray has backed up to the rear of his truck and is motioning at Daddy with both hands the same way he did when Olivia spooked as she walked out of the trailer. He's trying to calm Daddy, to make him settle down so he doesn't rear up. In four long steps, Daddy is standing face to face with Uncle Ray.

Shifting in her chair to hear more clearly through the open kitchen window, Celia smiles as Ray's truck finally quiets down. Next, one of the truck's doors opens, followed by heavy boots landing on the gravel drive. Another door opens.

"Help your Aunt Ruth." It's Reesa, probably calling out to Elaine. "She'll have a handful."

At the sound of her mother-in-law's voice, Celia presses her hands flat on the vinyl tablecloth, bracing herself, the smell of burnt chicken beginning to tug at her. Next to the chicken, which sizzles and pops,

99

though quieter now because its juices have burned off, broth hisses as it splashes over the sides of Reesa's iron pot onto the hot stovetop and disappears in a puff of steam. Celia presses her feet on the white linoleum and repositions herself on the vinyl seat cover, rooting her body so she won't be tempted to stand. The God damned chicken can burn for all she cares.

Sundays were pleasant in Detroit. It was the day she wore white gloves and her favorite cocoa velour pillbox hat with the grosgrain ribbon trim. The children wore their finest clothes to church and never worried about dust ruining the shine on their patent leather shoes. Arthur always wore a tie. Sundays in Detroit were properly creased and always well kept until the riots started and everything began to smell like burnt rubber and the Negro boys started calling Elaine. Now Sundays are dusty, filthy, wrinkled and spent watching Arthur pat his belly as Reesa fries up a chicken. Celia shivers thinking of Reesa's offer that next week she'll teach Celia how to pick a good fryer from the brood and wring its neck with a few flicks of the wrist.

"Look up at me, Ruth," Arthur says from outside the window.

Something about Arthur's voice makes

Celia stand. She slides her chair back and leans over the sink where she can see out the kitchen window. Ray and Ruth have both stepped out of the truck. Ray is standing on the far side, where only the top of his hat is visible, and Ruth is standing on the near side, her back to Celia, her arms dangling, her head lowered.

"This why you weren't at church this morning?" Arthur says, his voice louder.

Ruth doesn't move. Arthur takes two steps forward and Jonathon grabs his arm. Arthur yanks away, raises a fist in the air and slams it against the hood of Ray's truck.

Celia startles, her hand slipping off the edge of the sink.

"Tell me, Ruth."

Ruth lifts her face. Arthur closes his eyes and drops his head. A braid hangs down Ruth's back, tied off by a bright pink band. After teaching Ruth how to braid her own hair, Celia had promised to wash and trim it when she came on Saturday and she even bought honey for their biscuits. But Ruth never came.

The thick braid moves up and down, no more than an inch as Ruth nods her head yes.

Arthur slams his fist on the truck again and holds up his other hand to Reesa, who has started to walk toward him. He turns to Ray.

"You lay your hands on her face?"

Ray doesn't answer but instead backs toward the rear of the truck.

"Answer me. You lay a hand on her?"

"This is business between me and my wife, Arthur. No place for you."

Arthur shoves Jonathon away when he tries again to take Arthur's arm, and in four quick steps, he is standing face to face with Ray. Ray backs up a few more feet until they are clear of the truck and Celia can see them both. She pushes off the counter, ignoring the charred smell drifting up from Reesa's best cast-iron skillet and runs from the kitchen.

Evie hangs from the window ledge with both hands, her face pressed to the screen. Daddy grabs Uncle Ray's collar with one hand and hits him in the face with the other. Uncle Ray holds his fists up in front of his good eye, but Daddy pushes them away and hits him again. Uncle Ray tries to shove Daddy but Daddy won't let go. He holds on, shaking Uncle Ray like a rag doll and hitting him again and again. Evie pushes away from the window, stumbles over her handkerchief hem and something rips as she pulls the dress off her shoulders, steps out of it and throws it on the floor under the other dresses. She slams the closet door and as she runs out of the room, she hears Mama shout, "Stop, Arthur. Stop."

Daniel presses his face against the hole in the shed wall. Uncle Ray holds up both hands. His nose and mouth are red. Dad keeps hitting Uncle Ray even when his hat falls off, even when Uncle Ray's head quits bouncing back, even when Mama cries out for him to quit. Finally, Dad stops, holding his right fist over his shoulder, cocked and ready to hit Uncle Ray again.

"You ask Ruth," Uncle Ray says. "She'll tell you why I did it." Blood runs out of Uncle Ray's nose. "Out there sneaking around on me. All these months, taking food to those God damned Robisons. God damned people say I took their girl."

Dad lunges and hits Uncle Ray again, splattering blood across the gravel drive. Uncle Ray stumbles backward, tripping over his own feet and lands on his hind end. Dad stands still, watching and waiting while Uncle Ray props himself up on one elbow. Dad's shoulders lift and lower each time he takes a breath. Uncle Ray starts to stand but stops when Dad reaches into the truck bed and pulls out a whiskey bottle, grabs it by its thin neck and flings it at the shed. The bottle shatters. Someone screams, maybe Mama, maybe Elaine. Daniel falls backward, shuffling like a crab until he is pressed flat against the shed's far wall. Glass and warm bourbon splash up on the other side of the hole he had been looking through. The bits of glass sparkle in the cool sunlight for an instant before disappearing. The gravel driveway is silent.

Once the glass has settled, Celia turns to Arthur. He has not moved. Reesa reaches out to him but instead stops and walks inside. Ruth stands near the truck's front bumper, her head lowered, her arms hanging at her side.

"Ruth," Arthur says.

Ruth raises her head.

Celia gasps, covers her mouth again. Elaine and Jonathon lower their eyes.

"Oh, Ruth," Celia whispers.

"Go on with Celia," Arthur says, still staring at the shed, but Ruth doesn't move. "Now," he shouts.

Ruth's shoulders jerk.

"Go with Celia, now."

Celia wraps one arm around Elaine, both of them standing still, unable to move. Ray lies on the ground, blood smeared under his nose, down his chin, across his collar.

"Jonathon," Arthur says in a quieter voice.

Jonathon lifts his chin, pulls down his hat over his eyes and takes a step toward Arthur.

"Get them inside."

Jonathon nods, takes Ruth's forearm and, with his head lowered so that the brim of his hat hides his face, he guides her toward Celia and Elaine. Celia passes Elaine to Jonathon but shakes her head when he motions her to follow. She watches until the three have gone into the house and the screened door has slammed shut behind them.

"Gather yourself and leave," Arthur says to Ray. "Ruth isn't your concern anymore."

Ray pushes himself up, favoring his left side as if Arthur has broken a rib or two, picks up his hat, pulls it on so the front brim is cocked a little too high and limps toward his truck. "I don't see how you have any business between me and my wife."

"How many times, Ray?" Arthur says, picking up his hat and pulling it on. "How many times you lay a hand on her?"

Ray wipes the corner of his mouth, smearing the blood that drips down his chin. He spits red. A cut above his left brow drips blood into his bad eye.

Arthur throws open the truck door. "Not

105

your wife anymore."

"Arthur," Celia says, grabbing his arm and pulling him toward the house and away from Ray. "Please, let him be on his way."

Arthur pulls away and without looking at Celia, says, "Get inside."

"You're a man, Arthur. Same as me," Ray says, though he is looking at Celia when he says it, not in her eyes, but lower. "You wouldn't have me telling you about your wife, would you? Wouldn't want me telling you when you could or couldn't have her."

"Well, I'm telling you now," Arthur says, taking one step to the left so he blocks Ray's view of Celia. "Ruth is no longer your concern."

With his forearm, Ray wipes the blood from under his nose and steps up to Arthur. The brims of their hats nearly touch.

"You wait until they come looking for you," Ray says, "thinking maybe you're the one took that girl. You ought to know, people think it's strange, you all moving back right when that girl goes missing. People think it's strange, all right."

Arthur nods. "Folks'll think what they think," he says and Ray slips inside the truck.

Evie stops on the last step, holds onto the

banister and leans forward. The downstairs room is full of gray smoky air. Trying to see into the kitchen and beyond to the back porch, she listens for Daddy and Uncle Ray and wonders if they're still fighting. Mama shouted for them to stop but maybe Daddy and Uncle Ray won't listen to Mama. She blinks, clearing her tears. Not seeing anyone, she squeezes her nose closed with two fingers and steps down, touching the wooden floors with one toe. She holds that pose, trying not to breathe any of the smoky air and listens.

"Good Lord in heaven."

A crash follows Grandma Reesa's shout.

Evie presses her tiptoe foot flat on the floor and steps down with the other. Still pinching her nose, she walks through the living room and as she nears the front of the house, she covers her mouth and coughs. The gray smoke is thicker and swirls overhead. Waving it away, she steps into the kitchen. Grandma Reesa stands at the stove, her back to Evie, a silver potholder on one hand.

"Fine food charred to no good," Grandma Reesa says and, sliding the large iron skillet off the hot burner, she reaches into the sink, pulls out the cast-iron lid with the potholder, lifts it overhead and slams it back into the sink.

"What got burnt, Grandma?" Evie asks, her hands pressed to her ears in case Grandma throws anything else. She bites down on her lower lip when her chin wrinkles.

"Burned every last piece of chicken," Grandma Reesa says, holding the skillet up by its long thin handle. Black clumps of chicken stick to the bottom, even when she shakes it. "Help me, child. Get the bucket from the mudroom. We'll be scrubbing these walls for days."

Pulling a fan from under the sink, Grandma Reesa sets it in the kitchen window. "The mudroom, Eve. Get the bucket from the mudroom. My green bucket."

Evie runs into the large closet where everyone leaves their muddy boots on a rainy day, grabs the green bucket and hurries back to the kitchen. Grandma Reesa has begun pulling the white curtains off their rod. The fan drawing cool, outside air into the kitchen ruffles her gray hair and blows it across her blue eyes — the same color as Evie's, except older.

"Run the bathroom sink full of hot water and soak these," she says, brushing the hair from her eyes and handing the curtains to Evie. "Go on now. This mess will keep us busy all day if we let it."

"Daddy is fighting with Uncle Ray," Evie says, wrapping her arms around the bundle of curtains.

Grandma Reesa puts the green bucket in the sink and begins to fill it.

"I saw them," Evie says. "Outside. Fighting."

"Drop a bar of hand soap in the water." Grandma Reesa pulls a long-handled spoon from a drawer and points it at Evie. "No bleach. It will yellow the cotton."

"Daddy was hitting Uncle Ray in the face. Knocked him down and everything. I saw them from upstairs. I was in Aunt Eve's room, cleaning it for you. I dusted her dresser and fluffed her pillows. It'll be ready for her when she comes home."

Grandma Reesa stabs the spoon into a bowl. "Go on now," she says, yanking it out and jamming it back in. "This smoke will ruin my curtains. Go on now."

"Where's my daddy?" Evie feels her chin wrinkle again. She blinks as the air blown in by the fan parts her bangs. "He's hitting Uncle Ray."

"Run the water until it's good and hot. Get on with it."

"I saw them from Aunt Eve's room. I saw Daddy fighting." Evie stands in the middle of the kitchen, still hugging the curtains. "I wanted Aunt Eve's room to be nice for her. I wanted . . ."

Grandma Reesa lifts her white mixing bowl with both hands and slams it down on the counter. "Don't you speak to me about Eve, child. Don't you do it. Now get that hot water running. Get those curtains soaked."

Evie presses her face into the bundle of curtains. She lifts her eyes enough to see Grandma Reesa standing at the sink, her back to Evie, her right elbow jutting in and out as she scrubs the black skillet with a scouring pad. Evie nods her head, walks into the bathroom, breathing in the smell of the lemon-scented curtains, and closes the door behind her.

The devil's claws are waist high. Walking toward Mother's back porch, Jonathon guiding her by the elbow, Ruth brushes a hand over the pink, funnel-shaped blooms. The flowers are blurry through her one good eye. It still waters, as if she's been crying, but she never does. The tears will pool for a few more days. She licks her top lip, which is silky smooth where it has swelled to twice its normal size. Even though it hurts, she can't stop licking it. Sometime during the night, the shaking stopped. It always stops during the night. Ruth blinks her good eye and sees that some of the blossoms have died off, the tender petals shriveling and turning brown. The rest will follow and Arthur will mow them down soon. They won't bloom again until spring. Before walking inside, Ruth touches one of the woody claws that has dropped its seeds, and she knows she's pregnant.

CHAPTER 8

At the top of the hill, their warm breath turning to a frosty cloud that settles in around them, Celia and Elaine stop and wait for Ruth and Evie to catch up. The wind is quiet today and the sun is bright, almost blinding through the cold, dry air. In the surrounding fields below, perfectly spaced rows of green seedlings curve and roll with the flow of the land — the first stages of winter wheat. Their own land isn't fit for wheat because it's too hilly. Arthur says that someday they'll have a few more cows and put the pasture to good use.

Celia knows this land well. She knows that the hollowed-out spot used to be a pond, that two fence posts need mending a quarter mile up the road and that there's a patch of quicksand over the first ridge to the south. She knows these things because all of them, the whole Scott family, walked these grounds many times searching for Julianne

Robison. In the early weeks when she was first missing, they walked them almost every day, and then once a week and eventually in passing. Celia gasped the first time Arthur showed her the small patch of quicksand, thinking it had sucked poor Julianne to the bottom, but then Arthur stuck a stick in it and showed her it was only a few inches deep. As Evie and Ruth near the top of the hill, three olive, round-winged birds rise out of the thick bluestem growing along the road, glide across the red-tipped grass and settle in the ditch.

"Prairie chickens," Evie says, skipping up to Celia and pointing toward the spot where the birds disappeared.

Joining the others, Ruth nods but doesn't seem to have the breath to answer. She places one hand on her lower back and stretches.

"You feeling okay?" Celia says, motioning to the others to stop. "Did we go too far?"

Ruth shakes her head and signals that she needs a moment to rest. Before Ruth came to live with them, Celia took her walks along the dirt road, walking as far as County Road 54 before heading home. She needed fresh air, she would tell Arthur, and some time to herself. But what she really needed was a place to cry where no one would hear, a place where she could cry so hard that she choked and hiccupped and when she was done and her nose had stopped running, she would return home, saying her allergies were acting up or the wind and dust had reddened her eyes. She never told Arthur that she cried because she missed home and her parents, even though they were both dead. She never told him she missed walking Evie to school or visiting with the other ladies at Ambrozy's Deli. She never told him that she cried because in Kansas she is still afraid. She is afraid that he won't need her in the same way. She is afraid she'll never know how to be a mother in Kansas. And mostly, she is afraid of being alone. But now, she has Ruth. Thank goodness for Ruth, but having her in the family also means they must walk the pastures instead of the road where Ray might happen along in his truck.

"Hey, look," Evie shouts, holding one mitten to her forehead to shade her eyes and pointing with the other toward the fields south of the house. "There's Daniel. And that's Ian with him."

"Where do you suppose they're going?" Celia asks, knowing that it's Daniel not because she can see his face but because Ian's limp gives them away.

"Out for a walk, I suppose," Elaine says as the two silhouettes disappear over a rise in the pasture.

"Well," Evie says, swiveling on one heel so she can march back down the hill. "I hope they're not up to no good."

Celia pats the small of Ruth's back and gestures for everyone to follow Evie toward home. "I'll tell you what," Celia says. "No good will be had if we don't all get warmed up soon."

At the bottom of the hill, Evie stops, points toward the road straight ahead where a black sedan appears out of the glare of the late-day sun and shouts, "Look. It's Father Flannery's car."

Celia stops midway down the hill and pulls her jacket closed. "We don't have to go back, Ruth," she says. The prairie chickens rise up again as the car passes, kicking up dust and gravel. "Arthur can see to him."

Elaine nods. "Yes, we could stay out a while longer."

"They'll be waiting," Ruth says, tugging on the edges of her stocking cap and continuing toward home. "Can't hide from this forever."

Daniel stares down at Ian and thinks that even flat on his stomach, Ian is crooked.

Not as crooked as when he has to swing one leg over the bench seats in the school cafeteria, but crooked all the same. He is wearing his new black boots and even though his mother said they were only for church and school, Ian wears them all the time because they make things almost normal for him. One of the boots, the right one, has a two-inch heel while the other has a normal, flat heel. The thick heel is almost thick enough, but not quite and black boots don't do anything about a spine that looks like a stretched-out question mark. As Ian lifts up on his elbows, pressing his cheek to the stock of Daniel's new .22-caliber rifle, his shoulders sink under the weight of his head. Black boots don't do anything about Ian's oversized head, either. None of Daniel's Detroit friends had giant heads or lopsided legs. They were regular kids with regular-shaped bodies. Not knowing why but wanting to look somewhere else, any-where else but at Ian, Daniel turns toward the road as a black sedan drives over the hill to the north.

"That Father Flannery?" Ian asks, lifting his head up out of his shoulders for a mo-ment before letting it sink again.

"Yeah. How'd you know?"

"Everyone knows he's coming today." Ian

rests his right cheek against the rifle.

Pulling his jacket closed, Daniel exhales and squats next to Ian.

"Not too close," Ian says so Daniel scoots a few feet away, flipping up his collar and wrapping his arms around his waist. "Go there, behind the grass where they won't see you."

Daniel waddles a few more feet to the left where he'll be hidden by a clump of brome grass. "Won't my folks hear the shots?" he asks, still able to see the roof of his house. "I mean, we're not so far away."

"No one thinks anything about a gunshot this time of year. Hush and let me get the first one. The rest are easier." Ian inhales and lifts his head again. "There," he whispers. "Did you see it?"

Daniel stretches enough to see beyond the grass into the pasture on the other side of the barbed-wire fence. "I don't know. Maybe."

"It'll be back. Sit tight."

"How does everyone know? About Father Flannery, I mean."

"Everyone knows everything." Ian props the gun in his right hand and breathes short puffs of warm air into his left fist. A clump of brown hair has fallen out of his hat and across his forehead. "Everyone knows everything about everybody," Ian says, tucking the clump of hair back under his stocking cap with his warmed-up left hand.

In Detroit, nobody knew anything about anybody. They were too busy worrying about the Negroes who wanted to work side by side with the white people. They were too busy worrying about the color of their neighborhood and kids who couldn't play outside anymore. Nobody had time to care about someone like Father Flannery or why he was visiting on a Saturday afternoon. People in Kansas have nothing but time. That's what Mama says whenever Grandma Reesa shows up without an invitation.

"Know what else they say?" Ian says, crawling forward a few inches on his hips and elbows. The boot with the thick heel drags behind.

Daniel shakes his head. "Got mud stuck in your shoes," he says, pointing at the tread on the bottom of Ian's boots. Ida Bucher will know he wore them in the field. She'll whip him because money doesn't grow on trees and neither do black boots with extra-thick heels. "You'll need a nail to dig that out."

"They say your Uncle Ray went crazy from drinking."

Daniel stands and looks back at his house.

Though he can't see the driveway, he knows Father Flannery has parked his black car there. He will have gone inside and is probably sitting at the kitchen table. Mama will take his coat and serve him a piece of the apple pie that Aunt Ruth made after breakfast. Dad will drink a cup of coffee, cream and two sugars.

"He didn't even get his crop planted." Ian's head pops up, his legs go rigid and he fires.

Daniel stumbles backward, crushing a few feet of the new winter wheat and presses his hands over his ears. Beside him, Ian lifts up on his knees and watches his target. Wondering who or what may have heard them, Daniel scans the horizon.

"Got him," Ian says, flipping the safety and shifting the gun to the other side so he can pass it off to Daniel. "Now be real quiet. And get ready."

Keeping low to the ground where he'll stay out of sight, Daniel scoots toward Ian again and they switch places.

"Come on," Ian says, pulling back the bolt action. An empty casing pops out and flies over his left shoulder and after a new bullet has dropped into place, he pushes the rifle at Daniel. "Hurry up or you'll miss them."

"Who didn't plant his crop?"

"Your Uncle Ray," Ian says, flipping off the safety and pressing Daniel's right hand over the stock of the gun. "A lot of nice land going to waste. That's what Dad says. My brother says Ray got sick from all the drinking and the sheriff took him to Clark City. Says it's been coming for years. Says that's where people go to dry out."

"Dry out?" Daniel asks. Propping himself up on his elbows, he looks down the barrel of the gun and tries to balance it. The wooden stock is cold on his bare hands and against his cheek.

"Dry out. You know. Stop drinking. Your Uncle Ray is a drunk. Everyone says so. Says your Aunt Ruth is a married woman and belongs with her husband. Says he wouldn't be such a drunk if she'd go home."

With his lips pressed together, Daniel stares up at Ian.

"That's what they say. Not me. Hey, there's one."

Daniel flattens out so he can see under the barbed-wire fence. A hundred feet away, surrounded by unplowed ground covered with dry stubble, is the mound that had been Ian's target. One small head shaped like a giant walnut pops out of a hole in the center of the mound and then disappears. A few moments later, a prairie dog creeps out and lifts onto his hind legs. Its brown, furry body is plumper than the one Ian shot.

"Wait. Don't be too quick," Ian says.

"Who cares what they say about Aunt Ruth?" Daniel's breath warms the gun where it's pressed to his cheek. And then, remembering the words Dad used when he sent Uncle Ray away, Daniel says, "She's not my concern."

"Some people even say your Uncle Ray had something to do with taking Julianne Robison. Say that he is just that crazy. Even say he killed your Aunt Eve. But that was a long time ago."

"That's a lie," Daniel says, thinking that he'd know for sure if his own aunt was dead. "A God damned lie."

"I ain't saying it," Ian says. " 'Course it's Jack Mayer who took Julianne. But you ought to know that since you're the only one who's seen him." Ian kneels behind the same clump of grass. "Watch what you're doing. Careful." Before the new boots, Ian didn't squat or sit on the ground much because getting up was too hard. It's easier now but he still groans on the way down. "Wait another second. We might see more."

The prairie dog that Ian shot lies at the base of the mound, which, according to Ian, means he grazed it. A direct hit would blow the animal a foot in the air. Ian said it was best when that happened. Best for who, Daniel thinks, as the prairie dog starts to chirp — slow steady chirps as it drops down onto all fours. His stubby tail flicks in sets of three.

"Ready." Ian waddles a few feet closer, close enough that Daniel smells his moldy clothes and new leather boots, but the prairie dog won't smell him because Ian made sure they were downwind.

"Whoever said that about Ray, you tell them I don't care," Daniel says, pressing his cheek against the gun until it digs into his cheekbone and his eyes water. "I don't give one good God damn." Then he jabs his elbows into ground that is recently plowed and soft. Squinting through his right eye, he bites the inside of his cheek and tilts the barrel until the tip lines up in the sight.

"Don't talk. Take a deep breath, hold it, then fire."

The prairie dog crawls down the mound and begins to drag the injured one toward the hole.

"Not one good God damn bit," Daniel whispers.

"You got to be quick," Ian says, close enough that Daniel smells his breath. Slowly, Ian lifts his hands and covers both ears. "Now."

Daniel tightens his index finger, the trigger softening under the pressure. He inhales and squeezes his shoulder blades until his neck muscles ache and his lungs burn. The trigger collapses, and the gun fires. The prairie dog shoots up into the air and lands a few feet away. The chirping is gone.

"Got him," Ian shouts. He stumbles as he tries to stand, so stays put instead. "Now we have to wait. They'll be back. Be back for sure."

Peering through the rifle's sight, Daniel scans the field until he sees the dead prairie dog lying in the grass. Ian says prairie dogs are bad for the fields. He says they're rodents and that there will be lots more in the spring. Baby ones by June. They're the hardest to get. They don't come out like the others. Daniel drops the barrel of the rifle, flips the safety and pushes up on his knees.

"I'm not waiting around for another stupid prairie dog."

Being careful to step over the winter wheat, Daniel stands and walks toward home. Behind him, Ian stumbles with his old rhythm, the one he had before he got his new boots. God damn, Daniel hates that sound.

"Slow down," Ian calls out.

Holding the rifle at his side instead of over his shoulder, Daniel takes long steps toward home and doesn't look back.

CHAPTER 9

Trying to outrun the cold air that follows them onto the porch, Celia hustles everyone through the back door. Evie darts left, squeezes between Elaine and the doorframe and slips in front of Ruth.

"Sorry," she says, tripping over Ruth, and the two of them stumble into the kitchen.

"Evie." Celia grabs Evie's collar before she falls face-first on the kitchen floor. In a quieter voice, she says, "You be careful of Aunt Ruth. And mind yourself. We have company."

Celia pulls off her coat and tips her forehead toward Father Flannery, who sits at the head of the table. Arthur sits at the other end, and Reesa has taken a seat in between.

"So sorry to keep you waiting, Father," Celia says. "We lost track of time."

Evie steps up to Father Flannery, extends her hand the way she and Celia practiced in

125

the living room the night before and says, "Hello, Father Flannery."

Father Flannery pushes back from the table, his knees falling open to make room for the belly that hangs between them. He takes the tips of Evie's fingers in both hands. "Fine day to see you, Miss Eve."

"I'm Evie in our house, Father. Eve is only for Grandma Reesa's house. And church."

Father Flannery studies Evie over the top of his glasses. The tip of his nose and chin are still red from the cold. He finally nods and drops Evie's hands. "Your hair is cut," he says to Ruth.

"Yes." Ruth touches the ends of her new shorter hair and smiles up at Elaine. When she looks back at the Father, he isn't smiling. Ruth drops her eyes to the floor.

"Elaine cut it, Father," Evie says. "She's going to color it, too. Red maybe."

Reesa, who has made herself at home in Celia's kitchen, having already brewed the coffee and set out the cream and sugar, shakes her head and squeezes her eyes shut. "Good gracious," she says.

Arthur scoots up to the table, the squeal of his chair legs silencing Evie and Reesa.

To break the sudden silence, Celia opens the refrigerator and says, "Has Reesa offered you pie, Father?"

Reesa frowns, causing deep creases to cave in at the top of her nose, and shakes her head at Celia. "Didn't seem the time for pie yet."

Father Flannery, still staring at Ruth, says, "Pie'd be real nice, Mrs. Scott. Real nice about now."

Arthur waves off Celia's offer of pie and focuses on Father Flannery. "Seems there must be something the church can do for Ruth," he says. "Something that can help her out of this mess."

"It's not that easy, Arthur. They've been married a good many years."

Arthur exhales and runs a hand through his hair, pushing it off his forehead.

"What about 'inadequacy of judgment'?" Celia says, leaning into the refrigerator and pushing aside a carton of eggs. No pie. She stands, hands on her hips, and looks around the kitchen. Everyone at the table is staring at her.

"One of my aunts on my mother's side married quite young," she whispers.

"That's good, Celia," Arthur says, motioning for her to hand him the coffee pot. "Does that work for us, Father?"

Celia unplugs the pot and passes it to Arthur. Without even tasting it, Celia knows the coffee is strong, too strong, because

127

that's how Reesa makes it.

"That sounds like just what we need," Arthur says. "Inadequacy of judgment."

Father Flannery holds his mug out to Arthur and presses his glasses back onto the bridge of his nose. He sniffs as he does it, as if this will cement them into place. "That doesn't seem to apply, Arthur. Not after twenty years."

Reesa nods, closes her eyes and pats her forehead with a yellow handkerchief while pushing her mug across the table toward Celia to be refilled. Giving the pot a little shake to show that it's empty, Celia mouths the word "sorry" and steps to the counter to brew up some more.

"Sure it applies," Arthur says. "Inadequacy of judgment. We all had it."

He turns to Celia for help.

"They were very young when they married, right?" Celia says. "Young people don't always make good decisions." Then, dropping one spoonful of coffee into the percolator, shorting the batch by two scoops of grounds, she checks inside the stove. Still no pie.

"They were both adults," Father Flannery says, sipping his coffee. "Young, but adults. Both of sound mind. No undue force, I presume. How's that pie coming, Mrs. Scott?"

"Won't be but a moment, Father." Celia stands at the head of the table, her hands still on her hips. "I can't imagine what I've done with it."

Father Flannery leans back in his chair, his large stomach pushing against the edge of the table. "Did you try on top of the refrigerator? Some of the ladies like to keep their pies on top of the refrigerator."

"Father, there has to be something." Arthur rubs the heel of both hands into his eye sockets. "Undue force. There was undue force. You know what happened. We were all under undue force. That was a terrible time. For everyone."

Slipping behind Arthur, Celia grabs onto the top of the refrigerator and stands on her tiptoes. Nothing.

"I know. I know," Evie says, clapping her hands together. "The Clark City men took your pie."

"Please stop talking about Clark City," Celia says.

"But the kids at school say they escape all the time. Ian's brother says they catch rides on the backs of pickup trucks and jump off when they see the lights of the first house. Everyone knows that our house is the first house after the Brewster place. They take food. Like pie. They take food because they're hungry. Ian says a Clark City man cooked up old Mrs. Murray on the radiator, that radiator right over there in the corner. And Ian says a Clark City man stole Julianne Robison right out of her very own house."

"Good Lord in heaven," Reesa says. "Hush, child. No one took that pie. I put it on the front porch to cool."

Celia spins on her heel to face Reesa. "Reesa, why didn't you . . ." but Arthur gives her a look that tells her he's heard quite enough about the pie.

"So what about that undue force, Father?" Arthur says.

Father Flannery stands, staring at Ruth so hard that she can't lift her head. "I think we owe it to Ray to include him in these discussions. An annulment is no small matter."

"It damn sure isn't," Arthur says, also standing.

He is taller than Father Flannery by a good four inches but not nearly as round. Both men rest their fingertips on the edge of the table — Father Flannery on one end, Arthur on the other.

"Ray will not set foot in this house," Arthur says. "I'll make that perfectly clear."

"Understood," Father Flannery says. "We'll meet in the church, then. Or perhaps down at the café. When Ray returns, he'll have his thoughts heard." Father Flannery shakes his head as Elaine walks through the front door carrying the pie. "Thank you anyway, Mrs. Scott, but I'll need to be getting along."

"Twenty years this has been going on, Father. Where has the church been for twenty years?"

"And you, Arthur? Where have you been for twenty years?" The Father takes his coat from the back of the chair and drapes it over his arm.

Reesa pats her shiny, red cheeks with her handkerchief, the same one she carries into church every Sunday. Elaine sets the pie on the table and stands by Ruth, who is still staring at the floor. Celia crosses her arms and starts tapping her foot, but she stepped into her lavender slippers when they came back from their walk, so it doesn't make any noise.

"Thank you for the coffee, Mrs. Scott." The Father nods in Celia's direction. "Reesa," he says, giving Reesa the same nod.

"Father." From her spot near the stove, Ruth lifts her head, but not her eyes, and pulls her thin sweater closed as she wraps her arms around herself. "Maybe an annulment isn't called for."

"Ruth," Arthur says. "What are you saying? It damn sure is called for. That man beat you nearly senseless."

"Arthur," Celia says, holding up a hand, and then in a softer voice, "Ruth, you deserve some peace. I agree with Arthur. No matter what, that home is not safe for you."

Ruth touches the ends of her new hair. "I don't know if I can ever go back to him, Father." She turns toward Celia and Arthur. "And I'm so grateful that you've taken me in. But I can't have an annulment."

Father Flannery crosses his arms and rests them on his large stomach. "A married woman goes back, Ruth. She doesn't live in her brother's house."

"Yes, Father. I'll stay married, but I don't know if I can go back."

"Ruth, honey," Celia says, running a hand over Ruth's new hair. "You don't have to do this."

"Damn sure don't," Arthur says.

Reesa crosses her arms and frowns because Arthur cursed again in front of Father Flannery.

"They're right, Ruth," Father Flannery says, sniffing and pushing his glasses into place. He stands for a moment, fixing his eyes on Ruth as if the Holy Spirit will sort out the problem if he gives it time and a little silence. "Is there something more I should know?"

"No, Father. Nothing."

Still staring at Ruth, Father Flannery pulls on his black overcoat, tugs his collar into position and puts on his hat. "Reesa," he says, keeping his eyes on Ruth. "Anything I should know about?"

Reesa stretches her chin into the air and pats the folds of her neck. With her eyes closed and her face tilted toward the ceiling, she says, "No, Father. Nothing at all."

"What about you, son?" Father Flannery says.

Inside the back door, Ian and Daniel stand, their cheeks red, their noses shiny because they've just come in from the cold.

"Do you think there's anything else I should know about?"

Daniel steps into the kitchen and looks around the room. "I'm not sure what you mean, Father. We were out" — he pauses — "walking."

"Yeah," Ian says, stepping up next to Daniel and rubbing his right hip with the heel of his palm. "Out walking." Ian seems to shrink every time Celia sees him.

"Very well, then." Father Flannery steps away from the table, pushes in his chair and tips his hat. "It seems we've no need to discuss this matter again." He turns toward Ruth. "I'd like to see you in church tomorrow."

"She hasn't been in church, Father," Arthur says, "because Ray beat her face to a pulp."

Father Flannery ignores Arthur. "Tomorrow, then. You're looking well, Ruth, quite well. Doesn't she look pretty with her new hair, Eve?"

"I'm Evie, Father."

CHAPTER 10

Leaning against the kitchen sink, her arms crossed, Celia taps her lavender slipper. Reesa struggles out of her chair and shuffles after Father Flannery. Facing Celia on the opposite side of the kitchen, Arthur stands, his arms also crossed. He lowers his head, staring at her from under the hood of his brow, and as his mother passes, he steps aside to make room without ever taking his eyes off Celia. Daniel and Ian have disappeared down the basement stairs, and Elaine, pressing a finger to her lips so Evie won't speak, leads Evie out of the kitchen toward her bedroom.

Celia and Arthur stand facing each other, not moving and not speaking. The floor creaks as the two girls pass, and when they have closed the bedroom door behind them, the house falls silent. Ruth slips into the small space between the side of the stove and wall, puts her hands in her apron pockets, and lowers her head. Outside, Father Flannery's engine starts up. Arthur straightens to his full height and unfolds his arms.

"Put a pot of water on to boil. The big pot," he says and follows his mother outside.

Celia, thinking Ruth is no bigger than Evie tucked between the wall and the stove, turns toward her and smiles. When they moved into the house, the stove sat square in the corner, but Reesa moved it because she said a person would want to get a mop in there. She said Mrs. Murray wasn't much of a housekeeper, God rest her soul, so it wasn't any wonder the stove was pushed to the wall.

"I'll speak to him," Celia says, wrapping her arms around her own waist. "You don't have to go back, Ruth. We want you here. With us. It will work out. It will."

Ruth nods. "I have to tell him. Waiting won't solve anything."

"No," Celia says, as gently as she can, as gently as if she were talking to a sick child. "Let me."

Ruth nods again. She starts to slip back into her corner until Celia pulls out a chair from the kitchen table and motions for her to sit. In the months since they moved to Kansas, Ruth's skin isn't as pale as it once was and she lifts her eyes when she talks to a person. Now, after sitting for a few minutes with Father Flannery, she is back again, to the frail woman, carrying a cold strawberry pie, who stepped so carefully out of the truck on the Scotts' first day in Kansas.

"Thank you," Ruth says. "I'll put on Arthur's water and start supper."

Celia smiles, and walking onto the back porch, she grabs her blue sweater from the row of hooks near the door. She breathes in dry, cool air and presses the sweater to her face, smelling her own perfume. It reminds her of Detroit because she doesn't bother with perfume here in Kansas. Taking a few more deep breaths, as if the cold air will fortify her, she pulls on the sweater, straightens the seam of each sleeve and steps outside.

The sun has moved low in the sky, hanging barely above the western horizon. Soon the chilly afternoon will be a cold evening. She would have said it smelled like snow had she still lived in Detroit, but she doesn't know if Kansas snow smells the same. Pulling her sweater closed, she walks down the three steps toward Arthur, who is standing just beyond the garage.

"What do you need the hot water for?" she calls out when she thinks she's close enough to be heard. Crossing in front of the garage where she can see around the far corner, she stops and drops her arms to her side. Arthur and Reesa stand at the edge of the light thrown from the back porch. "What are you doing?"

"Ma brought it for supper," Arthur says, without looking up.

"I have soup and sandwiches," Celia says. "Ruth is laying it out."

"Now we have chicken."

Standing next to Arthur, Reesa tugs on a rope tied off to a beam jutting out a few feet from the garage's roofline. On the other end of the rope, a chicken hangs, suspended by its wiry, yellow legs. The bird is nearly motionless, seemingly confused by its upside-down perspective. Arthur grabs its head and Reesa steps back.

"I need to talk to you, Arthur," Celia says, buttoning her sweater's bottom two buttons and squinting at the bird. "Reesa and I both need to talk to you."

Gripping the chicken's head in his left hand, Arthur raises his eyebrows at his mother. Reesa dabs the folds on her neck with the corner of the yellow and white checked apron tied around her waist.

"Whatever it is can wait," Arthur says. He lifts the knife in his right hand as if inspecting the sharpness of the blade and rotates it slowly. It would have sparkled if there had been any sunlight.

"No," Celia says, glancing at Reesa. "It really can't."

In one seamless motion, Arthur rolls the bird's head slightly to the left and pulls the knife across its neck. He doesn't cut so deeply that the head comes loose in his hand. Instead, it dangles as if hanging by a hinge. Blood shoots out, a bright red, perfectly shaped arch. Celia lets out a squeaking noise and stumbles backward. After the initial gush, the blood slows and begins to flow in a smooth steam that lands in a bucket that Arthur kicks a few times until it is in the right spot. Then, with the knife still in his hand, he says to Celia, "Okay, what is it?"

Celia watches the bird, both of them motionless. Steam rises up where Arthur made his cut.

"Well," Arthur says. "Tell me. We've only got a few minutes. That water ready?"

"No, I, well . . . Ruth is putting it on."

Reesa tugs at the knot tied around the bird's legs, testing that it's strong enough and then walks to the house. "We need the water for scalding, Celia."

It is the kindest tone she has ever used

with her daughter-in-law.

"Ruth is pregnant," Celia says before Reesa can disappear into the house.

Arthur drops both hands to his sides and his chin to his chest. The porch light shines on the threesome, throwing a long thin shadow that falls at Celia's feet. Reesa stops at the bottom step leading to the back door. The bird, hanging upside down, its neck slit open, its blood slowing to a trickle, begins to beat its wings in the air. Celia jumps backward, Arthur doesn't move and Reesa dabs her neck again with her apron. The bird wildly flaps its wings one final time before hanging lifeless. Its heavy body sways on the end of the rope, but eventually, even that motion slows and stops. The only movement, tiny feathers, floating, spinning, drifting on the cold night air.

"What is it doing?" Celia asks, backing out of the yellow light.

"Dying," Arthur says. "What do you mean, pregnant?"

Celia glances at Reesa, who has taken her foot off the first step, and says, "Just that. She's pregnant."

"You knew?" Arthur asks Reesa.

She nods.

"How is she pregnant for God's sake? She's forty years old."

Celia takes two steps forward, back into the light, and cocks one hip to the side. "Forty is not so old."

"God damn it, Celia, this is not funny."

Reesa steps closer. "It's not meant to be funny, son. Ruth has carried three other babies over the years, but never more than a few months." She lowers her eyes and shakes her head. Her shoulders droop and roll forward, and her chin rests in the rolls of her neck. When she exhales, her breath shudders.

"Then why now?" Arthur asks. A dark shadow covers his lower jaw and his eyelids are heavy. He pulls off his leather gloves, and holding them in one hand, he shoves his knife in his back pocket and rubs his forehead.

"What do you mean, why now?" Celia says, holding up a hand to silence Reesa. "Why, it's not so hard to figure out. Look at her, after these months since we came back. She's happy. She's healthy. Thank God, she's healthy again. This baby has a chance."

"What chance does it have with a father like Ray?"

"Arthur," Reesa whispers.

Celia takes another few steps toward Arthur. "You will never call this baby an 'it' again. He or she will have everything. Love and a home and . . ."

Arthur leans forward, spitting his words in Celia's face. "What home? Our home? Christ, this is why she won't annul the marriage, isn't it? He'll be back, you know. You think this is how it'll be? Well, it won't. He'll be back and he'll want his wife and that baby."

"You don't know that. Maybe he'll stay in Damar."

Celia doesn't believe it even as she says it. She wishes the rumors were true. She wishes Floyd Bigler had shipped Ray off to Clark City where he'd rot and die behind those block walls. Instead, Arthur and William Ellis, Ray's other brother-in-law, threw Ray in the back of William's pickup truck. William, having had his fill of Ray's drinking over the years, agreed to keep him just long enough. When Arthur came home stinking of vomit and whiskey, Celia asked him what "long enough" meant. Arthur shrugged as he stripped off his clothes. "Let's hope long enough is long enough," he had said.

"He'll be back, Celia," Arthur says. "That's for damn sure. You think any father is going to let his son grow up in another man's house?"

"We don't know it will be a boy."

Arthur throws his gloves on the ground. He looks like he wants to kick something, but the only thing close enough is the dead bird. He seems to think about it but kicks the ground instead.

"God damn it, Celia. Boy or girl, it doesn't matter. You think I'll be able to keep Ray away? I have to work, you know. I can't be here every God damned second. You think I'll be able to keep Ruth and her baby safe?"

Celia closes her eyes but does not back away. She can smell the aftershave Arthur splashed on for Father Flannery, his worn leather gloves, his wool jacket. He is more of a man now that they are living in Kansas. She would never say it to him, imply that he was less before, doesn't even like to think it. Waiting until Arthur has finished shouting and the night air has fallen silent again, Celia opens her eyes.

"Yes," she says, hoping Arthur will protect them all, hoping he is stronger here in Kansas because he has to be. "Yes, I do."

Ruth stands on the back porch. Father Flannery's cologne hangs in the air, rich and spicy. She breathes it in, the same smell as Sunday morning mass. Waiting for her face to heal, she hasn't been to St. Anthony's for almost a month. Celia and Arthur were afraid of the things people might say if they saw the swollen eyes, blackened and bruised cheek and jaw, split lip. They wanted to protect Ruth. In the early years of her marriage, Ruth had been afraid, too. The first time Ray put a fist to her, she hid her cuts and bruises with powder and scarves, but then she realized that people knew the beatings were inevitable, and shouldn't Ruth have known the same?

Through the screened door, she listens for Arthur and wishes he would come inside so they could deliver the food to the Robisons. Going there takes her close to church, a half block away, takes her close enough to feel like she's still being a good Christian. Now that Ruth is living with Arthur and his family, she rides along on the deliveries to the Robisons and walks the food to Mary's front door, even puts it in the refrigerator and cleans out the spoiled leftovers, mostly things Ruth brought the week before. She hopes Arthur will still take her, that he won't be too angry.

Mary never asks why Ruth suddenly started coming along, but she knows. Everyone knows. And every week, as Ruth jots baking instructions on the notepad near the telephone, Mary Robison tells Ruth to stop troubling herself, that all this lovely food won't bring Julianne home. Nothing, nothing, will bring Julianne home. Ruth always smiles as best she can and continues to bake the pies and mix up the casseroles, because once, when they were so much younger, she and Mary Robison were friends, and Eve, too. The three of them, when they were young, when they had long, shiny hair and bright, clear skin, before husbands and children, they were friends. Because this is true, and because maybe, even though she can't let the thought settle in long before blinking it away, Ray did something awful to Julianne Robison, Ruth still takes the food.

Ruth's first lie to Floyd was a reflex. Standing in her kitchen, Ray watching her, Floyd slapping his beige hat on his thigh, she nodded yes, that Ray had been home all night. She lied out of reflex, the same as a person raises her arms to her face to fend off a fist. She lied because she was afraid not to. A hundred nights, Ray had gone off without telling Ruth where he was going, and a hundred nights, no little girl went missing. But the night Julianne disappeared was different. Ray remembered that once he had been happy. He remembered Eve because she skipped out of Mother's back door and stood right before him, smiling up with blue eyes and tender, flushed cheeks. Only it wasn't Eve, it was Arthur's youngest, and as deeply as Ray must have remembered what it was like to be happy, the moment he walked back into his own home with Ruth, he must have remembered that it was all gone.

"Daniel," Ruth says, when a set of footsteps stop at the top of the basement stairs. She turns toward the house. "Is that you?"

"I'm sorry, Aunt Ruth." He is about to close the door but stops when he sees her. "I didn't see you out there."

Ruth points across the porch to the gun cabinet in the back hallway.

"I think you didn't quite get things put away as you'd like," she says. "I thought you might want to tend to it before your father does."

Daniel scoots a small stool to the cabinet. He can't quite reach the top where Arthur keeps the key to the lock.

"Thank you," Daniel says, as the cabinet hinges creak and the lock snaps into place. He stands in the dark doorway, the kitchen light shining behind him. "I think your water is boiling. Do you want me to shut it off?"

"No, thank you."

Outside, Arthur and Celia's voices fade.

"You know, Daniel," Ruth says. "Your father, when he was a boy, he was a good shot. I'll bet you are, too. In your blood, you know. Are you a good shot?"

Daniel shuffles his feet and clasps his hands behind his back. "Yes, ma'am," he says. "I guess I am."

"So I thought."

"Is everything okay, Aunt Ruth?" Daniel asks, setting the stool back in its spot on the porch. "Aren't you cold out here? Do you want a coat or something?"

Ruth smiles into the darkness to hear Daniel's voice sounding more like a man's than a boy's. These children, Daniel and Evie, are ghosts of her childhood. Daniel so like his father, a young Arthur, working his way toward manhood, hoping nothing will derail him. Evie, resembling Eve so strongly, sometimes too painful to look at.

"I'm fine," she says, nodding toward the cabinet. "You take care."

"Yes, ma'am."

Beyond the screened door, Mother stands at the bottom of the stairs, her back to Ruth. As large as she is, Mother looks small there at the bottom of the steps, her head lowered, her shoulders sagging. Past Mother, on the far side of the garage where the porch light barely reaches, Celia and Arthur have started arguing again. Arthur's voice is tired and desperate, as tired and desperate as Ruth has felt for twenty years, while Celia's words have hope, the same hope that Ruth knows is growing inside her. She felt this hope with all three of her babies, but knew, even from the beginning, that none of them would live. Ray had beaten them out of her. Not literally. He never even knew they had been there, nestled inside Ruth's womb. Sadness killed those babies.

The first pregnancy had surprised Ruth. The baby didn't come in the beginning months of marriage. Ray had needed her, almost loved her in those early days. Together, they had mourned Eve, leaving no room for anyone else, not even a baby. Soon after, Arthur left to follow the best jobs in the country all the way to Detroit, but really Father drove him away, and Mother said no one should judge what's between a man and his son. Best to let things rest in peace. Arthur's leaving was the end of something for Ruth and Ray, or maybe it was the beginning of living with the truth, and this was when Ruth felt the smallest inkling of her first baby. She didn't arrive with a vengeance, this baby that Ruth was certain was a girl, but with a blush of nausea, a hint of fatigue, the tiniest shift in perspective.

And then she vanished, bled away in spots and smudges that Ruth bleached out in the bathroom sink while Ray slept in the next room. Then came the second and third. Something inside her, some glimmer of hope, sparked those babies that bled away like the first. Ruth knew that without hope, no more children would live or die, so she gave up on happiness and a future and that was the end of her babies — until now.

CHAPTER 11

Standing together in the small hallway between the kitchen and the back porch, Celia straightens Arthur's collar and centers his newly polished belt buckle.

"That should do it," she says, patting his chest with both hands.

"Do I have to go?"

Celia lifts up on her bare toes, kisses him once, but he pulls her back, and starts the kiss over. He smells like soap and the after-shave Celia insisted he splash on after she made him shave.

"Yes, you have to go," she says, wiping away the pink smudge on his upper lip and giving him one more quick kiss before ducking and slipping from between his arms.

"I shouldn't be leaving all of you alone." Arthur looks into the living room where Ruth and Evie are thumbing through a photo album, a table lamp throwing a warm circle of light on them. "Where's Daniel?

150

He should be in here."

"He's outside," Celia says. "Watering Olivia like you told him to. We'll be fine, Arthur. Everything will be just fine."

In the week since Celia told Arthur that Ruth is pregnant, he has begun locking doors, something he didn't bother with once they left Detroit and the smell of burnt rubber behind. He comes home every day now over his lunch break, has fixed the locks on two windows, and has started barking at everyone in the house, except Ruth, about things like scooting in chairs and shutting off lights.

Celia takes his wool coat from the hook near the back door, and in a whisper that won't carry to the living room, she says, "You go have fun. It'll be nice that you and Jonathon spend some time together."

"I see the boy damn near every day."

"That may be, but you're going all the same. Enjoy. You always fare well in poker. We'll all be fine, just fine."

"You lock up after I leave?"

"Good enough," Celia says, kisses him one last time on the cheek and locks the door behind him.

Evie runs a hand over the patchwork quilt lying across her legs as Aunt Ruth points to a pink satin square.

"This was your Aunt Eve's first Sunday dress," she says. "And this piece is from your father's favorite pair of jeans. He wore them until his belly was bursting through the buttons."

Evie snuggles into Aunt Ruth, laughing at the thought of Daddy having such a big belly and searching for another quilt square that might belong to Aunt Eve. "What about this?" she asks, tracing a line around a lavender calico patch.

Aunt Ruth shakes her head. "That was mine. An apron from a doll I once had."

Next, Evie points to a green velvet square, and as Aunt Ruth nods and smiles, Evie leans forward and brushes one cheek against the soft fabric. It doesn't smell like Aunt Eve should smell, sweet like a flower, but instead like Grandma Reesa's basement.

"Eve's favorite Christmas dress," Aunt Ruth says. "She tried to wear it to school once. Mother caught her at the back door because the hem stuck out from under her overcoat. My goodness, Mother was angry." Aunt Ruth pulls a red leather photo album back onto her lap and flips through the early pages. "Here. Yes, here is a picture of that dress."

Evie wraps the quilt around her shoulders

like a cape and presses closer to Aunt Ruth's side. "Do you think she looks like me?" Evie asks, staring down on a little girl standing on the steps of St. Anthony's, the same steps where Evie plays every Sunday morning while Daddy and Mama say their hellos.

Touching the little girl's picture, Aunt Ruth smiles through closed lips, nods but doesn't answer.

"Did Aunt Eve love the green dress as much as she loves the dresses in her closet?"

"Yes, I'm sure she did."

"Why does she have all of them?"

Aunt Ruth flips to the next page, and pointing out another picture of Aunt Eve, this one of a little girl sitting alone on Grandma Reesa's back porch, Aunt Ruth says, "They were to be for her wedding."

"Aunt Eve is getting married?" Evie pops up on her knees and pulls the quilt to her chin.

"Not now, sweet pea. A long time ago. She wanted each bridesmaid to have her own special dress."

"So she made all of them?"

"We all did. She and I and Mary Robison. Mrs. Robison was, is, a wonderful seamstress." Aunt Ruth flips to another page in the album. A picture pops loose as she lets the new page fall open. "Here we are," Aunt

Ruth says, tucking the picture back into the white corner tabs. "All three of us. Your Aunt Eve wanted to work with Mary one day, to be as good a seamstress."

Evie leans forward and squints into the face of Mrs. Robison. The picture was taken long before she grew up and had Julianne, long before Julianne disappeared. The kids at school say that since Julianne is gone, maybe the Robisons will take Evie in trade. Maybe since Julianne was the same age as Evie and had the same white braids, the Robisons will make Evie move in with them. That very Tuesday at recess, Jonah Bucher said he was going to change Evie's name to Julianne. He said everyone liked Julianne better than Evie anyway. Every other kid said the same and they called Evie by her new name all through recess until Miss Olson made them stop or else she'd call every mother and father of every kid in school.

"What about you, Aunt Ruth? Did you want to sew, too?"

Aunt Ruth pokes both of her thumbs into the air. "I'm all thumbs. Never as handy as those two."

"Which dress were you going to wear?"

"I hadn't decided. Whichever Eve chose for me, I suppose. But she was young when we made those dresses. Only dreaming of a wedding. Someday."

"And did she get older and get married?"

Aunt Ruth closes the photo album, patting the top cover three times and resting her palm there. "Sometimes things don't work out like we plan." She smiles down at Evie.

"Well, I think they're the most beautiful dresses. Maybe I'll use them when I get married one day."

"That would make Eve very happy."

In the kitchen, Mama is making cooking noises — pots and pans rattle and the gas stove goes *click, click, click* as Mama turns on the back burner that doesn't work so well. Elaine is off with Jonathon's mama, learning how to make piecrusts. Evie wonders if Mama's feelings are hurt because Elaine would rather learn about pies from someone else's mama. Smelling pot roast and roasted new potatoes, Evie lays her head on Aunt Ruth's shoulder. The radiator kicks on, making her think of old Mrs. Murray, but only until she remembers that Mama said Mrs. Murray died in a hospital bed. Mama said no one was cooked up on that radiator or any other. Evie closes her eyes and lays her right hand on Aunt Ruth's stomach.

"Too soon," Aunt Ruth says. "In a few

155

weeks, maybe."

Pressing her face into Aunt Ruth's arm where her nose and lips will warm, Evie knows the baby is too tiny to feel. Mama says it's like a bean now, like a lima bean, not a pinto bean. She says everyone has to take care of Aunt Ruth so her baby will have strong lungs and a healthy heart. Mama says when the baby comes, Aunt Ruth will move into Elaine's room and Elaine will move in with Evie, so Aunt Ruth and her baby can have a room all to themselves. Evie wants to ask Aunt Ruth if she will have a blue baby and will Daddy put it in the oven like they did Ian's baby sister. When Ian's dad first thought the baby was dead, he put her in the oven until the doctor could come. That's what Ian said. And then when they opened the door, she was kicking and breathing and all the way alive again. Instead of asking Aunt Ruth if her baby will be blue, Evie closes her eyes and imagines she is like the princess and the pea, except she will feel the lima bean in Aunt Ruth's stomach.

"Who was Aunt Eve going to marry?" Evie asks, thinking that she probably isn't a princess because she can't feel anything except the buttons on Aunt Ruth's dress.

Taking a deep breath, Aunt Ruth lifts her chin, and says, "A good man. She was supposed to marry a good man."

Daniel is glad Dad went out for the night. If he were home, he'd be yelling at Daniel about something. That's what Dad does most of the time now, yells at Daniel. Poking his potatoes and pushing them around the plate, he silently curses when one tumbles onto the red tablecloth Evie put out. Now he wonders if he'll have to confess to Father Flannery or does it not count if you only think the bad words without actually saying them. Waiting until Mama isn't paying attention, Daniel picks up the potato chunk and scoots his plate to cover the buttery stain. He glances up, wondering if anyone saw. Aunt Ruth winks and presses a finger to her lips.

Daniel tries to smile back, but every time he looks at Aunt Ruth since she caught him sneaking the rifle, he thinks she knows about the prairie dogs. He imagines that she saw him shoot that animal for no damn good reason, blow its head clean off. That's what Ian had said. He went back and found that prairie dog with its head blown all the way off and showed it to his brothers so they would stop calling Daniel a city kid. Ian said he lifted that dead prairie dog up by its tail and flung it as far as he could, and his brothers had said Daniel must be a pretty good shot to blow off the head but leave the rest. Biting his lower lip and stabbing a new potato with his fork, Daniel wishes he'd never shot that prairie dog because he can't ever take it back. But he did, and Aunt Ruth knows he has been taking the gun without permission.

"What was that?" Evie says, her mouth full of a buttered biscuit.

Daniel shakes his head at her. "Stop talking with food in your mouth."

Evie swallows, rocking her head forward to help the biscuit go down. "There's nothing in my mouth."

"There," Aunt Ruth says, staring past Daniel toward the kitchen window. "Is that what you heard?"

Mama pushes back from the table. "I didn't hear anything," she says, pressing out the pleats on the front of her dress. It's what she does when she's nervous, like when Dad went to meetings in Detroit about the Negro workers or the news showed pictures of burned-up cars and buildings. She hasn't done it much since they moved to Kansas where they haven't seen a single Negro or burned-up car. Also, Mama doesn't wear skirts with pleats much anymore.

Evie nods, wiping a crumb from her chin.

"That. What is it?"

Daniel turns in his seat, careful not to scoot his chair or make any noise. Through the white sheers, the window is black. "It's the wind."

"That's not wind," Evie says too loudly.

Daniel frowns and quiets her with a finger to his lips.

Again, as loudly as before, Evie says, "That was not wind. That was a thud. There it is again."

"Yes," Mama says, still pressing her pleats. "I hear it."

"I think Daniel's right." Aunt Ruth tucks her napkin under the lip of her plate and stands. "Probably the wind. But to be on the safe side, I'll check."

"No, Aunt Ruth," Daniel says, standing with a jerk and catching his chair before it tumbles over. "I'll go. I should go."

"Both of you stay put," Mama says. "I'll have a look."

Evie jumps out of her seat and leaps toward Mama. "Let Daniel go," she says.

Mama wraps an arm around Evie and kisses the top of her head. All four turn when something bumps the side of the house just below the kitchen window. The white sheers tremble.

"Someone's outside the window," Evie

says, her voice muffled because her face is pressed into Mama's side.

"Na," Daniel says, watching the curtains, waiting for another thud. "There's no one out there." But he's not sure now. The wind doesn't bump into the house or stumble around the side yard. He wishes his heart weren't beating so loudly because he can't hear over it. He hates his God damned beating heart when he can't hear over it, even tries to hold his breath to slow it down.

At the sound of another thud, Evie pulls away from Mama and points at the window. "It's a Clark City man," she says. "That's what it is." And then she whispers. "It's Jack Mayer. He's back and he's looking for food. Maybe he's even got Julianne with him."

"Shut up, Evie," Daniel says. "It's not a Clark City man. And it's not Jack Mayer. Shut up."

As the weather has turned colder, the pond near the curve in Bent Road has shrunk, dried up like every other pond around. Every time Daniel passes it, he looks for the tips of Jack Mayer's boots, thinking he might be lying at the bottom of that pond. Daniel has never seen him, and Ian says he won't because Jack Mayer has to be alive since he's the one who swiped Julianne Robison.

"Kids, please," Mama says. "Stop your bickering."

Aunt Ruth tucks Evie under her arm while Mama sidesteps toward the back door.

"I'm sure it's nothing," Mama says, but she's inching toward the porch like she definitely thinks it's something. "Evie, you stay here with Daniel and Ruth. I'll go . . ."

"No, Mama." Daniel walks around the table, tilts his head down and looks up at Mama from under his brow. "I'll give a look-see."

It's what Dad would have said.

Stepping onto the porch, Daniel pulls the door closed behind him and exhales a frosted cloud. He yanks on the knob again, listening for the click that tells him the door is latched good and tight, and once he hears it, he thinks he should feel more like a man. Instead, he slouches and pulls up the collar of Dad's flannel jacket because maybe whoever is stomping around their side yard will mistake Daniel for Dad. Mama says that by his next birthday, Daniel will be as tall as Dad. Keep eating Aunt Ruth's good cooking, she says, and you'll be as broad, too. He gives Aunt Ruth, Mama and Evie a thumbs-up sign through the window in the back door and walks across the screened-in porch. With the toes of his leather boots hanging over the first stair, he sees nothing or no one as far as the porch light reaches.

Ian had clipped out the latest story about Jack Mayer from page 3 of the *Hays Chronicle,* the shortest one yet, and one of many that didn't make page 1. After nearly four months, police now believe Jack Mayer has either left the Palco area or has died of exposure. Authorities at the Clark City State Hospital declined to comment on Jack Mayer's whereabouts, other than to say the hospital had successfully implemented new security measures. After Ian showed Daniel the article that he kept under his mattress along with a dozen others about Jack Mayer, he took Daniel out to the barn and showed him a wadded-up flannel blanket and empty tin can that were hidden behind three hay bales and an old wheelbarrow. Daniel kicked the can across the dirt floor. Ian stumbled after it, his right side lagging behind because he didn't have on his new boots, picked it up, and placed it back with the blanket because he thought the tin can and blanket were proof positive that Jack Mayer was alive and well and living in the Bucher barn. "No need to make a crazy man mad," Ian had said as he cleaned the brim of the can with his shirttail.

At the bottom of the stairs, Daniel tucks

his bare hands under his arms, stomps his feet, and looking toward the barn, he wonders if Jack Mayer might just be hiding in there. Mama found the pie that Aunt Ruth baked for Father Flannery and nothing else has gone missing in the house except the last piece of Evie's birthday cake, which Daniel knows Dad ate but won't admit. Ian said their food disappeared all the time. He said Jack Mayer stole it right off their kitchen counter. He said Jack Mayer crawled through their windows every night and helped himself to corn muffins, sliced pork roast and ham and bean soup. Daniel asked Ian how he could be sure Jack Mayer was eating all that food with so many brothers living in the house. Ian had said that no man alive could eat like Jack Mayer because Jack Mayer is a mountain of a man.

Walking into the center of the gravel drive, Daniel turns in a slow circle. Mr. Murray's old rusted car is still parked behind the garage. Mama complains about it, says it's dangerous to have around with young children in the house, but Dad says the children aren't so young anymore and he'll get to it when he gets to it. Next to the garage, near the fence line, stands the chicken coop that Dad and Jonathon started to build. Halfway through, Mama said no chickens because she saw the mess they left at Grandma Reesa's and because she didn't want to have any more dead chickens hanging in her yard. Dad told Jonathon he could have the wood if he'd tear it down.

Beyond the three-sided chicken coop, and opposite the garage, the barn seems to lean more than it did when they moved in. Wondering who or what is hiding out there, Daniel wishes he had grabbed his rifle. But what if it is Julianne? What if Jack Mayer stashed her in there? More than ever, Daniel wishes Mama would have slammed into Jack Mayer at the top of Bent Road. But Ian's right. Mama must not have hit him, at least not directly, because he swiped Julianne Robison and a dead man couldn't do that. If Mama would have hit Jack Mayer, Daniel wouldn't have to worry about accidentally shooting Julianne and blowing her head off like he did when he shot that prairie dog.

Twice, in the week since he killed that animal, Daniel has gone shooting with Ian. He can sneak the gun out and return it, tucked back in the gun cabinet, fingerprints wiped off the glass, lock snapped in place, before Dad gets home from work. Shooting tin cans and glass bottles instead of prairie dogs, Ian says Daniel is a good shot, a damn good shot. Ian says that if Daniel practices a lot, almost every day, he will be the best shot of any kid around. Daniel wants to run back to get that gun but it seems so far away now. He hears the sound again, a loud thud coming from the side of the house near the kitchen window.

Taking slow, quiet steps, Daniel slides one foot in a sideways direction and meets it with the other as he walks in an arch that will lead him around the side of the house. He looks behind and ahead, behind and ahead, and at the edge of the boundary laid down by the porch light, he stops and listens. In between wind gusts, he hears something crushing small patches of dry grass. There is a rustling sound, another thud, his own heartbeat. He leans to his right, peering around the side of the house without stepping outside the yellow light. He leans farther, bending forward and bracing himself with one hand on his knee. Something moves. A dark shadow. Daniel stumbles, stands straight and presses a hand over his heart.

He knows now that Sheriff Bigler didn't haul Uncle Ray off to Clark City but that he is living in Damar for as long as William Ellis will keep him, hopefully until he's dried out. When Daniel thought his uncle was locked up, he imagined Uncle Ray might escape like Jack Mayer and live off stolen leftovers. Before he knew Uncle Ray was living far away in Damar, Daniel would lie awake at night, listening for him. He would imagine opening his eyes and seeing Uncle Ray's face pressed against his window, his breath fogging the glass so Daniel couldn't quite see which way that bad eye was pointing. But Damar was a whole other town and Uncle Ray was with a whole other family. This is when Daniel began to imagine Jack Mayer's face pressed against his window. His breath would be cold and wouldn't fog the glass like Uncle Ray's. Then Christmas got closer, and Mama said the best store for wool fabric was in Damar, and since she needed a new dress for the holidays and Damar was only a few miles away, the whole family should go. Now, standing in the middle of the gravel drive, the thud ringing in his ears, Daniel doesn't know if he should be afraid of Uncle Ray, who isn't living so far away, or Jack Mayer.

His heart has begun to beat so loudly that Daniel isn't sure if he hears the next sound. If he had been sure, he wouldn't have looked around the corner again. Instead, he would have waited and listened or maybe run for the house, but his beating heart is like cotton in his ears, so he braces himself again and leans forward. Even though the maple that grows along the side of the house is bare, all of its leaves raked up and burned in the trash barrel, the moonlight shining through the empty branches is not enough to light up anything that might be hiding. The light from the kitchen throws shadows on the nearest branches but doesn't reach any farther. If the something is still there, hiding under the window, it isn't moving now, and Daniel can't tell it apart from the rest of the darkness. He takes a step forward, watching, listening, and the shadow shifts again.

Holding his breath, Daniel thinks he hears something. It sounds like metal clanking against metal, like a chain tangled up with itself. He crouches down, pressing both palms on the ground. The back door doesn't seem so far away now. He could run to it, reach it in a dozen steps, but he can't move. Yes, that is the sound of a tangled-up chain, broken handcuffs. He hears breathing — heavy, hot, long breaths — and footsteps crushing dry dead grass, footsteps kicking up gravel.

Hoping to see that Aunt Ruth and Mama are watching him through the screened door, he glances at the porch, but sees no one. Aunt Ruth's stomach is beginning to swell but she covers it with aprons and Elaine's skirts that she cinches up at the waist with safety pins. "You're in charge," Dad had said to Daniel before leaving. Mama had smiled and brushed the hair from his eyes. For a moment, Daniel imagines Julianne is sneaking around the side of the house. He could be the one to find her. He'd be a hero and kids would like him without even caring how good of a shot he is. Daniel drops his head again, knowing the breathing and chains and footsteps are closer even though his heartbeat has filled his ears. He decides it can't be Julianne because she wouldn't be wrapped in chains. He inhales, raises his eyes first and next his chin. Still crouched, his palms pressed to the ground, he cries out and falls backward.

"God damn," he says. "Good God damn already."

Standing at the corner of the house, her head inside the yellow cone of light, Olivia the cow looks down on Daniel. She seems to nod at him, and then she drops her snout to nuzzle the cold, hard ground. Her lead dangles from the red leather neck strap, the buckle and bolt-snap rattling like loose chain. Dad will be angry if he sees someone forgot to take it off.

"Good God damn."

CHAPTER 12

Over and over in her head and a few times aloud, Celia says, "It's the wind. Nothing but the wind." But she isn't sure. In Detroit, she feared firebombs, tanks and the Negro boys who called Elaine, none of which banged up against the side of her house. Being so new to Kansas, she isn't sure what she should be afraid of, but whatever it is, it is walking through her yard. Shivering because she is wearing only a thin cotton dress and no stockings on her feet, she leans forward. On the other side of the screened door, across the driveway, Daniel sidesteps around the house. If he goes much farther, she'll lose him in the dark. Behind her, Ruth and Evie huddle together inside the back door that Celia made them lock. She cups her hands together and blows hot breath inside them to warm herself.

"Can you see him?" Evie calls from inside. Through the frosty pane of glass, her voice is muted. She has wrapped both arms around Ruth's waist and must be standing on her tiptoes to see out the window.

Celia reaches to open the screened door, but Evie cries out and presses her face into Ruth's side.

"Okay, okay," Celia says, letting go of the cold handle and leaning forward until she feels the imprint of the mesh screen against her right cheek. "There he is. I see him." Exhaling a deep breath and motioning for Ruth to open the back door, she says, "It's Olivia. Olivia got out again."

Ruth flips the deadbolt lock, and Evie skips across the cold wooden floor and lands at Celia's side. Celia wraps one arm around her and opens the screened door so they can both see. A cold breeze slaps them in the face.

"See?" Celia says. "He's walking her back. Looks like her lead is on. Did you put it on without remembering to take it off?"

Evie shakes her head. "I took it off. I'm sure I did," she says through chattering teeth. "I walked her a little. But I took it off."

Celia watches Daniel until he and Olivia have disappeared through the gate and into the barn. When she can no longer see them, she steps back and motions for Evie to join her on a nearby wooden bench. Ruth flips a switch that floods the porch with light, then steps inside for a moment and reappears with Celia's lavender house shoes, one in each hand. She waves the slippers, which makes Evie giggle, tiptoes across the porch and slips the fuzzy shoes on Evie's bare feet.

"We shouldn't really walk Olivia," Celia says, wrapping both arms around Evie. "Left to her own, she could get hung up on that lead." Evie nods as Celia tightens the pink ribbon tied at the end of her single braid. "Be careful to always lock up the gate and take care to do as you're told. You know Daddy would be upset about this."

"Will we tell him?" Evie says, twisting and frowning.

"I don't see the need. I'm sure Daniel will slip it off and lock things up good and tight."

Evie smiles, nods, and lowering her head, she says, "I guess it wasn't Julianne out there, huh?"

Celia lifts Evie's chin with her index finger. "No, honey. It wasn't Julianne. Did you really think it was?"

"Just hoped, is all."

Celia glances at Ruth across the top of Evie's head. "Yes, I guess we all did. How about we say an extra prayer tonight? Especially for Julianne."

"Yes," Evie says. "An extra prayer."

"Good enough, then." Celia winks at Ruth and together they help Evie untangle her slippers from the hem of her robe so she can stand.

Evie giggles over the size of Celia's lavender slippers on her own small feet. "Thanks," she says once she has straightened out her legs and planted both slippers on the ground.

Celia smiles, gives a few tugs on the belt around Evie's terrycloth robe and, hearing footsteps on the stairs and the squeal of the screened door opening, she turns her smile toward Daniel.

"Ruth."

Ruth stands.

"Ray," she says.

In the beginning, in the very beginning, Ray felt badly for hitting Ruth. Over many morning cups of coffee, Ruth told Celia about the twenty years she had spent with Ray. When he would wake the day after, sober, he wouldn't remember the black eye he had given Ruth, the split lip, the bruised cheek. He would look at her, puzzled at first, and then apologize. "It's hard," he would say. "So damned hard." Ruth said she understood. She understood well enough to dab powder on those early

173

bruises, withdraw from cake sales with an upset stomach when her lips were split open and swollen, cancel lunches with her mother and father because of one of her headaches when Ray had blackened her eyes. As the years passed, Ray began to wake, sometimes before he was fully sober, and say, "This is your doing as much as mine." Finally, just, "This is your doing."

"Why are you here, Ray?" Celia says, stepping in front of Evie and gently pulling Ruth backward a few steps.

Ray glances outside at the sound of Daniel's footsteps on the stairs, and then turns back, placing one hand on the doorframe, one foot on the threshold. "Thought it might be around dessert time. Thought about a piece of Ruth's pie."

"We're not having pie tonight." Celia takes another backward step toward the house, keeping Ruth and Evie behind her. Daniel walks halfway up the outside stairs but says nothing because Celia shakes her head — a tiny movement, but enough.

"A cup of coffee maybe," Ray says, moving aside, and with the sweep of one hand, he motions for Daniel to pass by.

Slipping between Ray and the doorframe, Daniel stops next to Celia. He takes a half step forward, trembling.

"Too late for coffee," Daniel says, his voice barely more than a whisper.

"What's that you say?" Ray fills the doorway but doesn't cross the threshold.

Under his brown hat, Ray's hair is clean and the skin on his face is smooth. Standing beneath the light of the single bulb hanging in the center of the porch, his hat shading his face, he looks like a younger Ray, like the one Celia saw on her wedding day. Besides being clean-shaven, his face is swollen. She knows it's the alcohol, years and years of it, that makes his cheeks and jowls puffy and the lid over his bad eye droop. He is hanging on, probably by nothing more than his fingertips. He is sober, barely.

"I didn't hear your truck," Ruth says.

"Truck's dead. Walked up here thinking Arthur could give me a jump." Ray takes off his hat, holds it at his side and tips a nod in Evie's direction. "Thought about that pie, too."

"Arthur's not here." Celia takes Daniel's arm. "Try again tomorrow."

"Dan can help, can't he?" Ray glances at Daniel. "Arthur letting you drive a truck these days?"

The tips of Ray's boots hang over the edge of the threshold, teetering there, not quite

175

inside, not quite out.

"No, Ray."

Everyone turns toward Ruth. She is almost lost, wedged between Celia, Evie and Daniel. Celia glances down at Ruth's belly. She has wrapped both arms around her waist as if hugging herself for warmth.

"Daniel can't help," Ruth says. "You try tomorrow. When Arthur is here."

"Sure is a cold one tonight," Ray says, winking his droopy lid at Celia. His good eye travels from her face down to the white buttons on the front of her dress. It lingers there long enough to be too long, while his cloudy eye floats about. "I can wait maybe. Nothing wrong with waiting a spell. Arthur be home soon?"

Caught between two answers, Celia can't reply. It's something about the way he stares at her, taking his time, letting his eyes linger, maybe imagining something. Wondering if the others notice and feeling ashamed for it, she shuffles her bare feet and wraps her arms around her waist.

"Tomorrow," Celia finally says. "You'll see Arthur tomorrow and no sooner."

Daniel yanks off Dad's jacket, slings it toward an empty hook where one arm catches, leaving the jacket to hang lopsided, and stomps into the kitchen. Evie follows, still clutching Mama, while Aunt Ruth flips the deadbolt and waits in the window until Uncle Ray's footsteps go down the stairs. Then she hurries into the kitchen ahead of Daniel, Mama and Evie, and leaning over the sink, she stands on her tiptoes so she can see out the window.

"He's leaving," she says quietly, as if Uncle Ray might hear, and hoists herself onto the counter for a better view. "He's at the end of the drive now."

"Ruth," Mama says, dropping Evie in her seat at the kitchen table. "Please get down before you hurt yourself."

"He's gone for sure," Aunt Ruth says, holding her swollen belly as she slides off the counter. "I'm so sorry for the trouble. So sorry if he scared anyone."

"I wish it had been Julianne," Evie says, poking her cold potatoes with the tip of her butter knife. "I wish we would have found her."

Mama tilts her head, sighs and brushes the hair from Evie's forehead.

"I should have had my rifle," Daniel says.

Mama's head lifts straight up. "Daniel, no," she says, reaching out to him.

He steps back and doesn't take her hand.

"Don't say that. Don't you ever say that."

"A rifle would have stirred up a mess," Aunt Ruth says, moving to stand next to Mama. "A real mess."

"Would have made a mess of Uncle Ray."

"Daniel," Mama whispers. "That is never a good answer. Never. You did fine, just fine. Your father will be very proud of you."

Daniel leans a bit so he can see between Mama and Aunt Ruth. "You left that strap on Olivia," he says to Evie. "She's a cow, not a dog."

"Did not," Evie says, stabbing a potato and waving it at Daniel. "Did not. Did not. Did not. You left the gate open."

Daniel steps forward, wanting to grab Evie by the hair and fling her onto the porch, fling her all the way back to Detroit.

"It's done now, kids," Mama says, pressing a hand to Daniel's chest. And then in a quieter voice, as if she's afraid Uncle Ray might hear, she says, "Let's please not argue."

"Sorry, Mama," Evie says.

Mama smiles, but it isn't a real smile. It's the smile she gives when Grandma Reesa walks through the back door without calling first.

"Have a seat, Daniel," she says. "Our dinner has gone cold. I'll warm it up."

"I'm not hungry," he says.

As he walks across the kitchen, the floor-boards creak under Daniel's feet. Near the back door, he sees the gun cabinet. It's locked up tight. His rifle is resting just where it should be. Next time, he'll be thinking. Next time, he won't forget. Mama calls out again, offering to warm up a few extra rolls for him. He waves her off, doesn't bother with an answer, and once inside his bedroom, he pulls the door closed behind him. Waiting for the click that will tell him it has latched, he walks to his bed, lies down, pulls his knees to his chest and closes his eyes. Next time, he'll be ready.

CHAPTER 13

Holding her hands behind her back and taking small sideways steps, Evie edges toward Grandma Reesa's living room. Everyone else is sitting at Grandma's kitchen table, talking about how upset they are that Uncle Ray came to the house last night wanting Aunt Ruth's pie and a jump for his truck. Three times, Mama has told Daddy what a fine job Daniel did watching over all the ladies of the house, but Daniel is still feeling bad about it because he pulls away when Mama tries to brush back his bangs. In between chopping up a chunk of meat, Grandma Reesa keeps filling everyone's coffee cup, and Mama frowns every time Grandma drops another sugar cube in Daddy's. Aunt Ruth sits with her hands folded in her lap, not saying much of anything. Occasionally, she lifts her hands from her lap, wraps them around her coffee mug and takes a sip.

"Maybe you should go along and play upstairs, Evie," Mama says.

Evie unclasps her hands, bites her lower lip and says, "Okay."

"Mind the stairs in those stocking feet," Grandma Reesa calls out.

At the sound of Grandma's voice, Evie stops running and breaks into a slide that sends her floating through Grandma's over-stuffed living room. She sweeps past the coffee table, knocking over a frame, rattling a few of Grandma's knickknacks, and stirring up the sour, moldy smell that always hangs over Grandma's house. At the bottom of the staircase, she grabs the small plastic tote that usually holds her favorite doll's dresses, the ones that Aunt Ruth sews for her. With a running start, she takes the stairs two at time, slides down the narrow hallway on the second floor and is breathing heavily when she pulls Aunt Eve's door closed behind her.

Celia waits until she hears Evie's footsteps overhead before asking her next question. "You know him best, Ruth. Was he sober?"

Daniel stands. "Barely," he says, stepping away from Celia and leaning against the refrigerator.

"What do you know about being barely sober?" Elaine asks. She is sitting across from Celia, and as she speaks, she gazes up at Jonathon, who is standing behind her. She looks like a woman about to be proposed to and Jonathon like a man about to do the asking.

"I know plenty," Daniel says. "I know I was there and you weren't."

Jonathon takes Elaine's hand, pats it and says, "I'd guess Daniel knows what he's talking about."

"He was sober," Ruth says, nodding at Daniel. "Just barely."

"Well, that's it then," Arthur says. "He's back."

Reesa, standing near her kitchen sink, reaches into an overhead cabinet, and as she takes down the saltshaker and seasons the cubed steak she has laid out on a cookie sheet, she leans back and whispers to Celia, "You should salt the meat before you grind it. Not after." And then, in a louder voice, "I think Ruth should move here. Farther away has to be better. Let the dust settle for a while." She sets aside the salt and, as she takes a bag of bread crumbs from the freezer, she says, "You do know how to make bread crumbs, don't you?"

Celia takes a deep breath and smiles. "Yes, Reesa. I do."

"Ruth isn't moving here," Arthur says.

Ruth exhales a little too loudly, which makes Celia chuckle. She presses her lips together when Arthur glances at her.

"I'll help out however I can, Arthur," Jonathon says.

"What was that for?" Elaine asks because she, like Celia, saw Daniel roll his eyes at Jonathon.

"Nothing," Daniel says, studying his dirty, chipped nails when Arthur looks up at him.

Reesa finishes scattering the bread crumbs over the cubed meat. "Do you want to watch, Celia?"

From her seat at the kitchen table, Celia says, "I can see fine from here. Thank you."

"Can we forget about the meat for a minute?" Arthur says.

"When you do this yourself," Reesa says, leaning toward Celia as if no one can hear, "you should freeze the meat first, after you've cubed it. Makes the grinding easier."

Celia flashes another smile and the meat grinder begins to whine.

"Are we done with the meat, everyone?"

Reesa, breathing heavily from the effort it takes to turn the hand crank, ignores the question.

"We're done," Celia says.

"This is bad," Arthur says. "He's awful close now, and pretty soon, you'll be big as a barn."

Celia exhales, nodding as Reesa tilts the bowl of ground meat so Celia can see what it's supposed to look like. "She won't be big as a barn," Celia says. "We can still hide that peanut for a few months."

Nearly knocking Daniel to the floor when he stands, Arthur pinches his brows at him as if Daniel is somehow always in the way. "And what then? A half a mile away, Celia. What then?"

"Why are you angry with me? I didn't invite the man back."

"I didn't say I was angry with you. I said . . ."

"Please," Ruth says, pushing back from the table with one hand and holding the other over her stomach. "Don't argue. Maybe Mother is right. Maybe I should live here. It is a good bit farther away."

"You plan on staying locked up here for good?" Arthur says. "Never going to church again? Never going to the store? That," he says, pointing at her stomach, "will be hard to hide in a very short time."

"That's uncalled for, Arthur," Celia says, starting to stand, but Ruth holds up a hand that stops her.

"I understand what you're saying, Arthur. Really, I do. But I'm not your problem to solve. Let me move here with Mother. It will be easier. I've done it before. Lived here for a time." She pauses. "Lived here until things quieted down. Besides, Ray was sober. Maybe he'll stay that way."

Daniel, one foot crossed lazily over the other, clears his throat. "Ian says some folks think Uncle Ray did something to Julianne. He says folks think Uncle Ray is that crazy."

"Ray didn't do anything to that girl," Arthur says, leaning against the wall. "Man's a damn fool and a drunk, but he didn't take that child. Folks are just trying to piece together the past."

"How do you know that, Arthur?" Celia says, feeling that she should believe her husband, have faith in him, know that he'll protect his family. But since the moment Ray stood on her porch, his one good eye staring at the buttons on her blouse, she doesn't feel any of those things anymore. She doesn't believe. She's heard the murmurs when she and Ruth walk through the deli in Palco, seen the sideways glances. More and more, people believe it. They believe Ray is the reason Julianne Robison has never come home.

"How can you be so sure?" she says. "We should be cautious, more mindful."

Outside, a truck rambles down Reesa's

driveway, stops and idles near the garage.

"Think your ride is here, Dan," Jonathon says, stepping back from the table for a better view out the kitchen window. "Yep, it's Gene Bucher."

"Can I go, Mom?"

Celia nods, motioning for him not to forget his overnight bag.

"Your toothbrush is in the side pocket," she calls out as the screened door slams. "And mind your manners."

When the truck passes by on its way back to Bent Road, Arthur sits again, but this time, instead of pressing his back straight and sitting with one foot cocked over the opposite knee, he leans forward and rests his head in his hands.

"Ray didn't do anything to Julianne Robison." He looks up at Celia, holds her gaze. "He didn't do it." He stares at her until she lowers her eyes. "And please don't you start talking about leaving," he says, turning toward Ruth. "You know damn well I can't have you living in this house."

The meat crank stops.

"I'll stay," Ruth says. "But only if you promise to listen to Celia. Don't be so sure of what you don't really know."

"Fair enough," Arthur says. "And in the meantime, no one, I mean no one, breathes a word about this baby." He scans the table, fixing his eyes on each person for a moment before moving on to the next. "I need some time to figure this out."

Celia smiles until the meat grinder begins to squeal again.

Evie opens Aunt Eve's closet slowly so that it doesn't make any noise, lays her tote bag on the floor and walks across the room to make sure the bedroom door is latched. On the table near the closet, the Virgin Mary stands, holding out her new hands, the ones Daddy glued on after Evie told him that Aunt Eve would surely be upset if they didn't fix her statue. Daddy asked Grandma Reesa first. She looked sad about it, but nodded and handed Daddy a tube of glue from the kitchen junk drawer. Evie runs a finger over a tiny spot of glue that Daddy didn't wipe clean. It has dried into a hard, clear bubble. Pressing on the door twice, Evie tiptoes back to the closet, lowers to her knees and unhooks the buckles on her tote bag one at a time.

Evie tries to love all of Aunt Eve's dresses the same, thinks that if she has a favorite among them, it will hurt Aunt Eve's feelings but she can't help herself. She loves the blue one best. She loves the three soft ruffles and the silky sash. She loves the silver flowers embroidered on the lapel that feel cool when she runs a finger over them. Most of all, she loves it best because, as she slips the dress off its hanger and presses it to her face, she can smell Aunt Eve. After taking one deep breath to make sure the flowery sweet smell is still there, she holds the dress by the shoulders, folds one side toward the center and then the other. Next, she drapes the dress over her left forearm and again over her right, lays it in the bag and refastens the two buckles.

CHAPTER 14

Daniel exhales hot breath into his cupped hands. Even through the old green sleeping bag that Ian brought up from his basement, the wooden floor is cold. The Bucher house doesn't have a heater, only a parlor stove in the main room off the kitchen where Ian's two older brothers are sleeping. In Daniel's house, they have a radiator, the same radiator that cooked up Mrs. Murray. Mama says that never happened, but every time it clicks on, he thinks he can smell roasted skin.

Watching the Bucher brothers through the opened bedroom door, Daniel wonders if they are the lookouts for Jack Mayer. He pulls his knees to his chest and scoots farther down into the sleeping bag that smells like someone peed in it. Ian had said the cats did it, but Ian's brothers laughed like Ian was the one who did the peeing. Next to Daniel, Ian is sleeping, and by the dual snoring coming from the bed in the

189

corner, so are the two brothers who share Ian's room. Daniel breathes through his mouth so he can't smell the sleeping bag and covers his ears so he won't hear Jack Mayer climb through the kitchen window to sneak off with Mrs. Bucher's leftover brisket and mashed potatoes.

By morning, the house is warmer. The Buchers may not have radiators in every room, but they have enough people in their family to warm up the place quickly. Daniel pulls on a gray sweatshirt and the wool socks Mama packed for him and follows Ian into the kitchen. It smells like his kitchen, except for the pee smell that is stuck to him. Coffee bubbles up, bacon pops on the stove and dish soap foams in a sink of hot water. Daniel presses down on his hair and straightens his sleeves.

"Good morning, sir," he says when Mr. Bucher nods in his direction.

Ian nudges Daniel and muffles a laugh. "Something quick for us, Ma," he says, walking on one flat foot and one tiptoe. Since he got his new boots, he walks that way whenever he doesn't have them on, probably so he can forget about being crooked.

"Yeah, Ma," one of the older brothers says. He scoops a handful of potato peels out of the sink and tosses them in an old coffee can. "Daniel's going to show us all what a great shot he is. Okay we use your .22, Pa?"

Mr. Bucher nods over his coffee cup.

One of the brothers, the biggest, and the only one wearing a hat, turns in his seat. Mrs. Bucher doesn't seem like the type of mother who would allow hats at the table. Except when the man turns, it isn't a Bucher brother.

"Morning there, Dan."

Uncle Ray raises his cup and tips his hat.

Celia pretends to sleep as Arthur slips out of bed. She knows they'll be late to church if they don't get a move on, because the sun is high enough in the sky to fill their bedroom with light. Once Arthur has left the room, Celia pulls the blankets to her chin and tucks them under her shoulders. The front door opens, closes, and opens again and Arthur stomps his heavy boots. He only uses the front door when he is gathering wood for the fireplace from along the side of the house. When the night temperatures dip so low, the radiator can't keep up, but Arthur will have a fine fire going in no time. Newspapers crackle as he twists them into kindling and, after a few minutes, the sweet, rich smell of a newly started fire drifts into the bedroom. The house will warm quickly, but Celia wonders if even then she'll want to get up.

She pushed Arthur away last night, gently, but firmly, and this morning, she pretended sleep. She should tell him but won't because it'll only make things worse. She can't tell him how Ray looked at her out there on the porch the other night, how she can see what Ray is thinking and that it makes her ashamed. Or maybe Arthur would think her silly, or worse yet, selfish for thinking of herself instead of Ruth. Maybe she is silly and even selfish, too. Whatever this feeling is, shame or guilt, it'll pass. No, she can't tell Arthur, because if she really made him understand, if she made him appreciate that in the privacy of a single glance, a man can tell a woman that he is coming for her, he'd kill Ray. Just like that. He'd kill him.

"Morning, sir," Daniel says.

Uncle Ray looks at Mr. Bucher with his good brown eye, while the bad eye seems stuck on Daniel. He laughs and says, "Would you look at the manners on my nephew?" Then he stands and gives Daniel a solid pat on the back. "Thank you for the hot wake-me-up, Ida. Real kind of you."

Nodding to Mr. Bucher, he says, "Monday morning, then?"

Mr. Bucher stands and shakes the hand Uncle Ray has held out to him.

"Are you off so soon, Ray?" Mrs. Bucher says, poking her bacon with one hand and balancing her new baby on her hip with the other. "Bacon's almost done."

Uncle Ray holds up a hand and shakes his head. "No, thank you all the same. I'll leave you to your family, Ida."

"Will we be seeing you at church this morning?" Bouncing the baby so she won't fuss, Mrs. Bucher spears the fatty end of one piece of bacon with her fork, flips it and lays it back in the grease.

"Well, how about that. Today is Sunday, after all." Uncle Ray says it as if Sunday snuck up on him. "I guess I'll get along and put on something decent."

"We'll all be glad to have you back," Mrs. Bucher says.

Uncle Ray gives Daniel another pat on the shoulder. On the last pat, he holds on. "Nice manners. Real nice."

Mr. Bucher walks Uncle Ray outside and waits there until a truck engine fires up before walking back into the kitchen. Mrs. Bucher gives him a nod, or maybe she is taking a deep breath and they both turn to Daniel.

"Ray's going to be working with your father and me," Mr. Bucher says.

The clatter of silverware stops and chewing mouths go quiet. The brothers sitting around the table and the one scooping potato peels and the one poking through the cabinets and Ian pause to listen.

"Down at the county. Driving a grader, I suppose. Your pa called last night. Asked me this favor. Said he'd be sending Ray over this morning."

Mr. Bucher glances over at Mrs. Bucher again.

"Your pa's a smart man, Dan. Keeping that snake where he can see him." Mr. Bucher takes another sip of coffee. "Got a warmer-upper for me?" he says, holding his cup out for Mrs. Bucher to fill. "You understand that, Dan?"

"Yes, sir. A snake. I understand, sir."

After eating two biscuits dipped in maple syrup, something Mama would never let him do, Daniel follows Ian and four of his brothers outside. His gut hurts, maybe because Mrs. Bucher's biscuits were soggy in the middle, or maybe because he can still feel Uncle Ray's hand squeezing his arm, or maybe because he isn't as good a shot as

Ian says he is. Before they left the kitchen, Mrs. Bucher said they had only a half hour because everyone needed to wash up before church. She said the whole mess of them was a sorry sight, so a half hour and no more. Daniel pulls his coat closed and, slapping his leather gloves together, thinks that if the older boys go first there won't be time for him. Mrs. Bucher will call them inside and Daniel will shrug and say, "Maybe next time." Walking toward the barn, four Bucher brothers leading the way, Daniel wishes he had never seen Uncle Ray and that Ian hadn't told his brothers that Daniel is such a great shot — a good shot maybe, good for a city kid, but great means better than everyone else, better than every other brother.

"Who goes first?" Daniel whispers to Ian.

One of the brothers, the smallest, walks ahead of the group and lines up three cans on the top rung of the wooden fence that runs between the house and the barn. The wind blows down one of the cans. He kicks it aside, slaps his bare hands on his thighs and shouts, "All ready. Fire it up."

Ian nudges Daniel forward.

"Me?" Daniel says. "You want me to go first?"

"Sure," one of the brothers says.

The two oldest brothers didn't bother following everyone outside. Instead, they are watching from the porch. "Hurry up with it, already," one of them shouts.

"Here," says the brother who's two years ahead of Daniel in school. He hands Daniel a rifle. "You use a .22, right? This is a good one. Got a nice straight sight."

"Yeah, Daniel," Ian says. "Show them. Show them what a great shot you are."

Pulling off his gloves and tossing them on the ground, Daniel takes the rifle. The morning air is cold and wet, making his neck and arms stiff. He squints into the sun rising above the bank of trees on the east side of the house, shakes out his hands and bends and straightens his fingers. "Sure, I'll go first," he says. "Those cans over there?"

"Yeah," says Ian. "Get them both."

Daniel brings the rifle up to his shoulder, rests his cheek against the cold wood, and with one eye closed, his breath held tight in his lungs, his feet square under his shoulders, he fires, flips the bolt action and fires again. Both cans fly off the railing.

"Got them," Ian shouts.

"Na," says the youngest brother and the one with the loudest mouth. "The wind knocked them off."

"That wasn't the wind," Ian says. "Daniel

196

got them both. Clean shots."

"Na, just the wind," another brother says.

"Doesn't matter," Daniel says, flips on the safety and hands the rifle back to the brother who gave it to him.

"It was the wind," a brother shouts from the porch.

"I'll show you," Ian says, limping toward the spot where the two cans landed.

A few of the brothers laugh and mimic Ian's awkward gait, while the brother holding the rifle takes aim like he's going to shoot Ian.

"Told you," Ian shouts, holding up the cans. "Clean shots both."

The brother holding the rifle lowers it. "Okay," he says. "So maybe you are a good shot."

Ian limps back to Daniel's side. "Told you so."

The same brother says, "Maybe good enough to go hunting with us."

All of the brothers nod, including Ian.

"Pheasant. They're open season right now," the brother says. "So are quail. Or you might get yourself a prairie chicken."

"Sure," Daniel says, remembering the prairie dog's head that he blew off and the body he left behind. "I mean, not today, because it's church."

"Na, next time you come over. In a few weeks maybe," the same brother says. "What do you think, Ian? Maybe when we get a warm snap, so you're not so stiff."

"I'm not stiff. I'll go anytime."

The brother laughs. "Yeah, well, in a few weeks. Next time you're over. We'll all go hunting. Then we'll see what a great shot you are."

"Yeah, a few weeks," Daniel says. He looks at Ian and tries to remember if he is more crooked since it got so cold. "Anytime."

CHAPTER 15

Before sliding into the pew, Ruth genuflects, pulls off her stocking cap and smoothes her skirt. She winks at Evie as she does the same, and together, the Scott family sits. Celia and Elaine slide forward onto the kneeling bench and bow their heads in private prayer, and from their pew at the back of the church, Ruth scans the crowd. No sign of Ray's brown hat or his dark hair. No sign. He is home now and eventually he'll be back to church. But not yet. Not this morning. Ruth exhales, and feeling Mother's vibration through the wooden floor as she walks down the aisle, Ruth signals the family by waving one hand. Everyone scoots down one spot to make room.

"What a shame," Mother says, holding on to the back of the pew in front of them and groaning as she lowers herself. "What a darn shame."

"Mother, shhhh." Wondering if Arthur heard, Ruth looks down the line of Scotts.

Mother spreads out as she settles in, anchoring one side of the family, while Arthur anchors the other. She is angry because, once again, the Scotts are sitting in the last pew. One Sunday of every month, Father Flannery publishes a list that shows every family's contribution to the church, and Arthur's family remains at the bottom of that list, which means Arthur's family sits in the last pew. Arthur says the good Lord understands about a man starting his life over and tending to his family first. Mother says the Lord is good but that He's losing His patience.

"I thought I raised that boy to have some pride," Mother says, making the sign of the cross. Unable to kneel, she remains sitting, her hands in her lap as she bows her head.

Ruth shifts in her seat enough to shield Evie from the conversation. "Arthur has pride enough for ten men," she whispers, saying nothing more as Daniel peels away from the Bucher family, dips to one knee, makes the sign of the cross on his chest and slides past Mother and Ruth to take his place between Celia and Arthur.

Mother grunts, which means the conversation is over, so Ruth settles back into her seat. She turns and catches Elaine's eye. Elaine winks and gives a small nod of approval to the shiny pink lipstick she painted on Ruth's lips before church. Ruth, returning the smile, touches the corner of her mouth. When she looks back, Mother is frowning. Ruth lowers her eyes, slides forward onto the kneeling bench and with her forearms resting on the pew in front of them, she bows her head.

From this perspective, where she feels safe, she can see the two seats where Ray and she used to sit every Sunday morning. Ray always donated enough, barely enough, to keep their place in the third pew. Now, because Julianne is gone, the pew is empty except for Mary and Orville. Mary is thin, her shoulders frail and rounded, and Orville's hair has gone white.

Ruth has known Mary all of her life, but she didn't meet Orville until her thirteenth birthday. That was the day Orville stepped off a westbound train and walked into the Stockland Café. The café was crowded because dark clouds were rolling in from the south, the kind of dark clouds that meant rain. Every other dark cloud, for years it seemed, had been dust rolling in from Nebraska or maybe Oklahoma. Folks were tired of shoveling it from their homes and draping their babies with damp dish towels. The day Orville Robison arrived, folks were set to celebrate because those dark clouds meant rain. Finally, rain.

Wearing a tattered, old straw cowboy hat with a small red feather stuck in the black band, Orville walked into the café, carrying with him two leather suitcases. He had dark hair, almost black, and skin that made folks think he probably had some Indian blood in him. Sitting together at the booth nearest the front door, Eve, Ruth and Mary were sipping unsweetened tea, and the moment Orville Robison set down his suitcases, Mary smoothed her hair, bit into a lemon and said she liked that red feather. She said it meant good luck, said that feather was what brought the rain clouds. She said she'd marry any man with a feather like that tucked in his hat.

By the time Orville finished his first cup of coffee, he had noticed the three girls, just like they had noticed him. Leaning on the café counter with one elbow while a young Isabelle Burris dropped two cubes of sugar in his coffee, Orville Robison tipped the brim of his hat toward the girls' table. Even at thirteen, Ruth could see that he noticed Eve most of all. She had the kind of beauty that made people stop to stare at her as if they might never see such a thing again. Orville was no different from most folks who saw Eve for the first time. He looked at her once, at all of them sitting around the table, glanced away, and as if surprised, as if unable to trust his own eyes, he looked again. The second time, he looked only at Eve. But Eve was barely fifteen, so within the amount of time it took Orville Robison to finish that cup of coffee, he settled on Mary, the oldest of the three — nearly nineteen. Six months later, Mary Purcell became Mary Robison. Together, the three girls hand-stitched Mary's wedding gown and she wore a red feather tucked in her garter.

Lowering her eyes and pressing her hands together, Ruth prays that Julianne will come home to Mary and Orville soon. So many years, the two of them went without a child, but then, like the rain that came after so many years of dust, Julianne was finally born. Even after Mary's hair had started to gray and her friends were counting grandchildren, Julianne was born. Ruth finishes her prayer for Julianne with a silent "Amen," makes the sign of the cross to bless the Robison family in God's name, opens her eyes and there is Ray, sitting in the third pew.

Celia reaches across Elaine and Evie and

touches Ruth's forearm. Her face is pale again, like that first day she slid out of Ray's truck, a strawberry pie cradled in her hands. Ray nods in their direction. His eyes, even the bad one, rest on Ruth. With the tiniest motion, no more than raising one eyelid, he calls Ruth to him. Placing a hand on the back of the pew in front of them, Ruth turns toward Celia again. Celia squeezes Ruth's arm until she can feel the small, tender bone through her wool overcoat. Ruth lowers her head and scoots forward on the wooden bench.

"I can't believe he would sit right there next to Mary and Orville," Celia whispers and shakes her head. "You stay put, Ruth." And then to Arthur, she says, "Tell Ruth to stay put."

It seems that all through the church, in the pews in front of Ray and behind, people begin to scoot in whichever direction will take them farther away from the man they all think took Julianne Robison. Ever since the men from the state came to help Floyd search for Julianne, people have become more convinced than ever that Ray took the child and that he killed Eve all those years ago. Getting their first glimpse of him since he came back home, they raise their hands to their mouths so they can whisper unseen.

They take sideways glances. They turn away if Ray catches their eye. Some of them even give Ruth a fleeting look, just long enough to pucker their lips at the sour taste of it all and shake their heads, but Mary and Orville Robison seem to take no notice. Instead, they stare at the empty spot where Father Flannery will soon stand, without even a glance toward Ray.

"Arthur," Celia whispers again. "Tell Ruth to stay put."

Arthur tips his head in greeting to Ray, and with the smallest nod, he motions Ruth to go.

Celia sucks in a mouthful of air, and with Daniel caught between them, she hisses at Arthur. "What? What are you doing?"

Arthur, his eyes forward, says, "The man needs his pride."

Celia reaches across her girls, grabs Ruth's coat sleeve before she can stand, and says, "I do not care about his pride. How can you do this?"

Still staring straight ahead, as if he's not really talking to his wife, Arthur says, "He can't do her any harm here. It's only for the service."

Ruth places her hand over Celia's. "It's okay," she whispers, then smiles at Evie, kisses her on the cheek, and says, "See you after."

Evie reaches out to hug Ruth. "We'll make brownies still?"

"Yes, sweet pea."

Celia, now gripping only the very edge of Ruth's sleeve between two fingers, says, "Arthur, please."

Arthur says nothing else, and without even having to look at Ruth, he motions again for her to go.

Sitting with a rigid back, Celia turns away from Arthur. Ruth gives her a wink, stands and slips past Reesa. Once outside the pew, she wraps her frail arms around her waist, cinching her long coat closed, hiding her belly. All through the sanctuary, heads perk up. People shift in their seats, look from Ray to Ruth and back again as Ruth shuffles down the center aisle, her head lowered, her shoulders slouched forward. At the third pew from the front, she makes the sign of the cross and slips past Ray into her seat. As if she had been waiting for Ruth to be seated, the organist begins the hymn, calling them all to prayer. Ray drapes his right arm over the back of the pew and around Ruth's tiny shoulders.

After the organ plays its final note and the congregation closes and puts away their hymnals, Father Flannery steps to the pulpit. "The Lord be with you," he says.

"And also with you," the congregation responds in unison.

Several rows up, Ray is speaking the words along with the rest of the congregation, loudly, probably so that everyone can hear.

"My brothers and sisters," Father Flannery says. "To prepare ourselves to celebrate the sacred mysteries, let us call to mind our sins."

Celia doesn't look at Arthur, but listens for his voice. She hears every breath he takes, but he doesn't respond along with the others. "Lord have mercy," they all say.

Arthur is silent.

"Christ have mercy."

He says nothing. Even Daniel knows the words. He speaks them quietly.

"Let us pray," Father Flannery says, and Celia bows her head as he delivers the opening prayer.

"Amen," trickles across the church.

Arthur is silent.

Through the first and second reading, Celia watches Ruth and Ray, waiting for Ray to move or stand or take Ruth away. He doesn't. He sits motionless, his arm draped around Ruth, and as Father Flannery begins his homily, Ray slouches in the pew, pulling Ruth closer. A few seats down from Celia, Evie squirms, and Reesa quiets her by placing a hand in her lap. Next to Celia, Daniel slides down in his seat, settling in, probably tired from his sleepover at Ian's. Arthur sits straight, his feet planted squarely on the ground, his hands buckled into fists that rest on his thighs.

Finally, signaling that the end of mass is near, Father Flannery raises the host and breaks it. Several rows ahead, Ruth and Ray stand in tandem with Mary and Orville Robison, file out of the pew and walk to the front of the church. The other parishioners fall back and away from the awkward foursome, leaving a gaping hole in the procession. Orville holds Mary by the arm, helping her to walk, steadying her.

One by one, the parishioners step forward to receive the Eucharist, all the while keeping their distance. Celia stands to follow Reesa and Elaine. She pauses, waiting her turn, watching as Ruth steps up to Father Flannery, her head lowered, her hands cupped to receive communion. Though she can't hear them from the back of the church, Celia knows what they are saying.

"The body of Christ," Father Flannery will say, and Ruth will respond, "Amen."

Father Flannery lays the host in Ruth's hands. She places it on her tongue, bows to him and, with her head still lowered, she begins to follow the procession back to her seat. But before she can take a step, Father Flannery raises a hand, stopping her. He cups her chin in his palm, raises her face toward his, and smiles down at her. Ruth lifts her eyes to Father Flannery. Slowly, gazing down on her kindly, Father Flannery turns Ruth's head to show her profile to the congregation. Then he presses a thumb to her mouth and wipes away her pink lipstick.

Celia grabs onto the back of the nearest pew. Elaine stops.

"Mother," Elaine whispers, reaching for Celia's hand. "Did you see that?"

Celia takes Elaine's hand and looks back for Arthur, but he isn't behind her. He has returned to his seat and is staring straight ahead. A few of those having already received communion and returned to their seats close their eyes and shake their head, as if sorry to have seen such a thing but certain that it needed to be done. As Ruth passes by, closer now because Celia has made her way to the front of the church, a pink stain smears her lips and left cheek. She slips back into the third pew, kneels and, with her head lowered in prayer, takes a tissue from her coat pocket and wipes the lipstick from her face.

CHAPTER 16

Daniel grabs the back of Aunt Ruth's seat as Dad takes a sharp turn into Grandma Reesa's drive. He falls to the left, squishing Evie, and when the car straightens, they both sit up and Evie punches him in the arm.

"Get off me," she says.

In the front seat, Mama grabs the dashboard. "Are we in such a hurry?"

Dad doesn't answer until he has stopped near the garage and thrown the car into park.

"This family," he says, staring straight ahead, "will never go to St. Anthony's again."

The car is silent for a moment. Daniel watches for what Grandma Reesa might do because she is the one who cares the most about church. Instead, Aunt Ruth, whose lips are smeared with a pink shadow, speaks.

"That's not the answer, Arthur. Not on

my account."

Dad slams his hands on the steering wheel. Mama, who is sitting in the front seat, and Elaine, who is wedged between Aunt Ruth and Grandma Reesa, both jump. Aunt Ruth presses her hands over her mouth, Grandma Reesa lets out one of her groans and Evie's chin puckers. Then the car is quiet. Daniel closes his eyes so his chin won't pucker like Evie's.

"I think you should all hustle inside," Mama says quietly. "Evie, you and Elaine help Grandma set the table. Daniel, maybe you can start a fire. A fire would be nice."

Daniel nods. Aunt Ruth opens one door, Grandma Reesa the other. A blast of cold air shoots through the car as Evie and Daniel crawl out from the last seat in the station wagon. Before Daniel steps out of the car, he turns back. He wants to tell Dad that he saw Uncle Ray at the Buchers' and that he is going to drive a grader. He wants to ask him about hunting for quail and pheasant and if it's as easy to shoot a bird as it is to shoot a prairie dog. He wants to ask Dad to help him practice before the Bucher brothers take him hunting. But when Dad glares at him, Daniel knows not to speak. Instead, he climbs out of the car and closes the door behind him.

■ ■ ■ ■

Waiting until the others have gone inside, Celia inhales, filling her lungs with crisp, dry air, and lays her hands in her lap.

"You shouldn't have sent Ruth to sit with Ray," she says.

Arthur crosses his arms on the steering wheel and rests his chin there. "One good snow will bring down that roof," he says.

A few yards in front of the car, overgrown cordgrass, brown and brittle, has nearly swallowed up Reesa's small shed.

"Lot of good snows over the years, I suppose," Celia says. "And it's still standing. Help me understand, Arthur. Why do that to Ruth?"

Arthur is quiet for a moment, staring straight ahead. "Are you sorry I brought you here?" he says, still looking at the shed and not at Celia.

His dark hair has grown past his collar, making him look younger and somehow stronger. Celia stretches her arm across the back of the seat and weaves her fingers into the dark waves.

"No. Well, sometimes." She smiles but Arthur doesn't see. "I'm glad we're here for Ruth. And for our family. Elaine is certainly happy."

"Yeah, Elaine's happy." He nods but doesn't smile. "What about Evie and Daniel?"

Celia crosses her hands in her lap. "Happy enough. They'll make more friends along the way."

"That's where we found her," Arthur says, nodding toward the small shed.

"Who?" Celia says, sitting forward on her seat. "Do you mean Eve? You found Eve there?"

"Don't know why Mother keeps it around."

Celia falls back in her seat. "Right here. So close to home?"

Arthur nods and hangs his head between his arms. "The best I can do is to keep track of Ray," he says. "It's the best I can do. For now." He lifts his head and kneads his brow with the palm of his hand. "I'll take care of her."

Celia nods.

"I'll take care of Ruth," he says again, this time speaking more to himself than to Celia.

"Yes, Arthur, you will. I know you will." Wishing she meant what she said, Celia brushes her hand against his cheek. He leans into her touch. "People were different today. Did you notice? In church, they were different."

Arthur glances at her but doesn't answer.

"They think Ray did it." Celia pauses but no response. She looks back at the shed that seems larger now. "They really think he took Julianne, don't they?"

Still no answer.

"Because of what happened to Eve. Because Julianne was so like her."

"Small town. Nothing much else for folks to talk about."

"But what if he did? What if . . ."

"Ray didn't have anything to do with what happened to Eve."

"How do you know that, Arthur? How do you really, really know for sure?" Celia touches his hand. "You've always said how much Evie resembles your sister. Like Julianne did. If people really think . . . we have to consider it. For Evie's sake. My God, Arthur. You found Eve dead right here," she says, pointing across the drive toward the shed. "Right outside your mother's house. How can you be so sure? You promised Ruth, remember? You promised her you wouldn't be too sure of yourself."

Arthur nods and lays a hand over Celia's. "We'll go to Hays from now on. For mass, we'll go to Hays."

Celia needs to trust him. Now, more than

any other time, she needs to trust Arthur. And maybe she could have until she saw the looks on people's faces today. Most of them have probably known Ray all their lives. And all of them believe.

"I think it would be a nice drive for all of us," Celia says, trying to swallow the lump that has formed in her throat. "It's a lovely church."

Arthur nods. "Hays'll be fine."

Evie listens for Daniel in the hallway outside Aunt Eve's room. He is supposed to start a fire and that always takes him a good, long time. Grandma Reesa says the trees of Rooks County are plenty safe if the matches are in Daniel's hands. Hearing nothing, she opens her small plastic tote and lays it on the bed. She blows the dust out of the corners and looks around the room. The Virgin Mary won't fit inside the small case, and even if she did, Grandma Reesa would notice if Mary went missing. She is still mad at Daddy for gluing the hands back on, even though she said he could do it. Grandma says it's shameful to use plain old glue on the Virgin Mary and to leave clumps of it stuck to her wrists. Evie walks to the table where the statue sits and touches the seam where Daddy glued her left hand onto her left wrist. She lifts Mary, tilts her back and forth, feels the weight of her before gently placing her back on the table.

Pausing to listen for footsteps again, but hearing nothing except the faraway clatter of Grandma Reesa's pots and pans, she walks to the dresser next to the Virgin Mary's table, opens the small, center drawer and peeks inside.

"Are these your pictures?" she says.

She giggles, feels that she's done something naughty by talking to Aunt Eve like she's right here in the same room. Glancing around, she muffles another giggle with one hand and, with the other, lifts out a small silver frame with a picture of Grandma Reesa when she wasn't so big and a man, who must have been Grandpa. Evie holds the picture close to her face.

"He doesn't look so nice. Was he a nice dad?"

No one answers. After propping the picture up on the cabinet, she takes out another.

"Just look at you," she says, smiling down on a picture of Aunt Eve and Daddy. "Your hair is like mine. Look," she says, holding up one of her own thin braids. "Just like mine."

Evie sets the picture next to the first one

and pulls the drawer open a little farther.

"Who is this?" she asks, and then nods. "It's you, isn't it? You seem so happy. Look at how you're smiling."

Pulling one sleeve down over her hand, Evie wipes the glass in the last frame and holds up the picture. A young man, much younger than Daddy, is lifting Aunt Eve off the ground. His arms are wrapped around her waist and Aunt Eve is smiling and holding a wide straw hat on her head with one hand so it won't fall off. She is a girl, almost as old as Elaine, but not quite. The man is wearing a brown cowboy hat pushed high on his forehead. He has dark hair and is staring at Evie through the camera lens. Evie tilts her head left and right.

"He looks like Uncle Ray," she says, smiling. "He's so young and his eye is not so bad."

Then she remembers the Uncle Ray who came to the house wanting a piece of Aunt Ruth's pie and frowns. She looks around the room, at the closet full of dresses, at the Virgin Mary, at the window over the bed, wishing Aunt Eve would tell her the man isn't Uncle Ray, but she doesn't. Still hearing the clatter of Grandma Reesa's pots and pans, Evie puts the first two pictures back in the center drawer, closes it and lays the third picture, the one of Aunt Eve and the happy man, in her small bag.

CHAPTER 17

Sitting at the kitchen table while waiting for the potatoes to boil, Celia fans the book for a fifth time, stirring up a small breeze that fluffs Evie's bangs. On the count of three, Evie pokes a finger between the pages to mark the stopping point. The book, an early Christmas present from Ruth to Evie, falls open on the table. Celia takes a sip of spiced cider and stands to turn down the burner, leaving Ruth to study the book with Evie.

The family hasn't returned to St. Anthony's for a month of Sundays, and it is clear that mass in Hays doesn't suit the rest of the town, almost as if mass in a different church, even if it is catholic, isn't really mass at all. Even before the family had attended a single service at St. Bart's, the other ladies in town stared and whispered when they saw Celia and Ruth in the grocery store. Good Christians attended St. Anthony's every Sunday and good Christians didn't leave their husbands, for any reason. Arthur had promised Reesa that the family would go back to St. Anthony's for midnight mass on Christmas. Perhaps that would do a little something to make the town happy.

Though the rest of the town shakes their heads at the Scotts attending mass in Hays, it has kept Ruth out of Ray's sight and he seems content to see Arthur at work every day, at least the days that Ray makes it to work. Arthur says Ray is probably drinking again so he doesn't have time to worry about bringing Ruth home.

In the front room, Arthur struggles to force a crooked trunk into a straight tree stand, and out on the back porch, Daniel sifts through the boxes they moved from Detroit in search of the ones labeled CHRISTMAS DECORATIONS. The air smells of evergreen needles, sap and Ruth's home-made spiced cider, making the house warm and cozy even as the wind whips through the attic and the sky darkens with signs of snow.

Studying page 275 of Evie's book, Ruth wraps both hands around her mug, lifts it to her lips but doesn't drink, and makes a *tsk, tsk, tsk* sound as she shakes her head.

"Is that not a good one?" Evie asks.

"Very poisonous," Ruth says, glancing up

at Celia and tapping the page that lays open on the table.

Celia leans over the book and reads the caption beneath the picture — narrow-leaved poison wedge root. Ruth stops tapping and lays one hand flat over the picture, spreading her fingers so she hides the plant. She leans back in her chair, as if checking on Arthur and Daniel.

"It's good for her to learn about the poisonous ones, too, Ruth. To be on the safe side."

Ruth lifts Evie's chin so she'll look Ruth in the eye. "This is definitely a bad one. Very bad. One of the worst."

"Would it make me sick?"

"If you ate it, it would," Ruth says, swallowing and clearing her throat. "But you'd never, ever eat something you found growing outside."

"Except if it was in your garden."

"Yes, that's true." Ruth points to the white leaves that look like tiny tubes with pointed ends. "Cows eat them sometimes. Not often. They don't like the taste. But if they do, it makes them stagger and bump into things. The blind staggers. Very bad. You leave this one alone."

Evie nods and before Celia can sit again, the back door swings open followed by a gust of cold, dry air. Elaine and Jonathon stumble into the room, their cheeks and noses red, both of them breathing heavily.

"What's all the commotion?" Arthur says, pounding his leather gloves together as he steps into the kitchen.

Evie giggles at the pine needles stuck in his hair. Celia quiets her with a finger to her lips.

Elaine, still wearing her coat and mittens, sticks out her hand. "We're engaged," she says, gazing down at her brown mitten. "Oops." She pulls it off to show the new ring on her finger. "We're getting married."

With a sideways glance toward Arthur, Celia stretches her arms to Elaine. "Oh, sweetheart," she says, holding the tips of Elaine's fingers as she admires the new ring. "It's lovely." Then Celia lifts up onto her tiptoes and gives Jonathon a hug.

Celia had known this was coming. Not because of any secret Elaine had shared, but because of the speed at which Jonathon was building his scrap house. Every night at dinner, he came with news of his latest find — a load of two-by-fours, a few solid windows, a cast-iron tub. He was especially proud the day he finished the roof because he beat the first snow.

"Married?" Arthur says, holding his gloves

in one hand, both arms hanging stiff.

Ruth slides out of her chair, steps up to Arthur and, as she plucks the needles from his hair, she says, "Yes, Arthur. Married. Isn't it nice?"

Arthur makes a grunting noise but doesn't answer.

"Arthur," Jonathon says, sticking out his hand. "I intended to ask your permission. Planned to wait until Christmas day, but it snuck up on us this morning. I meant to ask you first."

Arthur brushes Ruth away and shakes Jonathon's hand.

"Have you talked about when?" Celia asks, wiping her hands on her apron. With her eyes, she motions to Arthur that he needs to hug his daughter. He doesn't seem to understand. "A date, I mean. Have you set a date?"

"Spring, I think. Before the baby," Elaine says, resting her hand on the small bulge in Ruth's stomach as the two share a hug.

"What do you mean, before the baby?" Arthur straightens to his full height. His shirt is lopsided because he has threaded his buttons in the wrong holes, his hair is spiked like a rooster's crown where Ruth pulled out the needles and his face is pale.

"I mean Aunt Ruth's baby," Elaine says,

her cheeks flushing red. "Before Aunt Ruth's baby comes along."

"Isn't that thoughtful, Arthur?" Celia says, also embarrassed at what Arthur was thinking, and also relieved. "But not until you've graduated." She turns toward Jonathon. "You understand, don't you?"

"I told her the very same."

"That doesn't leave us much of a window," Elaine says. "Aunt Ruth, your little sweet pea will be along in late June or early July, don't you think?"

Ruth smiles down at her stomach. "That's my best guess. But rest assured, she'll be along no matter when you plan this wedding, so you choose whatever date you like."

Evie leaps toward Elaine, grabbing for both of her hands. "I have a wonderful idea," she says. "The dresses. Aunt Eve's dresses. You can use them in your wedding. That's why she has so many. She made them all for her own wedding. Sewed them all by herself. With Mrs. Robison. Isn't that right, Aunt Ruth?"

Ruth looks between Celia and Arthur. "Yes, Evie, but . . ."

"She won't mind. She won't mind if Elaine uses them. Aunt Eve made them for her very own wedding. They're the most beautiful dresses ever. We'll go to Grandma

Reesa's. We'll go there and I'll show you. Can we go, Mama?" Evie stops jumping for only a moment. "And now that Elaine is getting married, Aunt Eve will come home again. She'll come to see Elaine get married. She'll come and see how much we look alike. She'll see that I'm little like her and I have braids like her. Won't she be surprised? Won't she?"

"Evie," Celia says, gripping Evie on both arms to stop her from bouncing. "There's plenty of time for wedding talk later. Let's not give Elaine too much to think about."

"I told her about Eve's dresses," Ruth says, stepping back to the table and lowering herself into her seat. "Told her what a wonderful seamstress Eve always was. She saw them in the upstairs bedroom and asked about them." She turns toward Arthur. "I hope you don't mind."

"Mama," Elaine says, nodding toward Evie. "Go ahead."

"Not today," Celia says. "It's your day."

Arthur lays his gloves on the table and runs both hands over his hair, smoothing it. "It's probably best," he says.

Taking a few deep breaths, Celia squats so she is Evie's size. "Evie, dear," she says. "I know Aunt Eve is very special to you."

Evie puckers her lips and nods. The very

225

roundest part of her cheeks and the tip of her nose are red, chapped from the cold dry winter air even though it's barely December. A lot of cold weather to go. The ends of her white, silky bangs catch in her eyelashes when she blinks. She tilts her head.

"She was very special to all of us," Celia says, inhaling and holding the air in her lungs to steady her voice.

"Aunt Ruth showed me her picture. So now I know what she looks like."

Celia takes Evie's hands. They are warm and soft and still smell like the pink lotion she rubbed on her arms and hands after her bath the night before. "We know how you love Aunt Eve's room and her dresses."

Evie nods and starts to smile, but then stops and nods again.

"Honey, Aunt Eve won't be coming to Elaine's wedding." Celia clears her throat. "Aunt Eve has passed on, Evie."

Evie crosses her arms and bites her lower lip.

"You know what that means, right?" Elaine asks, reaching a hand toward Evie.

Evie ducks away from Elaine, plants her feet shoulder width apart and rests both fists on her waist. "I'm not stupid. I know what it means."

"When she was quite young, Evie. She

died when she was quite young."

Celia glances at Arthur. He is leaning against the doorframe with his head lowered and his arms crossed. Less than five months in Kansas, and it must seem to Evie that everyone disappears or dies. First Julianne Robison and now Aunt Eve. In Detroit, Celia knew how to care for her children. She shut off the news when they came down for breakfast, locked the front gate, walked them to school. But here in Kansas, she doesn't know what to lock. Now her fears walk through her very own kitchen, stand on her back steps, sneak up on her at church. In Kansas, she doesn't know how to care for her children.

Celia stands from her squatting position and takes a few steps toward Evie. "We all miss Aunt Eve very much. We should have told you sooner, but we didn't know when it would be right."

"Why?" Evie asks.

"What, honey? What do you mean, why?"

"Why did she die?"

"No good reason why," Arthur says. "Never a good reason."

"Daddy's right," Celia says, tilting her head and smiling. "And we don't need to talk about what happened right now. That'll be for another day, but you should know

227

that she would have loved you very much."

"Is that why Aunt Eve didn't get married and wear the dresses?" Evie asks. "Because she was dead?"

Ruth presses a hand over her mouth.

"Evie, let's not talk about that," Celia says. "Let's just remember how much we loved Aunt Eve."

"That's why he hates Aunt Ruth," Evie says, pointing at Ruth. "Uncle Ray wanted to marry Aunt Eve, but she died. She died and he had to marry you."

Celia sucks in a quick breath, and Ruth closes her eyes.

"Evie Scott, that is a terrible thing to say," Celia says.

"I saw a picture. I saw Aunt Eve and Uncle Ray. Uncle Ray is happy. He is smiling in the picture and his eyes are almost normal. Aunt Eve is wearing a straw hat. I saw it."

Arthur steps into the kitchen and tosses his leather gloves on the table. "You will not say another word, young lady."

"Aunt Eve died and Uncle Ray had to marry Aunt Ruth. That's why he hates you."

"Stop it now," Arthur shouts, silencing the kitchen.

Evie pushes Celia's hands away and takes a step backward.

"Please, Evie," Ruth says. "I loved your Aunt Eve. I loved her so."

"You could have told me. I'm not a baby."

"No, honey," Celia says, reaching for Evie with one hand and for Ruth with the other. "We never thought you were a baby."

"Everyone thinks I'm too little."

"No, Evie," Elaine says, one arm still wrapped around Jonathon.

"No one thinks that, squirt," Jonathon says.

"I'm not a squirt either." Evie takes two more steps away. She is almost out of the kitchen. "I'm not too little. You could have told me she was dead. Dead, dead, dead. Dead like Julianne Robison." Two more steps and Evie stands where the living room meets the kitchen. "I don't even care. I don't even care about either one of them," and she runs across the wooden floors, into her bedroom, and slams the door.

Standing just inside the back porch and holding a box of Christmas ornaments, Daniel sees his reflection in the gun cabinet. Behind the glass, his .22-caliber rifle hangs next to Dad's shotgun. After Evie's door slams shut, he sets the box on the ground and bends to pull off his boots. Mama bought them at the St. Anthony's yard sale two weeks after they moved to Kansas. She said they were a good deal and would be plenty big enough to last a good long time. Now, a short five months later, Daniel's feet ache because the boots are too small. Small boots make crooked toes, God damned crooked toes that don't have room enough to grow. He sighs, thinking crooked toes are one more terrible thing about Kansas.

Dad and Mama never told Daniel that Aunt Eve was dead, just like they never told Evie. He never thought much about her, but if someone had asked, he would have said Aunt Eve moved away and was living somewhere else, probably with a husband and children of her own. Two probably, or maybe three. Had someone asked, he would have said Aunt Eve was like Mama. He would have said she wore aprons trimmed in white lace and had long blond hair. She probably smelled like Mama, too, and had soft, warm hands. But Aunt Eve is dead, and it makes Daniel feel the littlest bit like Mama is dead. Maybe that's why Mama and Dad never told Daniel and Evie.

Ian and some of the kids at school said Aunt Eve was dead. They said Uncle Ray killed her twenty-five years ago and now he's killed Julianne Robison — either he or Jack Mayer did it. One of them's guilty for sure, that's what the kids at school said. Daniel never believed them about Aunt Eve. Even though he never knew her, he didn't like to think about someone killing her, but now he knows it's true. Now he knows that his parents didn't tell him about Aunt Eve because they think he's a baby like Evie.

Still staring at the gun cabinet, Daniel wonders about the shotgun, wonders if it will be heavier than his .22. Maybe too heavy. Maybe too heavy for someone who doesn't have many friends and everyone thinks is a baby. But Ian says he needs it for pheasant hunting. A rifle won't work. Not even Daniel is a good enough shot to use a rifle. Ian has enough ammunition, but Daniel has to bring his own gun. The Bucher brothers say that if Daniel is really a good shot, he'll handle a shotgun just fine. He will use the key on top of the cabinet, take the gun before Mr. Bucher picks him up next Saturday afternoon, and hide it in his sleeping bag. Dad always takes a nap on Saturday afternoons. Mama says the week wears him out and that Dad needs a little peace and quiet. He'll take the gun while Dad is sleeping. Ian says the plan will work, that the sleeping bag will hide the shotgun. But Ian, who walked too slowly before he got his black boots, has never been pheasant hunting either and he's never stolen a shotgun, so how does Ian know what will work and what won't?

"Daniel," Mama calls out from the kitchen. "Is that you?"

"Yes, ma'am."

"Come in here, sweetheart. We have something to tell you."

Daniel hangs his coat on the hook closest to the gun cabinet. If he drapes it carefully, it almost covers enough of the cabinet to hide Dad's shotgun. It'll hide an empty spot, too. He will remember this for next weekend.

"Coming, Mama," he says and picks up the box of ornaments.

CHAPTER 18

Celia frowns across the table at Arthur as he drops a second sugar cube in his coffee. He is about to drop in a third but stops when Celia raises her chin and shakes her head. From the front of the café, the bell over the door rings, a blast of cold air floods their table, and Sheriff Bigler walks in. He pulls off his heavy blue jacket, which makes him shrink to half the size he was when he walked in, drapes it over a stool at the counter and sits. Arthur lifts a hand to greet him. Floyd nods in return.

"Wonder what brings Floyd out?" Arthur says.

"Having a little dessert like everyone else," Celia says, pulling off her coat and laying it over the seat back. "And I called him. Just in case."

Ever since the holidays ended, Father Flannery has been calling the house, saying he hoped the Scotts were a good Christian

233

family who hadn't forgotten about forgiveness since they started attending St. Bart's. Tired of the phone calls and thinking that maybe they could get that annulment after all, Arthur finally agreed to meet with Ray. Ruth shook her head at the idea and Celia said an annulment would never happen once Father Flannery found out about the baby. Still, Arthur wanted to try. Celia said she would approve only if they met Ray in the café because he certainly wasn't setting foot inside her kitchen.

"Shouldn't have done that," Arthur says, taking a sip of coffee and making a sour face as if it isn't sweet enough. He taps his teaspoon on the white tablecloth, leaving a small, coffee-colored stain.

"Why on earth not?"

"Just gonna get Ray riled up."

"He won't know Floyd is here for us."

"Man's not a fool, Celia."

Celia brushes him away with a wave of her hand. "Are you doing all right?" she asks, turning to face Ruth, who is sitting next to her in the small booth. She takes Ruth's hand with both of hers. "Are you feeling okay?"

"I'm fine," Ruth says. "Please don't fuss."

At the front of the café, the door chime rings again. Orville and Mary Robison walk in, stamping their feet and pulling off their coats. Arthur tips his head toward them as if he's wearing his hat and slouches back down into the wooden bench.

"What do you suppose brings them out?" Celia asks.

"They come every night," Ruth says, picking at the frayed end of her jacket sleeve. "Have ever since they first got married. Dessert and coffee usually."

The dinner crowd has cleared out and only the folks who, like the Robisons, have come for cherry pie and coffee are left. Half a dozen at most. At a table near the front counter, Orville Robison waits while Mary takes his coat and hangs it on the rack inside the door. She leaves on her own coat and as they sit, Floyd Bigler swivels around on his stool and walks over to them. He shakes Orville's hand and takes the seat that Mary offers him.

The two men begin to talk while Mary tips the white creamer, pouring milk into her coffee. The sleeves of her gray flannel jacket hide her hands, making it seem that she has shrunk in the months since Julianne disappeared, and the hair peeking out from under her tan hat is gray, almost white. How can she go on — standing, walking, sipping her coffee — now that no one is searching for Julianne anymore? There hasn't even been an article in the paper about the disappearance since before the holidays, and Father Flannery said a special prayer for Julianne at midnight mass on Christmas Eve, a prayer that sounded like good-bye. Maybe that's why folks stopped talking about it and writing about and searching for poor Julianne. They all thought good-bye meant Julianne would never come home.

The chime rings a third time, and Ray walks into the café. He takes off his hat, nods toward Isabelle Burris, who is folding napkins behind the counter, and lifts a finger in her direction.

"Cup of black coffee, Izzy," he says and, as he winks at her, he notices the Robisons and Floyd Bigler. He pauses for a moment, looks at them and at all the others in the café. Folks have laid down their forks, pushed aside their coffee and are watching. "Get back to it," Ray says to the room, glaring at them with his good eye while the cloudy eye goes off on its own, and without even a polite nod toward the Robisons, he walks past.

Isabelle follows Ray to the table with a pot of coffee and a white cup and saucer. She stays several feet behind him and only approaches the table after he has pulled a chair up to the booth and sat.

"I'll leave the pot for you folks," she says.

"How about a piece of your cherry pie, Izzy?" Ray says, scooting up to the table. "What about you all? Anyone else for pie?"

All around the café, folks pick up their silverware and go back to sipping their coffee.

"Nothing for us, Ray," Arthur says, sliding the creamer and sugar bowl to Ray's end of the table.

Ray takes off his hat and coat, fanning the table with a gust of the cold air he brought in from outside. It smells like campfire smoke and oil, but mostly whiskey. After draping his coat over the back of his chair and tossing his hat on the next table, he reaches for the coffeepot and, as he pours himself a cup, his hand shakes, causing a few drops to spill over the side and onto the white tablecloth. He fills the cup only halfway and glances at Ruth. Tiny red veins etch the yellow skin around his nose and mouth and his dark hair is matted against his forehead and temples. He is nearly the man he was twenty years ago — the strong square jaw, the heavy brow, the dark brown eyes. He still has these features, but they have wilted. He begins to drum one set of fingers and, under the table, where he occasionally brushes against Celia, his knees bob up and down.

"Arthur says things are going well for you at the county," Celia says, although this is not true. Ray has been showing up hours late and looking as if he hasn't slept. First, he said it was the flu, then trouble with the truck and finally food poisoning by that damned Izzy at the café.

"Things are good enough," Ray says, taking a sip of his coffee and wincing because his shaking hand spills too much into his mouth. He clears his throat and leans back when Isabelle sets his pie in front of him.

"Anything else, folks?" she asks.

"No," Ray says. "That's it." And he pushes the pie into the center of the table.

"Well," Arthur says, after Isabelle has walked away. "I guess you've been back about a month now." He pauses, taking a drink of coffee. "And things are working out. Working out fine the way they are."

"I think it's long about time Ruth comes home," Ray says, setting down his coffee and staring at Arthur, but not even his good eye can hold the gaze. "Time she gets back to church, too. Once on Christmas just isn't right."

"Ruth's been to church every Sunday.

Hasn't missed a one." Arthur shakes his head. "Nope, can't have her living with you."

"I'm sober, Arthur. Have been since the day I left."

"Fist hurts all the same," Arthur says, glancing at Ruth.

With her eyes lowered, Ruth touches the edge of her jaw.

"You want to come home, Ruth?" Ray's knees stop shaking for a moment, but they begin to quiver again before Ruth can answer.

Arthur holds up a finger to silence her. "Let's keep on like this for a short time more," he says. "Maybe consider whether staying married is the right thing for you two. Maybe you come for a few Sunday suppers so we can talk about it." Arthur nods at his own idea. "Yeah, maybe a dinner or two."

Ray presses both hands on the tabletop, steadying himself. He shifts in his seat, the cups and saucers rattling when his knees bump the table. "That's a damn fool thing to consider." His good eye lifts to look at Ruth.

She shifts in her seat, pressing back into the corner where the wooden bench meets the wall.

"You considering not staying married?" he says. "This how you start thinking when you quit the church?"

Celia ignores Arthur's signal to keep quiet. "She has every right to think as she pleases, Ray. You hurt her very badly."

Ray looks at Celia as if noticing her at the table for the first time. He never quite meets her eyes but instead looks at the individual parts of her. Tonight he studies her neck, the dimple where the two halves of her collarbone meet. After a long silence, Ray pushes back from the table. He stands and stumbles a few steps, knocking over his chair. The loud clatter silences the café again.

"Ruth is coming home tonight," he says, dropping two dollars on the table. "I've been patient enough." He leans forward, resting his palms on the table. "We'll fetch your things tomorrow, Ruth. Come along now."

Arthur tries to stand, but Ray, who is already on his feet, shoves him back down, reaches across the table and grabs Ruth's forearm. He tries to yank her from the booth as if she's no more than one of Evie's ragdolls. She cries out. Celia presses her body against Ruth's, pinning her in the corner. With both hands wrapped around one of Ruth's small wrists, Ray pulls. Across the table, Arthur struggles to his feet, tipping over the coffee and creamer. He grabs Ray's collar and drags him up and away. The weight pressing down on Celia is suddenly lifted. As quickly as Ray attacked, he is gone. Celia takes in a deep breath. With her body still pressed against Ruth's, she turns. Both men have stumbled over Ray's fallen chair. Arthur is first to scramble to his feet. He dives at Ray again but finds Floyd Bigler instead.

Even though Floyd is a much smaller man than either Ray or Arthur, he grabs Ray by his upper arm, shakes him and pushes him from the table. With the other hand, he stiff-arms Arthur.

"What's going on here, gentlemen?"

"Taking my wife." Ray wipes his forearm across his nose. "High time she comes home." He rocks from one foot to the other and shifts his eyes from side to side. "Ain't got nothing to do with you, Floyd."

Floyd tugs at his belt. "I guess if Ruth wants to go with you, she'll go on and do it." He looks at Ruth.

She wraps one arm around her midsection and shakes her head.

"All right then, I guess you're leaving alone."

Celia slides away from Ruth, pushes aside the table that has wedged them both in the corner and begins mopping up the coffee and cream that has spilled. The men in the café, the ones who had been eating dessert, including Orville Robison, are standing. Ray waves them off, grabs his hat from the nearby table and stumbles toward the door.

"It's wrong, what you're doing, Arthur Scott," he says, once he has reached the front of the café.

Standing with one hand on the doorknob, he sways a bit and seems to notice Orville Robison standing nearby. Orville crosses his arms over his chest. Still sitting, Mary stares down at her hands folded on the table. Ray leans forward to get a good look at her.

"Don't know a man who doesn't have a say when it comes to his own wife." Then he pulls open the door, letting in another blast of cold air. "It sure enough is wrong. Sure enough."

Once Ray is gone, Floyd motions for all of the men to sit.

"Everyone all right?" he asks, picking up Ray's chair and sliding it back to its original spot at a nearby table.

"Ruth, honey," Celia says, laying a hand on Ruth's stomach. "Is everything okay?" Ruth sits with one hand clutching her stomach and the other lying motionless in her lap. Her face has gone white and when Celia touches Ruth's hand, it is cold.

"You folks are in a tough spot, I'd say," Floyd says, nodding at Ruth. "You should probably shoot on over to the hospital. Let the doctor have a look."

Celia and Arthur exchange a glance, but neither one speaks.

"He doesn't know, does he?" Floyd asks.

Arthur shakes his head.

"Yep, that's a good enough mess, all right."

"Floyd's right," Celia says. Obviously, Floyd has figured out that Ruth is pregnant, and if he figured it out, so will others. "We need to get Ruth to the hospital. I think he hurt her arm."

Ruth slides across the seat. Arthur helps her to stand while Celia helps her on with her coat, pulls it closed and buttons it. With Arthur on one side, Celia on the other and Floyd following behind, telling folks to get back to Izzy's pies, Ruth shuffles toward the front of the café. Near the door, she stops and turns, her one bad arm dangling at her side.

"He wasn't home that night, Floyd," she says.

Celia starts to speak but Floyd holds up a

finger to silence her.

"Ray, he wasn't home like I said." And then facing Mary Robison, she says, "I don't know that he did anything, Mary. I don't know. But he wasn't home like he told Floyd. He wasn't home like I said."

Floyd nods as if he's always known.

"I'm so sorry, Mary," Ruth says. "I'm just so sorry."

Evie slowly opens her closet door so that it doesn't make any sound. Then she squats and crawls under the coats and dresses that Aunt Ruth brought when she first moved into Evie's room. The clothes smell like Aunt Ruth and, for a moment, Evie thinks Mama and Daddy and Aunt Ruth are home. She wiggles backward out of the closet and listens. They don't usually go out on a school night. Mama said they wouldn't be late and that Evie should mind Daniel and Elaine. Evie frowns to think she has to mind Daniel. Waiting until she is sure the house is quiet, she crawls back under the low-hanging hemlines, coughs as she reaches for the extra blankets that Mama stores in the closet, and so that they don't come un-folded, she pulls them out slowly, one hand on the bottom, the other on top. Next she drags out the box of photo albums that can't be stored in the basement because they might mildew and there, behind it all, she finds her hatbox. She pulls it from the dark corner, sits crisscross in front of it and, after checking the door one last time, she lifts off the lid.

"This is my favorite," Evie whispers, taking the perfume bottle from the box with two fingers.

The creamy white bottle has a short belly and a tall, thin stopper decorated with tiny red roses. Evie pulls out the stopper, and even though the bottle is empty, she smells Aunt Eve.

"I'm always afraid I'll break it," she says, and setting the stopper back in the bottle, she places it on top of the stack of blankets.

Dragging the box farther out of the corner and wrapping her legs around it, Evie takes out the picture of Aunt Eve and Uncle Ray and props it up on the closet floor. Next, she pulls out a compact, a brush and a hand mirror — all decorated with the same red roses — and lays them on top of the blankets. She took all four from Aunt Eve's room on the same day, but the pink heart-shaped brooch and purple scarf with gold stitching that she removes next, she took one at a time on separate days. Last, she slips one hand into the box and slides it under a carefully folded blue dress. She wiggles her fingers in the soft ruffles and rests her other hand on top of the dress, the silk sash feeling cool and smooth. Lifting the dress from the box, she takes it by each shoulder, holds it to her neck and lets it drape down her front as she stands.

"It's too long," Evie whispers, slipping the dress over her head and threading her arms through each sleeve.

The blue silky skirt flutters against her bare toes and the waist falls past her hips. At the neckline, six inches of blue piping left unstitched hang from the dress and the shoulder seam is torn because she tripped over the dress when Daddy and Uncle Ray were fighting. Evie gathers up the low hanging waist and ties it off in the proper place with the silk sash. The feathery sleeves tickle her elbows. Looking down, she thinks the dress is short enough, but without Mama's help, Evie can't do anything about the wide, torn neckline that slips off her shoulders or the dangling trim. Mama would pin it all up with safety pins, like she does the Halloween costumes that are too big, but Evie can't ask Mama for help.

"It'll be fine," she says. "Just fine."

Sitting in the backseat of Arthur's car, Ruth

recognizes the throb in her shoulder and the lopsided way her coat hangs. It's probably dislocated, has happened before. She lets her bad arm lie at her side and, sliding down in the backseat of the station wagon, she slips her good hand inside her jacket so she can feel her little girl. She hasn't told anyone that she can feel Elisabeth kicking or that she has named her baby. She deserved a name. From the moment Ruth felt she was a girl, Elisabeth deserved a name. A name would give the tiny new baby something to hold on to, a little more courage, or maybe it was Ruth who needed the courage. She smiles at the tiny flutter that stirs her insides and, laying back her head, she closes her eyes as the car rambles over the gravel road.

Up in the front seat, Celia and Arthur are silent. No one has spoken since Ruth told Floyd the truth about Ray. Not a word since they walked out of the café into a strong north wind, not as Arthur pulled away, the café's lights dwindling behind them, not now as they drive down Bent Road on their way to the hospital. Celia is no more than a shadow, occasionally checking on Ruth, reaching over the seat to pat her knee. Next to her, Arthur sits tall, stiffening and bracing his arms each time a truck passes and he has to ease the car toward the ditch. Celia is the first to speak.

"Will Floyd arrest him now?" she asks, her shadow turning toward Arthur.

"Don't suppose he has reason to."

"But he'll look into it, right?"

"Don't really know." Arthur rubs his palm against his forehead. Father used to do the same thing. "I suppose he'll ask Ruth some more questions, pay Ray another visit."

Celia reaches back and pats Ruth's knee again and probably smiles though Ruth can't see.

"Well, he's not coming to dinner. I can't imagine why you invited him."

"I didn't invite him, not for certain. Just suggested. Tried to ease my way in. Maybe buy a little time."

"Well, I don't want him around the kids. He did something to that girl. I just know it."

"I'm handling him the best I can for now," Arthur says.

Ruth closes her eyes again when another truck, driving in the opposite direction, flies past. The friction between the two automobiles and the heavy north wind rock Ruth from side to side. She closes her eyes and tries to hold her arm still.

"He's waiting him out," Ruth says into

the dark car.

Celia's shadow turns, stretching one arm across the back of her seat. "Waiting him out? What do you mean?"

"He thinks Ray will die soon. That he's drunk himself nearly dead."

A set of oncoming headlights outlines Celia with a yellow frame. "Is that true?"

Once the other truck has passed and its headlights have faded, Arthur shrugs. "Can't help what a man does to himself."

"I don't even know what to say about that," Celia says. "Besides being a horrible thought, what are the chances?"

"Pretty good from the looks of him." Fending off the wind and the rough gravel roads, Arthur's hands and arms shake on the steering wheel.

"I'm sorry, Ruth. I can't imagine what he's thinking."

"He's thinking he's seen a man nearly dead from drinking before and that Ray looks about the same."

Celia glances between the two of them.

"Papa," Ruth says. "Papa drank himself dead. But Ray's not that close yet, Arthur. Not like Papa. Not as bad as Papa was in the end."

Another car approaches. Ruth sits up. The more she talks, the more numb she feels inside. She didn't realize it in the café, or the night Ray came back from Damar, or the day Arthur asked Gene Bucher to give Ray a job, but sitting in the car, blinking against another set of approaching headlights, she knows that Arthur is counting on time because he doesn't know any other way.

"Arthur," Celia shouts. "Look out."

Arthur jerks the steering wheel, his shadow falling to the right. The car slides across the gravel road, throwing Ruth against the doorframe. Her head bounces off the window. Something jabs her side. Pressing her one good arm straight out, she braces herself against the front seat. The car grinds to a stop. Heavy tires spinning on the hard dry gravel fade in the distance. Outside the front window, a dust cloud settles like dwindling smoke in the headlights and a long winding tail and arched back appear — tumbleweeds caught up along the fence line on Bent Road. Someone had better clear them away soon, Ruth thinks, or they'll pull down the fence, and she closes her eyes.

Daniel lies in bed. Through his wall, he hears Evie fumbling about in her closet when she should be sleeping. Elaine told them lights out so she and Jonathon could sit on the couch and talk about flower arrangements, cummerbunds and the house that Jonathon will finish before they marry. Already, the wedding is the only thing Elaine talks about and already Jonathon is around even more, being Dad's extra set of hands. Daniel pulls his pillow over his head and rolls toward the window. He stares at the white sheers lit up by the porch lights so that they shine with an orange glow and wonders if Jack Mayer really stole Nelly Simpson's 1963 midnight blue Ford Fairlane.

Ian brought the newspaper clipping to school last Monday. He said that Nelly Simpson was married to the richest man in Hays and there wasn't a man, woman, or child in Rooks County who would dare leave a fingerprint on Nelly Simpson's Ford Fairlane. Never mind, steal it. No man except Jack Mayer. Ian said Jack Mayer wouldn't give two God damned cents about Nelly Simpson or any other Simpson.

"We got trouble now," Ian had said, sitting across from Daniel at the cafeteria table and propping up his short leg on the cross bar. He didn't need to do this with his new boot because both feet could touch the floor at the same time, but he did it anyway. "He's got himself a car now. He can get to anyone he damn well pleases."

"I thought he was living in your barn."

"Sure he was, but now he's got a car. It's trouble. Real big damn trouble." Ian glanced around as if Jack Mayer might be standing right behind him. "My brothers say maybe we can hunt him down." He lowers his voice. "After we go to shooting pheasant, maybe we'll go to shooting Jack Mayer. It'll be practice. Real good practice. We'll track him down."

"How we going to track a Ford Fairlane?" Daniel asked.

Ian opened his brown bag lunch, looked inside. "Dogs," he had said, pulling out a sandwich wrapped in waxed paper. "We'll use dogs."

When Daniel opens his eyes again, the white sheers still shine with an orange glow, his pillow is lying on the floor, Evie's room is quiet and the telephone is ringing. Outside his door, footsteps cross the living room floor and move into the kitchen. The phone stops ringing and Jonathon's muffled voice drifts into Daniel's room. He closes his eyes and opens them again when there is a tap on his door.

"Daniel," Elaine says. She knocks again, louder. "Daniel, wake up."

She cracks the door and the light from the

living room makes him blink. He lifts up on one elbow. "Yeah, I'm up. I'm awake."

"Get yourself dressed. That was Daddy. There's been an accident."

Daniel sits up, resting his hands on his knees.

"Get yourself going," Jonathon says, taking Elaine's place. Daniel wants to tell Jonathon to get his own damned self going, but instead he swings his legs over the side of the bed and puts both feet on the cold floor. In the next room, Elaine taps on Evie's door.

"No time for questions," Jonathon says. "Get a move on."

CHAPTER 19

Sitting in Elaine's lap, Evie wraps herself in a blanket and buries her nose in it. Elaine tightens her hug, kisses the top of top of Evie's head and says, "You try to sleep, pumpkin. Daddy will tell us when there's something to know."

Though she closes her eyes, Evie can't sleep because everyone's shoes make an awful noise on the tile floors and the hospital smells make her want to pinch her nose closed. She presses her hands over her ears as more people walk down the hall, their footsteps ringing off the gray block walls and shiny tile floors.

"Mama, you're here," Elaine says, lifting Evie and setting her on the ground. "You're okay."

Daddy wraps one arm around Mama while reaching out to Evie with the other. They both are as gray as the walls and Daddy looks smaller in the hospital than he does at home. Evie drops her blanket, letting it fall to the ground, and hugs Daddy's leg.

"I'm just fine," Mama says, kissing Elaine and Daniel's cheeks and hugging Evie as she drifts from Daddy's leg to Mama's. "Everyone is fine."

Mama's eyes are red, like she's been crying, and her hair is mussed on top. In Detroit, Mama's hair was never mussed. Every morning before they moved to Kansas, Mama backcombed her hair with a pink long-handled comb and sprayed it twice with hairspray. She always wore a dress and usually her tan shoes with the two-inch heel that she said were good for walking. She trimmed and buffed her nails every Saturday morning, rubbed petroleum jelly on her elbows every night and plucked the stray hairs that grew between her brows. Seeing Mama now, standing in the gray hallway, Evie thinks she doesn't do any of those things anymore. She looks sleepy and sad like maybe she's tired of being a mom in Kansas.

"Was it that curve at the top of Bent Road?" Jonathon asks, stepping up to Daddy and shaking his hand.

Daddy nods. It must have been the same monster that scared Mama off the road on the night they first drove to Grandma Reesa's house.

"Tricky spot," Jonathon says. "A little ice, a little wind and those trucks drive awful fast for that narrow road. Sure is a tricky spot."

"Threw us on the shoulder," Daddy says, turning again when the double doors at the end of the hallway open. "Shook Ruth up a good bit, but she's all right."

The overhead lights make Mama squint. "Doctor says Aunt Ruth bruised a rib or two and her shoulder was pulled out of place." Mama lifts Evie's chin. "But the doctor fixed her up. Aunt Ruth and her sweet baby are just fine."

Mama's hands are rough and cold. Not liking the feel of it, Evie pulls away. At the same time, Daddy lets go of Mama and marches down the hallway where two men are walking through the double doors. One man, wearing a long, dark coat, walks a few steps behind the other. The other man looks like Uncle Ray, except smaller. Daddy begins to walk faster, his footsteps tap, tap, tapping across the tile floor. The man without the coat stops in the middle of the hallway. He looks up at Daddy and then back at the dark coat man. Daddy walks faster.

"Oh, dear," Mama says.

Jonathon follows Daddy, and Daniel starts to tag along, but Mama grabs his arm and shakes her head at him. The dark coat man nods at Daddy. They are closer now and Evie knows the other man is Uncle Ray, even if he is smaller, even though he's shriveled up like someone left him in the drier too long and forgot to press out the wrinkles. Uncle Ray steps away from the dark coat man who Mama calls Father. Yes, it's Father Flannery all bundled up for the cold. Uncle Ray stumbles. He braces himself against one of the gray walls and points at Daddy. Uncle Ray may have shriveled up, but his voice hasn't.

"That woman," Uncle Ray says, pointing at Aunt Ruth's door. "That woman is none of your business now, Arthur. None of your concern. That's what you said. Now I'm saying it."

Daddy holds up two hands and, when Uncle Ray stumbles again, Daddy uses them to catch him.

"There's a God damned baby in there," Uncle Ray says, pushing off Daddy and falling on Father Flannery.

Father Flannery shoves Uncle Ray toward the wall and steps back.

"You told him about the baby?" Daddy

asks and Father Flannery nods yes as Daddy dances this way and that so Uncle Ray can't stumble into Aunt Ruth's room.

Jonathon slips behind Daddy, pulls Aunt Ruth's door closed and stands in front of it, his arms crossed over his chest and his feet spread wide as if he's bracing for a big gust of wind.

"I assure you that a man should know about his own child," Father Flannery says, backing away from Uncle Ray. "I assure you that is true."

"This was not your business," Daddy shouts at Father Flannery.

Mama scoots Evie off to stand with Elaine and walks down the hall but Jonathon waves her away. She stops when Daniel walks up to her side. He pats Mama on the shoulder, probably because he saw Jonathon do that and he wants to be grown up like Jonathon, and then he walks toward Daddy and Uncle Ray.

Nobody answers Daddy when he shouts out again wondering who told Father Flannery about Aunt Ruth's baby. Daddy stops searching for someone to be angry at and turns back to Uncle Ray.

"Go on home," he says, taking Uncle Ray by the shoulders and pointing him toward the double doors at the end of the hallway.

"You go home. Sleep it off. Jonathon'll drive you."

"No damn thing to sleep off," Uncle Ray says, pushing Daddy away. His cloudy eye is white under the bright lights. "I've been patient enough with you, Arthur Scott." He points at Daddy first, swings his arm around, stumbles and points next at Aunt Ruth's room. "That woman didn't get nothing wasn't coming to her. Feeding those Robisons after they aimed their God damned finger at me."

Uncle Ray sways a few steps and shoves Daddy with both hands. Daddy stumbles backward, trips over Daniel who didn't listen to Mama when she said to stay put, and falls on his hind end. Daniel falls, too, knocking his head against the gray wall. The crack his head makes when it bounces off the concrete is loud enough that Evie hears it. Mama hears it, too, and she jumps forward. This time Jonathon can't stop her even though he holds up the same hand that turned her around before. She rushes down the hall to Daniel as Jonathon shoves Uncle Ray away from Aunt Ruth's door. Daddy stands and tries to catch Uncle Ray as he staggers backward, but he misses and Uncle Ray trips over Mama and Daniel, who is trying to stand. All three fall to the shiny tile floor.

Elaine shouts out but it isn't loud because she has one hand pressed over her mouth. With the other hand, she tries to cover Evie's eyes, but Evie can still see. Daniel's legs are tangled up with Mama and Uncle Ray's legs. Mama lies flat on her back and Uncle Ray is spread out on top of her, his arms and legs straddling her, his chest pressing down on hers. Their noses would touch if Mama lifted her head an inch. Uncle Ray seems bigger again, lying face to face with Mama. She pulls her chin in tight and rolls her head away. Uncle Ray smiles down at Mama. Evie wishes he would go away. She wishes he were the happy man in her picture. She starts to cry as Daddy reaches into the pile and yanks out Uncle Ray.

"It's moving day," Uncle Ray says as Daddy shoves him. "You got no business doing what you're doing, Arthur Scott."

Evie chokes on her tears but she can still hear Uncle Ray shout. He doesn't stop, not even when Father Flannery walks back through the double doors with two more men. Daddy holds up one hand so the three of them stand back and watch.

"You go on home, Ray. Your time with this family is done."

The two men who came with Father Flannery push open the doors and Uncle Ray walks through, still mumbling. All four disappear.

Celia arches her back so Daniel can slip his arm out from under her but she doesn't stand. Focusing on a blank spot on the wall, she draws in full, deep breaths until the feel of Ray on top of her, the pressure that he laid down on her, is gone. It must have been her imagination, his hips grinding into her. He didn't have the time, couldn't have had the presence of mind, to take the opportunity. But she did feel him, pressed against her upper thigh and into her hipbone. She closes her eyes and hopes she doesn't cry. Next to her, Daniel sits up. She inhales, two deep breaths, pushes up on her elbows and reaches out to touch the spot where his head hit the wall. He pulls away and stands. At the end of the hallway, the double doors fall shut, swing back and forth and finally hang motionless. Above her, Daniel reaches down, offering a hand. Celia clears her throat, smoothes her hair and the gathered pleats on the front of her skirt and takes Daniel's help.

Once standing, Celia tugs at her waistline, straightens her collar, and when she looks at Daniel, she realizes she is looking up at him. Surely she has been for quite some time, but suddenly it strikes her how much he's grown, how close he is to becoming a man, and how, like a man, his ego is bruised. She smiles and reaches for him but he pulls away again and walks down the hall toward Elaine and Evie, where he sits in one of the chairs lined along the hallway and rests his head in his hands.

"My good Lord in heaven," Reesa says, her voice shattering the silence. Wearing her blue flannel housecoat, a pair of galoshes and the brown hat that she normally saves for Sundays, she shuffles through the doors. "What is going on here?"

"Everyone is fine, Reesa," Celia says, rubbing her tailbone. "We had a little car accident but everyone is fine."

"Well, from the sounds of Ray," Reesa says, motioning toward the closed doors, "things are not fine."

"Nobody's worried about Ray right now," Arthur says, shaking Jonathon's hand and slapping him on the back. "Ruth is in there." He nods toward her room. "Doctor checked her out. The baby's fine. She can come home in the morning."

"Seems that Ray plans on being the one to take her home. He knows, doesn't he?"

Reesa scans the room before finally resting her eyes on Celia as if she wears the most blame. "He knows about the baby?"

"He does," Arthur says, pulling a speck of fuzz from Celia's hair. "You okay?" he asks.

Celia swallows and nods.

Reesa snorts, shaking her head at Celia and scoots Jonathon away from Ruth's room, sending him back down the hall to stand with Elaine. "Well, I've said it before, and I'll say it again," Reesa says, taking Jonathon's position as guard. "I think Ruth should move in with me."

Arthur wraps one arm around Celia and rubs his forehead with his other hand. "No need for Ruth to move anywhere. She's fine where she is."

"Ray is going to come knocking now that he knows about the baby. She needs to live farther away. She needs to move home."

"Ruth is not living in that house." Arthur's voice is calm but his body is rigid, and the arm around Celia's shoulder is like a clamp.

"Maybe it's not such a bad idea," Celia says. "Only because you seem to upset Ray. Maybe he'd be less upset by Ruth living with your mother."

"And you think we should care about making Ray happy?" Arthur says.

Down the hall, Daniel sits alone, his

shoulders slumped, his head in his hands.

Shaking his head at Daniel, Arthur continues. "You think I give two God damned cents about making Ray happy?"

"I think nothing of the sort. But I do know we're trapped in a terrible place. All of us, but mostly Ruth and her sweet baby. You were the one who said you wanted to keep the peace. I want whatever will keep Ray away from them."

Celia doesn't want to say it, or even admit it to herself, but mostly she wants Ruth to move so Ray will never come near her house again. She doesn't want him near Evie. Doesn't want him to start thinking that Evie is close enough to Eve, something that he might have thought about Julianne Robison.

"I will keep Ruth and this family safe," Arthur says to Reesa. "And keeping the peace ended the second he found out about the baby."

Reesa takes a breath to say something back to Arthur but stops when the door opens behind her. Ruth peeks through the small opening, hiding her body with the door, and motions for Arthur to come inside.

Jonathon stands next to Elaine, one arm

wrapped around her waist, the other cocked on his hip as if he is wearing a holster and gun and is ready to draw if Uncle Ray returns. When Dad disappears into Aunt Ruth's room, Jonathon turns to Daniel.

"You okay, sport?" he says.

Elaine looks at Daniel, too, as if she were Mama and he were Evie.

"I'm fine," Daniel says and shoves away the hand that Jonathon holds out to him. "I can stand by myself."

Jonathon steps back. "Suit yourself."

Daniel stands from his chair and, crossing his arms over his chest, he leans against the wall. Ian says that the morgue is in the basement floor of the hospital and that's where the police will take Jack Mayer when he and Daniel shoot him dead. He says they'll take Julianne there, too, if they ever find her. He says that maybe he and Daniel will sneak into the basement morgue to see them both. Next time, Daniel will be ready for Uncle Ray. He is a good shot, a damn good shot, probably even better than Jonathon. Just like he told Mama and Aunt Ruth the night Uncle Ray showed up at the house asking for dessert and a jump start. He could make a real mess of Uncle Ray with Dad's shotgun. Next time, he'll damn sure be ready.

Ruth shuffles across the cold tile floor in her paper slippers and crawls into bed, using her good arm to hoist herself. Behind her, Arthur walks into the room and the door falls closed. With her head, she motions toward a wooden chair sitting in the corner of the room. Arthur moves it next to her bed and sits in it backward, straddling it with his legs — the way he sat as a boy. The moonlit room eases the creases around his eyes and because his hair has grown longer, like it was when he was a teenager, he looks younger. Tired, perhaps a little scared, but young again.

"We haven't talked much since you moved back, just you and me," Ruth says, wanting to touch Arthur's hand. "But I'm always around, aren't I?"

"Glad to have you. You know that."

"I do." Ruth rests both hands on Elisabeth and smiles when she feels a familiar flutter. "Do you remember how Eve used to tease you for having so little to say?"

Arthur nods.

"But when you did decide to talk, she always listened. She said you were worth listening to because you made darn sure you had something worth saying before you said it."

"Be nice if that were true."

"It is true, Arthur." Ruth reaches out and rests one hand on his. "I know you'll take care of us. If you say it, I know it's worth listening to."

Arthur drops his head into his folded arms.

"I know it's true. And I know if you could have saved Eve, you would have."

For a moment they are silent.

"What happened to Eve was not your fault," she says. "I know you think it was. I know Father made you think it was. But it wasn't. You were a boy, Arthur. No more a man than Daniel is now." Ruth touches Arthur's cheek and lifts his face. "I listened to you, Arthur. So now you listen to me. There was nothing you could have heard. Nothing you could have seen. It was a terrible thing, but you can't save her by saving me."

"I should have moved back home earlier. Shouldn't have left you alone for so long."

"All these years, I was afraid that you thought like the others. So many in town believing that Ray hurt Eve all those years ago. Like Floyd. All of them believing I married the man who killed my own sister. But he didn't, Arthur. I know he didn't. I promise that I'm certain of that. I hope you never believed like the others." Ruth lowers her eyes. "I hope that isn't what kept you away for so long."

Arthur drops his head, shakes it from side to side and exhales. "You're too forgiving of me. Far too quick to forgive."

"We all did the best we could," Ruth says, lifting Arthur's chin and smiling down on him. "I'll tell Floyd everything. I don't know what Ray was up to that night, I really don't. But I'll tell Floyd everything." She squeezes his hand. "I'd like to stay with your family, if you'll still have me, if you think it's best."

"Good enough," Arthur says.

She smiles and lays both hands over her stomach. "Her name is Elisabeth."

Arthur stands and nodding his head, he says, "Elisabeth, it is."

CHAPTER 20

Celia leans against the kitchen sink and rubs her tailbone. Two days since she fell in the hospital and it's still sore. The aches and pains won't last much longer but every time she kneads a sore spot, she feels Ray on top of her again, pressing into her thigh, smiling down on her. Wishing she had never suggested they meet Ray at the café, she swallows and tightens the belt on her robe. When Ruth asks if Celia is feeling all right, she smiles, embarrassed that Ruth would be worried about her, and turns to face her family. Arthur, wearing his denim coat and work boots, reaches up and catches the kiss that Evie throws from across the kitchen.

"You sure enough about me leaving today?" Arthur says, tucking the kiss in his pocket. Evie giggles.

"We'll be fine," Celia says and follows him to the back door. "Not much choice really." Standing together at the top of the base-

269

ment stairs, she kisses him and, as he climbs into his truck, she calls out, "We'll lock up tight."

Before walking back inside, Celia looks toward Ray and Ruth's house. Ruth says he'll drink for a good long time once he gets started but eventually he'll remember there's a baby to contend with, and he'll come again.

Back in the kitchen, sitting at the table, Evie breaks off a piece of biscuit and shoves it in her mouth. "When will the poppy mallows bloom again, Aunt Ruth?" she says before her mouth is empty.

Celia frowns and shakes her head at the bad manners.

The poppy mallows were the first flower Ruth taught Evie about because a thick patch grew every year in the ditches alongside their new house.

"We'll start to see them as early as April," Ruth says, snapping the lid back on the box of oatmeal with her good hand while keeping the sore arm tucked closely to her body. "But sometimes not until May. Depends on the rain. And how early spring comes."

Celia shouts for Daniel to hurry along or he'll miss the bus, and then she gently touches Ruth's hand. Ruth nods that she is doing fine.

"They're Aunt Eve's favorite, right?" Evie says, stirring her oatmeal and testing the temperature by touching a small spoonful to her upper lip.

"They *were* her favorite," Celia says. "A long time ago. Remember?"

Evie closes her eyes and takes a deep breath as if smelling a bouquet of flowers.

"You do remember, Evie. Don't you? You remember about Aunt Eve being gone?"

Evie smiles. "Sure," she says. "May I be excused?"

"You may. But hustle along or you'll miss the bus."

"Thanks," Evie calls out as she skates across the wooden floor and slides into her room.

Daniel pulls out his lunch and lays it on the cafeteria table. Ian does the same. Both boys have similar lunches except that since Aunt Ruth came along, Daniel has better desserts. He slides an extra oatmeal raisin cookie to Ian's side of the table even though he knows Ian won't eat it.

"Did you hear?" Ian asks, pulling the waxed paper off his sandwich and holding one half to his mouth. "About Nelly Simpson's car?"

Daniel shakes his head.

"Police found it near Nicodemus. It's all over the newspapers." Ian glances around the crowded cafeteria and whispers, "You know about Nicodemus, don't you?"

His mouth full of ham and cheese, Daniel shakes his head again.

"It's where all the coloreds live. Every one of them in the county. Proof positive Jack Mayer took that car. Took it and drove to Nicodemus where he must know pretty much everyone."

Daniel takes another bite.

"Folks there will help hide him."

"My mom says I can still come tomorrow," Daniel says because he doesn't know anything about Nicodemus and doesn't know what else to say.

Ian takes a bite of his sandwich and sets it aside. "You going to bring your dad's shotgun?"

Daniel nods.

"Your .22 won't do you any good. Not for pheasant hunting. My brothers say if you have a shotgun, we can be the pushers." Ian pokes his elbow into the center of an unpeeled banana. Its guts squirt out both ends. He does the same thing every day and throws it away so his mom will think he ate it. "You know about pushers and blockers, don't you?"

Daniel shakes his head.

"Blockers stand along the road, blocking the pheasant, and the pushers walk across the field, pushing the birds so they get squeezed between. Being a blocker is no good. Blockers get hit by buckshot if they're not careful. Pushing is best. Pushers flush out the pheasant, take an easy shot. We want to be pushers."

Daniel holds up a hand and shakes his head when Ian slides his uneaten sandwich across the table. A few months back, when Ian first started giving Daniel his leftovers, he took them. Ida Bucher made her sandwiches with double mayonnaise and extra thick slices of cheese, but when Daniel began noticing that he could see Ian's backbone through his shirt and that he wasn't growing like everyone else in the grade, he stopped taking Ian's sandwiches, no matter how much mayonnaise Mrs. Bucher used.

Ian wads up the sandwich in its waxed paper wrapper and drops it into his lunch bag. "My brothers say we'll be hunting late-season pheasant. They're the hardest to shoot. Early-season pheasant are stupid. They get shot straight away. But late-season pheasants, they're the smart ones. You got to be tricky to get the late-season birds. My brothers say that if we're smart enough to get us some late-season pheasants, we'll go hunting for Jack Mayer."

Daniel starts to ask why early-season pheasant are stupid but stops because a group of kids breaks out laughing. At first, he thinks they're laughing at Ian, but the kids are sitting two tables over and couldn't hear Ian talking about Jack Mayer and Nelly Simpson and late-season pheasant.

"What are they all laughing at?" Ian asks, putting the rest of his lunch back in the brown bag his mom packed it in and squishing it down with both hands.

"Don't know," Daniel says, thinking Ian looks a little blue. Or maybe it's the gray light from an overcast sky. He turns toward the laughter as a couple of kids at the next table stand. He leans to the left and sees her.

Two tables down, sitting by herself as she always does at lunch, Evie is wearing one of Aunt Eve's dresses — the blue one, the one with ruffles and a satin bow, the one she said was her favorite. The dress is too big and falls off her small, white shoulders. She tugs at it, gathering up the collar where it has torn away at the seam. She smiles as if she doesn't hear the kids laughing. She smiles as if Aunt Eve is sitting across the table from her. Daniel throws down his sandwich, jumps up and runs two tables over.

"Hi, Daniel," Evie says.

Turning to the kids sitting at the other end of Evie's table, Daniel says, "Shut up. All of you, shut up." Then he looks back at Evie. "What are you doing?"

"Eating lunch," she says, laying out two napkins — setting a place for two people.

"Why are you wearing that dress?"

Evie smiles and shoves a piece of peanut-butter-and-jelly sandwich in her mouth. "It's my favorite. Aunt Eve's favorite, too."

"You shouldn't be wearing that, Evie. It's all torn and it's not yours."

Two tables away, Ian is watching them. He still looks blue.

"You're going to get in trouble."

Evie takes another bite and dabs one corner of her mouth with her napkin. "No, I won't. Don't be silly." She stands to show Daniel how she rolled up the middle of the dress and tied it off with the sash. "See, I made it fit. I fixed it myself."

Daniel stands and holds out his arms, blocking the view of Evie modeling her dress. "Sit down already. Does Mama know you're wearing that?"

"Aunt Eve said I could."

"Aunt Eve said?"

Evie nods. "Yes, Aunt Eve said."

CHAPTER 21

The school bus hisses and slows near Daniel's house. Holding onto the back of the seat in front of him, he gathers his books and lunchbox, stands and waits until the bus has stopped before stepping into the aisle.

"Now, you're sure Evie wasn't meant to take the bus home today?" Mr. Slear, the bus driver, asks.

"No, sir. Guess my mama picked her up early."

The bus door slides open and Mr. Slear says, "She not feeling well?"

"Yes, sir. Not feeling well at all."

Daniel waits at the end of the gravel drive until Mr. Slear pops the bus into gear and drives away. Once it has disappeared over the hill, leaving behind a trail of gray exhaust, he walks up the drive. The tailgate of Dad's truck peeks out from behind the house. He has come home early. The only other time Dad came home early from work was when the first black boy in Detroit called Elaine. Now he's home because Evie wore Aunt Eve's dress to school.

After a few more steps, Daniel sees all of Dad's truck. It's parked in its normal spot. Mama's car is parked next to the truck and the spot where Jonathon normally parks is empty. Daniel smiles at the empty spot until he hears a low rumble. He takes a few more slow steps. There it is again. Almost a groan. Rounding the back of the house and seeing nothing, he stops and stomps his feet, trying to warm his toes. The cold air burns his lungs and the inside of his throat. Inching closer to the back of the house, he hears it again. He takes a few more steps. Aunt Ruth stands at the far end of the screened-in porch. She must hear it, too.

"What should I do, Arthur?" Aunt Ruth says. "What do you need?"

Aunt Ruth's voice is quiet as if she's trying not to scare something. Daniel shifts direction and walks toward the gap between the garage and the far side of the house. As he nears Aunt Ruth, she begins to sidestep toward the back door. She looks at Daniel. Her eyes are wide and she is shaking her head. She looks small, as small as Evie, as small as the day Uncle Ray came asking for pie and a jump for his truck. On his tiptoes now, so his feet don't crunch on the gravel drive, Daniel takes a few more steps.

Dad and Olivia are standing in the small alleyway between the house and garage, the space that Daniel always forgets to mow. But the grass has died off with winter and the ground is hard and bare. With one hand, Dad pats Olivia on the hind end. With the other, he waves Aunt Ruth away. Olivia is too large to turn around in the narrow space and she can't walk through and around the house because old Mr. Murray's rusted car blocks the far end. The only way out is for Dad to coax her to back up.

"There you go, girl," Dad says to Olivia in a quiet voice. He sounds like he's talking to Evie. "Get on back now, girl."

Step by step, Olivia backs out of the narrow passageway.

"Dan," Dad says, seeing Daniel standing in the driveway. "Get Evie inside. Get her inside now and get me my gun."

Blood is splattered across Dad's white work shirt, the one with the Rooks County patch that Mama sewed on the left pocket before his first day of work. Both sleeves are rolled up to his elbows, and his hands are shiny red like he dipped them in red paint. Olivia turns, leading with the top of her head, followed by her round, brown eyes.

Aunt Ruth said Olivia was a good mother to many calves, but she's too old now and she's apple-assed. No one wants her apple-assed calves anymore. Daniel gags into a closed fist and stumbles backward.

A gash runs the length of Olivia's neck and down into her dewlap and her jowls hang like parted curtains. Most of her blood is gone, drained out on the ground, soaked up by the dirt. What is left is thick and dark, almost black. A shadow grows out of the wound and spreads up and across her neck, staining her chestnut coat. She staggers, moans, barely more than a whisper. Dad pats her right haunch. Coughing and choking, Daniel thinks of Evie. Dad thinks Evie came home on the bus. No, she's with Mama. Mama came to school for her, picked her up early. The nurse was going to call Mama because Evie wore Aunt Eve's dress. The nurse was supposed to call.

"Get my gun," Dad says, starting to back up again and coaxing Olivia with his quiet voice. "Get on back, girl. Get on back now."

Daniel's legs won't move. He sees the steps leading to the back porch. He'll go up them, two at time, unlock the cabinet, grab the gun. Evie's already inside, hiding her face in Mama's apron, probably crying because Olivia is going to die. The gun is inside, too. But Daniel's legs won't move.

"My gun, Dan," Dad says, wiping his forehead with his shirtsleeve and leaving a red smudge. "I need a gun."

Daniel takes a step toward the porch. Only one. Another low rumble drifts up from Olivia. Dad yells again for him to get moving. He takes the stairs two at a time. Inside the back door, Mama and Aunt Ruth already have the gun cabinet open. They stand back as Daniel reaches in and grabs the shotgun. Dad said it once belonged to Grandpa Robert, but he's dead so now it's Dad's gun. It's heavier than his rifle, the weight of it pulling him forward. With one hand on the stock and the other on the double barrel, he swings around, careful to not hit Mama or Aunt Ruth, and runs back outside.

"Careful, Dan," Mama calls out.

Olivia and Dad stand in the driveway now, clear of the small space that had trapped Olivia. Dad has one hand on a leather lead that dangles from Olivia's neck strap. Evie left it on. Damn it all, she's always leaving on that lead. Olivia stomps her front feet, staggering from side to side as if she's frightened now that she is in the open. She starts to swing around, throwing her head to the left. Dad looks behind, measuring the distance between him and the garage because Olivia might crush him against it.

"There's a girl," he says, dropping the leather lead and coming at her from the front end where she can't hurt him. "There's a good girl."

Olivia staggers a few steps to the side and back toward Dad. Waiting until she staggers away again, he grabs at the strap and walks her in a half circle, coaxing her quietly until she is facing the opposite direction. Still talking to her, telling her she's a good girl, he backs toward the fence, and without taking his eyes off of hers, he wraps her lead around the nearest wooden post and ties it off. Olivia's blood is smeared across his face and his neck. Giving the lead a tug to test that it is good and tight, Dad sidesteps away from her.

"Go ahead on, son." He nods, and as he steps away, he pulls a handkerchief from his pocket and wipes the blood from his hands.

Waiting until Dad is clear, Daniel lifts the heavy gun and walks toward Olivia. With the wooden stock pressed to his cheek, he wraps his finger around the stiff trigger and stares down the wide barrel until Olivia is lined up in the sight. She is a Brown Swiss with long thin legs and dark lashes that trim her brown eyes. Akin to a deer, Dad had said. She'll be a jumper, quick and light on her feet. She'll be a good girl, a good cow. But a quick one. You'll have to take good care. She throws her head again, stumbling left and right, the lead pulling tight against her weight. Daniel's finger is numb on the trigger.

"Go on with it, son," Dad says. He stands with his back to Daniel and Olivia. "No need letting her suffer."

Daniel stares down the barrel at Olivia. She flicks one round ear and swats her long black tail.

Dad turns back to face Daniel. He exhales loud enough for Daniel to hear and reaches out as if wanting Daniel to hand off the gun. Instead, Daniel lines it up again and begins to pull the heavy trigger.

"Hold on there, Dan," Dad says. "Wait. Dan, no."

Daniel pulls. He thinks he pulls. And jumps when a shot fires.

It catches Olivia square between the ears, and the sound of her exploding skull seems to surprise her. She tosses her head, shaking away the echo, but the lead holds firm. Another shot. She drops her snout, nuzzles the ground, stumbles, her front feet crossing one over the other. Her back feet are rooted. The lead holds firm. A third shot. She falls. Daniel lowers the shotgun and turns. There, standing in front of his truck, ready to take another shot, Jonathon holds his position, but Olivia is already down. He had perfect aim with all three. He lowers his gun and leans against the hood of his truck. He's parked in his usual spot.

"Got herself caught up back there," Dad says. "Tangled up in her lead." He takes another deep breath and shakes his head. "Couldn't find her way out. Threw her head through the garage window."

Jonathon nods and wipes his brow with the palm of his hand like Dad always does. In the passenger side of his truck, Elaine sits, her face hidden in her hands.

Daniel looks down at his gun and back at Dad.

"Wouldn't want a shotgun for a job like this, son," Dad says.

Jonathon lays his rifle in the back of his truck. "Shotgun'll do the trick if something's coming at you," he says. "Good for protection and hunting. But if you have time to take aim, you want a rifle."

"Should have told you to get your rifle," Dad says. "Man'll always do right with his own gun."

Jonathon nods and Daniel wants to lunge

at him and beat him in the face for always being Dad's extra set of hands. Instead, he nods like he understands about shotguns and rifles.

"Hustle on in and get me some clean clothes," Dad says, noticing the blood smeared across his shirt and arms.

Unable to say anything, Daniel nods again, lays down Grandpa's shotgun and steps around it. At the top of the porch stairs, he turns. Dad has picked up the gun and he and Jonathon are looking at it, studying it. They stare at each other for a good long moment, like they are saying something without having to speak, and then propping the gun over one shoulder, Dad walks into the garage.

"Damn shame," Jonathon says, walking toward Olivia.

Daniel says nothing while he waits for Dad to come back out of the garage. When he does, he is empty-handed.

"Dad," Daniel says before opening the screened door. "Evie's home, right? Evie's already here."

Finding Mrs. Robison's house was easy. From school, Evie had only to follow the church steeple, and even though it wasn't a long walk, Evie's toes are cold and the tops of her ears burn. She knocks again, this time with the palm of her hand because knocking with her knuckles makes them sting. Mama will be angry if she knows Evie left the house without gloves and a hat. She forgot them because she was so worried about the hem of Aunt Eve's dress sticking out from under her winter coat where Mama might see it.

Standing at the front door, Evie pulls her coat closed so Mrs. Robison won't see the torn part of the dress before Evie can explain. It's Daddy's fault it tore some more. He hit Uncle Ray, and Evie tripped over the dress and the collar ripped. Maybe that's why Uncle Ray's red truck is parked down at the church. Maybe he is talking to Father Flannery about how Daddy hit him and how Aunt Ruth has his baby inside of her. That's Uncle Ray's truck for sure. It's parked in the same spot he and Aunt Ruth parked in every Sunday before Aunt Ruth came to live with Evie. As soon as Mrs. Robison answers the door, Evie will show her that Uncle Ray is at church because Daddy and he had a fight and made Evie tear her dress. Surely Mrs. Robison will fix it. She'll have the needles and thread and she'll sew it up tight, and maybe she'll fix the trim, too. Mrs. Robison might even be able to make the dress a little smaller so it will fit Evie better next time.

Knocking on Mrs. Robison's door again and hearing nothing, Evie walks to the picture window, cups her hands around her eyes, and tries to see inside, but the curtains are closed and the house is dark. She taps on the glass and presses her ear to it. Still nothing. Back at the door, she knocks again. The sun is starting to fall lower in the sky. The air is colder now than when Evie first left school, and soon, Mama will be thinking about supper. Mrs. Robison doesn't live far from school but Evie does. Her house is a long way away. Her house is so far from school that Mr. Slear drives them in the bus every day.

Not knowing why, except that the cold air and the gray sky make her think that she might never find home again, Evie starts to cry. She tries to stop by holding her breath and knocking with her knuckles so the sting will make her forget about how far away her house is, but the harder she knocks, the harder she cries. Mrs. Robison isn't home and she can't fix Aunt Eve's dress. Evie will have to go home with the torn collar and Mama will scold her for wearing Aunt Eve's dress and for ruining it. Laying one hand flat on Mrs. Robison's door, Evie drops her head, pulls her collar up and over her mouth and nose and walks away from the house.

At the end of the Robisons' sidewalk, with her face buried in her coat, Evie turns toward St. Anthony's. She knows to take Bent Road straight out of town. It will change from concrete to gravel, twist and bend, exactly like the name says, and after a good long way, it will break in two. One branch will lead to Grandma Reesa's house and the other will switch its name to Back Route 1 and lead toward home.

Crossing the street to the church, Evie sees that Uncle Ray isn't visiting Father Flannery. He is standing inside the white wooden fence that wraps around the grave-yard, staring down on one of the graves. The new graves, like the one dug for Mrs. Minken who died because she was 102, are way in the back of the cemetery, so Uncle Ray must be visiting an older grave, one for someone who died a long time ago. Three large pine trees stand over the grave Uncle Ray is looking at as if they are guarding it. He stands with those trees, his arms crossed, his feet spread wide like he's standing guard, too. In one hand, he holds his hat and his dark hair blows off his forehead. Evie calls out, good and loud so Uncle Ray will hear her over the wind.

"Hello," she says, and then is sorry for it. People are supposed to whisper in cemeteries.

Uncle Ray turns toward Evie. He watches her for a good long time, then pulls on his hat and looks back down on the grave.

The wind is colder once Evie steps onto the sidewalk and walks toward home. She pulls her sleeves over her hands, dips her head and tries to take long steps that will get her home quicker. Beyond the shelter of the church, the wind kicks up and dies down again when she passes Mr. Brewster's house. A light switches on. Mr. Brewster, carrying a plate, walks past the window. Mama says he's a widower because his wife died and that he doesn't get out much. Even Mr. Brewster, who is all by himself, is sitting down to supper. That's what Mama and the others are doing by now. Mama likes an early supper because going to bed on a full stomach never does anyone any good. Evie closes her eyes as she passes Mr. Brewster's house. He must be lonely in there all by himself and that makes Evie feel like she may never see home again.

At the last stop sign before the road changes to dirt, a car pulls up next to Evie. It rattles to a stop and exhaust swirls up, clouding the gray air around her. She unwraps her hands, lowers her collar and looks into the side of a big, red truck.

Celia clears her throat, and taking a deep breath to calm herself, she pulls a fresh shirt from the top drawer and a clean pair of pants from the closet. Out in the kitchen, Ruth is busying herself by setting the table and skinning the chicken for dinner. She's seen things like this before, probably much worse. If Arthur hadn't been able to come home in the middle of the day when Celia called to tell him that Olivia was out again and was apparently stuck between the house and garage, even with one bad arm, Ruth probably would have coaxed the cow out herself. Right this moment, she is probably planning how to best slaughter Olivia and where they will freeze so much meat. No, that's not true. Ruth wouldn't think those things. Reesa would, but not Ruth. Ruth will be thinking how to help the children understand that this is part of life on the farm. She would never tell them that Olivia will soon be wrapped in white butcher paper and stacked in the freezer.

Folding the blue and gray plaid flannel shirt for no reason other than to stall, Celia wonders if Arthur knew things would be this way when they moved from Detroit. Did he know that sometimes the eggs wouldn't be eggs when Celia cracked them into her skillet but that sometimes they would be the beginnings of a tiny, bloody chick? Did he know Daniel wouldn't have many friends and that Evie still wouldn't grow? Did he know Ray was beating Ruth all those years, beating the life out of her, and did he still stay away? Not wanting the answer to the last thought, Celia clears her throat again and walks from the bedroom with the clothes stacked neatly in both hands.

Standing at the kitchen table, one hand holding the back of a chair, Ruth doesn't look the way Celia thought she would. Her face is pale, her neck flushed. For a moment, Celia is relieved because Ruth is as upset as she by what has happened to Olivia. For a moment, Celia doesn't feel alone. Thank goodness for Ruth. Celia holds the clothes out to Daniel, who stands in the hallway leading to the back porch, but he doesn't reach for them.

"For your dad," Celia says, taking another step forward.

Daniel's arms hang limp and he steps aside when Arthur walks up from behind. Celia takes two quick steps backward and pulls the clothes to her chest, hugging them.

"Arthur, take this outside," she says, shoving his clothes at him. "You're an awful mess."

Reddish brown smudges that end with feathered edges travel from Arthur's right hip up to his left shoulder, as if Olivia threw her head against him, and dried blood is caked on his hands and forearms.

"Your shoes," Celia says. "Take those off. Outside."

Muddy tracks have followed Arthur into the house, bloody mud. Celia looks at Daniel's feet instead. He keeps telling her he needs new boots, that his toes are going to end up crooked if he doesn't get some bigger shoes.

"Please, take those off outside."

"Is Evie here with you?" Arthur says.

At this, Celia lifts her eyes.

"She's not outside," Jonathon says, walking up behind Arthur. Elaine stands next to him. She nods. "We checked the barn, the road. Elaine looked downstairs."

"She came on the bus," Celia says, looking Daniel in the eye. "With you. She came home on the bus. Like always."

"The nurse said she was going to call," Daniel says. "Because Evie wore the dress. I thought you came for her."

Ruth steps forward and takes the stack of clothes from Celia.

"The dress?" Celia says. "What dress? No one called."

"The school nurse." Daniel clears his throat the same way Celia does when she's trying not to cry. "She was going to call. She said maybe Evie should go home for the day."

Daniel looks up at Arthur. There's not so much difference anymore. They're almost the same height.

"Evie wore one of those dresses to school. One of Aunt Eve's dresses. From Grandma's house. I thought you picked her up." Daniel takes a deep breath. His chest lifts and lowers. "She didn't come home on the bus, Mama."

"Well, then she's still at school," Celia says, nodding. "Right. She's still at school."

"We'll go, Mama," Elaine says, pulling Jonathon toward the back door. "We'll check the school."

"I'll give them a call," Ruth says, setting the clothes on the table and taking care that they don't spill over and come unfolded. "I'm sure she's fine. Probably got caught up after class. Nothing to worry about."

"I thought you came, Mama," Daniel says. "I wouldn't leave her. I wouldn't."

Staring again at Daniel's boots, Celia thinks how much he's grown in the short time they've been in Kansas. And other things have changed, as well. His brow is starting to push out, the bridge of his nose is taking the same curve as Arthur's, his neck has thickened ever so slightly where it drapes into his shoulders. Celia cocks her head to the left and says, "Today at work, Arthur. Was Ray with you today at work?"

"Hasn't been in all week. Not since we saw him at the café. Not since Tuesday."

CHAPTER 22

The truck smells like a coyote wagon. That's what Mama would have said. Whenever Mama rode in Daddy's truck, she said it was becoming nothing more than a coyote wagon. After that, Daddy would take a leftover grocery bag and clean out the wadded-up newspapers, the half-eaten apples, which were half-eaten because Daddy only likes the bites that have red skin with them, and the cigarette butts that make Mama especially mad because she hates that he sometimes smokes in Kansas. Uncle Ray is a smoker, too, but he doesn't have anyone to tell him to clean out his butts so they spill over the small tray and some of them lie on the floor. Uncle Ray is an apple eater, too, but he eats his down to the core.

Wrinkling her nose and clearing her throat, Evie steps off the sidewalk and reaches for the inside door handle. It's cold in her bare hand. An old red and blue flannel sheet is draped over the spot where Evie is supposed to sit, probably because Aunt Ruth used to sit there and without the thin cover, the seats would be cold and hard. The sheet is tucked in tight where the back and the bottom of the seat meet. Aunt Ruth did that. She is always tucking and straightening. This makes Evie feel better, makes her feel that it is okay to get into Uncle Ray's truck. Bracing one hand against the doorframe and pulling on the inside handle with the other, Evie steps up into the truck, careful not to look at Uncle Ray's face because she can't help but stare straight into the bad eye and Mama says that's not polite. So instead, she keeps her head lowered, drops down on the flannel cover and swings her legs into the truck. Propping both feet on the toolbox that sits on the floorboard, she pulls the truck door closed.

"You call the school?" Arthur says, walking out of the bedroom and grabbing his keys from the table on his way outside. He has washed up and is wearing clean clothes. "She there?"

Ruth shakes her head and starts to speak, but Celia cuts her off. "No, she's not there. No one's there. No one to even answer the phone."

Standing face to face with Arthur, her hands on her hips, Celia suddenly hates him. She hates the way his hair curls when it is damp. She hates that he doesn't shave every day like he did in Detroit and that he can't be bothered with a tie on Sundays. She hates that he stretches and groans when he eats Reesa's fried chicken and doesn't use a napkin until he's eaten his fill. And most of all, she hates him for yelling at Daniel because he's not enough of a man yet. Arthur is the one who isn't man enough, and now, because of that, because he did nothing, because he isn't the man he is supposed to be, Evie is gone. Gone like Mother and Father. Gone like Julianne Robison. Gone.

"What about Jonathon and Elaine?" Arthur hops on one foot, pulling on a boot that has Olivia's blood caked in the tread. "They back yet?"

"No," Celia says, taking her own boots from the closet and reaching past Arthur for her coat. "Why would they be back?" She pushes him in the chest so he'll look her in the face. "It's a full thirty minutes there and home again. Thirty minutes at best. That's how far it is."

Cupping Celia's arms with both of his hands, Arthur says, "Take it easy. I'm sure she's fine. We'll find her. You stay here. You and Ruth. In case she comes home, you should . . ."

Celia shoves his hand away and yanks on her jacket. "This is your fault," she says, quietly at first, but then it feels so good, like beating on something with both fists, that she says it louder and louder until she is shouting. "I've been telling you, begging you to do something. I knew it. I knew it. He's angry. Angry that we kept the baby from him. First Julianne and now." But she can't say it. She can't say he has taken her Evie. "You brought us here. To this godforsaken place. This is your fault. All your fault."

It must be Ruth, laying a warm hand on Celia's back, and that must be Arthur, wrapping both arms around her, holding her to his chest. Someone is saying, don't panic. No need to panic. Won't do us any good. All these months that Julianne has been gone, Celia has thought of her every day, made herself think of the little girl she never met. If ever she found her day slipping away without a thought of Julianne, she stopped her scrubbing or ironing or weeding and looked up. If inside, she looked out a window. If outside, she looked to the horizon, always remembering, always searching, always hoping. Out of respect for the fear of losing her own children, she did these things every day, without fail. But no one ever found Julianne, and now Evie is gone and Celia is facing the same life Mary Robison must live.

The road under Uncle Ray's tires changes from asphalt to gravel. Evie feels the change in her stomach, the same tickle she gets when she rides with Daddy in his truck. Getting to Evie's house from church is easy. Now that the road has turned rocky, they will keep driving on Bent Road for a good long while, and when it breaks off to go to Grandma Reesa's house, they'll keep driving straight and the road will turn into Back Route 1. This is where Evie lives. Once Bent Road becomes Back Route 1, they're almost home. Except Uncle Ray turns before the twist in Bent Road that leads to Grandma Reesa's house. He turns on a road Evie's been on before but she can't remember when.

Daniel stands in the middle of the gravel drive, looking first toward the barn and next the garage, but he knows Evie isn't either place. He could check inside Mr. Murray's rusted old car, but she isn't in there either. Besides, he'd have to walk past Olivia to get to that old car, and he can't do that. Steam isn't rising from Olivia anymore. This must mean she's turning cold. Jonathon patted Daniel on the back before rushing off with Elaine to go to the school. He said he'd take care of the old gal when he got back. He said she'd keep just fine in the cold. Daniel doesn't want to think about what this means. There's a smell, too. Maybe it's Olivia's insides starting to rot out, or maybe it's mud and her wet, bloody hide.

Something is different now. It's the color of things. The sun is hanging on the horizon and its light is gray instead of clear. Everything is gray. It's almost night. It happens so quickly this time of year. Night didn't seem to settle in so fast in Detroit where there were streetlights and neighbors' lights and headlights. The gray air makes Daniel's stomach tighten and his chest begins to pound as each breath comes faster than the last. He backs away from Olivia. Evie isn't in the barn or the basement or Mr. Murray's old car. She's not anywhere. He takes another backward step and then another. Eventually, he'll run all the way to school. He'll find Evie there and bring her home. A few more steps, but he can't turn away from Olivia yet. She lies on her side, one rounded ear sticking up, one bright eye staring at him. He realizes he is waiting for that eye to blink, but it doesn't. It never will.

It's not quite dark yet. As soon as Uncle Ray turns off Bent Road, Evie sees a small group of men standing in the ditch. Uncle Ray must have seen them, too. They must be the reason Uncle Ray turned because he stops the truck in the middle of the road and shines his headlights on them. A few of the men hold a hand up to shield their eyes and they look at Uncle Ray's truck. Evie scoots to the edge of her seat.

"Those two men have dogs," she says.

Uncle Ray doesn't answer, but instead pulls down hard on the gearshift, backs up, rolling the steering wheel so the truck's tailgate swings around toward the ditch and throws the gearshift forward again.

"Do you know those men, Uncle Ray?"

Again, Uncle Ray doesn't answer. His hat sits high on his forehead, and even though his eyes have plenty of room to see, he doesn't look at Evie. Turning the steering wheel the other way, passing one hand over the other the same way Daddy does, Uncle Ray presses on the gas and the men and the two dogs disappear when Uncle Ray drives back onto Bent Road.

The sky is almost all the way dark now,

but even so, Evie remembers the place were they saw the men and dogs. She went there a time or two with Daddy when Uncle Ray was away with his other family in Damar. It's Mrs. Hathaway's farm, except Uncle Ray uses it because Mr. Hathaway died a long time ago. Evie slides back in her seat and grabs onto the blanket that Aunt Ruth left behind. For one quick second, something smells sweet and light like Aunt Ruth. Evie feels like she wants to cry again, though she doesn't know why. She grabs two handfuls of the rough quilt, wadding it up in both fists and watches for home.

Daniel is standing in the center of the gravel drive, staring down at Olivia, when Dad starts to beat on his steering wheel. Only then, does Daniel notice the empty sound of the truck's engine. It is rattling and choking but it won't turn over. Dad throws open the driver's side door.

"Go get your mother's keys," he shouts at Daniel.

Daniel doesn't move.

"Hurry up about it," Dad says, reaching behind his seat and pulling out a set of jumper cables. Next, the hood pops open. "The keys, Dan. Get your mother's keys."

Daniel backs away a few more steps. Dad

is going to search for Evie but his truck won't start. How will they find Evie if Dad's truck won't start? One more time, Dad shouts. Daniel jumps, spins around, takes two running steps and stumbles.

"Olivia," Evie says. "Is that Olivia?"

Daniel straightens and grabs Evie by the shoulders. Her cheeks and nose are red, her eyes watery. She steps to the side so she can see Olivia.

"What's wrong with her?" Evie says. "Her neck is bad. Her head isn't the right shape."

From a few yards away, Olivia's one eye is staring at them. It's big and black, and like a piece of polished glass, it shines where it catches the porch light. Daniel turns back to Evie and checks her over top to bottom, searching for missing parts. Two eyes, two ears, a whole head.

"Come inside," he says, stepping in front of her so she can't see Olivia. "Dad," he shouts, pulling Evie toward the house. "She's home. She's home." Stumbling up the stairs, across the porch and pushing open the back door, he shouts, "Mama."

Warm air meets them inside. It burns Daniel's cheeks and lips. He inhales, drops down to one knee and holds Evie's hands.

"Evie's here. Evie's home."

Mama rushes in like the hot air, sweeping

Evie up. She checks for missing parts, too. When she gets to Evie's hands, Mama presses them to her cheeks and rubs them between her own hands, warming them, softening them up.

From behind Daniel, Dad says, "Where have you been, child?"

But Mama quiets Evie, tells her that it doesn't matter. "You're home, sweet pea. You're so cold. So cold." And then to Daniel. "Where?" is all she says.

"I turned around and there she was." Daniel stands and whispers. "She saw Olivia. She saw what happened."

"I left her lead on," Evie says. "I did it. I left it on." She cries into Mama's shoulder. "I did it."

Mama looks over Daniel's head at Dad. Aunt Ruth wraps a blanket around Evie's small body. The old quilt smells sour and moldy like the basement. Mama hates drying clothes in the basement.

"No, Evie," Mama says. "It was an accident. No one's fault." Mama stretches out her arms, holding Evie where they can look into each other's eyes. "Where were you, Evie? How did you get home?"

"Uncle Ray brought me," she says. "We went to Mrs. Hathaway's farm, but there were men there so Uncle Ray brought me home."

CHAPTER 23

Celia cracks a third egg, cracks it so hard that the shell collapses in her hand leaving the yolk and white to slide through her fingers and into the dumpling dough. Dropping the shell into the sink and wiping her hands on the dishtowel tucked in her apron, she picks up a wooden spoon and stirs the thick dough. After a few minutes, she shifts the spoon to her other hand and continues to dig and grind until she's breathing heavily. Pausing once to roll her head from side to side, she shifts hands again, wraps her forearm around the bowl, drops the spoon and kneads the dough by hand. On the front burner, the chicken stock grows from a simmer to a rolling boil.

"Take it easy," Arthur says, leaning back in his chair and stretching.

Celia glances up at Arthur, but says nothing, and instead reaches for another egg. Reesa shakes her head. Celia grabs the egg anyway, cracks it as hard as the last and throws the empty shell toward the sink. She misses, and as it falls on the floor, she wipes her hands across the front of her white blouse.

Her right arm still in a sling, Ruth leaps from her seat to scoop up the shell. "A nice warm meal always makes things better," she says. "Always makes the house smell so wonderful." She talks as she picks up every piece of the slippery shell as if no one will notice the mess if she keeps talking.

"Making this house smell pretty good, that's for sure," Arthur says, leaning forward and resting his elbows on the table.

Celia takes a teaspoon from the drawer and begins to dip up the dough and drop it into the boiling broth, ignoring the fact that it's too runny because she's added one too many eggs. She clears her throat and chokes back a sob when Ruth, after cleaning the egg shell from her fingers, steps forward and whispers, "The kids are fine, Celia. Evie is fine. Safe and sound."

Pausing mid scoop, while Ruth kneads another cup of flour into the dough, Celia says to Reesa, "I've asked that Evie return all of Eve's things to you, along with an apology. I don't know what she was thinking. And getting in that truck with Ray."

She stops, swallows. "We need to call Floyd and report this."

"Report what?" Arthur says. "He gave the girl a ride home. Damn fool that he is, he just gave her a ride home."

"They are searching his farm," Celia says, stirring her broth. "Searching it with dogs. And he took Evie there. You know what that means."

Arthur brushes his hair back from his face and takes a deep breath before speaking. "For twenty-five years, Floyd has been thinking Ray had something to do with what happened to Eve." His eyes are swollen from his having rubbed them and from being tired. "That's the only reason he's keeping such an eye on Ray. Listen, I'll keep him clear of this family, that's for sure. And I know the man is up to plenty of no good, but I don't believe for a minute that he hurt Julianne Robison."

Celia throws her teaspoon into the broth, jumping back when it splashes up. "What about the night Julianne disappeared? He wasn't home. Ruth said so." Celia stands, hand on hips. "He could have done it. How can you know?"

"Evie doesn't have any friends."

Everyone turns. Daniel stands outside his bedroom, his hair tousled and his eyes red as if he woke up from having cried himself to sleep.

"At school. She doesn't have any friends at school. Neither do I, except for Ian. It's not like in Detroit. Nobody likes us here."

Celia, pulling off her apron, walks toward Daniel. He takes a few steps backward. "What do you mean, Daniel?"

"Just that. No friends. Except for Aunt Eve."

"Of course she has friends," Celia says.

Daniel shakes his head. "She did back home. Had plenty back then. But not here. They call her nigger lover. Have ever since we started school. Because we lived in Detroit. Called me one, too, until Ian started being my friend. The kids, they all tell Evie she's here because Jack Mayer stole Julianne Robison. Or maybe Uncle Ray took her. They say one of them's bound to steal Evie next."

"They say that to Evie?" Celia drops back against the kitchen counter.

Arthur shakes his head. Reesa makes a clucking sound.

"She sits by herself every day. At recess. Lunch. Everywhere. She's so small. They call her names. Tell her she's too small for Kansas. Sometimes Miss Olson sits with her at lunch. But Evie just pretends Miss Olson is Aunt Eve. Miss Olson isn't so small, though."

Ruth steps up to Celia's side. Her body is warm and she smells like Elaine's lavender lotion.

"How did I not know this?" she says to Ruth. "How could she be so unhappy and I not know?"

"She wasn't unhappy," Daniel says. "As long as she had Aunt Eve. That's why she took all that stuff. I guess that's why she wore the dress. But now she doesn't even have Aunt Eve. I think she's kind of scared about getting taken like Julianne. And she feels pretty bad about Olivia, too." He takes a few more steps away when Celia pushes off the counter. He shakes his head. "I understand though, about it being the kindest thing. To kill her, I mean. Just wish I hadn't left that gate open."

Arthur glances up at Celia before lowering his head to talk into the tabletop. "Cows like that get out all the time," he says. "They're jumpers. Could have jumped out."

Daniel stares at Arthur, not like a boy looks at his father, but like one man looks at another. Arthur tries to hold the stare long enough and hard enough that Daniel will believe Olivia was a jumper, but he can't manage it. He drops his eyes.

"I don't want to go to Ian's tomorrow," Daniel says, still staring at the top of Arthur's head.

Celia nods. "Certainly, Daniel. Whatever you want. Get some rest now. I'll call you when dinner's ready."

When Mama calls him to dinner, Daniel says he's too tired. Even when Mama opens the door a sliver and offers him a plate of Aunt Ruth's stewed chicken, Daniel rolls away and says no. Now, he can hear them, all of them, in the kitchen, their silverware clattering on the table, pots and pans being passed from place to place. They are probably talking about poor Evie and Daniel who have no friends. They probably think Evie is sick because she wore Aunt Eve's dress to school and that Daniel will never grow to be a man. He should have pulled the trigger and shot Olivia. No matter how stiff and heavy, no matter what kind of mess he would have made, he should have pulled it. That's what a man would have done. He would have carried the weight of that shotgun on his shoulder and pulled the God damn trigger.

Rolling over again and staring at the light shining under his door, Daniel hopes Ian will go pheasant hunting without him. He hopes Ian can be a pusher and that his black boots will help him keep up with his brothers. Maybe they'll do well, shoot a dozen birds or so, and then Jacob, the oldest Bucher brother, who only comes home on occasional weekends, will toss them all in his truck and drive to Nicodemus so they can flush out Jack Mayer. Maybe Ian will even get a shot at old Jack Mayer. Through the sight on his dad's shotgun, Ian will spot the man who's big as a mountain and black as midnight, and he'll take a shot. Even if he misses, even if Jack Mayer slips away because he's dark as night, Ian will have gotten off a shot and he'll never be quite as crooked again. And Daniel is Ian's friend, his best friend. Daniel will never be a city kid again if Ian gets off a good shot.

CHAPTER 24

Celia props the last dish in the drying rack, hangs her dish towel on the hook over the sink, and taking one last look around the kitchen to make sure everything is in its place, she flips off the light. Daniel and Evie's rooms are quiet, have been since dinner. Daniel didn't eat a bite. Celia will make pancakes for breakfast — his favorite. A light still shines in Elaine's room where she and Ruth are quietly talking, probably planning the bodice for Elaine's wedding dress or picking the flowers for her bouquet. Elaine thinks lilies but Ruth likes carnations. Checking that someone locked the back door and giving the deadbolt an extra tug, even though Arthur has twice done the same thing, Celia walks toward her bedroom and meets Arthur as he comes out of the bathroom, a towel wrapped around his waist, the steam from a hot shower following him.

His skin is thicker since they moved to Kansas, like a hide. His face and neck are dark, his hands rough, his back and chest broad. Celia touches his collarbone as she slips past him into their bedroom. He smells of soap. He takes her hand, stops her, makes her look up at him. She knows what he wants. He wants Celia to believe in him, to trust him. Laying her hand flat on his chest, she closes her eyes, breathes in the warm air about his body and prepares to tell him the truth. While he was in the shower, she called Floyd, even after Arthur said it would do no good, that it would only stir up Ray, stir up more trouble. She called Floyd and told him that Ray tried to take her little girl. She lied to Arthur and she was hateful to him, if only in her thoughts. Not once, not ever, in all their years together, has she been so hateful. Not even when Arthur brought home the new truck and lashed her Detroit life to it, did she have a hateful thought. She made herself trust him then and she wants the same now. More than anything, she wants to trust him.

Pulling their door closed, Arthur backs Celia toward the bed. As she lowers herself, Arthur standing before her, she lifts her hands and lays them on his stomach, bending her fingers, gently denting his dark skin with her nails. If he is more of a man now, then she is more of a woman. When they lived in Detroit, Arthur wore a starched shirt to church, shined his shoes once a week and sat for a haircut every fourth Tuesday. Celia wore pearls on Sundays and set her table with pressed linens. But here in Kansas, Arthur's shirts are fraying at the collars and cuffs and Celia's pearls are packed away in a box in her top dresser drawer. They are different, both of them.

Letting her hands slide down Arthur's flat stomach, Celia pulls apart the towel at his waist. She needs him to make her feel clean again because the showers and shampoo and soap did not. She needs Arthur to make her forget the way Ray looked at her or the feel of him grinding himself into her thigh, to make her forget the thought of Ray with her little girl, his dirty hands touching Evie's yellow hair. Clawing Arthur's back, she draws him down on top of her and buries her face in his shoulder where the muscle dips into his neck. He pulls her skirt up, presses aside the crotch of her cotton panties, and forces himself inside of her with one quick motion. The pain lasts only an instant. His movements are quick, fierce, almost angry. Pressing his face into the mattress, he muffles a groan. And then his breathing quiets. He shudders and is still. Celia needs something more, wants something more. But it's over.

Waiting until Arthur has rolled off her, Celia inhales a full breath, sits up, unbuttons her blouse and skirt and pushes them to the floor. The night air chills her damp skin where it was pressed against Arthur. Kansas has made her body harder, like it was when she was younger. Her stomach is flat again though marred by silvery white lines where it stretched for her babies. Her hips are soft and white, but narrow, slimmer than they were in Detroit. She reaches for Arthur's hand and places it on her left breast, holding it there until he begins to roll her nipple between two fingers. He breathes faster again, slips the same hand between her legs and presses apart her knees. Celia lies back, exhaling and not hearing the dry grass that crackles outside her window.

Evie rolls on one side, afraid to close her eyes because every time she does, she remembers the red silky inside of Olivia's neck and the black blood that she lay in. Daniel tried to cover her eyes before she saw but he was too slow. Evie always thought blood was red. Now she wonders why babies are blue and cows bleed black blood. She should have asked Uncle Ray. He is more of a cowboy than Daddy. Uncle Ray would know about blue babies and black blood, but he didn't want to talk much on the ride home. He didn't even ask about Aunt Eve's dress even though it stuck out from under the bottom of Evie's coat. She saw him looking at the blue ruffles. Mostly, Uncle Ray looked like he hadn't slept a single night in his whole life.

"Girl ought to wear trousers when it's so cold" is the only thing he said.

Thinking that next time she sees Uncle Ray she'll ask him about black blood, Evie rolls over and looks at the drawer where she hid the picture of Aunt Eve and Uncle Ray. Mama made her return the rest of Aunt Eve's things to Grandma Reesa and she has to write an apology letter on Mama's best stationery so they can send it through the mail. Mama doesn't know Evie kept the picture.

Across the kitchen, Mama's bed creaks. Sometimes, when the house is dark, Evie hears it. Mama always says they are making up the bed with clean sheets. Tucking in hospital corners, straightening the quilt, fluffing the pillows. Soon enough, Mama is done tucking her sheets and the house is quiet again. Maybe Evie can sleep without closing her eyes. Cows do that sometimes, or is it horses? Another question for Uncle Ray. But Evie isn't a cow or a horse. She tries closing her eyes. First one, then the other. Everything is black for a moment and then she hears a knock. Maybe Mama is making the bed again. Evie opens her eyes and sits up. She hears another quiet knock. Tapping on glass. *Tap, tap, tap.* Someone is at the back door.

Daniel wants to bang on his wall. He wants to punch a hole all the way through to Elaine's room and into her fat mouth. She and Aunt Ruth are still whispering about the wedding. All night long, probably all through dinner, and even now when they should be sleeping. Elaine doesn't care one damn bit that Olivia died. She doesn't care that Evie wore Aunt Eve's dress to school or that everyone calls Evie a nigger lover. She doesn't even care that Evie almost got swiped like Julianne Robison. All she cares about is studying and finishing high school so she can have the wedding that she spends all night, every night, planning with Aunt Ruth. Daniel sits up, lunges toward the wall he shares with Elaine, pulls back his fist, ready to punch a hole all the way into her room, when he hears a knock. The last time Mama checked on him, he pretended he was asleep so she left his door ajar. Unwrapping his fist and dropping his hand to his side, Daniel walks to his open door and listens. Yes, someone is knocking.

Ruth keeps talking, thinking that Elaine won't notice the quiet creaks coming from Celia and Arthur's end of the house. She gathers the fabric at Elaine's waist with the fingers that stick out of her sling and weaves a straight pen into the satin sash. "That should do it," she says as Elaine muffles a laugh. "Now, be still." Ruth ignores the giggle. With so much to be sad about that day, the laughter is sweet. "I can't keep taking this in. You need to eat better. You'll waste away to nothing by the wedding if you're not careful." She folds over another patch of loose fabric farther down Elaine's hip and this time when she smiles at the quiet creaks, it's because they make her feel that maybe things will be fine again. In these quiet moments, the house binds together.

"Will that do?" Ruth says, patting Elaine's hip and looking past her into the mirror on the back of the door.

Elaine so resembles Celia, though her features are dark like Arthur's. Still, she has her mother's long, soft waves, and even late at night, her eyes and cheeks shine the same way Celia's did when she smiled at Arthur through a cascading white veil.

"Perfect," Elaine says. "Just perfect."

The creaking stops and the house is quiet.

"Let me help you," Ruth says as Elaine wiggles out of her wedding dress.

"I need to use the restroom first," Elaine says, stepping off her stool and reaching for the doorknob as she hops from side to side.

She must have been holding it, waiting for the creaking to stop. They both begin with a smile before breaking into giggles.

"I can't wait anymore." Trying to muffle her laughter, Elaine opens the door a crack. "Did you hear that?" she says, turning toward Ruth.

"Sounds like someone is on the porch."

"Who would come so late?" Elaine says, and stepping out of her dress, she slips on a robe.

Ruth waves Elaine aside. With one hand pressed to her full, round belly, she says, "I'll have a look."

Celia opens her eyes. She rolls her head toward the dark window. No moonlight. No sparkling Battenburg lace curtains. Next to her, Arthur's eyes are closed. Covering her bare chest with one arm, Celia sits up and feels for the quilt. She finds it at the end of the bed and tugs but it is tangled in Arthur's feet. She tugs again, causing his eyes to open, and she hears it. A knock at the back door. She drops the quilt.

"Arthur," Celia whispers, poking his shoulder. Yes, she hears a knock. Louder now. "Arthur, did you hear that?"

Arthur rolls on his back to see Celia leaning over him, bare-chested. He lets out a quiet moan and reaches for both breasts.

She pushes his hands away. "Shhhh," she says. "Listen. I think someone's at the back door. Do you hear it?"

Reaching with one hand for the spot between Celia's legs, Arthur mumbles something about the wind. Celia slides off the end of the bed, yanks the quilt from under Arthur's feet, causing him to startle, and after wrapping it around herself and securing it by tucking in one end, she stands and looks straight into the eyes of a black silhouette standing in the window.

"Arthur," she says through clenched teeth.

Backing away from the window, she trips over the quilt and, as she stumbles, each step yanks down the blanket until she is naked again. The black silhouette still stands in the window.

"Arthur, someone is there," Celia says, squatting behind the bed and gathering up the quilt.

Arthur sits up, swings his legs around so that he is staring directly into the window. He is close enough to touch the glass. It's black. Empty.

"No one there, Celia," he says.

"Well, I saw someone. And I heard knocking."

Arthur exhales, loudly enough that Celia can hear, stands, pulls on the jeans draped over the end of the bed and walks past her, giving a playful tug on her quilt. She slaps his hand and gathers the cover under her chin with two fists.

"It's probably Jonathon. That kid might as well put his name on the mailbox."

As Arthur opens the bedroom door and steps into the kitchen, Celia whispers, "Jonathon wouldn't peek in our window."

"Suppose not," he says. "I'll give a look."

Evie pulls her robe closed and presses her face to the glass in the back door that leads onto the porch. With each breath, a frosty patch balloons on the window. Soon, she can't see outside. Rolling her head to the left, she presses her ear against the cold, wet glass. Quiet. She looks again and, seeing nothing and hearing nothing, she takes a step back, pulls the sleeve of her flannel nightgown down over her hand like a mitten and rubs a circle in the icy patch of glass.

"Evie," Daddy says.

A light switches on in the kitchen.

"Evie," he says again, taking a step toward her.

He fills up the small hallway that leads from the kitchen, past the basement stairs, to the back door.

"Step away, Evie."

Evie smiles at Daddy, turns back to the window and looks up to see Uncle Ray's face where it was dark before. She knows it's him because he wears his hat high off his forehead, but something about Uncle Ray isn't quite right. As Evie steps away, he steps forward. His head sways, like it's not screwed on tight enough, and one shoulder hangs lower than the other. Pressing both hands against the glass, he says something and smiles a crooked smile.

"What?" Evie says, stepping forward again and putting one hand on the door handle. It's cold but she squeezes it anyway. "Uncle Ray's out there," she says, looking back at Daddy.

Uncle Ray doesn't scare her like he used to, like he did on the night he asked for pie, because Aunt Eve loved Uncle Ray even if one of his eyes wanders off where it doesn't belong. She loved him so much she wanted to marry him but then she died and he had to marry Aunt Ruth. He wouldn't even be mean at all if Aunt Ruth had died instead.

"Don't open that, Evie," Daddy says, taking another step toward her. "Come away from there."

Uncle Ray looks over Evie's head. He sees Daddy standing behind her. Daddy isn't wearing a shirt and his feet must be cold, too. The handle is warm in Evie's hand now. Uncle Ray isn't smiling anymore, and in the dark, his cloudy eye is a black hole. With one hand, he knocks on the glass. With the other, he rattles the door.

"You tell Ruth to come out here," Uncle Ray shouts through the glass. "I should have left your girl to freeze."

Now Mama and Aunt Ruth are standing behind Daddy. All three of them creep closer, looking like Daddy and Daniel when they found a rattlesnake in the barn. Daddy snuck up on the snake with a long- handled spade. He hacked it in two and said to Daniel, "Careful, son. Rattlers never travel alone." They found another snake coiled up in the back corner of Olivia's stall, its tail shaking like a tin of dried beans. Daddy hacked it up, too.

"Evie, honey. Come on back to bed," Mama says, peeking around Daddy. "You must be so cold."

Aunt Ruth, standing at Daddy's other side, nods.

"You know they think I was taking their girl, Ruth? That what you think, too? That why Floyd's got his God damn dogs over at our house?"

Evie presses against the door, the knob still in her hand. She can feel Uncle Ray on the other side, jiggling the handle, wanting to come in. He shakes it harder. It sounds like the second snake when Daddy crept toward it, the dry hay snapping under his black boots. Evie frowns, imagining that Daddy is carrying a long handled spade.

"Go on home, Ray," Daddy shouts, taking another step toward Evie. "It's too late for this now."

Daddy must make Uncle Ray mad because he starts banging on the door. Just over Evie's head, his fist pounds into the glass. The door rattles in its frame. Evie knows what Uncle Ray is doing is bad. She can see it in Mama and Aunt Ruth's faces. Their eyes are wide and they are both leaning around Daddy like they want to scoop up Evie and wrap her in her favorite patchwork quilt. Evie presses against the door. The glass shakes overhead. Uncle Ray is pounding with both fists now, probably because he sees Aunt Ruth. He wants to talk to her and to see his baby. That's what he said in the hospital. That's all he wants. And now the men with dogs are at his house and he's mad about it. Daddy reaches to grab Evie's arm.

"Go on, Ray," Daddy shouts.

"What'd you tell them?" Uncle Ray keeps beating on the glass.

Evie pulls away from Daddy and wraps both hands around the knob. It's so warm now, almost hot. Daddy grabs both of Evie's shoulders. His fingers dig into her arms, like a snakebite, like a rattler bite. She cries out. Her breath fogs the glass. Uncle Ray looks fuzzy. Maybe he smiles, but Evie isn't sure because the glass is cloudy. He pulls back both fists in one motion and brings them down as Daddy lifts Evie up and away.

"What'd you tell them?" Uncle Ray shouts.

The glass shatters into tiny pieces and rains down like the fuzzy-tipped seedlings Evie and Daniel blew off the tops of dandelions when they first moved to Kansas. Dangling from Daddy's arms, Evie watches the feathery glass sprinkle down around her.

Daddy holds her, crouched over, shielding her so she can't see Uncle Ray or the door or Mama. Only the feathery glass. The house falls silent.

Because she can't breathe very well, Evie twists and squirms until Daddy stands. He turns away from the window, and after taking a few steps toward Mama and Aunt Ruth, his body tensing each time he steps on a piece of glass, he hands Evie to Mama like a cup of hot soup, carefully so none of her spills over. Laying her head on Mama's shoulder, Evie can see Daddy. He is staring at the broken window. Uncle Ray is there, his fists frozen where they hit the glass. He looks at Evie, or maybe he's looking at Mama. Mama sets Evie down, gathers the top of her robe under her chin with one hand and waves at Evie to go back into the kitchen. Yes, he's looking at Mama. He smiles.

Daddy stands still for a moment, watching Uncle Ray smile at Mama and then he lunges, leaping over the scattered glass. He grabs at Uncle Ray through the broken window, but Uncle Ray is gone, across the porch and down the steps. Daddy throws open the door.

"Arthur, no," Mama shouts. "Leave it be."

But Daddy doesn't listen, and he runs

after Uncle Ray.

Hearing the glass break, Daniel slips by Elaine, who has just hung up with Jonathon. She grabs for Daniel's sleeve, but he is too quick. A few short steps and he is across the kitchen and standing at the top of the stairs that lead to the basement. He reaches for the gun cabinet but it's locked, and the spot where Dad's shotgun usually hangs is empty. But Daniel's rifle is there, right where it should be. Aunt Ruth hears him, grabs his hand and shakes her head. He pulls away from her. This time, he'll take a shot. He'll have his own gun and the trigger won't be too heavy. He could shoot Uncle Ray, kill him dead just fine with his .22. And he'd do it, too, in three perfect shots, if the cabinet weren't locked. No time to fish for the key. He pushes between Aunt Ruth and Mama and follows Dad out the door.

Before Daniel crosses the porch, a light flips on. In the center of the gravel drive, near the garage, Dad catches up to Uncle Ray, whose legs can't keep up with his top half. He is stumbling and falling from side to side until Dad grabs his collar. For a moment, Uncle Ray is steady on his feet until Dad yanks him backward, causing Uncle Ray's boots to fly out from under him.

Landing flat on his back, he lets out a groan. As Dad kicks Uncle Ray in the side, wincing and bouncing on one leg after he does it because he is barefooted, snowflakes begin to fall, sparkling in the porch light.

Making no noise, Dad drops down and drives one knee into Uncle Ray's ribs. Something cracks. Sitting on Uncle Ray's chest, Dad holds him square with his left hand and beats him in the face with his right. Uncle Ray's shoulders bounce off the ground with each punch. He lets out muffled grunts, like Dad is beating all the air out of his lungs. The black tangled hairs on Dad's chest sparkle with wet snowflakes. He pounds Uncle Ray's face again and again until a set of oncoming headlights flash around the corner of the house. With one fist caught in midair, Dad stops. His sparkling chest lifts and lowers, and thick frost floats from his mouth, up and around his head and neck. Daniel turns and squints into the bright light. Stepping out of the truck and seeing Dad and Uncle Ray, Jonathon reaches back inside and flips off the headlights. He pulls on his hat and tugs the brim low over his forehead.

"How about I take it from here, Arthur?" Jonathon says.

Dad stands, his bare feet straddling Uncle

Ray. He nods and says, "Good enough."

Jonathon walks a few yards across the gravel drive, his footsteps the only sound, bends down and slips his hands under Uncle Ray's shoulders. Without saying anything to Elaine or Mama or Aunt Ruth, who are all standing at the top of the stairs, Jonathon drags Uncle Ray's limp body to his truck, his boots leaving two thin trails in the dusting of snow that has started to cover the gravel drive. Daniel runs to the passenger side of the truck and opens the door. He blinks away the snowflakes that catch in his eyelashes and watches Jonathon try to lift Uncle Ray, but when he can't quite get him into the truck, Jonathon looks to Dad for help. Dad, having not moved, stares at Jonathon for a moment before walking inside. First, the screened door slams shut, next the door off the kitchen. Mama and Elaine follow him but Aunt Ruth doesn't move. She stands, watching Jonathon try to lift Uncle Ray into the truck.

"Dan," Jonathon says. He breathes heavily and jostles Uncle Ray to get a better hold on him. "Can you give me a hand?"

Daniel glances back at Aunt Ruth, the only one left standing on the porch. She gives a nod, so Daniel steps up to Jonathon's truck and grabs one of Uncle Ray's arms.

"Should have left that girl to freeze," Uncle Ray mumbles. Both Daniel and Jonathon turn away from his breath. "God damn dogs. Even dug up my yard."

Clearing his throat and trying to suck in fresh air, Daniel slips under Uncle Ray's left arm and pulls it around his own shoulders so he can use his legs to lift. Together, he and Jonathon toss Uncle Ray into the truck.

"Tell your folks I'm taking him to the hospital," Jonathon says. Once Uncle Ray is inside the truck, Jonathon walks around to the driver's side. "From the looks and smell of it, he's mostly drunk. Nothing a few stitches won't take care of."

Daniel nods and steps back as Jonathon slides into the truck. Not certain why he does it, Daniel lifts a hand to wave good-bye. Starting the engine, Jonathon gives Uncle Ray a shove, causing his head to bounce off the passenger side door. He smiles and waves back.

Ruth counts out three tablespoons of coffee, plugs in the pot and watches, waiting for hot water to bubble up in the small glass lid. She startles, her shoulders and neck tensing, when Arthur begins to pound again. Each blow of the hammer vibrates through the floorboards. Soon, he'll have the broken window covered over with plywood and they can all go back to bed. Daniel is with him, fetching nails and scraps of wood, just like he did when the two worked together to repair the broken window in the garage. Elaine has gone to her room and Celia is taking a shower. Ruth didn't ask why she would shower so late at night when she's sure to catch a chill and maybe a nasty cold. She knew enough, had seen enough, to know the answer.

Soon, steam begins to leak from the coffeepot and it gives its first gurgle. Outside the dark kitchen window is the beginning of a good snowstorm. Making herself smile first, Ruth turns to face Evie, who sits at the kitchen table, swinging her legs because her feet don't reach the floor yet. With a creased brow, Evie watches Ruth. In the back of the house, Arthur begins to pound again.

"Your daddy and Daniel must be nearly finished," Ruth says, taking a loaf of sourdough bread from the top of the refrigerator and readjusting her sling. Her arm isn't so sore anymore. Tomorrow she'll take it off. "Do you feel it? The draft — it's almost gone. The house will warm up again soon. They'll be hungry, don't you think?"

Evie nods.

"And then it's off to bed with you."

Evie, still swinging her legs, leans forward and rests her chin in her hands. "Why does Uncle Ray hit you?"

Ruth stops in the middle of cutting a slice of sourdough and with her eyes lowered, she says, "I don't know, Evie. Except that life is harder on some people."

"Is it harder on Uncle Ray?"

"Yes," Ruth says, finishing one slice and starting another. "I'd say it has been."

"Because he wanted to marry Aunt Eve but she died and he had to marry you instead."

Ruth nods. "Yes. Yes, that's hard on a person."

"But he wouldn't hit you now. Since you have a baby in there." She points at Ruth's stomach. "He wouldn't hurt the baby."

Ruth lays down her knife and brushes a handful of crumbs off the counter into her palm, which she dumps into the sink. "No, Evie. He wouldn't hurt the baby." Ruth says it even though she's not sure it's the truth.

Evie stops swinging her legs and lifts her chin. She doesn't look like a little girl when she raises her eyes to Ruth. Her skin is pale and gray, her eyes old and tired and the fringe of white bangs that usually hangs softly across her forehead has been pushed back, sharpening her jawline and cheek-bones.

Tilting her head, Evie says, "Then maybe it's time you go back home with him."

Ruth smiles with closed lips. Her chin quivers. "Yes," she says. "I think it's time."

CHAPTER 25

When day breaks on Saturday morning, the snow continues, but because the wind that blew all through the night has stopped, it falls straight down, in thick, heavy clumps. Outside the kitchen window, where the maple tree sparkles with an icy skin, two sets of tire tracks cut through four inches of snow that blanket the drive — one set going, partially filled in now with fresh snow, and one set coming, deep ruts that still show the indentation of the chains on Jonathon's truck. Knowing the back door will swing open at any moment, followed by a blast of cold air, Celia slides her eggs off the hot burner and makes herself touch Ruth's sleeve. Something to comfort her. The only thing Celia can manage. Ruth sets aside the potato she is grating for hash browns and wipes her hands on her apron.

Arthur walks into the kitchen first. Jonathon follows, shaking out his blue stocking cap and brushing the snow from his coat. Arthur takes off his hat and sets it on top of the refrigerator. His dark hair is wet and matted on the ends, his nose and cheeks are red and his shoulders are dusted with snow.

"Smoke coming from his chimney." Jonathon slaps his hat against his thigh. "Someone must have driven him home from the hospital."

"I spoke to Floyd," Arthur says to Ruth. "He says they're done over at your place. Done all they could. Didn't find anything."

"Been so long," Jonathon says. "Since it happened, I mean. They didn't really expect to."

Ruth nods, and turning her back on them, she continues shredding her potato into a hot skillet, the paper-thin slivers sizzling and popping in melted butter.

After everyone has finished breakfast, Arthur asks Jonathon and Elaine to drive over to Reesa's and bring her back to the house before the storm strands her alone and he tells Daniel to get busy shoveling the snow off the roof.

"The flat roof over the porch," Arthur says. "That'll be the trouble spot. The rest should be fine. Just fine."

Daniel nods. "Yes, sir," he says, holding his fork in his left hand and his knife in his right. Like Arthur, like a Midwesterner. All night, Daniel stayed awake with Jonathon and Arthur, boarding up the broken window, listening for Ray, and from the three cups that Celia found on the kitchen table this morning, he even drank coffee with them.

Once Jonathon and Elaine have left for Reesa's, Arthur heads outside to bring more firewood up to the house and Ruth excuses herself to do some sewing, all of them leaving Celia alone in the kitchen. Even Evie shuffles back to her room, her head and shoulders slumped as if she's thinking about Olivia. Outside, there is a thud as Daniel drops the ladder against the house. His footsteps cross overhead. Warming her coffee with a refill, Celia pulls out a chair, sits and cradles her mug. After a few deep breaths, she stares across the room at Elaine's closed bedroom door, the one where Ruth and the baby were supposed to stay once the little one came along, except now Celia doesn't want them here anymore. After the snow stops and the storm has passed, Ruth can go home with Reesa. She can live there, anywhere, as long as it's away from Celia's family. She doesn't want Ruth and her baby in her home for one more day.

■ ■ ■ ■

In Elaine's room, Ruth pulls her suitcase from under the bed. The last time she touched it, she had just moved in with Arthur and Celia. She had been remembering the devil's claw growing outside Mother's house, the smell of it, the feel of the sharp pods. She had known she was pregnant, known it for sure, but didn't know how to be happy about it. Now, even though Ruth has lived in Arthur's house for nearly five months, even though she thought she had found a way to be happy, the moment she lays back the top of the blue suitcase, she smells home. She smells Ray. There was always something musty about him and that house. No matter that she scrubbed with bleach and washed with lye soap. No matter that she always hung out the clothes and towels to dry so they wouldn't mold. The house still smelled old and damp. Now she breathes in the smell, soaks it up, so she'll be ready.

Daniel pushes his shovel across the flat roof, clearing the last patch of snow. Standing straight, he plants his shovel like a pitchfork in a drift that has collected where the angled roof meets the flat. Up the road, Jonathon's truck creeps into sight. As he starts down the hill, his back end fishtails, leaving crooked tracks in the fresh snow, but then it falls back into a straight line. Watching the truck, Daniel arches his back and groans the way Dad would have. He thinks about Ian and all of his aches and pains. Mrs. Bucher says they're worse in this cold weather. Ian won't be hunting pheasant today. He won't be a pusher or a blocker, and he damn sure won't be hunting Jack Mayer.

As Jonathon's truck slows at the bottom of the hill and turns into the drive, Daniel looks back toward Uncle Ray's house. White smoke drifts up through the falling snow. Yep, Uncle Ray made it home, made it home in good enough shape to keep a fire going all morning long. Daniel stretches again, pulling his wool cap down over his ears, and leans on the shovel. The snow is falling straight down, harder since Daniel climbed onto the roof. A new layer of white has filled in where he already shoveled.

Walking to the edge of the roof, Daniel stands over the header board where he is sure not to fall through and squats to wait for Jonathon's truck to pull up. The chains on his tires make a crunching noise as he drives around the house. The truck stops and both doors fly open. Elaine steps out of the passenger's side, and Jonathon, the driver's side. Both hold out a hand, but Grandma Reesa takes Elaine's. Jonathon doesn't move, instead standing near the truck until Grandma Reesa has started up the stairs, leaning on Elaine with one hand and the handrail with the other. When she is at the last step, Jonathon slams his door, walks around the truck and, when he passes under the spot where Daniel squats, he calls up to him.

"I'll be needing a hand later today if you got one."

"Sure," Daniel calls down. He coughs and spits in a pile of snow on the ground below. "What do you need?"

"Ran into Norbert Brewster this morning," Jonathon says, removing his hat and shaking off the snow. "Said I'd better get what I want out of their old place quick. Said the roof is caving in on a good day. Won't hold up to this snow. Thought about driving out there. It's a decent road on toward Clark City. Things'll ice over tonight and we won't be going anywhere for a day or two." Jonathon glances back at his truck. "Says he's got some good hardware out there. And some cabinets might be worth

saving. Could use an extra set of hands rip-
ping it all out. Won't be any good if the
weather gets to it."

"Sure, I'll go." Daniel drops the shovel
into a mound of snow below. No sense staying at home. Once he goes back inside, even
before he can hang up his gloves and hat to
dry, Mama will be asking him how he's feeling. She'll press her hand to his forehead
like his not having any friends is a sign of
the flu and then she'll cock her head and
say once again how lucky they are that
Uncle Ray didn't get his hands on Evie.
She'll whisper that part so Evie doesn't hear.

"Hustle on in and put on dry clothes,"
Jonathon says, offering Daniel a hand as he
steps off the ladder. "We'll head out when
you're done."

CHAPTER 26

Route 60, leading Daniel and Jonathon fifteen miles southwest, was plowed sometime during the night, but as the snow continues to fall, a fresh layer, blowing like thick fog, covers the narrow road. Still, the chains on Jonathon's tires rattle over the hard, frozen ground. Outside, snowflakes fall in a heavy white curtain, larger and fluffier then they were at home. Squinting into the white haze, Daniel tries to follow one flake all the way to the ground.

"Here we go," Jonathon says, slowly rolling the steering wheel, his leather gloves stiff as he passes one hand over the other.

He pulls off the main road where a rusted mailbox hangs from a wooden post. The fresh, unplowed snow quiets the chains.

"Haven't seen this old place in years."

Daniel leans forward, both hands resting on the dashboard. The small two-story farmhouse has a flat roof and a wrap-around porch. Other than a single barren tree standing in front and to the side of the house, the landscape is empty. Flat, snow-covered fields stretch as far as the horizon in every direction. The snow makes everything crisp and new, tidy. It's as if Norbert Brewster and his wife never left the house, or perhaps it's as if they never lived there at all.

"Doesn't anyone live here?" Daniel asks.

"Not since Norbert lost his wife and moved to town. Couple years back, at least." Jonathon throws the car into park and leans over the steering wheel. "Let's have a quick look around. Doesn't seem to be much worth saving," he says and looks up at the thick white layer of snow on the flat roof. Grabbing his toolbox from the center seat, he climbs out of the truck.

The icy stairs creak when they walk up them to the porch. Standing at the front door, Daniel shoves his hands in his coat pockets while Jonathon fumbles with the key that Norbert Brewster gave him. The emptiness of the snow-covered fields surrounding the house makes Daniel think of Clark City. Jack Mayer would have come across this house first when he escaped, even before the Scott house, but if he did stop here, looking for food or anything else, he wouldn't have found it.

"Got it," Jonathon says. He steps inside, stomping his boots on the threshold even though no one lives here anymore, and Daniel follows closely behind, stomping his boots, too. Their heavy footsteps echo in the empty house and something scurries.

Jonathon winks at Daniel. "Rats, I suppose." He takes a few steps into the entryway, and stops. "Well, that's a shame," he says.

Daniel looks off to the right where Jonathon is looking. A snowdrift, littered with leaves and dirt, has spilled through a broken picture window into what was once the dining room.

"Might have pulled up those oak floors," Jonathon says, setting his toolbox on the third step of the stairway leading to the second floor. He opens it and hands Daniel a screwdriver. "Take a look around up there," he says, nodding up the stairs. "If you find a decent door, take it down. Give a shout if you need a hand. I'm going to see about the kitchen cabinets."

Daniel steps into the wide entry that leads into the dining room. A gust of wind catches him in the face. He shivers. Most of the glass in the picture window is gone. Only a few pieces hang from the top of the frame.

They are called shards. Daniel knows because that's what Dad called them after Uncle Ray broke their window. Dad knocked those shards loose with a hammer and boarded up the window with scraps of plywood from the basement.

"Looks to have been broken a long time," Daniel says, watching Jonathon rummage for another screwdriver. Maybe he isn't so bad. It's not his fault he's always the extra set of hands.

"No telling," Jonathon says and walks toward the back of the house. "Holler if you find anything worth keeping."

Evie sits on the edge of Aunt Ruth's bed, swinging her feet so the bedsprings creak and watching Aunt Ruth try to thread a needle. She is still sleeping in Evie's room, but once Elaine gets married to Jonathon, Aunt Ruth and her baby will live in Elaine's old room.

"You know your mother doesn't like you doing that," Aunt Ruth says.

Evie glances at Aunt Ruth, offers no response and the bed continues to squeak.

Aunt Ruth misses the needle's eye with her thread for a second time and smiles. "Light's not so good today," she says. "Would you like to try?"

"Daddy says Olivia won't die all the way until spring."

Aunt Ruth lowers the needle and thread. "What do you suppose he means by that?"

"He said things don't all the way die when it's so cold outside. He said she'll finish dying in spring. He said she'll sink into the ground and come back as a tree or something."

Aunt Ruth rests both hands in her lap. "I guess I understand that."

Evie nods. "Yeah, me, too." She stops swinging her feet. "Was it cold outside when Aunt Eve died?"

Aunt Ruth wraps her thread around the small bolt and lays it and the needle on her bedside table. "It was warm," she says. "A beautiful time of year."

"Is she all the way dead now?"

"Yes, she is."

Evie leans back on both arms and begins to swing her legs again so that her feet bounce off the box frame. "I saw Uncle Ray at church," she says. "He was visiting a grave." She stops swinging. "Is Aunt Eve's grave there? Was he visiting Aunt Eve?"

Aunt Ruth flips on the lamp near her bed, opens the small drawer in her nightstand and lifts out two round stones.

"Perhaps," she says, holding the stones in

the palm of her hand. "I suspect he was."

Daniel stops at the top of the stairs where a long hallway leads to the far end of the house. While the downstairs felt like a barn because of the wind blowing through the broken window and the leaves and dirt scattered about the wooden floors, the upstairs feels like a home, like he might find Mrs. Brewster living right behind one of the five doors that line the hallway. He takes a step toward the first room, slowly, carefully, leading with his toe and only rolling back onto his heel when the wooden floor doesn't bow underfoot.

Grabbing the knob on the first door with two fingers, he gently pushes and pulls, testing the hinges. They creak but swing freely. He takes one step closer, testing the floors again with his toe, and inspects each hinge. They are tarnished and black but Jonathon will want them. He'll scrub them with acid and a toothbrush and by the time he hangs them in Elaine's and his house, they'll be like new. Before continuing, he knocks on each of the door's six panels, happy to be doing something that doesn't involve Mama's rubber gloves and a bucket of soapy water. Solid. Yep, Jonathon'll want this one.

Pushing open the second door, Daniel

coughs at the dust kicked up and squints into the light that spills across the hallway. A bathroom. Better paint job on this door. Frame is in good shape. Hinges look the same. The third and fourth are keepers, too, making Daniel wonder how many doors Jonathon needs for his new house. The biggest bedroom, which was behind the first door, was empty, but the smaller two still have furniture in them — dressers, a rocking chair, two single beds — all covered with white sheets.

Daniel steps into the second small bedroom and carefully pulls the sheet from a rocking chair. He coughs and waves away the rising dust. Evie would like the red-checkered seat cushion, even if the rocking chair might be too big for her. Maybe, if Norbert Brewster doesn't want it anymore, Dad will come back with his truck after the snow melts and take the chair home for Evie. It might make her forget about Olivia rotting away in the back pasture and Aunt Eve being dead and Julianne Robison still missing. Before draping the sheet back over the chair, Daniel looks at the ceiling and hopes it won't cave in on Evie's chair before they can come back for it. Black mold seeps out from each corner and a single crack runs the length of the room. He backs away from the rocker, watching the snowfall through a dirty window.

Once outside the room, Daniel looks down the hallway to the last door. All of them are fine, and after Jonathon gets through with them, the hinges will be fine, too. Taking a few steps toward the staircase, Daniel calls down to Jonathon.

"Got five good ones up here," he shouts. "Hardware looks good, too."

"Did you say five?" Jonathon calls up. "Five? All in good shape?"

Daniel looks at the last door. "Yeah, five." He coughs.

"All have good hinges?" Jonathon calls back as he appears at the bottom of the stairs.

Daniel motions for Jonathon to come up and see for himself.

Celia takes two mugs from the cabinet overhead and fills them both with coffee. Reesa, sitting at the head of the kitchen table, stitches the belt back onto the body of a lavender and green plaid apron. The fabric is faded and frayed at the seams.

"I've never seen that one before," Celia says, setting one of the mugs in front of Reesa.

"Haven't worn it." Reesa drapes the apron

across her lap, demonstrating how little of her it protects. "Covered more of me when I was younger." She smiles, which makes Celia smile and realize that Reesa, after all these months, is making a joke. "Made from a feed sack," she says, holding the apron up again.

"From a feed sack?" Celia asks. "But it's such lovely fabric."

"Mother always picked the nicest ones for aprons. Different sack, different fabric."

"Do you have others?" Celia asks, looking at the bag sitting near Reesa's feet.

"Mmmm," Reesa says, meaning yes, and she lifts the bag into her lap. "Here's another." She holds up a blue calico bib apron with a solid blue ruffle sewn at the waistline. "Mother always liked ruffles. Here," Reesa says, handing the apron across the table to Celia. "This'll fit you still."

Celia frowns at the comment, thinking Reesa means that someday Celia will outgrow it, too.

"I couldn't, Reesa," Celia says. "Those are antiques. They're too special."

"Mmmm," Reesa says, again meaning yes.

While Reesa inspects the blue calico apron for torn seams, Celia takes a deep breath, and says, "Will you tell me about Eve?"

Reesa continues to run her fingers over

the worn cotton, pulling the thin belt through two fingers and tugging when she gets to the end. "What's there to know?"

"Well, I'm not sure."

Behind Celia, her bedroom door is closed. Having been up late fixing the back window and watching for Ray, Arthur is taking a nap.

"Arthur is getting more . . . well, more angry. Don't you think? I'm worried about him. And about Ruth. It seems that . . . there is something else. Something I don't know."

"The child is gone. Dead and buried. Not much more matters, does it?"

"No, definitely not. But something is eating away at him. You see that. I know you do. He stayed away from here for so long."

Celia waits, but Reesa doesn't respond.

"He thinks he should have saved her, doesn't he? His father thought that, too. He blamed Arthur. Blamed Arthur for Eve's death."

Reesa pulls a spool of blue thread from her sewing case, wets one end by dabbing it on her tongue and, lifting her hands to catch the light coming through the kitchen window, she pokes it through the eye of her needle.

"Reesa," Celia says, leaning forward. "Please tell me what happened. I'm worried about what Arthur might do."

"What happened twenty-five years ago won't change what's happening today."

"Maybe it won't," Celia says. "Or maybe it will." She stops talking when Arthur walks out of the bedroom, running a hand through his dark hair.

"The boys back yet?" he says, buttoning his flannel shirt and walking past them toward the bathroom.

Celia looks at Reesa as she answers. "No, but soon I hope."

Reesa pulls off a yard of thread and ties one end in a knot. The bathroom door closes.

"I just can't help but worry," Celia says.

Daniel steps back as Jonathon walks up the stairs, carrying with him a small paper bag filled with hardware from the cabinets. "Here," he says, handing the bag to Daniel. "Cabinets are no good, but I got all of the handles and knobs."

Daniel takes the bag, cradles it in one arm and points at the first door with his screwdriver. "Looks good to me," he says. "Scrape them and paint them. They'll be okay."

Jonathon nudges Daniel as he passes by. "You're finally learning something worth learning, aren't you, city boy?"

They start with the closest door. Daniels holds it while Jonathon unscrews it from its hinges. The job is easy until only the bottom hinge is left attached and Daniel has to hold the door square so it doesn't bend the hinge and ruin it. He uses his legs for leverage and tries not to grunt so Jonathon won't know how heavy it is for Daniel.

Once they have removed the door from its frame, the two of them carry it down the stairs and prop it up in the foyer where the wind and snow can't get to it. Then they go back upstairs and do the same thing three more times. At the second small bedroom, Daniel asks Jonathon if he thinks Mr. Brewster would let them have the rocking chair for Evie. Jonathon says that he thinks a bottle of bourbon for Mr. Brewster would be a fair trade.

By the time there is only one door left, both Jonathon and Daniel have pulled off their coats and hats. "Just one more," Jonathon says. "We'll get it downstairs, wrap them up in a tarp or two and head on home."

At the end of the hallway, Daniel opens the last door enough to grab onto the edge with one hand while holding the knob in the other. He waits while Jonathon unscrews the top hinge and braces himself as he pulls off the middle one. The door is instantly heavier. Daniel uses his legs to stabilize himself, and this time, he can't help the grunt that escapes him.

"Here," Jonathon says, taking part of the weight once he has removed the last screw. "Let's lay it down for a minute."

Daniel rests the bottom of the door on the floor and, following Jonathon's lead, he slowly lowers it, walking backward so it can lie down in the hallway.

"Good Lord," Jonathon says, dropping the door the last few inches.

The sudden movement makes Daniel stumble backward. When he catches his balance, Jonathon has already stepped over the door and taken two steps into the bedroom, blocking the entry. Daniel follows, slipping around Jonathon, stumbling again as he steps into the room.

"Jonathon," he says. "What is that? Is that . . ."

Sheets cover none of the furniture in this room. A dresser and chest of drawers stand on opposite walls and a lace curtain hangs in the room's only window. Bright white light spills inside, making the pale yellow walls shine. The snow is still falling. And there, its wrought-iron headboard centered on the largest wall, is a single bed made up with a white quilt that someone has carefully tucked around the remains of a very small person.

"Julianne Robison," Jonathon whispers. "After all these months. It's Julianne Robison."

CHAPTER 27

Celia steps back, giving Ruth more room to roll out the noodle dough. Soon the white floury clump is nearly paper-thin and Ruth is dabbing her neck with a dish towel. She smiles at Celia, only half a smile really, and after pulling a tea towel from the top drawer, she drapes it over the noodles.

"They have to dry a bit now," she whispers.

Celia nods, and she and Ruth sit at the kitchen table with the others.

"Part of the roof had collapsed by the time we got back with the sheriff," Jonathon says. "Fellows from Clark City came out, too."

Arthur stretches and rests one arm on the back of Celia's chair. Ruth sits next to Reesa; Daniel, across the table from them.

Jonathon continues. "They had a hard time of it, getting up the stairs to find her."

Reesa shakes her head and makes a *tsk tsk* sound. Daniel props his elbows on the table and rests his chin in his hands. His nose and cheeks are red and probably chapped, too. And Elaine, who was checking on Evie and making certain her door was shut tight, walks back to the table and stands behind Jonathon.

"Floyd brought her down. Couldn't do much looking around, though. Wrapped her up tight as he could in that quilt of hers and brought her on down. Nothing left. Not a damn thing of her left."

Celia presses her hand over her mouth. "Are they sure it's her?"

"Sure as they can be. She had blond hair. Looked more like dried straw, what was left of it. But Floyd, he said that means blond. And she was no more than a bit of a thing."

Ruth stands. Everyone stops talking.

"Just checking my noodles," she says, slipping behind Celia.

"So, what's next?" Arthur says. "Has anyone told Mary and Orville?"

"Floyd was going there straightaway from the house. Roads weren't so bad yet near town, so I'm sure he got there. Didn't want to bring them out to the house." Jonathon takes a sip of coffee that must have gone cold. "Funeral's next, I suppose."

Everyone around the table nods and Reesa makes her *tsk tsk* sound again. "How are those noodles coming along?" she asks Ruth, who is still staring at the counter.

"You know the strangest thing about it all?" Jonathon says, not really asking anyone in particular. "She's been there all along. The mattress, well . . ." He pauses, scans the table and whispers, "Floyd said it was stained, badly. From all the decomposition."

"Good Lord in heaven," Reesa says.

"But the quilt that was laid over her," Jonathon says, "it was clean. White as brand new. And the room. Spotless. Furniture dusted. Windows clean. But that quilt. That's the strangest of all. Clean as brand new."

Celia pushes back from the table and goes to stand with Ruth at the counter. "You all right?" she asks, touching Ruth's shirtsleeve.

Ruth nods that she is fine, and says, "Who would do such a thing? Who would do such a terrible, terrible thing?"

"Jack Mayer," Daniel says. "That's who."

A few days later, when the snowstorm has passed and the trucks have cleared all the roads into town, Evie has to go back to school. Miss Olson called Mama on Sunday night to say all the teachers decided it best not to disrupt the children's lives anymore than they already had been. Julianne had been missing for such a long time, after all. Mama shook her head after she hung up with Miss Olson and told Evie and Daniel to rustle up some clean, warm clothes because Monday was a school day.

On Evie's very first day of school in Kansas, everyone had known that she had to sit where Julianne Robison would have sat if she hadn't disappeared, because everyone had to sit in alphabetical order. Scott sat where Robison couldn't, but this morning, as Evie walks into class, pulling off her coat and mittens, Miss Olson has mixed up all the desks. Some point forward, some sideways, some toward the back of the room. Most are still empty.

"Today is crazy mixed-up day," Miss Olson says. "Pick a seat, Evie. Pick any seat you like."

Evie hangs her coat on one of the hooks inside the door and walks past Irene Bloomer and John Atwell, toward the back of the room, wondering why Miss Olson mixed up all the desks, but she doesn't wonder for long. Miss Olson doesn't want anyone to know which desk would have been Julianne's if she wasn't dead. But Evie knows. She knows because she sat in it for the whole first part of the year. The pencil holder in Julianne's desk is covered with black scribbles and someone carved a five-pointed star in the bottom right corner. At the very back of the room, in one of the desks turned sideways, Evie sits. She lowers her head as the rest of the kids walk into class, everyone giggling at the silly messed-up desks even though they're supposed to be sad about Julianne being dead. Some of them must remember this, because after they giggle a little, they cover their mouths and lower their heads, too.

After the second bell rings, Miss Olson tells everyone to settle down and turn their desks if they can't quite see the blackboard. Squeaks and squeals bounce around the room as everyone scoots until they can see Miss Olson. Once the room quiets again and Miss Olson begins to call attendance, Evie lays her index finger on the tip of the star, slowly traces each of its five points and wishes she could be dead like Julianne Robison. If she were dead, being small wouldn't matter because no one makes fun of a dead person. If she were dead, Julianne Robison could be her friend. If she were dead, she wouldn't have to miss Aunt Eve and Olivia.

Feeling tired, like he might never feel good again, Daniel walks into his classroom, hangs his coat and hat in the closet at the back of the room and sits. Ian is there, teetering on the edge of his seat, waving at Daniel from four rows over. He wants to tell Daniel something but since Mrs. Ellenton separated them on the third week of school, he'll have to wait until lunch. Daniel waves back and presses a finger to his lips when Mrs. Ellenton walks into the room, her high heels clicking across the tile floor. From the front of the classroom, she smiles at Daniel and tilts her head like people do when they feel sorry for someone.

At noon, Mrs. Ellenton dismisses the class for lunch. Daniel doesn't wait for Ian like he normally would. Instead, he takes his bag-lunch from the shelf near the door and races through the halls with his head down because every kid in school is staring at him — the kid who saw Julianne Robison dead. He hears Ian calling out but his crooked legs can't keep up. The cold weather seems to have made Ian stiffer, like every step he takes is painful. If it were possible, Daniel would say Ian looked even smaller, like he shrunk during the snowstorm. Everything except his head. It seems to have grown, and Daniel rubs his own neck thinking how heavy Ian's head must be to carry around all day. Once inside the cafeteria, Daniel sits at his usual table, which seems to be more crowded today, and opens his lunch. When Ian finally sits, he is panting for air. His eyelids are gray and sunken into his head and a bluish tint surrounds his mouth.

"Hey," he says, tossing his lunch on the table. "What are you doing?"

All around the cafeteria, kids watch Daniel. Not one of them has been his friend all year, but now they all want to hear about Julianne Robison.

"Doing nothing," Daniel says. "Eating."

"So you found her. You really found her." Ian smiles at the full table and leans forward. "What'd she look like?"

Daniel shrugs. He sees Julianne every time he closes his eyes, but he thinks he's really seeing only what he imagines. Once Jonathon realized what they were looking at up there on the second story of Norbert Brewster's house, he grabbed Daniel's arm and shoved him back into the hallway, telling him to stay put, stay damned well put, until he could figure things out.

"Come on," Ian says, cupping his mouth with both hands so no one can hear what he's saying. "You got to tell me."

"She didn't look like anything," Daniel says, taking a bite from his sandwich but thinking if he chews or swallows, he'll vomit.

"Did it smell bad?" Ian asks, but then answers his own question. "I guess not, because of the cold. Frozen, huh?"

Daniel lifts his eyes, looking out from under his brow without moving his head. "Yeah."

"You know, most folks say your Uncle Ray did it." He leans forward and whispers, "But I still say it was Jack Mayer. Swiped her up the second he broke out. Swiped her up and killed her there in Brewster's old house."

Ian leans back and studies his lunch like he's thinking about eating it, but he pushes it farther away instead and closes his eyes. He sits that way, taking in deep breaths for a good long minute before opening his eyes, ready to go again.

"She's the first person murdered around here in twenty-five years," Ian says. "The first in twenty-five years." He waves at two of his brothers sitting at the other end of the table. They both jump up and sit back down next to Ian. Once they are settled, Ian starts talking again. " 'Course you know who the last person murdered was."

Daniel shakes his head and keeps eating even though he feels sicker with every bite.

" 'Course you know."

Both of Ian's brothers nod but neither says anything.

"It was your own Aunt Eve. Your dad's sister. You know that? Murdered right there in your Grandma's shed. Everyone says your Uncle Ray did it but they couldn't ever prove it."

Daniel stops chewing.

"Say he killed her same as Julianne. You know, blond like Julianne. A girl. Older, of course. But blond just the same. Say he couldn't help himself." Ian looks at his brothers again, like he's making sure he's telling everything right. Both brothers nod. "But I say it was Jack Mayer killed them both. Killed your aunt before they locked him up. And now Julianne, just the same, twenty-five years later."

"Shut up," Daniel says, holding half of his sandwich with both hands. "You don't know anything about my aunt. You shut up."

"Jacob remembers," Ian says, talking about his oldest brother who is grown with his own two kids and lives in Colorado. "He remembers when it happened. Told us all everything. Ma told him to hush up about it, but he told us anyway. Says it was exactly like Julianne. Except they found Eve Scott before she rotted all away. All bloodied up between the legs. Just like Julianne Robison. Right?"

Daniel didn't see much of Julianne, but

he saw enough and heard enough from Jonathon to know Julianne didn't have any legs left to be bloodied up — nothing but bones.

"You knew about her, right?" Ian says. "You knew about Eve Scott?"

Daniel doesn't answer.

"Everyone else says it was your uncle. But I know it was Jack Mayer. I know it was. He bloodied them both up. Right there between the legs."

Daniel drops his peanut-butter-and-jelly sandwich, squishing it with his knee as he lunges across the table. He grabs Ian's collar and punches him square in the nose.

CHAPTER 28

Celia feels Arthur behind her, his body so much broader and taller, shielding her from the northern wind. No snow has fallen in four days, so while Arthur and the other county workers have cleared the roads and driving is easy enough, the temperature has continued to fall and not a flake has melted. Fourteen inches of snow covered the ground by the end of the day that they found Julianne, and the wind has stirred up the landscape, driving the snow into five-foot drifts in some spots and leaving frozen barren ground in others. Inside the cemetery, snow disguises the graves that lie in St. Anthony's shadow, making them almost beautiful. Someone, probably the two black men standing near the fence line, waiting and smoking, shoveled a path from the gate to Julianne's gravesite and the area around. Still, Celia's feet are cold and damp and beside her, tucked under one arm, Evie shivers. Celia pulls her closer, letting Arthur shield them both.

Beside Evie, Daniel stands with his hands folded and his head lowered. The entire town is here, a sea of dark coats and hats that surround a tiny grave, lying in the shade thrown by three large pine trees. The pines' branches are thick and white and clumps of snow drip when the wind blows. Celia tries to think it is a lovely spot for Julianne, so much nicer with the trees and the view of the church than the newer section of the cemetery where Mrs. Minken was recently buried. Here, Julianne lies near the grandparents she never met. Here, she lies in a grave that was probably meant for her mother.

From their spot near the back of the crowd, Father Flannery's voice, fighting with the heavy wind, is no more than a broken few words. "Tender young life . . . accept God's will . . . forbidden . . . we powerless sinners . . ."

Arthur touches Celia's arm and points to a closer spot, but Celia shakes her head and squeezes Evie. She is afraid to go closer, afraid that whatever took Julianne might find its way to her family. After a brief silence, the mourners around Julianne's grave say "Amen" in tandem and, following their lead, though she can't hear Father Flannery, Celia makes the sign of the cross, nudging Evie to do the same.

Behind her, Celia feels Arthur make the sign across his chest and his deep voice echoes "Amen." She leans into him, letting the sound of him comfort her. As everyone parts, filtering down the narrow shoveled path toward the gate, Evie tugs on Celia's sleeve. In a whisper, she asks to go to Elaine, who is standing a few rows up with Jonathon, Ruth and Reesa. Celia nods, and watching until Elaine has wrapped both arms around Evie, she turns toward Arthur. He is gone.

Daniel offers his arm to Mama because when Dad slipped behind him and started to walk away, he whispered for Daniel to take care of her. Mama takes Daniel's arm and smiles up at him. She does that now, smiles every time she has to crane her neck to see into his eyes, as if she's proud that he's finally become a man. Except maybe taller doesn't really mean he's a man yet. He hasn't fired a shotgun. He's still afraid of Jack Mayer and Uncle Ray, and he cries when he has to be alone at night and remember Julianne Robison lying under that white quilt. Being taller isn't all it takes to be a man. A man doesn't hit a crippled kid square in the nose. Only a boy does that, no matter how tall he is.

Watching the others leave, Daniel wonders if Ian told yet and if his pa will see Daniel standing there by Julianne's grave and come punch Daniel in the face for doing the same to Ian. Ian's brothers had picked him up from the ground after Daniel punched him, and one of them shoved a napkin under Ian's nose. Then they both looked at Daniel like they had never seen him before and dragged Ian, only his one good leg able to keep up, to the bathroom, where they cleaned him up so not even Mrs. Ellenton knew anything happened. Daniel doesn't see either of those brothers walking away from Julianne's grave. In fact, he doesn't see any Bucher brother, or Mr. or Mrs. Bucher or Ian. Maybe he should tell first. Maybe he won't get in as much trouble if he tells what Ian said about Aunt Eve getting bloodied between her legs and murdered in Grandma Reesa's shed. Watching Dad walk away from Julianne's grave, Daniel decides to tell because that's probably what a man would do.

Ruth reaches for Evie, but she slips into Elaine's arms instead and buries her face in

Elaine's wool coat. Jonathon begins to say something, probably words of comfort. Ruth pats his hand, silencing him, and nods as if she understands why Evie can't love her right now. Then she steps away from the crowd, not liking the feeling that everyone is leaving Julianne cold and alone, not liking the feeling that everyone is leaving her. Many of these mourners for Julianne have come from the country — farmers who have probably checked every abandoned barn and deserted tractor, fearing that another tiny body will turn up. Some of them stare at Ruth, at the swell she can't hide beneath her coat anymore, because they haven't seen her, only heard. They look at her as if they think Ruth should be with a husband. They stare as if she is sinning against poor little Julianne and her parents. Orville and Mary wouldn't squabble. Mary wouldn't keep her baby from Orville. Orville and Mary have to witness their baby in a casket, withered away to nothing but bones. Orville and Mary, standing at their daughter's graveside, withered away themselves, the life gone out of them, two people as dead as the daughter they're burying. They wouldn't waste time thinking a beating was so bad. Ruth closes her eyes and lifts her face into the icy wind, hoping it will be easier to breathe, and when she opens her eyes, she sees Arthur wading through the deep snow, away from Julianne's grave. She holds one hand over her baby girl and follows.

Ruth has come here every week for twenty-five years, and she's watched the pines grow, first standing with them to her back on the day they buried Eve. They were green then, not snow-covered, and thin and widely spaced. Now they've filled in and grown tall, their branches tangling together. The pines have always marked the way — two headstones to the north of the biggest pine, which was bigger than the rest even twenty-five years ago, and three headstones east. She doesn't have to count anymore, never really had to. Arthur must remember, too, or maybe he's been here to visit Eve since he came home. Maybe every week like Ruth. He seems to know the way as he steps through the smooth, clean snow and stops directly in front of Eve's grave. He looks back when he hears Ruth behind him and takes her hand. On the ground, a few feet ahead, stands a gray stone. EVE SCOTT. OUR DAUGHTER. OUR SISTER. OUR LOVED ONE. Ruth pulls off one of her brown gloves and reaches into her coat pocket. Pulling out two smooth rocks, she sidesteps along Eve's grave, through the snow, and lays them on top of the headstone.

"I always leave two," she says, stepping back to Arthur's side. "One for both of us, since you weren't always here. But you are now."

Arthur nods. "I couldn't come before," he says. "Before now."

"My stones were always missing," Ruth says. She feels Arthur watching her, but she keeps her eyes on Eve's headstone. "My two stones, every time I came to visit, they were gone. Strange. Don't you think?"

Again, Arthur nods.

"Ray was here that night, the night Julianne disappeared. He was here and he took my stones. All these years, I imagine. Why do you suppose he would do such a thing?"

"I hope to never know the answer to that," Arthur says and slips around Ruth to block the wind, taking her arm so that she won't fall.

But Ruth doesn't move to leave.

"He loved her," she says. "He would have been such a different man with her."

Arthur wraps an arm around Ruth. "Doesn't much matter what might have been."

"While she was here, while Eve was with us, she was happy because Ray loved her."

Ruth takes Arthur's other hand, presses it between both of hers. "He would have been a different man."

"But he's not, Ruth." In the dry, cold air, Arthur's voice is as deep and raspy as Father's ever was. "He's not a different man. I'm sorry for it, but he's not."

Ruth lifts her chin, turns her face into the wind and nods that she is ready to go. Together, she and Arthur step out of the snow onto the cleared space around Julianne's small grave. With all the other mourners gone, the tiny casket sits alone, waiting to be covered over by cold, frozen dirt. Two Negro men stand nearby, one of them stubbing out a cigarette in the snow, the other leaning on a shovel. Beside them lays a mound of dirt covered by a blue tarp. Ruth hadn't seen the open grave before because of the crowd of people, and seeing it now brings tears to the corners of her eyes.

"Come, Ruth," Celia says, stepping forward. "Let's get you home."

Standing near the gate, Jonathon holds Evie, who seems to be crying into his chest, and Daniel and Elaine stand next to him. At the head of the small grave, Reesa talks quietly with Father Flannery. As Arthur, Celia and Ruth walk past on their way toward the gate, Father Flannery steps forward.

"Ruth. Celia. Arthur," he says, bowing his head to greet them. "I was just mentioning to Reesa that we miss you fine folks at church."

"Been to church every Sunday, Father," Arthur says. "Haven't missed a one."

"I told Father Flannery that maybe we're getting tired of that drive to Hays. Don't you think, Arthur? Maybe we'll see him at St. Anthony's this Sunday."

Arthur continues on, holding Ruth's hand and reaching for Celia's. "St. Bart's is suiting me just fine. Nice to see you, Father. If you'll excuse us."

Reesa shakes her head.

"The gates to hell are wide," Father Flannery says. "Much wider than those to heaven."

Arthur stops.

Father Flannery looks back toward Eve's grave. The wind has started to fill in the footsteps Ruth and Arthur left in the snow.

Arthur drops Ruth's hand, steps up to Father Flannery, and in an instant, Ruth knows. She realizes that all along, all these many years, Arthur has known the truth. He's known the truth about what killed Eve.

"Is there something you want to say to

this family?" Arthur says to Father Flannery.

"My concern is for the child, Arthur. For the child and Ruth. I don't want to see things come to the same end."

"Arthur, he doesn't understand," Celia says, reaching for his arm. "Let's go."

"I understand that he's telling me Eve is in hell."

"Arthur Scott," Reesa says. "He's saying no such thing."

But he is. Ruth knows he is. Father Flannery thinks Eve is in hell because of what Ruth always feared Eve did to herself. Ruth presses both hands over her belly, protecting her sweet baby girl, sweet baby Elisabeth.

"That child died with a mortal sin on her soul. Would you have that for Ruth?"

Feeling as if Father Flannery can see inside her, Ruth takes two steps away. There was a moment, no longer than a blink, when she wondered if not having a baby would be best. This is what Father Flannery sees. Even now, all these months later, he can see inside and know that she once had the thought. She had considered it, for only a moment, in the very beginning, as it must have been for Eve.

"Eve died because of you and my father,"

Arthur says, jarring Ruth back to the present. "She died for fear of you and that church. For fear of her own father."

Celia is looking between Ruth and Arthur. As certain as Ruth is that Arthur knows, she is equally certain that Celia does not.

Father Flannery takes a step toward Arthur. "The gate is wide," he says, and after tipping his head at Reesa, he walks away.

Father Flannery walks down the narrow path, through the small gate and out onto the street in front of the church. When he has disappeared into his car, Celia turns to Arthur. He stands with his head down, shaking it back and forth, back and forth.

"I don't understand," Celia says. "Arthur. Ruth. I don't understand."

Ruth steps up to Arthur and takes his hand in both of hers. "You've always known?"

Arthur nods.

"Did she tell you who it was?"

This time, Arthur shakes his head no.

"I hoped she wouldn't do it," Ruth says. "I begged her not to. She was so young. So young and afraid."

"Ruth, what are you saying?" Celia says, trying to see Arthur's face because then maybe she'll understand.

Still holding Arthur's hand and ignoring Celia's question, Ruth says, "I'm so sorry, Arthur. It was my books. She must have read them. I think she used wedge root. I begged her. Really I did. I told her to tell Mother and Father. To tell them the truth. I told her we would all love her baby, no matter what."

Celia reaches for Arthur but he pulls away.

"She was pregnant," Celia whispers.

Beyond Julianne's grave, Elaine and Jonathon walk toward the car parked in front of St. Anthony's, Evie wrapped in Jonathon's arms. Daniel stands alone near the gate.

"And she tried not to be," Celia says. "But she was so young. Who? Was it Ray's?"

Ruth shakes her head. "No. She swore it wasn't. Ray loved her. Loved her so much. He wanted to marry her." She crosses her hands and lowers her head like she has done so many times before. "We never knew who. She'd never tell. Never really admitted to being pregnant. But I knew she was. I just knew it. Someone hurt her very badly. She was different after it happened. Never the same." Ruth is quiet for a moment and, as if she realizes something, she lifts her eyes. "Did Father know the truth?" she asks Reesa.

Reesa does not answer. Instead, she raises

her chin ever so slightly, just enough that the wind catches the wisps of silver hair sticking out from under her hat.

Ruth leans forward. "Did he know?" she shouts.

Arthur, still facing Eve's grave, says loud enough for everyone to hear, "He's the one who told her to do it."

Ruth's shoulders collapse.

"And you, too," Arthur says, turning to face Reesa. "You told her, too, didn't you?"

Reesa stands motionless, her chin in the air, gray wisps of hair blowing across her forehead.

"She was too afraid to do it alone," Arthur says. "So I helped her. I gathered up the wedge root. I boiled it in one of Mother's pans. I did it."

Daniel stumbles backward when Aunt Ruth screams at Grandma Reesa. Up until that moment, he had been planning what to tell Dad, how to tell him about Ian's nose and how Daniel almost broke it. But now, something else seems more important, and Aunt Ruth is shouting about Aunt Eve and how it wasn't Dad's fault that she died. She wasn't murdered and bloodied up by Jack Mayer. Something else killed her. Something that Daniel thinks a man should know, but he isn't a man yet. He takes a few steps backward until he feels snow underfoot, turns to follow Elaine and Jonathon, and there, in the shadow of a large pine tree growing near the fence line, stands Uncle Ray.

He must have been there all along, standing behind everyone who came to say good-bye to Julianne Robinson, because his collar is up and his hands are buried in his pockets making him look like he's been cold for a very long time. He probably hid back there because more than ever folks are talking about him being one of the rabble-rousers in town and how they think he must have taken Julianne Robison for sure. But he isn't causing any trouble now, only watching Mama and Dad and Aunt Ruth talk, but also he looks like he's not really seeing them. A blue bruise lies over one of his eyes and his bottom lip is still swollen from the beating Dad gave him. As Daniel takes a step to follow Jonathon and Elaine, his boot snaps the icy crust on the cleared path and Uncle Ray turns. Seeing Daniel seems to wake him. Daniel stops. He should call out, warn them, because none of them notices that Uncle Ray is coming at them from behind the pine.

Standing by the mound of dirt that will

bury Julianne, the two Negro men see Uncle Ray. One of them is leaning on a shovel and he pulls it out of the snow like he's ready to hit Uncle Ray with it if he needs to. The other man throws back his shoulders but doesn't have anything to hit with. Dad sees the men bracing themselves. He sees Uncle Ray.

"Ray," Dad says, which stops Uncle Ray. "Not today, Ray. This isn't the place."

"You knew all this, Ruth?" Uncle Ray says, ignoring Dad and looking straight at Aunt Ruth across Julianne's grave. "My Eve was pregnant?"

Aunt Ruth doesn't answer but instead wraps her arms around her baby.

"She did it to herself?" Uncle Ray asks.

"I said, not now, Ray," Dad says, louder still.

Again, Uncle Ray ignores Dad.

"That was a child bled out on the floor of that shed?"

No one answers. Mama turns away. Aunt Ruth looks down at her stomach. Grandma Reesa tips her face to the sky like heaven is up there and she can almost see it.

This time, Uncle Ray shouts as loudly as he can.

"That was a child?" His voice booms across Julianne's grave.

Mama presses a hand over her mouth, which means she is about to cry. Grandma Reesa turns to leave, and Dad starts toward Uncle Ray but Aunt Ruth grabs his coat sleeve, stopping him.

"Yes, Ray," Aunt Ruth says quietly, but the wind is to her back and it carries her voice for her. "That was a child, he or she — a baby."

Uncle Ray steps back when Aunt Ruth says it, almost like she slapped him, slapped him hard right across the face. Then he looks up at Dad. He looks directly at Dad and points at him. "And you did it," he says. "You killed my Eve."

The two of them stare at each other, waiting for something.

"Yes," Dad says. "I did it."

Uncle Ray's hat is cocked high on his forehead, showing off his tired eyes and gray skin. His face is thin and his cheekbones, like his hat, are cocked a little too high. His coat hangs on his shoulders and his pants bag around his boots as if he must have shrunk since he bought them. Dad once said too much drinking will wear heavy on a man. It looks like it has weighed Uncle Ray down about as far as he can go. After staring at Dad for a few more minutes, long enough that the Negro man with the shovel takes a few steps toward him, Uncle Ray walks away, down the cleared path, toward the station wagon where Elaine sits inside with Evie and Jonathon. He walks past the car without saying anything to Jonathon, who has stepped out probably because he heard all the shouting. He walks away, until he disappears down Bent Road without ever looking back.

CHAPTER 29

Celia takes Reesa's coat from the hook near the back door, hands it to Jonathon and steps aside as Reesa walks by. She fills the small hallway leading from the kitchen to the back porch, fills it with her size and with a sweet yeasty smell from the cinnamon rolls she mixed up that morning, intending to take them to the Robisons after the funeral. Now someone else will have to bake and deliver them to Mary Robison. Reesa says nothing as she sets her suitcase at Jonathon's feet and extends one arm so he can help her on with her coat.

"I'm sure the road home will be fine, Mrs. Scott," Jonathon says to Reesa. "Plows have had plenty of time to do their work."

Reesa makes a grunting sound and, after buttoning her top two buttons, she walks out onto the porch, leaving her suitcase for Jonathon to carry.

"She made her bed," Celia says to Jonathon. "Now she's got to sleep in it and try to make it again in the morning."

Jonathon shakes his head, signaling that he doesn't understand.

"Just a saying my mother liked to use." Celia swallows, something she does when she feels guilt. "And we have to think of them now, Ruth and the baby. They're most important."

Jonathon nods.

"You'll see to it that the house is warm before you leave her?"

He nods again. "Sure thing."

"Thank you, Jonathon," Celia says, reaching up to hug him. "And I know Arthur thanks you, too."

Overhead, footsteps pound across the roof. Arthur and Daniel climbed up there almost the instant they got home from the funeral to shovel more snow.

"He always goes to work when he's feeling bad. We'll have the cleanest roof in the county before this all settles." Celia hands Jonathon his coat. "You drive careful and come back for dinner."

"Yes, ma'am. I'll see Mrs. Scott home safe. Safe and sound."

Hearing the screened door open, Daniel stops shoveling and looks over the edge of the house. Behind him, Dad continues to scrape his shovel across the black roof.

"Grandma's leaving," Daniel says, slapping his leather gloves together. He looks over the edge again, the wind sweeping up and catching him in the face. He squints into the white sunlight bouncing off the snow below. "Jonathon's taking her."

Dad nods, lifts his shovel and begins to chip away at a patch of ice.

"Jonathon's carrying a suitcase," Daniel says.

Specks of ice sparkle as they fly off the end of Dad's shovel.

"Grandma's going home."

Jonathon's truck chokes a few times, rumbles, and then slowly starts down the driveway. Daniel watches, waiting for the truck to disappear, because once it's gone, he has to tell Dad. He has to tell because the weight of it is too much. Maybe a man could carry it around, but not Daniel. At the top of the hill leading toward Grandma's house, the truck fishtails.

"Dad," Daniel says. "I hit Ian Bucher. I hit him in the nose."

Dad stops hammering the ice.

"At school. In the cafeteria. I hit him."

Dad leans on his shovel. "You have good reason?"

Just like that. The weight of it is gone.

"Yes, sir. He said Aunt Eve was murdered. He said she was bloodied up between the legs and killed like Julianne Robison."

Dad nods, and lining up his shovel to take another whack at the ice, he says, "Bloody nose between friends never hurt anyone. But you be mindful of Ian's size. The boy can't help his size."

Daniel nods. "Sir," he says, and Dad stops again but doesn't meet Daniel's eyes. "I'm sorry Aunt Eve died. I'm sorry that happened."

Dad nods. "Yep," he says. "Me too, son."

Ruth sits on the edge of her bed, tulle draped across her lap and a small box of pearl beads on the nightstand to her left. She glances up when Elaine and Celia walk into the room, then continues trying to thread her needle.

"There's no hurry with that," Elaine says, sitting opposite Ruth on the other bed.

Ruth pulls the white thread through the eye of the needle. "The light's good today," she says. "Especially in here. We don't always have such good light."

Celia sits next to Ruth, lowering herself slowly and scooting close enough to drape part of the tulle over her own lap. "It is good," she says of the sunlight shining through the window. "This is beautiful work, Ruth. Did you see, Elaine? She's started to bead the pearl flowers." Celia lifts one edge of the veil so Elaine can see it, then lets it fall across her lap again. "Elaine, would you excuse us?"

"Certainly," Elaine says, standing. "It's beautiful work, Aunt Ruth. Beautiful." And she walks out of the room, leaving Celia and Ruth alone.

"Reesa is gone," Celia says, running her fingers along the veil's scalloped edge.

Ruth nods.

"She took her things. Jonathon is seeing her home." Celia pauses. "She'll be fine. Hardheaded as she is, she'll be fine."

"Why do you suppose we did this? Why so much hiding?"

"People get used to things," Celia says. "Without even realizing. We get used to the way things are." She reaches for the box of beads, plucks out one of the smooth, oval pearls between two fingers and passes it to Ruth. "Too afraid of the truth, I guess."

Ruth lays her hands in her lap and closes her eyes. Deep inside, Elisabeth shifts and flutters.

The elderberry was in full bloom by early

June 1942. Ruth's father, Robert Scott, was due to plant his soybean, and Ruth woke, thinking it would be a fine morning to make elderberry jam. Before the day turned hot, she decided to wake Eve so they could walk a quarter mile down the road to the ditch where the plants grew best. The exercise would do Eve good, maybe chase away the blue mood she had been carrying around for a few months. Whether it was a touch of dropsy or a lingering flu, the elderberries would clear it right up. Mother always cooked with too much salt, and the summer heat could make a person swell and feel out of sorts. That's all that troubled her — too much salt and humidity. That's all it was. After a day of fresh air, Eve would get her color back and feel like finishing the blue satin trim on her latest dress. Mary Robison said she could sell it if Eve would finish it, said she could sell all the dresses she and Eve had made together, but Eve never wanted to part with them. Until now. Now she said that once she felt well enough to stitch on the blue satin trim, she'd sell it and the rest, too.

Ruth stood at Eve's door and tapped on it, leaning forward to listen. "You up?" she whispered, even though the rest of the house was already awake.

Eve was always the last to get out of bed on the weekends, leading Mother to lecture her about laziness being an engraved invitation from the devil. Ruth tapped again, this time hard enough to push open the door that was not latched. She peeked through the crack, and seeing Eve's bed made, she walked downstairs.

At the bottom step, Ruth remembers that the air chilled, but it couldn't have. It had been June. Still, a shiver had slipped up her spine to the base of her neck. A pot boiled over in the kitchen, a heavy, rolling boil. Water hissed on a hot burner. Placing one foot flat on the wooden floor, holding tight to the banister, Ruth listened. Boiled eggs, probably, for Father to take along to the fields. He was quite precise — half a dozen eggs, fourteen minutes at a heavy boil, and Mother poked small holes in the large end of each one so they wouldn't crack. Father wouldn't eat a cracked egg.

Ruth walked across the living room, taking long slow steps because she knew something was wrong, and stopped inside the kitchen. She stood looking at the white, foamy water spill over the sides of Mother's cast-iron pot, and without turning down the flame or sliding the pot to a cool burner, she walked on toward the back porch.

At the top of the stairs leading down to the gravel drive, Ruth looked east, toward the patch where yesterday she had spotted the finest elderberries. She couldn't see them from the house, but Eve would know the spot. It was the same every year. The berries had a special liking for the odd stretch of ditch where Bent Road took a hard curve. Passing cars kicked up dust there. Maybe that's what the plants liked so well. It was the same stretch of road where the wind swept over the rolling hills, down into the valley, and where the barbed-wire fence scooped up all the tumbleweeds. She and Eve would have a nice bunch in no time at all, and they could pick some of the flowers, too, and dry them on the back porch for tea. If the jam wasn't enough, a nice tea with honey and sugar would definitely fight off whatever bug had slowed Eve down over the past several weeks. Ruth walked down the stairs one at a time and across the drive toward Bent Road.

"Ruth," Arthur said.

Only yesterday, it seemed, he had had a smooth, fresh voice that sometimes he sang with in the bath. Now, suddenly his words came from deep inside his chest and rattled like Father's.

"Ruth," he said again.

Ruth stopped in the middle of the gravel drive. Knowing they were there, she had been trying not to look. It was where Eve always went for privacy. She said a young woman needed quiet, even if it was in an old shed. Ruth turned. Arthur stood outside the small building. His arms hung at his sides, the Virgin Mary dangling from his left hand. Next to him, Mother kneeled inside the doorway. She shook her head as she fumbled with her apron strings, untying them and pulling off her apron. She passed it inside the shed. A hand reached for it, Father's hand, bloodied. Mother began to rock on her haunches. Back and forth. Back and forth. She breathed out a low, rumbling moan.

"She's gone, Ruthie," Arthur said, dropping the Virgin Mary.

Mother fell backward and scrambled for the two hands that broke off the statue and settled in the soft, dry dirt. She picked up each tiny hand and the rest of the Virgin Mary and started to slide them all into her apron pocket, but it was with Father now.

"She's gone," Arthur said.

The ditch was only a ten-minute walk. The elderberries were in full bloom. They'd have plenty for a dozen or more jars, and Eve would feel fit again, fit and fine.

■ ■ ■ ■

Ruth squints into the fading light, picks up a pearl bead but doesn't thread it onto her needle.

"Arthur thinks he did it," she says. "All this time, did you know?"

Sitting next to Ruth on the bed, Celia shakes her head but doesn't answer.

"He was about Daniel's age. When Eve died. Just Daniel's age."

Celia nods this time and holds a handkerchief to her nose.

"Everyone thought a crazy man killed her," Ruth says. "Everyone in town. That's what Father told them. I always assumed Arthur believed the same, but he never did. Even standing there in that shed, wiping up all her blood, he knew the truth. Mother knew, too. After Eve died, after we found her, I told Mother that I thought Eve had done it to herself, trying not to be pregnant. I told her about wedge root and blind staggers, told her that I was sure someone had hurt Eve, hurt her badly, but she'd never tell who. Mother said the truth didn't matter once a person was dead."

Ruth lifts her face into the sunlight spilling through the window. "Worst of all, we never told Ray. He was a good man back then. Really, he was. Why did we do that to him? We were so cruel."

"It wouldn't have brought her back," Celia says, her voice cracking at the end. "You were young, all of you. So young." Clearing her throat and taking out another bead, she says, "Let's get to work. We're going to lose this nice light soon."

"We wasted so many years," Ruth says, hooking the bead on the tip of her needle.

"It'll be better now," Celia says. "Now that everyone knows."

Ruth takes a stitch, securing the bead. "Yes," she says. "Better."

CHAPTER 30

Letting the powdered sugar frosting drip from the tip of the fork, Evie is sure Julianne would have liked these cinnamon rolls. When she was alive, she must have liked extra icing, too. But she's been buried underground for a whole day now, and she won't be eating these rolls or anything else.

Evie should be in school instead of sitting on the counter and stirring the icing for Mrs. Robison's rolls, but after Julianne's funeral and all the trouble with Uncle Ray, Mama said Evie and Daniel would stay home until Monday. Mama is afraid to let Evie out of the house ever since Uncle Ray brought her home. She's been to school only once since Jonathon and Daniel found Julianne dead in Mr. Brewster's house, and when Evie told Mama that she still got to sit in Julianne's desk, Mama cleared her throat and said that was enough of school for a while.

The only bad thing about missing school, Evie thinks as she stirs the powdered sugar and milk with a fork, is that the kids in her class will think she's scared to sit in Julianne's desk now that Julianne is rotted away and buried underground. But Evie isn't scared. She picked that desk, even after Miss Olson mixed them all up, because she wanted it especially for her own, and she told every kid at recess that she wasn't afraid one bit. They told Evie that she'd be next, that whoever killed Julianne, and everyone knew it was either Jack Mayer or her own Uncle Ray, would kill Evie, too. Evie put her hands on her hips and told every kid that she didn't care at all if she was next. That shut them up. That shut them up good and tight.

"Icing's done," Evie calls out, thinking that Aunt Eve would have liked the icing, too, but, like Julianne, she's dead. All the way dead. "I made extra."

Behind her, Aunt Ruth opens the oven a crack. "Rolls are too," she says.

She smiles at Evie, but Evie doesn't smile back. Grandma Reesa made those rolls. Yesterday, she mixed up the dough and punched it down twice when it rose up too high. Then Grandma had to go away because she made Aunt Ruth cry, and now

Aunt Ruth is baking the rolls that chilled overnight in the refrigerator and she's acting like she made them all the way from scratch. Aunt Eve is gone, too, and Uncle Ray thinks it was Aunt Ruth's fault. Now only Aunt Ruth is left, even though she packed up two suitcases.

"They smell good, don't they?" Aunt Ruth says, slipping on two oven mitts and pulling the pan out of the oven as Mama walks into the kitchen. "Would you like to come with me and your dad to take them to the Robisons?"

Mama takes a few steps toward the oven. "It's so cold outside, Ruth. And icy. You let Arthur and me take the rolls over."

"Grandma made those," Evie says, folding tinfoil around the edges of the bowl filled with white icing.

Mama and Aunt Ruth look at each other the way they did when Evie wore Aunt Eve's dress to school.

"Yes," Aunt Ruth says. "Grandma makes the best cinnamon rolls. I can never get the dough so nice." Aunt Ruth sets the hot pan on the table in front of Evie's spot on the counter. Thick sugary steam rises up. "We'll tell Mrs. Robison that Grandma made these."

"Please, Ruth. Let us take the rolls. You

need your rest. You and Elisabeth."

"I should go," Ruth says, wrapping her belly with both hands. "I really need to pay my respects."

"Cinnamon rolls won't make them feel better," Evie says.

"Yes, Evie," Mama says, pressing her lips together in a way that means Evie should stop talking. "You're probably right about that."

Evie hops off the counter. "I want to come, too," she says.

Someone definitely needs to tell Julianne's mom that Grandma Reesa made these rolls, not Aunt Ruth.

The pan of rolls is still warm on Ruth's lap when Arthur parks in front of the Robisons' house. Everyone else in town would have paid their respects yesterday after the funeral, but the Scott family didn't make it because they had a run-in with Ray. Ruth pulls on her mittens, cradles the pan with one hand and takes the frosting from Evie. Both Ruth and Arthur had decided that Mary Robison's house wasn't the place for Evie. She would be too much of a reminder. No sense stirring up more tears with Evie's blond braids and blue eyes. Before crawling out of the truck, Ruth looks back at Arthur, thinking she should say something, but not certain what that should be. He is staring straight ahead, lost in some thought. He turns. His eyelids are heavy, as if he can't quite hold them up. He looks tired, and suddenly so much older. He looks like Father.

"We'll probably visit a bit," Ruth says, sliding across the bench seat toward the door. "You two will be warm enough out here?"

He nods. "Go on and take your time. And watch the ice. Sidewalk'll be slippery."

Ruth holds tight to the truck's doorframe, steps onto the newly shoveled sidewalks, and walks toward the Robisons' house.

Celia hangs up the telephone, sits at the kitchen table and lays both hands flat on the vinyl tablecloth. She presses each finger into the table, holding on for a moment. After one final deep breath, she calls out.

"Daniel."

The house is silent.

"Daniel, come on out."

Daniel's bedroom door swings open and he steps into his threshold. His hair is matted on one side and his shirt is misbuttoned.

"Sorry if I woke you," Celia says.

Daniel glances at the telephone and at Celia.

"Come have a seat. I have some news,

Danny. Some sad news."

Ruth's shoulder isn't so sore anymore but still she favors it by balancing the dish on one hip. Someone has shoveled the sidewalk for the Robisons this morning, probably one of the men from church. Surely they didn't do it themselves. Even so, it's icy in spots. Ruth shuffles her feet, taking small steps and, at the bottom of the stairs leading to the Robisons' porch, she stares up at the black door. For a moment, she remembers being on the other side. A different house, a different day, a different death, but otherwise the same. Church ladies brought casseroles in porcelain dishes and biscuits wrapped in tinfoil. They tried to gather around Mother, to comfort her with hugs and gentle words, but Mother wouldn't have it. She sat them all down, served them coffee and crumb cake. The shirts that Father and Arthur wore that day smelled of starch and the cigars that the men brought and smoked on the back porch. Orville Robison is a smoker. The sweet smell meets Ruth at the top of the stairs. She breathes it in, raises her hand and knocks.

Celia pulls her hands off the vinyl tablecloth and lays them in her lap when Daniel walks from his bedroom into the kitchen. He has to duck now when he walks under the heavy beam that runs through the house.

"Have a seat," she says, gesturing toward the chair opposite her.

As Daniel sits, quickly at first and more slowly when he looks into Celia's face, the back door opens and Jonathon walks in. The sound of him coming home brings Elaine out of her room. They both walk into the kitchen and, like Daniel, they seem to feel that something is wrong. Celia motions to them and they both sit. She doesn't look at Jonathon or Elaine, just at Daniel. She reaches across the table and takes his hands.

Ruth knocks, lightly because she doesn't really want them to hear her. On the other side of the closed door, a set of footsteps approaches. The doorknob rattles. The door opens.

"Ruth," Mary Robison says. "Lord in heaven. What brings you out in this cold?"

Ruth lifts her pan. "Mother made them. For you."

"Her rolls?"

"Yes. She let them rise twice. Evie made extra icing. We're all so sorry for your loss."

"You're cold out there?"

Ruth shakes her head because the cold

doesn't matter. "We're all so very sorry," Ruth says, raising the pan again so Mary Robison can see it. "They're still warm," she says, though the pan has gone cold. "Would you like them in the kitchen?"

"Yes," Mary says. "Thank you." Then she steps back, ushering Ruth inside.

Mama's fingers are cold. Usually they're warm. Every other time, they've been warm. Daniel lets her hold his hands, but he doesn't hold back, and he wonders how he knows. Even before she tells him. By the look in her eye, or the sound of the phone ringing late in the day, or the smell in the air. He knows. He looks at Jonathon and Elaine. They don't understand. They don't see it or hear it or smell it. But Daniel does.

"That was Gene Bucher on the phone," Mama says.

Daniel nods. Yes, he already knew that.

"Ian has been ill, Daniel. Did you know? He's always been, well, fragile."

Mama thinks Daniel knows about Ian being sickly, but now she isn't sure. Yes, he already knew that.

"Daniel," Mama says, exchanging a glance with Jonathon and Elaine. "Ian didn't wake up yesterday morning. They expected it would happen. Eventually. Maybe it was this cold. Maybe it was too much for him. But he didn't wake up."

Daniel nods. Ian was more blue. Almost by the day. And shrinking away. He never got to be a pusher or shoot pheasant. He never found Jack Mayer's tracks or stared into the whites of his eyes. He said Aunt Eve died in the shed, bloody and murdered, and then he fell backward, off the cafeteria table, blood spilling down his chin and into the creases in his neck. Yes, Daniel already knew that.

"I thought they'd find her sooner," Mary Robison says.

After first laying a dish towel across the kitchen counter, Ruth sets down the rolls and puts the icing in the refrigerator. She is surprised to find it empty. When Eve died, Mother defrosted casseroles for weeks. She said not a single dish would go to waste. Waste was another invitation from the devil. Closing the refrigerator, Ruth steps to the sink, pushes open the curtains and raises the shade. She blinks at the late day light that spills into the room. Maybe folks weren't bringing food because Julianne first disappeared so long ago. Maybe they thought Mary Robison had had time enough for grieving.

Walking into the living room, Ruth tries to smile for Mary and says, "Pardon? What have you lost?"

"I didn't think . . ." Mary says. She sits in the center of her gold couch, facing an empty wall. ". . . it would take so long."

Ruth stands in the threshold between the kitchen and living room, her hands clasped under her belly. The chill she caught outside has stayed with her and she realizes the house is cold, too cold, as if the windows are open and the heat has shut down. She scans the room for rustling curtains and wonders what she should say to Mary. What did they all say to her when Eve died? They touched her, probably because, like Ruth, they didn't know what to say, and they brought chicken casseroles and apple cobbler. She should sit with Mary, touch her sleeve, pat her hand.

"We're all so sorry."

"Your baby is well?"

Ruth nods, pulling her coat closed and lowering her head.

"You should take care of yourself," Mary says, tilting her head as if looking at something on the empty wall. "I took care." Every few feet, at about eye level, nails stick out from the wall. "I took the best care I could. Waiting." Mary nods toward the corner where her sewing machine sets on a bare card table. When they were young, and Ruth and Eve came for sewing lessons, fabric and piping and measuring tapes had covered the table, leaving barely enough room for the three of them to huddle around the machine. Now it is bare, and the table droops in the middle.

"I even made new curtains while I waited. But it took so long."

Ruth steps closer, looking where Mary is looking.

"Can I do anything for you? Do you or Orville need anything? Anything at all?"

"I kept things nice, as nice as I could."

"Things are lovely, Mary." Ruth takes another step, watching the front door. She shouldn't be in a hurry to leave. Were they in a hurry to leave her and Mother and Arthur? "But you shouldn't work yourself like this. Where is Orville? Arthur is here. Outside. Do you need help with anything?"

"I did it myself, you know." Mary doesn't seem to see Ruth standing near the sofa, her coat wrapped tightly, hat and mittens still on. "All the cleaning. So much to take care of for one person."

"Too much really. You should rest now."

Mary tilts her head again, still staring at the empty wall. Ruth takes another step.

They are hooks to hang pictures. She remembers. Family pictures. A whole wall of them. Even a picture of Mary, Eve and Ruth when they were girls. They are gone now. The wall is empty.

"He wrapped her in feed sacks, you know."

Ruth turns on one heel to face Mary, stumbling and bracing herself against the bare wall.

"Before he buried her, I mean, so she was still beautiful when I got her back." Mary brushes gray wisps of hair from her eyes and smoothes them in place. "She was too beautiful to bury. Still so beautiful. I took care the best I could."

Evie curls up next to Daddy, laying her head against him. His hands are crossed on the steering wheel and he is resting his head. His breathing is quiet, not deep and loud like when he's sleeping. Evie scoots closer, snuggling up as best she can. His arm tightens around her shoulders. Still, Daddy doesn't look up. She wants him to lift his head to smile at her, and then maybe he'll notice. She could say something right out loud. She could pull on his shirt and point out the windshield so he would see, but Evie does nothing and Daddy doesn't move, not even to squeeze any tighter. She remembers the picture — Uncle Ray happy and lifting Aunt Eve high off the ground. Aunt Eve laughing under her straw hat, smiling and not dead.

Without moving in her seat this time, Evie glances at Daddy, quickly so he won't notice. Straight ahead, at the intersection of Main Street and Bent Road, sits a red truck. It is parked right in the middle where another car might crash into it. A white frosty cloud drifts up from the truck's tailpipe. Uncle Ray pushes his hat high off his forehead and the red truck rolls slowly through the intersection and disappears.

"After I took Mother's quilt to Julianne, I didn't go again." Mary Robison lays back her head and closes her eyes. "What with the weather blowing in. I worried about how long I'd be gone. Things get dusty so quickly."

Ruth swallows. The floor is uneven underfoot, and the front door seems to slip away. She coughs into a closed fist and walks across the room, sidestepping the coffee table.

"I'll call Arthur in," she says. "Maybe he can get the heat going."

"Orville, he never went. Couldn't bring himself to it."

"Arthur," Ruth says. "I'll get Arthur. He's right outside."

Mary lifts her head. "I threw away those nasty feed sacks. Orville left her and only I took care."

The front door opens slowly and Aunt Ruth slips outside. She stops at the top of the stairs, grabs onto her big stomach with both hands and hurries toward the car. Daddy doesn't look up until he hears her footsteps on the sidewalk. Then he throws open the door and jumps out. Aunt Ruth meets Daddy at the front of the truck, grabbing his arms, leaning on him. Daddy turns toward the house and, holding Aunt Ruth by the arm, he walks her to the truck and helps her inside.

"You two sit tight," Daddy says as Aunt Ruth crawls into the truck. "I'll go see about Mary."

Cold air sticks to Aunt Ruth and she smells like ice and snow.

"We'll be fine," she says, scooting closer to Evie, her knees bobbing up and down. "Just fine. Your daddy will be right back."

Evie scoots away, toward the spot behind the steering wheel, while Aunt Ruth watches Daddy walk up the stairs and onto Mrs. Robison's porch.

Hoping the red truck will drive past again, Evie says, "Did Aunt Eve die because her baby came out too early?"

"Where did you hear that, sweet pea?"

The sunlight bouncing off the white snow makes Evie squint. "I heard you all at Julianne's funeral. Will yours come out too early?"

Evie used to worry that Aunt Ruth would have a baby who was blue like Ian's baby sister and that they'd have to put her in the oven. Maybe the baby would wake up and cry. Maybe not. Maybe she'd die. Maybe Aunt Ruth will die, too.

"No, Evie," Aunt Ruth says. Her knees stop bobbing and she crosses her mittens on her lap. "I hope not."

Up on the Robisons' front porch, Daddy knocks on the door and pushes it open. Straight ahead, at the end of the street, the red truck is there again, rolling across the intersection. And then it is gone.

CHAPTER 31

Celia stands at her kitchen sink, her back to the conversation going on at the table, and dries the last dish from an early supper. Outside the window, as dusk falls, the light bouncing off the snow is gray. On the back porch, Jonathon is prying the wood from the window that Ray broke so he can lay in the new glass. Elaine is in her room, waiting for him to finish. Celia startles each time his hammer slams down. If only he would stop, for a moment at least, she could catch her breath. A piece of wood falls and clatters across the porch. Celia leans against the sink, and Arthur talks on, over the noise.

He called Floyd Bigler from Mary Robison's living room, relit her heater, and while they waited for the sheriff, Mary told Arthur that she had visited the house to tidy up for Julianne who lay dead there since summer. Mary had shined the windows with vinegar-water and swept the corners.

Before the weather turned, she laid a new white quilt over Julianne because the house carried a terrible chill. It didn't seem right to bury the girl. That's what Orville did at first. He wrapped her in feed sacks and buried her on Norbert Brewster's land. But Julianne was too lovely, too tender, and when she was dead, first dead, still too beautiful to be buried. So Mary dug her up, carried her inside the old house, and tucked her in tight. When the sheriff arrived, she retold the same story.

"Yes," Mary Robison said. "Orville killed her." She nodded toward the garage behind the house. "Done the same to himself."

Arthur and Floyd found Orville Robison on the garage floor, frozen solid, a hole blown out of the back of his head. Mary told Arthur and the sheriff that she thought to clean up after her husband, but then decided it wasn't her business to tidy up another one of his messes. She didn't know for sure how he killed Julianne, only that he said it was an accident, same as snagging a fish instead of catching it proper with bait and a hook. Didn't much matter how it got done — there's a fish on the end of the line either way.

"Some men don't know the difference between a daughter and a wife," she said.

"Don't let Ruth go back to that husband of hers. Don't let him have that sweet tiny baby like Orville had mine."

Arthur turns away from Ruth and chokes as he repeats Mary Robison's words.

"Don't let Ray have that sweet tiny baby like Orville had mine."

Celia slips behind Arthur's chair and kneels next to Ruth. "You're safe here. You and Elisabeth are safe." Holding Ruth's narrow shoulders, she raises her eyes to Arthur. "Is she not well? Has the sheriff taken her for help?"

"She didn't seem altogether aware. That's the only way I can put it. Not at all aware."

"That poor family," Ruth says. "That poor little girl."

Celia presses her palm to Ruth's cheek. "You should rest. This can't be good for you."

Celia says this because she has to. If she is to be a good person, she has to say it, and if she weren't so scared, she'd mean it. She reaches to touch Ruth's hand, but stops when Daniel's bedroom door opens. She doesn't want him hearing any of this conversation, doesn't even want him close to it. It's not fitting for a child to hear, but when he walks out of his room, he has become a man. Just like that. He is a man.

"You hungry?" Celia asks.

"Na," Daniel says. His voice, like Arthur's, is a low croak. When did his voice change? She thought she would hear it coming in cracks and squeaks along the way. His neck is thicker, too, and triangular muscles fix it to his shoulders, which are suddenly wide. Even his hands, they're larger. Just like that, when she was wasn't looking, he became a man.

"You should eat," Celia says, but he shakes his head and walks across the kitchen toward the back porch where Jonathon is still pounding. As she watches him walk away, tears well in the corners of her eyes.

He is gone.

"I won't have the children hearing any of this." Celia spits the words at Arthur as if it's his fault this has happened, his fault that the town will bury Julianne Robison and Ian in the same week and that Daniel grew up when her back was turned. Another funeral before Julianne's grave is even settled. Another small coffin, too small. Another child grown. What if it were one of her children instead of Julianne or Ian? How does a father kill his own child? How does a mother turn her back and find a man has taken over where once she had a boy?

She says it again. "None of it. Not a word."

Because Arthur is a good man, he nods and lowers his head, gladly taking the fault. Now the tears spill onto Celia's cheeks. She lays aside her dish towel and goes to him. He is stiff at first, not letting her feel him, but then his body warms, his muscles soften, and his shoulders fall. He leans into her for this moment.

Before he walks onto the back porch where Jonathon is pulling the last board off the broken window, Daniel stops in front of the gun cabinet. He takes his winter coat from the hook and sees the small gold lock hanging in place, snapped tight. Glancing back to make sure no one can see him from the kitchen and waiting until he hears Jonathon working at the back door, he stretches up and reaches for the key on top of the cabinet. He's never been tall enough before but Mama says he's growing like a weed. Dad says like a stinkweed. Lifting onto his toes, he reaches over the ledge. He stumbles, reaches again, his side starting to ache. He feels it.

Checking again and waiting until he hears Jonathon fumbling in his tool chest, he slips the key into the lock, turns it, thinking the click will echo through the house. No one hears. The lock falls open. But then he considers Jonathon working there on the back porch. There is no other way out. He won't let Daniel walk by with a rifle in hand. He'll tell him to put the damn fool thing away and then he'll tell Dad and Dad will hide the key somewhere higher. So Daniel snaps the lock closed and reaches overhead to replace the key. He stumbles again, not very steady in his leather boots because they cramp his toes. Bracing himself against the wall, he tries again and, as he slides the key back over the ledge, he knocks several coats off the crowded hooks. Pausing to make sure no one heard, he bends down to pick them up. Jonathon's, Dad's, Elaine's, another of Dad's. Then he stands and, as he begins to hang them up again, he sees the empty spot where Dad's shotgun usually rests.

Evie sits on the edge of her bed where she can see out her bedroom window. It is nearly dark, but through all the trees that have dropped their leaves, she can still see the road. A truck drives over the top of the hill. So many cars since everyone started to die. And phone calls. First Olivia the cow died. Evie doesn't like her anymore. She brought death to them and now it has settled in for a good long stay. She's probably not even all the way dead yet because of the cold. It will keep her for a while, that's what Ian said before he was dead. But not Julianne. She died all alone, all the way dead, in a little bed in a strange house, and now she's buried, still all alone. How did they dig it up, the frozen ground? Will the same two Negro men dig Ian's grave? They are small graves. Not so much digging. What if Aunt Ruth's baby comes too early and it's blue and it doesn't wake up in the oven? That will be a very small grave, but Aunt Ruth's will be regular sized, almost regular.

The truck is still driving down the hill toward their house. Daddy says there's black ice. It's the most dangerous. The truck knows it, too. It drives slowly, and at the bottom of the hill, it stops, white smoke spilling out of its tail end. Then the truck, the red truck, drives slowly past.

CHAPTER 32

Standing on the back porch, Daniel watches Jonathon, who is squatting near the door, a pane of glass balanced on his two palms. At first, Jonathon doesn't notice Daniel standing there. Daniel could push him down with one kick in the butt and he'd topple over and the glass would shatter all over him. It might even kill him, and he'd never find cabinets for his new house. Then there would be room for Daniel to be a man. Jonathon is a pocket clogger. That's what Dad called the men who worked in the car factories and made sure not to work too fast or too slow. Lots of the men complained about the Negroes taking jobs. Dad only complained about the men who did just enough to keep on working. Dad said they took a job from another man, a better man, who would take pride in his work. They were the pocket cloggers. Jonathon is a pocket clogger — clogging up the spot that

Daniel should have.

"Hey," Jonathon says. Balancing the glass on his two flat palms, he begins to stand. "You going out?"

Daniel nods but doesn't answer.

"Getting dark," Jonathon says, glancing outside. "Want some company?"

Across the porch and beyond the screened door, the gravel drive isn't white anymore. All the cars coming and going have ground it down to dirt again. One thing is for damn sure. This roof won't collapse because he cleaned off every speck of snow himself.

"Na," Daniel says to Jonathon because he most definitely does not want his company.

"Cold out there." Jonathon slides the glass into place. "Would you look there in that toolbox?" he says, motioning toward a silver box on the floor. "You see a small can in there?"

Daniel flips open the lid with his foot. He shakes his head.

"Well, damn it all. Forgot the glaze." Jonathon lifts the glass out again and lays it back on the cardboard box it came in. "A lot of banging around for nothing. You want to help me put this wood back up?"

Daniel shakes his head as he buttons his coat. Then he takes a hat from one of the pockets and pulls it down low on his forehead. Inside, a kitchen chair scoots across the wooden floor and someone walks through the house.

"I'm real sorry about Ian," Jonathon says, closing the cardboard flaps over the glass and looking at the ground instead of Daniel. It seems everyone is afraid to look at him. "Real sorry that had to sneak up on you."

"Didn't sneak up on anybody. I knew he'd die soon enough."

Jonathon lifts his eyes, one hand still on the pane of glass. "Well, so it wasn't such a surprise. Still sorry, though."

When Jonathon looks away again, Daniel wants to kick him hard, so hard that he flies through the door and lands in the kitchen at Elaine's feet. Instead, he says, "See ya," and starts to walk outside.

"Hey, Dan," Jonathon says. "Listen, I'll be taking off when I get this wood back up. But you ever need anything, just call. You know where to find me."

Daniel nods and walks across the porch.

By the time he reaches the last stair but before he steps onto the gravel drive, a thought starts to gnaw at him. He stops on the bottom stair and lets it gnaw all the way through. When it does, he looks toward the garage and smiles because now he knows where he'll find Dad's shotgun.

Celia offers Ruth a third cup of coffee when she excuses herself to go lie down, but she shakes her head and pats her stomach to signal a tired baby and Mama. At this, Celia smiles, but Arthur still can't look at Ruth. Celia nudges him for being impolite even though she knows it's not bad manners; it's fear. Mary Robison showed them all the truth about the very worst that a man can do to his own daughter. She made them all think, believe even, that Ray might do the same to little Elisabeth. She made them believe it so strongly that it still seems Ray is the one who hurt Julianne. It still feels like he is the one who wrapped that poor child in feed bags and dropped her in a hole.

"Rest well, Ruth," Celia says. "Things will be better tomorrow."

Daniel waits in the garage until Jonathon and Elaine leave, and then, thinking someone will put out the porch lights, he waits even longer. No one ever does, so taking a deep breath, he slips behind the oil drum, pushes aside an old woolen blanket and lifts the shotgun. He cracks it open and sees the brass end of two shells. Loaded. It's heavier than he remembered, and the barrel is cold, even through his leather gloves. He slaps his palm against the wooden stock, getting a good feel, a good God damned feel, and then props it on his shoulder, barrel pointing up like Dad taught him. After looking through two loose slats in the door and seeing no one on the porch, he slips outside and runs across the hard gravel drive, through the gate that used to hold Olivia before Jonathon shot her dead. High stepping it through the snow, he runs toward the spot where the prairie dogs once lived.

Evie crawls into her closet but scurries out when someone walks across the living room floor, footsteps rattling the floorboards all the way in Evie's room. Through her terrycloth robe, the floor is hard and cold on her legs. She sits back, pulling her knees to her chest, and listens. The footsteps pass by and Elaine's door opens. Aunt Ruth has moved into Elaine's room where she and the baby will live after the baby is born, so long as the baby isn't blue and dies in the oven. She switched rooms because Evie doesn't like her anymore. Aunt Ruth said it was because Elaine needed so much help with the wedding. Evie told her it didn't matter one bit and to go ahead and change rooms.

After Aunt Ruth closes her door, Evie falls onto her hands and knees, pushes through the hems of Mama's skirts and dresses, the ones she only wears in the spring, and drags out a wadded-up blanket.

Waiting and listening and hearing nothing more, Evie slowly untangles the blanket and pulls out the Virgin Mary. She holds her up, looking first into her ivory face and her tiny blue eyes and then at the seams where her wrists meet her hands. She thinks she'd like to talk to the Virgin Mary, but someone might hear. So instead, cradling the statue like a baby, she hops back onto her bed, scoots until she can see out the window, and together they watch the red truck, driving down the road from the other direction, drift over toward the ditch and stop.

Soon it will be all the way dark. Setting the statue on the bed next to her, Evie stands and presses her nose to the cold glass. Out on the road, beyond the bare trees where the red truck is parked, the driver's side door opens and a man steps out. He stands still, his hands on his hips, and looks up at the house for a good long minute. He wavers, like the tall wheat stalks on a windy day. He must be cold, even with his jacket. The brim of his hat rides high on his forehead. Tugging it down, Uncle Ray

reaches inside the truck and pulls out a
long, thin gun.

CHAPTER 33

Celia shuts off the hot water when the bubbles reach the top of the sink. Gathering her cardigan sweater closed and wrapping her arms around her waist, she stares out the dark window. The tree is there, holding out its bare branches, reminding her of the cold, harsh winter. In the dim light, its icy coating doesn't sparkle. The tree looks nearly dead, standing in the dark, making Celia doubt it will come to life again in spring, making her wonder if spring will ever come.

"It's been such a long few days," she says to Arthur, who is sitting at the table. "You should have something more to eat."

Arthur holds his head in his hands and nods, though to what, Celia isn't sure.

"I could make you a sandwich for now. Then you could sleep."

"I found her in the shed, you know," Arthur says, his head lowered as if talking to the table. "I did. I found her."

Celia slides into a chair without pulling it back or making any noise.

"I knew she was in there, even before I opened the door." Arthur presses both hands around his coffee mug. "How does a person know something like that? Even before I opened the door. I could feel it, feel something on the other side."

He looks up at Celia.

"How does a person know?"

Pressing a dish towel over her mouth, Celia shakes her head.

"She had Mother's statue with her, holding it in one hand. Must have thought it would help her." Arthur exhales, almost a laugh. "She was so tiny, lying there. More like she was sleeping, except for the blood."

"It's so long past, Arthur. It wasn't your fault. Wasn't anyone's fault."

"I dropped her, the statue. Broke both hands off. Mother lost them in the laundry. For days, Ruth searched for them. Long past the funeral. Through every sheet and sock and basket. Looked until she found them both."

From behind the cover of her dish towel, Celia nods because that is so like Ruth, hunting and searching — probably the only helpful thing she could find to do. Because there is nothing she can say, Celia reaches for Arthur's hand instead. He lets her touch his fingers. They sit this way, their fingertips intertwined, not speaking, until their coffee has gone cold. Celia wants to remind Arthur that he was a boy when Eve died. He did what his sister asked, thought he was helping. She wants to soothe him, but before she finds the proper words, a familiar sound outside the kitchen window distracts her. Olivia has gotten out again. Arthur will be so angry with Daniel. No, it's not Olivia. Olivia is dead. Celia slowly pulls her hands away and turns toward the dark window.

Arthur hears it, too, because he lifts up a hand to silence her when she begins to speak. A rustling. A snapping. The wind. Or a coyote. It's always a coyote. Whenever Celia is lying in bed late at night and hears something outside, Arthur wraps an arm around her, pulls her close and whispers that it is a coyote. Celia waits for him to say the same now, but instead, he holds up a hand to keep the silence and slides his chair away from the table. Celia mirrors his movement, pushing back her own chair, silently, slowly. Arthur steps up to the kitchen window, leans so he can see around the side of the house and exhales.

"Looks to be Mary Robison," he says,

walking toward the back of the house. "Awful cold night to be out and about."

Celia stands and presses out her skirt. "Well, heaven's sake, invite her in. I'll start some fresh coffee."

Dumping the stale grounds into a tin can near the sink, Celia shivers at the rush of cold air that spills into the kitchen when Arthur opens the back door. She spoons fresh coffee into the percolator and takes three mugs from the cabinet as Arthur and Mary walk into the kitchen, Arthur helping Mary out of her coat. Neither of them speaks. Mary is smaller here in Celia's kitchen then in St. Anthony's or the café or her own living room when Celia delivered Ruth's food. Her face is small enough to cup in one hand and, standing next to Arthur, she seems she might disappear in his shadow. Once Mary is seated, Arthur kneels in front of her, takes both of her hands and rolls them front to back. Then, he unlaces one of her boots and slips it from her foot. Celia steps forward. He sets the boot aside and begins to rub Mary's foot.

"Arthur," Celia whispers.

Shaking his head to quiet Celia, Arthur removes the other boot. Mary's small shoulders fall forward as he rubs her second foot. Celia sets down the coffee mugs, goes to the linen closet outside the bathroom and pulls out her heaviest quilt. As gently as she can, she wraps it around Mary, pulls it closed under her chin and tucks it around her narrow hips. Rubbing both feet at once now, Arthur glances up at Celia.

"She must have walked," he whispers. Then, leaning forward and inspecting Mary's eyes, he says, "Did you walk, Mary?"

Mary smiles down into Arthur's face but doesn't answer.

"Best you go wake Ruth," he says to Celia. "Think Mary'll be needing her about now."

Within five minutes, the glow of the porch lights has faded and Daniel is breathing hard, fogging the air around him though he can hardly see it. His thighs ache from running through the snow, throwing his knees waist high for every step, and his left side throbs. Deep in his chest, the icy air burns his lungs. His own breathing is the only sound he hears. When he reaches a low spot in the snow at the bottom of a drift, he stops, the shotgun still propped over his shoulder, leans forward, and rests with one hand braced against his knee. He is nowhere near the prairie dog mound, or where the prairie dog mound used to be. Ian went back there, flung that dead prairie dog for his brothers to see. The brothers said prairie dogs wouldn't live there anymore, not since Daniel killed one. Ian said, "Who the hell cares? It was a good shot, a damn good shot, so who the hell cares about some God damned old prairie dogs?"

Standing straight, Daniel lifts the gun. He braces the butt against his right shoulder and brings the stock to his cheek, keeping his head high. Ian showed him how with a sawed-off broomstick.

"Don't let your head sag," he had said. "Keep it straight. Point; don't aim. That's the big difference. Aim a rifle. Point a shotgun."

Problem is Daniel doesn't have anything to point it at. Staring down the barrel, he sees nothing but dark rolling fields. He listens hard, thinking that maybe he'll hear chains. Chains dangling from Jack Mayer's wrists. He'll see Jack Mayer, his black skin, his white eyes glowing bright as the snow in the dim light. He'll see those thick heavy arms again, pumping hard with every stride. He'll shoot Jack Mayer. He'll shoot him because Ian said Jack Mayer killed Julianne Robison. Except he didn't. Mr. Robison did, and he's dead already. So Daniel will point, not aim, because Ian is dead and Daniel doesn't have any friends left. He'll lead the target that will be running through the snow, high stepping under the weight of shackles and chains, and he'll spatter buck-shot across Jack Mayer's back. Daniel will shoot him dead and then he'll be a man.

But, in the fading light, on the distant horizon where the last of day is sinking, Daniel sees nothing. There is no Jack Mayer. He's dead somewhere, lying in a ravine or buried under a snowdrift, or maybe he escaped across state lines. For months, he's been gone, been gone all along. He didn't do any of those things that Ian read in the newspaper. Didn't live in Ian's garage or steal Nelly Simpson's Ford Fairlane. He's gone. Daniel lowers the gun and walks toward home, still a boy.

Ruth slips on her robe, pulls the belt tight and opens her bedroom door a crack so no one will see her packed suitcases at the foot of her bed. Celia peeks inside.

"So sorry to disturb you, Ruth," she whispers. "But Mary Robison is here and she isn't well. Arthur thinks maybe you could be of help."

"Goodness, it's awfully cold for her to be out."

Stepping aside so Ruth can pass, Celia whispers, "And it appears that she walked.

She's frozen. Frozen solid."

Ruth shuffles into the kitchen, her slippers sliding across the cold floor, and sits next to Mary. Until Ruth touches Mary's sleeve, she doesn't seem to notice Ruth. When she does, Mary lifts her head and smiles.

"So good to see you, Ruth."

Ruth takes both of Mary's hands and rubs them gently between her own. "You're like ice. Some coffee?"

"Milk, please, and one sugar."

Kneeling in front of Mary, Arthur wraps one end of the quilt around her feet. "That better?" he asks.

Celia pushes two mugs across the table and sits in a chair opposite Ruth and Mary. Arthur sits next to her.

"Nice of you to visit, Mary," Ruth says. "I hope you'll let Arthur drive you next time."

She holds up a finger to quiet Arthur when he starts to talk. After so many years, at least twenty, she feels like the big sister again.

"Did you mean to come here?" Ruth asks even though she knows the answer.

"We used to be such friends, didn't we?" Mary says, watching Ruth rub her hands over Mary's. "The three of us. When we were girls."

"We're still friends," Ruth says, beginning to knead each of Mary's fingers. Slowly, they are warming.

"Only two of us. And not like we were."

"Girls grow up, I guess," Ruth says. "Responsibilities and such. Not so much time for friends."

Making a humming noise, Mary presses her face toward her coffee cup as if letting the steam warm her cheeks and nose. "I remember when we stopped being such friends. The three of us. Do you remember?" Mary pauses and says, "The day Orville Robison got off that train."

Ruth lifts her eyes toward Celia and Arthur. "Yes, that was a long time ago."

She swallows. Her heart begins to beat against her chest. She tries to slow it by taking one deep breath after another. Massaging Mary's littlest finger, Ruth concentrates on the tiny veins that spread like frail blue vines across the back of Mary's hand.

"Do you remember?" Mary says. "It rained the day he came. First good rain in so many years. All the dust put to rest that day. Do you remember? Everyone in town thought Orville Robison brought us a miracle."

Ruth tries to lift her eyes to Mary but she can't. Instead, she lays Mary's hands in her lap and covers them with her own.

"I thought I was marrying a miracle worker. So carried away with him. Big and broad as a barn. And so handsome. Wasn't he handsome?" Mary lifts Ruth's chin with one finger. "He did it, Ruthie. He hurt your Eve. When she was so young. He hurt your Eve, did things to her no man should be doing to a child. And then your family came home again. After all these years, they haunted him like a ghost. Hurt him especially to see the little one." She cups Ruth's face with one hand. "I didn't know how to stop him."

Wondering if Arthur hears the rustling outside the kitchen window, Celia nudges him, but he is listening to Ruth and Mary Robison and he brushes her away. She has been trying to follow the conversation, but isn't able to because she can't shake the feeling that something is watching her. Outside the window over the sink, the maple tree's bare branches tap on the side of the house and the porch light throws long, thin shadows that skip into the corners of her eyes, startling her. She's a little jumpy, that's all. So much has happened. Celia takes a deep breath and exhales as she moves her chair closer to Arthur's.

"What is it you're saying, Mary?" Arthur asks, scooting to the edge of his seat.

Ignoring for a moment that it seems someone is lurking outside the kitchen window, Celia realizes that she missed something very important. She reaches for Arthur's arm, but he pulls away.

"Arthur," she whispers. "Let's not lose our tempers."

Again, Arthur ignores Celia. "Tell me, Mary," he says.

Keeping one hand on Arthur's forearm, Celia shifts in her seat to face Ruth. "I don't understand, Ruth," she says. "What's going on?"

Ruth doesn't answer. Instead, with her hands covering Mary's, she stares over Celia's shoulder. Celia slowly turns. There, in the dark window with the maple's bare branches bouncing in the north wind, a large shadow slips by. Celia jumps up, the back of her chair bouncing off the kitchen cabinets and catching her left ankle. She stumbles and cries out, but before she can steady herself, Arthur grabs her arm and yanks her backward.

"Go," he says, stepping in front of her and waving them all toward the front bedroom. "Get all the girls. Shut the door. Lock it."

Celia limps around the table, keeping her

eyes on the window even though the shadow is gone now and hurries Ruth and Mary toward the farthest bedroom — Ruth's room now that she stays with Elaine.

"What is it, Mama?" Evie calls out from her room.

"Here, Evie. Come here." Celia grabs Evie's arm like Arthur grabbed hers, hustles Ruth and Mary into the room, and pulling Evie in after them, she slams the door behind her.

"Mama," Evie says, jumping into the middle of Ruth's bed and tucking her knees up under her. "What is it?"

Celia presses her ear to the closed door as she waves at Ruth to back away. "Sit down," she says. "It's nothing. Nothing."

"Celia, did you see?" Ruth says, helping Mary to sit on the bed.

Celia glances around the room, which is brightly lit with two lamps and the overhead light. At the end of Ruth's bed sit two suitcases. "The lights," she says, though she doesn't know why. "Put out the lights."

"Why?" Evie says. "What is it?"

"Please, shut them off."

Ruth turns off the two lamps near the bed as Celia flips the switch on the wall. The room falls dark. The house is quiet. Celia stands at the door, listening but hearing

434

nothing.

"I know what it is, Mama," Evie says, her voice floating up out of the darkness.

Three silhouettes sit on the bed, smallest to tallest. The smallest sits up and lifts her head.

"It's Uncle Ray."

CHAPTER 34

Daniel stops in the shadow of the barn, his shotgun propped over one shoulder. His crooked toes are numb and his fingers have gone stiff. The cold, dry air burns his mouth and throat each time he inhales. The day was only warm enough to melt the very top layer of snow. Now, with nightfall, the slippery coating has frozen to an icy shell. With every movement, every step, the snow crackles underfoot. Trying to stand still, he breathes into a cupped fist to warm the air before taking it in again. He leans forward, out of the shadow. Straight ahead, between the house and the barn, the porch light glows in a perfect circle, and in its center, stands Uncle Ray.

Evie says Uncle Ray has shrunk since they moved to Kansas, that little by little, he has started to dry up. She showed Daniel the picture of Aunt Eve and Uncle Ray when they were young, not so long before Aunt

436

Eve died. Back then, Uncle Ray was tall and straight and strong. Like Dad. Looking at Uncle Ray now, his legs spread wide, a rifle braced against his chest and pointed straight at Dad, who is walking out of the house, his hands calming Uncle Ray the same way he calmed Olivia when she slit open her neck, Daniel thinks Uncle Ray looks plenty big.

Pressing back against the barn, Daniel feels suddenly hot. His jacket is heavy, so heavy that it's suffocating him. He rips off his stocking cap, takes a deep breath in through his nose and blows it out slowly through his mouth. He lets the cold burn his insides so it will wake him up, help him to think. Calm now. Calm. Breathe. In and out. Slowly. In and out. Watching the ground at his feet so that he steps only where he's already broken through the snow, he leans out again.

"I've had about enough," Uncle Ray says, his cheek lying on the stock of the gun. His head is hanging. Bad form, Ian would have said. "I've God damned had enough."

Uncle Ray shifts his weight, putting his left foot slightly forward and then his right as if he can't remember how to get off a good shot.

"Sure, Ray," Dad says, still trying to soothe Uncle Ray, and when Uncle Ray stumbles because he's still shifting his feet, Dad takes one quick glance at the house. "We've all had enough. Damn right about that."

"Ruth is coming home today. Ruth and that child of mine. And that'll be the end of it."

The porch light glows on the two men. Flakes of snow blowing off the roof sparkle in the air around them.

"Let's talk a bit," Dad says and begins to sidestep across the drive toward the garage a few yards away.

"No more damned talking." Uncle Ray stumbles again.

Dad stops, stands still.

"You call Ruth." Uncle Ray rams the gun toward Dad. "Call her now."

Continuing to sidestep away from the house toward the garage, Dad says, "She's not here. Left with Jonathon. Taking rolls on over to the Buchers."

Another step, farther away from the house. Closer to the garage.

"You heard about Ian, yes?" Dad says.

The closer Dad gets to the garage, the easier it is for Daniel to see him, but he can't see Uncle Ray unless he steps out of the shadow and around the side of the barn.

"You know how Ruth is. Always trying to

438

help out. She'll be back later. Soon enough, I'd guess."

Holding his breath and leaning as far as he can without stumbling outside of the shadow, Daniel listens for Uncle Ray's voice. He leans too far, and when startled by a loud bang, he falls forward through the icy crust on a patch of fresh snow. There is another bang. Metal against metal. Olivia's gate. He ran through it on the way to the prairie dog mound, and like he did when Olivia was alive, he left it open. Now it's banging in the wind that has stirred up since the sun set. Daniel jumps up, scrambles to his feet and falls back against the barn.

"What the hell?" Uncle Ray shouts.

He must be looking straight at the barn now, probably with his gun pointed at the dent Daniel made in the snow, except Daniel is standing in the shadows, not breathing, not moving, and Uncle Ray doesn't see him.

"Just that old gate," Dad says.

From the sound of his voice, Dad is almost to the garage. Daniel leans against the barn, breathing so fast and deep that he doesn't have time to think. He swallows and leans forward. Dad has taken a few more steps toward the garage, and Uncle Ray is following Dad with the tip of his rifle again, slowly turning his back on the house. Pressing against the barn, Daniel remembers the shotgun propped over his shoulder. Grandpa's old shotgun. Dad thinks he'll find it in the garage, behind the door, behind the oil barrel, under the blanket. He knew Uncle Ray would come one day. He knew it and was ready. Except he isn't ready because Daniel has the gun.

"Where you going, Ray?" Dad says. "I told you she's not here. Gone off with Jonathon."

Uncle Ray is backing toward the house, his rifle still pointed at Dad.

"I'm no damn fool, Arthur. You stay put. Stay right there."

Near the bottom stair leading up to the porch, Uncle Ray slips. He drops the tip of the rifle for a moment and grabs the railing to right himself before aiming the gun back at Dad. If he would turn slightly to his left, he might see Daniel, leaning out of the shadows, watching.

"Ruth," Uncle Ray shouts up the set of stairs. "Get your damn self out here."

"She won't hear you, Ray. She's gone off."

Uncle Ray backs up the stairs, stumbling but holding onto the railing with one hand and balancing the gun with the other. At the top of the stairs, he pushes the latch on the screened door with his elbow, kicks it open and disappears onto the porch. Before the door has slammed shut, Dad slips into the garage.

The path from the side of the barn through Olivia's gate is waist deep with snow. Daniel runs toward the garage, throwing his knees high, but before he reaches the gate where he can step onto the cleared gravel, the porch door swings open again and Uncle Ray walks out, dragging Aunt Ruth behind him. She carries two suitcases with her, causing her to stumble and trip.

"Ray," Mama shouts from inside the house. "The baby. Be careful of the baby."

By the time Uncle Ray and Aunt Ruth reach the bottom step, Dad is back outside the garage, looking left and right as if he might find his shotgun wedged there in a snowdrift. Daniel, having squatted behind a fence post outside the glow of the porch light, squints toward the house. Mama is there, standing inside the screened door. Ahead of him, Olivia's gate bounces in the wind, the slide bolt rattling and the strap hinges creaking.

"Ray, stop," Mama shouts. "Leave her be."

Really, it's more of a scream, something Daniel has never heard before. The sound makes his stomach tighten as if he might vomit right here in the snow. Mama's scream seems to surprise Uncle Ray, too, because he shoves Aunt Ruth away from the house and aims his gun at Mama. Dad takes two quick steps but then stops.

"Take it easy, Ray," he says.

"I'll go, Ray," Aunt Ruth says. "See. I'm packed. Already packed to come home." She is standing on the hard, cold gravel in only her slippers and she is wearing Elaine's beige housecoat. Her hair hangs loose and blows into her eyes. "Please. Let's go. Leave Celia be."

Uncle Ray jabs his gun at Aunt Ruth, but she doesn't flinch the way Mama did. She's seen a gun up close before, Daniel thinks. She's had one pointed right in her face.

"You think I should leave here, Ruth?" Uncle Ray says.

"Yes. Yes. I'm coming with you. Coming home with you now. I'm ready. See?" she says, lifting one suitcase. "I was waiting on the weather. Just waiting for it to clear."

Dad takes two more steps toward Uncle Ray.

"Come down here, Celia," Uncle Ray says, aiming his gun at Mama again.

At this, Dad backs up.

Mama stands at the top of the stairs, her eyes locked on Dad. She starts to cry.

"Get down here, now."

Mama presses both hands over her mouth and doesn't even bother to brush away the hair that blows across her forehead and eyes. She shakes her head and takes the stairs one at time.

"You've been drinking, Ray." Dad is trying to calm him and, at the same time, looking all around at the ground and in the air for anything that might help.

When Mama reaches the bottom step, Dad presses one hand in the air to make her stop right there. Behind her, the porch door opens again. Mary Robison and Evie step outside. Standing side by side on the top stair, Mrs. Robison holds Evie's hand.

"Did you tell him, Ruth?" Mrs. Robison shouts across the drive.

Aunt Ruth shakes her head. "Not now, Mary." She chokes before the words come all the way out. "Go back inside, Evie."

Mrs. Robison smiles down at Evie, nods and Evie runs down the stairs and grabs onto Mama's legs.

"I owe it to you, too, Ray," Mrs. Robison says, walking down the stairs.

Mama is trying to push Evie away, trying to make her go back inside but Evie won't let go.

"Shut up, the all of you," Uncle Ray

shouts, and waving the rifle tip at Mama, he says, "Get on over with Ruth."

Mrs. Robison walks past Mama and when Dad steps forward to stop her, Uncle Ray jabs at him with the gun and Dad stops.

"Don't involve yourself," Dad says to Mrs. Robison.

Ignoring Dad like she doesn't know he's there, Mrs. Robison keeps walking, slowly because she doesn't have anything on her feet. "I owe it to you most of all," she shouts over the wind.

Uncle Ray backs away as Mrs. Robison walks toward him. He staggers closer to Daniel. The weight of the gun seems to throw him off balance. He takes aim at Mrs. Robison, too, but she doesn't stop like Dad. With the rifle poised on his shoulder, Uncle Ray dips his head, presses his cheek to the stock and fires.

Celia must have screamed, maybe she is still screaming. Someone shouts at her. It's Ray.

"I said get your damned self over there." He waves his gun at her.

Celia starts to walk toward Ruth, but Evie has latched onto her legs, stopping her. She rips open Evie's arms and pushes her toward the stairs.

"Go. Go now," she screams.

Evie falls against the stairs and crawls on hand and foot toward the porch. Arthur is yelling, too, telling Celia to stay put, stay God damned well put.

"Don't you move, Celia," he tries to shout over Ray. "Don't you take one God damned step."

Behind Ray, Ruth stands in her robe and slippers. The hem of her robe slaps her legs. She shakes her head and presses both hands in the air as if she doesn't want Celia to come any closer.

With his rifle pointed at Arthur now, Ray walks forward, steps around Mary Robison's lifeless body, grabs Celia's arm and flings her toward Ruth. Stumbling backward and falling on her hind end, pieces of ice and gravel bite into her palms. Ray roots himself and points the gun at Arthur's head. Celia shuffles backward like a crab on her hands and feet until Ruth grabs her from behind and helps her to stand.

"Please, Ray," Celia says, wiping Mary Robison's blood from her cheek and drying her hand on her blue-checkered apron. "Enough. Please stop."

"Don't know who the hell you think you are," Ray shouts, aiming at Arthur. "Coming around after twenty years. God damned coward. How you like me taking your wife?"

Arthur lifts both hands, surrendering himself. Blood shines on his cheek and neck and stains one side of his shirt.

"Take it easy now, Ray," he says. "I should have told you. Should have told you about Eve. Christ, Ray, I was a kid."

Ray backs away, stumbling as he tries to step around Mary Robison's feet, and takes aim at Arthur again.

Celia grabs Ruth and guides her down the driveway. "We're going, Ray," she calls out. "Do you see? We're going. Wherever you want." She pulls Ruth backward, leaving the two suitcases. "Come on now," she calls out again. "Like you said." Ruth is stiff, but Celia knows they have to get clear. She needs Ray to back away a little more. "Come on, now."

They need to get clear. She sees Daniel there behind the fence post. He has a shotgun. They need to get clear.

Daniel drops his chin to his chest and rests his forehead against the wooden fence post. Without looking up, because he isn't ready for the sight of Mrs. Robison again, he sticks the index finger of his right glove between his teeth, bites down and pulls his hand away. Letting that glove drop into the snow, he does the same with his left. Maybe he only thought he saw blood splatter across Dad's chest and into Mama's face. Maybe blood didn't spray onto the snowdrift that runs along the back of the house. With the shotgun balanced on his lap, Daniel presses his bare hands between his knees and raises his chin.

"Don't do anything foolish now, Ray," Dad says. His hands are still in the air and Mrs. Robison's blood is a black stain across his shirt.

"I ain't no damn fool," Uncle Ray says, beginning to back down the driveway toward Aunt Ruth and Mama. "You're the fool. All of you." He staggers a few steps and his head wobbles. "You killed her," he says to Dad. "Same as if you put a gun to her head."

"Please, Ray. We're leaving," Mama says.

For an instant, she seems to look right at Daniel.

"Come on now." Yes, Mama sees him. "Ruth and I, we're leaving."

Uncle Ray backs away until he can see Mama and Aunt Ruth and Dad all at once. He seems to settle on Aunt Ruth. He points the gun at her and waves it like he wants her to come closer. "You tell me. You tell me that you knew what he did."

"Please, Ray. Don't do this," Mama says,

447

pulling Aunt Ruth away, farther down the driveway.

"Tell me now," he shouts.

Aunt Ruth lowers her head. She must be crying because her shoulders are shaking but she isn't making any noise. Uncle Ray swings around, presses the stock to his cheek and aims at Dad.

"You God damned well better tell me."

Uncle Ray pulls back the bolt action, presses his cheek to the barrel. He is steady now, lined up, ready for a solid shot.

Daniel slowly stands, his leg unfolding beneath him. Feet shoulder width, Ian had said with a sawed-off broomstick in hand. Left foot forward. Toes pointed straight ahead. Knees slightly bent.

Uncle Ray tilts his head an inch to the right the way a man does when he closes one eye and looks down the barrel of his rifle.

"No," Mama shouts. "Ray, stop."

Daniel lifts the shotgun. Brings the stock to his cheek. Back straight.

"Ray, please." Aunt Ruth is crying. She sounds far away, like she's inside a dream.

Daniel lines up the bead sight with the notch at the tip of the gun. Something snaps. A gun is cocked. Inhale. Exhale halfway. Just halfway, Ian had said. Hold steady. Be careful of the blockers. Give them twenty feet or so. Buckshot will scatter. The target will rise up between the pushers and the blockers.

"Now, Daniel," Mama shouts. "Now."

Uncle Ray squares his stance. Dad lunges. Daniel fires.

There is a crack in the air. A loud pop. Celia grabs for Ruth, pulling her so closely that together they nearly fall, tumbling and tripping over one another in their matted and muddy slippers. No matter what they see now, what they saw Ray do, he was Ruth's husband, a good man long ago. So many things led him to this moment, things set in motion twenty-five years earlier. What man would have taken a different path? Not even Arthur. Wouldn't he have started to drink? Wouldn't he have eventually hated the woman who could never be Celia? Wouldn't he have tried to kill the man who took her away? No, Ruth won't be able to live with the sight of what's happening to Ray.

She needs to remember him through pictures. A younger man, smiling, in love with Eve. She needs to remember that he would have been a good father had life turned a different direction. She'll love him because he loved Eve and she'll pass on

449

these memories, but none of that will be possible if she sees Ray now, his shirt tearing open, his blood spraying up toward the porch light, his lower skull ripped open. She could live with the knowledge, but not the sight. Holding Ruth's face against her side, Celia pulls her backward, down the drive as Arthur dives back and away. Daniel's shotgun echoes in the clear night air and ends with a sharp clap. There is silence.

The force throws Ray forward. He lands near Mary Robison's feet. Steam rises up from his torn body and, like Mary Robison's blood, Ray's splatters across the snow that drifts near the back door. It soaks in, leaving holes and dents in the soft white mound. At the top of the stairs leading into the house, Celia checks for Evie and exhales with relief when she isn't there, peeking through the screened door. She'll be in her closet, huddled under the skirts and dresses. Celia screamed at her to make her let go. She screamed at Daniel, too. She told her only son to kill a man. Had there been a kinder thing, she would have done it. Standing with the wind whipping at her skirt and blowing her hair from her face, her body harder and leaner than the day they arrived in Kansas, this is what she knows. Sometimes there is no kinder way.

Daniel is the first to move. He lowers the tip of his grandfather's shotgun and lets it slide off his shoulder. His movement pulls Arthur from the ground, slowly. He doesn't want to startle Daniel. He has that look about him, as if he's not quite inside himself anymore, as if he doesn't know his own father, as if he might fire again. Staring down at Ray, Arthur nods. He is dead. So is Mary Robison. Arthur knows dead. It takes him no time to see that. Then, he walks to his son, lays one hand on Daniel's wrist and the other on the barrel of the gun. Daniel lifts his eyes.

"It's what had to be done," Arthur says in a strong voice.

There was a time when Celia would have quieted him, asked him to lower his voice. Some things are best whispered, for the sake of fine manners. But she knows that Arthur speaks in a full voice so Daniel will never feel shame.

"You did a fine job, young man. Just fine."

Daniel turns to Celia and she nods.

Fine. Just fine.

CHAPTER 35

Evie closes her eyes, tilts her head toward the sky and inhales. This warm day, after so many cold, has a special smell about it. Aunt Ruth says things are greening up, so this must be what green smells like. With the sun warming her cheeks, Evie leans into Aunt Ruth, who pulls Evie close and kisses the top of her head. Aunt Ruth doesn't have to lean down as far anymore. Lately, most often at night when she lays in bed, Evie's shins and elbows ache. Mama says they are growing pains. Just that morning, she marked Evie's height on her bedroom doorframe with a black pen. Since moving to Kansas, she's grown almost an inch and a half. Mama has always said Evie would grow in her own sweet time.

Laying one hand on Aunt Ruth's hard, round belly, Evie cradles Aunt Eve's Virgin Mary statue in the other. In less than a month, Aunt Ruth will have a baby instead of a big belly. Evie holds her breath, waiting for a gentle nudge from Elisabeth.

"Get ready," Aunt Ruth says, squeezing Evie even tighter.

Evie clutches the statue to her chest, presses one ear against Aunt Ruth's stomach, and covers the other with her free hand. Near Grandma's barn, Daniel is wadding up old newspaper as kindling for the fire Dad asked him to start in the old trash barrel. Across the driveway, Jonathon sits behind the wheel of Grandpa's tractor, his hat pulled low on his forehead. Standing nearby, Daddy gives a nod and after a few chokes and coughs, the tractor starts up. Daniel leaves the barrel, smoke drifting up into the air and walks a few feet to stand behind Mama, Elaine and Grandma, his arms crossed, his hat pulled low like Jonathon's.

Aunt Ruth touches the Virgin Mary's head. "I'm glad you fixed her up," she says, leaning down and talking into Evie's ear so she can hear over the tractor.

Aunt Ruth wraps both arms around Evie as the tractor rolls across the drive. First, the wheels crush the tall grass that Daddy never lets Daniel mow, and when the tractor crashes into the small shed, Aunt Ruth's chest shudders. Daddy said the wood wasn't worth saving. He'd rather burn it and all the overgrown grass, too. He said what's past is past and it's time the Scott family puts it to rest. Aunt Ruth lowers her head, and when it's over, when Jonathon has backed away and turned off the tractor, she stands straight and takes a deep breath.

"Smells like green, doesn't it?" Evie says.

Daniel tugs on his hat when the dust settles and walks back to the barrel. Using one of the longer branches he gathered from Grandma's front yard, he pokes at his fire. It's going good now, burning strong, so he drops the branch, walks past Dad who is still staring at the empty spot where the shed used to be, and loads himself up with an armful of splintered wood. When he turns, suddenly feeling like he shouldn't toss the wood on the fire, Dad gives him a nod and a pat on the back.

"Thank you, son," he says and, lowering himself to his knees, he fills his own arms, stands and follows Daniel to the barrel. The two men stop a few feet from the fire and toss in the wooden planks. Soon their arms are empty. They stand together watching the ash and sparks float up into the air and disappear. Mama, Grandma Reesa and Aunt Ruth have gone inside to make Grandma's fried chicken. Dad still says it's the best in the Midwest, but mostly he says it when Mama isn't around to hear. Jonathon has gone off with Elaine, probably so Elaine can make him write his share of thank-you notes for their wedding gifts, and Evie is sitting on the top stair with the Virgin Mary at her side. When the sparks have settled and only smoke is drifting up, Dad and Daniel return for another load.

Celia sits across from Ruth, a paper bag placed between them on Reesa's table where she usually keeps the salt and pepper shakers. Grease sizzles and pops in the black skillet on the stove, and the chicken broth begins to boil, drops of it hissing as they splash on the gas burner. With a wooden spoon in one hand, Celia cracks an egg into the dumpling dough and starts to stir again. Reesa looks at Celia as if to tell her no more eggs but clears her throat instead and goes back to poking her chicken. Reaching across the table, Ruth touches the brown paper bag.

"I did think about it," she says. "In the very beginning."

"Anyone would have," Celia says, pausing for a moment before beginning to dig and stir again. "You thought you were alone."

"But I never would have done it. Not to Elisabeth."

Celia pushes aside the bowl, stands and takes the paper bag. "Do you want to me take care of this?"

"I never could have used it," Ruth says, crossing her hands on the table. "Don't even know why I kept so much." She looks up at Celia. "Things never seemed quite so bad when no one was around to see." She tucks her hair behind her ears, a motion that makes her look like a young girl again. "But then you all moved back, and I was so ashamed for you to know. All the drinking and the times he hurt me. You all made it" — she pauses — "more real. That's when I knew I could never let my own child see those things." She shakes her head and pulls two small brown bottles from her apron pocket. "These will need to go, too."

"Celia's right, child," Reesa says. With a teaspoon, she scoops a dumpling and dips it into the simmering broth. "Any sane woman would have done the same. You were taking care."

Celia picks up the bottles, holds them in one hand and raises her eyebrows because a smile doesn't seem appropriate. Ruth gives her a nod, and Celia carries the bottles and the bag from the kitchen.

Walking across the gravel drive toward Arthur and Daniel, Celia wonders when wedge root is in season. Ruth must have gathered it months ago. Surely it didn't grow under the cover of snow. No, she must have thought ahead. In the early weeks, when she considered how she could end her pregnancy, she could have found the plant growing along every ditch in the county, but by the time her plan changed and she needed to gather enough to kill a six-foot-four-inch 220-pound man, the wedge root must have been harder to come by. How much wedge root did it take to boil out enough oil to fill these two small bottles? When Ruth pulled the bag and bottles from her suitcase, Celia never asked her how she would have done it or if it mattered that Ray wasn't the one who killed Julianne Robison. Would she have seeped the wedge root with Ray's morning coffee over weeks and months until it eventually killed him? Would one strong dose of the oil, maybe mixed with the base of a nice chicken stock, have done the trick? No, Celia never asked.

Outside the screened door, Evie sits on the top step, cradling the Virgin Mary to her chest. As Celia passes by, she touches the top of Evie's head. Evie hugs the small statue with both arms and slips inside before the screened door falls closed. Walking toward Arthur and Daniel, she thinks that there was a time when she would have asked Daniel to step away. When he was a boy, just a year ago, afraid of the monster at the top of Bent Road, she would have asked him to leave. But not today, because now he is a man.

It's still there, that lazy bend in the fence line a quarter mile northeast of Reesa's house, except the fields are no longer empty like they were on the night that the Scott family arrived in Kansas. That spring, the short sprouts that had lain dormant all winter began to grow and when the weather warmed and the spring rains came, those sprouts grew and became shiny, green stalks that carpeted the fields. More time passed, and under the summer sun, the green stalks faded to yellow. The bristly heads are heavy and soon the farmers will harvest their golden crops, leaving the fields bare once again. As autumn draws closer, the tumbleweeds will begin to dry out. Their woody stems will turn brittle and break near the ground. They'll tumble and roll and the curve at the top of Bent Road will scoop them up.

Celia knows now to slow near the top of that hill. She edges toward the shoulder in case of oncoming trucks that she might not see in time. She knows where home is and which way to turn should Arthur's truck slip over the top of the next hill unseen.

Sliding in between Arthur and Daniel, Celia rolls down the top of the paper sack until it's closed good and tight. Heat spills out of the barrel, keeping the three of them at a distance. The wood crackles and hisses as it burns and smells of sweet cedar. Arthur slips an arm around Celia's shoulders, and saying a quiet God bless you to the memory of Aunt Eve, she tosses the bag into the fire.

ACKNOWLEDGMENTS

I owe tremendous thanks to Dennis Lehane and Sterling Watson. Together, they introduced the Eckerd College Writers in Paradise Conference to St. Petersburg, Florida, and have inspired and educated countless writers, myself among them. For your generosity and boundless commitment, I thank you. My deepest gratitude also to Christine Caya and the rest of the WIP writers group.

Thank you to my wonderful agent, Jenny Bent of The Bent Agency, for your professionalism and belief in this book, and many thanks to Judy Walters for plucking me from the slush pile. To my editor, Denise Roy: Your dedication to the craft of writing and commitment to your profession are an inspiration, and I thank you for your guidance. My appreciation also to the entire team at Dutton for their support of this book.

To my dear friends Karina Berg Johansson and Adam Smith, thank you for setting the high bar and for sharing so many laughs. Thank you to the following people who have inspired and supported me all these many years: to Kim Turner for being my first reader; to Stacy Brandenburg, for sharing stories over coffee; to Lisa Atkinson, Chris Blair, and Scotti Andrews, for your guidance in the early chapters; and to my parents, Jeanette and Norm Harold, and my in-laws, Evelyn and Orville Roy. Thanks, also, to my reading group of eleven years.

Finally, and most especially, thank you to Andrew and Savanna for understanding why dinner wasn't always on time. And to my dear husband, Bill, thank you for your quiet, unwavering, and steadfast belief over so many years.

ABOUT THE AUTHOR

Lori Roy lives with her family in west central Florida. Her work has appeared in the *Chattahoochee Review*. *Bent Road* is her first novel.

ANGLETERRE

DUNKERQUE
CALAIS
ARTOIS
LILLE
ARRAS
FLANDRE
BELGIQUE
PICARDIE
SOMME
AMIENS
ST-QUENTIN
OISE
LUXEMBOURG
ALLEMAGNE

MANCHE
LE HAVRE
ROUEN
SEINE
ILE-DE-FRANCE
LAON
REIMS
MARNE
METZ
LORRAINE
MEUSE
MOSELLE
RHIN

CAEN
NORMANDIE
PARIS
VERSAILLES
CHARTRES
CHAMPAGNE
TROYES
SEINE
NANCY
STRASBOURG
Vosges
ALSACE

MAINE
LE MANS
ORLÉANS
LOIRE
YONNE
BOURGOGNE
MULHOUSE
BESANÇON

ANGERS
ANJOU
TOURS
VIENNE
TOURAINE
BOURGES
DIJON
SAONE
SUISSE

POITIERS
VICHY
LOIRE
RHONE

LIMOGES
LIMOUSIN
CLERMONT-
FERRAND
ANGOULEME
LYON
ST-ÉTIENNE
SAVOIE
ITALIE
GRENOBLE

GUYENNE
DORDOGNE
AUVERGNE
Massif
Central
ALLIER
DAUPHINÉ

BORDEAUX
GARONNE
LOT
RHONE
DURANCE
PROVENCE
NICE
MONACO

GASCOGNE
TARN
LANGUEDOC
Cévennes
AVIGNON
AIX-EN-PROVENCE
CANNES

MONTPELLIER
NIMES
TOULON
TOULOUSE
MARSEILLE

CARCASSONNE
BÉZIERS

Pyrénées
PERPIGNAN
MER MÉDITERRANÉE

ANDORRE

Klaus Grutzka

Y0-CAR-436

LA CIVILISATION FRANÇAISE

LA

HARCOURT, BRACE & WORLD, INC.

New York   Chicago   San Francisco   Atlanta

CIVILISATION FRANÇAISE

Victor Duloup
Agnes Scott College

LA CIVILISATION FRANÇAISE
Victor Duloup

Title Page: (left) Maillol: *La Méditerranée*. (c. 1901). The Museum of Modern Art. (right) Rodin: *Le Penseur*. The Metropolitan Museum of Art. Gift of Thomas F. Ryan, 1910.

Drawings by Carol Robson

ACKNOWLEDGMENT

The author wishes to thank Éditions Gallimard for permission to use « Le Cantique des Colonnes » from *Charmes*, by Paul Valéry ; « Un homme de chez nous, de la glèbe féconde » from *La Cathédrale de Chartres* by Charles Péguy ; and the excerpt from *Exercices de Style* by Raymond Queneau. © Éditions Gallimard.

Acknowledgments and copyrights for illustrations appear on page 323.

ISBN: 0–15–548925–9

Library of Congress Catalog Card Number: 76–105691

Printed in the United States of America

A MA FILLE

PREFACE

Although French civilization is not a novel subject for a textbook, the unusual approach that has been used here warrants a few preliminary remarks.

The word "civilization" is not easily defined; it means many things to many people. It is not what Americans mean by "culture," nor what the French understand by *la culture*. In an attempt to avoid confusion, this text is restricted to one use of the term—with French connotations. *La civilisation* is regarded as closely related to the verb *civiliser* and to the adjective *civil*. It refers to the contributions of the best human talents participating in all fields of creative endeavor in a given geographical and historical setting. Given this definition, one must conclude that a civilization can be best apprehended only at its highest intellectual and social levels.

There are also important historical reasons for considering the highest levels instead of the average ones: They are more outstanding and hence more familiar to us; and they still live as part of us, while the others are dead and buried. In the pages that follow, the artist receives more attention than the gentleman and gentleman more attention than the peasant, who, although he has fed the others, cannot be said to have participated to the same extent in the events the book discusses. Groups of people, schools of thought, and institutions—painters, musicians, poets, philosophers, the press, the State, even haute couture—are also regarded selectively and from a distance, again more often through their successes than through their failures.

To attempt to depict the entire civilization of a thousand-year-old country in one small volume is an impossible task. The traditional approach to this problem has been the didactic one: the standard civilization textbook is little more than a superficial listing of four-figure numbers and a procession of Louis and Henris indistinguishable from one another. They mean little to the student and are forgotten by him as soon as examination time has passed. Even though this method might claim the advantage of being objective and unbiased, it is in fact highly subjective, for the author has impressed his personality on the work by the very acts of choosing and arranging his facts, names, and dates from the vast number available to him.

La Civilisation française contains, not a large number of facts, but a limited number of general ideas—for ideas govern every aspect of civilization from philosophy to gastronomy. These basic ideas may be easily compared with others that the reader is already familiar with. They can be accepted or disputed, and they make no pretense at being objective.

The ideas presented in this book are the author's. Although he has carefully contemplated them and has expressed them as clearly as possible, he does not wish to impose them on anyone. They may, indeed, be considered merely as hypotheses, as starting points for other creative views of the subject. The facts in the book appear as illustrations of the general ideas. By proceeding from the general to the particular, the reader will find that the particular, since it is in context, is more relevant and more easily remembered than if it had appeared alone. Nonetheless, names, dates, and places are given sparingly, for civilization is a matter not of craftsmen, villages, and years, but of geniuses, countries, and centuries.

The traditional attempts at objectivity are replaced by open opportunities for disagreement. Boxed quotations appear in each chapter; they often present views opposed to those of the author and may indeed contradict one another. The student is thus invited to reorganize the given facts in accordance with his own ideas, and discussion questions for each chapter enable him to express his views. The student may wish to initiate independent research to corroborate his ideas; in so doing he will penetrate even more deeply into this area of knowledge.

It is hoped that this creative approach will be consonant with the current student demand for more freedom in academic pursuits. Freedom should always be granted, but never without the corresponding responsibilities. In treating French civilization at its highest level, the author also has high expectations of the initiative, understanding, conscientiousness, and spirit of inquiry of the students who will read this book, in the belief that the greatest demand brings forth the greatest response.

VICTOR DULOUP

TABLE DES MATIÈRES

LA CIVILISATION FRANÇAISE

LA FRANCE: 1
ESQUISSE
POUR
UN PORTRAIT

IDÉE GÉNÉRALE

Un humoriste a dit : « Il faut se méfier de la première impression. C'est généralement la bonne. » Une journaliste française affirme que l'impression superficielle que produit un pays entr'aperçu n'est jamais contredite par les conclusions qu'on tire sur lui après en avoir fait une étude approfondie. C'est dans cet esprit que nous voulons commencer par dégager les traits généraux de la France : ce ne sera qu'une esquisse. Au lecteur de brosser le portrait plus complet, plus nuancé, dont nous n'aurons fourni que les mesures et les proportions.

Proportions, mesures : c'est à peine un hasard si ces mots se présentent déjà à notre esprit. Telle qu'elle se voit, la France est justement le pays de la modération et de l'harmonie. Non qu'elle soit ennemie des contrastes, mais elle aime à les équilibrer savamment. C'est un homme politique français qui a forgé l'expression « juste milieu » ; c'est un poète français qui a chanté « Midi le juste ». Ces notions de justice et de justesse ont été, pendant des siècles, au cœur même des préoccupations françaises.

Cet idéal, les Français ont longtemps voulu croire que la forme même de leur pays les destinait à le réaliser. Ce n'est pas sans naïveté que les professeurs de géographie du début du siècle commençaient toujours leurs manuels en déclarant d'un ton ravi que la France avait une forme géométrique presque parfaite. A les en croire, elle ressemblait fort exactement à un hexagone. Quoi d'étonnant, ajoutaient-ils, si un pays dessiné aussi harmonieusement a pour mission de fournir le monde entier en bon sens et en bon goût ?

Sans doute y avait-il là beaucoup de complaisance. Mais le terme d'*hexagone* est tout de même commode, significatif, stimulant : nous le retiendrons donc. Non pas immense comme les États-Unis, ni isolée comme la Grande-Bretagne, ni perpétuellement mouvante comme l'Allemagne, ni indéfinie comme la Russie, la France telle qu'elle se présente aujourd'hui constitue un bloc compact, dont la diversité n'a d'égale que la cohésion. *Foyer, creuset,* sont des mots qui lui conviennent bien. Entre ses frontières naturelles, tôt atteintes, souvent franchies mais rarement remises en question, elle a fait cuire et recuire les apports les plus variés dont elle a tiré son essence et sa civilisation.

Un visage, c'est, sans doute, une expression. Mais c'est d'abord une forme.

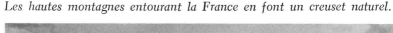

Les hautes montagnes entourant la France en font un creuset naturel.

Autant notre histoire est violente, autant notre géographie est douce. C'est un garçon guerel-leur et c'est sa petite sœur de sucre.

GASTON BONHEUR

Il n'est donc pas indifférent de savoir, lorsqu'on prétend faire le portrait de la France, que les Français eux-mêmes la définiraient volontiers comme un hexa-gone de dimensions moyennes situé au milieu du monde civilisé.

SITUATION

Au milieu du monde pour la latitude : à mi-chemin entre le pôle et l'équateur.

Au milieu du monde pour l'altitude : de 0 à près de 4000 mètres au-dessus du niveau de la mer.

Au milieu du monde pour le climat : zone tempérée, influences maritimes et continentales. Ni trop chaud, ni trop froid.

Au milieu du monde pour la politique : pendant des siècles, la France s'est trouvée au centre d'un triangle équilatéral ayant pour angles Londres, Vienne et Madrid. Les grandes puissances ne sont plus les mêmes, mais la situation géographique de la France la prédispose de nouveau à jouer les médiatrices : Paris, en effet, se trouve à égale distance du centre des États-Unis et de celui de l'U. R. S. S. Ne s'engageant ni dans un camp ni dans l'autre, la France se voit elle-même comme le fléau de la balance du monde, ainsi que le suggèrent les flèches innombrables de ses cathédrales.

FRONTIÈRES

On parle, pour la France, de frontières naturelles. « Fortifications naturelles » serait encore plus exact. Avec ses montagnes pour remparts et ses mers pour fossés, l'hexagone a l'air d'un château-fort dont le Massif central serait le donjon. Chacune de ces douves, chacun de ces bastions, a son histoire propre, et il convient de la retracer ici pour que leur mission apparaisse clairement.

Alpes   Les Alpes, encore qu'elles soient les plus hautes montagnes d'Europe, n'ont jamais été infranchissables. C'est par les sentiers de chèvres qui serpentent sur leurs versants abrupts que sont arrivés en France les enva-hisseurs — armés ou pacifiques — qui l'ont marquée le plus profondément. Jules César à la tête ses légions, les évangélisateurs chrétiens, plus tard les artistes de la Renaissance italienne, ont tous défilé au pied du Mont-Blanc. François Ier, Napoléon, à la recherche de conquêtes faciles, les ont traversées dans l'autre sens. Mais tous ces mouvements de troupes ou d'idées qu'elles n'interdisaient pas, elles les tamisaient du moins.

La France: esquisse pour un portrait   **3**

Pyrénées « Il n'y a plus de Pyrénées », aurait dit Louis XIV lorsque son petit-fils monta sur le trône d'Espagne, mettant fin à des guerres qui, pendant cent ans et plus, avaient déchiré ses deux patries : l'ancienne et la nouvelle. En fait, il y avait toujours des Pyrénées et elles n'avaient pas fini de jouer leur rôle. Sous Napoléon, elles permirent au peuple espagnol de résister victorieusement à l'envahisseur français ; pendant la guerre civile d'Espagne, au XXème siècle, elles consacrèrent la décision qu'avait prise le gouvernment français de ne pas intervenir dans les affaires de ses voisins. Il est vrai de dire, cependant, qu'elles ne furent jamais une barricade aussi efficace qu'aux XVème et XVIème siècles, pendant l'âge d'or du Saint-Empire romain-germanique. Avec un prince unique à leur tête, les tenailles Espagne-Autriche auraient sans doute écrasé la France si les Pyrénées ne les avaient pas empêchées de se refermer.

Est et Nord-Est Le Nord-Est, c'est le défaut de la cuirasse. Jura, Vosges, Ardennes, ce ne sont que montagnes à vaches, et qui ne compensent pas le déroulement des plaines de Flandre où soufflent depuis toujours les vents de l'invasion. Lorsqu'on regarde une carte de France faisant mention des batailles, on voit que toutes celles qui ont été livrées contre l'étranger se sont déroulées dans ces régions. C'est par là que sont venus les Germains, les Huns, les Anglais et même les Espagnols. La population y demeure attachée à ses patois ; les villes n'y ont guère de monuments historiques et présentent au touriste leurs façades uniformes érigées sous l'égide du ministère de la Reconstruction ; les cimetières militaires y abondent ; les noms des villages qu'on y trouve éveillent des souvenirs dans le monde entier : Azincourt, Malplaquet, Verdun.

Manche Ce n'est pas sans orgueil que les Anglais donnent le nom de « English Channel » à ce bras de l'Atlantique qui unit l'océan à la Mer du Nord. Les Français l'appellent simplement la Manche : ils peuvent se permettre quelque nonchalance. N'est-ce pas des côtes françaises que partit, il y a mille ans, cette armée normande qui devait conquérir et féconder toute la Grande-Bretagne ?

C'est de la Manche, semble-t-il, qu'est née la vocation maritime de la France. Ses pêcheurs, ses négociants et ses corsaires ont presque toujours eu des ports normands ou bretons comme lieux d'attache. Saint-Malo, base des partances les plus aventureuses ; le Mont Saint-Michel, sentinelle maritime du Moyen Age ; le Havre, l'un des ports les plus modernes du monde, donnent tous les trois sur le même bras de mer.

De même que les Pyrénées, la Manche joua un bon tour à Napoléon en l'empêchant d'envahir l'Angleterre comme il se le proposait. Protectrice naturelle de la France — elle porta jusqu'aux côtes françaises les libérateurs américains — elle a donc servi aussi à freiner ses appétits les plus démesurés.

Atlantique L'Atlantique, lui, n'est pas une protection, mais plutôt une sollicitation, un appel, peut-être une tentation. Longtemps, il ne fut qu'une limite. Ce n'est pas pour rien qu'on baptisa Finistère la pointe extrême de la Bretagne. Mais, aux temps modernes, il est devenu, au contraire, une façade

Le port de Marseille est, depuis 2500 ans, une porte ouverte sur la Méditerranée tour à tour phénicienne, grecque, romaine, chrétienne et musulmane.

largement ouverte pour l'exportation et l'importation. Ses ports, Nantes, La Rochelle, Bordeaux, aspirent les produits américains, distribuent les produits français entre le Canada, les États-Unis et l'Amérique du Sud qui, tous les trois, leur font face. Ce n'est qu'au cours des toutes dernières années — depuis l'avènement de la Cinquième République — que la France semble orienter de nouveau son regard vers ses créneaux continentaux. On peut en être déçu, mais il serait naïf de s'en étonner. La France est une personne : elle ne peut se tourner de tous les côtés à la fois. Si elle regardait sans cesse vers l'Atlantique, il lui faudrait vivre le dos tourné à l'Europe, ce qui n'est ni dans ses goûts ni dans ses intérêts.

Méditerranée   La Méditerranée n'est ni un moyen de défense ni une sortie : c'est une entrée. Par elle, avec la fondation du port de Marseille vers 600 avant Jésus-Christ, toutes les civilisations antiques se sont déversées dans la France. C'est par sa rive méditerranéenne que la France participe du miracle grec, et qu'elle a été amenée à jouer dans le monde arabe son rôle de conseillère plutôt que de conquérante.[1] C'est par sa rive méditerranéenne que la France a été amenée à disputer l'hégémonie anglaise en Afrique et en Asie ; c'est par là aussi qu'elle est demeurée perpétuellement en contact avec ce foyer civilisateur qu'est le Proche-Orient, inventeur de tous les dieux vénérés dans le monde moderne. Sans l'alphabet phénicien, la philosophie grecque, la législation romaine, la religion dite judéo-chrétienne, l'arithmétique arabe, que seraient l'Occident en général et la France en particulier ? Or, tout cela, c'est la Méditerranée qui le leur a donné.

L'HEXAGONE

Physiquement, l'hexagone constitue un bloc sans frontières intérieures. Les départements actuels ne correspondent à aucune réalité, géographique ou ethnique. Seules les anciennes provinces justifient les différences que l'on rencontre du Nord au Midi.

Ile-de-France, Anjou, Orléanais, Touraine, Poitou, Nivernais Si l'on regarde de nouveau une carte mentionnant les batailles et qu'on s'intéresse maintenant à celles que les Français se sont livrées entre eux, on s'aperçoit qu'elles ont presque toutes eu lieu dans les provinces qui s'étendent de part et d'autre de la Loire : Anjou, Touraine, Orléanais. C'est ici, en effet, que la France s'est forgée, et ce pays, avec la douce fermeté de son relief, la suavité discrète de sa lumière, le parler raffiné de ses habitants, constitue, de l'aveu de tous, la France idéale. La tête de la nation, c'est l'Ile-de-France, pas de doute là-dessus : c'est de là que sont parties les conquêtes, les lois, les réformes, les constitutions. Mais si la France a un cœur, il se trouve quelque part entre le Poitou et le Nivernais.

Normandie La Normandie est tout autre. Cadeau des rois de France à l'envahisseur normand au Xème siècle, elle a conservé une sorte de complicité avec tous les pays fécondés par la race prestigieuse des Vikings. L'écrivain Jean de La Varende a rendu, avec infiniment d'intuition, la communion mystique et sensuelle qui existe entre les Normands — peuple roublard, inquiétant, narquois — et le paysage — bocage, vallons, chemins creux, pommiers verdoyants, pâturages gorgés d'eau — qu'ils habitent depuis plus de mille ans.

Bretagne Les Bretons, avec leur langue gaélique, leurs velléités d'indépendance, leur passion toute celtique de la mort, et cette mer brumeuse qui encercle presque entièrement leur presqu'île, sont plus insaisissables encore. De tout temps, les Français les ont traités en parents pauvres. Au cours de la Première Guerre mondiale, c'étaient les divisions bretonnes qu'on envoyait dans les actions les plus meurtrières ; dans le peuple, on considère générale-

---

[1] *Historiquement* : traité entre François Ier et la Porte ; relations amicales entre Louis XIV et le Grand Seigneur ; protectorat au Maroc et en Tunisie ; mandat français au Liban. *Actuellement* : exploitation franco-algérienne du pétrole saharien ; compréhension mutuelle au sujet de la situation en Israel ; etc.

L'Atlantique, battant les côtes de Bretagne, ouvre à la France la route de l'Ouest et de l'aventure.

Si, comme l'a dit l'historien Michelet, la France est une personne et qu'elle ait une âme, cette âme est la cathédrale de Chartres émergeant des blés.

ment que les Bretons sont têtus et bornés. Cela tient sans doute à ce que le peuple français, dans son ensemble, n'est guère capable d'apprécier ce goût du surnaturel qui hante les imaginations bretonnes et qui donne à la civilisation française des racines mystiques sans lesquelles elle ne serait pas ce qu'elle est.

Picardie, Champagne « P'têt' ben qu'oui, p'têt' ben qu'non » (peut-être bien que oui, peut-être bien que non) passe pour être la devise des Normands. « Méfie-te » (méfie-toi) est celle des Picards. Froids, polis, toujours sur leur quant-à-soi, ils vivent par familles nombreuses et unies, groupés autour de leur noblesse à qui la Révolution n'a enlevé que peu de possessions et moins encore de prestige. Leurs voisins, les Champenois, s'adonnent à la culture d'un vin pétillant qui a fait leur réputation dans le monde et qui — depuis que le roi de France ne vient plus se faire sacrer dans Reims, leur capitale — demeure leur unique spécialité.

Lorraine, Alsace On met souvent l'Alsace et la Lorraine dans le même sac, sous prétexte que l'Allemagne a souvent revendiqué comme siennes ces deux provinces. En fait, tandis que l'Alsace parle un patois germanique et que toutes ses habitudes de vie (saucisses, bières et choucroutes) sont plus teutonnes que gauloises, la Lorraine, patrie de Jeanne d'Arc, appartient intégralement au bloc de civilisation française. Du reste, les deux provinces sont aussi patriotes l'une que l'autre ; maint Alsacien s'est battu avec conviction pour prouver que Schneider et Schumann sont des noms français, malgré leur origine évidemment germanique.

Bourgogne La Bourgogne — trait caractéristique — est à la fois le pays des vins et des cathédrales. La terre fertile qui recouvre ses coteaux aux modelés harmonieux, le soleil qui les échauffe, la pluie qui les rafraîchit, ont

Le Rhône impétueux et la Saône placide se marient. A leur confluent naît un des hauts lieux de la civilisation française : Lyon.

Rien de plus français que ce paysage du Massif Central que traversent à pied des enfants de paysans, au retour de l'école.

fait éclore cette merveille qu'est l'abbatiale romane de Vézelay ; ils font aussi éclore chaque année d'autres merveilles : un bon pommard ou même un beaujolais un peu raffiné. Les Bourguignons, personnages rustauds mais joyeux drilles, ne se sont ralliés qu'au XVème siècle à la couronne de France. Ils sont maintenant tout à fait amalgamés au reste de la nation.

Franche-Comté, Savoie, Dauphiné Régions montagneuses, la Franche-Comté conquise par la France sur les Francs-Comtois eux-mêmes, la Savoie longtemps disputée à l'Italie, le Dauphiné légué aux rois de France par son comte souverain, n'attirent les touristes que depuis que les sports d'hiver sont à la mode. Traditionnellement, la Savoie fournissait Paris en petits ramoneurs, assez minces pour se glisser dans les cheminées : les jeunes garçons débarquaient dans la capitale en portant dans leurs bras une marmotte somnolente qui leur rappelait leur pays.

Berry, Aunis, Angoumois, Saintonge, Bourbonnais, Lyonnais D'autres provinces s'étendent en demi-cercle autour du Massif central. Ce sont de vraies paysannes, attachées à leurs traditions, à leurs superstitions et à leurs spécialités gastronomiques. Il convient de faire une mention spéciale de la ville de Lyon, qui se considère elle-même comme une seconde capitale de la France. L'arrogance et la courtoisie également glacées dans lesquelles se complaisent ses habitants, l'accent particulier qu'ils affectent en parlant, les traditions littéraires et industrielles dont s'enorgueillit leur ville, toutes ces singularités

Le Midi, ce sont des villages escarpés dominant de leurs toits de tuiles des champs d'oliviers...

distinguent les Lyonnais des autres Français et même — du moins le croient-ils — du commun des mortels.

Auvergne, Limousin   Deux provinces se retranchent sur les pentes mêmes du Massif central : l'Auvergne et le Limousin. Les indigènes de ces pays reculés passent pour madrés et incroyablement avares. Les Auvergnats, en particulier, petits, trapus, consommant des quantités impressionnantes de « goutte »,[2] sont les héros de maintes histoires drôles. Leur accent (ils prononcent *ch* au lieu de *s*), leur exclamation favorite, qui est « Funérailles ! », leur métier de prédilection, qui consiste à faire des sabots, tout cela excite inlassablement la verve des autres provinciaux et des Parisiens. A Paris, du reste, les Auvergnats ont une profession bien à eux : sous le nom de « bougnats » ils tiennent des établissements où l'on peut acheter du bois et du charbon, mais où l'on peut aussi boire un petit verre de muscadet ou de rosé de Provence et quelquefois manger un morceau.

Midi   Plus au sud s'étend la vaste région qu'on appelle le Midi, où croît l'olivier, où fleurit le laurier rose, où les *e* muets se prononcent plutôt deux fois qu'une, où les voyelles nasales n'existent pas, où la vantardise est considérée

[2] alcool presque pur

comme un sport, le jeu de boules comme une occupation sérieuse, et le soleil comme une production régionale. Au Moyan Age, cette région s'appelait le Pays d'Oc. Sous des prétextes religieux, sa population, romanesque et nonchalante, fut soumise par le pouvoir central, au prix de quelques massacres et quelques décennies d'oppression. Elle ne semble pas en avoir gardé rancune aux originaires du Pays d'Oïl, qu'elle persiste néanmoins à trouver parfaitement ridicules, avec leurs airs graves, leurs soucis matériels et leur parler pointu.

Provence   La Provence, qui fut le pays de Pétrarque, est presque italienne déjà : par son paysage méditerranéen, orangers et cyprès ; par son architecture, mas roses et blancs exposés à la mer ; par ses indigènes à la bouche

... ou surplombant la mer violette *d'Ulysse, la* mère Méditerranée *de la civilisation occidentale.*

souriante et au verbe haut. Les vestiges romains se trouvent partout. Et certains écrivains, qui continuent à écrire en provençal, s'attachent à perpétuer les traditions de la littérature occitane, c'est-à-dire celle des troubadours. La Côte d'Azur ou Riviera — les Français disent « la Côte » tout court quand ils « savent vivre » — attire depuis le début du siècle les artistes et les gens fortunés de tout poil. Picasso cuit ses poteries à Vallauris ; Lanza del Vasto[3] distribue ses bénédictions à Tourettes ; Matisse a bâti sa chapelle à Vence-la-Jolie ; et tous les cinéastes se donnent rendez-vous sur le port de Saint-Tropez (défense de prononcer le *z* sous peine de passer pour un béotien !)

Languedoc Le Languedoc est plus tragique, plus secret. Ruiné par l'exode des campagnes au profit des villes, il dresse vers le ciel les tours en ruines de ses châteaux déserts et les charpentes sans toit de ses villages abandonnés.

Guyenne, Gascogne, Béarn Les provinces du Sud-Ouest, avec leurs vins de bordeaux, leurs foies gras du Périgord, et leurs cadets de Gascogne — dont

[3] penseur contemporain ; grand découvreur du spiritualisme de l'Inde

Sans le vin, la France ne serait pas la France. Bien des manoirs sont en fait des fermes viticoles produisant, par exemple, un bordeaux de la plus haute tenue.

le représentant le plus connu est le d'Artagnan d'Alexandre Dumas — donnent à la France ce qu'elle a de plus agaçant et de plus généreux à la fois. Ces somptueux produits d'un pays considéré comme pauvre déconcertent les Parisiens qui n'aiment pas l'accent rocailleux avec lequel les gens du Sud-Ouest exaltent leurs propres mérites. « Promesse de Gascon » signifie « promesse qui ne sera point tenue », et « offre de Gascon » veut dire « offre retirée aussitôt qu'acceptée ». Néanmoins, les Français n'oublient pas que c'est au Béarn qu'ils doivent le plus populaire de leurs rois, cet Henri IV auquel, dès sa naissance, son père frotta les lèvres d'ail et de vin pour faire fleurir en lui toutes les qualités viriles de sa race.

Pays basque   Le Pays basque n'est pas une province : c'est un monde. Les indigènes y parlent une langue sans aucune ressemblance avec le français. Leur passion est la pelote basque, sorte de tennis solitaire où le joueur, armé d'un long panier attaché à sa main, joue à la balle contre un mur ; leur divertissement est la contrebande. Outre quelques belles voix de basse, ils ont donné à la France la coiffure qui, pour tant d'étrangers, caractérise le Français : le béret basque.

Corse   La Corse, surnommée « l'Ile de beauté », a demandé elle-même son rattachement à la France, à la fin du XVIIIème siècle. Depuis lors, elle alimente la métropole en douaniers, en policiers et en gangsters. De même que l'Auvergnat avec son avarice et le Marseillais avec sa vantardise, le Corse, avec sa légendaire paresse, fait les frais de mille histoires drôles. La facilité avec laquelle les habitants de cette île, au tempérament et au dialecte italiens, se sont intégrés à l'hexagone dont, géographiquement, ils ne font même pas partie, en dit long sur les capacités d'absorption et la vocation universelle de la France. Qu'y a-t-il de commun entre un Celte de Bretagne, un Germain d'Alsace et un Latin de Corse ? Rien. Tout. Ils sont Français.

PAYSAGE

Le poète espagnol Machado a dit : « Le bon Dieu était dans la fougue de la jeunesse quand il a peint l'Espagne ; dans son âge mûr, quand il a peint la France. »

C'est que le paysage français est tout de modération et de compensation. Rien qui s'y puisse comparer aux perspectives immenses de la Russie ou de l'Amérique. Rien non plus qui y soit étriqué, minutieux, comme quelquefois en Hollande ou en Grande-Bretagne. Il serait absurde, à l'époque du film et de la diapositive, de faire des descriptions de paysages, mais il convient d'en noter les traits distinctifs : douceur, équilibre, variété. Rares sont les panoramas d'où l'homme soit tout à fait absent, et, s'il y est présent, c'est le plus souvent par le clocher d'une église ou un calvaire au bord d'un chemin. Aux calvaires et aux clochers, il sied naturellement d'ajouter les poteaux télégraphiques, les pylônes à haute tension et, quelquefois, des barrages, des cheminées d'usine et des derricks. Cependant, en plissant les paupières, on parvient souvent à effacer du paysage les traces hideuses de l'industrie, et à rendre ainsi leur fraîcheur première aux prairies, aux labours, aux bosquets, mouchetés seulement de quelques toits : ardoises bleues dans le Nord, tuiles roses dans le Midi.

POPULATION

On ne sombrera pas ici dans le piège que des guides plus savants que nous n'ont pas toujours évité. Il n'est pas question de nous donner le ridicule d'affirmer : les Français sont comme ci, ils ne sont pas comme ça. La France, pour paraphraser Daninos, est « divisée » en près de cinquante millions de Français. Son territoire correspond à celui d'un état moyen d'Amérique du Nord. Nous n'en dirons pas plus. Tous les Français naissent différents les uns des autres, et ils passent leur vie à cultiver ces différences. Dans ces conditions, quelle généralisation ne serait pas naïve, ou partiale, ou partiale et naïve à la fois ?

Ceux qui ont généralisé avant nous se sont souvent accordés à doter la France — avec ses dimensions, ses fleuves, ses montagnes, ses habitants, sa civilisation tout entière — d'une répugnance significative pour ce qui est excessif. Mais cette répugnance même, les uns l'intitulent « sens de la mesure », les autres la traitent de « goût de la médiocrité ». L'un et l'autre sont vrais, sans doute. A quoi bon conclure ? On ne conclut jamais que d'après son propre tempérament.

L'ÉTAT FRANÇAIS   2
DE LA FONDATION
À NOS JOURS

IDÉE GÉNÉRALE

La France a mille ans d'âge. C'est aujourd'hui l'un des États les plus anciens du monde.

Néanmoins l'histoire de l'État français suit de bout en bout une trajectoire *crossing* tendue pouvant être définie par la formule « centralisation croissante en fonction directe du temps écoulé ». *dispose z, sell*

NAISSANCE D'UNE PATRIE

Gaulois et Gallo-Romains   Lorsqu'ils évoquent leurs lointains ancêtres, les Français nomment généralement les Gaulois, pour lesquels ils ont conservé un attachement à la fois humoristique et sentimental. L'adjectif *gaulois* a diverses significations : appliqué à une moustache, il veut dire « abondante et

15

A la diversité de la France ancienne, succède la centralisation de Louis XIV, symbolisée par le château de Versailles...

... la centralisation napoléonienne, illustrée par l'Arc de Triomphe de l'Étoile à Paris se fait encore plus rigide...

tournée vers le bas » ; concernant une plaisanterie, il équivaut à « paillard ».
Des générations d'étudiants et de soldats ont chanté gaillardement « Les
Gaulois sont dans la plai-ai-ne », et des centaines de milliers de petits nègres
de l'Afrique francophone ont récité par cœur des manuels d'histoire s'ouvrant
par la phrase rituelle « Nos ancêtres les Gaulois avaient les yeux bleus et les
cheveux blonds. »

Dans la réalité, les Gaulois ne composent qu'une part du substratum
ethnique de la France. Mystiques, imaginatifs, querelleurs, ils se sont laissé
pénétrer par les Latins, forts de la redoutable organisation de l'Empire romain,
et par plusieurs peuplades germaines, guerrières de goût et de profession :
Francs (d'où le nom de « France »), Goths, Wisigoths et autres Ostrogoths.
Les Normands, ou Vikings, eurent aussi leur part du gâteau, et les Arabes
eux-mêmes laissèrent quelques traces dans le Midi.

Au premier siècle avant l'ère chrétienne, Jules César envahit, subjugue et
féconde une région correspondant à peu près à l'hexagone actuel et appelée
Gaule. Intégrée au système de provinces de l'Empire romain, cette région n'a
aucune unité interne, aucun caractère distinctif ; rien ne semble la désigner
pour le destin hors pair qui sera le sien. C'est cependant la conquête romaine
qui l'y prépare, car les Latins lui apportent l'une après l'autre les trois conditions de sa grandeur future : la paix intérieure, le droit romain et le
christianisme.

Celui-ci, devenant religion officielle avec le baptême de Clovis (VIème
siècle), se greffe sans difficulté sur le sauvageon des superstitions païennes :

... aujourd'hui, l'État français est un véritable vortex grâce aux mass-media mis
en œuvre par la Maison de la Radio.

les prêtres remplacent les druides ramasseurs de gui, les sources miraculeuses consacrées aux nymphes prennent des noms de saintes et conservent leurs vertus magiques, l'âme celte accepte avec enthousiasme le surnaturel chrétien.

Les bienfaits contradictoires de la Rome impériale se répandent indifféremment sur l'ensemble du territoire. Rien ne distingue Lutèce, bourgade appartenant à la tribu des Parisii, des autres bourgades gauloises. Cependant, lorsque les invasions mongoles conduites par le terrible Attila déferlent sur l'Occident (VIème siècle), la résistance semble se cristalliser autour de Lutèce sous l'inspiration de sainte Geneviève : c'est que Lutèce était en train de devenir Paris.

En revanche, lorsqu'au début du Moyen Age (VIIIème siècle), le grand rêve romain d'une Europe unie semblera se réaliser sous l'égide de l'empereur Charlemagne, le cœur de ce « Saint-Empire romain-germanique » se trouvera bien plus à l'est, dans la petite ville que les Allemands appellent Aachen et les Français Aix-la-Chapelle.

Charlemagne mort, toute unité européenne disparaît à nouveau, et un système complexe, original, naïf, obscur, lyrique, efficace, alliant la plus cynique brutalité au spiritualisme le plus pur, apparaît comme par sécrétion naturelle, pour la préservation d'un semblant d'ordre dans l'hexagone.

La féodalité   La féodalité repose sur une conception spiritualiste des relations humaines. Premier axiome : il n'est pas de puissance qui ne vienne de Dieu. Or, l'expérience montre que chaque homme a besoin de plus petits et de plus grands que lui : de plus petits pour le servir, de plus grands pour le protéger. Ainsi l'agriculteur se tourne tout naturellement vers le guerrier et le guerrier vers l'agriculteur. Quand le guerrier faiblit, il fait appel à un autre guerrier, dont la puissance repose sur une base terrienne plus étendue, sur le soutien d'un plus grand nombre d'agriculteurs. C'est la loi du plus fort, sans doute, mais nullement la loi de la jungle, car, plus on est fort, plus on a de responsabilités, puisque la force est distribuée par Dieu. Les obligations réciproques qui en découlent règlent les rapports du vassal (le plus petit) et du suzerain (le plus grand). *Grosso modo*, le vassal doit obéissance au suzerain qui lui doit justice et protection.

Seuls les commerçants — ou bourgeois — échappent à ce système, où la rigueur et l'honneur sont en fonction l'un de l'autre. De là, une certaine dépréciation morale attachée à la profession.

Le roi   L'ensemble forme une pyramide dont le sommet est occupé par le suzerain suprême, source de toutes les grâces et de tous les pouvoirs, Notre Seigneur Jésus-Christ. Son premier vassal se trouve être un seigneur de puissance moyenne, régnant sur un fief de petite étendue correspondant à l'Ile-de-France actuelle (capitale, Paris), mais qui s'est donné le titre de roi et a décidé de se faire sacrer, c'est-à-dire de souligner, de revendiquer hautement par le moyen d'une cérémonie religieuse, le caractère sacral de la puissance dont il dispose (Hugues Capet, Xème siècle).

Sa fonction devient ainsi une mission, presque un sacerdoce, qui lui permettra de demander des sacrifices plus grands à ses propres vassaux, de semer le doute parmi les vassaux des voisins auxquels il fera la guerre, et, en fin de compte, de réaliser autour de sa lignée l'unité de l'hexagone tout entier.

A l'origine, le personnage qui s'intitule « le roi de France » ne dispose, en dehors de ses propres terres, que d'une autorité purement spirituelle. En Bourgogne, en Artois, en Normandie, il n'est pas le maître, il ne peut lever ni troupes ni impôts. Et cependant, partout où l'on reconnaît sa suzeraineté, il est le protecteur et le justicier, c'est-à-dire qu'il possède un levier moral lui permettant de faire tomber les plus grands lorsqu'ils oppriment les plus petits — ou qu'ils en sont accusés. L'histoire de l'Ancien Régime[1] en France est celle de quarante rois qui, par la force, par la ruse, par le bien, par le mal, par la justice et par l'injustice, ont réussi à asseoir la puissance spirituelle dont ils disposaient déjà sur la puissance temporelle et territoriale correspondante. Pour ce faire, ils ont sciemment démoli le système féodal en soutenant le plus faible contre le plus fort, en égalisant par le milieu, en favorisant les bourgeois, en transformant vassaux et suzerains en sujets de la même espèce.

Surtout au début de la royauté, le roi de France était un personnage accessible à tous et particulièrement aux humbles. Il mangeait en public ; il se couchait, se levait en public. Ses enfants naissaient en public, quelque incommodité que cela présentât pour la reine. Il appartenait à son peuple, non pas à lui-même. Ayant été oint des saintes huiles lors de son couronnement, il disposait, croyait-on, de pouvoirs surnaturels : il guérissait les écrouelles[2] par simple attouchement. La continuité de la monarchie était si essentielle à l'unité de l'hexagone et à sa paix intérieure que, lorsqu'un roi mourait et que son héritier prenait sa place, on annonçait le double événement en ces termes : « Le roi est mort ; vive le roi ! »

L'une des figures les plus significatives de l'histoire de la royauté française est celle de Jeanne d'Arc. Sa légende comme son mystère sont encore vivants après cinq cents ans, comme le prouve l'abondante exploitation politique à laquelle le personnage donne encore lieu. L'extrême-droite[3] en fait le symbole de la France catholique et royale ; la gauche s'attendrit encore sur cette « fille du peuple brûlée par ses prêtres, trahie par son roi ».

Jeanne d'Arc   Au XVème siècle, cinq siècles après sa création, le trône de France est revendiqué simultanément par Charles de Valois, Français, et par Henri de Lancastre, Anglais. Les lois de succession sont peu claires, et il y a des honnêtes gens dans les deux partis. Henri semble devoir l'emporter. Alors une jeune fille originaire de la Lorraine, province qui ne fait même pas partie intégrante de la France, se met à avoir des visions : saint Michel, sainte Catherine, sainte Marguerite, lui apparaissent et lui commandent d'aller sauver le royaume de France. Jeanne d'Arc appartient à la menue bourgeoisie ;

[1] terme désignant les structures politiques et sociales de la France avant la Révolution de 1789
[2] maladie lymphatique, se manifestant d'ordinaire sur les glandes du cou
[3] tendance politique à sympathies nationalistes et traditionalistes

La sainte de la patrie, Jeanne d'Arc, brûle à Rouen, sur un bûcher inextinguible, dû au ciseau du sculpteur contemporain Maxime Real del Sarte.

rien ne la prédispose à porter les armes. Lorsqu'elle se confie à ses proches, ils la traitent de folle. Néanmoins, elle réussit à traverser la France infestée d'étrangers et de brigands, elle reconnaît Charles de Valois sous l'habit d'un page, elle lui confie, au cours d'une audience privée, un secret que nul historien n'a encore percé, elle le persuade de la prendre comme général, elle bat les Anglais à plate couture, et elle réussit à faire sacrer Charles roi de France. Dès lors la partie est gagnée. Les ennemis de Jeanne auront beau la capturer et la faire brûler comme sorcière, Charles VII est le roi légitime, le roi de droit divin : la France unanime se rallie à lui. Naturellement l'histoire est incroyable ; il se trouve seulement qu'elle est vraie.

Lorsque, grâce aux soins de Charles victorieux, Jeanne est réhabilitée par l'Église, la notion de patrie française est née dans les cœurs, en tapinois. Et cette « douce France », pour laquelle Dieu et ses saints ont un faible qu'ils ne cherchent même pas à dissimuler, ressemble trait pour trait à « la bonne Lorraine » qui fut, jusque sur le bûcher, fidèle à son souverain.

Quelques paroles historiques de Jeanne d'Arc donneront une idée de la foi dont était animée cette « grande fille toute simple ».

Pour encourager Charles : « Je vous dis que Dieu a compassion de vous et de votre peuple. Saint Louis et saint Charlemagne sont à genoux devant lui et prient pour vous. »

Dans une lettre aux Anglais : « Je viens, de la part du Roi du ciel, vous mettre hors du royaume de France. »

Défiant ses juges : « Quand il y aurait en France cent mille godons[4] de plus qu'il n'y en a, il n'en restera pas un. Excepté ceux qui mourront. »

---

[4] Anglais, par corruption des mots *God damn!* que les soldats anglais répétaient à tout propos

A propos de l'étendard sur lequel elle avait inscrit IESUS-MARIA entre les fleurs de lis, qu'elle brandissait dans les combats et qu'elle apporta en triomphe au sacre : « Il a été à la peine ; il est juste qu'il soit à l'honneur. »

Qu'on ajoute à cela l'intrépidité du soldat — Jeanne conduisait elle-même ses troupes à l'assaut — et toute la compassion d'une sœur de charité — des Anglais blessés moururent dans ses bras — et l'on aura une représentation véridique de l'image que les Français se faisaient alors de la personne France.[5]

Un dernier détail, qui n'est certes pas le moindre. Malgré tout son respect de l'Église catholique, Jeanne revendiqua toujours une certaine liberté de conscience et de jugement, ce qui lui attira les foudres de la hiérarchie. En fait, cette indépendance d'esprit à l'égard de la Papauté est conforme au génie de la France qui, « fille aînée de l'Église », ne s'est jamais soumise à Rome qu'à regret.

NAISSANCE D'UNE NATION

C'est une question de biologie et de philosophie à la fois de savoir si le besoin crée l'organe ou si l'organe crée le besoin. En France, il semble bien que le besoin d'un ordre stable à l'échelle nationale ait créé l'organe le mieux apte à traiter dans ce sens une situation en évolution constante : à savoir la royauté.

En effet, la France a eu sa bonne part de souverains stupides, cruels ou simplement fous. Et pourtant les moins doués d'entre eux ont tout de même poursuivi l'œuvre de longue haleine entreprise par leurs lointains ancêtres et que devaient achever les ennemis et vainqueurs de leurs lointains descendants.

Louis XI Dans le deuxième moitié du XVème siècle, le roi de France est au contraire l'un des personnages les plus astucieux et les plus pittoresques qui soient. Louis XI s'habille humblement, fréquente son barbier et son bourreau, va dîner en ville comme un bourgeois chez des bourgeois qu'il appelle « compères ». Quand il prie la Vierge, il l'appelle « ma bonne dame ». Quand il capture un de ses ennemis, il l'enferme — pour une période qui peut aller jusqu'à quatorze ans — dans une cage de fer où l'on ne peut ni s'asseoir, ni se coucher, ni se tenir debout. A qui refuse de payer ses impôts, il fait couper les oreilles. Il croit à l'astrologie, il ment comme un arracheur de dents, il ne prend jamais conseil de personne « que de son cheval ». Les chroniqueurs du temps le comparent à une araignée. C'en est une, et de taille : il meurt en laissant le France enrichie de sept provinces au nord, au sud et à l'est. Sans doute restera-t-il à ses successeurs à atteindre les frontières naturelles de la France, mais, la Bourgogne digérée, ils n'auront plus de rivaux à craindre à l'intérieur de l'hexagone. Il leur faudra affronter ceux de l'extérieur. Et ils y courent !

Guerres étrangères Pendant des siècles, la France fait éprouver *la furia francese* à tous ses voisins : Anglais, Italiens, Espagnols, Hollandais. Elle ferait la guerre à l'Allemagne, si l'Allemagne existait. Succès et revers se succèdent.

---

[5] Michelet a dit : « La France est une personne. »

Trois lis d'or dans un champ d'azur, c'étaient les armoiries de la France royale.

Mais cette histoire-là fait plutôt partie de la géographie. Bien avant la fin de l'Ancien Régime, la France aura établi ses frontières à peu près où elles sont maintenant. En fait, en essayant quelquefois de conquérir d'autres peuples, c'est elle-même qu'elle conquiert, qu'elle forge et qu'elle trempe tour à tour. Plus l'ennemi extérieur se fait menaçant, plus l'unité nationale devient indispensable, et chacun de se tourner vers le pouvoir central qui dispense la discipline et la protection.

Les troubles intérieurs aboutissent au même résultat. Ces troubles sont, à travers l'histoire de la royauté, de trois espèces.

Factions féodales   D'une part, les rois de France doivent faire face à leurs anciens rivaux, les seigneurs féodaux, qui s'unissent en factions armées. De chacun de ces conflits, le souverain — Louis XI, Henri IV ou Louis XIV — sort vainqueur, et chaque fois grandi de la paix bienfaisante qu'il rend à la nation.

Jacqueries   D'autre part, des troubles populaires appelés jacqueries éclatent de temps en temps et vont même jusqu'à ébranler la royauté (XIVème siècle). Mais les souverains, tant qu'ils ne se montrent pas trop délicats sur les moyens de répression, triomphent toujours en fin de compte et y gagnent la reconnaissance des éléments les plus stables de la population.

Conflits religieux   Enfin des problèmes religieux secouent profondément la nation française à plusieurs reprises.

Au XIIème siècle, au moment de l'apogée chrétienne du Moyen Age, une secte curieuse apparut dans le Midi de la France. Ses adeptes recherchaient la perfection spirituelle, refusaient d'avoir des enfants et se cantonnaient dans une vie contemplative que la Papauté déclara hérétique. Des expéditions punitives furent obligeamment envoyées par le roi de France, et les Cathares, ou Albigeois, massacrés sans pitié. On ne sait si la chrétienté y gagna beaucoup, mais la royauté s'enrichit de trois régions prospères qui, jusque là, méconnaissaient son autorité.

Au XIVème siècle, le roi constate que l'ordre des Templiers, strictement religieux à l'origine, est devenu une sorte de banque internationale, trop puissante et trop riche à son gré. Les Templiers sont accusés de tous les crimes. Sous la torture, ils en avouent quelques-uns. Ils sont condamnés — entre autres aménités — à la confiscation de leurs biens, dont bénéficie naturellement le trésor royal.

Au XVIème enfin éclate la Réforme. La majorité des Français demeurent catholiques, mais bon nombre adhèrent à la religion réformée. L'unité de la France, raison d'être de la royauté, est menacée.

Inutile de revenir ici sur les hasards des guerres civiles qui, sous le nom de guerres de religion, déchirèrent le pays pendant la seconde moitié du siècle. Tandis que protestants et catholiques s'étripaient de bon cœur, les souverains successifs, catholiques évidemment, hésitaient entre la tolérance et l'extermination. La situation se corsa lorsque le dernier prince de la dynastie des Valois mourut sans laisser d'héritier direct, et que le couronne échut à Henri de Navarre, protestant lui-même. Qu'allait-il se passer ?

Henri IV   La conduite d'Henri, en cette occasion, fournit une clef de ce phénomène de la nature que fut la royauté française. Le prince protestant commença par battre sur tous les champs de bataille ceux que des intérêts politiques ou personnels dressaient contre lui. Puis, avant de monter sur le trône de France, il « fit le grand saut », c'est-à-dire qu'il se convertit au catholicisme. A quelques incidents près, le cauchemar des guerres de religion était terminé, grâce à l'Édit de Nantes, qui garantissait la liberté de conscience aux protestants.

Henri IV est demeuré l'une des figures les plus séduisantes de cette galerie de portraits qu'est l'histoire de France. Le dernier souverain à conduire lui-même ses soldats au combat, ce fut un fameux gaillard et un fameux paillard, courant sans cesse le jupon quand il ne bataillait pas. Buvant ferme, jurant ferme, cognant ferme, il sentait l'ail à plein nez car il en consommait d'impressionnantes quantités. Il voulait que le plus pauvre paysan de son royaume pût « mettre la poule au pot le dimanche ». A ses ennemis, il pardonnait une fois — mais pas deux. Excellent père de famille, écrivain vigoureaux et enjoué, il est, comme Jeanne d'Arc, un de ces personnages-miroirs où les Français aiment à se reconnaître.

Richelieu   Le fils d'Henri IV, Louis XIII, fut un prince médiocre, mais la France ne s'en trouva pas plus mal, car il eut la sagesse de laisser les rênes du gouvernement au plus brillant des premiers ministres, le cardinal de Richelieu.

Depuis six siècles que les rois régnaient sur la France, ils avaient systématiquement affaibli la féodalité en favorisant les villes libres, les artisans et le petit peuple. En particulier, le droit de rendre la justice avait été enlevé à la noblesse et donné d'une part aux baillis et sénéchaux, d'autre part aux parlements. Richelieu poussa à fond la même politique et chercha à faire table rase autour de la royauté, qui y perdit en bonhomie ce qu'elle y gagna en puissance.

Alors que les provinces étaient encore aux mains de gouverneurs appartenant à la haute noblesse et se transmettant les charges à l'intérieur des familles, Richelieu créa les intendants, roturiers pour la plupart, et que le roi nommait

Rien n'est si dangereux que la faiblesse, de quelque nature qu'elle soit. Pour commander aux autres, il faut s'élever au-dessus d'eux ; et, après avoir entendu ce qui vient de tous les endroits, on se doit déterminer par le jugement, qu'on doit faire sans préoccupation, et pensant toujours à ne rien ordonner ni exécuter qui soit indigne de soi, du caractère qu'on porte, ni de la grandeur de l'État... Le métier de roi est grand, noble, flatteur, quand on se sent digne de bien s'acquitter de toutes les choses auxquelles il engage ; mais il n'est pas exempt de peines, de fatigues, d'inquiétude... Quand on a l'État en vue, on travaille pour soi ; le bien de l'un fait la gloire de l'autre : quand le premier est heureux, élevé et puissant, celui qui en est cause en est glorieux, et par conséquent doit plus goûter que ses sujets, par rapport à lui et à eux, tout ce qu'il y a de plus agréable dans la vie. Quand on s'est mépris, il faut réparer sa faute le plus tôt qu'il est possible, et que nulle considération n'en empêche, pas même la bonté.

LOUIS XIV

et révoquait à volonté. Quant aux fonctions de grand amiral et de connétable, jugées trop importantes, le cardinal les abolit simplement.

Malgré les progrès de l'artillerie, les châteaux-forts laissaient encore une certaine indépendance aux hobereaux[6] les mieux fortifiés : Richelieu rasa leurs fortifications.

Les gentilshommes tiraient une part de leurs qualités propres de l'usage du duel qui les pénétrait du sens de leurs responsabilités et les exerçait aux armes : Richelieu interdit le duel et punit de mort les contrevenants.

La centralisation du pouvoir devint de plus en plus exigeante, et la capitale, Paris, s'orna de quartiers tout neufs qui faisaient honneur à l'État. Cherchant à mettre la main sur les intelligences autant que sur les volontés, Richelieu créa l'Académie française, corps de quarante écrivains chargés de régenter la langue et la littérature.

Le grand politique qui, combattant les protestants à l'intérieur n'hésitait pas à s'allier à eux à l'extérieur, se trouva aussi être un grand guerrier. Ayant conquis plusieurs nouvelles provinces, il mourut au faîte de la gloire et un contemporain dit de lui : « Il s'est fait obéir de son roi même, faisant de son maître son esclave, et de cet illustre esclave un des plus grands rois du monde. »

Le terrain était préparé pour l'arrivée de Louis XIV, dont la minorité donna lieu à quelques troubles vite calmés grâce à un autre cardinal, moins brillant mais non moins efficace que le premier : Mazarin.

---

[6] gentilshommes campagnards

Louis XIV   Louis XIV a régné de 1643 à 1715. Son siècle porte son nom. Ce roi passe pour avoir été le type même du monarque absolu, ce qui ne signifie rien sinon qu'il n'avait de comptes à rendre à personne. Gouvernant dans le cadre d'une société traditionaliste dont il n'aurait pu transgresser les usages, Louis XIV avait moins de pouvoirs réels que, par exemple, le Président des États-Unis n'en a aujourd'hui. Un détail le montre clairement : il y avait des quartiers entiers de Paris où la police du roi n'avait pas accès et où les criminels pouvaient trouver asile.

Néanmoins, Louis XIV porta la royauté française à son apogée et put déclarer, avec autant d'assurance que de concision, « L'État, c'est moi. »

Il ne se trompait pas : il fut l'État. Non parce qu'il était irremplaçable, mais parce qu'il sut tirer le meilleur parti de cette fonction de roi qu'il occupait.

Sans doute commit-il de graves erreurs. La plus lamentable eut lieu vers la fin de sa vie, sous l'influence des bigots qui l'entouraient : ce fut la révocation des libertés que, sous le nom d'Édit de Nantes, son aïeul Henri IV avait consenties aux protestants. Résultat : 250 000 hommes, parmi lesquels les meilleurs artisans du royaume, quittèrent la France et allèrent féconder les industries étrangères.

Sans doute certaines de ses guerres contre la Maison d'Autriche ne furent-elles ni nécessaires ni heureuses et épuisèrent-elles le pays. Sans doute l'état d'impuissance où il réduit à dessein les nobles en en faisant des courtisans priva-t-il la nation d'énergies qui ne demandaient qu'à être employées. Mais c'est mal juger les gens en général et les souverains en particulier que de les juger d'après leurs fautes. Leurs réussites les caractérisent mieux.

I. Les hommes naissent et demeurent libres et égaux en droits. Les distinctions sociales ne peuvent être fondées que sur l'utilité commune.

II. Le but de toute association politique est la conservation des droits naturels et imprescriptibles de l'homme. Ces droits sont la liberté, la propriété, la sûreté, et la résistance à l'oppression.

III. Le principe de toute souveraineté réside essentiellement dans la Nation. Nul corps, nul individu ne peut exercer d'autorité qui n'en émane expressément.

IV. La liberté consiste à pouvoir faire tout ce qui ne nuit pas à autrui ; ainsi l'exercice des droits naturels de chaque homme n'a de bornes, que celles qui assurent aux autres membres de la Société la jouissance de ces mêmes droits. Ces bornes ne peuvent être déterminées que par la Loi...

DÉCLARATION DES DROITS DE L'HOMME ET DU CITOYEN

Louis XIV, entouré de son conseil que se réunissait dans ce salon, ne fut jamais aussi absolu que Napoléon dominant la France du haut de son trône isolé.

Louis XIV eut le plus grand talent que puisse avoir un roi : il se fit bien servir.

Bien servir sur les champs de bataille, où l'impétueux Condé et le prudent Turenne font triompher les armes françaises, où Vauban invente un système de fortifications qui fait école dans le monde entier.

Bien servir sur mer, car c'est sous l'égide du roi que sont créées de toutes pièces une marine marchande qui permet aux négociants français de commercer avec le monde entier, des Indes orientales aux Indes occidentales, et une marine de guerre qui va défier et battre la Hollande et la Grande-Bretagne, seules grandes puissances navales jusqu'à ce jour.

Bien servir de l'autre côté de l'océan : les colonies françaises, malgré l'indifférence du pouvoir central, s'étendent ; la Louisiane reçoit son nom.

Bien servir en ses conseils par des ministres tels que Colbert qui réorganisent les finances, l'agriculture, l'industrie et le commerce auxquels ils donnent une impulsion nouvelle et que, grâce à une économie protectionniste, ils placent pour ainsi dire dans la main du roi.

Bien servir enfin dans les domaines intellectuels : les écrivains, les artistes, tiennent à honneur de servir le roi. Guidé par un goût d'une sûreté remarquable, il sait s'entourer des mieux doués, les écoute, les protège, les pensionne. Aujourd'hui, l'on n'entend que gémissements sur le mal que les intellectuels ont à se faire connaître : sous Louis XIV, Racine était historiographe du roi ; Bossuet, précepteur de son fils ; Molière, chef de ses comédiens.

Louis XIV fut roi jusqu'au bout des ongles. Dans ses écrits, on trouve une noblesse de pensée et de style inégalable. Son courage physique, la courtoisie de ses manières (il saluait, dit-on, jusqu'aux femmes de chambre) le rayonnement de sa personnalité, étonnaient et charmaient Français et étrangers. Hélas ! Ce monarque si grand était de petite taille : aussi portait-il de très hauts talons et une perruque monumentale qui le grandissait.

Sous l'Ancien Régime de XVIIIème siècle n'ajoute pas grand-chose à l'œuvre de centralisation des rois de France ; un renversement spectaculaire des alliances sous Louis XV, quelques mesures financières sous Louis XVI, rien de plus. Ce fut à la Révolution française qu'il appartint de poursuivre l'œuvre des dynasties royales : les Capétiens, les Valois, les Bourbons.

La Révolution   Les Anglais le disent : la première qualité d'un système politique, c'est d'être viable. Aussi les régimes ont-ils le sort qu'ils méritent.

En fait — les historiens modernes commencent à tomber d'accord là-dessus — la Révolution française n'a nullement été faite contre la royauté, mais contre un système médiéval consistant en une mosaïque de provinces, de classes sociales, de corporations professionnelles, de relations fondées sur la tradition et non pas sur les réalités, système que la royauté elle-même avait sapé pendant mille ans mais que, après l'avoir rendu caduc, elle était impuissante à jeter à bas.

En 1789, le pays était toujours divisé en provinces, qui n'avaient plus de raison d'être organique mais pâtissaient de tous les inconvénients d'une indépendance dont elles avaient perdu les avantages.

Marianne, cette beauté rustique, symbolise la France révolutionnaire et républicaine.

La population était répartie en trois ordres : clergé, noblesse, tiers-état. Or, le clergé avait perdu une partie de son influence ; la noblesse, dont les privilèges se fondaient sur « l'impôt du sang » qu'elle était censée payer, ne faisait pas plus la guerre que les autres classes de la société. L'existence des classes bourgeoise et intellectuelle n'avait même pas été reconnue officiellement. En d'autres termes, la répartition réglementaire ne correspondait plus aux réalités.

L'unité nationale avait été réalisée, et cependant les législations, les usages, les poids et les mesures variaient de région à région.

La France était devenue un pays en pleine expansion économique, mais ses finances étaient gérées comme à l'époque où le trésor appartenait en propre au souverain.

La révolution industrielle avait éclaté depuis cinquante ans, mais toutes les structures de la France étaient demeurées agricoles.

Les ouvriers étaient toujours groupés en corporations rigides créées pour leur protection au Moyen Age, alors que mille nouveaux métiers s'étaient développés.

Bref, le fruit était mûr : monarchie ou pas, il allait tomber.

La Révolution elle-même eut lieu dans des circonstances tragi-comiques. La fameuse prise de la Bastille se déroula aux cris de « Vive le roi », et, la prison une fois ouverte, on n'y trouva que sept détenus, enfermés pour des raisons qui n'avaient rien de politique. Le défenseur de la Bastille, Launay, aurait pu repousser l'assaut sans difficulté, si seulement il avait fait tirer le canon, mais il ne voulut pas faire couler le sang des attaquants. Aussi, lorsqu'il se fut rendu, lui coupa-t-on la tête et la promena-t-on à travers Paris au bout d'une pique.

Le drapeau tricolore est bleu et rouge en l'honneur de Paris, blanc en l'honneur du roi : cela ne l'a pas empêché de devenir un symbole révolutionnaire. *La Marseillaise* fut composée par un officier royaliste et devint un chant jacobin. La guillotine, inventée sous la monarchie dans des intentions humanitaires, devint sous la Révolution la mangeuse d'hommes que l'on sait. Toute une province, la Vendée, qui demeurait farouchement royaliste, fut noyée dans le sang au nom du droit qu'ont les peuples à disposer d'eux-mêmes.

Tout cela est de la dernière incohérence car, en vérité, cela ne touche pas à l'essentiel.

L'essentiel, les diverses assemblées élues — États généraux, Constituante, Législative, Convention — y pourvurent rapidement, en reprenant l'œuvre de centralisation là où la royauté l'avait laissée.

Le vingt-un janvier
Sept-cent quatre-vingt-treize,
Capet, tyran dernier,
Qu'on nommait Louis XVI,
A reçu ses étrennes
Pour avoir conspiré ;
Ce fuyard de Varennes
Est donc guillotiné...
Les nobles orgueilleux,
Ses parents et ses frères,
Et, de la part des cieux,
Les prêtres réfractaires,
Lui disaient de mal faire,
Les ayant écoutés,
La loi le met en terre ;
Il l'a bien mérité...
Il pourrait être heureux
Étant roi sur terre.
Pour lui c'est malheureux
Qu'il fût sans caractère.
Faut avoir une tête
Pour être couronné.
Étant faible et trop bête,
Il fut guillotiné.
CHANSON RÉVOLUTIONNAIRE

La Déclaration des droits de l'homme fut publiée. En affirmant que les hommes naissent libres et égaux devant la loi, elle consacrait la rupture entre l'individu et les sociétés organiques autres que l'État.

Les provinces furent abolies, et remplacées par des départements sans raison d'être ethnique ni géographique, mais d'autant mieux maniables pour le pouvoir central.

Les classes sociales, ou plus exactement les corps sociaux, furent supprimés. Tous les citoyens devinrent égaux devant la loi.

Les prêtres durent prêter serment à l'État.

Le système métrique, avec le mètre, le litre, le kilogramme, l'hectare, devint obligatoire dans toute la France.

Un calendrier surprenant, dans lequel la proclamation de la République remplaçait la naissance de Jésus-Christ, les noms des mois avaient été inventés selon les principes de l'harmonie imitative et les semaines comprenaient dix jours numérotés, fut imposé à la population qui n'en voulut pas.

Les douanes intérieures, les péages, furent supprimés.

Les biens de l'Église et de la plupart des nobles furent déclarés biens nationaux et vendus à l'encan.

Les libertés du travail et du commerce furent établies.

En principe, furent établies également les libertés de pensée, de parole et de la presse, mais, sujettes à d'infinies restrictions, elles devinrent entre les mains de gouvernants avisés, des instruments de domination bien plus efficaces que les fameuses lettres de cachet du roi.

Dans la tourmente qui amena toutes ces réformes fut emportée non seulement la royauté, qui les avait préparées, mais aussi l'esprit du XVIIIème siècle, tout de claire raison et d'émotions suaves, qui les avait rendues possibles. Quel rapport, entre les philosophes pomponnés qui péroraient dans les salons sur les conditions idéales du bonheur humain et les sans-culottes qui massacraient à la guillotine ou au couteau ? Aucun, apparemment. Et cependant il est vrai de dire que les premiers amenèrent les seconds au pouvoir, mais les seconds n'y restèrent pas : ils s'entre-massacrèrent et laissèrent la place à une succession de régimes éphémères et grotesques (Convention, Directoire, Consulat) qui ne faisaient que préparer l'avènement de ce qu'on appelle aujourd'hui « l'homme fort » ou « l'homme de la situation », bref le bénéficiaire de ces cataclysmes : Napoléon Bonaparte.

NAISSANCE D'UN EMPIRE

On a longtemps cru, voulu croire ou feint de croire que le temps du despotisme s'achevait avec la Révolution et qu'avec elle s'ouvrait l'ère de la liberté. Cela est exact dans le sens très limité où la priorité des droits sur les devoirs fut reconnue aux citoyens. Mais, dans un sens également limité, le contraire est tout aussi vrai. Sous l'Ancien Régime, chaque individu était protégé contre le pouvoir central par une hiérarchie complexe de corps municipaux, profes-

Pour emblème, Napoléon choisit l'aigle...

sionnels, provinciaux et sociaux, par cent législations écrites ou coutumières, par une structure encore familiale de la société. Sous le nouveau régime, au contraire, il se trouve nu face à des autorités déshumanisées et qui n'ont plus ni tradition ni respect de l'opinion pour tempérer leur toute-puissance.

Napoléon A la fin du XVIIIème siècle, la confusion règne en France. Un jeune général se rend nécessaire au régime d'abord, puis à la nation, en pratiquant savamment la politique du prestige et le chantage de l'absence. De coup d'État en coup État, il devient dictateur (on disait « consul »), dictateur à vie, et se fait enfin attribuer le titre imprévu d'empereur, dont personne en France n'a entendu parler depuis Charlemagne. Empereur donc, et sacré de la main du Pape, s'il vous plaît, encore qu'il ait tenu à se poser de ses propres mains la couronne sur la tête, il plonge son pays dans une succession de conflits presque ininterrompus. En principe il gagne toutes ses batailles, mais toutes ses guerres, il les perd. Son empire a beau s'étendre de l'embouchure du Tibre à celle de la Vistule, il n'en laisse pas moins la France amoindrie et pantelante lorsqu'il est détrôné. Il revient pour régner trois mois, et la nation l'acclame. Il est renversé une fois de plus, et la nation le pleure. Après avoir rendu la France odieuse au monde entier et l'avoir fait battre par tous les peuples d'Europe, il meurt glorieux comme un grand serviteur de son pays.

C'est qu'en fait les massacres napoléoniens n'ont guère d'importance historique. L'œuvre de Napoléon est ailleurs, au cœur même de la nation. On peut l'aimer ou la détester, mais elle est cohérente, constructive, et elle s'oriente spontanément dans « le sens de l'histoire ».

L'œuvre de Napoléon est administrative, intérieure, pacifique. En premier lieu, c'est le Code civil.

Alors que l'Ancien Régime se contentait d'une justice fondée d'une part sur le droit romain, d'autre part sur la jurisprudence locale, Napoléon crée de toutes pièces un droit français qui, à l'heure actuelle, est encore la base de la famille et de la propriété, c'est-à-dire qu'il consacre et perpétue la victoire des milieux bourgeois par opposition aux classes aristocratique et populaire.

Sous l'Ancien Régime, le roi était la source théorique des trois pouvoirs, législatif, exécutif et juridique. Sous le nouveau, ils sont en théorie séparés. Mais en fait la justice, unifiée pour toute l'étendue du territoire, est désormais rendue conformément à la doctrine officielle, c'est-à-dire à celle du pouvoir central. Paris et le gouvernement qui y siège, quel qu'il soit, en recueillent les profits.

En vérité, on ne saurait surestimer l'importance du Code civil, qui fut un des instruments d'unification et d'égalisation les plus efficaces que le pouvoir central eût jamais inventés. Mais le système préfectoral, que l'Europe entière envia à la France, donna aussi, du point de vue du gouvernement, d'excellents résultats. Pour ces nouveaux départements que la Révolution avait découpés dans le sol de la France, Napoléon inventa les préfets, hauts fonctionnaires formant une police supérieure, à la dévotion du gouvernement. Une stricte hiérarchie imposée au corps préfectoral permit d'en faire une sorte de caste qui servit avec un impassible loyalisme les huit régimes différents qui se succédèrent en France au cours du XIXème siècle. Du reste, les préfets sont toujours en place.

A l'égard du clergé, la royauté avait observé une politique mal définie, extatique ou vaguement hostile tour à tour ; la Révolution l'avait persécuté ; Napoléon signa avec la Papauté un Concordat qui ne dura pas, mais dont l'esprit subsiste, dans la mesure où l'État français traite encore le Vatican en toute liberté, de puissance à puissance.

Comme il fallait récompenser les bons serviteurs de l'Empire, Napoléon créa la Légion d'honneur, qui demeure la plus haute décoration française. Et, comme il voulait gouverner les intelligences, il créa l'Université de France, qui concentre, au sein d'un organisme appartenant à l'État, tout ce qui ressort de l'enseignement public (primaire, secondaire ou supérieur). Lorsqu'on pense que Richelieu s'était contenté de l'Académie, on mesure tout le chemin

Louis-Philippe, plus modeste, préféra le coq gaulois et domestique.

parcouru — dans une direction qui n'a varié à aucun moment. Les finances ne devant pas plus s'égarer que les esprits, Napoléon institua la Banque de France, qui battit monnaie et émit des billets : elle le fait encore.

Pourtant, ce que Napoléon instaura de plus efficace et de plus durable, c'est sans doute sa police. Des pays dits libres, la France est encore aujourd'hui le plus policier : elle le doit, en partie du moins, à Napoléon et à ses ministres.

Sous l'Ancien Régime, la personne du roi était sacrée et les régicides punis des pires supplices. Mais aucune adhésion intellectuelle à la monarchie n'était demandée aux sujets, dont la plupart ne se mêlaient pas d'avoir des opinions politiques. Leur soumission de fait suffisait. La Révolution, au contraire, tout en proclamant la liberté de conscience, créait le délit d'opinion : sous la Terreur, un homme soupçonné de n'être pas républicain était tenu pour coupable *a priori*, puisque c'est le propre d'un bon citoyen de n'exciter les soupçons de personne. Intolérance typique de toute société puritaine, c'est-à-dire fondée, non pas sur une unité sociale organique, mais sur un idéal de vie.

De tout cela, l'Empire moissonna les fruits. De même que les régimes totalitaires actuels, dont il fut l'exemple, il était censé détenir le triple secret de la vérité, du bonheur et de la toute-puissance. Lorsqu'il croula, les régimes qui lui succédèrent renoncèrent à ces excès mais conservèrent une police politique.

La Restauration   On s'est étonné, voire scandalisé, que des hommes comme le grand diplomate Talleyrand ou le grand policier Fouché aient pu servir successivement la Première République, le Consulat, le Directoire, l'Empire et la Royauté restaurée. Mais c'est que la politique qu'ils poursuivaient demeurait la même : ces messieurs ne jouissaient peut-être pas d'une sensibilité raffinée, mais la suite dans les idées ne leur manquait pas.

Louis XVIII, en dix ans de règne, réussit à panser les innombrables plaies que la nation s'était faite en un quart de siècle. Vieux, malade, il ne figure pas parmi les séducteurs de l'histoire, mais il joua à la perfection le rôle ingrat qui était le sien. Ce prince méconnu fut en réalité l'un des plus grands que la France ait connus.

Son successeur, répugnant aux mesures violentes, se laissa chasser du royaume par un de ses cousins, dont l'ambition était de concilier les qualités de la monarchie et les vertus de la Révolution. L'ingénieux personnage se fit appeler « Louis-Philippe Ier, roi des Français », pour marquer qu'il tenait son pouvoir du peuple et non de la Providence comme ses prédécesseurs qui portaient le titre de « roi de France ». Il régna dix-huit ans, en s'appuyant sur les milieux industriels, commerçants et financiers, comme il était naturel en pleine révolution industrielle. Un de ses ministres lança au peuple un mot d'ordre caractéristique : « Enrichissez-vous ! » Devise peu exaltante en période romantique. Louis-Philippe tomba à son tour et dans les mêmes conditions que sa victime : il aurait pu écraser l'insurrection — abusivement dite Révolution de 1848 — en appliquant le plan de répression de son ministre Thiers, mais il préféra l'exil.

Le Second Empire   La Deuxième République fut proclamée et bientôt remplacée — grâce à un coup d'État — par le Second Empire, qui apporta à la France une ère de prospérité relative mais s'empêtra dans une politique extérieure incohérente et ne sut pas faire face à l'apparition d'une classe nouvelle, de plus en plus nombreuse : le prolétariat industriel.

La colonisation   En français, le mot *empire* est équivoque. On l'applique parfois à cette Europe unie que Charlemagne, Napoléon, Hitler, ont tour à tour rêvée, et qui s'est écroulée chaque fois en un monceau de ruines. On l'utilise aussi pour caractériser le régime de Napoléon Ier et de Napoléon III, espèce de totalitarisme militaire et bourgeois. Enfin, on se servit longtemps du même terme pour qualifier les colonies que quelques aventuriers avaient inaugurées sous l'ancien régime, et auxquelles Napoléon III et ses sucesseurs républicains consacrèrent efforts et crédits en abondance. A la fin du XIXème siècle, la France possédait les deux tiers de l'Afrique, un bon bout d'Asie, et d'innombrables îles un peu partout dans le monde. Grâce à une administration et des troupes spécialisées, Paris devenait le centre d'une immense toile d'araignée jetée sur la terre entière.

REPLI SUR LA NATION

La Commune   Comme le Premier Empire, le Second laissa la France amputée, exsangue. Dans un conflit incongru avec l'Allemagne dont elle avait naïvement favorisé l'unité, elle perdait non seulement son empereur mais encore deux provinces : l'Alsace et la Lorraine.

Ce fut la Troisième République, encore à l'état embryonnaire, qui dut faire face à la première révolution communiste au monde, celle de la Commune de Paris en 1871.

Or, de Restauration en Empire et d'Empire en République, le pouvoir de l'État s'était durci. Le ministre Thiers devenu président n'hésita pas à appliquer le plan qu'il avait proposé à Louis-Philippe vingt-trois ans plus tôt : le gouvernement et ses défenseurs quittèrent Paris où ils laissèrent la Commune donner libre cours à des utopies mêlées d'atrocités. Puis, ayant regroupé leurs forces, ils rentrèrent dans la capitale, fusillant au passage vingt mille révolutionnaires, ce qui, en décimant les partis d'extrême-gauche,[7] assura la paix sociale à la France pour vingt-cinq ans au moins. La bourgeoisie avait désormais les mains libres pour imposer sa loi à la nation.

Troisième République   On a dit de la Troisième République tout le mal qu'elle méritait. Il est vrai que les personnages qui gouvernèrent la France de 1871 à 1940 eurent plus souvent le sens de leurs intérêts personnels que celui de leurs responsabilités. Il est vrai que bon nombre d'entre eux furent mêlés à divers scandales. Il est vrai que les réformes sociales qui s'imposaient ne furent consenties que sous la pression croissante des syndicats, et toujours chichement, malgré les promesses électorales les plus démagogiques : « Allez tou-

[7] tendance politique à sympathies communistes, internationalistes ou socialistes révolutionnaires

Ce qu'il y a dans le peuple de plus peuple, je veux dire de plus instinctif, de plus inspiré, ce sont, à coup sûr, les femmes. Leur idée fut celle-ci : « Le pain manque, allons chercher le Roi ; on aura soin, s'il est avec nous, que le pain ne manque plus. Allons chercher le boulanger !... »

Sens naïf, et sens profond !... Le Roi doit vivre avec le peuple, voir ses souffrances, en souffrir, faire avec lui même ménage. Les cérémonies du mariage, et celles du couronnement, se rapportaient en plusieurs choses ; le Roi épousait le peuple. Si la royauté n'est pas tyrannie, il faut qu'il y ait mariage, qu'il y ait communauté, que les conjoints vivent selon la basse, mais forte parole du Moyen Age : « A un pain et à un pot. »

N'était-ce pas une chose étrange et dénaturée, propre à sécher le cœur des rois, que de les tenir dans cette solitude égoïste, avec un peuple artificiel de mendiants dorés pour leur faire oublier le peuple ? Comment s'étonner qu'ils lui soient devenus, ces rois, étrangers, durs et barbares ? Sans leur isolement de Versailles, comment auraient-ils atteint ce point d'insensibilité ? Le vue seule en est immorale : un monde fait exprès pour un homme !... Là seulement, on pouvait oublier la condition humaine, signer, comme Louis XIV, l'expulsion d'un million d'hommes, ou, comme Louis XV, spéculer sur la famine.

MICHELET

jours plus à gauche, conseillait un politicien de la Troisième à un de ses amis, *mais jamais au-delà !* » Il est vrai que les présidents de la République ne brillèrent à aucun moment par leur intelligence : « Je vote pour le plus bête », disait cyniquement Clémenceau en déposant son bulletin dans l'urne présidentielle. Il est vrai que la France fut déchirée en partis et en factions : croyants contre laïcs, Action française contre Front populaire, blouses blanches[8] contre bleus de chauffe.[9] Il est vrai enfin que, s'éclipsant en 1940, la Troisième République laissait la France non seulement vaincue et envahie par les Allemands, non seulement déshonorée par le manque de combativité de ses troupes, mais surtout inconsciente, ne comprenant pas du tout ce qui venait de lui arriver, et prête, semblait-il, malgré la résistance d'une partie de la population, à digérer avec complaisance la plus grande déroute de son histoire.

Cependant, si l'on y regarde de plus près, on constate qu'un régime qui put, sans commettre beaucoup d'abus de pouvoir, s'y maintenir pendant soixante-

[8] contremaîtres
[9] ouvriers

La République, elle aussi, voulut des armoiries.

neuf ans, qui imposa le service militaire et l'instruction obligatoires (brimades impensables quelques années plus tôt dans un pays considéré comme « libre »), qui soutint victorieusement une guerre comme celle de 1914–1918, qui sut s'adapter, tant bien que mal, à une situation sociale sans cesse en mouvement, n'avait pas que des défauts. En fait, son efficacité et son inefficacité provenaient l'une et l'autre de la même source : une centralisation toujours croissante des pouvoirs au profit d'un régime, d'une classe, d'une structure, dans lesquels les droits primaient toujours les responsabilités.

La République remplacée par une dictature : « l'État français »   Lorsque la France fut envahie et que les organismes républicains s'effondrèrent, un bouc émissaire fut trouvé : on chargea le maréchal Pétain de pactiser avec l'ennemi auquel le pays avait été livré pieds et poings liés et, en même temps, de reconstruire une France nouvelle à partir de décombres inutilisables. Comme on s'y attendait, il échoua. Cela permit, une fois la France libérée, de l'accuser de trahison, de le condamner à mort et même de se donner les gants de le grâcier (en commuant sa peine en détention à vie).

Quatrième République   Le régime dit de l'État français avait vécu. La Quatrième République, née de la Résistance à l'occupant et de la « France libre » du général de Gaulle, prit sa place, non sans qu'on eût exécuté sommairement quelque cent mille personnes accusées d'avoir collaboré avec l'ennemi. Ce fut une nouvelle version de la Troisième, revue et détériorée. A cette époque, une fabrique de peinture fondée depuis des générations adapta le slogan publicitaire « Les républiques passent, la peinture Soudée[10] reste. »

La constitution de la Quatrième République apportait à celle de la Troisième un certain nombre de modifications significatives. Le suffrage était rendu véritablement universel, car les femmes aussi recevaient le droit de

[10] marque de fabrique de la peinture

vote. La généralisation de la sécurité sociale consacrait le triomphe de classes nouvelles, issues du prolétariat et du syndicalisme, vernies de culture politique et ne déguisant pas leurs sympathies pour l'extrême-gauche. Mais, quelle que fût la valeur de cette constitution, son application donnait des résultats déplorables, un certain nombre de partis faisant la ronde autour des fauteuils ministériels qui étaient attribués de façon à satisfaire tout le monde, à la suite de marchandages infinis, et sans le moindre souci d'une politique viable et cohérente. De là de nouveaux scandales, une attitude contradictoire et stérile en face des principaux problèmes (la liberté de l'enseignement, l'Europe unie, la décolonisation) et une perte de prestige totale à l'étranger.

Pourquoi, demandera-t-on, le peuple ne réagissait-il pas ? Les partis multiples sont de tradition en France : que l'électeur A vote pour le parti X et l'électeur B pour le parti Y, ou que, mécontents du résultat, ils renversent leurs allégeances respectives, leurs votes s'annulent réciproquement, et les mêmes partis, tous minoritaires et tous compromis dans les mêmes scandales, se retrouvent à l'Assemblée, au Sénat et au gouvernement.

La décolonisation Sous la Quatrième République, l'empire colonial français, pour ménager les susceptibilités, était devenu l'Union française, puis la France d'outre-mer. En réalité, la France n'a jamais eu la vocation coloniale ou impériale ; toutes les aventures qu'elle a tentées dans ce sens ont toujours mal tourné pour elle ; les rois l'avaient pressenti, et il appartenait à la Cinquième République de ramener la France aux dimensions qui auraient toujours dû être les siennes : celles d'une nation, celles de l'hexagone. Dans le

---

Je fais don de ma personne à la France.
LE MARÉCHAL PÉTAIN (1940)

Il y a deux mots que je ne prononcerai jamais : République et démocratie.
LE GÉNÉRAL DE GAULLE (1940)

Dans l'ordre politique, nous avons choisi. Nous avons choisi la démocratie et la République.
LE GÉNÉRAL DE GAULLE (1944)

Ce qu'il faudrait à ce pays, c'est un roi. Un grand type qu'on sort comme cela de temps en temps dans les grands moments difficiles... C'est ce qu'il faudrait... Mais cela a été cassé, et cela ne se refait pas...
LE GÉNÉRAL DE GAULLE (1946)

Aujourd'hui, c'est par ce sceau que le peuple de France, représenté par le Chef de l'État, sanctionne ses volontés.

cas de l'Algérie, ce repli fut tragique, car il s'agissait de rapatrier un million de Français de souche européenne dont les familles étaient installées en Algérie depuis le siècle dernier, et de laisser à leur sort neuf millions d'Arabes et de Berbères[11] dont beaucoup étaient acquis à la présence française.

Néanmoins, au mépris des engagements contractés envers ces populations, la France se dégagea de la dernière de ses colonies qui avait pourtant été considérée comme faisant partie intégrante du territoire national. Ce faisant, le pouvoir central s'affranchissait d'obligations qui pesaient lourdement sur son budget et reprenait en main à la fois son armée, qui devenait turbulente, sa police, qui était pléthorique, et sa population, qui donnait des signes de lassitude. Porté au pouvoir par les partisans (minoritaires) de l'Algérie française, le général de Gaulle, en libérant l'Algérie, satisfaisait les partisans (majoritaires) de l'indépendance. Moralement douteux, ce n'en était pas moins un coup de maître.

Cinquième République   Une nouvelle constitution a été adoptée, constitution monarchique s'il en est, où tous les pouvoirs aboutissent indirectement au président en période normale, et directement dès que l'état d'urgence est appliqué.

Contrairement à la tradition républicaine française, qui voulait que le chef de l'État soit élu par « les grands électeurs » (députés, sénateurs, conseillers généraux), un amendement à la constitution a été voté, selon lequel le président est élu au suffrage universel.

Les structures préfectorales ont été maintenues, mais, pour que le pouvoir central les contrôle plus étroitement, les inspecteurs généraux de l'administration (igames) ont reçu des pouvoirs accrus : chacun d'entre eux dirige plu-

[11] population originelle d'Afrique du Nord

La République française, toujours hantée par la romaine, lui emprunte ses faisceaux, ses symboles et jusqu'à son costume.

sieurs départements constitués en « igamies » et correspondant à des régions économiques qui coïncident quelquefois avec les anciennes provinces.

La séparation des pouvoirs est toujours sacrosainte dans la lettre. Mais lorsqu'il s'est agi de juger des officiers qui avaient conspiré contre le général de Gaulle, chef de l'État, un tribunal spécial a été créé, dont les juges furent nommés par le gouvernement.

Le problème des écoles privées a été résolu : elles reçoivent maintenant des subventions de l'État et sont soumises à un contrôle officiel.

Les grèves, qui étaient constantes sous la Quatrième République, sont devenues plus rares sinon moins violentes, comme l'ont prouvé les évènements de mai 1968.

La police a reçu le droit d'appréhender des suspects et de les interroger pendant quinze jours consécutifs sans faire instruire leur procès.

Plusieurs affaires d'espionage ont révélé que les polices politiques et les services spéciaux se livraient à des activités peu conciliables avec le rêve démocratique (enlèvements, assassinats politiques).

Bref, les amis du régime ont beau jeu de déclarer qu'il unit enfin les avantages de la monarchie à ceux de la république, tandis que ses ennemis ont de bonnes raisons de lui trouver les inconvénients des deux systèmes, et ceux de l'Empire en plus.

Avantages et *inconvénients* sont des mots si naïfs qu'il convient de s'en méfier. De toute manière on juge l'arbre à ses fruits, et la Cinquième République n'en est encore qu'aux premiers boutons. Tout ce qu'on peut dire dès à présent, c'est que son esprit paraît conforme au destin de la France, et que, sur l'immense courbe de l'histoire, ce régime est venu tout naturellement occuper la place qui lui revient.

Ancien Régime

siècle	dynastie	principaux personnages
V	⎫	Clovis
VI	⎬ Mérovingiens	
VII	⎪	
VIII	⎭	Charlemagne
IX	⎫ Carolingiens	
X	⎬	Hugues Capet
XI	⎫	
XII	⎬ Capétiens	saint Louis IX
XIII	⎭	
XIV	⎫	
XV	⎬ Valois	Charles VII (Jeanne d'Arc), Louis XI
XVI	⎭	Henri IV
XVII	⎫	Louis XIII (Richelieu), Louis XIV (Mazarin, Colbert, Vauban, Condé, Turenne)
	⎬ Bourbons	
XVIII	⎭	Louis XV, Louis XVI

Nouveau Régime

date	régime	principaux personnages		
1789	monarchie « absolue », constitutionnelle			
1792	Première République		⎫	⎫
1795	Directoire		⎪	⎪
1799	Consulat	Napoléon Bonaparte	⎪	⎪
1804	Premier Empire	Napoléon Ier	⎬ Fouché	⎪
1814	Première Restauration	Louis XVIII	⎪	⎬ Talleyrand
1815	Cent-Jours	Napoléon Ier	⎪	⎪
1815	Deuxième Restauration	Louis XVIII	⎭	⎪
1824		Charles X		⎪
1830	« roi des Français »	Louis-Philippe		⎭
1848	Deuxième République			
1852	Second Empire	Napoléon III		
1871	Troisième République	Thiers, Clemenceau		
1940	État français	Pétain		
1944	Quatrième République			
1958	Cinquième République	de Gaulle, Pompidou		

ÉVOLUTION 3
DE LA PENSÉE
PHILOSOPHIQUE
ET RELIGIEUSE

IDÉE GÉNÉRALE

En 1949, le sujet de dissertation proposé aux candidats au baccalauréat de philosophie dans la région parisienne fit scandale. « L'amour est-il un moyen de connaissance ? » avaient demandé les jurés ; et les parents d'élèves — qui avaient oublié le sens philosophique des mots *amour* et *connaissance* — de provoquer un tollé général à propos d'une inconvenance qui n'était, bien entendu, qu'apparente.

Ce n'est pas le jeu de mots ni l'anecdote qui nous intéressent ici : c'est le sujet lui-même. Il est, si l'on ose dire, typiquement français.

En effet, si les philosophes allemands sont, avant tout, des métaphysiciens ; les russes, des moralistes ; les anglo-saxons, des psychologues, les penseurs français, eux, sont traditionnellement des logiciens. Ce qui les intéresse, c'est la connaissance. On chercherait vainement chez eux — du moins jusqu'à la fin du XVIIIème siècle — le moindre système, la moindre conception globale du monde, rien qui se puisse comparer à l'œuvre d'un Leibniz ou d'un Spinoza : ils ne se sont jamais préoccupés que de méthodologie.

A cela, rien d'étonnant. La France était un pays essentiellement chrétien. La vérité métaphysique apparaissait donc aux chercheurs comme révélée une fois pour toutes. Elle n'était pas de leur compétence ; elle les concernait comme hommes, non comme philosophes. Leur intelligence ne pouvait avoir d'autre objet que l'humain. C'est pourquoi la plupart des philosophes français sont des humanistes, quand ils ne sont pas de purs dialecticiens.

Lorsque, à la fin du XVIIIème siècle, on eut fait table rase de la religion, alors on put s'occuper à construire des systèmes, comme nous le verrons dans la seconde moitié de ce chapitre. Mais, jusqu'à une période qu'on peut approximativement faire coïncider avec la Révolution, les Français, sauf de rares exceptions, ne donnèrent libre carrière à la philosophie que dans les domaines qui n'étaient pas chasse gardée pour la foi.

Quant aux exceptions (et parmi elles on trouve quelques-uns des plus grands noms de la pensée européenne), leur premier souci fut toujours de situer la philosophie par rapport à la foi : pour, contre, grâce à ou malgré.

LE PRINCIPE D'AUTORITÉ

La débâcle de l'Empire romain avait emporté toutes les valeurs intellectuelles, à l'exception de celles qui s'étaient agglomérées à la valeur spirituelle suprême : le christianisme.

C'est à partir du christianisme que renaquirent philosophie, sciences et littérature. Elles n'apparurent tout d'abord que comme des moyens supplémentaires de louer Dieu, de le comprendre ou de l'expliquer. Les sciences exactes elles-mêmes consistaient en une étude attentive de la Création, donc en un acte de piété à l'égard du Créateur. Lorsque, soit par une lecture directe des quelques manuscrits antiques que préservaient les couvents, soit par une fréquentation de la civilisation arabe — remarquable véhicule de la civilisation grecque — les lettrés du haut Moyen Age eurent fait connaissance avec des modes de pensée qui n'étaient pas essentiellement chrétiens, ils s'efforcèrent à la fois de les « baptiser » et de leur appliquer les disciplines méthodologiques que la théologie leur avait, à eux-mêmes, inculquées.

Le cas de Platon et de sa pensée est représentatif. C'est dans un même mouvement d'amour et d'adhésion intellectuelle que l'Église essaya d'adopter le philosophe et de sauver l'homme, en lui accordant le bénéfice d'une pre-science miraculeuse du christianisme. Le haut Moyen Age vécut donc dans l'adoration d'un penseur qui, pour païen qu'il soit, est sans doute le plus lumineux de tous les temps. Mais Platon, trop peu dogmatique, fut bientôt supplanté par Aristote, dont les principes rigides cadraient mieux avec les habitudes de pensée des théologiens. Très rapidement — on veut dire en quelques siècles — Aristote devint un pape infaillible de l'intelligence.

L'Église avait raison *a priori* pour tout ce qui regardait la foi ; Aristote avait raison *a priori* pour tout ce qui concernait la philosophie.

Dans ce carcan, la raison humaine dut recourir aux abstractions les plus insaisissables pour avoir quelque chose à se mettre sous la dent. De là, la fameuse querelle des Universaux autour de laquelle s'organisa toute la pensée scolastique.

Universaux   On appelait alors Universaux les notions générales de l'esprit ; on en comptait cinq : le genre, l'espèce, la différence, le propre et l'accident. Il s'agissait de savoir si ces notions avaient une réalité transcendante — c'était la thèse des rationalistes ou réalistes — ou si elles n'étaient que des mots décrivant une expérience pratique — ainsi pensaient les empiristes ou nominalistes. La synthèse fut apportée par Abélard et le conceptualisme : les Universaux naissaient d'un contact de l'esprit humain avec l'expérience et leur appartenaient donc à tous les deux. Lorsque l'on pense que cette querelle occupa des centaines de penseurs pendant tout le Moyen Age, on mesure l'étroitesse du domaine réservé alors à l'invention humaine.

Saint Thomas d'Aquin   Le plus grand philosophe de l'époque fut, sans conteste, un Italien qui enseigna à Paris : saint Thomas d'Aquin (XIIIème siècle). C'était, comme par hasard, un théologien. Son propos fut d'organiser la connaissance humaine comme un tout. Il ne relevait aucune contradiction entre la raison et la foi pourvu que celle-là fut toujours subordonnée à celle-ci. En fait, sorte d'Aristote chrétien, il fonda la religion en philosophie et créa ainsi une doctrine officielle de l'Église catholique, extérieure au dogme mais complémentaire à lui, qui prit le nom de « thomisme », et où la mystique et la logique se tenaient réciproquement compagnie.

Dès lors, le scepticisme ne devait plus se faire attendre.

LA RÉACTION SCEPTIQUE

L'occasion en fut la Renaissance, qui, soudain, déversa dans les intelligences françaises toutes les valeurs païennes de l'Antiquité retrouvée. Coïncidant avec la lente déperdition de foi qui avait commencé dès le haut Moyen Age, ce fut comme une Révélation nouvelle, comme une anti-révélation. Aussitôt, devant tant de vérités également séduisantes, le doute — qui est le propre de l'intelligence — se mit au travail.

Réforme   La Réforme en est un exemple tragique. L'adhésion à la religion réformée fut, pour la minorité de Français qui s'y résolurent, une tentative pour sauver la foi par une compromission avec le doute. Ceux qui mettaient en question l'Église catholique, apostolique et romaine ne le faisaient en ce cas que pour préserver dans leurs propres cœurs une Église mystique qui leur paraissait plus essentielle. Il en va autrement des sceptiques de tempérament, tels Rabelais ou Montaigne, qui, au contraire, conservaient leur adhésion à l'Église catholique pour pouvoir, sans être suspects d'hérésie, *riddle*

passer au crible de l'intelligence toutes les notions humaines qui ne touchaient pas directement à la foi.

Montaigne L'exemple de Montaigne (XVIème siècle) est particulièrement représentatif. Voilà un homme qui, pendant que les guerres de religion déchiraient sa patrie, pendant qu'une monarchie vieille d'un demi-millénaire chancelait sur sa base, passait calmement son temps dans sa maison de campagne et *stagger* consacrait trois énormes volumes à faire, avec son propre portrait, celui de l'humanité tout entière. Sceptique dans sa vie, Montaigne ne le fut pas moins dans sa pensée. Non qu'il s'opposât sur aucun point à la religion admise ; sans doute croyait-il même croire en Dieu. Mais il n'en adopta pas moins pour devise le fameux « Que sais-je ? » de l'Antiquité. Ceux qui affirment « Je ne sais rien » lui paraissaient encore trop certains de leur ignorance : avec Montaigne, c'est l'agnosticisme intégral et souriant qui apparaît comme la seule sagesse accessible à l'esprit humain.

LA TABLE RASE

Montaigne était un aimable fantaisiste qui s'adonnait à un humanisme sans prétentions. Descartes (XVIIème siècle) posa les bases de toute la philosophie moderne et incarna à lui seul cet esprit français que les étrangers trouvent quelquefois exagérément « cartésien ».

Descartes Les portraits du temps le représentent foulant aux pieds un volume d'Aristote. Le symbole est patent : Descartes a, le premier, rejeté la tutelle du grand ancien et a revendiqué le droit d'aller plus loin dans l'étude de la logique et de la nature. Au principe d'autorité sous lequel avait vécu le Moyen Age, Descartes substitue le libre examen — en d'autres termes *l'esprit critique*.

Les enfants français jouent quelquefois à un jeu qui s'appelle « Jacques a dit ». Le meneur de jeu commande : « Levez la main droite ! » Personne ne bouge ; si un joueur obéit, il a perdu. Puis le meneur annonce : « Jacques a dit, levez la main gauche ! » Et tout le monde de lever la main gauche. Cette fois-ci, c'est celui qui ne le ferait pas qui devrait un gage. Avant Descartes, la philosophie française ressemblait à ce jeu, Aristote y tenant le rôle de Jacques. Après lui, elle put au contraire sembler exagérément destructrice, puisqu'elle refusait tout ce qui n'était pas strictement évident.

C'est en effet le principe de l'évidence (qui devait tenir en philosophie le rôle du postulat dans la géométrie euclidienne) que Descartes révéla au monde après avoir fait retraite dans des quartiers d'hiver qu'il appelait son « poêle ». Sur ce principe il édifiait sa *méthode*, et cette méthode, pensait-il, lui permettrait de percer les arcanes non seulement de la philosophie mais encore de la géométrie analytique qu'il inventa, de la physique et de la physiologie. En physiologie et en physique il ne fut pas aussi heureux qu'il s'y attendait ; mais sa méthode constitue aujourd'hui l'armature de toute recherche intellectuelle quelle qu'elle soit. Les articles nous en paraissent

Du haut de cette tour, Montaigne regardait avec amusement défiler le cortège des folies humaines.

simples, presque simplistes ; néanmoins, il avait fallu une révolution intellectuelle pour les dégager :

(1) N'accepter pour vrai que ce qui est évident.

(2) Morceler les difficultés pour les résoudre une par une.

(3) Aller du plus simple au plus compliqué.

(4) N'omettre aucune des données du probléme.

Le premier est sans doute le plus discutable et, partant, le plus intéressant. Évident ? Qu'est-ce à dire ? Ceci est évident pour vous ; cela, pour moi. Qui a raison ? Il ne s'agit pas d'évidences subjectives, mais objectives, répond en substance Descartes. « Le bon sens étant la chose la mieux partagée du monde », ce qui est vrai est évident pour tous, pour vous comme pour moi. Le type même de l'évidence universelle est le fameux axiome cartésien « Je pense, donc je suis. »

Il n'est pas indifférent de constater que cette méthode conduit Descartes à certaines conclusions d'ordre métaphysique, dont, entre autres, celle de l'existence de Dieu. Mais ces conclusions se situent sur un plan différent de celui de la religion, qui demeure pour lui affaire de révélation directe. Entre le Dieu qu'on adore à l'église et le Dieu dont la raison démontre qu'il ne pourrait pas ne pas exister, il n'y a plus guère de ressemblance. Encore un pas et, tout en tirant son chapeau au second, on trouvera le premier ridicule, démodé, plébéien.

Au lieu de ce grand nombre de préceptes dont la logique est composée, je crus que j'aurais assez des quatre suivants, pourvu que je prisse une ferme et constante résolution de ne manquer pas une seule fois à les observer.

Le premier était de ne recevoir jamais aucune chose pour vraie, que je ne la connusse évidemment être telle : c'est-à-dire, d'éviter soigneusement la précipitation et la prévention ; et de ne comprendre rien de plus en mes jugements, que ce qui se présenterait si clairement et si distinctement à mon esprit que je n'eusse aucune occasion de le mettre en doute.

Le second, de diviser chacune des difficultés que j'examinerais, en autant de parcelles qu'il se pourrait, et qu'il serait requis pour les mieux résoudre.

Le troisième, de conduire par ordre mes pensées, en commençant par les objets les plus simples et les plus aisés à connaître, pour monter peu à peu, comme par degrés, jusques à la connaissance des plus composés ; et supposant même de l'ordre entre ceux qui ne se précèdent point naturellement les uns les autres.

Et le dernier, de faire partout des dénombrements si entiers, et des revues si générales, que je fusse assuré de ne rien omettre.

DESCARTES

Est-ce modestie de l'intelligence ? Est-ce hypocrisie et goût de la sécurité ? L'enseignement de Descartes peut se résumer ainsi : la raison est le seul moyen de connaissance, mais elle ne s'applique pas à la religion, qui est du ressort de la foi.

LE PARI DE LA FOI

Pascal Infiniment plus moderne nous apparaît le personnage inquiétant de Pascal, mathématicien et philosophe comme son contemporain, mais aussi mystique et, en quelque sorte, « existentialiste » avant la lettre.

Descartes cherchait une méthode pour saisir la vérité ; Pascal en propose une aux athées pour découvrir Dieu. Cet infatigable raisonneur, parvenu à une rigueur dialectique exemplaire, la met tout entière au service de la foi. Sa pensée s'articule ainsi :

(1) L'homme est un mystère ; vivre, une angoisse insoutenable. Aucune des philosophies traditionnelles ne rend compte de la situation de l'homme dans l'univers, et l'athéisme moderne y échoue aussi, déplorablement.

(2) Au contraire, si le christianisme était vrai, le dogme du péché originel et celui de la rédemption justifieraient la condition humaine.

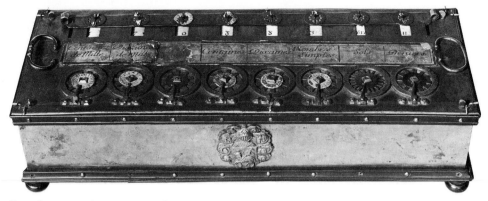

Pascal, ce mystique, inventa la première calculatrice; joli symbole de l'ambivalence de l'esprit français.

(3) Mais comment passer de l'état d'agnostique à celui de croyant? Il y faut la foi. Et si on ne l'a pas? Alors — et Pascal invente ici un procédé qui paraît emprunté à l'éthique existentielle plutôt qu'à l'enseignement chrétien — il n'y a qu'à parier. Parier sur Dieu, parier sur le Christ, puisque, après tout, on n'a rien à y perdre et tout à y gagner.

Le jansénisme   Tel quel, Pascal appartenait à une école de pensée dont les préceptes furent bien près de créer un schisme dans l'Église catholique du XVIIème siècle : le jansénisme. Comme si, dans l'attente des assauts matérialistes que tout faisait déjà prévoir, les plus croyants des croyants avaient voulu resserrer leurs rangs en durcissant leur doctrine, les disciples de l'évêque Janssen s'attachaient à interpréter les dogmes dans le sens de la prédestination et déniaient à l'homme la capacité de se sauver lui-même par son libre arbitre, s'il n'était déjà sauvé, de toute éternité, par le choix de Dieu. A ces rigoristes s'opposaient les Jésuites, qui, dans la subtilité de leur casuistique, réussissaient à excuser toutes les offenses et à rendre la religion accessible à chacun, pourvu qu'il y donnât un assentiment de principe. Cette attitude relâchée paraissait

---

Jésus dit :

« Je te parle et te conseille souvent, parce que ton conducteur ne te peut parler, car je ne veux pas que tu manques de conducteur.

Et peut-être je le fais à ses prières, et ainsi il te conduit sans que tu le voies. Tu ne me chercherais pas si tu ne me possédais.

Ne t'inquiète donc pas. »

PASCAL

Le pinceau austère de Philippe de Champaigne a dépeint, en Mère Angélique Arnaud, une des grandes jansénistes de son temps.

odieuse aux jansénistes, eux qui, dans un dernier effort pour reconquérir l'austère spiritualité du Moyen Age, représentaient le Christ crucifié avec les bras à peine écartés, pour symboliser la porte étroite de l'Écriture. « Il y a beaucoup d'appelés », citaient les Jésuites. « Mais si peu d'élus ! » insistaient les jansénistes. Les semi-persécutions dont ils furent l'objet de la part de la Papauté et du roi les renforcèrent dans leur croyance. Il fallut qu'ils mourussent un à un pour que leur influence disparût d'une église qui se voulait de plus en plus libérale, de plus en plus ouverte aux quatre vents.

LE MATÉRIALISME RÉVOLUTIONNAIRE

Le Moyen Age avait été une époque de foi ; le XVIème siècle, de doute. « Je crois », disait le Moyen Age. « Que sais-je ? » soupirait le XVIème siècle. Le XVIIème s'interrogea, « Comment faire pour savoir ? » « Il n'y a rien à savoir que ce que la raison peut enseigner », répond un siècle qui s'est surnommé lui-même celui des lumières.

Athéisme et déisme Raison, lumières, voilà les grands mots de Voltaire et de tous les Encyclopédistes. Ni croyants ni athées, la plupart d'entre eux sont déistes. Dieu a pour eux deux utilités : d'une part, horloger du monde, il en explique l'existence ; d'autre part, rémunérateur et vengeur, il incite les classes incultes de la société à respecter les règles de la morale. Nécessaire et inintéressant, Dieu occupe fort peu ces philosophes. A peine se soucient-ils davantage de la conscience et de l'inconscient humain. Ils consacrent toute la passion dont ils sont capables à deux objets d'études pratiquement inexplorés jusqu'alors : la nature et la société.

Sensualisme   Le réel, au sens le plus vaste du terme, y compris même l'action technologique que l'homme peut exercer sur lui, bref le monde extérieur tel qu'il nous est donné, voilà ce qui excite la curiosité des penseurs du XVIIIème siècle. A cela, rien d'étonnant. Ils croient que la perception physique est notre seule source de connaissance, et que le bien-être matériel et moral est le seul but qui nous soit proposé. De là, le sensualisme avoué du philosophe Condillac ; de là aussi, l'évolution des idées politiques qui demeure le principal apport du XVIIIème siècle à l'histoire de la philosophie française.

Idées politiques   Montesquieu fut le premier à essayer de codifier le *pouvoir* et la *souveraineté*, pour reprendre les termes du grand penseur moderne, Bertrand de Jouvenel. Il distinguait trois systèmes de gouvernement : le despotisme, fondé sur la crainte ; la monarchie parlementaire, fondée sur l'honneur ; la république, fondée sur la vertu. Comme il avait peu de confiance en la vertu, il préférait à la république une sorte de royauté constitutionelle. Aspect infiniment plus important de son œuvre, ce fut lui qui distingua le premier les trois pouvoirs — juridique, législatif, exécutif — et qui en réclama la séparation. En théorie, ce principe est le base de toutes les démocraties modernes.

Au demeurant, Montesquieu n'avait rien d'un révolutionnaire : il participait simplement à cette fermentation des esprits qui accompagnait l'apparition de l'industrie (dont on ne voyait encore que les avantages), qui se traduisait par la prolifération des laboratoires mondains où se formaient les physiciens et les chimistes du lendemain, et qui ne s'est jamais mieux exprimée que par la publication de l'*Encyclopédie*. Cette œuvre monumentale redigée sous la direction de d'Alembert et de Diderot, dont les dix-sept volumes mirent vingt ans à paraître, tendait à deux buts principaux : premièrement, mettre à la

Vieil athlète, à toi la couronne!... Te voici encore, vainqueur des vainqueurs ! Un siècle durant, par tous les combats, par toute arme et toute doctrine (opposée, contraire, n'importe), tu as poursuivi, sans te détourner jamais, un intérêt, une cause, l'Humanité sainte... Et ils t'ont appelé sceptique ! Et ils t'ont dit variable ! Ils ont cru te surprendre aux contradictions apparentes d'une parole mobile qui servait la même pensée !

Ta foi aura pour sa couronne l'œuvre même de la foi. Les autres ont dit la Justice, toi, tu la feras ; tes paroles sont des actes, des réalités... Tu as vaincu pour la liberté religieuse, et tout à l'heure pour la liberté civile, avocat des derniers serfs, pour la réforme de nos procédures barbares, de nos lois criminelles, qui elles-mêmes étaient des crimes.

Tout cela, c'est déjà la Révolution qui commence. Tu la fais et tu la vois... Regarde, pour ta récompense, regarde ; la voilà là-bas ! Maintenant tu peux mourir ; ta ferme foi t'a valu de ne point partir d'ici-bas avant d'avoir vu la terre sainte.

MICHELET, parlant de Voltaire

disposition du profane toute la science du monde, c'est-à-dire le libérer de l'ignorance ; deuxièmement, lui apprendre à penser conformément à la raison, c'est-à-dire le libérer de la superstition et de la foi.

L'*Encyclopédie*, elle, était directement *révolutionnaire*, ce qui, précisons-le, est loin de signifier *démocratique*. Ce que réclamaient ces réformistes, c'était la destruction d'un ordre de vie fondé sur les valeurs surnaturelles du christianisme, et la création d'un régime dont l'objectif serait le bonheur de l'homme. Ce régime, pour Voltaire, par exemple, n'était nullement républicain : un « despotisme éclairé » — c'est-à-dire le règne d'un monarque absolu et philosophe — voilà ce qu'il souhaitait. Certaines contradictions étaient inhérentes au système : sans doute tenait-il du paradoxe d'exiger qu'un despote vînt imposer la tolérance et la liberté, mais il ne semble pas que les Encyclopédistes s'en soient inquiétés outre mesure : leur principal adversaire, Jean-Jacques Rousseau, allait achever leur œuvre.

Nature et révolution   C'est que les Encyclopédistes étaient des rationalistes et que la raison est négative par nature. Rousseau, lui, était un passionné, et, en inventant le dogme de la bonté originelle, il fonda en nature le réformisme de ses aînés. « La nature, écrit-il en toutes lettres, a fait l'homme heureux et bon, mais... la société le déprave et le rend misérable. » Conclusion : il faut modifier la société, non pas pour la faire progresser vers un idéal qu'on atteindra à la fin des temps, mais pour la ramener à l'état primitif où elle était composée de « bons sauvages » et d'où elle n'aurait pas dû sortir. On

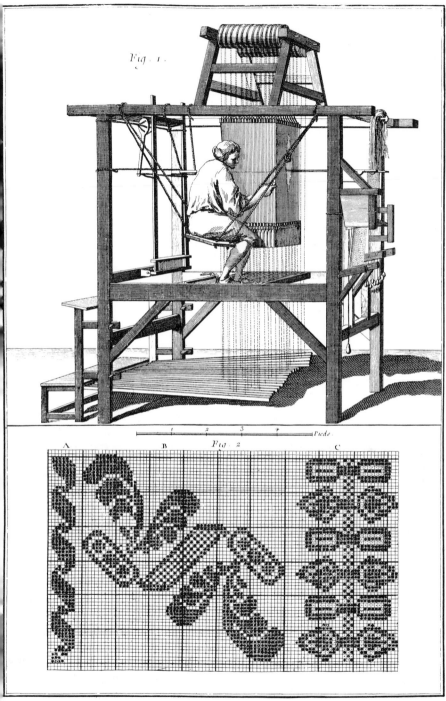

Les Encyclopédistes ouvrirent des yeux fascinés sur le monde de la technique qui leur paraissait un gage de progrès.

Montesquieu écrit, interprète le Droit. Voltaire pleure et crie pour le Droit. Et Rousseau le fonde...

Où prit-il son point d'appui, l'homme fort qui, frappant du pied, s'arrêta, tint ferme ?... Et tout s'arrêta.

Où il le prit, ô monde infirme, hommes faibles et malades qui le demandez, ô fils oublieux de Rousseau et de la Révolution ?

Il le prit en ce qui chez vous a trop défailli... Dans son cœur. Il lut au fond de sa souffrance, il y lut distinctement ce que le Moyen Age n'a jamais pu lire : un Dieu juste... Et ce qu'a dit un glorieux enfant de Rousseau : « Le Droit est le souverain du monde. »...

A un monde endormi encore, faible, inerte et sans élan, Rousseau dit et devait dire : « La volonté générale, c'est le Droit et la Raison. » Votre volonté, c'est le Droit. Réveillez-vous donc, esclaves !

« Votre volonté collective, c'est la Raison elle-même. » Autrement dit, Vous êtes Dieux.

Et qui donc, sans se croire Dieu, pourrait faire aucune grande chose ?...

Soyons Dieu ! L'impossible devient possible et facile... Alors, renverser un monde, c'est peu ; mais on crée un monde.

MICHELET, *parlant de Rousseau*

reconnaît une version païenne du mythe du Paradis terrestre. Condamnant en bloc tout ce qui a été inventé par les hommes — arts, sciences, morale, civilisation — Rousseau ne déclarait-il pas froidement : « L'homme qui médite est un animal dépravé » ? Conclusion : le pouvoir doit être remis aux mains du peuple qui, lui, ne médite pas, et auquel appartient la souveraineté nationale dont il ne peut se démettre même lorsqu'il passe un « contrat social » avec un gouvernement quel qu'il soit.

Découverte de la liberté   Ce vers quoi tendaient tous ces penseurs si différents par leurs méthodes, c'était tout simplement la liberté congénitale de l'homme, notion qui nous est si familière, et qui n'avait strictement aucune signification pour leurs prédécesseurs. Cette conclusion imprévue vaut qu'on la médite. Comment se fait-il qu'une race de philosophes dont le souci principal était l'élaboration d'une méthode de connaissance en soient arrivés à cette déduction métaphysique dont la portée, sans doute, leur échappait : « L'homme est libre » ?

Diverses explications peuvent être proposées. Ce qui paraît certain, c'est que l'appétit de connaissance des Français a peu à peu sapé leur sens du sacré : lorsque le sacré se fut écroulé, la liberté éclata aux yeux du monde.

Pour beaucoup de pays étrangers, la France apparaît essentiellement comme le pays où ont fleuri soudain les idées de la Révolution. Il y a là beaucoup de

Cette danseuse figure la déesse Raison. Un siècle plus tôt, Pascal avait dit : « Qui veut faire l'ange, fait la bête. »

confusion et quelque frivolité. La façon la plus objective de considérer la réalité est sans doute de la replacer dans son mouvement historique. Alors on voit que, pour les intellectuels du XVIIIème siècle (on disait « les philosophes » à l'époque), un texte comme la Déclaration des droits de l'homme était l'aboutissement unique et final d'une enquête commencée par la raison deux siècles plus tôt. Cette Raison — on n'écrivait plus le mot qu'avec une majuscule — était donc la libératrice de l'homme, la valeur suprême de l'humanisme, en quelque sorte une divinité.

Oui, une divinité, c'était bien ainsi que l'entendaient les révolutionnaires qui ne prétendaient défendre en même temps les droits du peuple et ceux de la Raison. Sous la Révolution, la Raison eut un temple, et pour jouer le rôle de la Minerve moderne, on engagea une danseuse de l'opéra.

C'est sur cette vision pour le moins paradoxale — une ballerine demi-nue recevant les hommages d'un peuple de pédants — que s'achève ironiquement l'évolution du cartésianisme.

Cependant, l'ascension des philosophes et le déclin du christianisme au XVIIIème siècle ouvrirent les portes, au XIXème, à une multitude d'écoles de pensée, les unes contradictoires, les autres complémentaires, certaines enfin sans relation entre elles. Les plus importantes, groupées en une suite où l'on a tenté de concilier la logique et la chronologie, paraissent être : humanisme, positivisme, bergsonisme, néothomisme, socialisme, nationalisme, existentialisme. A remarquer que cette liste n'est pas exhaustive et aussi que, selon la bonne vieille expression française, on y trouve à boire et à manger.

HUMANISME

Humanisme est un mot confortable, mais imprécis, qu'on emploiera ici avec le sens « d'intérêt porté à l'homme en tant que tel, système dans lequel l'homme en tant que tel est la valeur suprême ».

En France, l'humanisme est riche de toute une tradition. Les grands penseurs de la Renaissance sont souvent qualifiés d'humanistes ; ils l'étaient, dans la mesure où, moins passionnés de Dieu que leurs prédécesseurs du Moyen Age, ils accordaient à l'homme l'essentiel de leur attention. Parmi eux, Montaigne se place au premier rang.

Au XVIIᵉᵐᵉ, la première place était toujours, officiellement du moins, réservée à la religion. Cependant les écrivains — La Rouchefoucauld avec ses *Maximes*, La Bruyère avec ses *Caractères*, La Fontaine avec ses *Fables*, Mme de la Fayette avec son roman *La Princesse de Clèves*, et, bien entendu, les dramaturges Corneille, Molière et Racine — n'avaient d'autre objet d'étude que les passions humaines et, par ce biais psychologique, se comportaient en humanistes. Il est significatif que deux des ouvrages du grand Descartes lui-même s'appellent *Traité des passions* et *Traité de l'homme*.

Au XVIIIᵉᵐᵉ, que ce soit par la culture systématique de la vertu, comme la préconise Rousseau dans son ouvrage de pédagogie *L'Émile*, ou par l'étude approfondie de l'action du vice sur l'âme humaine, comme en traite Choderlos de Laclos dans ses *Liaisons Dangereuses*, la tradition humaniste était maintenue et confirmée.

Le XIXᵉᵐᵉ siècle, avec le romantisme, apporta à l'humanisme l'occasion de redoubler d'intensité. Le « culte du moi », le « mal du siècle », le « vague des passions » : autant de manifestations d'un culte morbide que l'homme commençait à se porter à lui-même. Les romans biographiques abondèrent avec, au premier rang, le plus révélateur d'entre eux : la *Confession d'un enfant du siècle* de Musset. L'étude psychologique acquit une précision presque clinique avec des essais comme *De l'amour* de Stendhal.

Dans la deuxième moitié du siècle, l'humanisme eut même des prétentions scientifiques : les sentiments humains étaient considérés comme des phénomènes naturels, comme des sujets d'expérience. Par la précision de l'observation, des romanciers comme Flaubert avec *Madame Bovary*, comme les Goncourt avec *Renée Mauperin*, entreprirent de rivaliser avec les médecins du corps : ils se considéraient eux-mêmes comme les experts de l'âme.

Au XXᵉᵐᵉ siècle, tous les barrages étant rompus, il était naturel que l'humanisme observateur devînt didactique et qu'il se trouvât un penseur pour prêcher un Évangile nouveau, selon lequel la valeur suprême de l'humanité devait être le libre développement de l'homme. *Prêcher, Évangile,* ces mots ne sont pas de trop : c'est en effet un ton de prophète que prit André Gide dans ses *Nourritures terrestres* pour réclamer la totale disponibilité de l'homme. L'œuvre de Gide tient dans son vocabulaire : *disponibilité, nouvelleté, acte gratuit,* en sont les grands mots. Il s'agit d'une libération totale à l'égard de la société (indifférente) : Je suis prêt à toutes les acceptations » ; à l'égard de la famille (hostile) : « Familles, je vous hais ! » ; à l'égard de la morale (tyrannique) : l'auteur de *L'Immoraliste* a fait du prosélytisme déclaré pour l'homosexualité, considérée comme un instrument d'affranchissement intellectuel.

En fait, Gide tirait les conclusions ultimes du grand axiome de Dostoïevski : « Si Dieu n'existe pas, tout est permis. » Axiome dont on n'a sans doute pas encore fini de mesurer l'effrayante portée, soit dit en passant. Le pédéraste-cambrioleur Jean Genet, qui est actuellement l'un des plus grands écrivains français, préconise le rejet de toute contrainte sociale, même les plus universellement admises, se vantant par exemple de trahir ses meilleurs amis s'il y trouve avantage.

A noter, bien entendu, que l'essentiel de l'humanisme de Gide réside non pas dans son plaidoyer pour l'inversion sexuelle mais dans sa revendication d'une liberté absolue de la personne humaine.

POSITIVISME ET SCIENTISME

Le positivisme organisé est mort depuis longtemps. Mais son esprit subsiste encore parmi ceux que Barrès appelait « les Barbares » et Simone de Beauvoir

La Sorbonne, siège de l'Université de France, est, comme toute école française, une école du doute.

La science positive ne poursuit ni les causes premières ni la fin des choses ; pour enchaîner une multitude de phénomènes par les liens d'une même loi générale et conforme à la nature des choses, l'esprit humain a suivi une méthode simple et invariable. Il a constaté les faits par l'observation et par l'expérience ; il les a comparés, et il en a tiré des relations, c'est-à-dire des faits plus généraux, qui ont été à leur tour, et c'est là leur seule garantie de réalité, vérifiés par l'observation, et par l'expérience. Une généralisation progressive, déduite des faits antérieurs et vérifiée sans cesse par de nouvelles observations, conduit ainsi notre connaissance depuis les phénomènes vulgaires et particuliers jusqu'aux lois naturelles les plus abstraites et les plus étendues. Mais, dans la construction de cette pyramide de la science, toutes les assises, de la base au sommet, reposent sur l'observation et sur l'expérience. C'est un des principes de la science positive qu'aucune réalité ne peut être établie par le raisonnement. Le monde ne saurait être deviné.

BERTHELOT

« les ingénieurs ». Au reste, son aventure est assez curieuse pour valoir la peine d'être racontée.

Le professeur Auguste Comte (XIXème siècle) se prenait pour un esprit scientifique. La science en général et la sociologie en particulier rendaient compte, croyait-il, de l'univers tout entier. L'histoire de toute société comprenait trois états successifs : le théologique, le métaphysique et le positif. La France en était au positif. En conséquence, elle devait adopter la « religion positiviste « dans laquelle l'humanité tout entière jouerait le rôle de divinité sous l'appellation de Grand Être, tandis que la terre y serait le Grand Fétiche, et l'espace le Grand Milieu. Le culte rendu au Grand Être serait à la fois personnel (adoration d'une mère, d'une fille ou d'une épouse), domestique (participation à neuf sacrements) et public. La France tout entière aurait pour patronne « sainte Clotilde », c'est-à-dire Clotilde de Vaux, la maîtresse d'Auguste Comte en personne.

Telle quelle, la religion positiviste était une magistrale caricature de cette passion pour la science qui posséda — au sens fort — le XIXème siècle. Le terme de *nouvelle idole* n'est certes pas trop fort. Les hommes croyaient d'une part que la science ne pouvait plus guère progresser et, d'autre part, qu'elle expliquait tout. Les écrivains se piquèrent d'être aussi scientifiques que les savants : de là le naturalisme, et l'idée d'Émile Zola : faire, sous forme romancée, l'étude clinique de toute une famille. Qu'un savant pût, par exemple, croire en Dieu paraissait parfaitement grotesque, et Pasteur, médecin illustre et sincère chrétien, passait pour une anomalie de la nature. Comment croire à une religion où les vierges sont mères ? L'évolution d'un Renan, séminariste dans sa jeunesse, historien athée écrivant *L'Avenir de la science* dans sa maturité, résumerait à elle seule celle de son siècle.

Répudiant la foi comme démodée, répudiant le rationalisme cartésien comme idéaliste, l'intellectuel positiviste du XIXème siècle se voulait délibérément empiriste. Il n'y avait pour lui qu'une méthode de connaissance : la *méthode expérimentale* mise au point par le médecin Claude Bernard, pour qui l'empirisme était le seul moyen de connaître le réel.

BERGSON ET LE BERGSONISME

Enfin Bergson vint et « brisa nos chaînes » s'écriait un écrivain fort peu positiviste. Bergson en effet — outre le système philosophique original qu'il créa — sut montrer que la méthode expérimentale était insuffisante même pour la science, et que, par conséquent, la logique, l'imagination et l'investigation intellectuelle avaient encore leurs chances. Pour tout ce qui savait réfléchir en France, c'en fut brusquement fini du cauchemar positiviste : l'intelligence pétrifiée reprenait ses droits.

De cette oppression que l'empirisme avait fait peser sur la pensée française date sans doute une certaine complaisance moderne pour les excès du surréalisme, et aussi cette vendetta qui oppose en France, dès leur plus jeune âge, les « littéraires » et les « scientifiques ». On ne relève rien de tel au XVIIIème siècle ; et, au XVIIème, les plus grands hommes étaient à la fois savants, philosophes et écrivains. Bergson, en tout cas, fit relever la tête aux « littéraires » en montrant à la barbe des déterministes que la conscience saisissait ses données « im-médiatement ». La méthode expérimentale elle-même ne serait rien sans « l'intuition créatrice ».

L'intuition créatrice, méthode de connaissance directe qui permettait de renvoyer dos à dos le rationalisme cartésien et l'empirisme positiviste, mit Bergson à même de sortir du dilemme dans lequel la philosophie était enfermée depuis l'Antiquité et qui consistait à opposer systématiquement l'être et le néant. Bergson répond : il n'y a ni être ni néant, mais un *devenir* perpétuel, dont le moteur est *l'élan vital* inscrit dans la *durée* concrète.

Cette notion de durée, outre qu'elle résolvait toutes les apories[1] logiques liées à l'idée de mouvement, faisait du mouvement la base même de l'univers et donnait à tous les autres systèmes philosophiques des airs de photographies statiques lorsqu'on les comparait au cinéma bergsonien.

Dans un essai sur *Le Rire*, Bergson alla jusqu'à montrer que l'hilarité était toujours causée par le contraste entre la mobilité essentielle de la vie considérée dans sa durée et la raideur des attitudes fixes : un homme qui trébuche est un homme dont les membres n'ont pas épousé les mouvements qu'il aurait dû faire pour garder son équilibre.

---

[1] impasses ; problèmes impossibles à resoudre

Teilhard de Chardin   C'est dans la lignée bergsonienne que se place la pensée du Jésuite Teilhard de Chardin, savant, philosophe et théologien. Il serait puéril de chercher à résumer la cosmologie teilhardienne en quelques lignes, mais on peut en donner une idée générale en disant qu'elle consiste à tenir l'univers pour la matière même de sa propre évolution, l'homme pour l'évolution devenue consciente d'elle-même, et le Christ pour le moteur de cette évolution dont le point de fuite est baptisé « point oméga ».

NÉOTHOMISME

A la fin de sa vie, Bergson, né juif, ne cachait pas qu'il était de plus en plus profondément attiré par le catholicisme. Mais le plus grand spécialiste français de Bergson, Jacques Maritain, qui se trouve être aussi le principal penseur catholique moderne, dénonce la philosophie bergsonienne comme une magistrale entreprise de nihilisme intellectuel. Pour Jacques Maritain, point n'est besoin d'invoquer l'élan vital et l'évolution teilhardienne pour concilier le christianisme et la science contemporaine : ils peuvent très bien voisiner dans le cadre — à peine agrandi — de *La Somme* de saint Thomas d'Aquin.

C'est là, à peu de choses près, la doctrine officielle de l'Église catholique qui a dû, au XIXème siècle, faire face à une attitude intellectuelle mais qui conserve encore des adeptes. « Nous voudrions croire, disent-ils, mais nous ne pouvons pas : la science l'interdit. »

A cette attitude s'ajoutait celle de la classe ouvrière, de plus en plus indifférente aux matières de religion, et une sorte d'indolence générale : « Dieu, même s'il existe, ne s'intéresse pas à nous : rendons-lui la pareille. »

Rome a essayé, essaye encore, de lutter — avec des succès divers — contre ce parti pris de détachement, et l'Église de France, qui a perdu, depuis la fin de l'ancien régime, toute tendance à l'autonomie, exécute fidèlement les consignes du Vatican. Ce fut d'abord (fin du XIXème siècle) l'abandon de la cause monarchique et le ralliement à la république ; ce fut ensuite la condamnation, par le Vatican, de l'*Action française*, le mouvement nationaliste de Charles Maurras ; ce fut la création de tout un catholicisme dit de gauche, qui s'intéresse plus au bien-être matériel et social des hommes qu'à leur salut éternel ; ce fut l'expérience d'abord tentée, puis interdite, puis partiellement reprise des prêtres-ouvriers, évangelisateurs des masses laborieuses ; c'est maintenant « l'Église nouvelle » avec la messe en français qui suscite des polémiques infinies. Malgré cette mise à jour, l'Église de Rome demeure toujours fidèle du reste à ses principes d'autorité.

SOCIALISME

A l'opposé de ces doctrines contradictoires mais, l'une et l'autre, spiritualistes, se trouve le socialisme français dont le maître fut, dans la première moitié du XIXème siècle, Proudhon.

Cet autodidacte barbu fut le contemporain mais aussi l'ancêtre spirituel de Karl Marx. Les relations entre les deux penseurs manquaient d'ailleurs d'aménité : Proudhon traitait son émule de « ténia du socialisme » et qualifiait le communisme « d'absurdité antédiluvienne ».

Certains socialistes modernes se réclament encore de celui qui, après tout, fut le père du socialisme européen. Le premier à dénoncer le profit capitaliste qu'il appelait « droit d'aubaine » et qui prend le nom de « plus-value » dans le marxisme, Proudhon réclamait essentiellement la suppression de l'intérêt, en d'autres termes l'instauration du crédit gratuit. Mutuelliste en économie, à la fois fédéraliste et anarchiste en politique, il rêvait d'une société idéale où la propriété serait pour tout le monde. Par une ironie du sort, la phrase qu'il a prononcée une fois et qu'on cite le plus souvent n'était, dans son esprit, qu'une boutade dépassant sa pensée au point de la contredire : « La propriété, c'est le vol. »

Il n'empêche que c'est avec cette plaisanterie pour slogan que furent menées la plupart des campagnes socialistes au XIXème siècle.

Au XXème siècle, les penseurs socialistes français se réclament plutôt de Karl Marx, dont ils affirment avoir conservé l'esprit avec plus de fidélité que les communistes.

NATIONALISME

La science était l'idole des positivistes ; l'homme, des humanistes ; l'humanité, des socialistes. La nation fut celle d'un groupe de penseurs, parmi les plus brillants de l'époque, qui se réunirent autour de Charles Maurras dans la première moitié du XXème siècle. Leur intransigeance, la grossièreté avec laquelle ils aimaient affirmer leurs opinions, peut-être bien la frayeur que causaient leurs menaces souvent exécutées, leur firent tant d'ennemis qu'il est difficile maintenant de parler d'eux avec sang-froid sans provoquer la colère, ou plutôt la hargne. Alors on tisse autour d'eux la conspiration du silence. Résultat : les tableaux que l'on peint de la France à l'époque sont déséquilibrés, et bon nombre d'événements historiques ne s'expliquent plus.

En fait, le nationalisme français coïncide mal avec les diverses caricatures qu'on en a quelquefois tracées. Il débouche sur le monarchisme, mais il le dépasse ; il a flirté avec le fascisme, mais sans en partager l'hypnose ni les rêves pseudo-scientifiques ; il a cherché à s'inspirer de certaines structures médiévales, en particulier dans le domaine de l'organisation professionnelle, mais c'était pour résoudre de façon moderne le conflit capital-travail.

Avant tout, comme c'est presque toujours le cas en France, le nationalisme, c'est une méthode. Il ne s'agit plus seulement de connaître, mais aussi de modifier, de mettre en ordre la réalité : cela s'appelle l'empirisme organisateur.

Ensuite, c'est une méditation sur le phénomène nation. Le raisonnement analogique montre que la nation n'est qu'une communauté moyenne, intermédiaire entre la province et la fédération. Mais rien n'est plus faux que certains raisonnements analogiques. Il se pourrait fort bien que les nations, unifiées par la langue, l'histoire et la civilisation, aient un destin propre, du moins dans une période donnée ; il se pourrait fort bien que, parmi toutes les valeurs humaines, la garde de certaines soit plutôt confiée à cette nation-ci qu'à cette nation-là; dans cette perspective, il se pourrait fort bien que le patriotisme soit réellement, comme le pensaient les Grecs et les Romains, un sentiment sacré.

Il n'est pas indifférent de noter que Charles Maurras, qui, personnellement, n'avait pas la foi, souhaitait tout de même que la nation France ne perdît rien de son engagement dans le catholicisme — fait pour elle à moins qu'elle ne fût faite pour lui.

EXISTENTIALISME

La doctrine dite « existentialisme » (le mot fut inventé par l'un de ses représentants, Gabriel Marcel) n'est une découverte ni moderne ni française. Mais les prix Nobel qui ont couronné ses représentants français et la diversité des formes par lesquelles ils se sont exprimés depuis quelque vingt-cinq ans (essais, traités, romans, pièces de théâtre) leur ont valu une réputation mondiale. Leur influence s'est exercée sur toute une génération de jeunes intellectuels, et, si elle n'est plus aussi forte maintenant, leur prestige n'en a guère décru.

Les Français distinguent trois existentialismes : l'athée (celui de Sartre), l'agnostique (celui de Camus), le chrétien (celui de Gabriel Marcel). Le représentant le plus typique du trio est indéniablement Sartre, et ce sont ses idées à lui que l'on a coutume d'exposer lorsqu'on prétend résumer l'existentialisme. Ici, nous essaierons de faire une synthèse de la doctrine, tout en la centrant sur son expression la plus répandue.

Pourquoi est-il absurde d'imaginer qu'un individu donné puisse démontrer l'existence de Dieu (alors qu'il n'y a rien dans la nature qui ne puisse être conçu comme pouvant être décelé par quelqu'un en particulier) ? — Ce dont l'existence pourrait être démontrée ne serait pas, ne pourrait pas être Dieu. L'impossibilité d'une preuve objective de l'existence de Dieu, l'absurdité d'une telle façon de poser le problème religieux : voilà ce qui est indubitable. Montrer notamment qu'établir que quelque chose existe, c'est l'identifier, le repérer — à moins que ce ne soit découvrir un rapport purement idéal...

Qu'on imagine une dépêche d'agence annonçant que M. X a découvert l'existence de Dieu. Pourquoi est-ce si radicalement absurde ?

GABRIEL MARCEL

> *Exister pour une conscience, c'est être en rapport avec d'autres que soi.*
>
> GABRIEL MARCEL

Axiome : « L'existence précède l'essence. » Comme Bergson s'échappait du dilemme être ou néant en imaginant le devenir, l'existentialisme s'en évade en posant comme principe que l'existence — pour parler concrètement, la vie humaine telle qu'elle est vécue par un homme naturellement libre mais toujours placé dans une situation donnée — détermine l'essence, qui naît de la série des choix successifs et existentiels assumés par la conscience.

La métaphysique qui en résulte paraît confuse au profane, et l'on assure même que, lorsque parut *L'Être et le Néant* de Sartre, les critiques ne s'aperçurent pas que l'ordre des pages avait été emmêlé, si obscur leur sembla le texte ! En revanche, toute une morale existentialiste vit rapidement le jour. Rien d'étonnant : dans le fond, l'existentialisme est surtout une méditation sur la condition humaine, débouchant sur l'angoisse et l'engagement dans l'action pour Camus, sur la responsabilité et aussi l'engagement dans l'action — plus spécifiquement politique — pour Sartre.

La morale existentialiste naît d'un conflit entre une situation et une liberté. Ce conflit est résolu par un choix. A force de choisir des attitudes, on se choisit soi-même. Le choix ne détermine donc pas seulement l'action mais aussi le sujet qui choisit. La liberté crée la responsabilité. Ceux qui refusent de choisir sont « de mauvaise foi ». Ceux qui choisissent mal — Sartre, en particulier, ne mâche pas ses mots — sont « des salauds. »

Une question se pose évidement. Qu'est-ce que choisir bien ou mal ? Quel est le critère du bien ? Serait-ce le tempérament de M. Sartre en personne ? Les augures de l'existentialisme restent muets sur ce point.

Sans s'égarer dans la nomenclature des en-soi (les objets) et des pour-soi (les consciences), il convient peut-être de faire un sort à une phrase de Sartre souvent citée et quelquefois mal comprise. « L'enfer, c'est les autres », dit l'un des personnages de *Huis clos*. Il faut entendre « les autres » dans le sens philosophique « d'autrui ». A mesure que nous choisissons nos attitudes et nos actions, nous pouvons toujours nous jouer la comédie d'être ce que nous ne sommes pas. Mais autrui nous observe ; autrui enregistre nos choix ; autrui voit notre essence s'édifier ; autrui nous enferme dans ce que nous sommes, c'est-à-dire dans notre essence, c'est-à-dire encore, si nous le méritons, dans notre enfer pour l'éternité.

La compagne de Sartre, Simone de Beauvoir, s'est faite en quelque sorte son disciple, et on retrouve dans son œuvre les mêmes thèmes de liberté d'engagement, de choix, de mauvaise foi. Dans un esprit semblable, elle a écrit un ouvrage plus qu'intéressant sur la condition de la femme et la femme elle-même : *Le Deuxième Sexe*. Il y a là un sérieux et en même temps un sens de la synthèse qui font de ce livre une somme de la question.

« L'existentialisme est-il un humanisme ? » On se demande cela chaque fois qu'on a lu plusieurs livres existentialistes d'affilée. On y trouve un tel sens du tragique de notre situation — généralement baptisé désespoir — qu'on a envie de répondre oui ; mais ils se signalent aussi par une telle absence de charité, un tel souci du système intellectuel cohérent, quand bien même faudrait-il couper tout ce qui dépasse, qu'on finit par répondre non. L'existentialisme apparaît alors comme une sorte de codification stérile de notre angoisse, une angoisse qui est déjà toute dans Pascal, si la codification n'y est pas.

FRANCS-TIREURS

Voilà pour les sept écoles de pensée que nous avons distinguées, non sans user d'un arbitraire certain. Restent les francs-tireurs qui opposent, à l'arbitraire du catalogue, une résistance opiniâtre. Les historiens, les critiques littéraires, les journalistes, ont sans cesse participé aux mouvements des idées, mais comme ils n'étaient pas proprement créateurs, nous les négligeons systematiquement. Les poètes et les romanciers ont souvent exprimé des idées, mais généralement elles appartenaient à quelqu'un d'autre, et c'est ce quelqu'un là que nous avons cherché à nommer. Cependant, un personnage du XXème siècle surnage encore et refuse d'être casé : Simone Weil.

Il y a quelque chose de satisfaisant pour un esprit tant soit peu paradoxal — et d'agaçant au contraire pour les intelligences systématiques — que ce soit une Juive non baptisée qui, face à toutes les idolâtries de son temps, face à l'Église même du Christ, dont elle ne faisait pas partie et que les préoccupations matérielles obsédaient déja, ait élevé la voix pour parler de l'amour de Dieu.

Elle n'a pas construit de système métaphysique : elle n'en ressentait pas le besoin. Mais, grâce à sa connaissance approfondie de la philosophie grecque et à sa propre expérience mystique, elle a, une fois de plus, rendu compte à l'humanité de l'essence même du christianisme.

BILAN TEMPORAIRE

On l'a vu, la pensée française, relativement homogène dans le passé, se caractérise aujourd'hui par une extrême fragmentation. Ayant explosé dans toutes les directions à la fois, il ne semble pas qu'elle apporte de solution exhaustive ni même satisfaisante aux problèmes de plus en plus nombreux, de plus en plus complexes qu'elle ne cesse pas de se poser.

ÉVOLUTION 4 DES STYLES DANS LA LITTÉRATURE FRANÇAISE

IDÉE GÉNÉRALE

Il n'y a pas de pays au monde où la littérature soit traditionnellement plus importante qu'en France. Les gens de lettres y ont fait la pluie et le beau temps, souvent les révolutions et quelquefois les régimes. Si, dans cet ouvrage, on donnait à la littérature une place proportionnée à son importance dans la vie française, on n'en aurait plus pour parler d'autre chose.

D'un autre côté, l'importance que la littérature française revêt dans son pays d'origine fait qu'elle est assez bien connue à l'étranger. En outre, comme la chose écrite est, par excellence, le sujet et l'objet de l'enseignement traditionnel, il est bien rare qu'on aborde l'étude de la civilisation sans avoir une bonne teinture des principaux écrivains.

C'est pourquoi, renchérissant sur notre propre principe qui est que l'idée prime le fait, nous réduirons notre survol de la littérature à quelques considérations sur l'évolution des styles et, accessoirement, de l'inspiration.

Aussi importe-t-il de dégager très nettement la différence de sens de ces deux termes que nous tiendrons pour radicalement opposés : l'inspiration, c'est la matière ; le style, c'est la forme. Les choix étant plus variés dans les questions de forme, ce sera, bien entendu, au style que nous consacrerons l'essentiel de notre attention. Quant à l'inspiration, il faut toujours la rapporter aux deux sources de la pensée française : l'esprit gaulois, dru, vert, truculent, collant à la terre, incarné en Rabelais ; et la raison romaine, sèche, analytique, exacte, translucide, personifiée par Voltaire. Bref, la truelle et le bistouri.[1]

Le style est une notion difficile à saisir. Souvent, on appelle ainsi l'écriture, mais c'est là une erreur, car l'écriture ne concerne que l'expression de la pensée, tandis que la pensée elle-même a un style. La citation — inexacte d'ailleurs — de Buffon, « Le style, c'est l'homme », rend mieux la liaison étroite qui existe entre un créateur et les formes qu'il choisit d'emprunter pour s'exprimer. En fait, le style est un rapport plutôt qu'une donnée, et l'on pourrait s'amuser à en donner une formule mathématique :

$$\frac{forme}{fond} = style$$

Il semble aussi qu'on arrive à caractériser de façon satisfaisante la plupart des écrivains en utilisant « la boussole des styles » :

classicisme

romantisme ⊕ préciosité

baroque

D'une façon générale, on appelle *précieux* les artistes pour qui la forme prend systématiquement le pas sur le fond, créant ainsi un déséquilibre dans le style. Leurs adversaires les trouvent affectés, efféminés, décadents ; de leur côté, ils prétendent avoir du goût, de la concision, du raffinement.

Au contraire, les *romantiques* se préoccupent relativement peu de la forme : ils veulent s'exprimer, à n'importe quel prix. On leur accorde du génie plutôt que de l'intelligence ; ils affirment, eux, que leur art ressemble à la vie. Du point de vue du style — et de celui-là seulement — le réalisme est un romantisme.

L'équilibre est l'idéal des *classiques* ; « rien de trop », leur devise. L'art leur apparaît comme une transcendance. Il y a du platonisme dans leur esthétique. Ceux qui ne les aiment pas les accusent d'être ennuyeux et guindés.

Le mot *baroque* en littérature comme dans les arts plastiques (il en va autrement pour la musique) signifie anti-classique. La recherche de l'effet, le désir d'étonner, le souci de l'ornement, caractérisent le baroque. Les grands mots des classiques sont nature et raison ; la baroque affectionne l'extraordinaire et l'élaboré. Si le classicisme est la sagesse du style, le baroque en est la folie.

Dans l'ensemble, le génie de la France est proprement classique, par opposition, par exemple, à celui de l'Espagne (baroque), de l'Allemagne (romantique), de l'Islam (précieux). Néanmoins, tant que l'expression artistique française demeure proche du folklore (soit, pendant une bonne partie du Moyen Age), la notion de style lui reste etrangère. Le style suppose un art conscient de lui-même ; le folklore ne l'est jamais. Dans l'art populaire, il n'y

[1] La truelle est l'outil du maçon ; le bistouri, celui du chirurgien.

a généralement aucun décalage entre le fond et la forme : le fond trouve sa forme tout naturellement et l'épouse sans que le choix intervienne à aucun moment. Aussi, parlant du Moyen Age, nous attacherons-nous moins au style proprement dit qu'à l'inspiration.

L'INSPIRATION AU MOYEN AGE

Les grandes époques se reconnaissent aux grands soucis. Dieu, le diable ; l'amour, la mort ; voilà ce qui préoccupe les hommes du Moyen Age et à quoi ils consacrent leurs poèmes épiques, les mystères joués dans leurs cathédrales, les fabliaux salaces[2] qu'ils se racontent à la veillée, les chroniques de leurs moines et de leurs hommes de guerre, les récits allégoriques qui guident leurs initiés vers le salut éternel.

Pour s'exprimer, le chant est peut-être plus naturel à l'homme que la parole, et toute littérature commence par la poésie. C'est donc en vers que, d'un bout à l'autre de l'immense scène médiévale, se répondent l'esprit et la chair, entre lesquels les hommes du Moyen Age se sentent déchirés. L'esprit — rien à voir avec l'intelligence — l'esprit parle le langage le plus raffiné qui soit accessible à l'âme humaine, et la chair glapit avec la crudité qui lui est propre. Point de milieu entre les extrêmes. Souvent, le conteur se plaît à décrire la vie courante, avec une verve satirique qu'on a rarement retrouvée depuis lors, mais ce qu'ici-bas a d'éphémère n'est jamais oublié : on sent, derrière chaque phrase, la présence d'un au-delà à la fois redoutable et désiré. Quelquefois, sa pitié pour les hommes, la noblesse de ses propres héros, ou la beauté de son héroïne donnent au poète un frisson qui le rend soudain très proche de nous, mais on sent toujours que, pour lui, tout se rapporte à un Dieu immuable, et parfaitement connu. Tous les jugements sont portés d'avance : l'esprit s'appelle sainteté ; la chair s'appelle péché, donc enfer. Sur tout ce qui concerne les questions essentielles — les seules qui l'intéressent — le Moyen Age déclare hautement : « Mon siège est fait. »

Avec ce qu'on a pris pour de la naïveté, mais qui est plutôt un sens aigu de la transcendance, les traîtres dans les romans du Moyen Age se désignent eux-mêmes en disant, « Moi, le traître. » Les jongleurs font des tours de passe-passe devant l'autel de la Vierge. Les rosiers plantés sur les tombes de deux amants entrelacent leurs branches. Les prêtres vendent quelquefois leur âme au diable (comme dans le mystère de Théophile), mais il leur suffit de prier Notre-Dame pour être sauvés. Bref, le monde tout entier est parcouru d'un souffle unique qui, emportant la vertu, le crime, la bêtise, la passion, la Création telle qu'elle est, chante le Créateur.

Romans bretons Ce qu'il y a de plus raffiné, au Moyen Age, c'est, sans conteste, le roman breton. L'aventure y est allégorique et mystique ; la femme, chaste ou non, une médiatrice entre l'homme et Dieu. La quête de l'amour ou celle de la pureté en tisse le fond ; les sentiments les plus pro-

[2] récits populaires d'une inspiration souvent libertine

— *Par sa grâce maniérée*, l'Amour se taillant un arc dans la massue d'Hercule, *de Bouchardon, appartient à l'art précieux* (XVIIIème).

— *L'harmonie sereine des formes, l'équilibre des volumes, sont les apanages du style classique, illustré par Maillol dans la Rivière* (XXème).

— *Avec ses corps nus, offerts à la pourriture sur ses draps chiffonnés*, le Tombeau de Henri II, de Pilon, est un chef d'œuvre de l'art baroque (XVIème).

— *Leur conception à la fois tourmentèe et méditative fait* des Portes de l'enfer *de Rodin une œuvre romantique*
(XIXème).

Vulgaire

L'était un peu plus dmidi quand j'ai pu monter dans l'esse. Jmonte donc, jpaye ma place comme de bien entendu et voilàtipas qu'alors jremarque un zozo l'air pied, avec un cou qu'on aurait dit un télescope et une sorte de ficelle autour du galurin. Je lregarde passque jlui trouve l'air pied quand le voilàtipas qu'ismet à interpeller son voisin. Dites-donc, qu'il lui fait, vous pourriez pas faire attention, qu'il ajoute, on dirait, qu'il pleurniche, quvous lfaites esssprais, qu'i bafouille, deummarcher toutltempts sullé panards, qu'i dit. Là-dsus, tout fier de lui, i va s'asseoir. Comme un pied.

Jrepasse plus tard Cour de Rome et jl'aperçois qui discute le bout de gras avec un autre zozo de son espèce. Dis-donc, qu'i lui faisait l'autre, tu dvrais, qui'i lui disait, mettre un ottbouton, qu'il ajoutait, à ton pardingue, qu'i concluait.

Précieux

C'était aux alentours d'un juillet de midi. Le soleil dans toute sa fleur régnait sur l'horizon aux multiples tétines. L'asphalte palpitait doucement, exhalant cette tendre odeur goudronneuse qui donne aux cancéreux des idées à la fois puériles et corrosives sur l'origine de leur mal. Un autobus à la livrée verte et blanche, blasonné d'un énigmatique S, vint recueillir du côté du parc Monceau un petit lot favorisé de candidats voyageurs aux moites confins de la dissolution sudoripare. Sur la plate-forme arrière de ce chef-d'œuvre de l'industrie automobile française contemporaine, où se serraient les transbordés comme harengs en caque, un garnement approchant à petits pas de la trentaine et portant entre un cou d'une longueur quasi serpentine et un chapeau cerné d'un cordaginet une tête aussi fade que plombagineuse éleva la voix pour se plaindre avec une amertume non feinte et qui semblait émaner d'un verre de gentiane, ou de tout autre liquide aux propriétés voisines, d'un phénomène de heurt répété qui selon lui avait pour origine un cousager présent hic et nunc de la STCRP. Il prit pour élever sa plainte le ton aigre d'un vieux vidame... Mais découvrant une place vide il s'y jeta.

Plus tard, comme le soleil avait déjà descendu de plusieurs degrés l'escalier monumental de sa parade céleste et comme de nouveau je me faisais véhiculer par un autre autobus de la même ligne, j'aperçus le personnage plus haut décrit qui se mouvait dans la Cour de Rome de façon péripatétique en compagnie d'un individu ejusdem farinae qui lui donnait, sur cette place vouée à la circulation automobile, des conseils d'une élégance qui n'allait pas plus loin que le bouton.

RAYMOND QUENEAU

fonds comme les plus délicats y trouvent une expression digne d'eux. *Tristan et Iseult* est à juste titre le plus illustre de ces romans.

Fabliaux   À l'autre bout, on trouve le fabliau, d'un réalisme qui va souvent jusqu'à la grossièreté, mais qui évite tous les pièges de la systématisation où tomberont les réalistes du XIXème siècle. C'est que le réalisme n'y est pas pris pour une fin, mais comme le moyen de faire rire le lecteur aux dépens du paysan naïf ou du mari trompé.

Villon   Bien des ouvrages du Moyen Age ne sont pas signés ; beaucoup le sont. Au-dessus de tous les noms qui sont restés d'une littérature s'étendant sur quatre siècles, il en est un qu'on ne peut pas ne pas citer. Dans une œuvre qui tient en un petit volume, dans un français déjà presque moderne pour le vocabulaire sinon pour l'orthographe, François Villon nous a légué un Moyen Age de poche : violence, truculence, piété, hantise de la mort, tout y est, sans la moindre enflure romantique, sans la moindre afféterie précieuse. Villon, qui mourut il y a quelque cinq cents ans, demeure un des poètes français les plus modernes. En fait, on pourrait affirmer qu'il est le seul poète existentialiste que la France se soit jamais offert.

LE BOUILLONNEMENT DE LA RENAISSANCE

Il n'y a guère d'écrivains français qui se situent sur la boussole des styles entre le baroque et le précieux, du côté où ils ne sont séparés que par un angle de 90°. Ils se promènent généralement sur les 180° restants. C'est ainsi qu'on peut dire que toute la littérature française tient entre ces deux génies extrêmes : Proust (comble du précieux), Rabelais (comble du baroque).

Rabelais   Rabelais, que l'on connaît mal parce que sa langue est encore difficile et que sa prodigieuse verdeur choque nos sensibilités malingres, compte parmi les plus grands écrivains français, dans la mesure où il utilise les moyens que la langue lui offre avec une puissance, un bonheur, un art qui ont suscité bien des émules mais pas un rival. Au XXème siècle, nul ne s'est soucié de ressusciter les traditions rabelaisiennes à l'exception de Jacques Perret, qui a retrouvé quelque chose de cette verve, de cette passion pour les inventaires grotesques, de cette respiration de géant des lettres.

Baroque Rabelais le fut, sans doute, parce qu'un grand écrivain choisit son style spontanément, par instinct. Qu'on s'arrête un moment sur l'inspiration de Rabelais — qui ne quitte guère les fonctions naturelles de l'homme et principalement le boire et le manger — et qu'on se demande quel autre style l'aurait mieux servie : est-ce la préciosité éthérée, le romantisme approximatif, le classicisme tout de mesure et d'harmonie qui auraient pu servir à faire passer dans l'imagination du lecteur tant de féroces ripailles, tant de joyeuses bagarres, tant d'homérique hilarité ? Non pas : il y fallait, outre un souffle éminemment vigoureux, une certaine absence de délicatesse, une aptitude résolue à utiliser tous les instruments, tous les projectiles du langage — de la rhétorique austère au coq-à-l'âne et au calembour — sans jamais faire la fine bouche. Styliste, Rabelais applique sans cesse le précepte qui forme la seule règle d'une abbaye de son invention : « Fais ce que tu voudras. »

Qu'on ne s'y méprenne pas : le baroque est loin de tenir tout entier dans l'œuvre de Rabelais, mais l'œuvre de Rabelais tient indéniablement dans le baroque.

La Pléiade   Rabelais, prosateur, s'amusait. Les poètes de la Pléiade qui vinrent après lui se prirent au sérieux. Fascinés par l'antiquité gréco-latine, tournant délibérément le dos au Moyen Age dont ils ne voyaient plus la grande lumière et qui leur paraissait une longue nuit, ils résolurent de créer de toute pièce une littérature française. Cela consisterait, pensaient-ils, à traiter en français les thèmes familiers aux Latins et aux Grecs. Cette vaste entreprise d'imitation nous surprend maintenant, parce que les modernes recherchent l'originalité à tout prix ; les hommes de la Renaissance — plus modestes, ou plus présomptueux ? — visaient la perfection.

En réalité, la perfection et l'originalité se passent difficilement l'une de l'autre. Si l'on est doué et qu'on poursuit l'une des deux, on trouve l'autre qui n'a pas voulu la quitter ; si l'on manque de dons, inutile de chercher celle-ci plutôt que celle-là : elles se déroberont toutes les deux.

De toute évidence, c'était le classicisme que les poètes de la Pléiade désiraient rencontrer. Mais comme la langue française elle-même en était à un stade relativement primitif d'évolution, il était impossible de deviner ce que le classicisme français pourrait bien être.

Ronsard, du Bellay   Ronsard, du Bellay, par leur désir d'enrichir le vocabulaire en utilisant des mots grecs, latins, techniques, archaïques, etc., et de l'assouplir en formant des diminutifs, en substantivant les infinitifs, en appliquant le dérivation systématique, servaient un idéal beaucoup plus proche du baroque que du classicisme auquel ils prétendaient. Et pourtant, comme si une langue était un organisme vivant, ce fut en réalité la cause du classique qu'ils servirent, car toutes leurs inventions linguistiques furent, en quelques années, rejetées par le français comme indigestes, à moins qu'elles ne pussent être adoptées par le classicisme, auquel cas elles furent digérées — comme, par exemple, la périphrase, qui ne fut abandonnée qu'à la fin du XIXème siècle.

Le classique tient au romantisme et à la préciosité par le haut ; le baroque y tient aussi mais par le bas. En ce sens, on peut considérer que le XVIème siècle fut comme l'envers, ou, si l'on préfère, comme l'image symétrique du XVIIème. Telle est la dialectique des styles.

NAISSANCE DU CLASSICISME

Le début du XVIIème siècle est l'une des périodes les plus riches, les plus nourrissantes, de la littérature française. Les contrastes y sont d'une violence exemplaire ; et puis, d'un mariage entre deux ennemis qui paraissaient irréductibles, le classicisme naît.

Il faut noter dès l'abord que, dans l'évolution des styles, les genres tiennent aussi leur place. On pourrait poser comme axiome que le style appelle le genre. Le Moyen Age s'exprimait naturellement en longs poèmes ; le baroque Rabelais écrivait en prose ; les plus belles réussites de la Pléiade sont des sonnets et des élégies ; les « parents » du classicisme chercheront en vain un genre qui leur permette de fournir une synthèse de leur esthétique ; mais le classicisme lui-même donnera naissance à une forme parfaite : la tragédie (ou comédie) en cinq actes et en vers alexandrins, dans laquelle il pourra couler son génie tout entier.

Le classicisme, préparé dans les tavernes (burlesques) et dans les salons (précieux), triomphera presque uniquement au théâtre.

Burlesques Au début du XVIIème siècle, le burlesque était en réaction contre le précieux : il y trouvait sa raison d'être. Mais le précieux était en réaction contre le burlesque : sans le burlesque, il n'eût point été du tout. Les deux tendances avaient existé depuis toujours, mais elles se côtoyaient peu. Un certain brassage social qui marqua la Renaissance les fit se rencontrer : elles s'exacerbèrent.

Les poètes ou romanciers dits burlesques étaient en fait des baroques, mais un même propos les unissait : ridiculiser les grands sentiments. Ils s'y employaient avec toute l'énergie dont leur verbe était capable, inspirés par l'ombre gigantesque de Rabelais. Cependant, la réalité étant souvent grotesque par nature, cherchant le grotesque ils débouchaient souvent sur la réalité. En tant que réalistes par la peinture des mœurs et du décor, ils se rapprochent de l'esthétique romantique. Ce n'est pas une simple coïncidence si, au *Roman comique* de Scarron (début du XVIIème) répond *Le Capitaine Fracasse* de Théophile Gautier (début du XIXème) : ces deux romans s'attachent à montrer la vie des comédiens errants et y réussissent par des moyens pittoresques qui se ressemblent sur plus d'un point. Toutefois, il faut retenir que le trait distinctif des burlesques est leur complaisance pour ce qui est bas, ridicule, et souvent répugnant.

Précieux Les précieux, au contraire, vivent dans un air raréfié, parlent un langage prétentieux, essaient de déguiser la laideur de la vie par le raffinement de l'expression — bref font preuve de ce qu'on appelle aujourd'hui la sophistication. Dans l'évolution des styles, ils jouent un rôle négatif mais de première importance : celui de filtre. Ce sont eux qui, leur snobisme rendant leur idéalisme efficace, ont rejeté dans les marges de la littérature proprement dite tout ce qui n'était pas digne de faire la matière du classicisme ; ce sont eux qui ont épuré la langue, raffiné la pensée, catalogué les sentiments. Il ne restait plus ensuite aux classiques qu'à déclarer leur attachement à la nature et à la raison pour y revenir : la voie était libre, nettoyée par Mlle de Scudéry et son entourage.

Si l'on veut, on peut considérer la comédie des *Précieuses ridicules* de Molière comme un apologue historique : Cathos et Madelon, précieuses, y sont ridiculisées par Mascarille et Jodelet, burlesques ; mais la victoire finale appartient à Du Croizy et à Lagrange, classiques, qui, ayant rossé leurs valets, demeurent maîtres du terrain.

Corneille   En un certain sens, Corneille est le classique le plus attachant parce que le moins classique. De tempérament, comme tous les écrivains français marqués par l'Espagne, il était éminemment baroque. Ses premières œuvres, datant de l'époque où il s'exprimait librement, en font foi. La langue en est colorée et brutale. Les passions les plus élémentaires s'y donnent libre cours : séances de magie, duels, viols en pleine scène, voilà de quoi se composent ces pièces qu'on nomme — le mot est caractéristique — des tragi-comédies.

Seulement, à mesure que Corneille devenait plus grand et plus connu, les théoriciens du classicisme s'occupaient de plus en plus de lui et lui imposaient de plus en plus leurs façons de voir qui ne s'accordaient nullement avec son tempérament. Il parvint à concilier le tout, l'espace d'un ou deux chefs d'œuvre, puis, se décolorant peu à peu par excès de bonne volonté, il finit par écrire des pièces tout bonnement ennuyeuses. Sa grande période est celle où, se rebiffant contre les unités de temps, de lieu, d'action et même de genre, il chevauche joyeusement par tous les champs ouverts à son génie.

L'Académie française critiqua violemment *Le Cid*, qui est la dernière œuvre de la première manière. Du point de vue classique, l'Académie avait raison : *Le Cid* est une chose bigarrée, violente. Mais, dans *Le Cid*, Corneille se montre unique. Il ne l'est déjà plus dans *Horace* : cette action resserrée, ce français lisse, ces unités respectées, on dirait que c'est déjà Racine, la musique en moins.

LE CLASSICISME

« Imiter la nature », voilà la grande idée des classiques. Du moins le croyaient-ils. Personne n'imite la nature : on s'imite soi-même. Cependant, on peut délibérément chercher la déformation des données naturelles, comme le font l'art baroque et l'art précieux, ou au contraire s'efforcer de les respecter et ne les modifier qu'inconsciemment : ainsi procèdent classiques et romantiques. Mais, là encore, il y a une différence. Les classiques pourchassent le *vrai* (ils veulent dire le général), et les romantiques le *réel* (ils veulent dire le particulier). Les classiques visent toujours l'abstrait, les romantiques le concret.

Racine   Les rois antiques de Racine dans ses tragédies *Phèdre*, *Athalie*, *Bérénice*, s'expriment comme des gentilshommes du XVIIème français, mais c'est parce que Racine parlait le français du XVIIème et que ses rois étaient des personnages universels. Les héros de Victor Hugo sont aussi empruntés à quelque époque reculée, mais il parlent comme Victor Hugo pensait qu'on parlait à cette époque ; les personnages d'un Henri Becque (réaliste du XIXème) sont des bourgeois contemporains de leur auteur et s'expriment comme tels. Cela revient à dire que Racine pensait à ce qu'il y a en l'homme d'éternel, tandis que les romantiques et les réalistes s'intéresseront au contraire à ce qu'il y a en lui de transitoire.

Molière   Le classicisme, en France, a duré cent cinquante ans. Qui dit
« classiques » pense Molière, parce que Molière avait du génie et que ses
chefs d'œuvre, vieux de trois cents ans, sont toujours aussi jeunes. Mais
Voltaire aussi était un classique, et Houdart de la Motte, et Jean-Baptiste
Rousseau,[3] et Veuillot. Leurs œuvres — celles de Voltaire comprises pour ce
qui est du théâtre — soufflent l'ennui, la froideur, l'artifice. C'est que le
classicisme n'était plus qu'une méthode, plus qu'un moule : la matière que
ses partisans y coulaient n'avait rien de vivant. Vivant ne veut pas dire nouveau
ni original. Certains créateurs, fort rares il est vrai, utilisent des formes à
moitié usées et en tirent des effets admirables, mais c'est qu'ils ont en eux
des ressources qui le leur permettent.

Voltaire   Voltaire a survécu, lui, en s'inventant des formes mineures qui
moulaient agréablement le classicisme un peu décadent dont il fut le principal représentant : la lettre, l'article de dictionnaire, le conte philosophique
ou satirique comme *Candide* ou *Zadig*, voilà les petits genres où il réussit
brillamment, les derniers rameaux qu'il fit pousser sur l'arbre du classicisme
auquel ses prédécesseurs avaient fourni le tronc et les grosses branches.

NAISSANCE DU ROMANTISME

Pendant plus de soixante-quinze ans, le classicisme expirant et le romantisme
embryonnaire ont cohabité en France.

Diderot, Rousseau   Diderot, avec ses romans comme *Le Neveu de
Rameau*, est le meilleur produit de cette cohabitation. Quel que soit notre
dégoût pour les dates, il peut être curieux d'en citer quelques-unes ici. En
1750, Jean-Jacques Rousseau publie sa première œuvre ; or, il est justement
considéré comme un précurseur du romantisme, à cause de l'intérêt passionné
qu'il se portait à lui-même et du ton plaintif sur lequel il parlait de sa
personne, particulièrement dans ses *Confessions*. En 1820 paraît la première
œuvre résolument romantique par l'inspiration : *Les Méditations* de Lamartine. En 1830, une bataille rangée, celle d'*Hernani*,[4] oppose encore les
romantiques à leurs adversaires classiques qui, jusque-là, tenaient le haut du
pavé. C'est dire que la naissance du romantisme ne se fit pas sans mal.

André Chénier   Si la Révolution ne lui avait pas coupé la tête, l'un des
plus grands poètes français aurait probablement été André Chénier, qui
s'apostrophait lui-même en ces termes : « Sur des pensers nouveaux, faisons
des vers antiques. » Apostrophe significative. Chénier ne ressentait aucuné-
ment le besoin de renouveler la forme du vers ; sa sensibilité méditerranéenne,
son vigoureux érotisme, étaient riches d'une énergie suffisante pour faire vibrer
d'une vie retrouvée les vieux modes époumonnés du XVIIIème siècle. Guillotiné, il céda la place à son cadet de vingt-huit ans, Lamartine.

[3] à ne pas confondre avec Jean-Jacques Rousseau
[4] drame de Victor Hugo

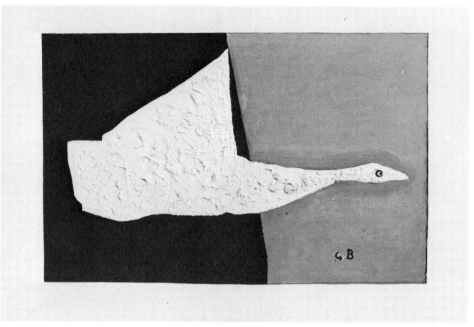

— *Elégance, simplicité — idéal classique :* Le Canard, *de Braque (XXème).*

— *Expressionnisme, pathétique — idéal romantique:* Le Vieux roi, *de Rouault (XXème).*

— *Sens subtil de la décoration* —
idéal précieux : Le Grand intérieur
rouge, *de Matisse* (XXème).

— *Recherche de l'im-
prévu, parfois même du
saugrenu* — *idéal ba-
roque* : Parade amour-
euse, *de Picabia*
(XXème).

Lamartine   Comme Corneille deux cents ans plus tôt, Lamartine cherche sa voie. Il est piquant de relever, dans ses poèmes dont la matière est toute personaliste, toute sentimentale, toute romantique, un amour de l'abstraction et une habitude de la périphrase encore purement classiques. Quand, pour ne pas nommer la lune, Lamartine l'appelle avec beaucoup de naturel « l'astre au front d'argent », on sent que l'époque n'est pas loin où, « mouchoir » étant un mot trop précis, trop grossier, on remplaçait par un billet celui de Desdémone dans les traductions d'*Othello* présentées en France (XVIIIème).

LE ROMANTISME

On a trop insisté sur le côté pleurard du romantisme. L'essentiel est ailleurs.

Victor Hugo   Premièrement, dans le renouvellement du vocabulaire. Lorsque Victor Hugo déclarait, « J'ai mis le bonnet rouge au vieux dictionnaire... J'ai nommé le cochon par son nom : pourquoi pas ? » sans doute se vantait-il. En fait, dans son œuvre on rencontre beaucoup plus de « pourceaux » que de « cochons », de « coursiers » que de « chevaux », de « glaives » que d' « épées ». Il demeure donc attaché par l'habitude au vocabulaire dit noble que les classiques avaient imposé à la poésie. Mais ce n'est que par l'habitude : consciemment, il cherche à donner leurs lettres de noblesse à tous les mots du dictionnaire français. Sans doute ne verse-t-il pas encore dans le vocabulaire ordurier, mais enfin il proclame la déchéance de la périphrase et l'avènement du *mot propre*. Qu'on nous permette un jeu de mots qui s'impose ici : les mots *sales* n'accéderont à la littérature que cinquante ans plus tard.

Balzac   Deuxième innovation du romantisme : les thèmes traités, les personnages évoqués, les idées remuées, ne sont plus les mêmes. A Racine, il fallait des rois ; à Victor Hugo, les grands seigneurs espagnols suffisent généralement. Balzac se satisfera des bourgeois de son temps. L'amour mis à part (lancé au Moyen Age, l'amour n'a pas cessé depuis lors d'être un best-seller), les sentiments aussi se sont modifiés : l'honneur était la grande affaire de Corneille ; l'arrivisme sera le sujet favori des romantiques. A noter que ce qui paraissait drôle au XVIIème devient tragique au XIXème. Ce serait à peine solliciter les faits que de voir dans le père Grandet, l'avare de Balzac, un descendant d'Harpagon, l'avare de Molière, et dans le « bourgeois gentilhomme » (Molière) l'ancêtre de l'arriviste Lucien de Rubempré (Balzac). A noter aussi le détail caractéristique des noms propres : dans Molière, qui vise au général, les personnages portent des noms de convention littéraire (Géronte, Léandre, Elmire), et cette tendance ne fait que s'accentuer à mesure que le classicisme se dessèche (Sylvia, Arlequin) ; chez les romantiques, au contraire, les personnages ont des prénoms modernes (Octave, René) et accèdent même quelquefois à la dignité concrète du nom de famille (Sorel, Bianchot).

Récit

Un jour vers midi du côté du Parc Monceau, sur la plate-forme arrière d'un autobus à peu près complet de la ligne S (aujourd'hui 84), j'aperçus un personnage au cou fort long qui portait un feutre mou entouré d'un galon tressé au lieu de ruban. Cet individu interpella tout à coup son voisin en prétendant que celui-ci faisait exprès de lui marcher sur les pieds chaque fois qu'il montait ou descendait des voyageurs. Il abandonna d'ailleurs rapidement la discussion pour se jeter sur une place devenue libre.

Deux heures plus tard, je le revis dans la gare Saint-Lazare en grande conversation avec un ami qui lui conseillait de diminuer l'échancrure de son pardessus en en faisant remonter le bouton supérieur par quelque tailleur compétent.

Composition de mots

Je plate-d'autobus-formais co-foultitudinairement dans un espace-temps lutécio-méridiennal et voisinais avec un longicol tresseau-tourduchapeauté morveux. Lequel dit à un quelconquanonyme : « Vous me bousculaparaissez. » Cela éjaculé, se placelibra voracement. Dans une spatio-temporalité postérieure, je le revis qui place-saintlazarait avec un X qui lui disait : tu devrais boutonsupplémenter ton pardessus. Et il pourquexpliquait la chose.

RAYMOND QUENEAU

Stendhal Troisième trait nouveau : les genres, une fois de plus, ont évolué. L'épopée, l'élégie et le long poème à digressions triomphent en poésie. Le roman donne enfin sa pleine mesure. Quelquefois courts (*Adolphe* de Benjamin Constant), généralement longs (*Le Rouge et le Noir* de Stendhal), s'emboîtant même l'un dans l'autre pour former des cycles (*La Comédie humaine* de Balzac), utilisant régulièrement l'artifice si commode du « narrateur omniscient » (*Indiana* de George Sand), recourant de temps en temps à l'artifice contraire, celui de la « première personne » (la *Confession d'un enfant du siècle* de Musset), les romans deviennent alors la production littéraire type : à un tel point que le mot *écrivain* n'est souvent plus qu'un synonyme de *romancier*.

Flaubert Le réalisme, on l'a dit, n'est qu'une succursale[5] du romantisme, du point de vue du style, précisons-le bien. *Madame Bovary*, histoire d'une

[5] au sens propre, établissement dépendant d'un autre et suppléant à certaines de ses insuffisances

petite bourgeoise qui, dans un milieu étouffant de réalité, rêve d'évasions romantiques, illustre bien la double inspiration qui hanta Flaubert.

Zola   Quant au naturalisme : avec Zola et son étude clinique de toute une famille, ce n'est à son tour qu'une variété de réalisme systématiquement orientée vers les sujets bas et odieux ; dans cette complaisance même éclate un romantisme patent.

En prenant de l'âge, le romantisme-réalisme découvrit — comme le classicisme l'avait fait avant lui — les petits genres : le conte, la nouvelle, la pièce en trois actes. C'est là une évolution intéressante et qui n'est pas terminée. En réalité, la France vit toujours en pleine époque romantique, et cela d'autant plus que le fossé s'élargit entre certains écrivains, qui cherchent à fomenter des réactions baroque, précieuse, ou classique, et le public, au sens large du terme, dont les goûts en sont restés à une esthétique une fois et demie centenaire.

RÉACTION PRÉCIEUSE

Sur la boussole des styles, la préciosité est à l'opposé du romantisme. D'après toutes les règles de la dialectique, il était donc naturel qu'une vague de préciosité suivît la vague romantique, et ce fut en effet ce qui arriva.

Gautier, Baudelaire, Verlaine, Rimbaud, Mallarmé   En raffinant indéfiniment sur les questions de forme — le sonnet de quatorze vers remplaçant pour eux les poèmes de leurs aînés qui en comptaient plusieurs milliers — les poètes montrèrent le chemin. La transition se fit aux cris de « l'art pour l'art », le slogan de Théophile Gautier, et il n'est que de lire *Les Fleurs du mal* de Baudelaire, et les divers poèmes de Verlaine et de Rimbaud, pour voir comment une inspiration toujours personnelle, toujours lyrique, toujours sentimentale, se coule dans des formes plus rigoureuses, plus exigeantes, plus raffinées. Cette évolution aboutit à Mallarmé, le précieux par excellence qui, lorsqu'il pleut, se refuse par principe à dire « il pleut ». Sa descendance est indéfinie et infinie à la fois ; à l'heure actuelle, elle sévit toujours.

Proust   En revanche, et contre toute attente, la préciosité déjà illustrée par Gide permit au roman romantique-réaliste d'atteindre un nouveau sommet : Marcel Proust, réalisant ce prodige d'être un précieux de tempérament et d'avoir le souffle d'un romantique de la grande époque, écrivit cette *Recherche du temps perdu* qui, par-dessus les siècles, fait face au chef d'œuvre baroque de Rabelais. De Proust se réclament généralement les auteurs du « nouveau roman », tels Robbe-Grillet ou Butor, qui se consacrent à ce genre, éminement précieux par le souci du détail, l'importance primordiale donnée à la forme et les airs ésotériques de ses auteurs.

Giraudoux   C'est aussi parmi les précieux qu'il convient de classer Giraudoux, dont les romans sont bien oubliés maintenant, mais dont le théâtre, infiniment raffiné, a pratiquement renouvelé la scène française.

RÉACTION BAROQUE

Le théâtre a également fourni la matière de la réaction baroque : Montherlant (*La Reine morte*), Claudel (*L'Annonce faite à Marie*), Anouilh (*Antigone*), ont cherché le salut de la littérature française dans des effets surprenants, inquiétants ou mystiques. Ils ont réussi chacun dans son genre, sans qu'il soit possible de prévoir s'ils auront une descendance littéraire.

L'anti-théâtre ou théâtre de l'absurde, où brillent les Ionesco, les Beckett, les Adamov, semble être au baroque ce que le nouveau roman est au précieux : peut-être une nouvelle aurore, peut-être un crépuscule.

RÉACTION CLASSIQUE

Le fantôme du classicisme hante les Français littéraires comme celui de la monarchie, les politiques. Mais quant à créer tout un mouvement stylistique cherchant à imposer des valeurs d'harmonie, de naturel, de proportions, qui le pourrait ? Ni les structures sociales ni l'internationalisme croissant des lettres ne s'y prêtent. Camus et Sartre ont contribué davantage au renouvellement des idées qu'à celui des formes. Saint-Exupéry, dans *Vol de nuit*, a bien tenté de tirer le meilleur parti des valeurs classiques, mais il est devenu le maître à penser d'une partie de la jeunesse plutôt qu'un novateur du style ; et le tempérament classique de Julien Green ne fait que souligner son isolement parmi les écrivains contemporains qui semblent plus dispersés qu'ils ne l'ont jamais été.

Ce morcellement des tendances, cette usure des styles, correspond aussi à un épuisement de l'inspiration. L'importance accordée aux écrivains en a considérablement baissé. Il y a quarante ans, des dizaines de milliers d'ouvriers saluaient, le poing levé, un André Gide dont ils n'avaient pas lu une ligne et qu'ils prenaient pour un socialiste. Aujourd'hui, les ouvriers sont à peine socialistes eux-mêmes et ils ne croient plus aux livres : ils ont la télévision. Les bourgeois, qui lisaient naguère, se sentent démodés s'ils lisent ce qu'ils comprennent et s'ennuient en lisant ce qu'ils ne comprennent pas. Quant aux intellectuels, ils n'ont plus le temps de lire : ils écrivent tous.

5   ÉVOLUTION DE L'ARCHITECTURE

IDÉE GÉNÉRALE

L'architecture, d'une façon très générale, peut être définie comme l'art de faire tenir un toit sur des supports verticaux. Deux considérations principales entrent dès l'abord en jeu. Premièrement, quel usage fera-t-on de l'édifice ? Deuxièmement, quels matériaux a-t-on à sa disposition pour construire les supports ?

L'avantage de l'architecture sur les autres arts, c'est qu'elle doit d'abord résoudre des questions pratiques, ce qui lui rend la fioriture, la rhétorique, la gratuité plus difficiles. Du moins était-ce vrai jusqu'à l'invention du béton armé, qui, affranchissant l'architecture de ses servitudes « fonctionnelles », rend toute les formes possibles et n'en justifie aucune.

En Gaule, à la fin de l'Empire romain, on construisait de grands bâtiments en petites briques collées les unes aux autres par une sorte de ciment et étayées par une charpente de bois. De tout cela, presque rien ne reste. Ce ne fut que lorsqu'on se décida à utiliser de nouveau la pierre (XIème siècle) et à lui obéir — car l'architecte doit obéir à son matériau pour le maîtriser — qu'on retrouva une architecture digne de ce nom.

En pierre, on construisit des forteresses appelées châteaux-forts et des églises. Les châteaux devaient être capables de résister à des machines de guerre d'où les tours rondes, les remparts, les donjons, que bâtirent à l'envi les seigneurs féodaux et les villes libres (château de Coucy, fortifications de Carcassonne), tant que l'artillerie ne les rendit pas caducs. Les églises, elles, devaient abriter un nombre toujours croissant de fidèles. Les formes que prirent ces édifices sont déjà contenues dans ces impératifs. La France était un pays chrétien. Chrétien signifie, entre autres choses, passionné de Dieu. Dieu se présentait aux Français contenu tout entier dans son Église. Il n'y a donc rien de surprenant à ce que, pendant quatre siècles, le peuple de France ait mis le meilleur de lui-même dans la construction de maisons pour y abriter l'Église de Dieu. Lorsque la foi baissa, l'intérêt pour l'Église baissa aussi, et les Français consacrèrent leurs chefs d'œuvre nouveaux à loger des princes, de jolies femmes ou des conseils municipaux.

L'ARCHITECTURE ROMANE

Permettre à plusieurs centaines de chrétiens d'entendre la messe en même temps, tel était l'objectif des architectes romans. Beaucoup d'entre eux travaillaient pour un ordre religieux et sous la surveillance des supérieurs de cet ordre. Il leur fallait trouver la meilleure solution pour ce problème qui ne datait pas de la veille, mais qui, à mesure que croissaient les populations, devenait toujours plus pressant.

Ils la trouvèrent. D'abord, comme on l'a dit, ils remplacèrent les constructions de petites briques par des édifices de pierre, ce qui leur permit de se débarrasser des charpentes de bois. C'était déjà une bonne chose de faite : en adoptant un matériau noble, ils choisissaient d'échouer ou de réussir glorieusement. Ensuite il leur fallut trouver un moyen de poser le toit sur les murs, ce qui n'était pas si facile s'ils ne voulaient pas renoncer à leur matériau. Ce moyen fut quelquefois *la coupole* et, dans la majorité des cas, *la voûte*.

Dans une architecture de pierre, tout tient dans la voûte, parce qu'il faut que la voûte tienne où elle est. D'où les piliers et, pour soutenir une poussée de plus en plus forte à mesure que les édifices devenaient plus grands, les contreforts.

Pour les piliers, on pouvait s'inspirer des colonnes romaines, mais on les voulait plus robustes. Aussi leurs bases furent-elles élargies, et seuls les chapiteaux eurent-ils droit aux ornements sculptés.

Les murs eux-mêmes portaient toujours une bonne partie de la poussée : il en fallait donc de solides, sans trop de fantaisie. On percerait des fenêtres où on pourrait, et généralement le plus haut possible, dans les parois de la nef centrale, plus haut que le toit des bas-côtés. De là, ces églises noyées d'ombre dans leur partie inférieure, et pleines de lumière dorée filtrant par les vitraux dans les hauteurs.

À l'extérieur, comme il était nécessaire d'appeler régulièrement à la prière des fidèles qui n'avaient pas de montre, et que le seul moyen qu'on connût pour ce faire était la cloche, on avait besoin d'un clocher. Et ce clocher, généralement carré ou octogonal, rarement rond, fut incorporé à l'église, se dressant soit au-dessus de l'entrée, soit au croisement du transept et de la nef, soit sur le côté.

Il est bon quelquefois de jouer aux adjectifs : sobre, pesant, harmonieux, noble, mâle, lyrique, foisonnant, le roman est un art de haute époque qui ne daigne pas mépriser la rhétorique et l'effet : il les ignore. Devant un édifice roman, on songe à la musique grégorienne et au ciel étoilé. C'est que l'austérité en est radieuse et comme royale.

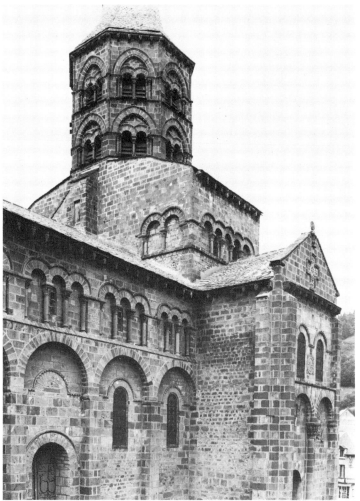

*Noblesse du roman :
Orcival.*

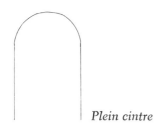

Plein cintre

Arc en berceau brisé ou en ogive (déjà connu du roman, mais surtout utilisé par le gothique)

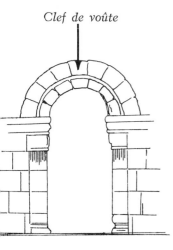

Clef de voûte

Voûte en plein cintre

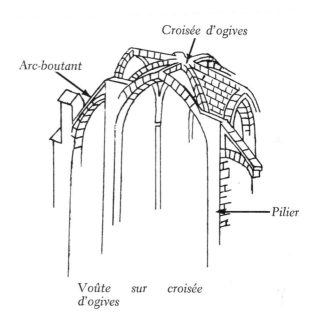

Croisée d'ogives

Arc-boutant

Pilier

Voûte sur croisée d'ogives

Gothique flamboyant

Gothique de haute époque

Gothique rayonnant

Outre les joies esthétique et spirituelle qu'on en retire, on ne peut s'empêcher de constater que sa rondeur plaisante, son équilibre un peu lourd, l'organisation simple et puissante de ses masses et de ses volumes, bref ce qu'il a de majestueux et de débonnaire à la fois, en font un des meilleurs témoins de l'ancienne France — celle, par exemple, de Louis VI dit le Gros, dit aussi l'Éveillé, dit aussi le Batailleur.

L'ARCHITECTURE GOTHIQUE

Le temps passait ; les villes croissaient et multipliaient. Permettre à plusieurs *milliers* de chrétiens d'entendre la messe en même temps devint le problème de l'heure, et il se posait au clergé séculier plutôt que régulier. Autrement dit, il fallait agrandir les églises. On s'y employa. La voûte sur croisée d'ogives fut découverte, ou plutôt — car on la connaissait déjà — on en constata les mérites techniques : puissance, souplesse. Le gothique était né.

Selon les romantiques du XIXème siècle, qui ont remis le gothique à la mode, ses aiguilles effilées exprimaient un élan vers Dieu qu'on n'avait pas connu jusqu'alors ; ses clochers ressemblaient à des index pointés vers le ciel ; ses nefs, à des forêts chantant le Seigneur. Actuellement, les amateurs éclairés vouent à ce style une admiration moins rhétorique et pensent qu'il vaut

Lyrisme du roman : Vézelay.

Roman : rustique harmonie des formes les plus simples.

Roman : symbolisme religieux de l'anecdote, imagination plastique déchaînée.

Gothique : élégance recherchée, jaillissement des lignes.

Gothique : utilisation concertée des motifs décoratifs.

mieux expliquer le gothique esthétiquement, par la voûte sur croisée d'ogives, plutôt que littérairement, par une religiosité passionnée.

L'idée en était simple. Au lieu de faire porter le poids de la voûte par deux murs, ou deux piliers, étayés de contreforts, on allait répartir cette poussée entre quatre points d'application placés en carré.

De là, l'utilisation généralisée de l'ogive avec tous les motifs d'ornementation que cette forme géométrique nouvelle portait en elle.

De là aussi, assouplissement du système de contreforts, par l'adoption des arcs-boutants, qui transmettaient la poussée de la voûte par voie aérienne, sans prendre d'espace au sol.

De là encore, suppression radicale — ou presque — des murs, qui n'avaient plus de mission de portance, et qu'on pouvait avantageusement remplacer par des surfaces de verre.

De là enfin, la possibilité de construire des églises beaucoup plus hautes, beaucoup plus larges, beaucoup plus longues, et d'y loger autant de monde qu'on voudrait. La nef de Beauvais a 47 mètres de hauteur ; celle d'Amiens en a 145 de longueur. Vastes, claires, élancées, les nouvelles églises étaient prêtes à prendre dans le monde la place qu'elles y tiendraient pendant des siècles et qu'elles y tiennent encore, sous le beau nom de « cathédrales ».

Verticalité du gothique : Amiens.

*L'architecture
gothique se couvre de
sculpture : Amiens.*

L'IDÉE DE CATHÉDRALE

Plus que les églises romanes, les églises gothiques, du fait même qu'elles étaient urbaines, gigantesque et construites pour les laïcs, participent du mythe de la cathédrale, chef d'œuvre collectif.

Malraux ne s'y est pas trompé, lui qui écrit dans *La Condition humaine* que l'usine doit devenir la cathédrale du communisme. Il s'agit là, sans doute, d'un espoir frivole : l'usine a pour but de produire des biens de consommation, tandis que la cathédrale ne produit que des biens spirituels — d'où sa capacité d'unir les hommes.

« Si tu veux unir les hommes, disait Saint-Exupéry, donne-leur une tour à construire ensemble. » Oui, ou une cathédrale.

L'absence d'architecte — le maître d'œuvre ordonnait moins qu'il ne coordonnait — et la succession des générations qui travaillaient au même édifice auraient pu, auraient dû, se traduire par une discordance profonde

Un homme de chez nous, de la glèbe féconde
A fait jaillir ici d'un seul enlèvement,
Et d'une seule source et d'un seul portement,
Vers votre assomption la flèche unique au monde.
Tour de David, voici votre tour beauceronne.
C'est l'epi le plus dur qui soit jamais monté
Vers un ciel de clémence et de sérénité,
Et le plus beau fleuron dedans votre couronne.
Un homme de chez nous a fait ici jaillir,
Depuis le ras du sol jusqu'au pied de la croix,
Plus haut que tous les saints, plus haut que tous les rois,
La flèche irréprochable et qui ne peut faillir.
C'est la gerbe et le blé qui ne périra point,
Qui ne fanera point au soleil de septembre,
Qui ne gèlera point aux rigueurs de décembre,
C'est votre serviteur et c'est votre témoin.
C'est la tige et le blé qui ne pourrira pas,
Qui ne flétrira point aux ardeurs de l'été,
Qui ne moisira point dans un hiver gâté,
Qui ne transira point dans le commun trépas.
C'est la pierre sans tache et la pierre sans faute,
La plus haute oraison qu'on ait jamais portée,
La plus droite raison qu'on ait jamais jetée,
Et vers un ciel sans bord la ligne la plus haute.

PÉGUY

dans les styles, ou alors par un froid attachement à la lettre de la première conception. Il n'en est rien. Une cathédrale gothique est à elle seule un monde fourmillant de variété, sans que cette variété détruise jamais l'harmonie de l'ensemble. Depuis les labyrinthes inscrits dans son pavage et que les pénitents avaient coutume de suivre à genoux, jusqu'à la fine dentelle de son aiguille déchirant les nuages, et en passant par les sculptures de ses portails, le mystère de ses chapelles latérales dédiées à des saints différents et ornées de la façon la plus bigarrée possible, les petits escaliers en colimaçon qui, à l'intérieur des murs ou des piliers, grimpent vers les clochers ou le triforium, les tombeaux sculptés des évêques, les grilles ouvragées du chœur, les immenses vitraux historiés filtrant et colorant la lumière avec un raffinement inimitable, les fûts de ses colonnes filant d'un seul jet pour aller soutenir les fines nervures de la voûte, tout, dans la cathédrale gothique, participe d'un même esprit, baigne dans la même lumière et sert la même fin. Ce qu'on pourrait appeler la « tolérance stylistique » du gothique est si grande que la plupart des ornements qui ont été ajoutés tardivement dans ces églises (grilles, chaires, bas-reliefs polychromes, crucifix de diverses époques, peintures souvent regrettables) n'en rompent pas l'ardente méditation. Il faut attendre le XVIIIème siècle pour que des bronzes tordus et des bois dorés importés dans les églises y triomphent comme des témoins de Lucifer en terrain conquis.

Au reste, le gothique, qui fut tant décrié dès que la Renaissance eut remis les valeurs classiques à l'ordre du jour — « gothique » fut alors utilisé pendant trois siècles comme un mot péjoratif signifiant barbare, inculte, grossier — portait en lui-même la semence de sa propre destruction. La Renaissance l'acheva peut-être, mais il se mourait déjà, sous les formes exagérées du « rayonnant » et du « flamboyant ».

La Guerre de cent ans, les guerres de religion, la Révolution française, ont gravement détérioré l'héritage gothique français, et quelquefois les architectes chargés des restaurations (XIXème siècle) ont fait encore pis. Il est arrivé à un Viollet-le-Duc de modifier l'original pour, croyait-il, l'améliorer. C'est tout de même à ce romantique que l'on doit d'avoir en quelque sorte ressuscité bien des cathédrales et d'en avoir répandu la vénération. Toutes étant, en une certaine façon, des variations sur un même thème, il a voulu réunir leurs perfections en dessinant une cathédrale idéale, qui a la nef de l'une, le clocher d'une autre et l'abside d'une troisième. Huysmans, lui, a consacré tout un roman à celle de Chartres et Victor Hugo en a dédié un autre à Notre-Dame de Paris.

L'architecture religieuse, en France, est essentiellement démocratique : tous les éléments de la société y ont participé, dans un élan qui, par parenthèse, semble donner un démenti au postulat marxiste concernant la lutte inexpiable des classes. L'architecture laïque, au contraire, est éminemment aristocratique et royale.

Si l'histoire de l'architecture religieuse est aussi celle de la foi, l'histoire de l'architecture laïque est celle de l'art de vivre dans les classes dirigeantes.

LA FRANCE NOBILIAIRE

Les guerres d'Italie (XVIème siècle) — on a tendance, à notre époque, à oublier la profonde influence civilisatrice de la plupart des guerres — révélèrent l'utilité décisive de la poudre à canon et par conséquent l'inutilité de construire des châteaux-forts. Mais elles révélèrent aussi aux Français toute une architecture qu'ils ne connaissaient pas encore : celle des palais italiens.

Première découverte : la fenêtre. Les façades du Moyen Age étaient aveugles, sourcilleuses sous leurs mâchicoulis. Et soudain voilà que, tant pis pour les jours d'arquebusade, on les perce de hautains rectangles aux nobles proportions. L'air entre, et la lumière : la vie en est transformée.

Deuxième découverte : l'espace. Au Moyen Age, l'espace était l'ennemi : il fallait le circonscrire, le mater, le colmater. Maintenant, on l'organise. Au

L'architecture laïque médiévale est, avant tout, fonctionnelle, comme le montrent les lourdes formes du donjon de Loches.

lieu des gigantesques pans de pierre dont les créneaux seuls rompaient la monotonie, on élève des murs dont on fait moduler la surface de toutes les façons possibles : par des vides (fenêtres), par des changements de matériau (brique et pierre), par des modifications de forme (corniches et bandeaux pour découper l'édifice en bandes horizontales, colonnes et pilastres pour en scander le rythme vertical).

A vrai dire, le sens de l'espace n'avait jamais fait défaut aux architectes français, et les églises romanes, en particulier, sont là pour en faire foi ; mais, en attendant la Renaissance, ils n'avaient guère l'occasion de le prouver que dans des édifices de caractère religieux. Aussi, dès qu'ils le purent, s'en donnèrent-ils à cœur joie, et l'arrangement intérieur des salons en enfilade de même que la disposition extérieure des corps-de-logis, ailes, tours et pavillons traduisent-ils un engouement passionné pour ce qu'on pourrait appeler « l'aménagement du vide ».

Troisième découverte : l'Antiquité. Tantôt par l'intermédiaire de l'architecture italienne, tantôt en en prenant le contrepied, les Français accèdent au prodigieux univers de beauté plastique de l'Antiquité. Plastique et païenne, bien entendu. C'est d'un même amour dévorant que les artistes français se prennent pour les nymphes et pour les colonnes antiques, et la sensualité entre pour autant dans leur extase que la géométrie. Simultanément, ils découvrent la radieuse splendeur du corps féminin où ils ne voient plus seulement la beauté du diable, et les trois ordres architecturaux qui les attendaien, dans un rendez-vous immuable, sur les bords de la Méditerranée : le grave dorique, l'ionique souriant et le corinthien luxurieux.

Alors, dans un étonnant mouvement de renouvellement, la France se met à construire — du moins les rois, et les nobles les plus riches du royaume. Les hobereaux demeurent toujours perchés dans leurs nids d'aigle d'Auvergne ou du Limousin, un œil collé à la meurtrière, regardant le monde se transformer à leurs pieds.

Châteaux de la Loire   Comme la Loire est le séjour favori des princes, et que les rois ont déjà une cour importante, sans compter les maîtresses et les mignons, la Loire se couvre de châteaux « modernes ». Il faut en connaître les noms, parce qu'ils sont si français et qu'ils chantent si bien : Chenonceaux, Chambord, Amboise, Azay-le-Rideau...

Étrange à dire, leurs architectes ont immédiatement découvert tout le pittoresque des anciens châteaux-forts et n'ont abandonné ni la tour, ni le créneau, ni le mâchicoulis ; mais ils n'en utilisent que les formes élégantes, ne se souciant plus d'aucune utilité martiale. Ainsi les chemins de ronde deviennent des galeries couvertes, et les douves, de clairs miroirs d'eau.

Paris   Les mêmes transformations atteignent Paris. Le vieux Louvre médiéval et lugubre disparaît, remplacé par un palais dont les nobles proportions ne sont pas déparées par le chatoiement de ses façades de pierre jaune, dont les sculptures, les moulures, les balustrades, les frontons, reflètent avec bonheur la lumière subtile de l'Ile-de-France.

A Amboise, au massif donjon médiéval, s'accole la façade plus riante du château Renaissance.

Aux XVIIème et XVIIIème, on continua bien à construire des châteaux en province — en brique à coins de pierre sous Louis XIII, en pierre sous Louis XIV et Louis XV ; mais l'influence croissante de la royauté concentra dans les villes une bonne partie de l'architecture française.

Vauban les entoura de ses fortifications en dents de scie : il fallut deux siècles et demi de progrès militaire pour que ce type de fortification fût depassé.

Dans les cités elles-mêmes, l'architecture religieuse, en déclin depuis la fin du Moyen Age, éleva des églises néoclassiques à coupoles et à frontons de style dit jésuite.

L'urbanisme fut découvert. Sous Louis XIII, l'aménagement systématique du quartier du Marais à Paris en donna le signal : des hôtels, c'est-à-dire des maisons de ville d'une élégance distinguée, y furent construits pour les grandes familles.

Les plus grands architectes construisirent des *places*, ces ouvrages où le génie latin se révèle d'une manière si spécifique. De la place des Vosges, d'un style Henri IV rustaud mais chaleureux, à la place de la Concorde, d'un style Louis XV à la fois majestueux et exquis, on peut suivre le raffinement progressif du goût. Après tout, il est plus facile de faire des pleins que d'organiser des vides. Qu'est-ce qu'une place ? Un espace rond ou carré où se rencontrent plusieurs rues et que limitent des édifices harmonieux. Mais un grand architecte peut en faire un chef d'œuvre. Sauf erreur, le dramaturge Sacha Guitry disait que le silence qui suit une œuvre de Mozart est de Mozart aussi : de la même façon, l'air qui flotte place de la Concorde est signé Gabriel.

Versailles C'est pourtant en dehors de toute agglomération que s'élève le principal monument du classicisme : Versailles. D'un petit pavillon de chasse qui servait à Henri IV, son fils Louis XIII fit un agréable château à quelque distance de Paris. Flanqué de marais d'un côté, mais de forêts de l'autre, il était à la fois insalubre et commode. De ce passé campagnard, aristocratique et bon enfant, l'actuel palais conserve ce qui est son corps-de-logis central, une gentilhommière à peine plus riche, à peine plus vaste que des centaines d'autres construites en France à la même époque. Tout le reste est l'œuvre de Louis XIV et symbolise parfaitement ce spectacle grandiose que fut la royauté sous le roi-soleil : il n'était plus question que la demeure du souverain ressemblât à celle de ses sujets.

Du côté de la ville, les diverses ailes s'organisent assez mal ; les styles successifs s'y accordent heureusement mais les masses se chevauchent, et il faut bien connaître le château — l'immense palais porte le nom distingué et modeste de « château » — pour reconnaître son visage dans l'enchevêtrement des lignes et des plans. La ligne des toits est rompue par celui de la chapelle et celui du théâtre ; les ailes des ministres manquent de grâce ; ce n'est qu'une fois dans la cour d'honneur qu'on a tout loisir pour admirer l'exquise cour de Marbre qui, entre ses trois façades Louis XIII, forme une scène parfaitement décorée, où fut jouée plus d'une comédie de Molière.

Du côté des jardins, c'est tout autre chose, c'est le triomphe du Louis XIV dans toute sa splendeur : c'est la gageure, tenue et réussie, de concilier le simple, l'orné et le grandiose, car à une époque où toute l'Europe était plongée dans le baroque, la France seule s'en tenait à un classicisme non moins somptueux.

La façade est composée sur un rythme ternaire : un corps-de-logis central avancé, de vingt-trois fenêtres ; deux ailes placées en retrait, de trente-quatre fenêtres chacune. La supériorité de l'impair sur le pair donne une prééminence mathématique au logis central. Le rythme ternaire y est repris par des groupes de trois fenêtres, séparés soit par des pilastres, soit par des statues, soit par des fenêtres isolées, elles-mêmes encadrées de colonnes. A la verticale, le rythme est également ternaire, puisque la façade comprend trois étages,

> *Douces colonnes, ô*
> *L'orchestre de fuseaux !*
> *Chacune immole son*
> *Silence à l'unisson.*
> *Que portez-vous si haut,*
> *Égales radieuses ?*
> *— Au désir sans défaut*
> *Nos grâces studieuses !...*
> *Vois quels hymnes candides !*
> *Quelle sonorité*
> *Nos éléments limpides*
> *Tirent de la clarté !*
> *Si froides et dorées*
> *Nous fûmes de nos lits*
> *Par le ciseau tirées,*
> *Pour devenir ces lys !...*
> *Un temple sur les yeux*
> *Noirs pour l'éternité,*
> *Nous allons sans les dieux*
> *A la divinité !...*
> *Filles des nombres d'or,*
> *Fortes des lois du ciel,*
> *Sur nous tombe et s'endort*
> *Un dieu couleur de miel.*
>
> VALÉRY

celui du milieu étant orné avec plus de pompe que le supérieur et l'inférieur. Tous les intervalles verticaux sont couronnés par un vase ou une panoplie sculptée dressés dans le ciel : il y en a vingt-quatre, et le logis central apparaît ainsi, pourrait-on dire, comme un distique d'alexandrins à la prosodie exemplaire.

Toute cette géométrie, toute cette mathématique, est d'ailleurs musicale et symbolique à la fois. La chambre de Louis XIV est placée au centre de l'édifice, de telle façon que les premiers rayons du soleil viennent frapper la tête du roi dans son lit, après avoir couronné la statue d'Apollon, au fond du parc. Il y a tout un ésotérisme solaire de Versailles, que le paganisme classique autorise et qui s'oppose à l'ésotérisme chrétien des cathédrales. Seulement, les cathédrales étaient l'œuvre d'une collectivité au service d'un Dieu-Homme ; Versailles est l'œuvre d'un homme-dieu qui se glorifie lui-même. Mansart, Le Nôtre, ont bien construit le château et dessiné les jardins, mais toute la conception, mystique et royale, en est de Louis XIV.

Les jardins   Les jardins méritent des volumes à eux tout seuls. Le Nôtre, génie complet, utilise toutes les ressources de l'architecture, de la géométrie, de la botanique, de la sculpture, de la physique, de l'optique et de la douceur de vivre. Il mêle avec un art consommé ces éléments de *surprise* et de *sécurité* que connaissent bien les poètes classiques : les grandes avenues rectilignes offrant la sécurité, et ce qu'on trouve au bout, la surprise. Il compose la nature des bosquets avec l'humanisme des statues. Il accapare l'eau, immuable et verte dans les bassins, jaillissante en poussière dans les fontaines ; la terre, d'où sourdent les grands arbres, les massifs de fleurs, les bordures de buis, le tout taillé, mesuré, ordonné ; l'air, qu'il découpe en longues perspectives, qu'il colore des reflets de ses pièces d'eau et de ses gazons. Il ne restera plus, les soirs de fête, qu'à lancer le feu d'artifice sur le Grand Canal, pour que tous les éléments naturels se mettent au service du roi. On a beaucoup parlé du mariage de la verdure et de la pierre : ce n'est qu'un des aspects de cet art des jardins, qui créa de tels chefs d'œuvre pendant un siècle ou deux et qui a complètement disparu depuis lors.

Le Grand Trianon   Le « château » de Versailles avait été construit pour le roi, sa famille, ses quelque trois mille courtisans et leurs dix mille domestiques. La plus haute noblesse se piquait d'y habiter : le roi était plus heureux ailleurs, à Marly, ou dans ce Grand Trianon qu'il tenait pour villégiature. L'art classique s'y est fait plus aimable, moins pompeux ; les marbres gris et roses y ont une délicatesse de coloration qui suggère la douceur de vivre, mais l'ordonnance en est toujours solennelle ; maison de campagne, si l'on veut, c'est celle du roi de France, il n'y a pas à s'y tromper.

Le Petit Trianon   Du baroque, l'Europe versait dans le rococo. La France, classique de tempérament, adopta, du moins pour la décoration intérieure, le *rocaille*, baroque aussi mais moins agressif. Au contraire l'architecture proprement dite, délaissant la pompe pour la grâce, évoluait dans le sens d'un goût de plus en plus pur, sans la moindre mièvrerie. Le Petit Trianon, du

Le classicisme du Grand Trianon proclame encore les conceptions de grandeur du XVIIème siècle, avec ses grilles, son marbre rose, ses pilastres, ses fenêtres en plein cintre couronnées de guirlandes.

Au XVIIIème, les proportions et le rythme sont déjà presque seuls à composer l'élégance du Petit Trianon, dont la façade sobre aux angles droits n'a pas d'autre ornement que ses quatre colonnes corinthiennes.

même Gabriel que la place de la Concorde, est aussi parfait de proportions, aussi ambitieux de pureté, qu'un temple grec. En fait, avec ses fenêtres rectangulaires, sa façade dépourvue d'ornements, sa toiture plate que masque une balustrade sans sculptures, il est encore beaucoup plus « classique » que le château de Versailles.

Mais la taille en est révélatrice : cinq fenêtres de façade au lieu de quatre-vingt-onze : quelque chose avait changé dans la monarchie française.

Sans doute, comme tous les chiffres, ceux-ci sont-ils naturellement menteurs. Versailles est la résidence du roi ; Trianon, d'une de ses maîtresses. Mais l'idée même de construire petit indiquait une nouvelle conception de la vie : le Moyen Age n'avait connu ni confort ni vrai luxe ; la Renaissance avait apporté le goût du luxe italien ; le XVIIIème commençait à s'intéresser au confort anglais : la décadence n'était pas loin.

Hameau   Non contents de s'intéresser, sous l'influence de Voltaire, à la civilisation des Anglais et de leur emprunter leur sens, tout relatif, du confort, les hommes du XVIIIème prétendirent aussi imiter leurs jardins, dont le faux naturel contrastait avec le vrai artificiel de la tradition française. Sous Louis XVI — voir le Hameau de Marie-Antoinette — on fit serpenter de petites rivières entre des berges dessinées par des paysagistes, sous des ponts de bois d'un goût champêtre ; on leur fit tourner des moulins qui ne moulaient rien ; on y mit à nager des carpes qu'on ne pêchait pas. On s'organisa pour rêver commodément : le romantisme — le moins architectural des styles et le moins aristocratique — approchait à pas de géants.

LA FRANCE BOURGEOISE

Quoi qu'on en dise, la noblesse française survécut fort bien à la Révolution, mais non son génie. Sous la Renaissance, aux XVIIème et XVIIIème siècles, l'air était si bien pénétré soit de grandeur soit de raffinement, que les financiers eux-mêmes se faisaient construire des châteaux qui avaient de l'allure. Au XIXème, on construisit encore quelques belles maisons, auxquelles l'austérité du style Empire seyait bien ; mais ce n'étaient plus que des maisons bourgeoises, à qui qu'elles appartinssent. Et de celles-là même le secret s'évapora bientôt.

Ce qui est simple est toujours tolérable, même dénué de grâce, d'intelligence et de charme. Mais si l'on cherche à faire pompeux, il faut se garder de tomber dans le pompier[1] : le XIXème s'en garda fort mal.

Sans doute est-on toujours tenté de parler plus longuement de ce qui est beau, en escamotant les laideurs d'une civilisation ; sans doute trouverait-on agréable de pouvoir dire : le XIXème français ne bâtit rien. Hélas, il bâtit beaucoup. Et tout semblait conspirer pour lui faire bâtir les édifices les plus laids possibles.

[1] terme d'argot artistique désignant ce qui est prétentieux, solennel, de mauvais goût

D'une part, la révolution industrielle en égalisant les fortunes restreignait le sens aristocratique du luxe. Il est bien évident qu'un château se prête mieux à des effets d'élégance noble qu'un immeuble d'appartements locatifs,

D'autre part, on ne saurait nier que le goût avait baissé, que, par un de ces phénomènes d'épuisement qui se rencontrent dans l'histoire de tous les peuples, les architectes français se voyaient abandonnés par l'inspiration.

Qu'on ajoute à cela la disparition progressive de l'artisanat et l'introduction des méthodes industrielles, donc approximatives, et l'on verra que les perspectives de l'architecture française au XIXème siècle n'étaient rien moins que riantes. Mais il y avait pire.

Le XIXème correspond à l'avènement des classes bourgeoises, dont la grandeur ne s'appuyait que sur l'argent. « Faire riche » était donc une de leurs préoccupations essentielles. Souvent, elles voulurent faire riche en imitant les excès du baroque étranger qui, au siècle précédent, avaient eu l'excuse de la nouveauté et d'une sorte de folie. Le baroque rassis du XIXème n'en avait aucune : de là tout ce qu'on peut voir à Paris et qui a été construit sous Louis-Philippe, sous Napoléon III et sous la Troisième République. La province ne fut guère épargnée non plus. Du moins y voyait-on moins grand.

L'Opéra de Paris, avec ses colonnes, ses dorures, ses frises, ses arcades, ses statues, son fronton, sa coupole (rien n'y manque), est un bon exemple de ce qui passait pour beau en 1875.

Façade surchargée de l'Opéra de Paris, dans le goût bourgeois du XIXème siècle.

Deux éléments ont révolutionné l'architecture française à partir de la fin du XIXème siècle : premièrement, l'introduction du fer et d'autres matériaux nouveaux dans l'industrie du bâtiment ; deuxièmement, l'amélioration rapide du niveau de vie des classes dites laborieuses et, par conséquent, la nécessité de construire des logements décents en grand nombre mais à prix réduit.

Si les architectes du Moyen Age avaient su utiliser le fer à des fins de construction, le problème de la voûte ne se serait pas posé à eux, et c'eût été bien dommage. Avec le fer, en effet, le problème fondamental de l'architecture (mettre un toit sur deux supports) est immédiatement résolu. Or, quand il faut produire beaucoup, la facilité devient indispensable : d'où le succès du fer dans le bâtiment.

Perret   L'architecture de fer pur n'a du reste, à son actif (ou à son passif comme l'on voudra), que la seule Tour Eiffel, assemblée pour prouver que le

Façade du Théâtre des Champs-Elysées, dans le goût épuré et sophistiqué du XXème.

métal était bien un matériau de construction. Le fer servit surtout enrobé de béton. D'abord on coula des façades de fausses pierres ; puis, sous l'impulsion des frères Perret, on se mit à construire en pans de béton, directement. Alors, toutes les formes devinrent possibles : l'architecture moderne prenait corps.

Les frères Perret eux-mêmes ont signé, entre autres œuvres importantes, le Théâtre des Champs-Elysées, à Paris. Par le plan, comme par la décoration, c'est là un monument typique du début du XXème siècle; le goût en est indéniablement plus raffiné que celui de l'Opéra : la France intellectuelle était en train de remplacer la France bourgeoise.

Le Corbusier   Les destructions provoquées par les deux guerres mondiales, le poussée démographique qui suivit la seconde, stimulèrent la construction et la reconstruction. Tandis que Perret se chargeait du Havre, le Suisse Le Corbusier s'occupait de Marseille. Il y construisait, sur pilotis, une cité moderniste qu'il baptisa « La Cité radieuse », mais que les Marseillais s'obstinent à appeler « la cité du fada » (c'est-à-dire du fou).

C'était sans doute méconnaître les vertus de la folie dans tout ce qui touche à l'art. Le Corbusier a tenté de créer une mystique architecturale, à l'échelle de son siècle et même de la postérité. Apôtre du gratte-ciel habitable, prédicateur des espaces verts, il a laissé des milliers de disciples et de rivaux auxquels se posent les mêmes problèmes qu'à lui : (1) loger des

Pas d'ornements ; guère de rythme ; une forme subtilement galbée : la façade de l'UNESCO à Paris montre que l'architecture contemporaine se conçoit comme une sculpture géante.

millions de personnes ; (2) tenter de faire une œuvre d'art avec un ouvrage utilitaire ; (3) découvrir des formes nouvelles.

Artistiquement, on retrouve chez la plupart d'entre eux la même idée : se passer de toute ornementation, faire que l'édifice soit beau en lui-même, que sa masse seule suffise à ravir les yeux. D'où les lignes sobres de l'Unesco, les courbes audacieuses du Palais de la Défense. On ne peut qu'approuver cet idéal résolument classique et s'étonner de la platitude relative des réalisations.

Vues de loin, les résidences modernes construites autour de Paris ne manquent pas d'une certaine grandeur apocalyptique, créneaux immenses suggérant les cosmodromes des temps futurs. De près, elles ressemblent à leurs propres maquettes et alors le cœur se serre à l'idée de tant d'êtres humains parqués Résidence Joie de Vivre, bloc 38, escalier S, appartment 179.

Bref, l'équation

$$\text{gigantisme} + \text{facilité} = \text{beauté}$$

n'est pas encore résolue.

Quant à l'architecture religieuse — qui s'était contentée, au XIXème siècle, d'appliquer sans bonheur les recettes usées du néogothique et du néoroman — elle connaît un certain renouveau. Cathédrales et chapelles de béton armé s'élèvent de tout côté. Il est permis de considérer comme une réussite — de l'art sinon de la dévotion — la chapelle du peintre Henri Matisse dont le toit bleu de roi met une note stridente dans le paysage méditerranéen (ocres et jaunes brûlés) de Vence-la-Jolie.

PEINTURE 6
ET SCULPTURE

IDÉE GÉNÉRALE

Depuis trois quarts de siècle, les idées du public ont été à dessein brouillées, pour tout ce qui concerne les arts plastiques en général et la peinture en particulier.

On commencera donc par rétablir certaines évidences sur lesquelles on fondera tout ce qu'on dira par la suite. Dans cette façon de préambule, on parlera toujours de la peinture, pour simplifier, étant bien entendu que les mêmes réflexions peuvent s'appliquer à la sculpture (ronde-bosse, haut-relief ou bas-relief).

La peinture peut être définie comme une fonction consistant à tracer des lignes et à déposer des couleurs sur une surface.

Dans l'exercice de cette fonction, trois buts peuvent être poursuivis :

(1) *Créer* des assemblages de lignes et de couleurs à partir de sa propre imagination, sans se référer à la nature.

(2) *Reproduire* la nature.

(3) *Représenter* une fraction du réel par des symboles.

Plusieurs remarques s'imposent à ce sujet. Dans le premier cas, il arrive rarement, jamais peut-être, qu'un artiste parvienne à faire de la *création* pure. La plupart du temps, il s'inspire de la nature, ne serait-ce que pour la déformer, et son œuvre participe donc de la *reproduction*.

Dans le second cas, l'artiste ne dispose pas des mêmes moyens que la nature. Par exemple, sa toile n'a que deux dimensions, alors que la nature en a trois. Il se voit donc obligé de recourir à des procédés optiques, tel l'emploi des règles de la perspective ou, au contraire, de contredire le témoignage de ses propres yeux en appliquant à sa peinture d'autres modes de connaissance (tactile ou géométrique) : s'il adopte cette dernière solution, il dessinera un cube avec six faces alors que l'œil humain ne peut en voir que trois généralement, cinq au maximum. Amené à tricher avec la fausse réalité optique, l'artiste est donc conduit à utiliser, même si ses intentions sont de *reproduction* pure, certains éléments de *symbolisme*.

Dans le troisième cas, il arrive sans doute que le symbole n'ait aucun rapport avec la réalité visuelle de l'objet symbolisé : les croix que les jeunes filles anglaises mettent à la fin de leurs lettres pour représenter des baisers appartiennent à cette catégorie. Mais, plus fréquemment, le symbole retient dans son apparence une part de l'aspect de son double réel : ainsi, le troisième cas participe plus ou moins du second. C'est ce qui se passe pour les hiéroglyphes.

Allons plus loin, et, sacrifiant l'exactitude à la clarté, prenons des exemples.

Un motif géométrique, tel qu'on en voit sur les papiers peints, voilà un assemblage de lignes et de couleurs dans lequel l'élément humaniste tend vers zéro et où l'élément décoratif prédomine nettement.

Une photographie, voilà la reproduction la plus fidèle que l'homme sache réaliser de ce qui s'offre à ses propres yeux et à ceux de ses appareils.

L'écriture : qui pourrait rêver un système de symboles visuels plus complexe et plus cohérent ?

Et cependant, les papiers peints, les photographies et les caractères d'imprimerie, ce n'est pas de la peinture.

En d'autres termes, lorsqu'une production à apparence picturale entre parfaitement dans une des trois catégories prévues sans que rien ne dépasse,

---

Quelle vanité que la peinture, qui attire l'admiration par la ressemblance de choses dont on n'admire pas les originaux !

PASCAL

> *La peinture tend bien moins à voir le monde qu'à en créer un autre ; le monde sert le style, qui sert l'homme et ses dieux.*
>
> MALRAUX

il faut conclure que l'apparence est trompeuse, et qu'il ne s'agit pas de peinture proprement dite. Pour qu'il y ait peinture, il faut ambivalence ou ambiguïté, comme on préférera.

La confusion des valeurs dans laquelle nous vivons pour tout ce qui concerne les arts plastiques est encore renforcée par la difficulté de porter un jugement qualitatif simple sur une œuvre qui — nous venons de le voir — est équivoque par définition. Une fois de plus, prenons des exemples. Un portrait entre de toute évidence dans la deuxième catégorie prévue. Prenons-le très ressemblant à son modèle : c'est un bon portrait. Mais est-ce une bonne peinture ? Pas forcément. Pourquoi ? Parce que le dessin peut être grossier, la composition gauche, la couleur terne. Prenons un autre portrait, qui ne ressemble pas, visuellement, à son modèle. Mauvais portrait, soit. Mais peut-être les harmonies de couleur rendent-elles sensible le tempérament du personnage, et ce portrait est-il peint dans un esprit symbolique (troisième catégorie) ? Plus simplement, peut-être le peintre s'est-il simplement inspiré d'un modèle vivant, mais avec le dessein de créer une œuvre originale ? Va-t-on chicaner un créateur sur quelques millimètres de nez ? Si l'on peint une femme de profil et qu'on lui fasse deux yeux parfaitement semblables à l'original mais vus de face, est-on un génie, un farceur, ou doit-on être soupçonné d'avoir le don d'ubiquité ?

Inutile de poursuivre dans cette direction, si le lecteur a compris notre propos : montrer l'origine de l'hébétude qui règne actuellement dans les milieux d'honnêtes gens, et que les critiques entretiennent savamment par des articles écrits dans un jargon délibérément incompréhensible.

Il est d'usage de dire que, traditionnellement, la peinture française vise la vérité. Mais laquelle ? En art, il y en a tant ! C'est ce qu'on s'efforcera de débrouiller ci-dessous.

ARTS PLASTIQUES ROMANS

L'art carolingien, qui précède le roman, nous séduit parce que nous sommes avides de barbarie ; nous aimons ses reliquaires et ses ciboires d'or, éclatant de pierres précieuses grosses comme des œufs. Mais il s'agit là d'œuvres simplettes malgré leur somptuosité, et d'où la notion concertée de création artistique est absente. Passons donc directement au roman.

La peinture romane est constituée essentiellement de fresques. Sur les murs aveugles des basiliques, des peintres anonymes badigeonnaient leurs visions qui, au même titre que les mosaïques byzantines ou les icônes russes, participent de la troisième catégorie (la symbolique) bien plus que de la deuxième (celle des reproductions). En revanche, c'est surtout pour son originalité plastique (première catégorie) que nous l'apprécions, tout en rendant hommage à sa richesse spirituelle qui nous échappe quelque peu.

La Colère, fresque romane, en est un bon exemple. Ces lignes échevelées, ce visage qui ressemble à peine à un visage, cette lance infiniment cruelle, ces couleurs rendant un accord si lugubre, tout cela forme un ensemble d'une extrême audace artistique. La notion de représentation pseudoréaliste est totalement étrangère au peintre roman : il veut peindre « la colère » et se trouverait ridicule de dessiner le portrait d'une dame ou d'un monsieur plus ou moins fâchés. Ce qu'il vise, c'est l'essentiel et non le particulier.

On a conservé peu de vestiges de la peinture romane française. En revanche, la sculpture abonde. C'est une sculpture essentiellement ornementale, qui ne se prend pas pour une fin en soi, qui veut seulement décorer tel édifice religieux : elle est la servante attentionnée de l'architecture.

De là, ces formes figées ; de là, ces garde-à-vous de saints verticalement noyés dans la muraille de pierre ; de là, ces draperies de granit qui sont si belles et qui ressemblent si peu à des draperies de drap. Il s'agit de placer un roi dans cette voussure. Parfait. Que sait-on des rois ? Ils ont une couronne, une barbe et un manteau. C'est leur essence. Surtout la barbe et la couronne,

Se refusant à tout réalisme, la Colère, fresque romane, *joint le symbolisme mystique à une audace plastique peu ordinaire.*

évidemment : on les fignolera donc. Mais qu'on ne s'y trompe pas. Le sculpteur roman, loin d'être naïf, est au contraire un petit malin. Ce n'est pas à lui qu'on ferait prendre un pan de pierre pour un pan de tissu. Il ne méprise pas son public au point d'espérer faire passer du caillou pour de la moustache. Le roi lui-même n'étant qu'un objet décoratif, sa moustache, sa couronne, son manteau, seront eux aussi des objets décoratifs, stylisés à outrance en accord avec leur rôle symbolique plus qu'avec leur apparence physique. Collées quelquefois aux fûts des colonnes avec lesquelles elles ne font qu'un, les sculptures romanes vont, plus souvent encore, se jucher sur les chapiteaux. Là, les sculpteurs-décorateurs sont vraiment à leur affaire. Avec un sens exemplaire de l'espace, ils bourrent ces cônes tronqués et renversés de scènes édifiantes réduites à leur plus stricte, leur plus éloquente expression de pierre. Comme il faut bien changer de sujet, et sous prétexte d'expliquer aux illettrés ce que sont les péchés capitaux, les sculpteurs retracent parfois d'autres scènes, beaucoup moins édifiantes, respirant la verdeur la plus gauloise, et dont cependant le spiritualisme médiéval — qui n'avait pas encore inventé le puritanisme — s'accommodait fort bien.

En d'autres termes, l'art plastique roman, sculpté aussi bien que peint, est résolument expressionniste : il est destiné à représenter des vérités d'ordre général, telles qu'elles sont conçues par l'artiste.

ARTS PLASTIQUES GOTHIQUES

L'art gothique, prenant le contrepied de son prédécesseur et ancêtre, tendra à représenter des vérités particulières, telles qu'elles sont vues par l'artiste et par son public. On pourrait parler d'impressionnisme, si cette vision n'était pas, le plus souvent, marquée d'une certaine idéalisation dûe au sujet et qui sauve le gothique des platitudes du réalisme.

Sculpture   En sculpture, le changement est frappant. Ces rois, ces saints, ces patriarches, qui n'étaient que des blocs de pierre, deviennent troncs, arbres, se détachent de leurs murs et de leurs colonnes, tournent la tête, lèvent le bras, avancent le pied. C'est toute une façade de cathédrale qui, dans un immense frémissement, vient de faire un pas en avant.

Cette métamorphose suppose évidemment un progrès énorme non pas du sentiment artistique mais de la technique. Les artistes gothiques peuvent risquer de faire ressemblant : ils sont sûrs de réussir. Ils réussissent en effet, et, grâce à l'inspiration qui anime leurs doigts, ils créent des formes admirables par elles-mêmes, indépendamment de leur similitude avec le réel. Ivres de lumière, ils composent les modelés les plus savants, jouent avec l'expression du visage autant qu'avec l'équilibre du corps, et peignent, à la pointe du ciseau, de miraculeux sourires de granit.

Les ornements proprement dits, géométriques ou végétaux, envahissent les chapiteaux, tandis que les sujets humanistes sont réservés aux portails et, principalement, aux tympans. Avec une utilisation de l'espace qui ne le cède

*Un réalisme noblement idéalisé carac-
térise la sculpture gothique en général
et le* Beau Dieu d'Amiens *en particulier.*

en rien ni aux maîtres antiques composant des frontons triangulaires ni aux artisans romans meublant leurs pleins cintres, les gothiques tirent des effets saisissants de la disposition en ogive. Loin de servir les architectes, les sculpteurs se servent d'eux maintenant : tout leur est prétexte à tailler dans la pierre de la chair qui ressemble à de la chair, et de la soie qui ressemble à de la soie.

Bien entendu, cette réussite porte en elle-même le germe de sa propre décadence : dès que l'inspiration créatrice fera défaut, on sombrera dans l'académisme et la virtuosité.

Peinture　L'évolution de la peinture est, chose curieuse, plus lente.

A la fin de la période romane, les murs des églises disparaissent et les fresques avec eux : les vitraux les remplacent. Les peintres se réfugient donc dans l'enluminure de manuscrits et dans le travail sur panneaux de bois servant d'ornements pour chaires ou pour retables : deux peintures aussi dissemblables par la technique que par le propos. En effet, les enlumineurs ont pour premier objectif de décorer le manuscrit : ils ne représentent des scènes ou des paysages que pour varier les motifs d'ornementation. Le but des peintres sur bois est surtout de raconter la vie d'un saint ou un incident dans la vie d'un saint : la peinture n'étant pas, en soi, un genre favorable au récit, l'artiste utilise tour à tour le vocabulaire de la représentation visuelle et celui de la représentation symbolique, celui-ci plus souvent que celui-là, et s'efforce d'en obtenir des effets complémentaires.

Aucun souci de réalisme, au sens moderne du mot, ne vient gêner l'imagi-nation des peintres gothiques, qu'ils travaillent dans la miniature ou dans le gros. Le fond du tableau est fréquemment une feuille d'or qui ne représente rien. L'Enfant Jésus, étant Dieu, ne ressemble pas du tout à un enfant d'homme. Le portrait du personnage contemporain qui paie le tableau est introduit dans une scène antique sans aucun scruple d'authenticité. La perspective encore très hésitante permet un aménagement beaucoup plus artistique de l'espace pictural. Bref, le peintre gothique cherche à faire un tableau avec les moyens dont il dispose (souci de première catégorie) beaucoup plus qu'à imiter le réel.

Mais, comme peindre ne suffit pas — il faut bien peindre quelque chose — l'artiste gothique, avec une humilité exemplaire, décide de s'inspirer du réel, dans la mesure où le réel ne contredit pas ses intentions religieuses et esthétiques. Ainsi les saints de l'Antiquité seront représentés avec des visages, des vêtements, des outils contemporains, sans que l'artiste s'inquiète jamais du mythe de la couleur locale.

En fait, la peinture gothique française est une des plus complètes qui soient, et il y a quelque chose de piquant à voir ces artistes, dont les intentions étaient d'abord purement religieuses, réaliser des chefs d'œuvre plastiques sans s'en douter.

Tels furent Jean Fouquet, le Maître de Moulins, l'auteur plus ou moins anonyme de la *Pietà d'Avignon*, tous soucieux de vérité religieuse, passant tous par la vérité psychologique et aboutissant tous à la vérité esthétique.

La Pietà d'Avignon, *tragédie religieuse transmuée en chef d'œuvre plastique.*

La Renaissance arrive, et la France se met à l'école de l'Italie. Pour les peintres français, il s'agit tout d'abord de se débarrasser de leur héritage religieux, ce qui ne va pas sans difficulté ; puis de se familiariser avec les sujets nouveaux, surtout mythologiques et nus ; enfin de digérer les techniques nouvelles, étincelantes et complexes, qui, en Italie, progressent constamment. Cela fait, ils pourront créer un style bien à eux, mais au XVème et au XVIème siècles ils n'en sont encore qu'à l'imitation sauf pour ce qui est du portrait.

Dès le XIVème siècle, avec le portrait du roi Jean le Bon, les artistes français ont trouvé un mode d'expression qui leur convient parfaitement. Sobre, incisif, humaniste, nécessitant de la délicatesse et de la fermeté, exigeant plus de précision dans le dessin que dans la couleur, le portrait est chez lui au pays de Racine et de Voltaire. Il permet à l'art français de s'affirmer dans ce qu'il a de plus spécifique, du moins dans une certaine direction.

Clouet   Rien d'étonnant, par conséquent, à ce que, sous la Renaissance même, une œuvre de Clouet ne pâlisse nullement devant les Italiens. A l'aise dans un sujet exploité depuis deux cents ans, le perfectionnement et l'assouplissement des techniques sont tout profit pour lui — on devrait dire pour eux, car les Clouet sont père et fils, mais ils poursuivent leur exploration dans le même sens, aussi les confond-on facilement.

Goujon   La sculpture, elle, ignore le portrait, sauf le portrait funéraire, en pied et généralement idéalisé. Mais elle met moins de temps que la

Finesse du dessin, justesse du trait, font du portraitiste Clouet l'égal d'un Holbein.

peinture à trouver son style propre, dans le cadre des innovations de la Renaissance. Goujon, par exemple, assimile avec une prodigieuse voracité les découvertes italiennes et les transmute en un art bien à lui. Le souffle qui parcourt les draperies de ses nymphes peuplant la Fontaine des Innocents à Paris, la lumière qui se joue sur leurs plis, ne sont ni un vent ni un soleil d'Italie. Ce lyrisme organisé, chaleureux mais retenu, c'est Ronsard, c'est du Bellay, c'est toute la France païenne qui se redécouvre avec étonnement dans les moules rigides du christianisme.

LE CLASSICISME AU XVIIÈME

La France a toujours produit de grands sculpteurs. Il est bien dans son génie de faire chanter les pierres. Chose curieuse, ce fut au XVIIème siècle, c'est-à-dire à l'apogée même de la culture française prise dans son ensemble, que la sculpture est la plus décevante. Non que les Girardon et les Coysevox manquent de grâce, de grandeur, de souffle ou de bon goût. En un certain sens, ils sont parfaits, et, dans les jardins de Versailles, ils agrémentent merveilleusement la promenade. Mais cette perfection demeure froide, d'un charme quelque peu convenu. Tous ces empereurs romains, tous ces dieux de l'Olympe, même tous ces rois à cheval et toutes ces nudités, on dirait qu'aucune inspiration ne les soulève, qu'aucune sensualité n'animait le bras qui les sculpta. La sculpture du XVIIème ressemble à la littérature du XVIIIème : elles sont l'une et l'autre d'un classicisme époumoné.

Quoi qu'il en soit, c'est plutôt dans la peinture qu'il faut chercher au XVIIème une expression de la fameuse vérité française.

Caïlot, Le Lorrain, Poussin   La prodigieuse invention de Callot, en fait de monstres et de personnages fantaisistes, correspond très exactement à l'inspiration littéraire des burlesques, ses contemporains. Les deux peintres classiques français qui ont le mieux utilisé l'influence italienne sont Poussin et Le Lorrain ; Le Lorrain, avec cette lumière idéale qui coule comme du miel sur ces *Ports au lever du soleil* qu'il ne s'est jamais lassé de peindre ; Poussin, avec cette composition infiniment savante des masses et des volumes, cette sensualité mélancolique, cette gamme de tons raffinés, qui sont les attributs principaux du classicisme pictural en France (*Orphée et Eurydice*).

Philippe de Champaigne   Parmi les portraitistes qui sont légion, il faut faire une place à part à Philippe de Champaigne : sa palette austère (blancs, bruns, gris, noirs, quelques rouges légèrement déteints), sa psychologie sans défaut, son dessin impitoyable, son sens imprévu de l'espace, en font comme le Pascal de la peinture. Qu'on examine le portrait très janséniste de *Mère Angélique Arnauld*, et l'on verra que le vrai théâtral s'y moque du théâtral comme, d'après Pascal, la vraie éloquence se moque de l'éloquence.

Le Nain   Les frères Le Nain, qui ont souvent travaillé collectivement, avaient bien du talent ; l'un d'eux, Louis, avait du génie. Non seulement ses compositions ne le cèdent en rien à celles de Poussin ; non seulement son

Composition raffinée du paysage, personnages savamment distribués, sérénité de l'atmosphère : Orphée et Eurydice, *de Poussin, est une toile classique type.*

dessin est impeccable, sa palette exacte et sobre, ses masses noblement organisées ; mais encore il a ouvert la voie à bien des successeurs en s'intéressant à des sujets picturaux qu'on avait complètement délaissés depuis le Moyen Age. En un temps où l'on ne peint que des princes et que des ministres, sur commande bien entendu, Le Nain fait, pour son propre plaisir, des paysans, des charrettes, des verres de vin renversés sur des nappes (*Repas de paysan*). Non que le sujet soit l'essentiel d'un tableau, certes non ; mais, en choisissant des sujets humbles et qui lui plaisent, Le Nain invente une vérité artistique plus intime et plus authentique parce qu'elle s'accorde exactement avec son propre tempérament.

La Tour Georges de La Tour, qui traite des sujets religieux dans un esprit d'humilité voisin à la fois de Le Nain et des peintres gothiques, et que le XXème siècle a remis à la mode alors qu'il était presque oublié, est un des meilleurs représentants de ce mysticisme français, qu'on trouve chez les sculpteurs romans, chez des musiciens comme Delalande, chez des écrivains comme Bernanos (*Dialogue des Carmélites*, XXème siècle). Mysticisme de l'immédiat, sans enflure, sans déchirure, sans ésotérisme. Ce n'est même pas de mysticisme religieux que l'on veut parler ici, mais d'un certain sens des rapports entre les données du réel — couleurs, formes, visages — d'un certain regard attentif dans lequel le monde baigne comme dans une lumière. La lumière, justement, et toute sa sorcellerie, voilà ce qui passionne La Tour, ce Rembrandt français.

Falconet, Houdon   Au cours du XVIIème siècle, la sculpture française avait mis une chose au point : la représentation du mouvement. Les sculpteurs du XVIIIème siècle en usèrent abondamment. C'est dans le mouvement que leurs successeurs trouvent même l'essentiel de leur génie. Tel Falconet, par exemple, dont le Pierre le Grand chevauche encore au-dessus de la Néva, et, à un moindre degré, tel Houdon, qui tira du bronze, aussi bien dans le portrait (Benjamin Franklin, Voltaire, Rousseau) que dans le nu (*Diane chasseresse*), des effets plastiques d'une noblesse que seul le marbre avait fournie jusqu'alors.

Mais la peinture, qui était en retard au Moyen Age et sous la Renaissance,

Au sommet de la perfection technique, la Diane chasseresse, de Houdon, joint l'élégance des formes à la grâce du mouvement.

garde l'avance acquise au XVIIème siècle. Elle n'en est pas moins féconde pour être devenue un art d'agrément. Le portrait s'est affiné, féminisé ; il a maintenant quelque chose de moins positif, mais de plus frémissant. Pour le reste, les petits sujets sont de rigueur. Cela pourrait être insupportable par la fadeur et l'artifice ; au contraire, c'est charmant par l'enjouement, le coloris, la fougue de l'exécution. Deux très grands noms : Watteau et Chardin ; deux noms de moindre importance : Fragonard et Boucher ; une multitude d'autres noms dont l'énumération couvrirait des pages. La France entière semble s'être armée de pinceaux, et il y a beaucoup d'esprit à la pointe de ces pinceaux-là.

Chardin   Chardin est le Vermeer français, en ceci que la peinture seule lui importe, que ses sujets lui sont indifférents, que la littérature n'a aucune part dans ses préoccupations. C'est un pinceau fait homme. Il peint des enfants (*Le Toton*), des ménagères (*Le Bénédicité*) ; il invente la nature morte ; il détaille une raie à un étalage de poissonnier : il fait, avant la lettre, de la « peinture pure ». Avec une palette plus bleue et plus subtile, il se situe néanmoins dans la lignée de Le Nain. Reproduire le réel avec le dernier scrupule est pour lui le meilleur des prétextes pour faire de la bonne peinture.

Watteau   Watteau, coloriste d'une finesse inconnue jusqu'à cette époque — les Italiens eux-mêmes avaient alors une touche plus lourde, plus grasse, moins naturelle — invente quelque chose lui aussi : l'humeur appliquée à la peinture. Exquis produit de son temps, témoin mélancolique d'un monde consacré à la recherche du plaisir, il est bien naturel que, à un siècle et demi de distance, Watteau ait inspiré le poète Verlaine et, indirectement, les musiciens impressionnistes Fauré et Debussy. Il y a, dans ses *Fêtes galantes*, non seulement un pressentiment de la technique impressionniste par touches juxtaposées mais encore toute une langueur, toute une tristesse d'un romantisme contenu où ces post-romantiques devaient trouver une pâture à leur goût. Au demeurant, son art du dessin et de la composition, une certaine noblesse dans la présentation du sujet, en font encore un classique — un peu bien poétique, un peu bien fantaisiste, mais un classique tout de même.

Fragonard   Dans Fragonard, ce qui éclate, c'est la joie de peindre, la fougue d'un virtuose en pleine possession de ses moyens, et qui, parvenu aux limites d'une certaine technique, s'en amuse franchement, sans chercher à la dépasser. Ses touches fiévreuses, ses couleurs fraîches, sa joyeuse sensualité, en font un des peintres les plus agréables de son siècle (*Les Hasards heureux de l'escarpolette*).

Boucher   Boucher, lui, est le chef de file des polissons. Son grand souci, c'est le nu (*Diane au bain*), et non pas le nu académique fait pour permettre au peintre de déployer sa science du modelé et de la nuance, mais le bon vrai nu de chair rose, rondelet, potelé et appétissant, destiné à donner au public d'aimables sujets de contemplation. Un siècle plus tard, Boucher aurait choqué les bourgeois ; sous l'Ancien Régime, il fit rire les gentilshommes.

Comme Vermeer, Chardin, avec son Bénédicité, *fait de la « peinture pure ».*

Greuze   Greuze, le plus moral, le plus vertueux des peintres, se propose non pas d'exciter les sens, mais d'attendrir les âmes en montrant le vice puni et la vertu récompensée.

Bref, la peinture avait atteint ses limites dans les directions déjà explorées et ne pouvait plus rien produire qui valût ce qu'elle avait produit déjà. La sculpture se survivait. Mais il fallait que de grands bouleversements vinssent donner aux artistes de nouvelles sources d'inspiration, pour qu'ils découvrissent de nouvelles techniques et fournissent au public l'occasion de redécouvrir les beaux-arts en tant que tels.

LES NÉOCLASSIQUES

A un moment qu'on peut faire coïncider approximativement avec la Révolution française, les artistes vont prendre conscience de la notion de style et, par conséquent, de celle de choix. Au lieu de *faire* « de leur mieux », ils vont décider de *faire* « classique » ou « antique » ou « vertueux » ou «révolutionnaire ». Ce point de vue transcendental, qui fait de l'artiste un intellectuel au lieu d'un artisan, nous semble être le trait distinctif de la création artistique moderne. D'où prolifération d'écoles obéissant à des manifestes exprimés ou non, et auxquelles il faut rattacher les artistes, presque autant d'après leurs idées que d'après leurs œuvres, ce qui ne va pas sans un certain arbitraire dont il importe d'être bien conscient.

David   Tout commença avec David, qui, conformément aux idées révolutionnaires, voulait rendre à la peinture une simplicité antique. En fait de simplicité et de Révolution, il déboucha sur la grandiloquence et l'Empire, mésaventure politico-esthétique qui ne manque pas de piquant. Peintre officiel de Napoléon Ier, du moins put-il satisfaire son goût du théâtral, des grandes ordonnances artificielles (*Le Sacre de Napoléon*). Peut-être croyait-il toujours faire simple alors qu'il faisait de plus en plus solennel. Avec tout son talent, il demeure le père spirituel des divers académismes qui, depuis lors, se sont succédés en France.

Ingres   Son descendant direct, et plus doué que lui, fut le paradoxal Ingres. Paradoxal, car son tempérament le poussait à toutes les trépidations du romantisme, tandis que ses préférences intellectuelles le vouaient à l'idéal classique. Alors que David s'était spécialisé dans les grands sujets historiques, Ingres fit aussi du portrait, du paysage, des sujets religieux, et surtout des nus. Dans toute sa production, il se conforma à des théories qu'il énonçait avec dogmatisme et qu'il imposait d'autorité à ses élèves. Aussi

Le Sacre de Napoléon, *de David, illustre l'aspect solennel du néoclassicisme...*

tous les académiques du XIXème se sont-ils pieusement réclamés de lui, lui rendant par là un mauvais service, car il avait plus de valeur comme peintre que comme théoricien. Nul ne songe à déprécier ses admirables *Odalisques,* dessinées avec une sûreté, une maîtrise, un sens de la masse et du volume dont des peintres anti-académiques au possible (Degas, Cézanne) s'inspireront dans la seconde moitié du siècle. Mais que d'austérité, que de froideur dans ces corps de femmes disciplinés par l'art ! Il entendait régenter son propre talent comme celui de ses disciples, avec une férule de fer.

Généralement on obtient ce que l'on désire passionnément, si l'on est prêt à faire les sacrifices correspondants. Sacrifiant une part de son talent, Ingres devint ce qu'il souhaitait être : une incarnation du classicisme dans la France du XIXème siècle. C'est par rapport à lui que se classent tous les peintres venus après lui, aussi bien que ses contemporains.

Puvis de Chavannes   Avec Prud'hon, le peintre des *Funérailles d'Atala,* Puvis de Chavannes est le plus heureux des déscendants spirituels d'Ingres.

De tout tableau qui procure une impression morale, on peut dire, en thèse générale, qu'il s'agit d'un mauvais tableau.

GONCOURT

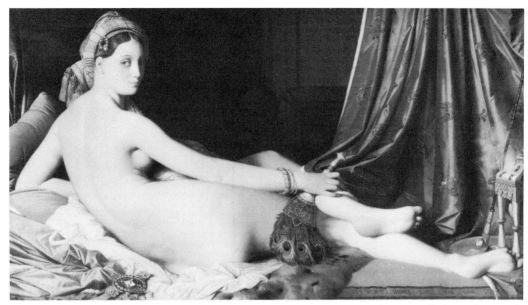

... tandis que la Grande Odalisque, *d'Ingres, montre le souci de beauté pure de cette école.*

Ne se mêlant à aucun des mouvements qui agitèrent la seconde moitié du siècle, ayant su créer un style bien personnel, fait d'une idéalisation systématique du réel, d'un aplatissement volontaire de la perspective et de l'utilisation généralisée des couleurs les plus pâles sinon les plus nuancées, Puvis demeure sagement dans la lignée d'Ingres, dans la mesure où sa peinture reste statique, sereine, grave (telle *Sainte Geneviève veillant sur Paris*), et se refuse à un renouvellement organisé des formes.

LE ROMANTISME

Delacroix   C'est aussi par rapport à Ingres — comme son ennemi le plus irréductible — que se situe le grand peintre romantique Delacroix. Son goût pour les compositions mouvementées, son amour d'un exotisme un peu clinquant (il n'est que de voir *la Mort de Sardanapale*), sa façon nerveuse de poser la couleur, ses couleurs mêmes, d'une agréable violence et d'un chatoiement sans modération, font de lui le romantique type, le Berlioz ou le Victor Hugo de la peinture. Ingres le haïssait, et il ne portait pas Ingres dans son cœur. Heureusement, nous pouvons goûter les œuvres de l'un et de l'autre sans nécessairement souscrire à leur esthètique.

Ce que l'on s'accordera à reprocher à Delacroix, d'un point de vue moderne, c'est l'abus de littérature sur ses toiles, un expressionnisme facile et pas mal de grandiloquence. Mais le peintre demeure étincelant par la

Exotisme, sens du drame, contrastes accusés, toutes les valeurs romantiques éclatent dans la Mort de Sardanapale, *une des œuvres les plus chatoyantes de Delacroix.*

fougue du dessin, l'emportement de la composition, la rage savante du coloris.

LE RÉALISME

Courbet   Naturellement, comme il est d'usage en France, Ingres peignait classique pour « faire vrai ». Delacroix peignait romantique pour « faire vrai ». Et Courbet, qui avec son *la Rencontre* leur tourna le dos à tous les deux, s'engagea dans le réalisme pour « faire vrai ». Comme tous les réalistes, c'était un romantique de cœur ; autrement dit, il aimait le dramatique, le sombre et, quelque peu, le sordide. Comme tous les esprits systématiques, il parvint lui aussi à fonder un académisme, toujours le même, à peu de noms près. C'est là le malheur des artistes en France : ils trouvent toujours des épigones qui font survivre leurs idées, alors que leurs œuvres seules devraient rester. Au demeurant, la peinture de Courbet ne manque nullement de qualités solides, d'une technique approfondie, d'une inspiration certaine, encore que nous soyons gênés aujourd'hui par sa complaisance pour ses sujets.

Millet   La même complaisance se retrouve chez Millet, qui s'obstine à exprimer des sentiments alors qu'on ne lui demande que des formes et des couleurs. C'est néanmoins un peintre de très grand talent, qui vaut surtout par un dessin d'une exemplaire fermeté. Il faut oublier sa prédilection sentimentale pour des sujets d'une humilité un peu démagogique et ne voir que les qualités propres de son travail : elles éclatent mieux qu'ailleurs dans ses esquisses et croquis.

Cependant, on ne saurait passer sous silence la fortune extraordinaire que connurent deux de ses œuvres, *l'Angélus* et *les Glaneuses*, qui, sous forme de gravures, de lithographies, de reproductions, ont orné tous les salons de la petite bourgeoisie française pendant cent ans. Bien entendu, personne ne songeait à les aimer pour leurs qualités picturales : elles étaient, à la sensibilité du XIXème, ce qu'à la sensualité du XVIIIème étaient les espiègleries d'un Boucher ou d'un Fragonard.

Daumier   A l'opposé de Millet pour la sensibilité, mais non pour l'esthétique, on trouve Daumier, plus lithographe que peintre, et dont le réalisme, du genre impitoyable et drôlatique à la fois, crée en fait la caricature. Sa série de gravures la plus connue, qui s'apparente à Goya par la verve tragique et l'humour noir, concerne les hommes de loi.

Dans la Rencontre, *Courbet cherche comme toujours à reproduire le réel.*

Souvenirs de Mortefontaine, *de Corot : modestie du sujet — grandeur de l'exécution.*

LES SANS-PARTI

A côté de tous ces peintres affiliés à des écoles, il en est quelques-uns qui demeurent indépendants, et dont l'esthétique ne permet pas de les enfermer dans tel tiroir plutôt que dans tel autre. C'est le cas de l'un des plus grands peintres français du XIXème siècle : Corot.

Corot Paysagiste avant tout, Corot a joui longtemps d'une popularité de mauvais aloi. Le sens de la grâce, l'amour des beautés naturelles, qui abondent dans les tableaux comme *Souvenirs de Mortefontaine*, étaient faits pour rassurer le client bourgeois : ni audaces picturales, ni femmes nues, quelle aubaine pour décorer son salon ! Le client bourgeois ne se découragea que lorsqu'il constata enfin combien cet art était tout de même raffiné, et presque insolent dans sa modestie. Aucune littérature, aucune recherche apparente au profane, rien à se mettre sous la dent. Vivent les sympathiques paysans de Millet, décide le bourgeois, et il libère Corot, que des amateurs plus éclairés ne craignent plus d'admirer maintenant.

En réalité, Corot, qui patronna quelque peu l'école de paysagistes-réalistes de Barbizon dont Millet est le principal représentant, vaut par ses qualités picturales pures. Il appartient à ce que nous avons appelé la première catégorie : il peint pour peindre. Les paysages voilés d'une brume dorée qu'il s'obstine à reproduire avec une telle exactitude ne sont que des prétextes. S'il cherchait à en tirer le moindre effet, ce ne serait pas tant le paysage que sa propre facture qu'il trahirait. Il appartient à cette caste de très grands artistes qui, tel Chardin en France, tel Vélasquez en Espagne, ne daignent même pas dédaigner leur sujet.

Boudin Bien au-dessous de Corot, mais dans la même lignée, il faut placer Boudin, qui avec ses *Vues d'Honfleur* jouit actuellement d'une mode apparemment aussi excessive que l'oubli où il fut plongé près d'un siècle. Paysagiste délicat, il préfigure, de même que Corot, l'avènement de l'impressionnisme, c'est-à-dire d'une peinture où le visuel pur l'emporte sur toutes les autres considérations (doctrine, composition mathématique).

L'IMPRESSIONNISME

L'impressionnisme est le phénomène le plus important de l'histoire de la peinture moderne, et cela pour un nombre considérable de raisons hétéroclites cristallisées autour de lui, au moins autant qu'à cause des œuvres auxquelles il a donné naissance. Se plaçant dans la même ligne que la révolution philosophique du XVIIIème siècle et le romantisme littéraire au début du XIXème, l'impressionnisme, avant toute autre considération, *conteste l'autorité établie*. Cette contestation — qui, en l'occurrence, était indéniablement légitime — crée autour de lui deux courants d'opinion, l'un pour, l'autre contre, aussi éloignés l'un que l'autre de l'objet même de la querelle, qui était d'ordre principalement technique. Le tourbillon créé par ces deux courants dessert les Impresionnistes pendant leur vie, mais leur fait, après leur mort, une publicité à laquelle le bon public est encore sensible : le mythe du peintre maudit charme le petit bourgeois du XXème siècle en lui donnant bonne conscience, car il peut se dire : « Moi, je ne suis pas comme mes arrière-grands parents ; moi, j'aime Manet et Pissarro ; moi, j'ai des goûts artistes. »

Ce que les Impressionnistes revendiquent en fait, c'est l'indépendance totale de l'artiste — indépendance à l'égard des règles morales (libre choix du sujet), indépendance à l'égard de la doctrine officielle en peinture (libre choix des techniques). Ces revendications se résument temporairement à la formule suivante : « Je peins comme je vois. »

Peut-être n'y avait-il pas de quoi crier au scandale : nous ne serions pas choqués qu'un daltonien nous propose sa vision du monde. Mais c'est que nous avons une conception plus sacrée — à moins qu'elle ne soit plus frivole — de l'art. Au XIXème, il s'agit toujours de faire vrai, et un daltonien qui peindrait apparaîtrait comme un menteur. D'ailleurs, les détracteurs de l'impressionnisme avaient raison de s'inquiéter : le « Je peins comme je vois » n'était qu'un slogan éphémère qui ne pouvait servir qu'à la peinture de reproduction, celle que nous avons classée dans la deuxième catégorie. Aussitôt que cette catégorie-là ne fut plus à la mode, les descendants spirituels des Impressionnistes remplacèrent le « Je peins comme je vois » par le « Je peins comme je veux », car ils affirmaient que la peinture n'était pas uniquement visuelle, mais aussi intellectuelle, symbolique, etc. Autrement dit, par la brèche que les Impressionnistes avaient ouverte, tout l'art moderne se déversa sur le monde, toujours au nom de la vérité. Reprenons notre exemple du daltonien. « Tu mens, lui dit-on ; cette robe est verte, pas rouge. — Mais je la vois rouge, répond-il ; c'est si je la représentais verte que je mentirais. » Et le symboliste, descendant du daltonien : « Pour moi, l'idée de robe est noire ; je ne veux donc peindre que des robes noires. » C'est à cela que se ramène un conflit qui a commencé il y a cent ans et qui n'est pas encore résolu.

Pratiquement, quelles furent les innovations des Impressionnistes ?

Ils firent passer au second plan la notion de composition, alors que les toiles de leurs prédécesseurs étaient organisées comme des ouvrages d'architecture.

Ils plantèrent leurs chevalets en plein air et renoncèrent à peindre des paysages en atelier.

Ils bannirent le noir de leurs palettes, en affirmant que les ombres mêmes étaient colorées.

Ils récusèrent l'art traditionnel du modelé, préférant procéder par juxtaposition de taches de couleur.

Ils s'interdirent, du moins en principe et au début, de mélanger les couleurs sur la palette, faisant tout le travail sur la toile.

Manet fit scandale avec son Olympia : pour la première fois, un peintre tentait de faire un nu qui fût beau bien que représentant un modèle qui ne l'était pas.

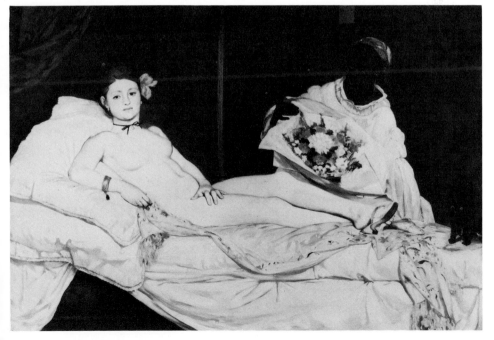

La sensualité de l'homme Renoir servit celle du peintre : tous ces sujets — par exemple ce Torse de Femme au Soleil — *il les peignit en amoureux.*

Il fallait une société bien conservatrice, et des académiques qui tenaient bien fort à leurs places, pour que ces réformes soulevassent les tempêtes qui conduisirent à la création des Salons des Indépendants et des Refusés. Ce fut cependant ce qui arriva, et toute la peinture française contemporaine vit encore sur les souvenirs héroïques de cette guerre où, pour une fois, tous les bons (peintres) étaient d'un côté et tous les mauvais (peintres) de l'autre.

La démagogie mise à part, ce qui reste de l'impressionnisme, c'est une vision nouvelle des choses, beaucoup plus fraîche, colorée, spontanée, une sorte d'ivresse de la lumière qui demeure parmi les grandes réussites de l'humanité.

Les principaux Impressionnistes français sont Manet, Monet, Degas, Renoir. Il n'entre pas dans notre propos d'étudier tous ces peintres individuellement, mais seulement de donner quelques indications permettant au profane de s'y reconnaître.

Manet   Manet est l'aîné de la bande ; sa façon de poser la couleur par aplats plutôt que par juxtaposition de taches ou par dégradés causa moins de scandale que les sujets de ses tableaux. *Le Déjeuner sur l'herbe* fut trouvé indécent par Napoléon III en personne, parce que l'on y voyait des femmes nues et des hommes habillés ; ç'aurait sans doute été moins choquant si tout le monde avait été nu. *Olympia* n'indigna pas moins le bourgeois, parce que la femme nue qui s'exhibait sur cette toile n'était pas précisément jolie et que sa chair, loin d'avoir les tons nacrés et roses de rigueur pour un corps de femme, était d'un jaune quelque peu malsain.

Renoir A l'opposé de Manet, Renoir avec son *Torse de Femme au Soleil* apparaît comme le plus impressionniste des Impressionnistes par la technique, sinon par les idées. Les petites femmes qu'il adore peindre sont aussi roses qu'on peut les désirer, dodues à point et parcourues de charmants frissons de sensualité. On peut être agacé par tant de mièvrerie, tant de complaisance, un dessin si peu ferme, un désir de plaire aussi insistant. Mais cela n'enlève rien aux mérites du coloriste étonnant que fut ce peintre que ses camarades — jaloux probablement — considèrent déshonoré parce qu'il avait accepté la Légion d'honneur, pactisant ainsi avec les académiques. Mainte-

Les Danseuses Roses de Degas : une extrême précision dans le flou et le vaporeux.

On ne voit pas les choses mais seulement la lumière qu'elles réfléchissent : c'est la doctrine de l'Impressionnisme qui doit son nom à Impression, de Monet.

nant, cette Légion d'honneur nous rassurerait plutôt sur la pureté d'un artiste qui préférait la gloire aux idées, réaction qui nous paraît pleine de santé et de bon sens pour tout autre qu'un philosophe ou un révolutionnaire. De Renoir est ce mot, l'un des plus intéressants qu'on ait prononcés au sujet de l'art en général : « Le modèle n'est là que pour allumer le peintre. »

Degas, Monet   Degas avec ses danseuses, Monet avec ses poudroiements de lumière sur ses locomotives, complètent le quatuor — ou le quarteron — central de l'impressionnisme.

Seurat   Seurat, dont le tempérament était classique et le portait aux grandes compositions un peu solennelles, telle *la Grande Jatte,* tenta d'utiliser dans ce sens la technique impressionniste et même pointilliste (juxtaposition de points de couleur minuscules, dans un esprit de système passablement pédant). Aussi le range-t-on généralement parmi les peintres de cette école. En fait, il annonce déjà des recherches qui ne sont plus exclusivement visuelles, et l'intelligence a autant de part que l'œil dans son travail.

RÉACTIONS ANTI-IMPRESSIONNISTES

Après l'impressionnisme (il faut entendre cet « après » d'une façon plus logique que chronologique), deux évidences éclatèrent aux yeux de tous : (1) en peinture, tout est possible, (2) mais aussi terriblement compliqué.

En effet, on avait maintenant le droit moral de faire ce qu'on voulait, mais un pinceau n'y suffisait plus : il y fallait des idées. Avant les Impressionnistes, on peignait avec ses doigts ; ils le firent avec leurs yeux. On eut recours ensuite à sa tête, à son cœur, à son inconscient, à je ne sais quoi encore. La notion de « travail bien fait », qui avait été celle de Fouquet, de Poussin, de Chardin, disparut pour faire place à celle des catégories que nous avons exposée au début de ce chapitre et qui se fit peu à peu un chemin dans les esprits. *Peindre* cessa d'être un verbe transitif (je peins une toile) et se mit à exiger des prépositions (je peins *pour* m'exprimer, *selon* mes conceptions, *malgré* ma famille, etc.).

Conformément à la dialectique inhérente à l'histoire des idées, et puisque les Impressionnistes avaient mis l'accent sur la deuxième catégorie (l'aspect visuel de la peinture), leurs successeurs exploitèrent de préférence la première et la troisième. Ainsi les uns voulurent que le tableau fût non pas la représentation d'un objet mais un objet par lui-même, trouvant dans ses conditions d'existence une esthétique propre (première catégorie), et les autres, qu'il exprimât non plus leur vision mais leur conception du monde et, par la même occasion, leurs états d'âme (forme moderne de la troisième catégorie, l'expression prenant la place de la signification).

Trois tendances apparurent alors, remontant toutes à des contemporains de l'impressionnisme qui, pour des raisons diverses, étaient toujours restés séparés de ce groupe. A noter que cette classification a, bien entendu, tous les défauts des classifications : certains peintres, par exemple, ont pu appartenir successivement ou même simultanément à deux groupes opposés. Néanmoins, elle nous semble rendre compte des faits d'une façon à peu près satisfaisante.

LES EXPRESSIONNISTES

Toulouse-Lautrec   En pleine période impressionniste, un grand seigneur nain, Henri de Toulouse-Lautrec, donna du réel une vision hilarante et dramatique où la curiosité, la passion, le mépris, avaient certes plus de part que l'impression produite par la lumière sur la rétine. Autodidacte et dilettante à la fois, il semble qu'il ne soit jamais parvenu à la maturité de son génie, qui était grand. Ses lithographies, ses affiches, ses croquis, sont d'une maîtrise et d'une liberté de facture remarquables. La mauvaise littérature qu'on a suscitée autour de lui ne doit pas faire oublier, par-delà le bohème et l'original, l'artiste indépendant et le père de l'affiche moderne (*La Goulue*).

Rouault, douanier Rousseau, les Surréalistes   Au XXème siècle, le grand peintre religieux Rouault utilisa également la peinture pour exprimer ses

L'expressionniste Toulouse-Lautrec créa l'affiche artistique.

sentiments ; ce fut aussi le cas de tous les « naïfs » avec, à leur tête, le douanier Rousseau, petit fonctionnaire un peu véreux qui trouvait dans l'art une évasion presque mystique, ainsi que celui des Surréalistes, qui répandirent plus d'idées qu'ils ne créèrent d'œuvres, mais qui eurent le mérite d'enquêter sur les possibilités de l'insolite dans les arts plastiques.

C'est également parmi les Expressionnistes qu'on range d'ordinaire Waroquier et Gromaire, pour ne parler que des Français. Mais il faut bien constater que, à la fin du XIXème siècle, le prestige des Impressionnistes était tel à l'étranger que la France était devenue la patrie de la peinture mondiale. Ne parler que des Français, c'est oublier les Hollandais, les Italiens, les

Anglais, les Russes, les Espagnols, qui étaient venus former l'École de Paris et qui, par l'air qu'ils respiraient et les toiles qu'ils peignaient, peuvent sembler aussi français que leurs voisins.

Soutine, Modigliani, Van Gogh, Chagall Ainsi le Russe Soutine, l'Italien Modigliani, sont aussi des Expressionnistes, et ils ont peint en France beaucoup plus qu'ailleurs. Le grand Van Gogh lui-même, en qui certains voient le père de l'expressionnisme, avait quitté sa Hollande natale pour venir hanter les paysagse et les asiles d'aliénés français. Et Chagall, ce Juif russo-polonais qui a passé toute sa vie en France, faut-il le renvoyer dans ses foyers ou le naturaliser ? La même question se posera plus loin à propos de peintres plus illustres encore. Nous opterons ici pour une solution moyenne, en citant à leur place les noms des artistes d'importation, mais sans évoquer leur œuvre.

LES « DÉCORATIFS »

Deux groupes parallèles, les « Fauves » et les « Nabis », ont poursuivi la réaction anti-impressionniste dans un sens également anti-expressionniste.

Gauguin Leur ancêtre est Gauguin, dont la vie pathétique ne devrait pas faire oublier l'originalité de sa peinture. Aussi bien dans sa période bretonne que dans sa période polynésienne, il s'est attaché à créer des composi-

Avec Gauguin et ses Femmes de Tahiti, *la ligne, la forme et la couleur servent à des fins décoratives : la reproduction du réel n'est plus qu'un prétexte.*

tions, des formes et des couleurs auxquelles le réel sert simplement de support. Son art, qui rebutait ses contemporains, nous paraît un peu trop séduisant, au contraire, un peu trop flatteur pour les sens.

Matisse Cependant, ce désir de « faire décoratif » lui est commun avec la plupart des « grands Fauves », en particulier avec Matisse, dont l'élégante sobriété cache d'infinies recherches de forme et de couleur. Dufy, peintre d'extérieurs traités avec humour, Marquet, attentif et modeste, Vlaminck, non dénué de romantisme, Derain et Van Dongen, telle est la liste à peu près complète du groupe des rugissants. Sans doute y a-t-il quelque injustice à citer des peintres dont la postérité oubliera peut-être les noms à côté d'autres, qui sont immortels. Mais notre propos dans ce livre est culturel ; et, pour l'instant, tous ces peintres font encore partie de la culture française.

La grande affaire des Fauves était « le transformé imaginaire de la couleur », comme ils le déclaraient dans leur langage très fin de siècle. Ils entendaient par là que les couleurs qu'ils utilisaient n'étaient pas censées reproduire les couleurs du réel mais, au contraire, projeter sur la toile leur propre « réalité intérieure ».

Bonnard C'est aussi l'idée des Nabis, dont le plus grand est incontestablement Bonnard, l'un des plus clairs de tous les peintres français, dont les scènes intimes, extérieurs et intérieurs, baignent toutes dans une lumière d'une intense douceur. La « réalité intérieure » d'un Vuillard, d'un Denis, d'un Sérusier, est nettement moins lumineuse, mais le même idéal de création pure rassemble ces quatre peintres.

LES CUBISTES

Les Expressionnistes en voulaient au cœur ; les Fauves et les Nabis, aux sens. Les Cubistes proclamèrent hautement que l'intelligence seule les intéressait : ils voulaient reconstruire le réel à partir de la géométrie, entreprise dont l'idéalisme didactique semble avoir échappé à beaucoup de commentateurs.

Cézanne Les Cubistes avaient eux aussi un père spirituel : Cézanne, qui avait commencé par appartenir au groupe des Impressionnistes, mais qui s'était bientôt retiré dans une retraite provençale pour y faire son salut artistique tout seul. N'étant jamais satisfait de son travail, mais hanté par le besoin de peindre, il fit de sa vie une longue ascèse : cent fois, il recommençait la moindre nature morte, cherchant non pas à *reproduire* des pommes mais à *faire* des pommes, à atteindre par sa peinture l'archétype platonicien de la pomme universelle. On peut ne pas goûter cette production laborieuse, et qui se ressent des peines qu'elle a coûtées (surtout lorsqu'il s'agit de nus, car ses convictions religieuses interdisaient, paraît-il, à Cézanne d'en peindre d'après nature) ; mais il est impossible de ne pas y voir l'origine du plus idéaliste des mouvements artistiques modernes.

Trouver des figures géométriques dans le réel, les mettre à nu, et les

L'Homme au Gilet Rouge, *de Cézanne : méditation sur l'architecture des choses.*

recouvrir ensuite, ç'avait été jusque-là le travail des sculpteurs, procédant par plans. Mais les peintres s'y mirent à leur tour.

Picasso, Braque Le plus illustre d'entre eux est, sans conteste, l'Espagnol Picasso ; le plus grand des Français, Braque. Marcoussis, Villon, Léger, forment le gros des troupes. La plupart d'entre eux ont rapidement abandonné ce que le cubisme avait de systématique pour accéder à un art purement

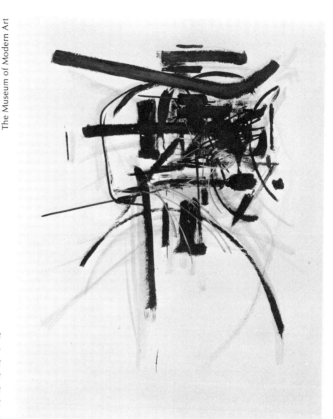

Le dynamisme de Mathieu — qui prépare longuement ses tableaux et puis les exécute en quelques minutes — apparaît dans Peinture, *1947.*

formel, où le jeu intellectuel tient la première place, et pour déboucher quelquefois (on pense à Braque principalement) sur des espaces idéaux où la création pure paraît enfin accessible à l'homme.

LES ABSTRAITS

L'art abstrait, le mal nommé,[1] n'a guère trouvé d'adeptes en France : Delaunay, Picabia, Manessier, Mathieu, les Russes Kandinsky et Lanskoy, et c'est à peu près tout. Il n'y a rien d'étonnant à cela : l'art abstrait reposant sur un malentendu (ni décoratif, ni représentatif, ni significatif) n'a pas encore trouvé sa vérité et n'intéresse donc pas directement les artistes français. Beaucoup de jeunes peintres travaillent cependant dans cette direction, tandis que d'autres font des efforts rarement heureux pour revenir à l'art figuratif. Tout cela, dans l'ensemble, ne paraît guère concluant, ce qui est dommage, car l'aventure d'un art plastique absolument pur méritait des réalisations plus satisfaisantes.

[1] Il s'agit en réalité d'art concret, puisque la toile colorée y est simplement une toile colorée et non la représentation d'une bataille ou d'un potiron.

CAVALIER SEUL

Un très grand peintre français refuse de se laisser classer dans nos ingénieuses petites boîtes. Résolument figuratif et alcoolique, il a passé sa vie à s'intoxiquer et à se désintoxiquer, ce qui l'a sauvé des écoles et des académies. Par son application, non pas rageuse comme celle de Cézanne, mais plaisante, comme celle de Chardin, il appartient à cette lignée de peintres-peintres parmi lesquels nous avons rangé Corot. Entre deux ivresses, entre deux séjours à l'hôpital, il peignait de petites toiles précises représentant des paysages parisiens. Son nom est Utrillo.

LA SCULPTURE AUX XIXÈME ET XXÈME SIÈCLES

La peinture est facile : une surface vierge (tissu, papier, bois, carton) et quelques couleurs qu'on n'a même plus besoin de savoir mélanger depuis qu'on utilise les couleurs pures, et voilà : on peut se prendre pour un génie.

La sculpture est difficile : il y faut de la glaise ou du plâtre, du bronze ou du marbre, un ciseau solide, beaucoup de place, du biceps et même du poumon. Ce n'est pas un art pour petite nature. Rien d'étonnant, par conséquent, à ce que les déchets y soient minces, sauf parmi nos contemporains, qui ont inventé de sculpter dans des matières faciles comme l'alumi-

Rodin « entre le diable et le bon Dieu » : montage photographique de Steichen, associant le sculpteur à deux de ses œuvres, Victor Hugo *et le* Penseur.

nium. Au XIXème et au début du XXème, seuls les artistes qu'emportait une grande certitude de leur génie trouvaient l'énergie nécessaire pour sculpter.

Rodin, Maillol Certains se trompaient : ils n'avaient que du talent. C'est le cas d'un Rude, d'un Carpeaux, d'un Barye, d'un David d'Angers — peut-être même d'un Bourdelle, dont les soucis décoratifs, proches du fauvisme, l'ont détourné de la voie austère du sculpteur pur. Mais ce n'est certes pas celui des deux géants barbus qui se dressent à l'orée du XXème siècle, Rodin et Maillol.

On a pris l'habitude de les opposer l'un à l'autre, et c'est commode, pour mieux faire ressortir leurs qualités propres. Rodin est tourmenté, angoissé, colérique, tout en mouvement ; Maillol est placide, rayonnant, serein, tout en rondeurs. Rodin fait passer dans la pierre et dans le bronze tous les frissons de son âme inquiète ; Maillol contemple avec une joie sensuelle la beauté du monde. Il y a de la passion dans Rodin ; dans Maillol, il n'y a que des formes. Rodin, c'est l'élan ; Maillol, la plénitude.

De là à prétendre, comme on l'a fait, que Maillol est classique et Rodin romantique, il y a une distance considérable et qu'on ferait mieux de ne pas franchir. Si le classicisme de Maillol ne fait de doutes pour personne, Rodin est fort classique aussi par son art de composer les masses, romantique peut-être par son inspiration, mais également baroque par son culte de la puissance en mouvement, proche de celui de Michel-Ange.

Ces deux personnalités si contradictoires en apparence sont comme les deux faces du génie propre de la France, et, pour ainsi dire, ses deux vérités.

Vérité « gothique » de Rodin : art de la verticale, de la danse, du labeur, parent de l'art d'un Balzac, d'un Berlioz, d'un Cézanne Vérité « romane » de Maillol : art du cercle, du repos, de l'accomplissement, à rapprocher de l'art d'un Rabelais, d'un Rameau, d'un Renoir. Ce n'est certes pas un hasard si Rodin est né à Paris, et Maillol sur les bords de la Méditerranée.

Ce n'est pas un hasard non plus si nous avons choisi de conclure cet exposé sur les arts plastiques en évoquant ces deux prestigieuses figures qui n'ont guère laissé de descendants dignes d'eux. A travers toute l'histoire de leur art et des arts connexes, ils sont comme deux phares, par rapport auxquels il peut être commode maintenant de situer leurs prédécesseurs. Chez l'un comme chez l'autre, les trois impératifs des arts plastiques (être, représenter, signifier) se réconcilient dans un équilibre d'éternité.

MUSIQUE 7

IDÉE GÉNÉRALE

La musique française est souvent méconnue.

C'est assez pour donner envie d'en parler d'abondance et dans le détail, car, en réalité, la France a donné au monde certains de ses plus grands musiciens. On aimerait commencer par caractériser la sensibilité musicale des Français, puis raconter tout au long l'évolution de la chanson populaire (son mariage avec le chant liturgique, la naissance de leur prolifique progéniture, l'influence que cette progéniture eut sur les musiques voisines), expliquer les découvertes harmoniques et instrumentales des théoriciens français, opposer nom à nom les compositeurs qui ont appliqué leurs théories à ceux des autres pays, et conclure à l'inanité des préjugés qui font de l'Italie ou de l'Allemagne la patrie d'Euterpe.[1]

[1] muse de la musique

Mais il faut résister à cette tentation : analyser des œuvres inconnues du lecteur ne servirait à rien ; débiter des chapelets de noms qui n'évoqueront pas un seul accord serait ennuyeux et stérile. Il faut transiger. On essaiera tout d'abord d'expliquer en quoi consiste l'excellence de la musique française et de montrer comment cette excellence même a créé un malentendu difficile à dissiper ; puis, à grands traits, on peindra l'évolution des styles musicaux en citant au passage des noms d'œuvres et de compositeurs et en espérant que le lecteur se précipitera au concert ou sur son catalogue de disques pour illustrer lui-même un exposé nécessairement squelettique, puisque le papier d'imprimerie, qui reproduit si bien les images visuelles, n'a pas encore appris à chanter.

Le Français distingue — assez naïvement — la « grande » musique de l'autre, qu'il ne sait pas comment appeler. On rappelle des mots de compositeurs, déclarant fort justement qu'il n'y a pas de « grande » ni de « petite » musique, mais seulement de la bonne et de la mauvaise. Mais ce n'est pas là le sentiment de l'auditeur. Il tient à ce qu'il y ait de « grands genres » (symphonie, concerto) et des genres négligeables (opéra-comique, ballet). Pour ceux-ci, le Français a entière confiance dans les compositeurs de son pays, ce qui explique la fortune extraordinaire que connurent au siècle dernier des compositeurs faciles, parfois sans le moindre talent, parfois gentiment doués mais dépourvus de véritable invention. Pour les «genres nobles », au contraire, le Français fait preuve d'une xénophilie singulière : il trouve ses compositeurs nationaux sans génie et n'a d'amour et d'admiration que pour les Italiens, les Allemands et les Russes.

Pourquoi ? C'est que, nous semble-t-il, la « grande » musique française, bien qu'essentiellement mélodique, est aussi essentiellement raffinée et, pour tout dire, intellectuelle. D'un goût classique, raisonnable, quelquefois un peu froid, elle répugne de Couperin à Ravel aux effets faciles, à l'expressionnisme, aux répétitions. Elle n'est nullement conçue pour favoriser le vague à l'âme ; elle n'est pas « humaniste » ; elle n'est que musique. Ceux des Français qui l'aiment la qualifient volontiers d'un terme qui, en l'occurrence, ne signifie pas grand chose mais correspond à leurs sentiments : ils la trouvent « aristocratique ».

Au demeurant, la musique française ne déçoit pas moins les amateurs de grands mots que ceux de sensations fortes. Si les recherches techniques de ses compositeurs étaient affichées avec quelque affectation, elles auraient de quoi séduire les pédants. Mais, au contraire, obéissant au mot d'ordre de Rameau, l'un des plus grands d'entre eux, ils s'attachent à « cacher l'art par l'art ». Cette formule, inoffensive en apparence, est en réalité une des clefs du grand art français. Il est piquant de la rapprocher de la réflexion — souvent mal interprétée — de Pascal : « La vraie éloquence se moque de l'éloquence. »

De ce qui précède, il ne faut pas déduire que la musique française est affaire de chapelles et de préciosité. Le seul nom de *Carmen* suffirait à montrer le contraire.

Cependant, tandis que la musique italienne tend toujours vers un certain lyrisme, la germanique (au XIXème du moins) vers un style narratif, la russe vers un expressionnisme descriptif, la française se refuse le plus souvent à être autre chose qu'une musique tout court. Les exceptions — Berlioz, Franck — ne font que mettre en valeur cette tendance générale.

LA POLYPHONIE

Les trouvères dans les châteaux, les moines dans les couvents, chantaient des monodies généralement non accompagnées. Les trouvères inventaient leurs compositions ; les moines disposaient depuis le VIème siècle d'un système modal admirable, dit « grégorien ». Les moines avaient en outre un tempérament contemplatif et beaucoup de temps. Les trouvères étaient solitaires : la monodie constituait donc leur expression naturelle. Les moines étaient nombreux : logiquement, ils devaient, tôt ou tard, aboutir au chant à plusieurs voix. Ce fut ce qui arriva, dès le IXème siècle, soit deux siècles avant l'apparition du grand art dés trouvères.

La mélodie grégorienne fut bientôt doublée d'une mélodie identique, chantée à l'octave supérieure par les ténors : ce n'était déjà plus l'unisson primitif. On y ajouta ensuite une troisième mélodie, toujours pareille, mais chantée à la quinte, puis à la quarte. Les voix de « dessus » en prirent de l'importance. Pendant que la basse continuait à chanter la mélodie primitive, le ténor put faire des variations, en passant tout d'abord de l'octave à la quinte et retour. Ces variations ne s'appliquaient pas seulement à la musique, mais aussi au texte : la basse chantait, le ténor commentait. Dès lors, le grégorien était mort : les barrages de quinte et d'octave furent vite rompus, et la polyphonie, c'est-à-dire l'art de faire chanter plusieurs airs différents à la fois, put éclore librement.

L'origine religieuse de la polyphonie ne fut pas oubliée aussitôt. Tandis que les monodies des trouvères devenaient des chansons à une voix, accompagnées par un luth et rythmées à peu de choses près comme nos chansons modernes, l'Église, abandonnant le grégorien aux besoins liturgiques, s'enrichissait d'innombrables motets, morceaux de musique vocale polyphonique composés librement sur des paroles latines. L'infini entrecroisement des lignes mélodiques, la beauté grave et constante qui résulte de leur superposition, ont fait comparer les compositions polyphoniques à leurs contemporaines architecturales : les cathédrales romanes et gothiques. Cette longue époque marque le triomphe de l'écriture dite horizontale, dans laquelle il n'y a pas

L'imagination gracieuse, la sensualité vibrante, la fougue picturale de Fragonard, font de sa Leçon de Musique *un aimable morceau de virtuosité.*

d'harmonie proprement dite : plusieurs mélodies chantent simultanément, c'est ce qu'on appelle le contrepoint. Cependant le grégorien était déjà loin : la musique, partie du mode, évoluait vers le système tonal que nous connaissons.

Sous la Renaissance, il n'y eut pas de modification radicale de la musique : la polyphonie continua à évoluer dans le même sens, mais elle s'enrichit de thèmes profanes. Il faut ici prendre le mot *thème* dans les deux sens : d'une part, bien des compositions polyphoniques furent consacrées à des sujets mondains ; d'autre part, la matière musicale en fut souvent empruntée au monde de la chanson et même du cri lancé par les marchands de Paris pour attirer la pratique.

La polyphonie complexe commence vers le XIIème siècle. Elle est remplacée par l'harmonie classique au XVIIème. Cinq siècles de musique. Qu'en reste-t-il pour le mélomane non spécialisé ? Quelques noms comme Pérotin, Machaut ou Josquin des Prés. Or, il suffit d'entendre un de leurs motets pour se persuader de la qualité profonde et sûre de leur musique. Mais elle est austère, ferme, sans concessions. On n'en fait pas ce qu'on veut : on la subit ou on s'en détourne. La subir même nécessite des capacités d'attention que n'ont pas la plupart des habitués de concerts. Résultat : cette musique ne s'est guère jouée pendant les trois siècles qui ont suivi sa disparition, et se joue à peine aujourd'hui.

LE CLASSICISME

La monodie engendra le contrepoint ; le contrepoint engendra le ton ; le ton engendra l'harmonie ; l'harmonie engendra l'écriture verticale, par accords. L'écriture verticale avait besoin d'instruments capables de produire plusieurs sons à la fois : l'orgue d'abord, puis le clavecin et le violon, apparurent et triomphèrent chacun dans leur domaine. En utilisant plusieurs violons ensemble, on avait déjà un petit orchestre. Ces instruments nouveaux, ces orchestres en pleine croissance, qu'allaient-ils jouer ? Jusque-là, la musique instrumentale avait servi uniquement à la danse. Les compositeurs écrivirent donc des suites de danses, parce qu'ils en connaissaient bien le rythme, mais ces danses ne se dansaient plus. Autrement dit, ce que nous appelons prétentieusement « musique pure » était en train de sortir de la chrysalide polyphonique. Le classicisme[2] était à deux pas.

Au XVIIème siècle, la France connut une floraison de compositeurs qui, au moins autant que les Italiens et les Allemands, contribuèrent à fonder la musique moderne. Au XVIIIème, elle en eut d'autres, qui exploitèrent les richesses créées par leurs aînés. De 1650 environ (début de la carrière de Lully) jusqu'à 1764 (mort de Rameau — disons jusqu'au milieu du XVIIIème siècle pour arrondir), se situe ce qu'on peut appeler le premier âge d'or de la musique française (si l'on considère que l'ère polyphonique appartient à l'Europe chrétienne tout entière).

Lully   Lully, musicien d'origine italienne, qui vint se fixer à la cour de Louis XIV, créa la musique française moderne proprement dite. Ses opéras sont un modèle de déclamation : avec un bonheur que, Rameau excepté, aucun musicien ne retrouvera plus jamais, Lully fait chanter la langue française conformément à sa prosodie intérieure.

En outre, Lully crée une forme dans laquelle certains voient l'origine de la sonate et, par conséquent, de la symphonie : *l'ouverture*. L'ouverture dite française, dite lullyste, dite pointée, est née de la suite de danses en honneur au début du siècle : mais elle a sa structure et ses règles propres. Constituée d'un mouvement lent (de rythme généralement pointé) suivi d'un mouve-

---

[2] A noter que, en France, le nom de « classiques » s'applique à des musiciens du XVIIème et du XVIIIème siècles, tels Charpentier ou Delalande, qu'ailleurs on aurait appelé « baroques ».

Georges de La Tour, le Rembrandt français, apparaît, avec son Joueur de Vielle, *comme un peintre austère, dédaignant les effets faciles, utilisant avec sobriété les ressources de la composition, du dessin et de la couleur.*

ment rapide, elle s'oppose à l'ouverture à l'italienne, où les mouvements sont inversés.

Campra, Charpentier Parmi les contemporains et successeurs de Lully, alors que Campra triomphe dans l'opéra, Charpentier se donne entièrement à des sujets religieux : son austérité, sa puissance, son art du contrepoint, en font un des maîtres du classicisme français.

Delalande Delalande, à peine postérieur, est aussi un compositeur religieux. Sans jamais chercher ses effets, avec un naturel pleinement classique, ses motets atteignent, par la seule noblesse de son style, au tragique le plus profond et le moins complaisant. A travers lui, on saisit une autre France que celle qui jouit à l'étranger d'une popularité de mauvais aloi : une France de vigilance intérieure et non de panache et de distraction.

Couperin Plus recueilli encore est l'art de Couperin le Grand, le représentant le plus doué de toute une dynastie de musiciens. Essentiellement claveciniste, Couperin, sans jamais élever le ton, sans jamais céder à la moindre facilité, tire, d'un instrument considéré à juste titre comme sévère, une géométrie de sons à laquelle on ne trouve à comparer que celle de Jean-Sébastien Bach.

Rameau Bien d'autres noms se présentent à la pensée ; le plus grand est, sans conteste, celui de Rameau, qui, quand on ferait abstraction de ses compositions instrumentales ou de ses opéras, tel *les Indes galantes*, demeurerait encore un des musiciens les plus « constructifs » que le monde ait connu. Toute l'harmonie moderne se fonde sur le traité où il organise en quelques principes clairs les connaissances éparses qu'on avait amassées avant lui. Et l'histoire de l'opéra — qu'il soit italien, allemand, russe ou français — remonte à lui, avant d'aller trouver sa source dans Monteverdi. Son récitatif, infiniment plus subtil que celui de Lully, élève le français au niveau d'une langue musicale de premier plan, qualité qui lui a été si souvent contestée depuis lors, non sans justes raisons. Toutes les qualités les plus raffinées, celles auxquelles se reconnaît l'artiste de très haut vol — précision, mesure, art des liaisons, générosité, capacité de choisir la solution la meilleure parmi une multitude d'autres — appartiennent à Rameau dont on citait, en tête de chapitre, le mot révélateur.

Après Rameau, rien qui vaille la peine d'être mentionné, et cela pendant trois quarts de siècle.

La querelle dite des Bouffons, qui opposait « le coin du roi » (c'est-à-dire les partisans de la musique française) au « coin de la reine » (formé de ceux qui défendaient le *bel canto* naissant) et parmi lesquels Jean-Jacques Rousseau militait en bonne place), présente un intérêt plus historique que musical : elle marque la dernière étape du classicisme, le combat où les défenseurs du bon goût, de la raison et du naturel tirèrent leurs dernières cartouches. Ensuite, c'est le pathos et la virtuosité qui s'affrontent : l'art véritable n'a plus rien à dire ; il se tait.

LE ROMANTISME

Berlioz La bannière fut relevée dans le second quart du XIXème siècle par Berlioz. Non pas la bannière de l'art classique, mais celle de l'art tout court, et sous les couleurs du romantisme le plus « échevelé » (c'est le mot rituel).

L'œuvre de Berlioz, toute de drame, d'agitation, de violence, en un mot d'expressionnisme, a très longtemps été mal jugée : les uns l'aimaient, les autres la détestaient, pour de mauvaises raisons. Certes, les sous-titres pompeux de la *Symphonie fantastique* (*Marche au supplice*, par exemple) agacent copieusement les dents des amateurs modernes, après avoir fait battre le cœur de leurs arrière-arrière-grand-mères. Certes, la grandiloquence des cymbales peut surprendre, et l'étrange dessein d'exprimer ou de décrire quelque chose par la musique peut-elle indisposer au plus haut point. Mais nous aurions tort de boucher nos oreilles à la suite d'un réflexe de mauvaise humeur. En réalité, malgré — et non pas à cause de — toute la littérature romantique qu'il a lui-même échafaudée autour de son œuvre, Berlioz est un compositeur de premier plan et, pratiquement, le créateur de cette orchestration moderne que l'on compare toujours à la peinture, les timbres des divers instruments y tenant lieu de couleurs. Cette notion de coloration, si difficile à définir, il l'introduit même dans sa structure harmonique, lui qui, n'ayant pas l'oreille suffisamment juste, cherchait tous ses accords à la guitare, un à un...

Non content de créer une œuvre originale, Berlioz fut le premier représentant de cette renaissance de la musique française qu'on peut, si l'on aime les expressions toutes faites, appeler son second âge d'or, et qui correspond plus ou moins à la seconde moitié du XIXème siècle.

Franck　César Franck, Belge d'origine, Français d'adoption, fut l'un des représentants les plus graves, les plus austères de cette renaissance. Son amour de la musique instrumentale, son goût pour les poèmes symphoniques, en font aussi le plus « germanique » des romantiques français.

Bizet　C'est un romantique d'un tout autre genre que Bizet, compositeur de plusieurs opéras dont l'illustre *Carmen*. Nietzsche, après s'être brouillé avec Wagner, voyait dans Bizet l'incarnation du génie méditerranéen, donc classique, par opposition au génie proprement romantique de son ex-ami. Mais il pourrait bien y avoir là une systématisation outrée due à un accès de bile. Bizet est tout mouvement, tout flamme, tout couleur. Il bouillonne. Il a une exubérance juvénile, un tempérament violent, auquel les épithètes qu'on utilise pour qualifier les œuvres classiques siéraient mal. C'est en fait un cas unique dans son genre. N'est-il pas pittoresque que ce musicien français ait fait un opéra typiquement espagnol auquel les Espagnols eux-mêmes ne trouvent rien à redire ? Il est déjà rare qu'une semence étrangère puisse féconder un artiste et lui faire produire un chef d'œuvre ; mais que ce chef d'œuvre soit accepté dans le pays qu'il est censé représenter, c'est là une exception dont on trouverait malaisément un deuxième exemple.

François Mauriac dit, fort justement, que *Carmen* est un piège à cuistres.[3] Les gens qui, par snobisme, prétendent aimer la musique affectent de mépriser *Carmen* pour ses mélodies trop expressives et trop colorées ; les vrais amateurs savent reconnaître une grande œuvre sous les oripeaux qui plaisent au vulgaire.

Sous-produit du romantisme, le réalisme n'a abouti à aucune réussite notable. Mais des tentatives ont été faites dans cette direction par Gustave Charpentier.

---

[3] Un cuistre prétend avoir une supériorité intellectuelle sur le commun des mortels, mais cette supériorité est imaginaire.

L'ACADÉMISME

Certains musiciens, sans rien inventer de nouveau, ont tout de même collaboré à l'édification de la musique française dans un esprit conservateur qui ne devrait pas les faire totalement méconnaître, même si, à tel ou tel moment, ils ont joui, auprès du grand public, d'une extrême faveur.

Gounod, Massenet, Saint-Saëns — Gounod avec son *Faust*, Massenet avec sa *Manon*, font partie de cette catégorie. Il est permis d'y ranger aussi Saint-Saëns, amateur de belles sonorités un peu creuses.

Avec son Concert Champêtre, Watteau *n'est-il pas le Mozart de la peinture ?*

L'IMPRESSIONNISME

La peinture dite impressionniste a fait la guerre à la peinture dite académique. Par analogie, on a pris l'habitude de désigner sous le nom d'impressionnistes des musiciens tels que Claude Debussy ou même, avec quelques réserves, Gabriel Fauré ; par analogie aussi, nous avons qualifié d'académiques Saint-Saëns et Gounod. Mais que veut dire « académique » ? « Attaché à une certaine esthétique » (ajouter « périmée », ou « décadente », ou « sclérosée », si l'on veut rendre la définition péjorative). Et que veut dire « impressionniste » ? La définition philosophique, qui s'appliquait en peinture, ne signifie plus grand chose en musique. Il faut bien reconnaître que nous entrons ici dans le royaume mystérieux de la correspondance des arts, où l'on parle de coloration des timbres et de stridence des couleurs. Avançons prudemment.

En musique, « impressionniste » signifie à peu près « procédant par suite d'accords aux harmonies très fouillées ». Berlioz partait d'une mélodie, qu'il enrichissait par des accords. Les impressionnistes tendent à procéder à partir d'accords qui s'agrègent en mélodie. A l'oreille, cette technique donne une impression de nuancé (pour les partisans), de confus (pour les détracteurs), qui n'est pas sans rappeler le fouillis de petites touches juxtaposées d'un Renoir ou d'un Pissarro.

Debussy Il y a quelque chose d'agaçant et de rassurant à la fois à penser aux petits travers des hommes de génie. Les plus grands manquent souvent de cette qualité qui est si importante pour les moins grands : le bon goût. Balzac s'écriait lyriquement, « Mozart, à genoux devant Rossini ! » Claude Debussy se fit longtemps appeler Claude-Achille de Bussy. Il serait mesquin de le lui reprocher, mais ce genre de détail peut nous éclairer sur son esthétique.

Berlioz peut se comparer à Victor Hugo ; les musiciens académiques, aux poètes parnassiens (par exemple, Saint-Saëns à Sully-Prudhomme). Debussy, qui a choisi d'illustrer par un poème symphonique le texte de Mallarmé *l'Après-midi d'un faune*, n'est pas sans rappeler le chef des symbolistes. Mais il ne faut pas pousser ces analogies trop loin. Par-delà les esthétiques décadentes, les intentions biscornues, les snobismes salonnards, Debussy demeure l'un des plus grands musiciens connus, car ce qui l'intéresse vraiment, c'est la musique « en soi », comme on peut le voir dans ses dernières études pour piano, d'où toute littérature est absente, où l'art, seul et nu, règne en maître. Les titres parlent pour eux-mêmes. Entre *Rêverie* (1890) et *Étude pour les sonorités opposées* (1915), Debussy avait parcouru un bon bout de chemin. Cependant, c'est le drame lyrique *Pelléas et Mélisande* qui nous paraît être l'œuvre la plus significative de Debussy. Composée sur un livret symboliste et prétentieux, elle introduit, dans la musique française, une déclamation nouvelle dans le style récitatif, imitant dans les moindres détails le langage parlé, non plus en vers, mais en prose. En disant adieu à l'opéra traditionnel par airs et par numéros, Debussy se plaçait, dans la lignée wagnérienne ; d'un autre côté, en conservant toujours un ton contenu, en utilisant de petits écarts et en cherchant à imiter scrupuleusement le rythme du discours naturel,

La peinture de Braque, qui utilise des méthodes chères à Picasso, consiste en une reconstruction picturale du monde, comme l'atteste cet Homme à la Guitare.

Debussy prenait la tête des anti-wagnériens. Même opposition dans son orchestre : comme chez Wagner, l'orchestre ne sert plus d'accompagnement pour les chanteurs ; il devient l'élément fondamental du poème et les voix gardent à peine plus d'importance que les violons ; en revanche, alors que Wagner procède par leitmotivs, Debussy crée son atmosphère par des accords et — c'est affaire de tempérament — fait donner les cuivres bien moins souvent.

C'est surtout par cette façon de mettre à profit les innovations wagnériennes, mais, en même temps, de s'y opposer résolument au nom de la grâce, de la finesse, de la limpidité, de la modération, que Debussy a mérité son surnom de « Claude de France ».

Fauré, Duparc   Plus français encore, à la vérité, nous paraît Gabriel Fauré, moins inventif peut-être et en quelque sorte plus académique, mais d'une tenue plus stricte et plus souriante à la fois. Auprès de lui, il convient de placer un Duparc, qui s'est fait un nom avec quelques mélodies pour voix et piano révélant un talent dont la production demeure malheureusement restreinte.

LE NÉOCLASSICISME

Ravel   Encore qu'il ait adopté le coloris impressionniste, Maurice Ravel est, sans conteste, le prince des néoclassiques. C'est l'intelligence faite musique.

Mélodiste avant tout, il oppose aux effusions harmoniques d'un Debussy la rigueur un peu sèche de ses thèmes impeccablement entrelacés. Tout ce qui est son le passionne. Il crée des rythmes nouveaux, des accords insolites. Il s'attache en particulier aux problèmes d'orchestration pure. Le *Boléro* n'est jamais qu'un seul thème exposé successivement par tous les instruments de l'orchestre ; les *Tableaux d'une exposition*, une suite de Moussorgsky, écrite originellement pour piano, et que Ravel fait chanter par l'orchestre entier. S'étonnera-t-on qu'un aussi grand musicien s'amuse à travailler sur des thèmes qui ne lui appartiennent pas ? Outre de nombreux précédents musicaux, il convient d'evoquer ici les réflexions de l'écrivain anglais Charles Morgan dans *Sparkenbroke* : la traduction, dit-il, peut être une œuvre d'art plus satisfaisante que la création pure, car seuls les problèmes de forme s'y posent, et l'artiste est ainsi débarrassé de tout souci anecdotique.

Au reste, Ravel s'orchestre lui-même aussi brillamment. Et, dans ses œuvres les plus importantes (par exemple, le *Concerto pour la main gauche*), dévorant sa propre virtuosité, il atteint un niveau d'expression musicale qui, la géométrie de l'art étant non pas dépassée mais assimilée, se prête au langage de la poésie la plus tragique et la plus élevée.

Ce sens du tragique joint à un sens aigu de l'humour, cette possession complète des moyens les plus difficiles, voilà de quoi faire réfléchir ceux qui trouvent Ravel décadent et qui aiment à rappeler qu'il préférait jouer sur des pianos un peu désaccordés, par un raffinement excessif d'oreille.

Dukas, Vincent d'Indy, Roussel   Paul Dukas, étincelant et comme métallique ; Vincent d'Indy, fondateur de la Schola Cantorum et grand admirateur de la tradition musicale française ; Albert Roussel, compositeur d'une rare vigueur, ne regimbent pas trop si on les fourre dans la boîte aux néoclassiques. Un même souci de perfection les unit ; leur puissante vitalité les oppose aux académiques ; leur sens de la mélodie fait d'eux des adversaires directs de l'impressionnisme.

Quand les mélomanes français peu avertis parlent de musique moderne (avec un froncement de sourcil), ils pensent à Ravel et à Debussy, à qui ils reprochent leurs dissonances ; ces derniers ne s'en inquiètent guère, car ils sont morts depuis un tiers de siècle. On peut s'irriter de cette attitude retardataire ; on peut aussi s'interroger sur ses raisons.

C'est qu'en fait, dans le monde musical proprement français, il n'y a pas eu d'événement marquant depuis la bataille de *Pelléas* en 1902.

Certains musiciens ont poursuivi solitairement des recherches aboutissant à une œuvre individuelle de valeur, mais ne donnant pas le branle à un de ces grands mouvements qu'on avait connus plus tôt. C'est le cas d'un Eric Satie, d'un Florent Schmitt et surtout du plus intéressant d'entre eux, le compositeur religieux Olivier Messiaen.

Certains, pendant le second quart du siècle, se sont groupés au sein d'un cénacle appelé « les Six » (à l'imitation du groupe des Cinq Russes au siècle précédent), mais aucune unité de doctrine ne les unissait. Poulenc, Milhaud, le Suisse Honegger, semblent les plus universellement connus.

Boulez D'autres, tel Boulez, se sont intéressés, sous la forme sérielle aux recherches atonales que poursuivaient les musiciens allemands. La notion de *ton* leur paraissait tout à fait relative ; ils souhaitaient revenir à des modes différents. Il ne semble pas que, en France, leurs recherches aient produit des résultats notables.

D'autres encore voudraient explorer le domaine du quart de ton. Mais quel public les suivra ? Leurs explorations demeurent pour l'instant plus théoriques que pratiques.

Schaeffer La musique concrète — c'est-à-dire faite de bruits non timbrés et non plus de sons — a ses adeptes. Son grand maître est Pierre Schaeffer. Pour le moment, les réalisations dans ce domaine paraissent plus piquantes que constructives, mais c'est peut-être parce que nous n'avons pas encore l'oreille faite à ce genre de productions. Après tout, la tierce paraissait bien insupportable au public du Moyen Age qui n'y était pas habitué.

Sans doute pourrait-on citer des noms de compositeurs de talent, jeunes ou vieux, qui s'efforcent de renouveler l'opéra, la suite symphonique, la littérature d'orgue, l'oratorio, etc., en appliquant quelquefois une écriture par « cellules sonores » dite non plus horizontale ni verticale, mais oblique. Mais on ne saurait le faire sans partialité, car aucun d'entre eux — à l'exception de Poulenc, suprêmement délicat, sophistiqué, précieux — n'a encore émergé de la masse.

Cela tient peut-être à l'absence, en France, d'une élite musicale suffisamment écoutée pour imposer des choix. Cela pourrait tenir aussi à un « creux de l'histoire » comme ceux qu'elle a déjà connus en d'autres occasions. Essoufflée par tous les talents qu'elle a produits à la fin du siècle dernier, elle est peut-être en train de récupérer ses forces, en attendant l'an 2000.

8 COSTUME ET
ARTS DÉCORATIFS

IDÉE GÉNÉRALE

Il serait plaisant pour l'esprit d'établir une correspondance rigoureuse entre l'évolution des arts tout court et celle des arts décoratifs. Au classicisme en littérature ferait pendant un goût sévère et sobre dans l'habillement ; les précieuses auraient des franges de perles à leurs abat-jour ; les peintres et les modistes s'engoueraient en même temps pour l'Antiquité.

Dans la réalité, il n'en est rien. Et il y a à cela une raison bien simple : c'est que les grands artistes sont toujours en avance sur leur temps et qu'ils ne s'occupent pas d'arts décoratifs.

Nous imaginons le XVIIème siècle comme une époque « classique ». En réalité, quelques dizaines d'hommes à peine étaient attachés au classicisme dans ce qu'il a de plus idéal, mais, pour leurs usages vestimentaires et mobiliers, ils vivaient avec leur temps, c'est-à-dire dans un foisonnement qui tenait du baroque et du précieux.

Nous prenons le début du XIXème siècle pour une période romantique. Nullement. Ce fut une période éminemment bourgeoise, pendant laquelle plusieurs exaltés — ceux dont nous avons retenu le nom — ont créé ce que nous appelons le romantisme. La mode n'était rien moins que romantique, et les fabricants de meubles dessinaient des fauteuils pour douairières[1] et non pour jeunes gens tuberculeux.

Cette notion de décalage entre l'art et le goût est de première importance dans une enquête comme celle que nous poursuivons. On ne peut pas généraliser et simplifier à la fois sans tomber dans la contre-vérité systématique. Donc, dans la mesure où nous généralisons, ne simplifions pas.

La France a longtemps été considérée comme la patrie du goût et de l'art de vivre. C'est dire que les arts décoratifs y ont toujours eu une place de choix, non seulement pour leur valeur plastique, mais aussi parce qu'on les fréquente chaque jour et que, pour cette raison, ils ont une influence directe sur notre vie. C'est donc dans cette perspective qu'il faut considérer leur évolution.

LE MOYEN AGE

Epoque du raffinement le plus délicat et de la barbarie la plus crue, le Moyen Age, que nous considérerons pour cette fois dans son ensemble, nous a légué, en fait d'arts décoratifs, peu de choses, mais sublimes.

Pendant cette succession de siècles mi-religieux mi-guerriers, l'ameublement et le costume tinrent dans la vie une place relativement restreinte. Les salles immenses des châteaux recevaient un tapis de paille uniformément distribué, qu'il était facile de changer lorsqu'il sentait trop mauvais. Cette paille servait de lit à la plus grande partie de la mesnie.[2] Seuls le seigneur et sa dame avaient droit à un lit véritable, qui ressemblait à un monument : escalier pour y accéder, colonnes pour en soutenir le baldaquin, rideaux pour en abriter l'intimité. Cette couche sacrée était une maison dans la maison. Quelquefois, les serviteurs les plus proches y dormaient avec leurs maîtres. Quelques tables rustaudes, quelques lourdes chaises plus féodales que confortables, quelques bancelles pour le menu fretin, d'énormes bahuts de bois sculpté, à ferrures ciselées, et voilà tout le mobilier d'un grand seigneur médiéval.

Tapisseries, vitraux   En revanche, les murs recevaient des ornements qui demeurent parmi les plus beaux du monde et que, comme tels, on trouvait plus souvent dans les églises que dans les châteaux : tapisseries et vitraux. Accrochées à même les grosses pierres grises des tours, les tapisseries racontaient des histoires allégoriques, mystiques ou historiques : conquête de

[1] au sens propre, veuves de personnages importants ; ici, dames d'un certain âge, imposantes, solennelles jusqu'au ridicule
[2] ensemble comprenant la famille du seigneur, ses cousins, ses pages, ses domestiques et ses hommes d'armes

L'imagination plastique éclate dans la tapisserie médiévale de l'Apocalypse...

l'Angleterre, Apocalypse, capture d'une licorne.[3] Surfaces translucides posées entre les fidèles et le soleil pour en colorer la lumière dans les églises, les vitraux illustraient des sujets religieux. Vitraux et tapisseries du Moyen Age sont admirables non seulement à cause de leur beauté propre mais parce qu'ils représentent l'aboutissement suprême d'une technique qui se mue en art, soit le point culminant de la pureté artistique.

Plus tard, au XVIIème siècle en particulier, bénéficiant de l'encouragement royal et de la création de la manufacture des Gobelins, les tapisseries, de plus en plus complexes, de plus en plus achevées, ne seront plus qu'une sous-peinture. La même aventure arrivera aux vitraux au XIXème siècle.

Au XXème, les tapisseries renaîtront, principalement sous l'influence de Lurçat ; mais les vitraux semblent être bien morts, d'autant que toutes les tentatives faites pour retrouver leurs secrets de fabrication ont été vaines. Sans doute peut-on encore faire des vitraux, mais rien qui puisse se comparer pour la richesse et la finesse du coloris aux chefs d'œuvre du XII[éme] et du XIII[éme] siècles, l'époque des rouges et des bleus foncés, quand le vitrail était encore une mosaïque de verre maintenue en place par un réseau de plomb.

[3] bête fabuleuse symbolisant la chasteté

C'est à dessein qu'on a réuni dans un même paragraphe deux expressions presque contradictoires du même besoin de couleurs aux murs ; en réalité, le vitrail, art essentiellement français, entre en décadence quand la tapisserie, importée de Flandre, commence à produire des chefs d'œuvre.

Costume Les miniatures du temps nous ont conservé l'image des costumes, qui ne manquaient pas de grâce. Les braies — c'est-à-dire le pantalon — étaient traditionnelles chez les Gaulois, et, après un intermède gallo-romain à l'antique, pendant lequel hommes et femmes portèrent tuniques, ces messieurs revinrent au pantalon, qu'ils portaient long, collant et quelquefois de couleurs différentes pour les deux jambes. Ces dames s'amusaient surtout avec des chapeaux de formes et de dimensions démentielles qu'elles appelaient hennins.

LA RENAISSANCE

Costume La puissance croissante de la monarchie, ce désir d'épater leurs vassaux par un étalage de richesses qui s'empara alors des rois de France (ils avaient, en ce temps-là, des naïvetés de parvenus), la révélation des costumes italiens, la prolifération de la cour, la disparition progressive des armures, ces vêtements de fer, tout cela fit de la Renaissance une des grandes périodes vestimentaires de l'histoire de France. Tandis que les femmes s'en donnaient à cœur joie avec les riches étoffes qu'on importait d'Italie et les dentelles que

... comme dans les tapisseries modernes, qui sortent de l'atelier de Jean Lurçat.

produisait la Flandre, les hommes faisaient résolument peau neuve. Leur collant coupé en deux devenait *haut de chausses* (culotte bouffante couvrant le bassin et le haut des cuisses), et *bas de chausses* (plus ou moins semblables aux bas de femme actuels mais plus gros). Le *pourpoint* (c'est-à-dire la veste) s'enrichit de superbes manches à crevés faisant apparaître, par des ouvertures dans l'étoffe, une somptueuse doublure. Le linge s'exhibait fièrement avec la *fraise*, qui forçait à porter haut la tête et donnait grand air.

Décoration   Parallèlement, l'intérieur des maisons se transformait. Les murs de pierre n'étaient plus tolérables : on les cacha, soit en les recouvrant de lambris de bois sculpté, soit en les tendant d'étoffes uniformément rouges. Finis, les plafonds à solives : on les fit à caissons, on les sculpta et on les dora. Le luxe fleurissait partout, et l'ornementation proprement dite se donnait libre cours. Les motifs les plus courants étaient encore empruntés au bestiaire héraldique, telle la fameuse salamandre de François Ier. Les cheminées devenaient des pièces montées, avec des cariatides pour en porter le manteau. Il ne restait plus qu'à fabriquer des meubles dignes de figurer dans ces salons. On les fabriqua.

Le bois sculpté dans la masse distingue tout particulièrement la Renaissance. On fit ainsi des tables, des chaises, des lits et, les bahuts, ces gisants, s'étant enfin décidés à se lever, des buffets. Avec leurs colonnes, leurs torsades, leurs moulures, leurs motifs géométriques ou représentatifs, avec toute leur luisance de bois poli, les meubles Renaissance ont actuellement mauvaise presse. Mais c'est qu'on les juge surtout d'après les mauvaises imitations qu'on en fit au XIXème siècle.

LOUIS XIII

On ne niera pas cependant qu'ils n'atteignent pas à l'inimitable grandeur du Louis XIII, ce style dans lequel le moindre fauteuil a l'air d'un trône, mais qui ne pèche jamais par ostentation. Dossiers perpendiculaires en tapisserie ou en cuir repoussé souvent importé d'Espagne, accoudoirs imposants faits pour porter les avant-bras d'un Richelieu, pieds vigoureusement torsadés mais encore reliés entre eux par des barres transversales pour plus de solidité, voilà de quoi faire rêver toutes les maîtresses de maison de Paris devant les vitrines des antiquaires.

LOUIS XIV

Ameublement   Les meubles ont leur dialectique. Après la richesse de la Renaissance, la sobriété du Louis XIII ; puis, la pompe du Louis XIV.

Non seulement les fauteuils deviennent encore plus vastes, encore plus ornés et, si l'on peut dire, encore plus perpendiculaires, mais de nouvelles catégories de meubles apparaissent. On fait des divans, des secrétaires, des armoires, des commodes, des pendules, et non plus seulement des lits, des sièges, des tables et des buffets. Le bronze triomphe partout ; il sert, le plus souvent, à représenter des sujets mythologiques. La marqueterie fait fureur. Les plus grands fabricants se mettent à signer leurs meubles : Boulle est le plus illustre d'entre eux.

Décoration   La décoration proprement dite ne le cède en rien à l'ameublement pour la splendeur. Des parquets au dessin compliqué luisent de toute leur cire. Les murs, qu'au début du siècle on avait déjà commencé à décorer d'étoffes de couleurs variées, ne sont plus maintenant que tapisseries des Gobelins, marbre, miroirs, lambris sculptés, et peinture. Peintures au-dessus des portes, peintures au-dessus des cheminées, peintures même au plafond, avec perspective appropriée.

A voir tout cela, ce ne sont certes pas les mots de grâce ou même de bon goût qui viennent à l'esprit. A vrai dire, on s'étonne surtout que malgré la débauche de dorure et de mythologie, malgré cette rage d'utiliser le moindre espace à fins de décoration, l'ensemble ne soit pas vraiment laid : il conserve une unité dans le propos et une qualité dans le détail qui imposent des idées de noblesse et de grandeur.

Costume   Hélas, la grâce manque aussi tragiquement aux costumes de l'époque, et c'est plus grave, car qu'est-ce donc qu'un costume sans grâce ? On ne parle pas ici des femmes : elles tiraient leur épingle du jeu en conservant plus de sobriété. Mais les hommes ! Ce n'était que plumes, que nœuds, que rubans, que dentelles, et qu'espèce de petits volants. La tête disparaissait sous une perruque qui avait l'air d'un catafalque, et le corps, sous des ruissellements de faveurs. Pas une ligne verticale dans tout le costume : rien que des horizontales et des diagonales enchevêtrées. La culotte, beaucoup plus longue qu'au siècle précédent, se cache sous le gilet, qui se cache sous la jaquette, qui se cache sous les rubans. Et s'habiller ainsi, c'était, ce que l'on appelait au XVIIème, « être propre ».

LOUIS XV

Costume   Au XVIIIème, tout changea. En fait, tout avait déjà commencé à changer un peu plus tôt, mais c'est au siècle de Louis XV qu'il appartenait de créer des vêtements, masculins et féminins, d'une élégance qu'on ne retrouvera jamais plus. Les robes prennent, par le bas, une ampleur admirablement proportionnée, mettant en valeur la taille corsetée au bon endroit et la gorge généreusement découverte. Les paniers qu'on porte sous des étoffes de plus en plus délicates, le rouge, les mouches, la poudre, tout cela ne brille

Renaissance : sculpture sur
bois.

Louis XIII : torsades.

Louis XIV : solemnité de
bon goût.

Louis XV : courbes et
contre-courbes.

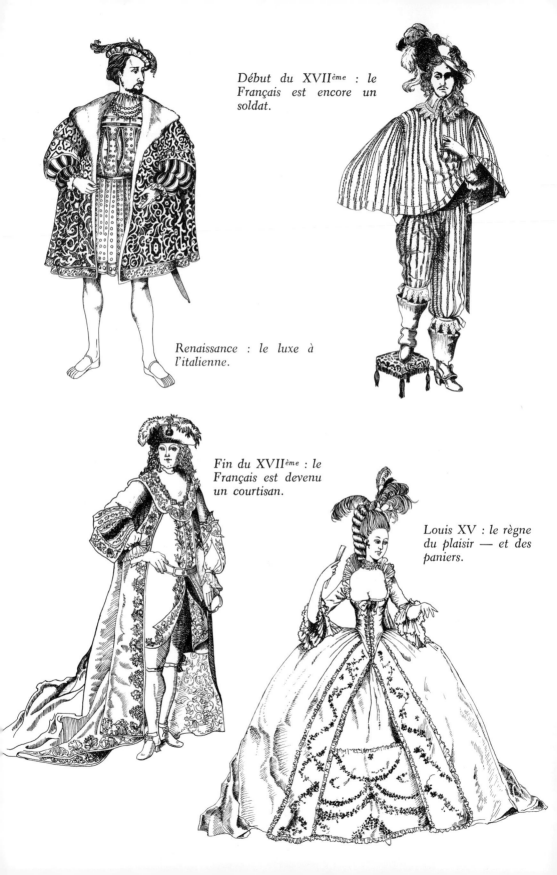

Début du XVIIème : le
Français est encore un
soldat.

Renaissance : le luxe à
l'italienne.

Fin du XVIIème : le
Français est devenu
un courtisan.

Louis XV : le règne
du plaisir — et des
paniers.

sans doute pas par le naturel. Mais quelle réussite plastique ! Quel art fastueux dans la simplicité de la conception ! Quelle révélation sur un monde où l'on savait vivre et où le mot *plaisir* n'était pas encore entaché d'infamie !

Le costume masculin est plus réussi encore. De la perruque poudrée, moulant la tête et nouée derrière en forme de queue, aux fins souliers à boucles et à talons, en passant par le jabot de dentelle, le gilet court, la jaquette longue aux basques insolemment échancrées, aux manches à revers d'où sourdant les explosions de dentelle des manchettes, la culotte à la française s'étranglant au-dessous du genou, les bas galbés sur des mollets avantageux (et quelquefois rembourrés d'ouate), la petite épée de cérémonie à poignée de nacre, sorte de point d'exclamation accentuant la distinction du personnage, le costume Louis XV est parfait en tout point. Il est encore porté de nos jours — l'épée en moins — par les valets de grande maison dits « habillés à la française » que l'on voit dans les principales réceptions parisiennes.

Décoration　En revanche, ce n'est pas par la sobriété que brille la décoration Louis XV. L'engouement des décorateurs pour « les chinoiseries », le désir de faire suave, gracieux et luxueux en même temps, l'influence de l'Europe dont les décorateurs français adoptent le rococo sous la forme assagie du rocaille, font du Louis XV un style précieux jusqu'à l'afféterie.

Ameublement　Cela se voit surtout dans l'ameublement. La ligne droite du siècle précédent est remplacée par la ligne tordue, avec courbe et contre-courbe. Ce n'est pas pour cela qu'il y a moins de dorures : le Louis XV est un Louis XIV dépravé. Il y a davantage d'amours joufflus que de Minerves austères sur les pendules ; les panneaux héroïques ont fait place aux scènes langoureuses ; les fauteuils aux pieds incurvés ne sont plus calculés pour porter des ministres mais d'insignifiants abbés de cour. Cependant, tout cela demeure surchargé, et seule la légèreté de la surcharge en autorise l'excès.

LOUIS XVI

Le Louis XVI est à la décoration ce que le Louis XV est au costume. Brusquement l'aristocratie française semble avoir trouvé un goût réellement classique, par lassitude de tous les semi-baroques dans lesquels elle vivait depuis cent ans. La ligne droite reparaît soudain, avec le rond et surtout l'ovale ; la forme s'épure ; la dorure passe au troisième plan ; on recherche l'harmonie des nuances ; les motifs de décoration deviennent des pastorales : toutes les tapisseries de France se couvrent de bergers sentimentaux qui n'ont rien à envier à leurs ancêtres, sortis du roman de *L'Astrée* au XVIIème siècle. Sous prétexte de vertu, la sensualité des thèmes devient plus subtile ; c'est le règne du médaillon, du nœud plat, de la cannelure, et la rayure apparaît déjà. Il y a tout un enseignement artistique dans cette splendeur digérée qui s'épanouit en bon goût.

DIRECTOIRE

En France, chaque fois qu'on veut faire simple, on annonce qu'on va « faire Antique ». C'est là une pose plus qu'une illusion, car qu'y a-t-il de moins simple que le « corinthien » grec ou le « composite » romain ? Le Louis XVI, le Directoire et l'Empire avaient des prétentions antiques tous les trois, mais ils se ressemblent fort peu.

Le Directoire accentue la prédilection du Louis XVI pour les lignes droites, met des bouts carrés à ses bras de fauteuil, enroule les dossiers de tous ses meubles, les tapisse d'étoffes à rayures et commence à les fabriquer en acajou, mode anglaise. Il y a de la provocation dans cette simplicité. Elle était censée convenir aux mœurs austères de la République romaine dont on se réclamait hautement tout en pataugeant dans la débauche. De là peut-être cette froideur feinte, ce refus des rondeurs, et en même temps cet amour des divans intimes, si caractéristiques d'un style qui porta à son comble le *naturel artificiel*.

EMPIRE

L'Empire lui aussi prétend retrouver la gravité antique. C'est pourquoi il fait lourd, massif, cubique. Il affectionne l'acajou, bois foncé et dur qui se prête mal au ciseau de l'artisan et qu'on décore en conséquence de moulures en cuivre. Le bronze n'est pas oublié. Ces bronzes, ces cuivres vert-de-grisés, mettent des reflets verts dans les surfaces polies de l'acajou rougeoyant. Les fauteuils imitent les chaises curules ; il leur faut supporter maintenant le poids de maréchaux qui furent palefreniers : ils sont taillés en conséquence. Le meuble qui s'appelait secrétaire devient prosaïquement bureau et ressemble à un arc de triomphe. La ligne droite demeure au pouvoir, avec quelques complaisances pour le cercle. Les motifs d'ornementation sont soit militaires soit égyptiens : casques, trophées, panoplies, sphinx, etc. Dans la décoration le vert forcé, le jaune pâle, le violet, sont à la mode. On a prétendu que l'Empire était le style d'un homme : Napoléon. C'est beaucoup plus celui d'une classe : la bourgeoisie, qui vient d'arriver au pouvoir et qui entend montrer qu'elle y restera.

LE COSTUME DE LOUIS XVI A NAPOLÉON IER

Sous Louis XVI, le costume demeura, à peu de choses près, ce qu'il était sous Louis XV. La jaquette se simplifia encore, et les gentilshommes oublièrent quelquefois de porter l'épée ; les dames se mirent des tournures par derrière au lieu de paniers sur les côtés et se dressèrent des échafaudages sur la tête. La Révolution allait changer tout cela, en faisant rouler les têtes et en supprimant la cour qui donnait le ton à celles du monde entier. Jamais les vêtements n'ont autant changé qu'entre 1789 et 1815.

Louis XVI : l'apogée de l'élégance masculine.

Empire : la taille quitte sa place naturelle.

Restauration : tous les hommes s'habillent en bourgeois.

Second Empire : la crinoline est aux bourgeoises ce que les paniers furent à la noblesse.

Louis XVI : le sommet du goût français en art décoratif.

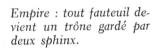

Directoire : les influences anglaises apparaissent.

Empire : tout fauteuil devient un trône gardé par deux sphinx.

... avant de sombrer dans le goût pompier du Second Empire.

Restauration : l'art décoratif se guinde une dernière fois...

En 1789, les Françaises étaient en forme par devant et plus qu'en forme par derrière. Dix ans plus tard, elles sont devenues normales par derrière ; par devant, elles ne s'habillent plus : elles se déshabillent. La gorge est presque nue et le reste, enveloppé d'une mousseline si transparente que c'est comme s'il n'y avait rien. Elles prétendent que c'est la mode antique et républicaine ; on les appelle gentiment « merveilleuses ». Encore dix ans, et voici que, la vertu logeant aux Tuileries, les étoffes redeviennent opaques, et la taille fait un bond vers le haut tandis que la poitrine s'efface chastement, comme par enchantement. C'est la robe Empire.

Les hommes, eux, renoncent à tout ce qui a fait leur élégance jusque-là. Ils remplacent la culotte par le pantalon à sous-pied, la jaquette par la redingote et l'habit ; ils abandonnent peu à peu les couleurs variées qu'ils avaient aimées. Coupés en deux horizontalement au niveau de la taille, recoupés, toujours horizontalement, au niveau de l'aine ou de la cuisse, ils deviennent en peu de temps ce qu'ils sont encore : de tristes oiseaux au plumage noir, gris et blanc, chez qui la couleur passe pour une audace de goût ou pour une manifestation d'opinions non-conformistes. Ici comme ailleurs se faisait sentir l'influence de l'Angleterre — « cette nation de boutiquiers », disait Napoléon.

LA RESTAURATION ET LE SECOND EMPIRE

Costume   Il est inutile de traiter l'évolution du costume masculin de la Restauration jusqu'à nos jours. Cette évolution n'a rien de typiquement français. A Londres, à Saint-Pétersbourg et à Berlin, on s'habillait exactement comme à Paris. On préférait les tailleurs français mais les étoffes anglaises ; on n'était pas tout à fait certain que les huit-reflets parisiens eussent tout le chic des londoniens : ce n'était plus qu'une question de snobisme. Les lignes, les éléments, étaient fournis une fois pour toutes, et l'on en jouait avec une extrême prudence. Qu'on y songe : en plein romantisme, il suffisait que M. Théophile Gautier mît un gilet rouge pour affoler Paris !

Pour les femmes, il en va à peine autrement. Seule l'apparition de la haute couture sous le Second Empire sauva le costume féminin du marasme[4] d'où les complets-vestons ne se relèveront sans doute jamais. Mais, comme alors le monde entier se mit à copier la France, l'histoire de la robe française est trop connue pour la raconter ici. Contentons-nous de dire qu'elle sut s'adapter à l'évolution des mœurs et que la nécessité d'habiller, de façon plus ou moins semblable, les milliardaires et les trottins en raccourcit la longueur, en supprima les éléments postiches et en ramena la variété au jeu perpétuel des deux horizontales : emplacement de la taille et hauteur de la jupe au-dessus du sol.

C'est sans doute du Second Empire que date la notion moderne d'une correspondance secrète entre la façon dont un homme (ou une femme) s'habille et ses penchants, sa conception du monde, sa personnalité. La raison en est évidente : la disparition d'une classe dirigeante qui imposait un certain

[4] décadence tragique

goût (le sien) à toute la nation, a favorisé, pour un certain temps, l'initiative personnelle. Bien entendu, le conformisme vestimentaire de nos contemporains, la production industrielle du prêt à porter et, d'une façon générale, le nivellement par le milieu auquel nous assistons, auront raison un jour ou l'autre de cette fantaisie que permettait l'existence des couturières et des petits tailleurs.

Ameublement   Les vêtements, au XIXème, ont encore du chic sinon de la grâce. Les meubles sont bien pires. Pendant près de cent ans, les artisans français sont incapables d'inventer et se contentent de superposer des ornements de styles différents, espérant faire une création de ce mélange. C'est le Restauration guindé ; le Louis-Philippe pataud ; le Napoléon III tape-à-l'œil. De cette époque — toujours l'influence anglaise — date la naissance d'une pièce nouvelle : la salle à manger, qui contredit toutes les traditions françaises en fait d'aménagement de l'habitation. Jusque-là, on dressait une table volante dans tel ou tel salon, au choix, et l'on changeait souvent. La Varende cite même le cas d'un duc qui fit un jour dresser sa table à l'écurie, pour avoir des commensaux[5] aussi nobles que lui. Mais, à partir du XIXème siècle, une solennelle salle à manger va faire pendant au salon unique.

C'est au XIXème aussi qu'apparut l'usage de meubler son appartement en styles différents d'après les pièces : la chambre, en Louis XV ; le salon, en Louis XVI ; la salle à manger, en Henri II ; le bureau, en Empire ; etc.

Rustique   Cependant, malgré la laideur ambiante, on continuait à fabriquer des meubles assez élégants du style dit « rustique ». Il s'était comme spontanément créé en province au siècle précédent, et les connaisseurs commençaient à apprécier cette aimable synthèse paysanne du courbe et du rectiligne. Hautes armoires normandes, lits bretons en forme de buffets, chaises et tables de noyer, ces meubles-là, construits pour durer jusqu'au Jugement dernier, ont une distinction simplette de fort bon aloi et coûtent à présent de petites fortunes. On en refait maintenant, industriellement, comme on refait du Louis XV, du Louis XVI et de l'Empire industriel : c'est là ce qu'on appelle des meubles « de style » par opposition aux meubles « d'époque ».

LE MODERN STYLE[6]

Décoration   A la fin du XIXème siècle et au début du XXème, il se passa tout de même un phénomène nouveau : la banquise bougeait. Le public découvrit tout à coup qu'il ne pouvait plus respirer dans l'atmosphère écrasante du pseudo-style régnant : il réclama (c'est là une façon de parler,

[5] invités partageant la table de leur hôte ; il s'agissait évidemment de chevaux de très grande race
[6] nom donné en France avec cette orthographe curieusement anglo-saxonne au mouvement que les Anglo-Saxons, eux, appellent du nom français d'*art nouveau*.

Le métro est là pour témoigner des outrances du style « nouille » du début du siècle... et (à droite) de son épuration au cours des décennies suivantes.

car en réalité le public ne réclame que ce que les artistes lui proposent) du naturel. Oh ! ce fut encore un naturel bien contourné, bien sophistiqué, bien fin de siècle. Du moins, principal avantage de la chose, disait-on définitivement adieu au composite surdoré du Second Empire. On découvrit que, pour mettre un ornement en relief, il fallait un espace vide autour : c'était simple, mais il fallait y penser. On se laissa intriguer une fois de plus par les arts orientaux et, pour la première fois, par l'art nègre. On s'aperçut avec surprise que la végétation terrestre ne produit pas que des feuilles d'acanthe, et l'on mit partout des fleurs stylisées et des espèces de lianes. Tout cela ne paraissait pas venir très spontanément aux artistes ni aux artisans : ils y consacraient des efforts qu'on sent toujours dans la torsion des lignes, dans l'allongement vermiculaire des formes. C'est ce qu'on appelle familièrement le style *nouille* ou le style *métro* : les plus anciennes stations de métro parisiennes ont en effet été traitées dans ce genre.

LE STYLE RECTILIGNE DES ANNÉES 20

Décoration   Le Modern style triompha jusqu'en 1914, avec ses courbes insidieuses, sa laborieuse frivolité, son apparence générale de liquide solidifié. Après 1918 on ne voulut plus que des droites, mais, de préférence, sans angles droits. Ce fut l'apothéose de l'hexagone. On mit des hexagones partout. Le mobilier devenait de moins en moins cher et de plus en plus hideux — comme d'habitude, par désir de simplicité. Le désir de simplicité des Français les entraîne aux plus étranges complications.

Ce n'est guère que dans le domaine de la vaisselle et de certains ustensiles que le bon goût se faisait jour peu à peu. Comme en architecture, les décora-

teurs recherchaient là des formes belles par elles-mêmes, sans souci d'orne-mentation. Et peut-être réussissaient-ils mieux que les architectes...

LA DÉCORATION CONTEMPORAINE

Aujourd'hui, la décoration est devenue un art mineur mais indépendant, alors que, au siècle dernier, elle ne se distinguait guère de l'architecture. Elle y a acquis certains dénominateurs internationaux qui ne permettent plus de l'étudier dans les mêmes conditions. En outre, l'apparition d'innombrables matières nouvelles semble la dominer, plus que le respect d'un style donné. Enfin, l'optique contemporaine a changé du tout au tout : alors que, pour le XVIIème siècle, nous nous contentons généralement de savoir comment étaient logés le roi et les grands seigneurs, pour le XXème, nous avons sans cesse sous les yeux, par le moyen de la presse, les intérieurs les plus divers, des plus pauvres aux plus riches. Par conséquent, il ne semble pas que nous puissions risquer des généralisations qui ne correspondraient qu'à une moyenne abstraite, donc inexistante.

Les décorateurs à la mode sont anglais ou scandinaves, et ce sont eux qui décorent les appartements de Paris, aussi bien que ceux de New York ou de Londres. Les petits bourgeois aiment bien acheter des meubles espagnols dans les grands magasins. Les industriels se plaisent à décorer leurs bureaux dans un style futuriste pour impressionner leurs concurrents, mais ils achètent du rustique pour leur maison de campagne et du Louis XIII pour leur apparte-ment parisien. Bref, une sorte de confusion règne dans le domaine du goût. Du moins peut-on dire que le mauvais ne prédomine plus.

LA NATION 9
FRANÇAISE

IDÉE GÉNÉRALE

A l'origine, les États-Unis ont été une fédération. La Russie a toujours été un empire. La France est une nation.

C'est même la nation-type, car la Grande-Bretagne est insulaire avant d'être nationale ; l'Allemagne, l'Italie, sentent encore l'amalgame récent ; l'Espagne, malgré l'admirable relèvement des dernières années, demeure l'ombre d'elle-même ; les pays d'Amérique du Sud n'ont pas encore atteint leur propre originalité. La France, elle, est redevenue, après avoir fait quelques expériences impériales, une nation au sens le plus étroit du terme.

On se propose d'analyser le phénomène « nation française » en étudiant d'abord le moule dans lequel elle s'est coulée, c'est-à-dire ses institutions ; ensuite sa matière politique, économique et sociale ; enfin son état actuel, c'est-à-dire la Cinquième République telle qu'elle se présente face aux problèmes intérieurs et extérieurs qui se posent à elle.

Marx, en une page admirable, a déclaré que jusqu'ici les sociétés humaines n'avaient été gouvernées que par la fatalité, par l'aveugle mouvement des formes économiques ; les institutions, les idées n'ont pas été l'œuvre consciente de l'homme libre, mais le reflet de l'inconsciente vie sociale dans le cerveau humain. Nous ne sommes encore, selon Marx, que dans la préhistoire. L'histoire humaine ne commencera véritablement que lorsque l'homme, échappant enfin à la tyrannie des forces inconscientes, gouvernera par sa raison et sa volonté la production elle-même. Alors son esprit ne subira plus le despotisme des formes économiques créées et dirigées par lui, et c'est d'un regard libre et immédiat qu'il contemplera l'univers. Marx entrevoit donc une période de pleine liberté intellectuelle où la pensée humaine, n'étant plus déformée par les servitudes économiques, ne déformera pas le monde. Mais, à coup sûr, Marx ne conteste pas que déjà, dans les ténèbres de la période inconsciente, de hauts esprits se soient élevés à la liberté ; par eux l'humanité se prépare et s'annonce. C'est à nous de recueillir ces premières manifestations de la vie de l'esprit : elles nous permettent de pressentir la grande vie ardente et libre de l'humanité communiste, qui, affranchie de tout servage, s'appropriera l'univers par la science, l'action et le rêve. C'est comme le premier frisson qui dans la forêt humaine n'émeut encore que quelques feuilles mais qui annonce les grands souffles prochains et les vastes ébranlements.

JEAN JAURÈS

LA DÉMOCRATIE FRANÇAISE

Traditionnellement, du moins pour les étrangers, la France est le pays démocratique par excellence, puisqu'elle est la patrie de la révolution. Et sans doute peut-on dire, dans la mesure où ce genre de généralisation a un sens, que le tempérament français — irrespectueux, frondeur, individualiste, envieux, libertin — ne saurait s'accommoder que des structures politiques, économiques et sociales les plus lâches. En réalité, il n'en est pas ainsi. Moins un tempérament est naturellement discipliné, plus il a besoin de discipline ; moins les Français sont capables de se gouverner eux-mêmes, plus ils sentent le besoin d'être gouvernés. De là tous les paradoxes de la démocratie française.

La souveraineté, en principe, appartient entièrement au peuple, qui l'exerce de trois façons.

Démocratie municipale   Elle s'exerce, premièrement, à l'échelon municipal, autrement dit celui de la commune, fraction de base de la nation fran-

La démocratie française commence dans les petites mairies des villages...

çaise, pour le territoire et la population qui l'habite. Tous les six ans le peuple élit au suffrage universel direct un *conseil municipal* d'une vingtaine de membres, lequel choisit dans son sein le *maire* de la commune. Le maire devient à la fois un représentant de « sa » commune et un agent de l'État. Il prépare le budget, exerce la police administrative, applique les lois, sert d'officier d'état civil à ses administrés. Ses fonctions sont étendues ; ses responsabilités, considérables. L'originalité de son rôle consiste dans le fait que, élu par le peuple, ce n'est pas devant le peuple qu'il est responsable mais devant l'autorité de tutelle, dont on parlera ci-dessous.

Démocratie parlementaire   Deuxièmement, toujours au suffrage universel direct, le peuple élit le *Parlement*, composé de deux chambres. Le *Sénat*, élu pour neuf ans et doué de pouvoirs limités, représente les valeurs de stabilité et de continuité. Il est d'ailleurs sans doute appelé à se voir remplacé par un conseil consultatif mieux adapté aux besoins de la démocratie présidentielle d'aujourd'hui. L'*Assemblée nationale*, ex-Chambre des députés, a une durée de vie normale de cinq ans et forme la source principale du pouvoir législatif, l'incarnation concrète de la souveraineté populaire.

En fait, du moins sous la Troisième et la Quatrième Républiques, l'Assemblée nationale faisait beaucoup plus qu'incarner la souveraineté populaire : elle la détenait. Le Français, paresseux et sceptique, ne prenait guère la peine (comme le font souvent les Anglo-Saxons) d'aiguillonner et de brider tour à tour ses députés par des lettres, des entrevues, des appels téléphoniques. Le

... s'élève jusqu'au Sénat et à l'Assemblée Nationale logés respectivement au Luxembourg et au Palais-Bourbon, et se transmue finalement en autorité...

... au Palais de l'Élysée, résidence du Président de la République, Chef de l'État.

député faisait ce qu'il voulait jusqu'au jour des élections prochaines, où il risquait sans doute de ne pas être réélu si l'on était mécontent de lui. Mais comme personne n'avait suivi de très près les débats de la Chambre, il suffisait généralement au député sortant de faire des promesses mirobolantes pour l'avenir, et de confiance on lui renouvelait son bail. En d'autres termes, la crainte de la dissolution de l'Assemblée avant l'expiration de la législature normale était la seule forme de responsabilité que connussent les députés : ils avaient donc intérêt à s'entendre avec le gouvernement pour éviter ce risque majeur.

Démocratie présidentielle   Troisièmement, le peuple élit maintenant son président au suffrage direct. L'un des résultats de cette innovation de la Cinquième République c'est que l'Assemblée nationale ne peut plus prétendre représenter la totalité de la souveraineté populaire. L'avenir nous apprendra si le sens des responsabilités des députés a crû en raison inverse de leurs prérogatives.

> *La politique, la grande, la vraie, celle qui change le cours des événements, le destin des peuples, l'avenir des Nations, c'est le Verbe. In principio erat verbum. Le 18 juin,*[1] *j'ai changé l'Histoire par un appel de quarante lignes.*
>
> *LE GÉNÉRAL DE GAULLE*

[1] 1940

La démocratie parlementaire n'a jamais cessé d'être ridiculisée en France : témoin ce Ventre Législatif de Daumier, grand peintre realiste et caricaturiste du XIXème siècle.

A noter que le démocratie française est d'origine bourgeoise et non populaire. C'est en effet la bourgeoisie qui a fomenté la Révolution de 1789, organisé les diverses républiques qui ont suivi et, au cours du XIXème siècle, écrasé les mouvements populaires à tendances socialistes et communistes, en particulier la Commune de Paris. Aussi les multiples constitutions qui se sont succédé en France visaient-elles à grandir le législatif aux dépens de l'exécutif. On sait en effet que, depuis les Grecs et les Romains, ce sont les classes populaires qui préfèrent un exécutif fort et les classes moyennes qui profitent le mieux sous un législatif puissant. Il a fallu le prestige personnel du général de Gaulle et son mépris total de la tradition républicaine, sans compter le coup d'État du 13 mai 1958 qui le ramena au pouvoir, pour que l'exécutif, en France, devînt ce qu'il est maintenant, c'est-à-dire pratiquement tout-puissant. Encore fallut-il quatre ans de préparation pour que le chef de l'État osât faire voter le référendum modifiant la Constitution et selon lequel le Président de la République est maintenant élu directement par le peuple et non plus par les grands électeurs. Cette réforme éminemment démocratique a paru foncièrement anti-républicaine aux Français, car elle risque de favoriser les engouements de la masse pour les aventuriers de tout poil.

Quoi qu'il en soit, le *Président de la République* est actuellement, plus encore que l'Assemblée nationale, l'incarnation de la souveraineté populaire, et ses pouvoirs ne connaissent pratiquement d'autre limite que celles que l'article 16 de la Constitution lui permet de supprimer à volonté. Il nomme le premier ministre ; il signe les ordonnances et décrets ; il commande l'Armée ; il dissout l'Assemblée nationale ; il recourt au référendum s'il le juge bon. Bref, il est réellement *le chef de la France* et se situe aussi bien au-dessus du législatif (qu'il tient en laisse) que de l'exécutif proprement dit (qui tire ses pouvoirs de lui).

L'AUTORITÉ EN FRANCE

C'est là en fait qu'on débouche sur l'un des paradoxes de la démocratie française. Toute cette puissance que le peuple a forgée par ses votes, il doit maintenant la subir sans disposer contre elle d'aucun moyen de recours : il l'a lancée vers le haut, et elle redescend sur lui.

Au niveau du gouvernement, le premier ministre et les membres de son cabinet peuvent avoir été députés, mais, le plus souvent, ce sont des administrateurs, des financiers, des technocrates, quelquefois même des écrivains. Investi par un vote de confiance de l'Assemblée, le cabinet n'est plus responsable, en pratique, que devant le Président de la République.

Les grands corps de l'État — Conseil constitutionnel, Conseil économique et social, Conseil supérieur de la magistrature, Conseil d'État — sont formés de membres nommés et non pas élus.

Au niveau des régions administratives les super-préfets (ou « igames »), et au niveau fondamental du département les fameux préfets eux-mêmes, sont des agents nommés par l'État dont ils dirigent la police. Tous ces hauts

La peine capitale est toujours en usage en France. On fusille les condamnés politiques, mais on « guillotine » les criminels de droit civil. L'aimable machine que l'on voit ici a été surnommée « La Veuve » par le peuple.

fonctionnaires, et le million de fonctionnaires moyens et petits qui servent sous leurs ordres, émargent au budget et exécutent les ordres de l'État, ou, plus exactement, ceux du gouvernement.

Au niveau du département, il existe bien un Conseil général élu pour six ans au suffrage universel, mais son rôle est essentiellement consultatif : en fait, c'est le préfet qui prend toutes les décisions importantes.

Au niveau de l'arrondissement, subdivision du département, les sous-préfets exercent l'autorité de tutelle citée plus haut, c'est-à-dire qu'ils dirigent les maires dans l'exercice de leurs fonctions. Cette tutelle, relativement légère dans les grands centres où les maires se sentent forts de l'appui d'une population active et nombreuse, est presque une dictature lorsqu'il s'agit de petites communes rurales dont les maires sont des paysans satisfaits de se voir guidés dans l'accomplissement de leur mission.

Bref, lorsque l'on pense que, à l'entrée du système, le peuple est censé détenir la souveraineté absolue, on est bien forcé de constater que, à la sortie, il a pratiquement perdu tout ce qu'il avait. Il ne s'en plaint guère du reste. Le Français n'est pas un animal politique comme l'Anglo-Saxon : il lui paraît naturel d'être gouverné par des autorités supérieures, et tout ce qu'il demande en échange, c'est le droit de les chansonner.[1]

[1] Le peuple de France compose et écoute volontiers des chansons ridiculisant systématiquement ses hommes politiques : les « chansonniers » parisiens se spécialisent dans cette forme de satire.

LES GRANDES ADMINISTRATIONS

La façon dont le Français considère les députés qu'il élit et les administrations qui lui sont imposées par l'État est particulièrement typique. Pour lui, les députés sont méprisables *a priori* et, pour ainsi dire, d'office : ce sont tous des « vendus » qui ne cherchent qu'à « faire leur beurre ». En revanche, les fonctionnaires ne lui paraissent odieux que dans la mesure où il les connaît, où ils ont pour lui la figure bourrue de l'homme-derrière-le-guichet. Dès qu'il s'agit de personnages plus importants, investis d'une réelle autorité, et par conséquent rarement visibles, le Français s'emplit pour eux d'un respect presque affectueux. Ce sont, dit-il, « de grands commis » ; ce sont eux qui dirigent le « pays réel », tandis que le Parlement n'est là que comme la coûteuse garantie de certaines libertés fondamentales.

Il faut voir avec quelle fierté les Français parlent de leurs postes et de leurs chemins de fer, qui sont effectivement parmi les mieux organisés du monde. Il en va de même du corps, perpétuellement raillé mais profondément respecté, des pompiers. En revanche, ils se méfient de leur propre justice, détestent leur police (l'une des plus nombreuses du monde), récriminent contre leur sécurité sociale, se plaignent du fisc, de la radio, de la télévision, des téléphones et des travaux publics. Quant à leur Armée, ils se prétendent presque tous anti-militaristes mais se déplacent en masse pour voir un défilé militaire, phénomène qui traduit bien les sentiments d'inimitié amoureuse qui unissent les Français à leurs défenseurs professionnels.

Le facteur matinal fait partie de « tout ce p'tit monde 'là qui fait marcher la France », comme dit la chanson.

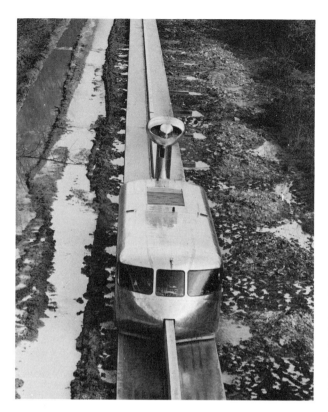

Le monorail experimental montre que l'intérêt des Français pour les moyens de transport les plus modernes demeure aussi vif que lors des premiers chemins de fer, automobiles et avions.

Paradoxes ? Sans doute. Nous avions bien dit que la démocratie française en était tissue. Dans l'ensemble, on croit pouvoir affirmer que le public français ne manque pas d'un certain bon sens, et qu'il applique, à la réalité quotidienne, le principe cartésien de l'évidence avec un certain bonheur. Il est bien évident que les trains français sont rapides, ponctuels et généralement confortables (grâces en sont justement rendues à la haute administration) ; il est bien évident aussi que les contrôleurs qu'on rencontre dans les wagons sont arrogants, discourtois et mal renseignés. (Ah ! ces petits fonctionnaires, tous des planqués !) Il est certain que les postes françaises livrent le courrier avec une admirable précision et une inépuisable bonne volonté ; il est non moins certain que les Français attendent deux ou trois ans pour qu'on veuille bien leur installer le téléphone. Il est vrai que les préfets font régner l'ordre dans les départements sans que leur présence se fasse sentir par le moindre abus ; il est également vrai que la police française n'est pas ennemie des « passages à tabac ».[2] Il est indéniable que la sécurité sociale assume la presque totalité des frais médicaux des salariés, tout en leur laissant la possibilité de choisir leurs médecins ; on ne saurait nier non plus que la gabegie[3] et la

[2] correction appliquée par des policiers à un prisonier récalcitrant
[3] fraudes et négligences administratives

bureaucratie sévissent dans ses bureaux. On a raison d'affirmer que l'Armée française est le plus sûr soutien de la nation mais aussi la menace la plus redoutable pour la démocratie.

L'un de ces grands corps que nous venons d'évoquer doit être étudié de beaucoup plus près, car, par sa vocation autant que par la place qu'il tient traditionnellement dans la nation française, il participe bien plus profondément que tous les autres à la civilisation : sécante magistrale à travers toutes les couches de la société, il sert à la fois de précipité à la France passée, de creuset à la France actuelle et de moule à la France de demain : nous voulons parler de l'Université.

L'UNIVERSITÉ DE FRANCE

Ici encore, il sied de commencer par un paradoxe : il n'y a sans doute pas de pays au monde où la formation de l'intelligence soit tenue pour aussi essentielle qu'en France, et il n'y a pas de pays au monde non plus où le métier d'enseignant soit plus décrié. En réalité, pour peu qu'on y regarde avec attention, les raisons de cette attitude s'éclairent d'elles-mêmes.

Premièrement, la conception de la culture est, en France, assez particulière : « c'est ce qui reste quand on a tout oublié », disait un homme d'esprit. Or, le rôle des professeurs, c'est justement de ne pas oublier mais, au contraire, de rappeler perpétuellement les mêmes notions, avec une insistance qui tient forcément du pédantisme. En d'autres termes, un homme cultivé, un « honnête homme », conserve toujours une certaine rancune à l'égard des maîtres qui l'ont rendu ce qu'il est, par des moyens qui répugnent à son raffinement.

Deuxièmement, l'attitude rationaliste, libérale, sceptique, du corps enseignant, si elle flatte les tendances abstraites de l'intelligence française, rebute son réalisme foncier : les pions[4] lui apparaissent non pas comme des êtres de chair et d'os mais comme des jardiniers d'abstractions, vivant, aux frais du contribuable, dans un monde artificiel.

Troisièmement, tout l'enseignement français repose sur la négation du principe d'autorité, sur le développement systématique du sens critique, du libre arbitre, du raisonnement personnel ; néanmoins, pour dispenser cet enseignement, les maîtres sont quelquefois obligés de recourir à l'autorité même qu'ils ne cessent de nier : de là une contradiction qui leur nuit.

Enfin, et c'est là un argument qui ne peut manquer de compter dans une société bourgeoise, le corps enseignant est fort mal payé, ce qui lui ôte tout droit au respect de ceux — et ils sont nombreux — qui honorent les gens en fonction de ce qu'ils leur coûtent.

Malgré cela, l'Université de France, qu'il faut considérer comme un tout — à une exception près — constitue un corps profondément homogène encore que bigarré, et peut-être la machine-à-apprendre-à-penser la mieux conçue du monde.

4 terme péjoratif pour désigner les surveillants et les professeurs

Enseignement privé L'exception, c'est l'enseignement privé, payant, et généralement catholique, qui recrute ses membres dans des milieux traditionnellement religieux et qui place l'esprit au-dessus de l'intelligence. Cet enseignement, dit « libre », dont les résultats ne sont pas négligeables, s'est vu en butte, pendant plus de cinquante ans, aux attaques de l'État laïc. Il semble que la Cinquième République ait réussi à résoudre, sinon à apaiser, les inimitiés et à faire entrer, par un système de subventions, l'école libre dans le plan général de l'éducation nationale.

L'Université proprement dite, organisme d'État, gratuit à tous ses niveaux, et qui est en pleine réforme suite aux troubles estudiantins de mai 1968, se divise en trois degrés principaux.

Primaire Au sortir de la maternelle, soit vers sept ans, l'enfant français entre dans une école primaire, où il reçoit un enseignement général (lecture, écriture, langue, calcul, sciences naturelles, histoire et géographie) qu'il continuera jusqu'à seize ans par un enseignement technique, s'il ne désire pas poursuivre ses études plus avant. Il sera alors apte à devenir un ouvrier spécialisé. La partie technique de cet enseignement est de création moderne et n'a pas encore fait ses preuves ; mais la partie générale est une véritable éducation intellectuelle qui apprend au petit Français à juger des choses par l'expérience et la déduction, au rebours de l'enseignement médiéval, et de celui de certains autres pays, où l'on cherche à inculquer aux enfants une vérité toute faite élaborée par une église, une société ou un État.

Secondaire Si l'enfant veut faire des études plus poussées, il subit dès onze ans un examen spécial et accède à l'enseignement secondaire, qui fait à juste titre l'orgueil de l'Université française. Un seul défaut, et de taille : la culture du corps y est systématiquement négligée au profit de celle de l'intelligence, et tous les efforts faits par l'État pour imposer des normes physiques plus proches de celles, par exemple, de l'enseignement anglais, se heurtent à l'apathie générale et au mépris où « le sportif » a toujours été tenu par tout ce qui pense en France. En revanche, les intelligences sont prises en charge par un système parfaitement adapté à sa tâche et reçoivent pendant sept ans un enseignement approfondi comprenant des langues mortes, des langues vivantes, des mathématiques, des sciences naturelles, de la physique, de la chimie, de l'histoire, de la géographie, de la littérature, des notions de philologie, de dessin et de musique, le tout étant couronné, en classe terminale, par une teinture de philosophie plus ou moins complète d'après la section choisie, et reposant sur un système d'émulation continuellement entretenue par des distributions régulières de notes, de places, de prix et d'accessits divers, ainsi que « d'heures de colle ».[5] Il est bien évident que les jeunes Français oublient rapidement une bonne partie de tout ce qu'ils apprennent ainsi, mais cela n'est pas considéré comme un inconvénient car, dans l'entre-temps, ils ont appris à raisonner, à réfléchir, bref à *douter*.

---

[5] heures supplémentaires à passer au lycée

L'enseignement secondaire français peut être défini comme une école systématique du doute, considéré comme l'élément de base de la connaissance. Cet enseignement est sanctionné, à dix-huit ans, par un baccalauréat, sans utilité pratique en soi, mais ouvrant aux futurs étudiants les portes des facultés ou des grandes écoles qu'ils choisiront.

Sans doute, le niveau des bacheliers est-il fonction de leurs qualités propres. Néanmoins, l'examen final étant administré par l'État, sous forme écrite d'abord, sous forme orale ensuite ; les candidats étant interrogés par des examinateurs qui ne les connaissent pas et jugés uniquement sur leurs réponses (et non, par exemple, sur leur assiduité en classe) ; toutes les villes de France offrant des épreuves d'une difficulté égale, il est possible de tracer, à grands traits, le portrait culturel du bachelier. Il a généralement une excellente connaissance de la littérature, de l'histoire et de la géographie françaises ; il possède de solides notions sur la culture antique ; il a appris à raisonner en « construisant » ses versions latines ; il a abordé, en mathématiques, les logarithmes et le calcul intégral ; il connaît les éléments de la biologie, de la chimie et de la physique ; sans avoir approfondi aucun philosophe, il est instruit des buts et de l'histoire de la philosophie. Tel quel, le bachelier accède à l'enseignement supérieur.

Supérieur L'enseignement supérieur est dispensé par des organismes qu'on peut grouper en deux catégories : d'une part les facultés (lettres, droit, médecine, beaux-arts) qui préparent, par un système souple de conférences, de travaux pratiques et d'études personnelles, les membres des professions libérales ; d'autre part les grandes écoles (Polytechnique, Normale, Centrale), qui, dans un cadre beaucoup plus rigide, forment les futurs spécialistes, ingénieurs, pédagogues, agronomes, militaires, administrateurs, technocrates.

L'enseignement supérieur est nécessairement spécialisé et, en grande partie, didactique. Par là, il exprime moins bien le génie national que l'enseignement secondaire. Néanmoins, il est aussi en grande partie critique, et les grades universitaires successifs qu'obtiennent les candidats traduisent moins une érudition croissante qu'une aptitude croissante à exploiter une érudition considérée souvent comme un mal nécessaire.

Ces grades varient selon les facultés et les écoles. Prenons, par exemple, un étudiant en lettres. Une fois bachelier, il lui faudra trois ans pour obtenir sa licence d'enseignement (comprenant des études détaillées sur la littérature et la philologie française, grecque et latine), un ou deux ans de plus pour la maîtrise, un temps indéfini pour réussir au concours de l'agrégation, et une demi-douzaine d'années encore pour présenter les deux thèses qui lui vaudront, s'il les soutient avec succès, le titre de docteur. Résultat : ce n'est peut-être pas tout à fait à tort que, après être sortis de cette longue filière, les universitaires français ne pèchent généralement pas par modestie.

Mais, surtout s'ils ont réussi à sauter tous ces obstacles, ils considèrent souvent — du moins les plus brillants d'entre eux — que l'enseignement ne peut constituer pour eux qu'un gagne-pain : leurs véritables intérêts sont ailleurs, dans la recherche personnelle, à laquelle ils s'adonnent alors avec une passion qui fait progresser le niveau des études nationales, plus peut-être que celui des étudiants dont ils ont la charge. On rencontre ici l'un des aspects les plus caractéristiques de l'esprit français. L'apostolat de l'enseignant existe en France comme ailleurs, mais seulement aux degrés inférieurs de la hiérarchie intellectuelle ; passé un certain seuil, l'esprit missionnaire apparaît comme primaire, ridicule, et même odieux : seule la recherche désintéressée semble noble et digne d'un grand esprit. En fait, les seuls professeurs à échapper au mépris général sont ceux qui n'enseignent plus.

Au-delà de l'Université proprement dite, les intellectuels les plus féconds — ou les plus adroits — peuvent accéder à des consécrations encore plus élevées. Le Centre national de la recherche scientifique est un organisme de travail et de coordination de la science française, dont les réussites ont récemment été sanctionnées par plusieurs prix Nobel. L'Institut, lui, est le temple même de la science gratuite. Organisme mondain plus qu'universitaire, il consacre essentiellement les mérites d'écrivains, d'artistes et de savants qui ont œuvré dans un sens traditionnel et conformiste. Ce n'est pas sans un pincement de vanité et d'angoisse à la fois qu'un romancier vieillissant écrit pour la première fois après son nom la mention « de l'Académie française » : sans doute a-t-il consacré vingt ans de sa vie à conquérir ce privilège, mais, d'un autre côté, il sait bien qu'à partir de maintenant tout le monde dira qu'il « sent le naphtaline », ou qu'il « s'est fait faire un enterrement de première classe ».

A ce point de vue, l'Institut peut être considéré comme la plus caractéristique des institutions françaises : décrié et ambitionné, envié et ridiculisé, il dresse au bord de la Seine sa silhouette tricentenaire et radieuse heureusement rajeunie par les bons soins de M. Malraux. A l'intérieur, on trouve des salles de réunion où se pressent les immortels en habit vert, l'épée au côté, de vieilles cours poétiques aux murs couverts de lierre, et une bibliothèque un peu sombre où viennent travailler des étudiants. Leurs jeunes visages au sourcil froncé, penchés sur de vieilles reliures de cuir sentant le moisi, à la recherche non pas d'une vérité mais d'une pierre de touche, reflètent san le savoir une tendance profonde de l'esprit français : la culture individuelle d'une intelligence qui, systématiquement, dit « non » d'abord, réfléchit ensuite, et ne finit par conclure « oui » qu'à son corps défendant.

RÉALITÉS ÉCONOMIQUES

Dans les institutions qui forment l'armature de la nation France se coulent ses réalités économiques, sociales et politiques qui en sont la matière même. Des institutions aux réalités, le rapport est celui qui unit le squelette à la chair, ou plus exactement l'armement du béton au mélange de sable et de ciment dont il est enrobé.

Les possibilités économiques de la France sont étendues mais insuffisantes. En d'autres termes, la France exporte beaucoup mais importe encore plus. En d'autres termes encore, elle a une balance commerciale régulièrement déficitaire, mais ce déficit, relativement faible (5 à 10 pour cent), est ordinairement

La France, grosse productrice d'uranium et de gaz naturel, exploite activement
ces deux sources modernes d'énergie : l'une à Pierrelatte, l'autre à Lacq.

compensé par les exportations invisibles (tourisme, revenus de capitaux à l'étranger, etc.). Bref, du point de vue économique la France vit dans un équilibre approximatif.

Cet équilibre s'établit grâce aux industries de transformation, sans lesquelles la France serait devenue depuis longtemps un pays de dixième ordre. En effet, elle produit relativement peu de matières premières et relativement peu d'énergie : elle est donc amenée à importer un peu de houille, beaucoup de pétrole, beaucoup de laine, tout son caoutchouc et tout son coton. A noter que ses réserves en fer, en bauxite et en potasse la mettent complètement à l'abri du besoin sous ce rapport, qu'elle n'a pas besoin d'importer d'énergie électrique, que de récentes découvertes de gaz naturel dans son sous-sol l'aident à résoudre ses problèmes énergétiques et enfin qu'elle est la première puissance d'Europe pour la production de l'uranium. Dans ces conditions, on prévoit que sa balance commerciale deviendra de moins en moins déficitaire et peut-être même excédentaire dans un proche avenir, d'autant plus que la France produit la presque totalité de ses produits d'alimentation.

Les exportations françaises comprennent essentiellement des produits manufacturés : pétrole raffiné, fonte, acier, aluminium, automobiles, acide sulfurique, engrais, produits caoutchoutés, verre, laine et coton travaillés.

Les principaux clients et fournisseurs de la France sont l'Allemagne fédérale, les pays du Bénélux (Hollande, Belgique, Luxembourg), l'Algérie, la Suisse, la Grande-Bretagne et les États-Unis.

L'agriculture, traditionnellement, est non seulement la nourricière, mais l'inspiratrice de la France. Maintenant encore 27 pour cent des Français cultivent la terre ou élèvent du bétail et déterminent pour une large part la politique économique de la France. On verra plus loin les conséquences de ce phénomène pour le Marché commun et pour les relations qu'entretient la France avec ses voisins proches et lointains.

Du point de vue de ses structures officielles, l'économie française est de type capitaliste, dans la mesure où les moyens de production appartiennent à des sociétés anonymes, et où les investissements sont libres. Néanmoins, l'existence d'un Commissariat au plan et à la productivité et la nationalisation de certaines grandes firmes, comme les Usines d'automobiles Renault, donnent une allure plus socialiste à certains aspects de la vie économique française. En effet, les diverses administrations travaillant pour et avec le Commissariat au plan parviennent, par des pressions généralement indirectes, à imprimer à l'économie nationale la direction souhaitée par le gouvernement. C'est là un exemple intéressant de compromis entre le libéralisme et le dirigisme économiques.

RÉALITÉS SOCIALES

La population française se répartit de façon équilibrée entre les trois secteurs de la vie économique : 27 pour cent pour le secteur primaire (agriculture), 38 pour cent pour le secondaire (industrie), 35 pour cent pour le tertiaire

Citroën Pallas.

Simca 1501.

Peugeot 204.

Renault 8.

(commerce, professions libérales, fonction publique, etc.), soit trois tiers à peu de chose près.

Les agriculteurs, classe traditionaliste, mal organisée pour défendre ses intérêts, d'ailleurs attachée à des valeurs difficiles à concilier avec les impératifs des luttes sociales, ont toujours fait figure de parents pauvres dans la République française ; leur influence, citée plus haut, ne pesant que sur l'attitude économique extérieure et non sur l'équilibre social intérieur. Ils sont en pleine évolution ; les violences quelquefois pittoresques auxquelles ils se livrent à l'instigation de leurs syndicats (barrages sur les routes, enlèvements de touristes, souvent suivis d'invitations à des dégustations de crus), tout autant que la modernisation de leurs méthodes de culture, sont en train de leur donner dans la société une place qu'ils y méritent depuis longtemps.

Les ouvriers, employés et petits fonctionnaires, sont depuis longtemps groupés en syndicats, et c'est l'action virulente de ces organisations qui a forcé l'État à appliquer une politique sociale grâce à laquelle la France se trouve maintenant à l'avant-garde du progrès social dans le monde. Les conventions collectives protègent les salariés en temps normal ; le conseil des Prud'hommes arbitre leurs conflits individuels avec leurs employeurs ; la grève est le moyen extrême qu'ils utilisent pour exiger des augmentations de salaires ou d'autres avantages sociaux. Avec leurs quarante heures de travail par semaine, leur quatre semaines de congé payé, leur salaire minimum interprofessionnel garanti, les ouvriers français font figure de bourgeois et commencent de plus en plus à se considérer comme tels. De là un certain

---

Apprendre. Comprendre. Je parle à la première personne. Je suis un homme donné, et non un autre. J'ai mon métier. Je suis défini socialement par là. Et à ceux qui me demandent : « A la fin, qu'êtes-vous d'abord : communiste ou écrivain ? » Je réponds toujours : « Je suis d'abord écrivain, et c'est pourquoi je suis communiste. » Les choses, pour moi, ont pris ce tour logique. C'est parce que, dans mon métier, là où je sais mieux qu'un autre, j'ai touché les limites imposées, que je suis devenu ce que je suis. L'ouvrier aussi devient communiste parce qu'il était ouvrier. On appelle alors cela le sens de classe. Mais quand tout l'avenir de ce qui est la pensée, la culture, l'art, passe des mains d'une classe dégradée à celles d'une classe nouvelle, ces mains fussent-elles rudes, inexpérimentées encore, ces mains laborieuses et blessées, ces mains honnêtes qui accouchent l'avenir, l'écrivain aussi, c'est par le sens de classe, qu'il change, car sa classe à lui, alors, c'est celle que voici, celle des bâtisseurs, celle de ces ouvriers qui ont gardé leur fusil pour se tenir en sentinelles à la porte de leurs usines.

LOUIS ARAGON

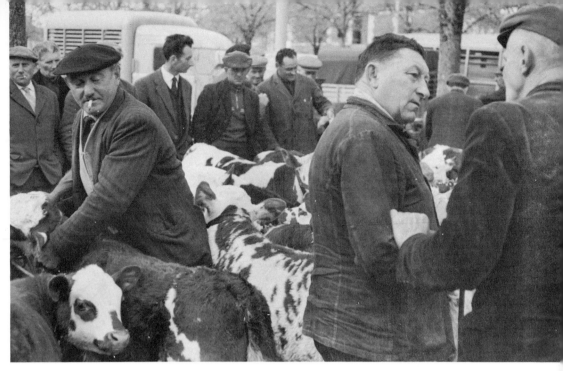

Aujourd'hui comme hier, l'élevage demeure une des grandes richesses de la France.

affaiblissement des syndicats, d'ailleurs déchirés par des luttes politiques qui diminuent leur prestige social. Du reste, la plupart des revendications justifiées concernent maintenant l'habitat, toujours insuffisant aussi bien en quantité qu'en confort, et non plus les avantages professionnels qui vont croissant, y compris un certain intéressement pécuniaire à la gestion de l'entreprise, de plus en plus souvent appliqué.

Tandis que les ouvriers et petits fonctionnaires agissent le plus souvent par l'intermédiaire de syndicats ouvertement ou moins ouvertement inféodés au communisme (et souvent accusés, par conséquent, de mieux défendre les intérêts de la Russie soviétique que ceux de leurs membres), les cadres et même les patrons ont leurs propres associations professionnelles qui, sans être rattachés à des organismes politiques, font bénéficier leurs adhérents d'une protection efficace dans le domaine social.

RÉALITÉS POLITIQUES

L'Anglo-Saxon prend la politique au sérieux. Le Français la prend au tragique. Ou alors au comique. Ou alors il ne la prend pas du tout. Le plus souvent, il se passionne pour elle — sans y croire. Depuis cent cinquante ans, il règle les problèmes du monde et sauve la France, mais le plus souvent « au café du Commerce » en prenant l'apéro,[6] ou bien au cours de bagarres homériques

[6] terme familier pour vin, apéritif

contre la police — rarement dans les bureaux de vote, car les jours d'élection il préfère « aller à la pêche ». C'est que, d'une façon générale, les problèmes politiques chatouillent l'imagination et le rationalisme complaisant du Français, qui cependant ne se fait guère d'illusions ni sur l'influence toute-puissante des « princes qui nous gouvernent » (c'est-à-dire, en l'occurence, des puissances d'argent) ni sur le manque d'initiative du peuple dit souverain.

Deux types, deux personnages tour à tour héroïques et caricaturaux, se partagent en tous cas la scène politique française : ce sont l'homme de droite et l'homme de gauche.

L'homme de droite   L'homme de droite est conservateur à l'intérieur, protectionniste, voire nationaliste à l'extérieur. Il considère que, en politique, la fin justifie amplement les moyens et éprouve même une certaine sympathie pour les plus douteux, qui lui inspirent confiance dans la mesure où ils lui semblent « réalistes ». Partisan de l'autorité, il ferait volontiers sien le mot de Gœthe : « Une injustice vaut mieux qu'un désordre. » Ses ennemis l'accusent d'avoir « des vues bornées » ; de « porter des œillères » ; il est volontiers obstiné, rageur, voire violent. *Ordre* et *nation* sont ses grands mots. Souvent catholique, il se méfie néanmoins du Vatican ; ses ancêtres spirituels sont Louis XIV, mais aussi Robespierre, et surtout Napoléon. Ses ennemis ont été, sous la Troisième République, les Juifs et les francs-maçons ; ce sont maintenant les Juifs et les « cocos ».[7] Son plus grand défaut est d'avoir mauvaise

[7] terme familier pour communistes

conscience. En effet, à l'exception des extrémistes, qui se prétendent ouvertement réactionnaires, les hommes de droite français ne se reconnaissent jamais pour ce qu'ils sont : ils se veulent « indépendants », « libéraux » ou « modérés ».

L'homme de gauche L'homme de gauche, au contraire, fait carrière — ou campagne — dans l'idéalisme et dans la vertu. Chevaleresque défenseur de tout ce qui peut passer pour opprimé, il place au-dessus des impératifs nationaux les exigences humanitaires de sa conscience, chrétienne ou laïque, il n'importe pas. Anti-colonialiste, anti-impérialiste, il milite contre la peine de mort, contre les États-Unis, contre la bombe atomique, contre la police, contre tout ce qui lui paraît menacer la dignité de l'homme. Sa qualité d'homme de gauche, il la proclame hautement, ce qui lui donne un panache mérité et rémunérateur. Ses ennemis jurés étaient les jésuites — jusqu'au moment où les jésuites ont eu l'astuce de passer à gauche eux-mêmes. Maintenant ses injures favorites sont « fasciste » et « réactionnaire ».

PARTIS POLITIQUES

Les étrangers sont toujours surpris de la multiplicité des partis politiques en France. Mais c'est que, pour des Anglo-Saxons, par exemple, un parti est un élément, virtuel ou actuel, de la machine étatique ; il a, au gouvernement ou dans l'opposition, un rôle fonctionnel bien défini ; il se présente comme essentiellement positif, réservoir d'hommes, d'idées et de solutions. Au contraire, en France un parti est simplement un groupe de personnes qui ont des opinions politiques ressemblantes, et peut-être faudrait-il même parler de sentiments plutôt que d'opinions.

On s'est mille fois interrogé sur l'origine de cet état de choses, et l'on a mille fois répondu que « c'est la faute de l'individualisme français ». Peut-être. Il serait probablement non moins exact d'affirmer que « c'est la faute d'un certain cynisme, traditionnel en France, pour tout ce qui concerne la politique ». Peu de Français croient sérieusement qu'il dépend d'eux de changer quelque chose à la politique de l'État, sauf dans la mesure où elle les concerne directement (salaires, avantages sociaux, etc.). En revanche, beaucoup sont attachés à une certaine précision intellectuelle et ne sauraient souscrire à un programme qu'ils n'approuveraient pas entièrement, ni s'intégrer si peu que ce soit à un groupe d'hommes dont la sensibilité politique serait différente de la leur.

S'intégrer, d'ailleurs, est un bien grand mot. La « chaleur humaine » répugne aux Français ; le « coude à coude » leur fait peur. A l'exception des formations extrémistes (de gauche ou de droite), les partis n'enrégimentent pas leurs membres, et la plupart des citoyens, même s'ils votent fidèlement pour leur parti, trouveraient déplaisant d'avoir à y adhérer.

Le P. C. Commençons par la gauche. Le Parti communiste est le seul groupement politique français de quelque importance à posséder des structures puissantes, une police intérieure et une doctrine cohérente. Il vise ouvertement à l'instauration de la dictature du prolétariat et ne se cache pas de recevoir ses ordres de Moscou. Sa participation active à la Résistance pendant la Deuxième Guerre mondiale a fait espérer aux uns et craindre aux autres qu'il parviendrait à faire basculer la France dans le camp des démocraties populaires. Mais trois événements successifs l'ont sérieusement atteint dans sa popularité, et même dans ses effectifs proprement dits.

Au lendemain de la Deuxième Guerre mondiale, il a été découvert que les premiers camps d'extermination créés dans le monde n'avaient pas été inventés par les fascistes de Hitler mais par les communistes de Staline. D'où une certaine confusion parmi les bonnes gens qui croyaient à la pureté angélique de l'extrême-gauche. Ensuite, la révolte hongroise (1956) et son écrasement ont confirmé cette impression : le visage impitoyable du communisme apparaissait à découvert. Enfin, la querelle russo-chinoise, faisant éclater les failles intérieures du communisme, jeta le doute parmi ceux qui, par sympathie ou par panique, croyaient à la victoire inéluctable du prolétariat marxiste.

Le P. S. U. De là, dans une certaine mesure, le succès intellectuel des groupes formant la Fédération de la gauche démocratique et socialiste et, en particulier, du Parti socialiste unifié, d'inspiration marxiste mais qui, ne disposant pas de troupes de choc, ne fait peur à personne. Défenseur de toutes les causes qui peuvent séduire les cœurs sensibles, s'exprimant soigneusement dans un jargon politique qui donne du sérieux à ce qu'il dit, l'électeur du P. S. U. bénéficie à la fois de sa propre bonne conscience et de l'existence inquiétante des démocraties populaires : c'est, en un mot, le « marxiste gentil ».

La S. F. I. O.   La Section française de l'internationale ouvrière n'est pas aussi terrible que son nom paraît l'indiquer : la plupart des Français ont d'ailleurs oublié la signification du sigle[8] par lequel ils l'appellent. Marxiste en théorie, le socialiste se conduit généralement comme un nationaliste lorsqu'il parvient au pouvoir. Il suffira de citer deux exemples de cette attitude : ce sont les socialistes qui ont conduit avec le plus d'énergie la répression de la révolte algérienne ; ce sont les socialistes qui ont ordonné l'expédition franco-anglaise de Suez (1956), interrompue sur l'initiative du gouvernement conservateur britannique.

Les radicaux   Il y a en France toute sorte de radicaux, portant des étiquettes diverses. Cependant les partis radicaux n'ont guère de doctrine politique, pas de troupes de choc et fort peu d'adhérents. Dans ces conditions, on pourra s'étonner qu'ils aient exercé sur la politique française une influence déterminante, mais ce n'en est pas moins un fait. Ils ont réussi par une utilisation systématique des idées de gauche, avec tout ce que le terme comporte de vague, à se donner une réputation de vertu, tandis que leurs relations de famille et d'affaires — les radicaux sont, pour la plupart, issus de milieux bourgeois — leur permettaient de peser sur les sphères extra-parlementaires où la vraie politique du pays se décidait. Leur influence était caractéristique du régime parlementaire — compromis et négociations — que la France a connu sous les Troisième et Quatrième Républiques : les structures actuelles leur conviennent moins et ils sont appelés à disparaître comme tels de la vie politique du pays.

Le front populaire   Les partis dont on vient de dire quelques mots se groupent épisodiquement en une masse hétérogène mais unique, dite front populaire. Si la Cinquième République en arrive là où elle semble vouloir en venir, le front populaire deviendra un grand parti travailliste, où les communistes seront minoritaires et qui, tout en demeurant attaché à un idéal essentiellement social, ne sera pas suspect de travailler en sous-main pour le compte d'une puissance étrangère. Tel qu'il est actuellement, le front populaire n'a d'existence que par rapport à ce catalyseur qu'est un Président de la République élu au suffrage universel.

En face du front populaire, il n'y a pas de front national, mais, au contraire, des partis encore plus morcelés que ceux de la gauche.

---

[8] lettres initiales employées comme appellation abrégée

Le P. D. M. Les groupements du centre se sont amalgamés en une masse hybride baptisée Progrès et démocratie moderne, sans racines dans la nation.

Le R. I. Les « indépendants », « paysans » et autres « modérés » ont bien des sentiments relativement nationaux, mais, outre qu'ils ont accepté sans trop regimber l'indépendance algérienne, et qu'ils ne protestent que mollement contre la création d'une Europe dénationalisée, leur « Rassemblement » ne représente guère que des communautés d'intérêts et non d'opinions. De programme, ils n'en ont pas. De quoi sont-ils « indépendants » ? En quoi sont-ils « modérés » ? Quel « paysan » parmi eux a-t-il jamais touché une charrue ? On se le demande.

L'extrême-droite On groupe sous la désignation imprécise d'extrême-droite toute une variété d'éléments divers, parmi lesquels se trouvent quelques-uns des esprits les plus brillants et aussi quelques-uns des plus faux — ce sont les mêmes quelquefois — que la France ait eus. Il faudrait un volume entier pour distinguer clairement entre les diverses tendances qui les divisent,

Violence estudiantine, répression policière, sont de tradition au Quartier Latin.

et auxquelles la guerre d'Algérie a donné une dimension tragique. Si le nationalisme était la grande idée de l'Action française, aujourd'hui beaucoup de personnes qu'on rangea dans l'extrême droite sont favorables à l'Europe intégrée ou à la satellisation de la France autour des États-Unis. Ceux qui se déclarent attachés à la monarchie ont généralement des idées sociales très avancées ; ceux qui exigent l'instauration d'un régime autoritaire viennent souvent des classes les plus modestes. Bref, il y a là un mélange inextricable de passions qui ne pèsent guère sur la vie du pays en temps ordinaire mais avec lesquelles il faut compter en période de crise — comme l'ont montré les événements de mai 1968.

L'U. D. R.   Quant à l'Union démocratique de la Cinquième République, est-ce vraiment un parti ? Certains en ont douté. Fondée sous l'impulsion personnelle du général de Gaulle, n'ayant que sa personnalité pour programme, pour slogan et pour porte-drapeau, l'U. D. R. avait été portée au pouvoir par un mouvement où la panique avait autant de part que l'enthousiasme. Depuis lors, elle a été amenée à assumer toutes les responsabilités du gouvernement, et la démission du Président de Gaulle a consacré, pour ainsi dire, son affranchissement intellectuel.

Groupée autour du Président Pompidou, l'U. D. R. remplace peu à peu ses fidélités sentimentales par une cohésion politique fondée sur un réalisme — pour ne pas dire un opportunisme — certain.

CINQUIÈME RÉPUBLIQUE

On a comparé les institutions de la France à une armature ; ses réalités politiques à un béton, armé par les institutions. Avec ce béton armé, il appartient à la Cinquième République de construire un édifice. Lequel ? C'est là la question à laquelle on essaiera de répondre maintenant.

Ici, une note liminaire est indispensable. La Cinquième République vient de naître ; elle a atteint chaque Français dans sa vie personnelle ; elle est

---

Le gaullisme a été, est, restera la loi de l'effort, l'école da la politique qui refuse et refusera toujours que la France soit une puissance de second ordre. Le gaullisme est la négation du fait accompli. C'est le refus du pessimisme, du défaitisme, de l'abdication et du renoncement. Voilà ce qu'est le gaullisme ! C'est un réflexe national — non la faction, la coterie, que l'on a décrite. Ce n'est pas un expédient provisoire : c'est une immense foi en la France. Un grand peuple qui cesse de croire en son destin, qui abandonne à d'autres le sort des armes, n'est plus un pays. Il devient un territoire géographique. Cela, je ne l'accepterai jamais, je ne capitulerai jamais !

LE GÉNÉRAL DE GAULLE

---

encore très loin d'avoir réalisé ses projets ; une certaine dialectique historique peut faire que les apparences d'aujourd'hui soient détruites par les vérités de demain. Décrire la Cinquième République à travers ses réalisations de l'heure, ce serait faire œuvre de journaliste, dans l'éphémère, et par conséquent sortir du cadre de ce livre. Porter sur elle des jugements de valeur serait encore plus saugrenu, soit qu'on lui reproche ses fins mêmes (comme la gauche), soit qu'on critique ses méthodes (comme la droite), soit qu'on l'admire béatement comme elle s'admire elle-même.

Non, le seul moyen, nous semble-t-il, de rendre à la Cinquième République ce qu'on lui doit, c'est de la considérer dans sa virtualité, dans ses intentions, dans ses possibilités, compte tenu du fait que les prophéties de ses ennemis ne se sont pas réalisées et que l'abdication — le mot n'est pas trop fort — du Président de Gaulle n'a pas été suivie d'un effondrement général : au contraire, il est avéré désormais que ceux-là mêmes qui avaient juré la perte de l'homme acceptent dans l'ensemble le régime qu'il a légué au pays.

Au reste, s'il fallait résumer les intentions du pouvoir, on pourrait le faire ainsi : les hommes de la Cinquième République se proposent de donner une nouvelle jeunesse à la nation française.

Ce renouveau souhaité se présente sous une triple forme : (1) revalorisation de l'État, (2) revalorisation de la nation, (3) revalorisation du rôle joué par la France sur le plan international.

REVALORISATION DE L'ÉTAT

La Constitution de la Cinquième République — constitution que les Français considèrent volontiers comme « américaine » parce qu'elle instaure un régime présidentiel contraire à la tradition française — a été conçue pour rendre à l'État tous les moyens nécessaires pour se faire respecter, au besoin en se faisant craindre. La répression brutale des agitations d'extrême-droite, suite à la guerre d'Algérie, la multiplication des polices secrètes, une stabilité ministérielle qui semble renouvelée de l'ancien régime, tout cela doit rappeler aux Français qu'ils sont gouvernés par un pouvoir qui n'entend rien négliger de ses prérogatives. Entre les deux guerres, les monarchistes avaient coutume de se moquer de la République en l'appelant « la femme sans tête » : ces quolibets ne seraient plus justifiés sous la Cinquième. Il n'importe guère que ce changement ait pu avoir lieu grâce à la personnalité du général de Gaulle : une fois acquis, il est douteux qu'il puisse laisser la place à des oligarchies occultes renouvelées des régimes précédents.

Cette revalorisation de l'État devrait être suivie, du moins en principe, d'une revalorisation du gouvernement — actuellement en cours — et d'une revalorisation de l'opposition, qui paraît plus problématique, étant donné les habitudes politiques négatives des Français. Néanmoins, le nombre forcément réduit de candidats à la présidence de la République a déjà cristallisé quelques rassemblements, éphémères il est vrai.

Enfin, toutes les réformes qui profiteraient d'une façon ou d'une autre à la nation rétabliraient la confiance des Français à l'égard de l'État : c'est ainsi qu'il faut entendre les grands efforts de renouvellement qui sont faits — avec plus ou moins de succès — dans tous les domaines de la vie publique.

REVALORISATION DE LA NATION

Il n'y a guère de domaines où la Cinquième République n'ait cherché à rajeunir la France. Le symbole de cette politique, c'est sans doute le ravalement des façades parisiennes, dont la blancheur rappelle tous les jours à cinq millions de Français que la France est en train de changer, dans un effort profond pour retrouver le visage qu'elle a eu pendant des siècles : changer, pour se ressembler mieux...

La première réforme apportée par la Cinquième République est symbolique également. D'un jour à l'autre, le vieux franc a été remplacé par le nouveau, cent fois plus lourd, sans qu'aucun avantage financier en découlât pour personne ; mais le fait était là : systématiquement dévalué depuis des siècles, le franc cessait brusquement d'être une fraction infime de la livre ou du dollar pour en devenir le pendant sinon le rival. Sa dévaluation, en août 1969, indique peut-être une façon un peu plus pratique, un peu moins sentimentale,

Le plus grand avion commercial du monde, le Concorde, est le fruit d'une collaboration franco-britannique qui fera date dans l'histoire de l'Europe contemporaine.

de considérer les réalités économiques. Elle ne modifie pas l'essentiel de la volonté de relèvement de la France.

D'autres bouleversements suivirent la première réforme symbolique : heureux ou malheureux, ils indiquent en tout cas un regain de vitalité. D'abord, l'État pèse plus lourdement dans des domaines où la tradition républicaine voulait qu'il n'eût rien à dire.

Pressions　Les activités du Commissariat au plan sont quotidiennement taxées de dirigisme par la droite et d'insuffisance par la gauche (puisque — c'est là un paradoxe de plus — en matière économique c'est la gauche qui est autoritaire et la droite libérale). Les pressions du gouvernement sur le Centre national de la recherche scientifique, sans être comparables à celles qui sont exercées sur les organismes scientifiques dans les pays totalitaires, n'en deviennent pas moins certaines. L'autorité de l'État sur les moyens de masse, en particulier sur la radio et la télévision, est absolue ; les promesses de libéralisation sont plus souvent données que tenues. Les postes privés, dit périphériques, demeurent en principe libres, mais, de fait, ils suivent d'assez près les postes nationaux dans leur œuvre de propagande et d'endoctrinement. Plus significatives encore sont les ouvertures faites par l'État aux hommes de lettres, dont certains lui sont désormais attachés à des titres divers, tandis, que d'autres ont préféré l'indépendance.

Passons au domaine propre de l'État.

Armée　L'Armée a été transformée de fond en comble, aussi bien par l'adoption des armes nucléaires que par le rajeunissement des officiers, la formation d'officiers et de sous-officiers plus spécialisés, la modification des marques extérieures de respect et enfin la suppression du « service militaire » au profit d'un « service national », qui doit permettre d'une part une meilleure utilisation des compétences, d'autre part un plus grand rayonnement de la France dans les pays de la Communauté.

Décentralisation　Du point de vue économique et administratif, la Cinquième République vise à une décentralisation croissante qui doit redonner vie aux provinces encore somnolentes. Cette décentralisation (superposition des régions économiques et des régions administratives) ne nuit d'ailleurs en rien à la centralisation politique qui, on l'a vu, va toujours croissant. Ainsi les projets d'aménagement routier — le réseau actuel est très insatisfaisant — serviront à la fois à la décentralisation des moyens et à la centralisation des fins, dans la France de l'avenir où les distances ne compteront plus.

Le même souci d'aménagement apparaît dans les efforts qui sont faits pour éviter la congestion dans les principales agglomérations : création du district de Paris, construction de grands ensembles.

Agriculture　En ce qui concerne l'agriculture, l'État cherche à imposer une politique de remembrement des terres, car la plupart des propriétés françaises, même les plus petites, sont morcelées : recoller ces parcelles de terrain pour augmenter la productivité prendra sans doute des dizaines d'années, compte tenu de l'attachement du paysan français pour les terres de ses aïeux, mais certains résultats ont déjà été obtenus. Et la mécanisation de l'agriculture d'une part, l'organisation de l'enseignement agricole de l'autre, vont dans le même sens. Il serait exagéré d'attribuer les bienfaits de cette évolution à la Cinquième République en tant que telle, mais il importe de bien montrer qu'il y a une sorte de convergence entre les intentions des hommes au pouvoir et le progrès technique. En 1939, la France produisait 50 pour cent de sa consommation agricole ; maintenant elle exporte 20 pour cent de sa production.

Civile, militaire, politique, répressive, officielle, officieuse, secrète, omniprésente, la police française est bien nombreuse pour un pays « démocratique ».

Formation   La Cinquième République, se flattant de voir loin, s'intéresse particulièrement aux problèmes de formation de la jeunesse, qui se posent d'une façon de plus en plus dramatique. La réforme de l'enseignement — bonne ou mauvaise — en fait foi, elle qui, contrairement à toutes les habitudes humanistes françaises, essaie de mettre l'accent sur l'enseignement technique et même sur les sports.

L'exemple des sports est typique. Il y a peu, les sportifs français ne triomphaient que dans les domaines réservés de l'escrime et de l'équitation, arts aristocratiques par excellence, et comme passéistes. Au contraire, ce sont aujourd'hui les nageurs et les skieurs français qui remportent des victoires internationales : c'est que la France est sortie de sa tour d'ivoire intellectuelle ; elle accepte la compétition moderne sur le terrain d'aujourd'hui.

REVALORISATION DE LA FRANCE SUR LE PLAN INTERNATIONAL

La France était en train de devenir un pays sans importance et supportant à peine lui-même la conscience de son individualité. Le but de la Cinquième République est d'en refaire une nation pesant de tout son poids dans la balance du monde et fière de ses différences.

Résultat : nous assistons en ce moment à l'une des tentatives les plus intéressantes de l'histoire, et qu'il importe de considérer précisément comme une expérience, au sens scientifique du terme, sans préjuger des résultats. En effet, la France — avec pour moteur l'équipe de la Cinquième République — essaie de remonter le courant qui, jusqu'à présent, a toujours emporté dans la décadence et la confusion les pays qui avaient déjà connu leur apogée. On notera que cette tentative est faite contre le sentiment de la majorité des Français, qui pensent que la France devrait abdiquer mais qui ne sont pas d'accord pour déterminer entre les mains de qui (les États-Unis ? l'Europe unie ? l'U. R. S. S. ?) : cela seul permet à une minorité — d'ailleurs puissante, et disposant des moyens d'information officiels — de tenter la gageure. On notera aussi que deux éléments d'une importance primordiale jouent en faveur des ambitions de cette minorité : d'une part la poussée démographique de la France — la population de la France s'accroît plus vite que celle de tous les autres pays d'Europe (33 pour cent des Français sont des enfants) ; d'autre part le progrès scientifique contemporain qui, allant à rebours de celui du XIXème siècle, donne à nouveau leur chance aux puissances moyennes.

La force de frappe   Le point primordial du programme de la Cinquième République a été la création d'une arme atomique française, qui a eu autant de détracteurs en France qu'à l'étranger. Ces dépenses sont absurdes, disait-on : quand même la France y consacrerait tout son budget, elle ne parviendrait pas à se munir d'un armement nucléaire comparable à celui des États-Unis ou de l'U. R. S. S. Alors, à quoi bon ?

La doctrine officielle se présentait ainsi : premièrement, si une nation prétend à l'indépendance, elle doit être capable de la défendre elle-même par ses propres moyens, et l'on ne peut rien défendre au XXème siècle sans arme nucléaire ; deuxièmement, l'arme nucléaire la moins puissante est néanmoins d'une puissance telle qu'elle ne peut que faire réfléchir à deux fois des agresseurs éventuels, peu soucieux d'obtenir une victoire qui leur coûterait presque autant qu'une défaite ; troisièmement, le progrès joue en faveur de la France — lorsque les États-Unis et l'U. R. S. S. disposeront de bombes pouvant faire sauter cent planètes Terre, et la France une seule, ils seront en fait à égalité ; quatrièmement, la création d'une industrie atomique militaire stimulera l'industrie atomique civile, et ainsi les dépenses encourues seront rapidement compensées.

La Communauté   L'équipe de la Cinquième République n'a pas été moins critiquée par les Français pour l'aide à la Communauté, qui pèse lourdement sur le budget, non seulement sous forme d'investissements et de prêts, mais même sous forme d'assistance directe. « En échange de quoi, nous ne trouvons qu'ingratitude dans nos anciennes colonies », grognent certains.

En fait, ce que la France cherche à sauvegarder — principalement en Afrique — c'est d'une part une zone d'influence et d'autre part des marchés pour l'avenir, lorsque l'Afrique deviendra une grande consommatrice. Sans doute la France est-elle amenée à tenir là un pari qu'elle n'est nullement certaine de gagner. Du moins mise-t-elle sur l'avenir ce qu'elle n'avait pas fait depuis bien longtemps. Pour l'instant, seule l'Algérie, le troisième client de la France dans le monde, illustre brillamment l'idée de créer des marchés dans les pays en voie de développement.

L'étalon or   Les financiers sont comme les graphologues : on en trouve toujours un pour dire, dans un jargon incompréhensible, le contraire de ce qu'un autre vient d'affirmer dans un langage hermétique. Loin de nous l'idée de chercher à départager les grandes autorités qui déclarent que l'étalon or est « dépassé » ou qu'il est « éternel ». On se bornera ici à faire remarquer, à propos de cette question âprement débattue, qu'il eût été absurde, dans le cadre de sa politique d'indépendance actuelle, que la France demeurât attachée à « l'étalon dollar ». Dans la mesure où toute son attitude, à l'égard du bloc des États-Unis, est de dégagement, il est logique qu'elle revienne à un étalon international, qui lui permet de limiter les investissements américains en France et qui lui donne une position intéressante à l'égard du plus important rival économique des États-Unis, qui est aussi le second producteur d'or dans le monde, à savoir l'U. R. S. S.

La France et les États-Unis   Un mouvement d'indignation s'est répandu aux États-Unis lorsque cette attitude de dégagement aussi bien économique que militaire s'est dessinée. Sans doute est-il vrai de dire que la France a joyeusement accepté l'aide militaire et économique américaine quand elle en avait besoin (intervention au cours des deux Guerres mondiales, plan Marshall), et l'on pourrait parler d'ingratitude à cet égard si, appliqué à une

Pour un pays, une politique indépendante est celle qui lui appartient en propre, qui ne lui est pas imposée de l'extérieur. L'indépendance n'est autre que la « propriété », au sens philosophique du terme. C'est le refus de recevoir la vérité toute faite, le jugement tout préparé, c'est-à-dire dans les conditions actuellement données de la politique internationale, le refus d'accepter telles quelles les positions prises par un super-État chef de file, Amérique ou Russie...

La France n'a pas de moyens militaires suffisants pour s'opposer où que ce soit aux U. S. A. ou à l'U. R. S. S., mais elle n'en a pas l'intention. Nos moyens cependant ne sont pas inexistants et ils ne sont pas dérisoires. Notre force serait insuffisante par rapport à des objectifs que nous écartons, elle est suffisante pour nous donner une autorité que n'aurait pas, en effet, une puissance trop chétive, même si elle parlait le langage des dieux. Il y a là, en somme, un mélange d'éléments moraux et d'éléments matériels qui ne nous désavantage pas. Tel est plus particulièrement le rôle que l'on peut attribuer à notre force de frappe, à notre place comme membre du club atomique. Nous sommes assez forts pour garder un minimum de prestige, nous sommes assez faibles pour mériter un maximum de confiance. Nous sommes la plus petite puissance de cette académie de destruction, mais nous sommes aussi la seule dont les intentions pacifiques ne puissent en aucun cas être mises en doute. C'est, en somme, la posologie appliquée à la politique. La vertu de la « dose moyenne de puissance ».

EDGAR FAURE

nation, le mot même n'était pas déplacé. Les premiers devoirs d'une nation sont envers elle-même, il n'y a pas de doute là-dessus.

Or, il est bien clair que les États-Unis forment une puissance productrice de premier plan et que, comme tels, ils ne peuvent pas avoir avec la France, nation productrice moyenne, de relations d'égalité : ils ne peuvent que chercher à l'absorber économiquement. La balance export-import montre bien l'inégalité des forces : les importations américaines en France sont près du double des exportations françaises vers les États-Unis. Lorsque cette inégalité — qui ne peut que s'accroître dans l'avenir — se compliquait d'une sorte d'occupation militaire de la France par les forces de l'O. T. A. N. (sans compter les investissements américains, toujours énormes), on assistait indéniablement à une satellisation du plus petit pays autour du plus grand. Pour éviter ce phénomène, il fallait que le premier sortît de la zone d'attraction du second. Il faut se garder de transporter ce débat mercantile sur le plan sentimental.

Sans doute peut-on réprouver les volontés d'indépendance de la France ; mais, une fois ces volontés acquises, sa politique extérieure en découle logiquement, non seulement à l'égard des États-Unis, mais aussi envers l'U. R. S. S.

La France et l'U. R. S. S. Entre ces deux géants, la France indépendante ne peut chercher qu'à maintenir l'équilibre, sous peine d'être dévorée par l'un ou gobée par l'autre. Personne, et les hommes de la Cinquième République moins que quiconque, ne doutent que l'invasion militaire par les Soviétiques ne soit infiniment plus pénible à supporter que l'invasion économique par les Américains ; mais, du seul point de vue de l'indépendance de la nation France, le résultat serait le même : la disparition pure et simple.

Ajoutons à cela que le bloc oriental consiste en un ensemble de pays où les produits manufacturés font défaut depuis trente ou cinquante ans selon le cas et que, la France étant exportatrice dans ce domaine, il est logique qu'elle se cherche de ce côté de nouveaux débouchés. Parler d'un rapprochement idéologique, comme certains l'ont fait, semble curieux. De par sa situation géographique, comme de par sa puissance relative, la France est amenée à jouer les fléaux de la balance.

Les mêmes considérations commandent l'attitude de la France à l'égard de la Chine : débouchés possibles, perspectives variées, contrepoids de rechange, la Chine offre tout cela, et il faudrait s'étonner bien davantage si la France négligeait les possibilités qui lui sont offertes de ce côté.

La France et l'Europe A l'Europe, la France est liée étroitement par le Marché commun. Du moins à ce qu'on appelle l'Europe, et qui tend en fait vers une alliance bicéphale France-Allemagne de l'Ouest, avec quelques appoints. Il est bien clair que, dans une association de ce genre, chacun cherche à se tailler la part du lion et à empêcher son partenaire d'en faire autant. Puissance industrielle de premier plan, l'Allemagne ne courait pas, dans l'aventure, les mêmes risques que la France — ce qui explique la modération, la prudence, avec lesquelles la France s'est engagée dans la voie européenne, craignant surtout pour son agriculture arriérée la concurrence des pays nordiques, plus modernes sous ce rapport. Maintenant que l'agriculture française a fait des progrès considérables, ce problème-là ne se pose plus. En revanche, deux autres se présentent : faut-il que la France nationale disparaisse dans le bloc européen ? faut-il que la Grande-Bretagne entre dans le Marché commun sans renoncer à ses attaches avec les États-Unis et le Commonwealth ?

A ces deux questions la Cinquième République a systématiquement répondu « non ». Si la France renonçait à son individualité historique, elle se renierait elle-même : argument moral. D'ailleurs, une telle fusion ne profiterait qu'à l'Allemagne, plus agressive sur le plan économique : argument pratique. Si la Grande-Bretagne était entrée dans le Marché commun avec toutes ses attaches extérieures, ou bien ce serait elle qui s'y serait taillée la part du

> *Si la France ne peut accomplir cet acte d'énergie, si elle ne peut faire cet acte de foi qui conditionne sa résurrection... alors, tant pis pour elle ! C'est qu'elle ne sera plus digne de subsister.*
>
> LE GÉNÉRAL DE GAULLE

lion, ou bien ce serait la vocation proprement européenne de l'association qui aurait été sacrifiée.

Tel, ramené à ses grandes lignes, semble être le rêve de la Cinquième République.

Depuis que cette politique est systématiquement appliquée, le prestige de la France est allé croissant d'une part dans les pays sous-développés et en voie de développement (Afrique francophone, monde arabe, Amérique du Sud) et d'autre part dans les deux grands blocs rivaux. Prestige ne signifie pas « capacité d'inspirer l'amitié » : il peut même signifier le contraire. On ne se tromperait pas beaucoup en affirmant que, dans plus d'un pays, la politique de la Cinquième République a ressuscité un sentiment oublié depuis longtemps : la haine de la France. C'est que, entre nations, on ne hait que celles qu'on a des raisons de redouter.

LES MOYENS 10
D'INFORMATION

IDÉE GÉNÉRALE

L'Anglo-Saxon aime être renseigné ; le Français aime modifier ce qu'il apprend. De là son dégoût traditionnel pour la géographie, par exemple, parce que la géographie ne saurait être modifiée.

Le Français « bricole » son information.

Tous les moyens d'information français traditionnels sont conçus pour autoriser et encourager ce bricolage. Il en va autrement de la radio et de la télévision, qui, étant entre les mains de l'État, sont bricolées au départ et non à l'arrivée. Il est possible que, par voie de conséquence, le caractère du Français évolue, et que le peuple le plus méfiant au monde devienne, comme les autres, un consommateur de vérités officielles débitées au mètre ou au kilo.

Pour l'instant, il n'en est pas encore là, et l'on peut distinguer très clairement deux sortes de publications dans la presse française : celles qui sont constituées de faits arrangés pour favoriser le rêve et celles qui sont composées d'idées montées pour aider la réflexion.

197

LES DÉBITS DE VÉRITÉS OFFICIELLES

L'État français ne dispose pas d'une presse officielle, comme les États totalitaires. Sans doute influence-t-il directement les journaux les plus conservateurs, qui ont tout intérêt à entretenir de bons rapports avec le pouvoir, mais cette influence est trop subtile pour qu'on puisse tenter d'en rendre compte ici. Bornons-nous donc à considérer le seul O. R. T. F. (Office de radiodiffusion et télévision françaises) comme l'organe du gouvernement.

Les quatre chaînes de radiodiffusion et les deux chaînes de télévision présentent aux « chers auditeurs » et aux « chers téléspectateurs » des programmes variés, comprenant des émissions documentaires, des concerts, des jeux, des bulletins d'information, des commentaires, des comptes rendus d'événements sportifs, à l'exclusion de toute publicité privée. Le temps consacré aux émissions de valeur est réduit ; le niveau de la plupart des programmes est adapté aux publics les plus étendus et par conséquent les moins exigeants. Cela est surtout vrai de la télévision, qui demeure en France une distraction populaire (tous les ouvriers disposent d'un poste TV, alors que la plupart des intellectuels se refusent à s'en procurer un). Les débats d'idées sont un peu plus fréquents à la radio qui, tard le soir, présente quelquefois des confrontations intéressantes.

Le rôle principal de l'O. R. T. F. est, bien entendu, de présenter au public les faits politiques sous le jour sous lequel ils sont vus par le gouvernement. Son influence, comme organe de propagande, va croissant. Le général de Gaulle faillit lui-même être battu aux élections présidentielles de 1966 parce qu'il avait dédaigné de paraître à la télévision : une apparition *in extremis* renversa la situation.

Un aspect négatif mais important du rôle de l'O. R. T. F. est la transformation qu'il provoque dans la presse écrite : les événements étant rapportés par la radio et par la télévision beaucoup plus vite que par les journaux, les éditorialistes de la presse écrite ont tendance — beaucoup plus encore que par le passé — à commenter, à présenter, à organiser, une réalité qu'ils supposent déjà connue de leur public.

Comparée à l'importance des moyens de masse dans des pays intellectuellement plus unifiés (comme, par exemple, les États-Unis), celle de l'O. R. T. F., bien qu'en progrès, demeure faible. Répugnant à l'image particulariste et toujours esclave de son cadre, le Français préfère la parole aux résonances illimitées ; et il préfère la parole écrite, qui ne peut plus s'envoler, aux déclarations volatiles des ondes.

LA PRESSE DU RÊVE

Dans la presse quotidienne, deux éléments favorisent le rêve : c'est le fait-divers — les plus sanglants, les plus sordides, sont les plus demandés — et le potin — les plus croustillants concernant les personnalités les plus en vue sont les mieux venus.

Quotidiens   Les rêveurs du matin emplissent le métro aux heures où les voitures ressemblent à autant de boîtes de sardines ; ils sont au nombre d'un million à peu près, à en croire le tirage de leur principal fournisseur : *Le Parisien Libéré*.

Les rêveurs du soir, qui disposent de plus de temps pour s'emplir l'imaginative, sont naturellement plus nombreux (un million et demi approximativement), et leur traiteur de prédilection est *France-Soir*.

Ces journaux, où les photos, la publicité et les petites annonces occupent les trois quarts de l'espace, sont lus, on l'a dit, pour leurs faits-divers et leurs potins. Ils comprennent pourtant aussi des éditoriaux et même des articles de fond, qui donnent un semblant de sérieux à la publication, mais personne ne se soucie d'en prendre connaissance, sauf ceux de leurs lecteurs dont le parcours en métro est particulièrement long.

Il y a on ne sait quoi de pathétique dans l'image de ces millions de citoyens souverains emportés par des trains brinquebalants[1] vers leurs usines et leurs bureaux respectifs, et ajoutant une petite tartine de rêve à leur café au lait du matin ou à leur apéritif du soir. Les rêveurs de la fin de semaine sont bien mieux lotis : la presse hebdomadaire qu'ils consomment en bâillant leurs dimanches leur apporte des rêves confortables et parfaitement adaptés à leur personnalité — ou à son absence.

Périodiques   Les femmes disposent de deux gammes de journaux féminins, les uns mettant l'accent sur la mode et destinés à toutes les classes de la société sans exception (*Elle*, *Marie-Claire*), les autres consacrés essentiellement aux rêveries sentimentales et visant au plus bas, aussi bien du niveau social qu'intellectuel (*Nous Deux*, *Intimité*). Leurs tirages tournent autour du million d'exemplaires et permettent à un grand nombre de Françaises de se pourvoir — en imagination — de toute une garde-robe de haute couture, ou de tout un sérail d'admirateurs passionnés et brillantinés.

Les jeunes gens possèdent, depuis quelques années, une presse bien à eux, d'un ton qui intéresse le sociologue de plus près que l'historien de la civilisation : il y a en effet dans cette exaltation collective systématiquement entretenue, dans cet ésotérisme yéyé, dans ce bain bon enfant de violence organisée, des semences inquiétantes qui ne manqueront pas de germer d'ici quelques années et dont les effets sont imprévisibles. Le seul titre de *Salut les Copains* est déjà significatif par son populisme[2] agressif.

Les hommes faits, rêveurs du dimanche, se classent généralement en deux catégories. Ou bien ce sont des sportifs en chambre, incapables de faire cent mètres au pas gymnastique mais s'intéressant aux records battus par les champions internationaux : ceux-là lisent la presse sportive. Ou bien, amateurs de sensationnel et de grivoiserie, ils ont besoin que des journalistes avertis viennent leur émoustiller l'imagination : ils trouvent tout ce qu'il leur faut dans des publications de l'ordre de *France-Dimanche* (près d'un million

[1] secoués violemment

Paris-presse l'intransigeant

TOUTE DERNIÈRE — France-Soir

BOURSE COMPLÈTE

IL SE MÉFIE DU « TRIOMPHALISME » ET RESTE CONVAINCU QU'IL DOIT « ALLER AUX FRANÇAIS » ET POURSUIVRE SES DÉPLACEMENTS EN PROVINCE

LA NOUVELLE CAMPAGNE QUE VA FAIRE POMPIDOU

Il y associe tous les chefs de sa « probable » majorité et reçoit aujourd'hui Giscard d'Estaing et Jacques Duhamel

M. Edgar Faure face aux drapeaux rouges d'Orsay

L'or baisse brutalement

LE P.C. S'ABSTIENT MAIS PRÉVIENT :

« Attention aux rendez-vous sociaux »

La Convention Mitterrand hésite entre l'abstention et Poher

De Gaulle change de résidence une nouvelle fois

L'EXPRESS

N° 966 - 12-18 janvier 1970

LES COMMUNISTES CONTRE-ATTAQUENT

MM. ROGER GARAUDY, GEORGES SÉGUY, ROLAND LEROY, MEMBRES DU BUREAU POLITIQUE DU P.C. • « Tout devient légitime à qui défend l'Église, » (Voltaire)

et demi d'exemplaires), rendez-vous de la vulgarité française dans ce qu'elle a de plus cru et de plus éculé.

Enfin, la majorité des Français est devenue, malgré qu'elle en ait, friande d'images. Elle s'en méfie tant, qu'elle préfère ne pas les voir à la télévision, où elles bougent ; mais sur photo, elles participent encore de la dignité du tableau de maître et, par conséquent, effarouchent moins. De là le succès des magazines du genre de *Paris-Match* (près de deux millions d'exemplaires). Servi par des photographes ayant plus de talent que de délicatesse, et par des journalistes plus doués pour le titre (que tout le monde voit) que pour l'article (que la plupart n'ont pas le temps de lire), *Paris-Match* réussit la gageure de satisfaire tous les goûts : documentaire, humoristique, pittoresque, édifiant, il milite toujours pour les causes gagnantes, qui, à l'en croire, sont invariablement les causes justes. C'est peut-être trop beau pour être vrai, mais c'est un triomphe commercial : la firme de textiles et de sucrerie qui finance ce magazine n'en demande pas plus.

LA PRESSE DE L'IDÉE

Le consommateur français ne se nourrit pas que de rêve : aussi fréquemment, sinon plus, il suit un régime d'idées qui le confirme régulièrement dans ses partis pris, car, le parti pris n'étant pas un parti dont il lui faudra porter l'insigne et fréquenter les réunions, le Français est fermement attaché à ceux que ses parents, son éducation, le hasard d'une rencontre au service militaire ou, plus rarement, une profonde conversion intellectuelle lui ont donnés. Non seulement le Français a les idées qu'il préfère, mais il préfère aussi les idées qu'il a. C'est-à-dire qu'il en change le moins souvent possible — lui qu'on a pourtant accusé de frivolité — et ce qu'il demande à son journal, ce n'est pas du tout de lui fournir un assortiment d'opinions, mais de l'équiper en arguments pour défendre celles qu'il a déjà.

Quotidiens du matin. — Le consommateur d'idées du matin se nourrit à l'un des cinq principaux râteliers de l'opinion, dont la plupart lui entonnent quotidiennement la même proportion de vitamines, de calories, d'excitants et de tranquillisants.

A l'extrême-droite — car toute la presse française à idées est une presse politique — on trouve *L'Aurore*, journal qui satisfait les besoins de méfiance et de colère d'un demi-million de petits bourgeois français pour qui *différent* est synonyme d'*étranger* et *étranger* d'*ennemi*. Une exception, toutefois, dans cette xénophobie : les Américains ont droit aux bonnes grâces de *L'Aurore* car ils sont résolument anti-communistes, et il n'y a rien que les petits bourgeois craignent plus que le partage des biens matériels auxquels ils tiennent par-dessus tout.

Le Figaro (même tirage) fait l'objet d'un mot charmant dans une des comédies de Jean Anouilh. « Où avez-vous lu cette mauvaise nouvelle ? demande un personnage. — Dans *Le Figaro*, répond son interlocuteur. —

Impossible ! » s'écrie le premier. En effet, *Le Figaro* a pris l'habitude de dorloter ses lecteurs bourgeois : tout ce qu'ils trouvent dans ses colonnes soignées est de nature à leur faire plaisir.

Étrange histoire que celle de ce journal, qui fut lancé au XIXème siècle pour servir de tribune aux monarchistes frondeurs et impénitents, et qui est devenu l'un des plus solides monuments du conformisme républicain. Car c'est vraiment une institution que *Le Figaro*, plus qu'une publication. Depuis ses éditoriaux politiques écrits sur le ton d'une gravité aimable jusqu'à ses chroniques gastronomiques soi-disant amusantes, en passant par ses critiques théâtrales d'une violence glacée, ses feuilletons passéistes, ses articles pour la défense de la langue française, ses mots croisés érudits, etc., *Le Figaro* apparaît à certains comme les dépendances de son propre carnet mondain. C'est là, dans ce carnet, que se rencontrent les grands noms de France et surtout tous ceux que leurs propriétaires voudraient faire passer pour tels : fiançailles, mariages, naissances, décès, décorations, tous les événements de quelque importance dans la société française sont signalés ici (contre rétribution), si bien que plus d'un acheteur du *Figaro*, qui ne le lit pas, le laisse traîner dans son salon, ouvert à la page du carnet, pour faire accroire à ses visiteurs qu'il a besoin de se tenir au courant des activités « mondaines ».

Combat est un journal d'un tout autre ordre. Avec un tirage dix fois inférieur à celui du *Figaro*, il est le seul organe de la presse française à accueillir des articles contradictoires, le seul à défier les conformismes de droite et de gauche. Fondé par des intellectuels de gauche à l'époque de la Résistance, il n'a pas de position officielle sur les problèmes politiques : il suffit d'en lire quelques numéros pour sentir toute la diversité de l'opinion populaire, pour prendre conscience de la multiplicité des vérités possibles.

Le Populaire est le porte-voix du socialisme S. F. I. O. ; *L'Humanité*, celui du communisme. Le tirage de *L'Humanité* (200 000 exemplaires) et l'obstination avec laquelle ce journal rabâche la propagande et les mots d'ordre de Moscou lui donnent un certain poids que ne mérite pas son niveau intellectuel, volontairement primaire.

Quotidiens du soir   Les journaux « à idées » du soir sont moins nombreux que ceux du matin. *La Croix* dessert une clientèle de catholiques relativement limitée ; *Le Monde* est aux intellectuels ce que *Le Figaro* est aux bourgeois. Deux cent quarante mille exemplaires de cette feuille documentée, qui s'arrange pour être de gauche avec tant de sérieux que beaucoup la prennent pour une publication de droite, fournissent tous les jours à un public fait de professeurs, d'étudiants, d'industriels à la page, d'écrivains ouverts aux problèmes du jour, une information soigneusement tamisée à travers le fin réseau du conformisme de l'intelligence. Plus qu'un journal, *Le Monde* est une école de pensée, qui enseigne à raisonner sur des faits statistiques et économiques quelquefois incomplets mais présentés dans un ordre dialectique, souvent inspiré du marxisme. *Le Monde* possède aussi un carnet, qui rend à la bourgeoisie tout ce que ses éditoriaux tentent de lui prendre.

LE FIGARO

ÉDITION DE PARIS

MERCREDI 4 JUIN 1969

LA COMPÉTITION PRÉSIDENTIELLE

LES DEUX CANDIDATS DRESSENT MAINTENANT LEUR PLAN DE BATAILLE

• MM. Duhamel et Giscard d'Estaing participent activement à la campagne de M. Georges Pompidou

• M. Alain Poher a expliqué hier après-midi le sens de son maintien.

Éviter au second tour un affrontement entre gaullistes et communistes

LE ROLE DU CENTRISME

De l'élection primaire à l'élection présidentielle

par Valéry GISCARD D'ESTAING

DÉSACCORD FONDAMENTAL ENTRE SAIGON ET WASHINGTON

sur la question d'un éventuel gouvernement de coalition

Le prochain sommet de Midway présente au Sud-Vietnam comme un affrontement

De notre envoyé spécial J. GUILLEME-BRULON

Triomphe des conservateurs pro-soviétiques à Prague

M. Strougal nommé premier secrétaire adjoint du P.C.

par simple décision du praesidium

HYGIÈNE DES MOTS

par Jean D'ORMESSON

LE GÉANT "BOEING 747" A RÉUSSI SON ENTRÉE... MALGRÉ LA PLUIE

AUTO-INTERVIEW

CONSÉQUENCES DE L'INCLUSION D'UN VACCIN

• PAUL VI À GENÈVE LE 10 JUIN

VINGT-SIXIÈME ANNÉE — Nº 7585   32 PAGES   MERCREDI 4 JUIN 1969

Le Monde

Rédaction, Administration: 5, rue des Italiens, Paris-IX. — Directeur: Hubert BEUVE-MÉRY

Après le premier tour de l'élection présidentielle

Un « moindre mal » pour l'étranger

• Le parti socialiste se prononce pour M. Alain Poher

• Le parti communiste invite ses électeurs à s'abstenir

A LA SUITE DE MULTIPLES INCIDENTS

L'échec de la mission de M. Rockefeller risque de compromettre la négociation globale entre Washington et l'Amérique latine

Au Brésil le 18 juin

LE NOUVEAU VISAGE DE LA GUERRE AU LAOS

I. — Un pays qui s'essouffle

par JEAN-CLAUDE POMONTI

AU JOUR LE JOUR

Promesses...

Hebdomadaires On rangera dans une catégorie à part la presse hebdo-madaire littéraire et artistique, avec *Les Nouvelles Littéraires et Le Figaro Littéraire*, qui ont une clientèle étroitement délimitée : de grandes fresques historiques, des documents et des reportages leur permettent d'étendre un peu leur public, qui demeure néanmoins intellectuel d'une façon quelque peu vieillotte. Tout le reste de la presse hebdomadaire est politisé et représente une véritable presse d'opinion.

A l'extrême-gauche, *L'Humanité-Dimanche*, strictement doctrinaire comme sa consœur quotidienne, et *Les Lettres Françaises*, dont le prétexte littéraire voile à peine les tendances politiques.

A gauche tout court, *Témoignage Chrétien*, d'un catholicisme « em-marxisé » ; *France-Observateur*, qui voudrait être à la semaine ce que *Le Monde* est à la journée ; *Le Canard Enchaîné*, journal satirique d'une violence peu commune, utilisant tour à tour le sarcasme le mieux aiguisé et le calem-bour le plus vulgaire, servant d'ailleurs de carquois anti-gouvernemental à la droite aussi bien qu'à la gauche ; enfin *L'Express*, à peine moins répandu que *Le Canard* — 300 000 contre un demi-million — mais qui, par sa présentation imitée des magazines américains du style de *Time*, par le ton agressivement intellectuel de ses chroniques, par ses pages féminines, par tout son côté « parisien », « snob », « dans le vent », représente des tendances françaises très profondes et très modernes à la fois.

Au centre, *Le Nouveau Candide*, très proche des milieux gouvernementaux, et qui, sans avoir les prétentions intellectuelles de *L'Express*, cherche néan-moins à atteindre les couches supérieures de la population, en flattant ce qu'elles ont quelquefois de moins recommandable : un certain appétit du scandale couché en bon français.

A droite, une pléiade de publications diverses, où l'on trouve du pire et du meilleur et dont l'ensemble représente une partie non négligeable de l'opinion. *Carrefour* demeure fermement attaché aux valeurs nationales pures et sim-ples ; *La Vie Catholique* compte par ses tirages (près d'un demi-million) et par son attitude imitant fidèlement celle de l'Église ; *Rivarol* ressasse indé-finiment les souvenirs d'un temps où une certaine droite collaborait joyeuse-ment avec l'occupant allemand ; *Minute* fouille la vie privée des grands hommes de la Cinquième République pour en monter en épingle les détails les plus scabreux ; *Aspects de la France* milite pour un rétablissement de la royauté en France.

L'énumération de toutes ces publications peut donner une idée de la bigarrure de l'ensemble, bigarrure profondément conforme au génie même de la France, que n'ont pas encore étouffé des publications massives défendant non plus un style de pensée mais un genre de vie : à savoir *Sélection du Reader's Digest* (près d'un million et demi d'exemplaires) et *Constellation* (plus d'un demi-million).

Si l'on place ces deux magazines populaires au bas de l'échelle intellectuelle de la presse périodique française, et toutes les publications énumérées précé-demment au milieu de la même échelle, c'est à son sommet qu'il conviendra de situer les feuilles et revues mensuelles, qui s'adressent aux publics les plus réfléchis.

Mensuels On rangera d'un côté les feuilles d'information politiques, publiées à titre privé par certaines personnalités bien renseignées et fréquemment par le gouvernement pour divulgation d'informations confidentielles. A la même catégorie — encore qu'il s'agisse d'une série de mises au point politiques, économiques et sociales plutôt que d'informations proprement dites — appartient le *Bulletin* du bureau politique de Mgr le comte de Paris, prétendant au trône, qui, lui, demeure toujours en excellents termes avec le pouvoir.

D'un autre côté, on mettra toutes les revues culturelles. En France, la plupart de ces revues meurent aussi vite qu'elles naissent ; quelqu'unes au contraire paraissent résolues à survivre. *La Revue des Deux Mondes* alimente depuis plus de cent ans une clientèle de « vieilles barbes » de tous âges ; *Le Mercure de France* représente une certaine avant-garde poétique, vieille de cinquante ans ; *La Nouvelle Nouvelle Revue Française* demeure la revue littéraire par excellence, à laquelle la plupart des grands écrivains donnent des articles et des nouvelles ; *Esprit* séduit les bonnes âmes par son catholicisme de gauche ; *Les Temps Modernes*, l'organe personnel de Jean-Paul Sartre et de son équipe, fournissent le lecteur en considérations marxistes existentialistes aptes à donner bonne conscience aux bourgeois honteux.

A noter que la situation de la presse française évolue sans cesse. Des nouveaux venus comme *L'Express* ont fait fortune en quelques années ; leurs tirages demeurent cependant réduits (environ un quart de million) à côté de ceux dont disposent des publications spécialisées comme *L'Auto-Journal* ou *Modes et Travaux* (qui, pour sa part, dépasse le million). Cette situation fluide paraît être significative de l'époque actuelle qui représente, indéniablement, une transition. Il est difficile de prévoir ce que sera la presse française d'ici quelques années. Des facteurs aussi divers que le coût du papier, la popularisation de la télévision, l'attitude de l'État, modifieront nécessairement son évolution.

Presse provinciale On a sciemment fait la part belle à la presse parisienne — qui, seule, rayonne à l'étranger — et négligé la presse de province, qui la dépasse pourtant pour le nombre d'exemplaires vendus. C'est que la France, on l'a dit, souffre d'une centralisation exagérée dans le domaine intellectuel : consciemment ou non, les Français sont convaincus qu'il ne se passe rien d'important qu'à Paris, et le résultat, c'est qu'effectivement Paris est la seule ville où les personnalités de premier plan trouvent à s'exprimer. Si le provincial achète le journal de sa province, il achète généralement aussi celui de Paris : dans l'un, il lit les nouvelles locales, mais pour affûter ses opinions, il a besoin de l'autre.

SITUATION DE LA PRESSE

Dans l'ensemble, la presse française, face à la concurrence de la radio et de la télévision, se porte mal. Elle qui, pendant un siècle et demi, a tenu tête à tous les pouvoirs successifs et exercé une mission civilisatrice auprès de ses lecteurs en raisonnant avec eux sur les problèmes de la nation, semble se contenter maintenant de satisfaire leurs besoins intellectuels les plus élémentaires à n'importe quel prix.

Pour la quantité, les chiffres sont éloquents : en 1939, 220 quotidiens étaient vendus à 11 millions d'exemplaires ; en 1963, alors que la population avait considérablement augmenté, 150 quotidiens n'en vendaient que 12 millions.

Pour la qualité, les statistiques sont encore bien plus accablantes. Quels sont en effet du point de vue du tirage les « cinq grands » de la presse française ? *L'Écho des Françaises* (publication catholique sans intentions intellectuelles), *Paris-Match, Sélection du Reader's Digest, France-Dimanche* et *France-Soir.*

Le succès de ces feuilles suivant de près de grands efforts pour la démocratisation de l'enseignement — c'est-à-dire l'accession des masses populaires au niveau de clientèle de la presse — devrait faire réfléchir ceux qui ont tendance à s'exagérer soit l'intelligence naturelle du Français, soit la valeur de son système d'enseignement.

En France comme ailleurs, la presse est un reflet grossier mais véridique du public qu'elle sert. Le Français est peut-être « né malin », mais pas plus qu'un autre il n'a le goût naturellement bon. Le goût, comme l'alcool, a besoin d'être raffiné.

LES SPECTACLES 11

IDÉE GÉNÉRALE

« Du pain et des spectacles », hurlaient les foules romaines. Ces spectacles consistaient alors en combats de gladiateurs et en crucifixions d'esclaves. Nous avons perdu le goût de ces plaisirs, à moins que nous ne manquions tout simplement d'esclaves et de gladiateurs, mais nous n'avons pas perdu le goût des spectacles, et nos spectacles nous jugent. Si « du pain » n'exprime qu'un besoin, « des spectacles » implique déjà un désir, c'est-à-dire un choix, c'est-à-dire un luxe.

Le jugement par le luxe s'applique à tous les pays ; mais il ne saurait mieux s'appliquer qu'en France, où le frivole est rituellement sérieux, et le sérieux frivole.

LE THÉÂTRE

Paris, avec ses quarante théâtres pouvant recevoir tous les soirs quarante mille spectateurs, demeure — malgré les efforts de décentralisation dont on parlera plus loin — bien plus que la capitale du théâtre en France : en vérité, presque tout ce qui se fait de significatif, à l'exception de quelques festivals, se fait à Paris, sous les yeux d'une critique et d'un public qui ont un goût distinctif (sinon distingué) et qui l'imposent au reste de la France.

Un trait significatif apparaît à quiconque réfléchit un instant au rôle joué par les théâtres parisiens : c'est que les uns ont pour but de poursuivre une tradition ; les autres, d'en fonder de nouvelles.

LES THÉÂTRES CONSERVATEURS

Parmi les théâtres « conservateurs », les subventionnés ont une place à part. L'État ayant reconnu que la qualité ne faisait pas ses frais, il a décidé de lui fournir, aux frais du contribuable, une assistance financière. Les résultats sont quelquefois positifs (il est excellent qu'on puisse voir du Molière, du Corneille et du Racine à Paris chaque fois qu'on en a envie) et quelquefois désastreux (il est désolant que le théâtre devienne une sorte de bureaucratie).

Comédie-Française Le théâtre subventionné par excellence est la Comédie-Française (les Parisiens disent simplement « le Français »), qui,

La mode veut qu'on joue les pièces du XVIIème à sujet antique en costumes du XVIIème, comme au temps de leur création. La Phèdre de Racine en est un exemple typique.

L'École des Femmes, *de Molière, ancêtre de toutes les pièces de boulevard.*

malgré les efforts de renouvellement de divers administrateurs, demeure un véritable musée consacré au XVIIème (tragédie et comédie classiques) et au XIXème (drame romantique, comédie bourgeoise). On y accueille bien quelquefois des auteurs modernes, mais ils apparaissent déplacés parmi tous ces lustres dorés, ces fauteuils en peluche rouge, ces rideaux en trompe-l'œil, qui évoquent une autre époque et un autre style. Il serait contradictoire de demander à la Comédie-Française des mises en scène originales, puisque tout son esprit consiste à sauvegarder du passé ce qui peut l'être : aussi n'y voit-on rien de nouveau, de « révolutionnaire ». Mais l'impeccable formation technique de ses comédiens, recrutés parmi les plus brillants élèves du Conservatoire d'art dramatique, leur diction parfaite, leur connaissance de toutes les ficelles du métier aussi bien que leur culture classique, font de la troupe même du Français une des meilleures troupes parisiennes, à la fois la plus professionnelle et la plus désintéressée, celle où — chose remarquable pour un organisme d'État — la médiocrité n'est jamais tolérée.

L'Opéra L'autre pilier de la tradition française, c'est l'Opéra, que complète, pour les programmes plus légers, l'institution jumelle de l'Opéra-Comique.

L'Opéra a si souvent été accusé de demeurer courbé sous le poids de son passé que des tentatives frénétiques ont récemment été faites pour le mettre sur un nouveau pied, en utilisant toutes les techniques modernes du « grand spectacle ». On n'y a réussi que partiellement, car, malgré l'abondance des décors, des éclairages, des machines et de la publicité, il demeurait impossible de compenser la pauvreté des voix. L'orchestre cependant est nettement supérieur aux chanteurs, et les chefs d'orchestre quelquefois remarquables. Le ballet reste l'un des premiers dans le monde et conserve, avec une piété qui n'a rien de démodé, la tradition classique léguée par le siècle dernier et faite d'un sens aigu de la perfection appliqué aussi bien aux ensembles qu'aux détails.

Le boulevard   A côté de ces salles subventionnées, vouées au théâtre de conservation, on trouve ce que l'on appelle « le boulevard », conservateur aussi, mais qui, loin de recevoir des subventions de l'État, vit de succès d'affiches qui tiennent quelquefois pendant plusieurs années.

Le théâtre de boulevard est moins un art qu'un produit de consommation ; son public est constitué de bourgeois parisiens et surtout de provinciaux en goguette. Un certain nombre de recettes sont utilisées par les auteurs et les metteurs en scène pour flatter ce public sans jamais le surprendre. De jolies comédiennes, des acteurs maniant le ridicule avec un semblant de légèreté, des décors réalistes, des situations agréablement grivoises, une mise en scène discrète, quelques mots d'auteur destinés à la fraction la plus raffinée du public, voilà de quoi est constituée une pièce de boulevard. Quant au sujet, il est le même depuis près de cent ans : un mari trompe sa femme ou une femme trompe son mari, et ce qui s'ensuit. Molière ne pensait pas que l'Arnolphe de son *École des femmes* aurait une telle descendance !

L'opérette   A quelques degrés au-dessous du théâtre de boulevard, on trouve l'opérette à grand spectacle, qui jouit d'une faveur constante auprès des publics populaires les moins avertis. Dans des Espagne de convention (et non de fantaisie), des chanteurs sans voix ronronnent des scies lamentables après s'être déguisés en hussards ou en toreros. Aucun rapport entre ces productions des théâtres du Châtelet ou de Mogador et les *musicals* américains au rythme fracassant. La Gaîté lyrique, subventionnée depuis peu comme la Comédie-Française, a pour but de faire revivre les opérettes du passé où pétillaient la malice et l'espièglerie d'Offenbach et de Messager ; mais il semble bien que ceux des Français qui aiment encore l'opérette la veuillent avec jets d'eaux sur la scène, carrosses renversés, et corps de ballet de cent sujets : dans ce cas, les tentatives plus modestes de l'État sont vouées à l'échec.

LE THÉATRE DE RENOUVELLEMENT

Au début du XXème siècle, le théâtre a été envahi par des hommes qui avaient des idées sur la mise en scène. Ils n'ont pas toujours réussi à les mettre en pratique, et il n'est même pas certain qu'elles aient toujours été bonnes, mais maintenant le public averti trouve plat un spectacle qui ne correspond pas à une prise de position sur les questions théâtrales. D'une pièce présentée à des spectateurs intellectuels ou se croyant tels, on exige toujours ce que l'on appelle « une certaine recherche ».

Cette tendance avait commencé avec Antoine, qui, partisan du réalisme intégral, imposa avec son Théâtre libre, les « tranches de vie » et, sur la scène, la vraie nourriture, les vrais arbres. Dès la fin de la Première Guerre mondiale, le réalisme se compliqua d'impératifs plus subtils, avec Lugné-Poe, qui accueillit au Théâtre de l'Œuvre des écrivains français et étrangers à la recherche d'eux-mêmes. Jacques Copeau, lui, devait être, pendant l'entre-deux-guerres, le maître à penser de toute une génération d'hommes de théâtre, estimant encore que tous les moyens du spectacle devaient être mis au service d'une fin : la pièce que l'on jouait.

En revanche, ses successeurs voient souvent dans la mise en scène une fin en soi. Les principaux formèrent ce qu'on appela le Cartel. Dullin, à l'Atelier, donnait la préférence à l'acteur, objet de tous ses soins ; Baty mettait la mise en scène proprement dite au-dessus de tout ; Pitœff versait dans le symbolisme ; Jouvet bâtissait ses spectacles autour de sa propre personnalité. Ils présentaient tous les quatre des pièces de qualité, anciennes ou modernes, et ont donné au théâtre français une réputation dont il jouit encore maintenant, sans toujours la mériter.

Théâtre de France   C'est de l'Atelier qu'est sorti l'un des plus grands metteurs en scène contemporains, Jean-Louis Barrault, qui a longtemps dirigé le Théâtre de France, salle subventionnée, dont l'organisation date de l'avènement de la Cinquième République. Tournant résolument le dos au naturalisme et au symbolisme, Jean-Louis Barrault est partisan du « réalisme poétique ». C'est dans cet esprit qu'il a monté nombre de pièces françaises, depuis *Bérénice* de Racine jusqu'au *Partage de midi* de Claudel, ainsi qu'un *Hamlet* inoubliable. Amoureux du théâtre sous toutes ses formes, Barrault n'a pas hésité non plus à monter des pièces sans prétentions intellectuelles mais auxquelles sa mise en scène donnait une nouvelle dimension artistique : ainsi du *Bossu* de Paul Féval et de la *Gaîté parisienne* d'Offenbach. Les événements de mai 1968 ont contraint Barrault à abandonner son théâtre, et il a perdu sa situation de metteur en scène officiel. Son œuvre n'en demeure pas moins irremplaçable.

Théâtre national populaire   La plupart des metteurs en scène français modernes partagent la méfiance de Barrault à l'égard du décor réaliste, qu'ils tiennent pour un mensonge inutile, auquel personne ne croit. Ils s'attachent au contraire à suggérer les atmosphères par des éclairages étudiés et ne recherchent l'authenticité que dans les accessoires. C'est là un retour à la tradition classique, retour qui paraissait exagérément intellectuel à certains, mais que le Théâtre national populaire a fait sien, sans que cela paraisse le desservir auprès du grand public. Subventionné aussi, et dirigé d'abord par

Jean-Louis Barrault, mime, acteur et metteur en scène, a créé un Hamlet bien à lui.

Jean Vilar puis par Georges Wilson, le T. N. P. — qui date de la Quatrième République — avait pour but d'éveiller les masses ouvrières aux réalités théâtrales. A vrai dire, il n'est pas certain que ce résultat ait été atteint, et l'on peut supposer que ce sont surtout les étudiants qui profitent des tarifs réduits du T. N. P. pour aller au théâtre à peu de frais. Mais quand sa réussite se limiterait à cela, sa création serait déjà justifiée. Le T. N. P. présente des tragédies classiques françaises et étrangères et aussi des œuvres modernes, d'un caractère généralement poétique et que l'on croit aptes à séduire « le peuple ». L'influence de Brecht s'y fait sentir et une certaine politisation abîme la pureté de ce théâtre, dont les réalisations sont d'ailleurs remarquables, aussi bien au Palais de Chaillot à Paris que dans le cadre du festival d'Avignon.

Il est heureux que l'État subventionne ces deux creusets de théâtre que sont le Théâtre de France et le T. N. P., car les salles privées semblent réussir moins bien dans le renouvellement que dans le conservatisme. Un ou deux théâtres de la rive gauche et l'Atelier repris par André Barsacq sont presque les seules salles d'importance à présenter des spectacles un peu ambitieux, aux frais de leurs producteurs. Il faut évidemmnt faire une exception pour les théâtres d'avant-garde qui, bénéficiant d'une vogue curieuse, font triompher dans des locaux exigus et inconfortables des pièces qu'on groupe généralement sous l'appellation de « Théâtre de l'absurde » ou « anti-théâtre ». Ce phénomène a acquis une telle importance dans la France actuelle et a eu une telle résonance à l'étranger qu'il est bon de s'y arrêter.

L'anti-théâtre   Pendant l'entre-deux-guerres, Antonin Artaud avait inventé un théâtre « différent » qu'il appelait « le théâtre de la cruauté », qui mourut à peine avait-il vu le jour et dont, sur le plan pratique, il ne reste rien, comme il arrive chaque fois où, en art, l'idée précède l'action. Mais cela ne signifie pas que l'idée soit fausse en soi, et il nous paraît essentiel de rapprocher l'anti-théâtre actuel des rêveries d'Artaud.

Le théâtre, disait Artaud, ce n'est pas du tout une pièce plus une mise en scène. C'est une communion du public seul, dans laquelle la pièce ne joue que le rôle de catalyseur. Elle pourrait avantageusement être remplacée par telle ou telle invention nouvelle, comme elle a remplacé elle-même les cérémonies religieuses de l'Antiquité. Aussi préconisait-il l'emploi de méthodes qu'il considérait propres à séduire les masses, à rapprocher le théâtre du peuple, et qui tenaient plus du *happening* américain que de la littérature. A ces méthodes les masses demeurèrent insensibles ; elles continuèrent à hanter le cinéma dominical, préférant apparemment les spectacles où le maximum de passivité est demandé au public. Mais, vingt ans plus tard, sinon les masses, du moins une certaine élite assez nombreuse s'intéressa à l'anti-théâtre, qui ne réclamait pas de participation active de ses spectateurs mais qui les adoptait en quelque sorte, puisqu'il leur parlait d'eux-mêmes dans un langage ésotérique, inintelligible aux non-initiés.

Dans Mère Courage *de Bertolt Brecht, le T.N.P. s'en est donné à cœur joie avec une mise en scène à la fois artistique et populiste et avec des éclairages-décors.*

D'où une autre forme de communion, encore très littéraire sans doute mais intimiste, facilitée par de petits théâtres qu'animaient de semi-amateurs, et qui prenaient figure de chapelles, comme on les a toujours aimées en France, depuis les cours d'amour du Moyen Age jusqu'aux cénacles romantiques en passant par les salons du XVIIIème siècle.

Ionesco, Beckett, Adamov, tous d'origine étrangère, ayant tous librement choisi de s'exprimer en français, réussirent ainsi à faire éclater dans le pays du bon sens une réaction de saine folie : leurs clochards attendant un Dieu qui ne vient pas au rendez-vous (*En attendant Godot* de Beckett), leurs déchets humains achevant de mourir dans des boîtes à ordures (*Fin de partie* de Beckett), leurs professeurs ineptes assassins de leurs propres étudiants (*La Leçon* d'Ionesco), expriment autant de protestations contre le monde moderne.

Les cafés-théâtres   Les cafés-théâtres, de création plus récente, sont une autre forme de renouvellement théâtral ; assurant leur survie matérielle en servant du whisky, utilisant des acteurs qui exercent généralement une autre profession, ne payant pas leurs auteurs, ils représentent, pensent certains, l'espoir du théâtre de demain. Peut-être y a-t-il là quelque exagération. Il est possible que les cafés à spectacles intellectuels disparaissent en quelques mois, comme ils ont apparu. Mais il est certain qu'ils échappent aux diverses tyrannies qui pèsent sur les théâtres proprement dits : tyrannie de l'État pour les subventionnés ; du producteur, pour les commerciaux ; d'un metteur en scène paranoïaque, pour les artistiques. Il est certain aussi qu'ils trouvent un nouveau public et dénouent par là ce que l'on appelle « la crise du théâtre en France », expression savante signifiant « tout le monde veut faire du théâtre et personne ne veut y aller ».

La décentralisation   D'autres espoirs sont permis par la décentralisation théâtrale, qui, en province, en banlieue et dans les festivals, jouit d'une assistance systématique de l'État.

Les grandes troupes provinciales existent depuis la fin de la Deuxième Guerre mondiale. Animées par des metteurs en scène pleins d'idées — les leurs ou celles de Brecht — elles ont leur base dans les principales villes de province et font des tournées dans les régions environnantes. Lyon, Toulouse, Saint-Étienne, Aix, Rennes, Tourcoing, Strasbourg, Beaune, ont leur troupe, et produisent, avec des comédiens recrutés sur place, des spectacles classiques ou modernes d'un intérêt indéniable. Leurs tournées les conduisent jusqu'à Paris, où les connaisseurs les apprécient à leur juste valeur.

C'est depuis quelques années seulement que la politique de décentralisation théâtrale a gagné la banlieue parisienne. Des théâtres ont été créés dans les banlieues populaires et ont pour mission de mettre les chefs d'œuvre éternels à la portée des classes laborieuses. Initiative passionnante, conduite dans un véritable esprit d'apostolat.

Les festivals, eux, sont une forme beaucoup moins populiste du renouvellement théâtral. Ils ont simplement pour but d'utiliser les décors réels offerts

Dans une cave séculaire, un théâtre ultra-moderne : des semi-amateurs jouent l'Intervention *de Victor Hain au café-théâtre* Les Deux Ponts *dans l'Ile Saint-Louis.*

par certains sites historiques, soit pour permettre de les restaurer, soit pour en exploiter les possibilités artistiques cachées. Certains se tiennent dans les vieux quartiers de Paris — le Marais, la place Furstenberg, etc. ; d'autres en province — à Nîmes, à Avignon, à Aix-en-Provence. Le festival d'Aix, en particulier, présente d'admirables opéras, avec des chanteurs internationaux. On peut trouver dans ces festivals un lointain écho de ce que furent les « fêtes » du grand siècle, auxquels participaient des génies comme Molière et Lully, et que subventionnaient des Mécènes comme Louis XIV.

LE CINÉMA

Dans certains pays — les États-Unis, par exemple — le cinéma est considéré par le public comme un art de consommation et non comme un art tout court. Cependant, les moyens financiers dont disposent les producteurs d'une part, le talent naturel des metteurs en scène d'autre part, font du cinéma américain le plus grand du monde. Un producteur décide de faire un film qui lui rapporte de l'argent ; pour cela, il engage un metteur en scène qui est un artiste : résultat, le film commercial est un bon film, sans que personne n'ait songé à prononcer les mots de « septième art » ou de « responsabilité du créateur ». Le procédé est, comme on le voit, absolument *démocratique*.

En France, il n'en va pas ainsi. Le Français croit inconsciemment à une certaine prédestination de la qualité. Il distingue très nettement les « bons films » des « films commerciaux » et n'admet pas que les deux catégories puissent coïncider. Un producteur décide de faire un film qui lui rapporte de l'argent ; pour cela, il engage sciemment un metteur en scène voué aux productions à succès et qui, la plupart du temps, se considère lui-même comme « vendu ». Des vedettes sont embauchées, non pour leurs qualités mais pour leur cote. On tourne le film et on le présente à grand renfort de publicité. Tout le monde se précipite pour le voir, sauf les « vrais » amateurs de cinéma, qui boudent. Ils ont d'ailleurs raison de bouder : le film est mauvais, il doit son succès aux procédés les plus bas, il sera oublié aussitôt qu'il aura quitté les salles d'exclusivité et fait la tournée des quartiers.

Autre procédé. Un metteur en scène décide de faire un film qui lui plaise. Il va trouver des dizaines de producteurs et mendie auprès d'eux les fonds nécessaires. Les producteurs finissent par se laisser fléchir — ils savent qu'ils jouent perdants. Ils ont raison. Le film est excellent, mais il fait à peine ses frais : le grand public boude à son tour une œuvre qui, il le sait, n'est pas faite pour lui. C'est un système typiquement *aristocratique* : les revendications socialistes qu'on trouve dans les films intellectuels n'y changeront rien.

Sans doute y a-t-il une part de caricature dans le tableau qu'on vient de brosser : tous les bons metteurs en scène français ne couchent pas sur la paille ; tous ceux qui gagnent de l'argent ne sont pas des imposteurs. Mais c'est ainsi du moins que le public voit les choses, et un honnête homme, avant d'aller au cinéma, s'interroge pour savoir ce qu'il va voir : un film populaire, ou un film de qualité. La distinction est inévitable.

RÉTROSPECTIVE

Le cinéma est une invention française datant de la fin du XIXème siècle. Si les projections animées de l'inventeur, Louis Lumière, ne passent plus que pour des expériences de laboratoire, les courts métrages de Georges Méliès, farces rudimentaires durant à peine quelques minutes mais déjà tournées en studio et utilisant les premières possibilités de trucage, reparaissent périodiquement à l'écran et suscitent l'attendrissement du public. Non pour leur qualité technique s'entend, mais pour la nostalgie qu'ils éveillent à l'égard d'une époque demeurée « belle » dans le souvenir et l'imagination ; plus encore peut-être, par une sorte de reconnaissance pour le chemin parcouru en si peu de temps et pour les joies — artistiques ou sentimentales — que le cinéma a procurées à ses spectateurs.

Avant la guerre de 1914, la France était la reine incontestée du septième art. Dès le début de l'après-guerre, elle perd sa suprématie au profit des États-

Unis, qui, avec Charlie Chaplin, créent les premiers films véritablement classiques, tandis que l'Allemagne se consacre à un expressionnisme baroque ne manquant pas d'intérêt. La France, elle, ne produit que des « comédies dramatiques » de caractère sentimental, sans chercher à utiliser les moyens propres du cinéma qu'un Chaplin découvrait comme sans y penser. C'est l'époque, en France, du théâtre filmé, des histoires policières et des interminables feuilletons pleurards, réalisés quelquefois en une douzaine d'épisodes.

L'avènement du parlant ne change pas grand chose au cinéma français. Du moins pas immédiatement. Cependant, plusieurs cinéastes qui, dès la fin de la Première Guerre mondiale, essayaient de faire des films de qualité, commencent à conquérir leur public et surtout à imposer au monde intellectuel l'idée que le cinéma est bien un art et non pas un divertissement. De cette époque date le divorce dont on parlait plus haut. Georges Auric, faisant de la musique pour les films de Jean Cocteau, était encore accusé de « se vendre », alors que ces films étaient réalisés avec un minimum de moyens matériels. Mais cette situation n'allait pas durer : bientôt les « bons » cinéastes eurent droit à toute la considération entourant un véritable artiste.

La Deuxième Guerre mondiale, le triomphe d'un certain naturalisme, le retour au réalisme poétique qui avait marqué les années 30, puis le déferlement de la nouvelle vague, toutes ces époques se chevauchent et s'enchevêtrent de telle façon que les synthèses en apparaissent comme gratuites. Aussi, pour une fois, essaierons-nous une autre méthode : après avoir réglé son compte au cinéma commercial, dit « de compensation », nous consacrerons de brefs paragraphes aux principaux metteurs en scène en les nommant par leurs noms et en les rattachant *a posteriori* — et seulement lorsque cela semblera rationnel — aux principales tendances du cinéma artistique français.

LE CINÉMA DE COMPENSATION

Le cinéma de compensation peut se présenter sous plusieurs formes : théâtre filmé, permettant aux publics les moins fortunés de voir sur l'écran un succès de la scène ; films comiques, conçus pour apporter une heure et demie d'euphorie aux spectateurs les moins raffinés ; films sentimentaux, ayant pour but de faire pleurer les âmes sensibles ; films de violence, satisfaisant sans risques les instincts guerriers des petits bourgeois ; grandes reconstitutions

Ce que la cathédrale gothique avec ses pompes et ses richesses était à l'imagination du Moyen Age, le truc l'est au rêve du titi. Au ciel du faubourg Saint-Antoine, le corps de ballet remplace les Anges et les Dominations.
GONCOURT

historiques, avec costumes chatoyants, personnages célèbres et maîtresses royales.

Le théâtre filmé joue un rôle d'une certaine importance dans les activités culturelles, mais, comme il n'y a pas là de création proprement dite, il est inutile de s'arrêter sur cette catégorie de films, sinon pour remarquer que Sacha Guitry a filmé quelques-unes de ses pièces avec un talent cinématographique certain (*Mon Père avait raison*).

Les films comiques, sans comparaison possible avec les chefs d'œuvre américains, dans lesquels la folie du rire atteint à une sorte de grandeur, sont généralement consacrés aux prouesses de tel ou tel acteur dont l'apparition seule provoque l'hilarité générale : c'est le cas, par exemple, d'un Fernandel ou d'un Louis de Funès. Quant aux metteurs en scène, ils ne comptent gurère dans ce genre-là.

Les films sentimentaux — on pense à la version filmée de *La Dame aux camélias*, ou de tel roman du siècle dernier — forment les mélodrames de notre époque. A noter que beaucoup d'entre eux consistent en des reprises d'œuvres du XIXème adaptées pour l'écran, ce qui étaierait notre opinion, selon laquelle la sensibilité des masses est généralement en retard d'un siècle environ sur celle des créateurs.

Les films de violence jouissent d'une faveur certaine, soit que la violence y soit prise au sérieux, soit qu'il s'agisse d'une satire où l'on affecte de ridiculiser

Avec Napoléon, *Abel Gance apparaît comme le premier classique du cinéma français.*

les bagarres homériques, tout en en montrant de plus homériques encore. D'âpres polémiques entourent la projection des œuvres de ce genre, que beaucoup tiennent pour des écoles de meurtre, tandis que d'autres y voient l'occasion pour la jeunesse de dépenser par procuration son trop-plein d'agressivité.

Les grandes reconstitutions historiques plaisent généralement à des spectateurs d'âge plus mûr, ravis de retrouver sur l'écran de lointains souvenirs de classe. Quelquefois, ces reconstitutions s'enrichissent d'une atmosphère sensuelle passablement simplette. Le *Si Versailles m'était conté* de Sacha Guitry, déjà nommé, est un bon exemple de ce genre de production.

LE CINÉMA ARTISTIQUE

Gance   Entre les deux guerres, pendant que Marcel L'Herbier faisait des recherches de symbolisme cinématographique avant de créer l'I. D. H. E. C. (Institut des hautes études cinématographiques), où sont formés la plupart des metteurs en scène français, un grand réalisateur tournait résolument le dos aux producteurs de comédies dramatiques à la mode et tentait de créer au cinéma un style épique, auquel le petit écran de l'époque ne se prêtait guère à première vue. C'était Abel Gance. En fait, et comme beaucoup d'artistes américains, ses contemporains, il parvint à tirer du petit rectangle muet des effets plus saisissants que bien des réalisateurs plus tardifs n'en tirèrent du cinémascope et de l'écran panoramique et rugissant. Le *Napoléon* (1927) de Gance peut passer pour le premier film classique français.

Cocteau   Le poète Jean Cocteau, lui, considérait le cinéma comme un véhicule poétique, au même titre que le poème, le dessin ou la pièce de théâtre. Sa Mort en chignon, qui passe à travers les miroirs et se déplace en Rolls, suivie de deux motards en casques apocalyptiques ; son poète qui écoute les émissions d'une radio mystérieuse située on ne sait où (*Orphée*) ; ses beaux jeunes gens qui se transforment en bêtes monstrueuses parmi de longs rideaux de mousseline agités par un vent furtif (*La Belle et la bête*) ; ses cadavres parfaitement conservés qui, au premier souffle, s'effondrent en poussière (*Le Baron fantôme*), appartiennent à un monde poétique où tout est signe et correspondance, et où la pensée préexiste à la réalisation.

Clair   En France, René Clair est sans doute le premier cinéaste pur, c'est-à-dire le premier artiste français qui n'aurait pas trouvé à s'exprimer si le cinéma n'avait pas été inventé.

Loin de la poésie consciente et hermétique de Cocteau, la sienne consiste en une interprétation de la réalité par le moyen de l'humour et de la grâce. Chez Clair, tout est léger et immatériel, mouvement et fantaisie. L'odyssée de deux bagnards évadés (*A nous la liberté*) ; les mésaventures — mi-rêve mi-réalité — d'un jeune compositeur amoureux de la fille d'un garagiste, mais que d'étranges houris visitent dans son sommeil (*Belles de nuit*) ; les ennuis d'un fantôme dont le château écossais est racheté par un millionnaire améri-

A Nous la Liberté, de René Clair, peut passer pour un exemple de cinéma pur.

cain qui lui fait traverser l'océan pour le reconstruire dans son parc (*Fantôme à vendre*) ; les avatars d'une sorcière brûlée au Moyen Age et renaissant à l'époque moderne (*Ma Femme est une sorcière*) ; l'histoire même de Faust et de Méphisto remise au goût du jour (*La Beauté du diable*), tout est prétexte à variations plaisantes pour René Clair, chez qui la légèreté voulue du dessein ne nuit jamais à la fermeté de l'exécution. Le premier cinéaste à accéder à l'Académie française, René Clair est aussi le premier à avoir utilisé sur l'écran les qualités traditionnelles de l'artiste français.

Becker   Plus réaliste, plus sombre, mais aussi plein de verve, d'imagination, aussi doué pour la finesse et le doigté, Becker s'est fait connaître par une production hélas moins abondante, mais de la meilleure qualité. L'un de ses derniers films fut consacré au fameux gentleman-cambrioleur Arsène Lupin : il n'y a rien d'étonnant à ce que ce gentleman-illusionniste qu'était Becker ait traité ce thème avec autant de délicatesse et de brio.

Renoir   Renoir, descendant du peintre, a aussi quelquefois prétendu à la légèreté, mais peut-être avec moins de raison. Fasciné par la couleur dès son introduction au cinéma, par le mouvement, par une certaine forme d'absurde cinématographique, il se veut artiste avec tant de conviction qu'il indispose une fraction de son public, alors qu'une autre fraction le croit sur parole et lui fait crédit. De toute façon, et de même que Cocteau, que Clair et que Becker, il a voulu que ses films baignassent dans une certaine poésie, souvent sordide d'ailleurs, et que la réalité n'y fût présentée que sous un certain jour délibérément déformant, que, dans le cas de Renoir, on a appelé — non sans pédantisme — « la caractérisation par le milieu » (*Les Bas-Fonds*, *Éléna et les hommes*).

Clément   Pour qu'un véritable naturalisme s'emparât de l'écran français, il fallut attendre la Deuxième Guerre mondiale, la Résistance, et le film de Clément *La Bataille du rail*. Retraçant la guérilla des cheminots pendant l'Occupation allemande Clément utilisait la réalité toute crue pour en faire un objet d'art, à la façon de certains metteurs en scène italiens, dits véristes. Mais Clément ne laissa pas de traces très profondes, et la plupart des films français censés être réalistes demeurent pénétrés d'une inspiration plus subtile — on pourrait presque dire d'un certain sens de l'au-delà.

Autant-Lara   Il y a cependant des exceptions tel Claude Autant-Lara, qui paraît résolu à serrer la réalité au plus près, quitte à l'étouffer un peu. Cette sorte de sadisme, que ferait accepter un souffle poétique s'il y en avait un, se retrouve aussi bien dans *Le Diable au corps*, mélodrame assez raffiné, que dans *En cas de malheur*, où Autant-Lara a tenu et réussi la gageure de faire de Brigitte Bardot une actrice dramatique et larmoyante.

Clouzot   Il y a du sadisme aussi, mais plus brutal, plus direct, chez Clouzot, le metteur en scène du *Salaire de la peur*. Imitant les réalisateurs américains dans leur art de l'impact immédiat, Clouzot est essentiellement un peintre de la méchanceté humaine. Fasciné par les possibilités du roman policier et du roman d'espionnage, il en a porté certains à l'écran, avec un art du suspense, un souci du détail, un goût de la publicité bien faite (*Les Diaboliques*), qui feraient penser à Alfred Hitchcock si Clouzot n'était pas totalement dépourvu d'humour, ce qui, pour ainsi dire, aplatit son art. Au reste, personnage pittoresque, il est connu pour brutaliser ses acteurs et surtout ses actrices, avec une intransigeance qui lui sert beaucoup à faire parler de lui.

Cayatte   Dans le cinéma français, le réalisme est plus souvent un moyen qu'une fin. C'est pour présenter au public des plaidoyers et des réquisitoires de caractère humanitaire que Cayatte réalise des films soi-disant réalistes comme *Justice est faite*, où il aborde les grands problèmes de l'euthanasie, de la peine de mort, etc. Là où Becker met en scène des cambrioleurs qui l'amusent, Cayatte présente des hommes qui se croient vertueux et qui lui répugnent. Bien entendu, les deux attitudes exigent un traitement particulier de la réalité, qui y perd des plumes.

Tati   Ce traitement peut aller jusqu'à la déformation systématique, jusqu'au parti pris de dérision : c'est là le programme de Jacques Tati, qui dans *Les Vacances de M. Hulot* montre un sens du *gag* généralement étranger aux metteurs en scène français (Tati, d'ailleurs, est d'origine russe).

Carné Le cas de Carné, l'un des réalisateurs les plus justement célèbres, est bien différent. Son œuvre entière apparaît comme une quête d'un certain équilibre artistique entre le rêve et la réalité, qu'il cherche, trouve, perd et cherche à nouveau.

Dans *Les Visiteurs du soir*, il met le diable en scène, arrange le Moyen Age à son goût, et plaide pour l'amour. Dans *Les Enfants du Paradis*, grande fresque sur la vie des comédiens sous le Second Empire, il superpose et juxtapose une série de réalités différentes, qu'il a, au préalable, transposées sur un plan artistique. Le ton de ce film est on ne peut plus faux, mais dans ce décalage même on trouve un charme difficile à imiter, et l'utilisation d'acteurs qui se présentent avec leurs tempéraments, avec leurs tics naturels, apparaît, même avec le recul du temps, comme profondément originale. Dans *Juliette ou la clef des songes*, Carné perd tout contact avec le réel et le monde même du rêve qu'il dépeint en souffre, car il n'est plus vraisemblable (or qu'est-ce qu'un rêve qui n'est pas vraisemblable ?). Dans *Les Tricheurs*, c'est au contraire la réalité qui prend le pas sur le rêve, mais une réalité quelque peu truquée, de façon à justifier les thèses de l'auteur.

Bresson Entre ces metteurs en scène de la « vieille génération » et ceux de la « nouvelle vague », une place à part revient à Bresson, le réalisateur du *Journal d'un curé de campagne* et d'un certain nombre d'autres films dont chacun a constitué un événement cinématographique. Les impératifs artistiques sont les seuls qui comptent pour Bresson, qui s'interdit d'engager des vedettes et ne tourne jamais qu'avec des amateurs ; son parti pris de sobriété, consistant à refuser systématiquement tous les « effets » qui se présentent, finit par devenir une affectation, particulièrement gênante lorsqu'elle se complique d'un symbolisme assez primaire et d'une sentimentalité commune, comme c'est le cas dans *Balthazar*. Il est vrai de dire, néanmoins, que Bresson, qui travaille toujours avec des budgets réduits et dans une indépendance absolue, demeure le type même du « bon » metteur en scène par opposition aux « mauvais » — c'est-à-dire aux commerciaux. On aura compris que des réserves s'imposaient sur cette classification élémentaire, dont les catégories éthiques ne correspondent pas toujours aux catégories esthétiques, les seules qui devraient nous intéresser.

Cela dit, abordons les metteurs en scène de la nouvelle vague, ou, plus exactement, ceux de la « jeune génération », car le terme de *vague* est tantôt appliqué, tantôt refusé à une bonne moitié d'entre eux.

Malle Louis Malle, par exemple, le plus hautain et peut-être le plus doué des réalisateurs de l'après-guerre, ne saurait être mis dans le même sac qu'un Godard. La complaisance de Malle pour son propre talent lui a joué un certain nombre de tours, mais il n'en reste pas moins le poète des *Amants*, d'un style à la fois lyrique et désabusé d'une haute tenue. Surtout, l'on sent chez Malle — comme chez un Fellini, par exemple — le désir d'aller jusqu'au

J-L. Barrault, *dans* les Enfants du Paradis, *de Carné : du sordide au romantique.*

Jeanne Moreau, *dans* les Amants, *de Louis Malle : du romantique au quotidien.*

bout de ses propres qualités artistiques et non pas l'ambition vulgaire d'épater le bourgeois.

Godard   Godard, en revanche, est le type même du réalisateur « nouvelle vague », c'est-à-dire qu'il tourne avec un budget limité, utilise un personnel quelquefois peu qualifié, affectionne, dans ses dialogues, un vocabulaire particulièrement grossier, et ne se gêne pas pour condamner la société bourgeoise, à grand renfort de citations philosophiques. L'espèce d'angoisse sordide dans laquelle il se complaît ne manque ni d'intérêt ni de vie : elle est l'expression — toute négative, mais véridique — du désarroi d'une génération.

Truffaut   Alors que les prétentions de Godard sont du genre intellectuel, celles de Truffaut s'appliquent au cinéma seul, ce qui est un bien. Il y a sans doute quelque masochisme dans son penchant pour ce qui est bas, malheureux, raté ; mais une certaine tendresse compense cette complaisance, et des films tels que *Jules et Jim* ou *Les Quatre Cents Coups* constituent des recherches cinématographiques originales, bien qu'inspirées des maîtres américains.

Lelouch, Resnais   Tandis que Lelouch poursuit dans *Un Homme et une femme* une forme de romantisme épuré, avec (comme chez Bresson) un gommage systématique de tout ce qui peut ressembler à un effet de choc, Resnais apparaît comme le principal apôtre du cinéma « difficile », qu'on compare au « nouveau roman » et à « l'anti-théâtre », alors qu'il s'agit plus

Pour la nouvelle vague (Les Quatre Cents Coups, de Truffaut), le monde et les hommes sont laids. La beauté, cette fugitive, n'est accessible qu'aux petits enfants.

simplement d'un nouvel essai de cinéma symbolique, avec quelques résonances surréalistes. *L'Année dernière à Marienbad,* en plongeant les publics non-avertis dans une sorte de stupeur, a plus fait pour la gloire de Resnais que des œuvres plus aisément intelligibles ne l'auraient pu. *Hiroshima mon amour,* malgré quelques portes ouvertes bravement enfoncées, malgré quelques longueurs et quelques passages d'une sophistication légèrement puérile, demeure une très belle œuvre, au sens le plus strictement artistique du terme.

Vadim   On a laissée pour la fin l'autre Russe du cinéma français, à savoir Vadim, businessman excellent, homme brillant, metteur en scène sans originalité, mais découvreur de génie, puisque c'est à lui que le monde entier doit cette déesse du paganisme contemporain qu'est Brigitte Bardot.

LE PUBLIC

Les frais de la production cinématographique sont si exorbitants que les cinéastes, plus qu'aucun autre artiste, dépendent de leur public. Aussi ne saurait-on conclure cette brève étude sans dire un mot des consommateurs de cinéma.

Grosso modo, on peut les classer en deux catégories : ceux qui, formés par les nombreux ciné-clubs d'étudiants, par d'innombrables veillées à la cinémathèque ou par des sorties fréquentes et intelligentes, ne vont jamais voir un film sans demander le nom de son metteur en scène ; et ceux qui, au contraire, sans se soucier de connaître le principal responsable de l'œuvre qu'ils vont applaudir ou siffler, sans savoir même qu'un film a un *auteur* au même titre qu'un roman ou qu'un tableau, ne se préoccupent que du sujet. Ils affectionnent tour à tour « ceux où on rigole » et « ceux qui ont du fond », et des acteurs, « beaux gosses » ou « jolies mômes ».

Bien entendu, la deuxième catégorie l'emporte par le nombre : les samedis soirs, les dimanches après-midis, les cinémas sont pleins de petits bourgeois qui y vont religieusement une fois par semaine, comme à la messe. Quelquefois ils ne choisissent même pas leur film mais seulement leur salle (confort des fauteuils, distance cinéma-chez soi, etc.). Mais la première catégorie est la plus active. C'est elle qui, peu à peu, impose sinon ses goûts du moins son vocabulaire ; c'est elle qu'il faut remercier — ou blâmer, comme l'on voudra — de l'évolution du cinéma français dans la lutte qu'il mène, amoureuse et rancunière, contre la réalité du monde d'aujourd'hui.

SPECTACLES ÉPHÉMÈRES

Le théâtre et le cinéma sont les principaux témoins de notre procès imaginaire de la civilisation française : le cinéma a l'inestimable avantage de conserver ses pièces à conviction ; le théâtre, plus difficile à saisir, présente celui d'avoir mis le public en contact direct, charnel, avec des œuvres que nous possédons encore. Mais il est d'autres spectacles, dont rien ne reste — ou si peu — et qui traduisent pourtant des moments importants encore que fugitifs de la civilisation que nous examinons. Ce qu'ils ont de périssable ajoute quelquefois à leur valeur, même quand ils ne représentent que des « alibis » de la civilisation.

Alibi, les cirques provinciaux et parisiens ; alibi, les grands championnats sportifs ; alibi, les rencontres de boxe et surtout de catch, où l'élément spectacle l'emporte nettement sur l'élément compétition et où un certain sadisme populaire trouve un exutoire comique ; alibi, le fameux musée Grévin, où la prestidigitation et les mirages artificiels tiennent autant de place que les statues de cire ; alibi, les hercules de foire, qu'on trouve sur les grands boulevards parisiens, discourant pendant des heures, faisant des quêtes périodiques, et ne soulevant jamais les énormes haltères déposées à leurs pieds.

Mais est-ce un alibi que le music-hall, le cabaret, la boîte à chansonniers, ou « la boîte » tout court ? Nous n'en croyons rien. Il y a sûrement des éléments de civilisation proprement dite dans ces établissements.

Au fait, certaines de ces institutions sont envahies par des spectacles internationaux et, comme telles, ne nous intéressent guère ici. Nous ne citerons que pour mémoire le Lido, où dansent des Anglaises ; le Crazy Horse Saloon, où des Allemandes se déshabillent ; le Concert Mayol, le Moulin Rouge, et même les Folies Bergères, où sinon les spectacles du moins les publics sont aux trois quarts étrangers. Et lors même que des Français vont s'asseoir sur

Mireille Mathieu, réincarnation contemporaine d'Édith Piaf, triomphe au music-hall.

ces fauteuils usés par des Allemands et des Anglo-Saxons, ils obéissent à des sollicitations rudimentaires où la civilisation française a moins de part que la nature humaine. Il en va de même des boîtes de Pigalle, comme de celles des Champs-Elysées, et des music-halls de la rive gauche (Bobino), comme de ceux de la rive droite (Olympia), du moins jusqu'au moment où un chanteur s'approche du micro, car alors, s'il chante en français une musique composée par un Français, il franchit soudain, sans s'en douter, la frontière qui sépare le divertissement international d'un certain folklore industrialisé mais encore vivace.

Chanson d'amour au Moyen Age et sous la Renaissance, chanson politique pendant les guerres civiles qui déchirèrent la France au XVIème siècle, chanson satirique au XVIIème, chanson révolutionnaire sous Louis XVI, chanson royaliste sous la Révolution, chanson bonapartiste sous la Restauration, chanson populiste sous le Second Empire et la très bourgeoise Troisième République, chanson à boire, chanson de soldats, chanson d'étudiants, il y en a toujours eu pour tous les goûts, et ce n'est pas pour rien que le proverbe dit, « En France, tout finit par des chansons. »

Il y a à peine une génération, le peuple de France, que l'on dit si peu musical, fredonnait en travaillant ; certaines corporations se piquaient de chanter même des airs d'opéra ; les peintres en bâtiment se croyaient obligés de faire résonner les chantiers de leurs ténors et de leurs basses, et si le peuple ne composait plus ses propres chansons, du moins répétait-il volontiers les romances de Béranger au XIXème siècle, les bluettes de Delmet au XXème.

Le progrès a détruit tout cela et maintenant les Français ne font plus qu'écouter, mais ils écoutent plus attentivement que les autres peuples, demeurent sensibles aux paroles autant qu'à la musique, s'intéressent aux rétrospectives de chansons, et vont même quelquefois jusqu'à préférer des chansons de qualité à la production courante. Déplorons que la technique moderne ne nous permette pas encore d'incorporer des disques à ce volume, pour que des illustrations sonores viennent justifier un texte nécessairement abstrait.

LES CHANSONNIERS

On l'aura sans doute deviné d'après l'énumération historique qui précède : la chanson est un terrain d'élection de l'anti-conformisme français. Pour une *Marseillaise*, pour un *Chant du Départ*, qui trouvent d'ailleurs le meilleur de leur inspiration dans l'appel au combat *contre* les ennemis et non *pour* la patrie, combien de chansons satiriques, ridiculisant tour à tour les princes, les

---

Le Français, né malin, forma le vaudeville.
BOILEAU

---

rois, les députés, les ministres et les présidents ! Jadis, on affirmait, « En France, le ridicule tue. » Peut-être, mais pas en musique. En réalité, être conspué par les chansonniers politiques était non seulement la contrepartie mais la garantie d'une certaine popularité en France.

Actuellement, on constate une certaine décadence de la chanson politique. Toujours très écoutés dans leurs divers repaires (Dix Heures, Caveau de la République, Deux Anes, Trois Baudets), les chansonniers semblent avoir épuisé une bonne partie de leur verve sur les hommes de la Troisième et de la Quatrième Républiques : non qu'ils ne trouvent plus de traits contre les politiciens de la Cinquième, mais ils semblent appartenir à une époque révolue, celle du Café du Commerce, où personne ne voulait s'occuper de politique mais où tout le monde s'y intéressait. Maintenant les citoyens pénétrés du sens de leurs responsabilités ont bien autre chose à faire qu'à écouter chansonner leurs amis et leurs ennemis indifféremment ; quant aux au tres, ils plantent leurs choux ou participent à des mouvements de masse, mais dans une atmosphère de sérieux où l'esprit éculé des chansonniers n'a décidément plus sa place.

LE MUSIC-HALL ET LES BOITES

Les chansonniers étant classés à part, il y a trois sortes d'établissements dans lesquels les chanteurs peuvent se produire : les boîtes de nuit, élégantes ou non, souvent désignées sous l'appellation de « cabarets » ; les music-halls, où le populaire vient applaudir les vedettes les plus connues ; enfin les cabarets de la rive gauche, antres intimes où se préparent les succès les plus estimables du lendemain.

Les boîtes de nuit ne participent guère au processus de création de la chanson française ; elles entérinent plutôt les décisions des publics intellectuel et populaire, et celles surtout des marchands de disques.

Quant au music-hall, pour autant qu'une classification de ce genre puisse signifier quelque chose, disons qu'on y rencontre des chanteurs de six catégories, et que ces catégories intéressent, trois par trois, deux sortes de public : les « croulants » d'une part, les jeunes de l'autre, toutes les interférences étant possibles et encouragées, bien entendu.

Voyons d'abord les catégories les plus classiques.

Réalisme   La chanson réaliste, ou dite telle, remonte aux ballades populistes de Bruant, à la fin du siècle dernier. Elle dépeint généralement, en couleurs émouvantes, la vie des classes les plus deshéritées de la population et fait un constant appel à la sensibilité de l'auditeur, qu'elle entretient tantôt d'orphelins portant des roses sur la tombe de leur mère ou mourant de froid dans les rues, tantôt de femmes de petite vertu mais au grand cœur ; depuis quelque temps, les femmes l'emportent beaucoup sur les orphelins. Plusieurs grandes artistes ont illustré ce genre, qui semble réservé aux femmes et dont la vogue semble aller en s'affaiblissant, les publics devenant de plus en plus cyniques, de plus en plus axés sur la sexualité et de moins en moins capables d'apitoiement. Edith Piaf demeure la grande chanteuse réaliste française par excellence.

Charme   La chanson de charme est une autre spécialité française encore que, depuis la Première Guerre mondiale, elle se pare régulièrement de pacotilles exotiques pour mieux séduire ses fidèles auditoires. Corses comme Tino Rossi, Grecs comme Guétary, Espagnols comme Mariano, Basques comme Dassary, Américanisants comme Jean Sablon, les chanteurs de charme rugissent ou ronronnent des sérénades ou des complaintes qui leur assurent les applaudissements de publics en majorité féminins. Non qu'il n'y ait pas de chanteuses de charme, et qui réussissent fort bien ; mais les publics masculins semblent généralement préférer des séductions plus corsées, et la sensibilité pseudo-romantique de ces chanteuses ne les satisfait pas.

Fantaisie   Enfin viennent ceux qu'on appelle d'un mot vague à souhait : les fantaisistes, parmi lesquels, une fois de plus, on compte plus d'hommes que de femmes, mais c'est que la bouffonnerie — dont ils font un usage fréquent — n'est pas un article féminin. Certains d'entre eux, à cheval sur le charme et la fantaisie, ont atteint la gloire internationale d'un Maurice Chevalier ; d'autres ont su trouver des accents réellement poétiques encore que bien faciles, comme Charles Trénet ou Mireille ; certains ont monté des équipes travaillant dans un esprit de complicité réglé comme un système d'horlogerie : c'est le cas des Frères Jacques. Le but des fantaisistes est plus souvent d'amuser ou de surprendre que de charmer ou de faire pleurer. Ils ont une longue tradition derrière eux, remontant aux beaux jours des cafés-chantants, et n'ont pas de difficulté à se trouver encore des publics ; néanmoins, ils sentent bien que leur poésie fleur bleue ainsi que leur vulgarité bon enfant commencent à se défraîchir, et de même que l'on voit certains chanteurs de charme devenir fantaisistes pour renouveler leurs auditoires, on peut observer tel fantaisiste évoluant vers un style plus moderne, par lequel un public plus jeune se sentira mieux « concerné ».

Sautant d'une catégorie à l'autre, et se rétablissant avec un talent de gymnaste égal à son talent de chanteur, citons Yves Montand, tour à tour charmeur, comédien, populiste et bouffon.

Après la Deuxième Guerre mondiale, et surtout vers le milieu des années 50, l'évolution du public et l'influence croissante du disque causèrent un profond bouleversement du monde de la chanson. On vit apparaître, dans l'ordre chronologique, les chanteurs que nous appellerons « intellectuels », les « sexy » et les « yéyé ».

Charles Aznavour, fantaisiste, sentimental, « sexy » : un chanteur-compositeur doublé d'un comédien de talent.

Sexy Commençons par les sexy, qui ont pris, auprès des publics plus jeunes, la place que les chanteurs de charme tenaient auprès de leurs aînés. Compositeurs, paroliers et interprètes à la fois, essayant d'utiliser toutes les séductions depuis les plus sensuelles jusqu'aux plus humoristiques, ils ont généralement renoncé aux ronronnements sentimentaux de leurs prédécesseurs et chantent à pleine voix, avec force vibratos et trémolos. A la chanson-histoire et à la chanson-état d'âme ils ont substitué la chanson-tableau, où ils se plaisent à décrire une situation qui leur paraît pittoresque : tragique ou comique, elle est généralement violente, et les nerfs de l'auditeur — plus peut-être que son sens de la poésie ou de la musique — assurent le succès de Charles Aznavour et de Gilbert Bécaud. Aussi bien par leur façon de traiter les thèmes musicaux que par le renouvellement qu'ils ont apporté au pathétique, ils participent à l'évolution de la civilisation française : créateurs au petit pied, ce n'en sont pas moins des créateurs.

Yéyé Le cas yéyé est bien plus étrange : il s'agit là d'une invasion de la barbarie, intéressant l'ethnologue ou l'anthropologue plus que le modeste observateur d'une civilisation humaniste. Sur des rythmes trépidants généralement importés d'Amérique, des jeunes gens déchaînés se livrent à des crises d'hystérie collective qui ne sont pas sans rappeler certaines pratiques pseudo-

Deux « idoles des jeunes »,
créatures d'une maison de
disques, chantant dans le
style yéyé : Sylvie Vartan...

... et son mari intermit-
tent : Johnny Halliday,
paré d'un costume aussi
inattendu que ce pseudo-
nyme américain.

religieuses, et dont les grands prêtres s'appellent Johnny Halliday ou Hugues Auffray. Le yéyé ne peut se comparer au jazz, qui constituait une véritable création artistique, du moins dans les meilleurs cas, car il ne s'agit plus maintenant que d'une répétition indéfinie d'éléments thématiques simplifiés à l'extrême et créant à la limite un vertige purement physiologique. Les textes des chansons yéyé, d'un caractère sentimental extrêmement primaire, ne comportent généralement aucune intention d'auteur : ils fournissent simplement des paroles à glapir aux divers chanteurs qui se les empruntent. Il paraît essentiel de remarquer ici que ces chanteurs, qui se laissent complaisamment appeler « les idoles des jeunes » et prennent soin de placer tout l'argent qu'ils gagnent par l'hystérie dans de bonnes affaires sûres, confections de vêtements ou de sous-vêtements, sont tous d'un âge proche de celui de leur public, ce qui les rend sans doute plus malléables dans les mains de leurs maîtres occultes, les marchands de disques.

Intellectuel   A l'autre bout de l'échelle, on trouve les chanteurs « intellectuels » tels Jacques Brel et Serge Gainsbourg, qui composent souvent leur propre musique et écrivent leurs propres paroles, à moins qu'ils n'utilisent des poèmes de grands écrivains, de Victor Hugo à Raymond Queneau.

Juliette Gréco, au lendemain de la Libération, fut la première chanteuse à prétentions artistiques sérieuses. Le pessimisme de ses couplets, son chandail noir, ses longs cheveux droits, la rangèrent au premier plan de ce qu'on appelait alors les « existentialistes ». L'étiquette a disparu, mais le talent de l'interprète demeure et le goût exigeant dont elle fait preuve dans le choix de ses chansons.

Georges Brassens, avec sa grosse moustache, sa guitare, sa poésie tendre et gaillarde, puise aux sources les plus authentiques de la véritable chanson française.

Évanescente, insaisissable, travaillant sur des textes et des musiques de qualité qu'elle détaille d'une voix mourante, Barbara est le type même de la chanteuse poétique.

Léo Ferré, qui fit fortune dans les rodomontades anarchiques, s'imposa un peu plus tard, aussi bien par la qualité de ses textes que par la grâce de ses musiques et par ses dons vocaux, d'un charme indéniable. Il avait d'ailleurs su s'entourer d'une littérature à la fois ésotérique et populiste qui lui permit d'asseoir solidement sa publicité.

Enfin Georges Brassens, dont certains font l'égal d'un François Villon, ce qui est tout simplement burlesque, n'en apparaît pas moins comme un poète véritable, qui a su élever le non-conformisme au niveau de la création artistique. Sa profonde connaissance de la langue française, aussi bien la très verte que la très littéraire, son talent mélodique, son utilisation raffinée des possibilités expressives de la modulation, son courage dans la polémique, son anticléricalisme spiritualiste, la bonhomie bourrue de sa grosse moustache, certaines affectations soigneusement étudiées (comme, par exemple, le mépris du public), lui ont valu un succès largement mérité. On a remarqué, dans un chapitre précédent, que les Français aimaient à se reconnaître dans tel personnage historique, Jeanne d'Arc ou Henri IV : eh bien, ils se plaisent aussi à se mirer dans la poésie de Georges Brassens, qui incarne un certain réalisme inspiré, faisant voisiner la plus saine grossièreté avec la plus évanescente délicatesse, ce qui est bien conforme à la grande tradition française.

LES CABARETS RIVE GAUCHE

Ce qu'il y a de mieux dans la chanson française s'élabore dans les caves et autres cabarets de la rive gauche, où, devant un public de noctambules peu nombreux mais fidèles, les gloires de l'avenir viennent chercher leur style, tandis que certaines gloires présentes ou passées y trouvent leur dernier lustre. A l'Écluse, à la Galerie 55, à l'Échelle de Jacob, on pouvait entendre Brassens avant qu'il ne fût illustre ; c'est toujours là qu'on entend Barbara, Mouloudji ou Cora Vaucaire. Certains des chanteurs qu'on rencontre ici n'accéderont jamais à la renommée internationale parce que leur art, tout de finesse, exige une certaine intimité pour se révéler pleinement : aussi est-ce dans ces cabarets-là qu'il faut les chercher pour jouir de leur talent. Diseurs de qualité, ce sont souvent des mimes remarquables : aussi les marchands de disques les boycottent-ils sysématiquement, sachant qu'ils ne leur rapporteront jamais autant qu'un hurleur professionnel. On pense par exemple à France Gabriel, héritière de la tradition presque séculaire d'Yvette Guilbert, cette diseuse caustique immortalisée par Toulouse-Lautrec.

C'est aussi dans les cabarets de la rive gauche qu'on assiste à des spectacles éphémères par définition, comme les sketches comiques, dont certains atteignent, par les détours du surréalisme, du jeu de mots ou de la loufoquerie pure, à une grandeur indéniable dans l'absurde. Leur style est généralement pessimiste et grinçant ; la satire politique n'en est pas absente ; tandis que certains artistes y attaquent sans se lasser l'Église, l'État, l'Armée et la magistrature, d'autres, plus originaux, s'en prennent à la démocratie elle-même et aux idées reçues en général.

Il est vraisemblable de supposer que la vogue des cabarets de ce genre passera dans quelque temps. Sous l'action des moyens de masse, du progrès technique, de la stabilité intérieure et extérieure (les exceptions ne faisant que confirmer la règle, comme il se doit), le public français perdra probablement son goût pour la corrosion intellectuelle qu'il a tant aimée jusqu'à présent. Mais nous n'en sommes pas encore là. Pour l'instant, on peut toujours trouver, dans les cabarets de la rive gauche sinon ailleurs, une survivance de l'esprit français, fait de gouaille, de poésie et d'indépendance.

Conflits   Revenons à l'idée d'où nous étions partis : nos spectacles (ou, pour mieux dire, nos arts de représentation), dans la mesure où ils trahissent un choix, donc une préférence, sont des révélateurs indiscrets de nos tendances profondes. Que nous ont-ils donc révélé au sujet de cette civilisation française dont nous sommes en quête ?

Rien de définitif, certes, mais tout au moins un certain nombre de conflits, dont l'énoncé seul nous apprend plus qu'un inventaire détaillé des auteurs, des acteurs et des œuvres : conflit entre le réalisme et la poésie, conflit entre le conservatisme et l'évolution, conflit entre la qualité et la quantité. C'est dans les trois dimensions de ces trois conflits, exacerbés par le progrès technique et l'avènement de publics plus étendus et moins avertis, que s'agite pour l'instant la civilisation française, vue sous l'angle des arts de représentation.

L'ART 12
DE VIVRE

IDÉE GÉNÉRALE

L'homme cultivé ne saurait penser à la Grèce antique sans ressentir un profond mouvement de gratitude : c'est à elle que nous devons notre philosophie, nos arts, nos sciences, notre humanisme et, pour une grande part, notre religion.

Toutes proportions gardées, la France ne mérite-t-elle pas le même frisson de reconnaissance ? N'est-ce pas elle qui nous a « appris à vivre » ? C'est à dessein que nous employons cette expression ambiguë : « apprendre à vivre » signifie non seulement « enseigner la politesse » — et c'est ce que la France a fait pour l'Europe au cours du XVIIIème siècle — mais aussi « apprendre à profiter de la vie », et sur ce point également les Français ont longtemps été les précepteurs des autres peuples.

Que l'on ne s'y trompe pas. « Profiter de la vie » n'est pas à la portée de tout le monde : il y faut — comme pour peindre, pour écrire, pour composer

L'homme est né pour le plaisir : il le sent, il
n'en faut point d'autre preuve.

PASCAL

— non seulement des instruments mais aussi des capacités et de longues études. Sans doute n'importe qui peut être un noceur ; un jouisseur, c'est déjà plus difficile ; quant à devenir un épicurien, cela nécessite du génie, plus une véritable ascèse.

Toutes les civilisations européenes modernes sont nées d'un mariage entre le christianisme et la civilisation antique. Mais tandis que la paternité du christianisme est relativement homogène, chaque peuple a retenu de l'Antiquité ce qui convenait le mieux à son tempérament. Ainsi l'Espagne est stoïcienne-chrétienne ; l'Angleterre aussi, à sa façon ; la Russie, platonicienne-chrétienne ; la France, épicurienne-chrétienne. L'épicurisme, ne l'oublions pas, est une doctrine exigeante et humble, qui apprend à se passer de beaucoup de choses pour mieux apprécier les autres : elle exige que l'on sache toujours choisir la meilleure part ; elle tend à faire de la vie humaine une musique ; dégradée quelquefois en théorie de la jouissance à tout prix, elle n'a en fait que des rapports lointains avec l'hédonisme et vise essentiellement à un développement harmonieux de la personne humaine.

Bien ou mal compris, bien ou mal utilisé, l'épicurisme chrétien-français a longtemps fait l'envie du monde entier, et maintenant encore, lorsque certains étrangers, l'œil pétillant de sous-entendus, vous parlent du « gay Paree », ils ne font que renouveler le baron de Gondremarck, ce personnage d'Offenbach qui, arrivant de Suède en France au XIXème siècle, chantait éperdument, « Je veux m'en fourrer jusque-là ! »

Il est bien évident que le baron de Gondremarck ne pensait qu'aux aspects les plus vulgaires de cet épicurisme et, par là, en condamnait peut-être, sans le savoir, les aspects les plus élevés. Mais les uns et les autres sont solidaires. Il fallait sans doute le même genre de tempérament — grossier à un bout, raffiné à l'autre — pour inventer le French cancan et la *Musique pour les soupers du roi*, les guinguettes[1] de Nogent et le château de Versailles, le gros rouge et le Heidsieck Monopole,[2] les tripes à la mode de Caen et le pâté de foie gras ; pour enfanter Gavroche[3] et Voltaire, Nini Peau d'chien[4] et Ninon de Lenclos. Et le christianisme, que fait-il dans tout cela ? Eh bien, il bénit, il sourit, il pardonne ; après tout, il n'y a pas que la Passion, dans l'Évangile : il y a aussi les Noces de Cana. Le christianisme, vu sous un certain angle, n'est-il pas un épicurisme de l'au-delà ?

[1] bals populaires
[2] excellent champagne
[3] type de gamin parisien dans *Les Misérables* de Victor Hugo
[4] héroïne d'une chanson populaire

Il y a mille façons d'examiner l'art de vivre d'une nation, et ce n'est pas sans avoir considéré celui de la France d'une multitude de points de vue que l'on a décidé d'adopter ici la méthode suivante : on observera d'abord le Français considéré comme un animal social ; ensuite on étudiera ses relations avec ses proches ; enfin on s'interrogera sur son art de vivre individuel, et, chemin faisant, on essaiera de montrer en quoi les détails de la vie française participent de la notion de civilisation et en qui, par conséquent, ils appartiennent à l'humanité tout entière.

L'ART DE VIVRE : IDÉE ARISTOCRATIQUE

La notion d'art de vivre, épicurienne en soi, est également *aristocratique*. Il convient de préciser ici le sens que nous donnons à ce mot d'usage scabreux. *Aristos*, en grec, signifie le meilleur : le choix d'un meilleur suppose qu'on

Depuis cent ans et plus, la plage de Deauville est le rendez-vous des vacanciers parisiens qui croient s'y distraire à force de s'y entasser comme harengs en caque.

accepte au départ de faire des différences entre les hommes, qu'on accepte de les tenir, à un moment quelconque de leur évolution, pour inégaux entre eux et qu'on entend faire usage de cette inégalité. Il ne s'agit pas nécessairement de différences sociales : nous avons déjà utilisé le mot d'*aristocratique* au chapitre précédent pour qualifier (et critiquer) le système français de production de films, fondé sur une *différence* entre les bandes commerciales et les bandes de qualité. Nous dirons de même que le système universitaire français, où le meilleur élève de la classe reçoit des prix dans chaque discipline et un prix d'*excellence* pour l'ensemble de ses études pendant une année donnée, est un système *aristocratique*.

L'idée de vivre selon une certaine esthétique, en s'astreignant à obéir à un certain code, est *aristocratique* en soi, car elle suppose des choix, donc des différences. En outre, l'art de vivre à la française exige certains moyens (si réduits qu'ils soient), certains loisirs et une certaine distance entre l'individu et les instruments de son bonheur — éléments « aristocratiques » au sens le plus large du terme. Notons qu'on peut parler d'art de vivre pour le paysan, qui travaille dans ce champ-ci ou dans celui-là à son gré, qui prend son café quand il l'entend, qui fabrique son calvados comme il lui plaît, qui va aux vêpres ou qui n'y va pas, qui fréquente le voisin de droite mais méprise le voisin de gauche, etc. Cela, bien entendu, était encore plus vrai lorsque l'artisanat paysan était plus développé, que le folklore existait encore et que les provinces avaient toutes leurs coutumes particulières, élaborées au cours des siècles, de préférence à d'autres. En revanche, il serait absurde de parler d'art de vivre pour un ouvrier qui passe sa vie à visser le même boulon, à boire le même ordinaire, à regarder le même programme de télévision.

Notons encore que l'évolution actuelle fait de l'art de vivre une notion de plus en plus aristocratique, car la prolifération des moyens de masse remplace, auprès de la majorité, les éléments d'*art* de vivre existant encore par des *recettes* industrielles, appliquées mécaniquement et ressemblant à l'art de vivre proprement dit autant qu'un meuble de style à un meuble d'époque. C'est donc auprès d'une minorité qui se différencie délibérément de la masse que l'art de vivre se réfugie de plus en plus souvent.

Cela étant posé, on ne s'étonnera pas de voir le principe aristocratique éclater à tous les niveaux de la société française, puisque la France peut être considérée comme le pays de l'art de vivre par excellence, le professeur d'art de vivre des autres nations. A tous les niveaux, c'est-à-dire aussi bien dans les classes possédantes que dans les classes laborieuses, aussi bien dans les organismes d'État que dans les entreprises privées, aussi bien dans les nominations que dans les élections, dans les travaux comme dans les divertissements.

> *Le mauvais goût mène au crime.*
>
> MARESTE cité par Stendhal

Ainsi, en France, on s'inquiète de connaître les origines d'un homme avant sa profession, et sa profession avant son salaire ; les missions, quelles qu'elles soient, sont confiées à des individus et non à des comités ; la notion d'exemple forme la base même de l'éducation ; on fréquente généralement des gens qui ont reçu la même éducation et non pas ceux qui gagnent autant d'argent ; on aime assez à porter des signes distinctifs signalant la qualité de sa famille (chevalière armoriée) ou les siennes propres (décoration à la boutonnière) ; on éprouve de la méfiance à l'égard des autres milieux que le sien (par exemple, le plus pauvre se méfie du plus riche, le bourgeois du gentilhomme, le paysan de l'ouvrier, etc.) ; on a créé tout un système — on pourrait presque dire tout un code — de conventions permettant de situer rapidement l'origine sociale d'un inconnu (prononciation, vocabulaire, manières, maintien); enfin, et ceci malgré le caractère naturellement envieux des Français, la plupart des milieux ayant une réalité organique ont aussi un orgueil propre, et leurs membres, si on le leur offrait, hésiteraient à accéder à un milieu supérieur mais différent.

Il est bien clair que ces structures et ces habitudes vont en s'amenuisant, à mesure que ces deux classes anonymes que sont le prolétariat et la bourgeoisie remplacent les castes plus rigides et plus colorées du passé. D'ici quelques décennies, les citoyens français seront peut-être devenus aussi semblables les uns aux autres que ceux des véritables démocraties. Mais alors la base même de la civilisation française aura changé, et la France participera d'une civilisaton internationale. Ce qui nous intéresse ici, c'est la civilisation française proprement dite, avec toutes ses singularités. D'ailleurs, si les différences de classes s'estompent de plus en plus, le principe aristocratique, changeant de monture, a enfourché maintenant les professions organisées et refusera encore longtemps, croyons-nous, de se laisser distancer par l'idée égalitaire : les médecins, les avocats, les officiers, les cultivateurs, les garçons de café, sont tous persuadés de la supériorité essentielle de leur ordre, possèdent leurs signes de reconnaissance, leur jargon secret, leur façon spécifique de frauder le fisc,[5] et s'offrent le luxe innocent de se mépriser réciproquement. Jusqu'aux gangsters et aux souteneurs, chez qui les vrais professionnels ont droit à l'appellation honorifique d'« affranchis », tandis que la plèbe de leurs victimes est formée de « caves ».

C'est dans cette perspective de différences sociales délibérément entretenues que nous allons faire un tour d'horizon de la société française : le plus grand compliment qu'on puisse faire à un homme en France, n'est-ce pas de dire qu'il est *distingué,* c'est-à-dire différent ?

[5] payer moins d'impôts qu'on ne devrait ; c'est là un sport national auquel s'adonnent tous les Français

Non seulement la noblesse joue un rôle indéniable[6] dans la société française par son prestige, par ses traditions, par l'envie dont elle fait l'objet, mais encore elle pèse toujours d'un poids léger mais certain sur les destinées mêmes de la nation. Une partie importante des terres, surtout des terres fertiles du Nord-Est, appartient encore à des hobereaux ; beaucoup de grandes sociétés anonymes ont pour présidents généraux des personnages titrés, qui, s'ils n'administrent pas ces sociétés, en touchent du moins les dividendes et les réinvestissent comme il leur plaît ; la noblesse fournit encore une partie des cadres de l'Armée, surtout dans la cavalerie ; dans les milieux intellectuels traditionnels — par exemple, à l'Académie française — certaines grandes familles sont toujours présentes et le gouvernement républicain n'hesite pas à percevoir des impôts sur les titres nobiliaires. Quant au snobisme qui entoure les noms nobles, on n'en veut pour témoin que la prolifération des particules postiches que tant de roturiers attachent abusivement à leur nom, s'imaginant — à tort — que le *de* est un signe de noblesse.

Historique   Dans le passé, la noblesse française était essentiellement foncière et militaire, c'est-à-dire formée de propriétaires terriens dont les fils passaient leur jeunesse à servir dans l'Armée. C'était ce que l'on appelait la noblesse d'épée. Pour affaiblir cette caste trop puissante à leur gré, les rois créèrent des charges civiles dans la magistrature et dans l'administration municipale, que l'on pouvait acheter et qui conféraient la noblesse à leurs acquéreurs : ainsi se formèrent les noblesses de robe et de cloche. La noblesse d'Empire créée par Napoléon s'unit par des mariages à son aînée mais ne put réussir à s'y mêler comme elle l'eût voulu. Actuellement, lorsque les Français parlent de noblesse, ils pensent à la plus ancienne, authentique ou non.

Un trait distinctif de la noblesse française, c'est qu'elle constitue une caste fermée, qui prétend remonter à une race guerrière, les Francs, conquérants et seigneurs de la Gaule. C'est pour cela, affirment certains historiens, que la plupart des nobles français sont blonds. Ce n'est pas le lieu ici de faire des statistiques pour prouver le contraire ; en réalité, s'il y a jamais eu une différence raciale entre les seigneurs et leurs serfs, elle s'est effacée depuis longtemps. Mais la notion de caste fermée — accentuée encore par la disparition de l'ancien régime, c'est-à-dire par l'établissement d'un *statu quo* de fait dans les armorials — n'en demeure pas moins. L'usage anglais veut qu'on puisse être un *gentleman* par la naissance, la fortune ou l'éducation ; un proverbe français, au contraire, dit que « le roi même peut faire un noble, non un gentilhomme ».

Cette qualité de gentilhomme se perdait, sous l'ancien régime, par la pratique d'un métier lucratif — du commerce, par exemple. Un gentilhomme

---

[6] Ce rôle est souvent minimisé par les commentateurs, par suite d'un parti pris démocratique peut-être fort louable mais assurément démenti par les réalités françaises.

Le mariage du comte de Clermont, fils de Mgr le comte de Paris — qui serait roi de France si la France avait un roi — contraste avec un mariage populaire et bon enfant.

ne pouvait que servir dans l'Armée, dans l'administration, dans l'Église, ou cultiver ses terres : sinon, il *dérogeait*, et perdait les privilèges moraux et matériels de sa naissance.

Professions   Actuellement, il n'en est plus de même, et bien des garçons de familles nobles suivent des carrières commerciales (san parler de ceux qui deviennent médecins, avocats, journalistes). Condamnée par certains, cette pratique est justifiée par d'autres en vertu d'une idée selon laquelle un gentil-homme se doit de vivre noblement, de sauvegarder le prestige de son nom, et que cela ne se peut sans des revenus considérables que le commerce seul peut assurer aujourd'hui : un officier touche une solde dérisoire ; un gentleman-farmer vit la plupart du temps comme un paysan.

Conclusion : on trouve des nobles dans toutes les branches du secteur tertiaire, aussi bien que dans le secteur primaire ; dans le secondaire, il y en a moins qu'ailleurs, car c'est là un fief de la bourgeoisie.

Le monde   Mais, à vrai dire, le métier qu'ils exercent leur paraît générale-ment secondaire : ils appartiennent, de par leur naissance, de par leur éduca-tion, de par leurs attaches familiales, à un certain milieu, et à l'exception de ceux qui « tombent en roture », c'est dans ce milieu qu'ils vivent constam-ment. Une minorité appartient à ce que l'on appelle le *monde* et qui réunit, autour de quelques familles d'origine provinciale mais généralement fixées à Paris, quelques centaines de gentilshommes qui se connaissent tous entre eux, membres pour la plupart du Jockey Club et trouvant dans la fréquentation les uns des autres leur véritable raison de vivre. Quelques roturiers, pourvu qu'ils sachent se tenir et n'aient pas de prétentions nobiliaires, sont admis dans ce cercle fermé et traités, bien entendu, comme des égaux.

Le *monde*, que l'on pourrait comparer à une cour sans roi, a ses exigences, ses usages, ses grandeurs et ses ridicules. Constamment imité par d'autres groupes, nobles ou bourgeois, que l'opinion publique distingue mal du *monde* réel, cette cour oligarchique a régenté longtemps, et régente encore partielle-ment, le goût français grâce à un phénomène souvent dénigré — et d'ailleurs odieux dans certaines de ses manifestations — mais que nous n'hésiterons pas à considérer comme une des forces vitales de la France : le snobisme.

Snobisme   Le snobisme consiste à imiter ce que l'on juge élégant ou de bon goût. Aussi le *monde* est-il le milieu le moins snob qui se puisse imaginer, car c'est lui qui détermine ce qui est élégant et de bon goût. En revanche, tous les autres milieux — nobles, bourgeois ou intellectuels — sont-ils possédés par divers snobismes, les pires et les meilleurs, consistant tous à imiter, directe-ment ou par intermédiaire, des gens tenus pour être raffinés, de bon ton, comme il faut, distingués, de goût, bien, à la page, dans le vent.

Naturellement, il y a aussi des anti-snobismes, qui consistent à faire le contraire de ce qui se pratique dans tel groupe, mais c'est généralement au nom d'un snobisme supérieur, se rattachant à un autre groupe, jugé préférable pour telle ou telle raison.

Je n'accorde guère de créance à quelqu'un qui me declare :

— Je ne suis pas snob pour deux sous.

La vérité, c'est qu'il y a des snobs partout, depuis le mendiant jusqu'au milliardaire, depuis le riche-armateur-grec jusqu'au dernier des mousses...

Ainsi cet aristocrate qui m'a avoué : « Mon snobisme à moi, c'est de ne pas appartenir au Jockey Club alors que je pourrais en être... »

Le service du « Sceau de France » que notre ministère de la Justice abrite en son sein, place Vendôme, estime à 35 000 le nombre de nobles authentiques en France et à 350 000 celui des nobles se prétendant tels.

PIERRE DANINOS

Ce jeu des snobismes et des anti-snobismes, innocent dans le domaine des usages et des vêtements, a rendu de grands services aux écrivains et artistes inconnus qui devenaient célèbres d'un jour à l'autre parce que telle fraction de l'opinion — et quelquefois le *monde* lui-même — leur devenait subitement favorable et entraînait à sa suite des centaines d'imitateurs et des milliers d'imitateurs d'imitateurs.

L'autre face du snobisme, c'est le mépris ou, plus exactement, le *dédain*. *Snober* quelqu'un, c'est lui faire entendre qu'il appartient à une sorte d'hommes inférieure et y appartiendra jusqu'à la fin de ses jours. « Quoi de plus cruel ? » se récrieront les âmes sensibles. Mais aussi, dans certains cas, quoi de plus juste ? A une époque où le duel ne se pratique plus guère, où l'on ne peut plus faire bâtonner un mufle par ses laquais, quelle défense un homme de quelque éducation a-t-il contre un malotru ? On ne cause point de tort à quelqu'un en le snobant : on prend simplement ses distances à son égard, en « le remettant à sa place ». Dans cette punition tout à fait platonique, et pourtant cuisante, réside la preuve de ce que le snobisme est une forme — décadente, pas de doute, là-dessus — d'un certain *spiritualisme appliqué*.

LA BOURGEOISIE

Le terme de *bourgeois* est injurieux par quelque bout qu'on le prenne. « C'est un bourgeois », disent les nobles avec arrogance. « C'est un bourgeois », disent les intellectuels avec mépris (et envie parfois). « C'est un bourgeois », disent les ouvriers, avec une rancœur soigneusement entretenue par le mythe marxiste de la lutte des classes.

En réalité, le terme de *bourgeois* devient de plus en plus vague à mesure que la noblesse se défait et que les classes laborieuses accèdent à un niveau de

*Face au noble qui est de naissance et garde la
qualité conquise de haute lutte par le courage
physique d'un ancêtre (le bourgeois), part
d'un manque qu'il s'emploiera à compenser
en expiant le péché originel de sa classe...
Les bourgeois ne sont pas : ils ont, ils font.*
                                    HENRI LEFEBVRE

vie supérieur. Il y a en France plusieurs milieux différents et même contradictoires qui, par certains côtés, appartiennent à la bourgeoisie.

Bourgeoisie de tradition   D'abord, il existe une véritable caste bourgeoise,
composée de vieilles familles qui remontent parfois jusqu'au XVIIème siècle,
qui tirent une véritable fierté de leur ancienneté et ont tenté, au XIXème, de
constituer une noblesse nouvelle. Elles y ont échoué, dans la mesure où toute
base spirituelle manquait à leurs prétentions. N'ayant pas, comme l'avaient
fait les nobles, porté l'épée, servi leur prince, protégé leurs paysans, participé
à cet apostolat que fut la chevalerie, les bourgeois s'étaient enrichis en faisant
tisser des toiles, en prêtant de l'argent, plus tard en exploitant des mines : il
aurait fallu que le peuple de France eût perdu toute notion de valeur supérieure pour trouver à ces occupations mercantiles le moindre prestige. La
bourgeoisie de tradition ne parvint donc pas à remplacer, dans l'imagination
du peuple, la noblesse ancienne, mais elle n'en forma pas moins une aristocratie soucieuse de se maintenir au pouvoir que la Révolution française lui
avait donné. Elle y a partiellement réussi, et c'est elle qui, en grande partie,
fournit les cadres de la haute administration, de l'industrie, et de la banque
française.

Bourgeoisie protestante   A côté de cette bourgeoisie traditionnellement
catholique, on en trouve une autre, quelquefois plus influente et plus unie, du
fait même qu'elle forme une minorité : c'est la bourgeoisie protestante, que
des snobismes pointilleux partagent en H. S. P. (haute société protestante) et
T. H. S. P. (très haute société protestante).

Bourgeoisie israélite   Se mêlant à peine aux autres classes aussi fortunées,
la bourgeoisie israélite continue à régenter les finances françaises, quelquefois
avec la complicité de certaines familles nobles, qui ont eu, au XIXème siècle,
suffisamment de présence d'esprit et d'absence de préjugés pour s'allier à
des dynasties de banquiers juifs.

Le tout Paris   C'est aussi dans les classes bourgeoises que nous classerons
ce milieu saugrenu qu'on appelle le tout Paris et qui, formé de personnages
appartenant à la haute couture, au monde artistique, au monde intellectuel,
au monde du jeu et quelquefois même au monde tout court, hante les pre-

mières et les vernissages, s'exhibe à la Journée des drags,[7] et fournit aux journaux la plupart de leurs échos.

Les intellectuels   Les intellectuels en France se défendent comme de beaux diables d'être des bourgeois, sous le prétexte marxiste qu'ils ne possèdent pas les moyens de production de la nation. Il est d'ailleurs exact de dire que, suite à la démocratisation de l'enseignement, beaucoup d'entre eux viennent de milieux populaires : mais ils en viennent, ils n'y retournent pas. Qu'ils le veuillent ou non (et ils le veulent, mais ils ne veulent pas le reconnaître), ils appartiennent, par leur formation sinon toujours par leur salaire, aux classes privilégiées. L'attitude des ouvriers à leur égard, distante et souvent hostile (les événements de mai 1968 l'ont prouvé une fois de plus), montre bien d'ailleurs que les intérêts des uns et des autres sont amenés, tôt ou tard, à diverger.

Grande, moyenne, petite bourgeoisies   Pour le reste, la bourgeoisie se classe essentiellement d'après ses revenus, avec cependant une exception qu'on trouvera plus bas. La *grande bourgeoisie* est formée d'industriels et périodiquement agonie d'injures par les journaux de gauche sous l'appellation « les deux cents familles », certaines statistiques approximatives démontrant, paraît-il, que l'essentiel de la fortune française appartient à deux cents tribus bourgeoises. La *moyenne bourgeoisie* est constituée de commerçants, de cadres, et des membres des professions libérales. La *petite bourgeoisie* est pratiquement indéfinissable, car on y classe pêle-mêle les épiciers, fort à l'aise, les instituteurs, généralement pauvres, et en général toutes les personnes qui ne travaillent pas de leurs mains et cependant n'appartiennent à aucune des catégories citées précédemment.

Nouveaux riches   L'exception, ce sont les *nouveaux riches* ou B. O. F. (beurre, œufs, fromages). Honnis par tous, raillés par tous, les nouveaux riches — qui ont généralement fait fortune par des moyens douteux, au cours d'une guerre ou de telle autre crise — sont hors de toutes les classes, hors de tous les milieux. Si l'on refuse de les « recevoir », ce n'est pas pour des raisons morales : la société française n'a rien contre les escrocs bien élevés. Ce n'est pas les méthodes d'acquisition de leur fortune qu'on leur reproche, c'est ce qu'elle a de récent et, pour ainsi dire, de cru. Ils finissent bien généralement par se caser, cependant, sous l'aile tutélaire de telle famille noble ou bourgeoise qui se résout à « redorer son blason » ou, selon l'expression moins élégante mais plus pittoresque de Mme de Sévigné, à « fumer ses terres ».

LES CLASSES LABORIEUSES

Les classes laborieuses d'un pays participent rarement à son art de vivre : elles en profitent moins que les autres ; certes elles y collaborent, mais indirectement. Sans doute y a-t-il eu une civilisation paysanne française au cours

[7] course de chevaux élégante ayant lieu une fois par an

des siècles écoulés, mais à part quelques chansons, quelques dentelles, quelques faïences, qu'en reste-t-il ? Quant aux ouvriers, ils n'accèdent jamais à la civilisation en tant que tels, mais seulement dans la mesure où ils font des études et cessent d'être des ouvriers. Nul, depuis la fin du XIXème siècle, ne songe à prétendre que c'est leur faute ; au contraire, il faut compter la prolétarisation des masses sans défense au nombre des grands crimes historiques des divers régimes nés de la révolution industrielle. Mais le fait est là : il ne sert à rien de s'attendrir sur le port de la casquette, les syndicalistes barbus ou même les très belles expressions d'artisan, telles que « le métier lui entre dans le corps » pour dire qu'un apprenti s'est blessé en travaillant. Il n'y a rien dans tout cela qui ressemble à un art de vivre. Du reste, les ouvriers le savent très bien eux-mêmes, et de manœuvres en ouvriers spécialisés, de spécialisés en qualifiés, de qualifiés en contremaîtres, ils n'aspirent qu'à devenir de petits bourgeois, avec maison de quatre pièces en banlieue, jardin potager, rosiers, poulailler plein de poules et clapier plein de lapins. On reconnaît dans ce rêve — d'ailleurs souvent réalisé lors de la retraite — l'ascendance paysanne encore toute proche et le refus de s'amalgamer à un prolétariat correspondant à une situation artificielle et, espérons-le, transitoire.

On l'a vu plus tôt : pour un Français, l'art de vivre consiste à *se distinguer*, beaucoup plus qu'à *se conformer*, du moins dans l'ordre social. De là, peut-être, une cellule familiale plus rigide, car « se distinguer » signifie souvent « se défendre, défendre ses différences », et aussi des rapports plus riches et plus harmonieux entre les sexes, car la notion même de diversité, voire d'opposition, qui paraît choquante à des peuples plus graves, semble au contraire au Français un gage de qualité, de fécondité, de divertissement.

LE SAVOIR-VIVRE

Épicurien dans toutes les classes de la société qui offrent assez de liberté pour le développement de l'épicurisme — on pourrait presque dire épicurien dans toutes les classes de la société sans restriction, si un certain prolétariat n'échappait temporairement à cette règle générale — le Français considère la recherche du plaisir comme une caution de sa dignité humaine et de sa liberté politique.

Ce mot de *plaisir*, injustement dénigré au XIXème siècle, demeure néanmoins l'un des plus beaux et des plus pénétrants de la langue française. *Plaisir* est à rapprocher de *bon plaisir*, donc de choix, donc de liberté ; *plaisir* est à rapprocher de *s'il vous plaît*, donc de politesse, donc de respect.

Recherche du plaisir par conséquent, mais pas n'importe comment : à l'intérieur d'un cadre, dans des limites librement acceptées, et dont la seule présence ennoblit leur contenu. Tout le secret est là.

Quel cadre ? Quelles limites ? Le cadre est double : chrétien d'une part, c'est-à-dire moral ; social d'autre part, c'est-à-dire aristocratique. Les limites, elles, ne sauraient être définies dans un ouvrage didactique. Elles sont fluides, et l'intuition seule les détermine pour chaque situation : elles appartiennent à l'ordre de l'harmonie.

Le cadre chrétien, il faut le reconnaître, est assez extensible et autorise toute sorte d'accommodements : en France, la vertu est souvent ridicule. Ce cadre existe bien, mais c'est pour qu'on en sorte avec élégance.

Le cadre social apparaît encore, et surtout apparaissait au cours des siècles écoulés, comme bien plus rigide. On plaisante avec la vertu, pas avec l'honneur. S'il y avait conflit entre les deux cadres, comme cela se produisait souvent, le second avait la priorité : les maris chrétiens tuaient en duel les amants de leurs femmes sans le moindre scrupule. Aujourd'hui, le mot *honneur* semble grandiloquent, excessif, mais il est clair qu'un Français bien élevé et normalement constitué souffre davantage d'avoir commis une gaffe qu'un péché.

Le jeu incessant de ces deux cadres complémentaires et contradictoires a créé le (ou, mieux, les) savoir-vivre français. C'est qu'en effet il y a plusieurs savoir-vivre en France, et surtout il y en avait plusieurs sous l'Ancien Régime, quand les paysans, les artisans, les bourgeois provinciaux, inculquaient à leurs enfants les usages du milieu dans lequel ils vivaient, qui était fermé (donc aristocratique par définition) mais fort différent des salons de la noblesse de Paris et de la cour de Versailles. Au XIXème siècle, ces différences persistèrent : ce qui était décent pour un dandy ne l'était pas pour un savetier, et ils le savaient tous deux. Actuellement, malgré le brassage social qui s'opère, on

La présentation des débutantes est une des manifestations au cours desquelles le tout Paris artistique et commercial emprunte au « monde » un peu de son prestige.

constate encore souvent l'existence d'usages distincts d'après l'appartenance sociale des individus : les cultivateurs bas-normands s'excusent avant de vous parler de *cochons* ; les petits bourgeois vous tournent le dos pour se moucher.

Néanmoins, l'évolution sociale moderne, dans ses grandes lignes, aboutit à former trois milieux principaux : les gens sans éducation, les gens prétentieux, les gens bien élevés, lesquels nous intéressent principalement, dans la mesure où ils sont les seuls à apporter des éléments positifs à la civilisation proprement dite.

Le savoir-vivre des gens bien élevés vivant au XXème siècle, à quelque classe qu'ils appartiennent (noblesse, haute, moyenne ou petite bourgeoisie), provient en droite ligne de celui qu'élaborèrent les courtisans de Louis XIV et de Louis VX, qui logeaient, au nombre de trois mille, dans une seule maison, vaste il est vrai — le château de Versailles a un kilomètre de façade — mais néanmoins limitée, et où, s'entassant les uns sur les autres, ils se voyaient contraints à d'infinis ménagements réciproques, sans quoi la vie y fût devenue impossible.

Ce savoir-vivre, qui a évolué sur plus d'un point, dans le sens d'un plus grand laisser-aller et en même temps d'une plus grande hypocrisie, est demeuré le même sur les points principaux : il consiste essentiellement à traiter les gens comme ils ont envie d'être traités, à les mettre à l'aise, à leur témoigner du respect s'ils en méritent, en un certain sens à les rendre heureux — à charge de revanche, bien entendu, et toujours dans le double cadre cité plus haut.

Le respect est dû — et c'est là un des traits les plus spiritualistes et les plus réalistes à la fois de ce savoir-vivre — à la force et à la faiblesse, à la puissance et à l'innocence, à la grâce et à l'autorité, pourvu qu'elles aussi, bien entendu, respectent le même code. La tradition veut que Louis XIV se découvrît devant les femmes de chambre de son palais. Authentique ou non, l'anecdote est intéressante : elle montre le respect que le roi voulait qu'on témoignât aux femmes, en tant que représentantes du sexe faible ; mais, en tant que chambrières, il attendait d'elles les services professionnels que leur fonction les amenait à lui rendre. Autrement dit, le respect consiste à placer les êtres à une certaine distance de soi, distance calculée intuitivement en fonction de leur sexe, de leur âge, de leur état, et qui peut varier d'après la perspective dans laquelle on se place. Autrement dit encore, le savoir-vivre français repose, comme on le faisait pressentir plus haut, sur la notion de différence et de distinction.

Cette caractéristique apparaît clairement dans l'infinie variété de formules de politesse que les Français utilisent à la fin de leurs lettres. Depuis les « Daignez, Monsieur le Président... » jusqu'au « Recevez, Monsieur le Percepteur... », quelle variété de sentiments respectueux, cordiaux, sincères, dévoués, de salutations distinguées, empressées, de considérations, de respects, de prières, de demandes, d'assurances, d'expressions, chacune correspondant très exactement à la relation qui existe entre l'expéditeur et le destinataire ! Que l'on compare cette richesse à la sobriété impersonnelle des formules anglo-saxonnes, et l'on aura immédiatement un aperçu de ce que le savoir-vivre français, avec son art subtil de la « distanciation », a de spécifique.

Il ne saurait être question ici d'exposer en quoi consistent les usages français, mais quelques exemples peuvent être utiles. Un Français marche à la gauche d'un homme plus âgé que lui s'il veut lui témoigner de la déférence. Un Français entre dans un lieu public avant la dame qu'il accompagne, pour s'assurer que rien, dans cet endroit, ne pourra l'offenser. En sortant d'une maison, un Français précède également une dame, pour la même raison. Un Français cède le haut du pavé non seulement aux dames mais aussi aux hommes plus âgés, et même aux hommes plus jeunes, s'ils se trouvent être ses invités. Un Français s'habille pour sortir, mais le moins possible pour recevoir, afin de ne pas gêner des invités qui pourraient arriver moins habillés que leur hôte.

Cette délicatesse a une contrepartie : l'insolence. L'insolence entre dans l'éducation d'un Français. Ne pas savoir être insolent, c'est risquer de devenir « bourgeois » ou même « vulgaire ». On est insolent avec les supérieurs, lorsqu'ils le méritent ; avec les égaux, lorsqu'ils deviennent ennuyeux ; avec les inférieurs, lorsqu'on décèle chez eux la moindre tendance à la prétention. L'insolence française est un art ; la première condition à satisfaire pour y exceller, c'est de savoir insulter sans manquer à la politesse. Plus l'injure est courtoise, plus elle est insolente. Il ne faut pas confondre l'insolence, considérée comme une haute qualité, avec l'impertinence, qui n'est que de l'insolence utilisée mal à propos et constituant donc l'un des vices les plus vulgaires.

Vulgaire est d'ailleurs un de ces mots dont l'utilisation classe un Français : aucun homme bien élevé n'est jamais « vulgaire » ou « commun ». En revanche, et les circonstances s'y prêtant, il peut se révéler *grossier* avec complaisance, avec brio, avec génie, pour peu que la langue verte qu'il emploie ne trahisse aucune petitesse dans l'inspiration, aucune hésitation dans le vocabulaire. La grossièreté alors devient un art à son tour et l'apanage des classes les plus raffinées, car les bourgeois n'aiment guère à se risquer sur ce terrain glissant, qu'il faut savoir quitter au bon moment.

Cet appétit de distinction aristocratique des Français, ils l'affichent en prêtant à telle profession telle vulgarité spécifique. Des écrivains aux convictions les plus démocratiques diront froidement qu'Untel « parle comme ma *concierge* », « a une mentalité de *valet* », « s'habille comme un *garçon coiffeur* ». Le mépris devient alors un instrument de « distanciation » au même titre que le respect et participe intimement de l'art de vivre à la française.

Toutes ces subtilités et ces contradictions apparentes font quelquefois accroire aux étrangers que les Français bien élevés sont formalistes. C'est le contraire qui est vrai : l'intuition d'un homme bien né et convenablement éduqué le guide dans le dédale des usages sans aucun risque d'erreur possible. Ces usages il n'a même pas besoin de les apprendre : il les pressent, car ils correspondent à son tempérament, à son tact innés. Les éducations rigides et simplifiées des autres peuples semblent au contraire formalistes aux Français, qui se considèrent comme les gens les plus simples du monde.

Les deux cadres — chrétien et social — qui limitent cette recherche du plaisir (certains préfèrent dire, du bonheur) à laquelle s'adonnent la plupart des Français forment la base même de la famille.

Notons ici que cette famille est en pleine évolution, surtout dans les classes laborieuses, où une tendance au matriarcat apparaît très nettement, soit influence de la société américaine, soit affranchissement de la femme par le travail à l'extérieur et domestication de l'homme par l'aide qu'il est obligé d'apporter à l'intérieur du ménage. En fait, plus une famille française est ancienne, ou fortunée, plus elle est attachée au patriarcat traditionnel, soit par culte du passé, soit parce que l'essentiel de ses revenus lui est fourni par le chef de famille, dont le prestige en bénéficie.

L'image stéréotypée du *pater familias* français régnant sur sa femme et ses enfants par la terreur n'est fausse que lorsqu'elle est interprétée littéralement. Il est vrai que les parents français ont généralement la main leste — quand ce n'est pas le pied : les punitions corporelles forment la règle générale dans les familles, et plus d'un père ou d'une mère français applique chaleureusement l'adage « Qui aime bien châtie bien ». La gifle est monnaie courante dans les familles. Le coup de pied au derrière, pittoresque et expressif, se

La table est le centre autour duquel la famille se regroupe deux fois par jour.

... C'est déjà autour d'une table que Le Nain (XVIIᵉᵐᵉ) assemblait sa Famille de Paysans.

pratique encore dans les repaires des patriciens provinciaux. Généralement, les enfants n'en veulent nullement à leurs parents de ces châtiments bien mérités et, lorsqu'ils ont grandi, auraient plutôt tendance à se plaindre s'ils ont été traités avec une indulgence excessive.

Il est d'usage de considérer que le père est l'apôtre de la sévérité dans la famille ; la mère, de la douceur. Mais c'est là affaire de convention plus que de réalité : bien des pères ont avec leurs enfants des relations de complicité où les mères ne participent pas.

Dans l'ensemble, l'évolution se fait dans le sens d'un abandon des responsabilités du côté des parents et d'un affranchissement toujours plus grand du côté des enfants. « Je suis le camarade de mes enfants » est la devise de bien des pères, et quelques mères préfèrent même que leurs filles les appellent par leur prénom. Le tutoiement d'enfant à parent devient la règle générale, à l'exception d'une assez importante minorité de vieilles familles, où le vouvoiement — qui n'exclut nullement la tendresse mais souligne le respect — demeure habituel et le demeurera encore sans doute pendant de nombreuses générations.

Les oncles, tantes et grands-parents considèrent d'un œil sceptique l'évolution moderne. Dans les classes laborieuses, où l'on n'a rien à attendre d'eux, on se préoccupe peu de leur opinion ; là, le grand-père ancien combattant, qui raconte sa guerre de 14–18, est désormais un personnage assommant et ridicule. Il n'en va pas tout à fait de même dans les classes aisées, où oncles et tantes distribuent des étrennes le premier janvier, ce qui vaut bien qu'on les écoute radoter un peu.

Les cousinages, que le proverbe qualifiait de « dangereux voisinages », comptent de moins en moins, sauf en province et dans les milieux les plus traditionnalistes. Dans la majorité des cas, la famille moderne se referme sur la cellule élémentaire : papa, maman et les enfants.

Cette cellule même entretient des rapports intérieurs très différents de ceux qu'on trouve dans les autres pays. D'une façon générale, les Français ne raffolent pas des enfants et préfèrent les tenir à distance. S'ils en ont, c'est souvent moins pour satisfaire l'instinct de pouponner que pour obéir aux recommandations de l'Église (cadre chrétien) ou pour avoir à qui léguer leur fortune et leur nom (cadre social). S'ils les élèvent sévèrement, c'est pour remplir leur mission sur terre (cadre chrétien) et pour n'être point déshonorés dans le monde (cadre social). S'ils penchent maintenant vers un libéralisme désordonné, c'est seulement parce que les cadres se lézardent et se disjoignent. Il est indéniable que les enfants français actuels paraissent mal élevés en comparaison avec leurs aînés, mais c'est justement parce que la civilisation française est en train de craquer. « Il n'y a pas d'enfants qui dégénèrent, faisait remarquer l'existentialiste Gabriel Marcel. Il n'y a que des parents qui démissionnent. »

Le « père noble » transformé en copain, la « pauvre mère » en sœur aînée, les « affreux Jojo » remplacent « les petites filles modèles ». Nul ne songe à le nier. Cependant, si dans certains milieux, à quelque classe sociale qu'ils appartiennent, l'art de vivre français subsiste encore, c'est que, dans ce milieu-là — paysan, bourgeois, militaire, universitaire — les cadres ancestraux « tiennent encore le coup ».

LES SEXES ENTRE EUX

La situation est bien différente pour les rapports entre les sexes où les tendances contemporaines semblent l'emporter haut la main, parce qu'elles correspondent aux tendances profondes de la race.

Dans certaines tribus gauloises, les femmes étaient en commun et les enfants, ne connaissant pas leur père, étaient confiés aux druides pour éducation. Le christianisme commença bien par asservir chaque femme à son mari, mais pas pour longtemps, surtout dans les classes dirigeantes : au contraire, la courtoisie chrétienne fit bientôt de la femme l'inspiratrice de l'homme, presque la médiatrice entre l'homme et Dieu. A partir du XIIème siècle, les rapports entre les sexes furent donc conditionnés par deux sentiments masculins : l'attirance physique d'une part, la vénération religieuse de l'autre. Les femmes, elles, profitaient de la situation au mieux de leurs capacités.

Cette attirance et cette vénération — il importe de ne pas se tromper là-dessus — ne s'excluaient nullement. La dame du chevalier pouvait être une amie platonique ou une maîtresse : cela ne changeait rien à l'essentiel de leurs relations, et pour ce qui était du péché, au sens religieux du terme, il était largement excusé par les prouesses que l'amour inspirait au chevalier.

Au XVIème siècle, les rapports entre les sexes semblent avoir été extrêmement libres. Brantôme consacre un chapitre de ses admirables *Dames galantes* à déterminer si les jeunes filles, les femmes mariées ou les veuves sont les plus faciles à séduire. *Séduire* d'ailleurs semble un bien grand mot, car il était d'usage, en ce temps-là, que les dames entretinssent les messieurs. Elles n'en conservaient pas moins un sens de l'honneur social qui peut nous sembler paradoxal, mais qui n'en est pas moins révélateur : le même Brantôme précise que les femmes mariées vraiment distinguées ne prennent d'amants que lorsqu'elles se savent enceintes, afin d'être certaines de ne pas donner à leur mari d'enfants d'un autre sang.

Au XVIIème, les précieuses tentèrent d'imposer à leurs soupirants une courtoisie platonique, mais sans grand succès. Au XVIIIème, tandis que la bourgeoisie cultivait la vertu, la noblesse organisait le libertinage avec un art de vivre consommé. Une jeune fille noble sortait dans le monde à quatorze ans ; à seize, elle se mariait, vierge généralement. Son mari avait trente ou trente-cinq ans ; il avait vécu. Le mariage avait été arrangé, pour des raisons de fortune et de convenance mondaine. Si les époux se plaisaient, ils passaient une lune de miel agréable ; sinon, ils se traitaient en étrangers. Être amoureux de sa femme ou de son mari paraissait le comble du ridicule bourgeois. Après la lune de miel, Monsieur retournait à ses amours et Madame apprenait à connaître les siennes. La discrétion qu'ils observaient l'un et l'autre n'allait même pas jusqu'aux limites de l'hypocrisie ; elle ne sortait pas de celles de la politesse.

Au XIXème, tout changea sous l'influence de la bourgeoisie et, en particulier, du Code Napoléon, qui prenait l'adultère au sérieux. Alors que, sous Louis XV, les relations conjugales n'avaient été réglées que par le jeu tout spontané des libertés réciproques, un véritable droit de propriété exercé par les maris sur leurs femmes fut codifié par les législateurs de l'Empire. Traitée en mineure, devant l'obéissance à son mari, incapable de tester ou d'ouvrir un compte en banque, la femme fut condamnée au mensonge systématique par des juristes bourgeois qui traînaient, depuis le fabliau médiéval, l'obsession ridicule du cocuage. Le brassage social avait commencé ; il devenait beaucoup plus difficile de trouver pour sa fille un mari convenable ; en outre, les filles commençaient à étudier : elles se marièrent donc plus tard, ce qui faussa encore la situation, car pour conserver à vingt ans l'innocence qu'on avait à seize, il fallait violenter la nature. Le résultat ne se fit pas attendre : le personnage même du mari, qui attendait de sa femme une virginité prolongée et prétendait lui imposer une chasteté qu'il n'avait garde d'observer, devint grotesque. Au jeu des adjectifs obligés (Albion ? perfide ; bosquet ? riant ; tyran ? sanguinaire), le mot *mari* allait désormais appeler le qualificatif inévitable *trompé*. Ce fut l'époque où l'on s'imagina que l'honneur d'un homme était attaché à la conduite de sa femme, conception évidemment esclavagiste et qui peut avoir été noble dans d'autres pays mais qui, en France sentait son bourgeois d'une lieue.

A la fin du XIXème siècle, la poussée des forces laïques amena l'autorisation du divorce à volonté. Il fallut bientôt abroger cette loi, car tout le monde voulait divorcer, tant le joug du mariage à la Napoléon paraissait insupportable. Actuellement, le divorce est réglementé ; néanmoins un mariage sur dix y aboutit, malgré l'opposition, toujours aussi ferme, de l'Église catholique, qui considère qu'une union contractée devant elle l'est pour l'éternité. Un sur dix, ce serait beaucoup pour un pays aux mariages heureux ; c'est peu, comparé aux chiffres correspondants pour les pays où le divorce est vraiment passé dans les mœurs (un pour quatre mariages, aux États-Unis).

C'est que, favorisés à la fois par la régression de l'Église catholique, par un relâchement très net des contraintes sociales, par le dégoût général qu'inspirent aujourd'hui les mœurs bourgeoises, par l'emploi de plus en plus admis des anti-conceptionnels, les rapports entre les sexes sont en train de retrouver leur liberté originelle.

La France a longtemps été considérée comme la patrie de l'amour libre. Le Baiser de Rodin semble en effet exalter un amour profane et sacré tout à la fois.

A la différence des jeunes gens anglais ou américains du même âge, les garçons et les filles sortent peu en France jusqu'à dix-huit ans ; et ils ne sortent pas du tout avant d'en avoir au moins seize. Mais dès vingt ans, vingt et un tout au plus, ils se considèrent libres d'agir comme il leur plaît, et les parents modernes ont tendance à sanctionner ce jugement. Alors que l'entre-deux-guerres fut l'époque du flirt à outrance et des « demi-vierges » (les garçons semblant encore soucieux de la virginité de leur future épouse), une certaine égalité entre les sexes semble se généraliser maintenant. En France, une femme sur deux travaille ; cela lui donne une autonomie matérielle sur laquelle elle asseoit l'autonomie morale qu'elle est en train de conquérir : quand une jeune fille indépendante a envie de prendre un amant, elle hésite de moins en moins, et bien sot le garçon qui lui reprochera d'avoir usé d'une liberté dont il va profiter.

Assurément répréhensible du point de vue de la religion, la liberté sexuelle n'en donne pas moins des résultats positifs sur certains points. Au lieu de débaucher des filles du peuple ou d'utiliser la prostitution, les jeunes hommes des classes aisées s'attachent, pour plus ou moins longtemps, à des jeunes femmes de leur propre milieu, ajoutant ainsi une communauté d'intérêts et

Quel Parisien serait choqué par « les amoureux qui s'bécotent sur les bancs publics » ?

de goûts aux plaisirs sensuels qu'ils en retirent. Cela aussi est conforme au tempérament français, pour lequel les sens et les sentiments sont indissolublement mêlés : le beau mot d'*amour*, qui recouvre la tendresse, la passion et la sexualité, et qui est le seul que les Français utilisent couramment, en est la preuve. De plus, l'affranchissement sexuel de la femme favorise son affranchissement social, et vice versa. Dans cette perspective, il est même possible d'imaginer qu'un jour le mariage retrouvera son sens, dans la mesure où il sera contracté par des partenaires désireux de fonder une famille solide et non par des jeunes gens énamourés mais soucieux du qu'en dira-t-on.

Il apparaît en tout cas que le mariage civil, créé par la Révolution bourgeoise et qui précède obligatoirement le mariage religieux, s'est soldé par une faillite totale : le cadre social n'était pas suffisamment robuste pour sauvegarder une institution intéressant aussi profondément les individus.

En revanche, le cadre social joue à nouveau dans les relations libres : ne pouvant plus compter sur les contraintes extérieures, l'homme et la femme retrouvent certaines délicatesses, certaines courtoisies, que l'ombre du commissaire de police (que le mari pouvait convoquer pour faire rentrer sa femme dans l'obédience conjugale) avait bannies du mariage bourgeois du XIXème siècle. C'est qu'en effet dans la mesure où la liberté est acquise, l'usage français exige qu'on la limite aussitôt, car c'est la seule façon de s'en rendre digne, sans quoi l'on tombe dans le domaine des désordres vulgaires.

Sans doute serait-il exagéré de parler d'une *morale* des relations libres, d'une morale de l'amour, qui est immoral ou du moins amoral par définition. Peut-être le mot d'*éthique* serait-il plus exact. Il est certain, par exemple, que l'adjectif *honnête* appliqué à une femme a toujours un sens, bien que très différent de celui qu'il avait il y a trente ans. Une honnête femme, naguère, demeurait chaste à tout prix ; maintenant une honnête femme obéit à ses sentiments quoi qu'il en coûte à ses principes. Un certain respect réciproque apparaît aussi dans les relations libres nouvelle manière : au XIXème, un homme avait des maîtresses, mais il les méprisait, soit qu'elles appartinssent à un milieu social inférieur au sien, soit qu'il leur reprochât, par une injustice abominable, d'avoir pour lui les bontés qu'il leur avait demandées. Aujourd'hui, au contraire, un homme n'aura de mépris pour une maîtresse que s'il la juge vénale : femme libre, elle lui inspirera autant de respect que légitime.

On s'est interdit, dans ce volume, d'utiliser aucune citation invérifiable, aucune anecdote personnelle. Mais le moment est venu de manquer à cette règle, car la formule qu'on veut mettre à la fin de cette section résume mieux qu'aucune autre ce besoin de *distinction morale* qui régit le comportement des Français : c'est celle qu'a employée un homme bien élevé d'une quarantaine d'années, jugeant de son devoir de donner quelques conseils à sa fille qui commençait à sortir dans le monde et ailleurs : « En ce qui concerne les garçons, ma petite fille, tu feras ce que tu voudras, mais fais-le *comme une dame*. »

LES PLAISIRS 13

IDÉE GÉNÉRALE

Cet art de vivre aristocratique qui s'affirme dans la structure de la société et dans les relations humaines en France ne serait pas complet si la vie même, dans ses détails journaliers, n'était pas réglée pour obéir à la même inspiration raffinée, pour servir le même épicurisme qui, pour les Français, est synonyme de civilisation : ne traitent-ils pas régulièrement de « sauvages » tous ceux qui ne mangent pas, ne boivent pas, ne s'habillent pas comme eux ?

Pour rendre entière justice au raffinement français, il faudrait ici étudier toutes les industries d'agrément, en consacrant des paragraphes séparés aux cristaux de Baccarat, aux porcelaines de Limoges, aux faïences de Rouen. Il faudrait citer les fleuristes, les coiffeurs, les confiseurs ; il faudrait parler des grands bals, des fêtes mondaines et populaires, des réceptions de tout genre. Il faudrait traiter dans un chapitre à part la bijouterie, l'horlogerie, la sellerie, en citant les noms des artistes qui donnent de la *distinction* à la vie française.

On doit cependant se limiter, et on le fera en respectant la vocation universelle de la France, c'est-à-dire en s'attachant à donner une idée des arts d'agrément pour lesquels la France est, de l'aveu de tous les étrangers cultivés, inimitable : la haute couture, les parfums, la cuisine et les vins. On essaiera de montrer en même temps que, dans tous ces domaines, le principe de différenciation, d'aristocratie, prévaut toujours, et cela, comme on l'a dit plus haut et comme on ne le répètera jamais assez, à tous les niveaux de la société.

HAUTE COUTURE ET PARFUMS

Qu'on ne nous fasse pas dire ce que nous ne disons pas : la haute couture est indéniablement réservée à un très petit nombre de femmes fortunées ; mais de même que les hommes, plutôt que d'acheter des vêtements de confection, s'habillent chez des tailleurs (extrêmement chers, très chers ou simplement chers), les femmes même les moins riches choisissent leurs robes au lieu de se contenter, comme cela se fait dans d'autres pays, de suivre la mode plus ou moins aveuglément. Certaines se font faire leurs toilettes par les couturières de quartier, en voie de disparition ; d'autres achètent des patrons, taillent et cousent elles-mêmes ; d'autres s'adressent aux grands couturiers qui font aussi du prêt-à-porter ; d'autres achètent la confection soignée d'un Lempereur ; d'autres enfin s'habillent dans les prisunics, mais exigent une telle variété dans l'assortiment qui leur est offert qu'elles peuvent toujours penser qu'elles sont mieux habillées que leurs voisines, parce que, au moins, elles le sont différemment.

Néanmoins, le ton de ces collections mises à la portée de toutes les Françaises et donné par les grandes collections présentées deux fois l'an dans les salons de couturiers au renom international, ayant chacun un style personnel, faisant et défaisant la femme à leur fantaisie, et profondément convaincus de l'importance primordiale de leur art.

Sans énumérer les quelques vingt grands-maîtres de la haute couture, on fera ici une brève étude de quatre d'entre eux qui paraissent les plus représentatifs.

Balmain   A un bout, l'on trouve Balmain, le couturier des princesses. Sa coupe est constamment élégante et sobre, et cet artiste s'interdit scrupuleusement tous les effets faciles, tous les excès. Quand les jupes deviennent très courtes, les siennes paraissent un peu longues ; quand la taille change de place, la sienne demeure où elle est. Balmain travaille en finesse, avec des ampleurs étudiées, de légers évasements, un dessin ferme mais souple et comme retenu, laines et soieries attentivement dosées. Bref, une simplicité de très haute tenue.

Chanel   Coco Chanel passe également pour conservateur — ou plutôt pour conservatrice. Chanel est d'ailleurs plus qu'une couturière qui se contenterait de dessiner des robes — aux clientes de les porter ! Elle se préoccupe des conditions dans lesquelles ses modèles seront utilisés ; elle prétend qu'une

*Balmain : la coupe la plus re-
cherchée.*

*Chanel : les vêtements les
plus portables.*

femme n'a pas besoin de renouveler sa garde-robe trop souvent, qu'au contraire des robes trop nombreuses, trop bien adaptées aux circonstances, trop neuves, trop à la mode, trahissent des goûts de nouvelle riche — ce qui est, comme l'on sait, la pire injure de la langue française. Bel exemple de snobisme à rebours : comme le snobisme numéro 1 réclame des robes du matin, de l'après-midi, de cocktail, de dîner, de soirée, etc., le snobisme numéro 2 affirme que tout cela est un peu vulgaire et recommande le tailleur pour (presque) toutes les occasions. Le trait dominant de Chanel est sans doute la sobriété : Balmain était sobre aussi, mais là où les robes de Balmain nécessitent tout un décor pour que leur sobriété — du genre luxueux — ne soit pas ridicule, celles de Chanel sont éminemment *portables*. Si Chanel affectionne les tailleurs, avec ce que cela suppose d'un peu rigoureux, d'un peu austère, c'est justement parce que le tailleur est, par excellence, ce qu'une femme met pour *être vêtue* et non pour *s'habiller*.

Courrèges A l'autre bout on trouve les novateurs, et tout d'abord Courrèges, qui à ses débuts a créé une véritable révolution dans la haute couture. Ses collections sont géométriques, dessinées avec plus d'énergie que de subtilité et recourant à des ornements typiques tels qu'incrustations et volants festonnés quelque peu imprévus sur les toiles et cotonnades qu'il utilise généralement. Portables ses créations le sont, pour peu qu'on soit jeune, bronzée, musclée, et qu'on réduise son maquillage au strict minimum. Sinon, on a l'air de retomber en enfance, ce qui n'est pas précisément l'effet désiré.

Ungaro L'Italien Ungaro dessine également pour des femmes très jeunes qui n'hésitent pas à s'habiller en petites filles sophistiquées. Ses coupes douces, ses couleurs tendres, composent un style personnel, d'autant mieux qu'Ungaro est fort difficile pour ses tissus : des crêpes de laine, des jerseys

Courrèges : pour filles jeunes ou se prétendant telles.

Ungaro : pour sympathiques fofolles.

gaufrés, des organdis rebrodés, voilà pour la sophistication ; des chaussettes blanches jusqu'au genou, voilà pour l'allure petite fille. Trait distinctif : Ungaro fait imprimer lui-même des tissus aux motifs tachistes artistement fondus les uns dans les autres.

D'un bout à l'autre de l'éventail haute couture, on trouve donc le même culte de la différence, ou, si l'on préfère, le même individualisme. Il n'en va pas autrement au royaume des parfums : certains sont produits par des parfumeurs spécialistes, telle l'Heure bleue de Guerlain ; d'autres viennent de chez les grands couturiers et portent des noms de fantaisie traduisant, plus ou moins bien, les intentions. Prenons pour exemple le fameux *Numéro 5* de Chanel, chaud mais aussi sobre que le suggère son austère appellation, ou *Jolie Madame* de Balmain, coquet, espiègle, d'une langoureuse et fine sensualité.

Voilà bien des noms, bien des styles, bien des frais pour satisfaire la coquetterie des femmes (et le goût des hommes) : c'est là l'impression un peu écœurante qu'on retire d'un inventaire nécessairement succinct et spécialisé comme celui que l'on vient de lire. Mais tout cela prend une autre signification lorsque l'on réfléchit qu'il s'agit en réalité d'un aspect unique de ce plaisir de vivre auquel tendent toutes les activités d'un peuple chez qui le luxe est un besoin. Les midinettes elles-mêmes ne vont-elles pas s'acheter pour quelques sous de fleurs afin de décorer leurs chambres sous les toits ?

Hermès : tous les accessoires de la vie moderne pour l'homme et la femme de goût.

Lasserre : un des temples de la gastronomie française.

GASTRONOMIE

D'abord une remarque significative : alors que la cuisine française jouit dans le monde de la réputation que l'on sait, il serait probablement difficile de trouver des collectivités plus mal nourries qu'en France. Pensionnaires dans les collèges, employés déjeunant en cantine, soldats en caserne, peuvent à peine manger ce qu'on leur donne, tant les légumes sont mal cuits, les sauces grasses, les viandes repoussantes. Pourquoi ? Parce que la cuisine française n'est elle-même que dans des conditions « aristocratiques », c'est-à-dire individuelles.

Prenons pour premier exemple la journée d'un simple paysan normand et nous verrons combien de raffinement il introduit dans son ordinaire.

Levé avant le jour, il commence généralement par un petit verre de calvados pour se mettre en train. Après avoir nourri ses bestiaux, il mange une soupe qui pendant des heures a mijoté sur le feu, et qui est rendue épaisse non seulement par les légumes qui la composent mais surtout par les morceaux de pain qui y ont trempé : il s'agit d'un pain de croûte, cuit spécialement pour cet usage. Ensuite notre paysan va aux champs. Vers dix heures du matin ses enfants lui apportent une collation, constituée de pain entier, de beurre baratté à la maison, de lard fumé, d'un de ces fromages que le monde entier envie à la Normandie, et de cidre. Pour « dîner » à midi il rentre chez lui, à moins que le champ ne soit trop loin ou que le travail ne presse. Il mangera probablement une omelette à la crème, avec des morceaux de jambon dedans, et travaillera encore jusqu'à l'heure du goûter (cinq heures), à laquelle une tartine de beurre et de confiture lui rendra des forces. Il tiendra ainsi jusqu'au « souper » de sept heures, composé par exemple de châtaignes fendues et grillées sur feu de bois, dans une poêle spéciale à trous, et d'une bouillie de sarrazin servie au beurre ou bien, s'il s'agit de restes de la veille, grillée aussi dans une poêle et formant une sorte de galette croustillante. Après chaque repas, notre paysan a pris, bien entendu, une ou deux tasses de café noir, très fort, additionné d'une bonne rasade de calvados.

Ces menus sont, comme on le voit, extrêmement simples, mais ils supposent en même temps des ingrédients de qualité et une expérience assez raffinée dans la préparation. On ne s'étonnera donc pas que certains des plats

Les ouvriers déjeunent d'une gamelle soigneusement préparée par leur femme.

> *Dis-moi ce que tu manges et je te dirai ce que tu es.*
>
> BRILLAT-SAVARIN

français les plus caractéristiques et les plus savoureux, tels les pâtés et terrines, innombrables dans leur variété, soient d'origine directement paysanne.

L'ouvrier, on l'a dit, ne dispose des possibilitées de l'agriculteur dans aucun domaine de l'art de vivre. Néanmoins, lorsqu'il ne peut rentrer pour déjeuner, il emporte généralement sur le chantier ou à l'usine une *gamelle* préparée par sa femme et qu'il réchauffera comme il pourra, p'.utôt que de se fier à une cuisine collective qu'il méprise à juste titre.

Au demeurant, ce qu'on appelle la cuisine française, ce n'est pas, bien entendu, la préparation des plats populaires — encore qu'ils soient succulents — mais le véritable art que pratiquent les chefs des grands restaurants, les cuisiniers de quelques rares mais heureux particuliers, et la plupart des Françaises qui y passent de longues heures quotidiennes, avec la profonde conviction de faire une des deux ou trois choses qui, sur terre, valent vraiment la peine d'être faites. Il faut voir avec quelle avidité elles se précipitent sur les recettes publiées par les journaux, et surtout avec quelle jalousie elles gardent celles que leur mère leur a confiées sous le sceau du secret. Des recettes de famille, en France, ce sont presque des lettres de noblesse !

Dédaignant le petit déjeuner qui ne se prête pas aux effets culinaires, c'est au déjeuner (entre midi et deux heures), au dîner (entre sept et neuf heures) et au souper (en rentrant du théâtre) que sont réservés les raffinements de la cuisine française, la seule, disent les spécialistes qu'on puisse prendre au sérieux, à l'exception de la cuisine chinoise. Ce qui ne signifie pas que les Russes, les Espagnols, les Italiens, n'aient pas des plats traditionnels et délicieux, mais que la France et la Chine sont les seuls pays à avoir un *style* gastronomique.

Le style de la France, c'est la sauce.

Ce n'est pas le lieu ici de donner un inventaire des sauces françaises ni de leurs ingrédients : il y faudrait des volumes. On préfère insister sur cette notion de *style*, ou, si l'on préfère, d'ordonnance générale d'un repas. Il a été dit et redit qu'un repas français était une pièce en cinq actes (hors d'œuvre, entrée, viande garnie de légumes, fromages, dessert), mais cela n'est pas tout à fait exact pour plusieurs raisons. D'abord les déjeuners ordinaires (ceux que découvrira le touriste) et les soupers, même fins, se conçoivent en trois actes ; les banquets au contraire en ont au moins sept. Ensuite, parler d'une *pièce*, c'est donner une importance exagérée au dessert, qui correspondrait au dénouement, alors que le dessert n'est jamais qu'une sorte d'épilogue, complétant le plat de résistance lequel, à la rigueur, pourrait se suffire à lui-même : or, que dirait-on d'une pièce où l'acte du milieu signifierait quelque chose à lui tout seul ? Enfin, parler d'actes suppose un enchaînement logique alors qu'il vaut mieux penser à un rythme, c'est-à-dire à une alternance de temps forts et faibles, alternance que souligne la grande tradition française qui exige que l'on serve successivement des plats contrastant non seulement par le goût mais aussi par la couleur.

Précisons cette notion de contrastes. Si le hors d'œuvre est une terrine (faite de viande, donc de couleur rose), l'entrée pourra être un poisson (goût opposé, couleur différente). Le plat de résistance sera une viande rouge, qui rappellera de loin la terrine, et à laquelle succèdera une salade verte. Après la salade verte viendront les fromages, jaunes et blancs, dont le goût soutenu servira d'antithèse à la fraîcheur de la salade.

Somme toute, le mieux serait peut-être de dire qu'un repas français est *dialectique*.

Précisons encore qu'un repas français ne se conçoit pas non seulement sans vin — ce qui est connu — mais aussi sans conversation. Le vin et la conversation sont comme des sauces accessoires mais nécessaires, comme des compléments indispensables : des usage de politesse en règlent l'emploi, et il serait aussi incongru de boire du vin blanc avec un fromage que de parler de procès perdu en mangeant des huîtres.

Ayant un style, la gastronomie française a aussi une géographie — chaque province se nourrissant de ses propres spécialités — et une histoire. Elle a beaucoup évolué depuis un siècle, et toujours dans le sens d'un certain allégement des repas, qui deviennent moins copieux, moins sucrés et moins abondamment arrosés.

Au XIXème siècle, et encore aujourd'hui dans certaines provinces, on n'aurait jamais servi un seul hors d'œuvre ou un seul plat de viande. Personne ne se fût étonné de voir apparaître, après le poisson, une volaille, un gibier, et ensuite seulement le rôti ou le gigot. De même, après les fromages, on servait un entremet, un plat sucré, des fruits et finalement le dessert. Comment les estomacs résistaient à ce régime est une question de médecine que nous ne saurions trancher ici !

De cette tendresse passée pour les sucreries s'est conservée la tradition des bonbons fabriqués en province par des maisons spécialisées : truffes, pralines, chardons bleus, nougatines, bêtises, cassissines, calissons, griottes, sucres d'orge, ou violettes confites. Leurs goûts variés et doux, qui nous paraissent maintenant un peu écœurants, recèlent encore quelques traces de ce que Talleyrand appelait « la douceur de vivre ».

Aujourd'hui, la disparition de certaines traditions familiales et de bien des grandes fortunes fait que la *haute cuisine* ne se trouve plus — à quelques exceptions près — que dans les restaurants parisiens ou provinciaux les plus sérieux qui sont aussi, naturellement, parmi les plus chers, sans que le prix soit une garantie de raffinement. Lasserre, le Grand Véfour, Prunier, Lapérouse, Drouant, sont parmi les hauts lieux de la gastronomie française, tandis que d'autres restaurants, aussi illustres et aux additions aussi exorbitantes, ne seront jamais que d'excellents relais pour touristes, nouveaux riches et autres profanes. En revanche, certains petits restaurants à portée des bourses plus modestes — de plus en plus rares, il est vrai — entretiennent, au profit des initiés qui les fréquentent, la tradition du « bien manger » et de la *cuisine bourgeoise*.

VINS ET BOISSONS

Si un certain snobisme existe en matière de cuisine, il y a toute une gamme de snobismes en matière de vins, et ce qui importe au Francais, c'est de savoir démêler les snobismes distingués des snobismes vulgaires.

Réglons d'abord leur compte aux vulgaires : ils consistent en une application injustifiée d'un certain nombre d'usages mal compris, en un formalisme prétentieux, en un respect de la lettre morte de l'œnologie et non de son esprit. N'importe qui peut ouvrir un dictionnaire et y apprendre, s'il ne le savait déjà, qu'un vin rouge se boit avec de la viande et un vin blanc avec du poisson ; mais si, au goût, il n'est pas capable de distinguer un rouge d'un blanc, à quoi lui sert d'obéir aux règles ?

Les vrais snobismes, eux, ont trait à l'appréciation d'un vin pour ses qualités propres (les moins connus étant, naturellement, les plus distingués), à l'intuition d'une harmonie profonde existant entre tel vin et tel plat, et surtout au *sérieux* avec lequel il convient de traiter les vins en toutes circonstances, un sérieux qui serait tout à fait déplacé s'il s'agissait d'une question de métaphysique ou d'une vie humaine.

Le goût d'un vin dépend du raisin dont il est tiré, de la terre dans laquelle la vigne est plantée, de l'exposition de cette terre au soleil, de l'ensoleillement et de l'humidité de l'année, de la période et des conditions de vieillissement. Aussi les véritables dégustateurs se vantent-ils, souvent à juste titre, de pouvoir reconnaître au goût non seulement le cru mais aussi le millésime.[1]

Un vin se juge d'abord à la vue, pour sa limpidité et pour sa robe ; ensuite à l'odorat, pour son arôme (parfum dû au cépage et à la fermentation) et son bouquet (parfum dû au vieillissement) ; en troisième lieu seulement au goût, exprimé par trois facteurs : le corps (plein, racé, corsé, charnu, élégant, étoffé, charpenté, équilibré, ou au contraire mince, maigre, étriqué, commun) ; la douceur (vin rond, gras, tendre, souple, soyeux, mœlleux, coulant, velouté, à moins qu'il ne soit vert, dur, pointu, mordant, acide, astringent) ; la vinosité (vin chaud, nerveux, puissant, généreux, capiteux, dans les meilleurs cas, et froid, mou, plat, dans les plus mauvais).

Il existe trois qualités principales de vins en France : *l'ordinaire* est formé de vins de coupage, généralement originaires du Languedoc et mélangés à des vins d'Algérie dont la teneur en alcool est beaucoup plus forte ; les *vins délimités de qualité supérieure* consistent aussi quelquefois en mélanges, mais strictement surveillés (la plupart des Français s'en servent comme vins de table) ; enfin les *vins d'origine contrôlée*, correspondant à des crus dont

[1] Le millésime est un nombre de quatre chiffres indiquant l'année. Pour les vins, il s'agit de l'année au cours de laquelle le raisin a été cueilli. Exemple : un beaujolais 1962.

l'authenticité est garantie et consistant en plus ou moins grandes bouteilles, l'adjectif s'appliquant à la qualité et non à la quantité, comme dans « grande famille » et non comme dans « grande maison ».

Pour l'origine, on distingue principalement :

le bourgogne rouge, type même du vin « généreux »

le bourgogne blanc, qui est sec (c'est-à-dire non sucré)

le bordeaux rouge, moins capiteux que le bourgogne mais plus nerveux, avec une robe transparente, qui l'a fait surnommer « claret » par les Anglais

le sauterne, bordeaux blanc très doux (c'est-à-dire sucré)

le graves, bordeaux blanc relativement sec

le côtes-du-rhône, vin rouge apparenté au bourgogne

le muscadet, vin blanc apparenté au graves

les blancs d'Alsace, très secs

le champagne, qui peut être demi-sec (c'est-à-dire sucré), sec (un peu sucré) on brut (pas sucré du tout)

Il n'y a pas de très grands vins parmi les rosés ; on distingue cependant les rosés d'Anjou, plus doux, et ceux de Provence, plus secs.

Le service de ces vins à table se fait non pas, comme certains le croient, suivant les règles du savoir-vivre mais selon des méthodes éprouvées, garantissant aux connaisseurs un maximum de satisfaction. Cet empirisme épicurien apparaît clairement avec le champagne, que ses talents variés permettent de boire, quoique blanc, aussi bien avec du caviar qu'avec du foie gras. Le

Les Français ne boivent ni ne mangent : ils *dégustent* et *savourent* — *tout en conversant.*

même empirisme enseigne, dans un repas comprenant plusieurs vins, à les servir dans un ordre croissant de qualité — les plus corsés succédant aux moins charnus, et les plus puissants aux moins capiteux. Au reste, l'usage moderne, qui fait peu à peu disparaître les vins les plus doux, aura bientôt fait justice des repas à cinq vins différents : un blanc sec pour commencer, un rouge puissant pour finir, et voilà, on a assez bu.

Sauf dans les provinces qui ignorent la vigne, et où l'on boit du cidre ou du poiré, les Français consomment tous une grande quantité de vin, et ils veulent tous passer pour experts dans ce domaine si frivole qu'un peu de pédantisme y est permis. Il faut voir de quel ton un ouvrier demande « un petit muscadet » ou « un petit beaujolais » au bougnat du coin ; il faut voir avec quelle crainte religieuse un vigneron de Beaune vous apporte une bouteille « de derrière ses fagots ». Une grande différence néanmoins : les gens raffinés ne boivent guère de vin qu'en mangeant, ne serait-ce que des noix ou du fromage ; les gens simples boivent leur vin tout seul. Mais, dans tous les milieux, certains Français coupent leur vin d'un peu d'eau, sauf s'il s'agit d'une grande bouteille, cela va de soi.

Pour être la plus connue, le vin n'en est pas la seule boisson qu'on consomme en France. Citons l'eau minérale (Vichy, Vittel, Évian), que l'on préfère à l'eau du robinet ; le thé, d'introduction relativement récente et qui fut d'abord le breuvage des snobs et des anglomanes ; le café, qui est généralement pris « noir comme la nuit, chaud comme l'enfer et doux comme l'amour », pour citer Talleyrand ; et enfin les eaux-de-vie, liqueurs, cognacs et marcs, qui méritent des mentions à part.

Faites à partir de fruits (mirabelles, framboises, prunes ou pommes), les eaux-de-vie se boivent après le café, dans les milieux cultivés ; mélangées au café, dans le peuple ; et dans la même tasse que le café, mais le café une fois avalé, chez certains connaisseurs. C'est aussi après le repas que l'on boit les liqueurs (Chartreuse jaune ou verte, Vieille Cure), distillées à partir d'herbes diverses, d'après des secrets de fabrication soigneusement gardés. Souvent sucrées, alors que les eaux-de-vie sont sèches, les liqueurs ont, dans l'ensemble, passé de mode. On leur préfère maintenant les cognacs et l'armagnac, préparés à partir des vins correspondants et qui plaisent par leur saveur plus sèche et, pour ainsi dire, plus aérée. A noter que la France exporte exactement autant de cognac vers la Grande-Bretagne qu'elle n'en importe de whisky.

Les marcs (de champagne, de bourgogne, etc.) sont un sous-produit des vins : on utilise pour les faire les résidus du raisin, et leur goût très puissant, joint à leur forte vinosité, en fait d'excellents pousse-cafés (comme on disait naguère) ou digestifs (comme disent maintenant les petits bourgeois).

Du digestif, sautons brièvement à l'apéritif, pour préciser qu'il n'y en a pas de bon, et que tous ces vermouths que consomment les Français des classes moyennes par hectolitres entiers avant leurs repas ne sont qu'un signe indéniable hélas d'une certaine décadence de l'art de vivre.

Ah ! comme elles étaient plus raffinées, les tisanes et infusions de nos aïeules — camomille, tilleul, quatre-fleurs, verveine — dont les noms seuls évoquent de vieilles tantes provinciales, coiffées d'un bonnet de dentelle et le cou orné d'un ruban de velours ! Rares sont les familles où le souvenir s'en conserve encore.

C'est que, peut-être, pour connaître la vraie douceur de vivre française, il aurait fallu — comme disait Talleyrand, toujours lui — vivre dans la France de l'ancien régime. « Comment ? douceur de vivre ? objecteront immédiatement les gens les mieux intentionnés. Ah ! oui, pour les classes privilégiées, peut-être ; mais les autres ?... »

C'est que l'expression « douceur de vivre » aura été mal comprise. Talleyrand pensait sans doute à une certaine liberté, à un certain goût désintéressé du plaisir. Maintenant, en le citant, les Français pensent surtout à ce goût d'authenticité que la vie avait encore — et pour les moins privilégiés plus que pour les autres, peut-être — il y a seulement vingt ou trente ans, quand le pain était cuit au feu de bois, quand le beurre se vendait à la motte sans être pasteurisé, et qu'il coûtait moins cher de faire des confitures chez soi que d'en acheter au prisunic.

Une tartine de beurre et de confiture — une vraie tartine, s'entend — c'était cela, la douceur de vivre ; et le goût qu'on lui trouvait, c'était l'art de vivre ; et la manière de la manger, c'était le savoir-vivre. Et sous ce triple rapport, les Français privilégiés ou non étaient tous des épicuriens aussi raffinés, aussi aristocrates, les uns que les autres. Maintenant, le vrai pain, le vrai beurre, la vraie confiture, sont réservés à un petit nombre de personnes privilégiées qui ont le temps de les chercher dans les magasins diététiques.

PARIS 14

IDÉE GÉNÉRALE

Gœthe appelait Paris « la capitale du monde ». Il exprimait ainsi, à la fin du XVIIIème siècle, l'admiration passionnée que tous les hommes civilisés ressentaient pour une ville qui était réellement le centre de la vie culturelle dans le monde occidental.

Aujourd'hui, d'autres villes disputent à Paris cette suprématie. Londres, Rome, New York, sont devenues elles aussi des éprouvettes pour bouillons de culture. Mais Paris n'en garde pas moins certains attraits inégalés.

Au physique, c'est une ville âgée qui est restée jeune. Les ruines romaines y voisinent avec les immeubles en aluminium. Le passé et le présent s'y croisent à tous les carrefours. A la différence de Londres, où presque tout date du XIXème siècle, Paris est le meilleur témoin de sa propre histoire.

Au moral, le rôle de Paris dans la vie française est demeuré prépondérant. Malgré les sérieux efforts de décentralisation industrielle et culturelle qui ont été faits depuis vingt ans (exil des usines d'automobiles Renault en Normandie, création des centres de théâtre périphériques), Paris est resté « la grosse tête » de la France, ce pays exagérément intellectuel. Le terme *Parisien* peut être une insulte ou une flatterie, mais il désigne dans tous les cas une espèce d'êtres à part. *Provincial* demeure l'un des mots les plus injurieux du vocabulaire intellectuel français.

Dans le monde, on tient encore Paris pour la capitale de la légèreté. C'est faire beaucoup d'honneur à une ville qui a secrété une doctrine aussi pédante que l'existentialisme, où les critiques d'art parlent le langage le plus prétentieux qui soit, où psychanalystes et voyantes font aisément fortune, où chacun croit savoir à seize ans ce qu'il faut faire pour sauver la France.

En réalité, la haute couture, les parfums et les cabarets ne sont que les sous-produits de cette usine à intelligence.

LES ILES

Lorsqu'on regarde un plan de Paris avec les arrondissements bien distincts et portant leurs numéros de 1 à 20, on voit que la capitale a l'air d'un énorme colimaçon ou d'une gigantesque marelle. En effet, les arrondissements s'enroulent en spirale les uns autour des autres, et à quelques écarts près cette spirale correspond au déroulement chronologique de la construction.

La Cité — Paris est né du fleuve Seine. Il ne fut d'abord qu'une petite forteresse sur une petite île, celle qu'on appelle maintenant l'Ile de la Cité. C'est là que fut le cœur de la ville au Moyen Age, et il en reste la cathédrale Notre-Dame, qui veille sur Paris depuis huit cents ans. La vénérable église a abrité toutes les passions les plus effrénées de l'histoire de France. Toutes les défaites y ont été pleurées ; toutes les victoires y ont éclaté en *Te Deum*. C'est là que, maintenant encore, se rend le Président de la République pour les messes officielles. C'est là qu'aboutissent symboliquement toutes les routes de France, les kilométrages comptant à partir du parvis.

De l'autre côté de l'île, immense et poussiéreux, se tapit le Palais de justice. Il est aussi vieux que la ville — ou presque. Il contient dans ses murs l'ancien palais des rois de France, les sinistres cachots de la Conciergerie où des centaines de prisonniers furent massacrés pendant la Terreur, les locaux où siégea le tribunal révolutionnaire, les sombres cellules où furent enfermés avant leur exécution la reine Marie-Antoinette, le poète André Chénier et tant d'autres. Il recèle aussi une des plus éblouissantes merveilles de l'art gothique : la Sainte-Chapelle, érigée par le saint-roi Louis IX pour abriter la couronne d'épines de Jésus-Christ.

Le reste du palais, construit sous Napoléon III et toujours utilisé pour y rendre la justice, ne présente aucun intérêt artistique, mais il peut être amusant de s'y promener : dans d'immenses salles à colonnes, sans grâce ni élégance, dans un labyrinthe infini de couloirs et d'escaliers, on est sûr de croiser d'innombrables hommes de loi, portant une robe noire et un rabat

blanc souvent crasseux et, de déceler sur le visage de certains d'entre eux, les expressions d'astuce, d'avarice, de vanité et de perfidie qui n'ont pas changé depuis qu'elles ont été fixées par Daumier, peintre et graveur.

La plupart des grands procès de l'histoire de France ont été plaidés dans ces lieux. C'est ici que, récemment, la Cinquième République a réglé ses comptes avec son Armée révoltée.

A l'extrême pointe de l'île, au-delà de la Préfecture de police, qui voisine cocassement avec le Marché aux fleurs, se trouve l'exquise place Dauphine, parfaite de proportions et d'asymétrie. De petits restaurants modestes où l'on dîne aux chandelles se nichent dans des rez-de-chaussée datant du XVIIème.

Ile Saint-Louis   L'Ile Saint-Louis est séparée par un pont de celle de la

Paris, ville de la flânerie, avec les bouquinistes de ses quais...

Cité. On y trouve de beaux hôtels du XVIIème et du XVIIIème siècles, en particulier le Palais Lambert, qui fend la Seine comme l'étrave d'un vaisseau.

Les deux rives   Les îles mises à part, Paris s'étend sur les deux rives de la Seine. Ce sont deux rives ennemies, qui représentent des façons de vivre et de penser opposées et complémentaires.

La gauche est la plus ancienne ; ele fut la plus aristocratique ; elle est la plus intellectuelle aujourd'hui.

La droite a plus de prospérité et moins d'imagination ; c'est la rive bourgeoise par excellence.

Il existe un accent rive droite, que l'on tient pour snob, et un esprit rive gauche, qui se veut frondeur.

LA RIVE GAUCHE

Les vrais parisiens ne parlent jamais d'arrondissements ; s'ils en connaissent l'existence, ce n'est que pour en faire figurer les numéros dans leurs adresses. Seul le XVIème (rive droite) est généralement nommé par son numéro. Tout le reste de la capitale vit par « quartiers ».

Quartier latin   Le Quatier latin est l'un des plus anciens, du moins par son emplacement, car il ne reste plus rien des tavernes où les joyeux *estudiants* du Moyen Age festoyaient avec leur camarade, le poète Français Villon, ni de la Sorbonne primitive, qui fut d'abord une école de théologie. La Sorbonne moderne date en partie du XVIIème, en partie du XIXème. Elle est vaste, sombre et morose d'aspect. Des milliers d'étudiants de tous les sexes et de toutes les couleurs s'entassent dans des amphithéâtres surdorés et surpeuplés. Par les nuits de printemps, le Groupe de théâtre antique interprète sur le parvis de la chapelle des tragédies grecques. Certains jours éclatent des manifestations politiques. Des bagarres ont lieu entre étudiants d'extrême-gauche (communistes) et d'extrême-droite (royalistes). Des cars de police grillagés, pittoresquement surnommés « paniers à salade » arrivent sur les lieux, et les combattants, assommés à coups de matraques et de pélerines, sont emmenés au poste. Les événements de mai 1968 sont partis de ce quartier traditionnellement mouvementé.

Si l'on remonte le boulevard Saint-Michel, qui sous le nom de « boul' Mich' » sert d'artère principale au Quartier latin, on arrive à la Faculté de droit, où les futurs juges et les futurs avocats s'initient aux subtilités du Code civil dit Code Napoléon, tandis que, dans les coins, leurs camarades du sexe féminin attendent en bâillant un mari providentiel.

Le Panthéon, qui fut une église et où sont ensevelis actuellement les grands hommes de la patrie (ou les amis politiques des gouvernants), domine la rue Soufflot, qui débouche sur l'un des plus anciens et des plus charmants jardins de Paris : le Luxembourg. C'est là que, dès les premiers jours de printemps, les étudiants viennent « bûcher » leurs cours ou s'embrasser sur les bancs publics, sous le regard indulgent de vieux messieurs nourrissant à la becquée des moineaux apprivoisés.

Ville de la tendresse, avec ses vieux messieurs nourrissant les pigeons des Tuileries...

Saint-Sulpice   Le Quartier latin voisine avec Saint-Sulpice. Là, autour d'une église de style « jésuite », prolifèrent des magasins d'articles de piété appelés péjorativement « saint-sulpiceries » ou « bondieuseries » : statues de saints polychromes, médailles religieuses, ornements sacerdotaux, crucifix de mauvais goût, etc.

Saint-Germain   Par Saint-Sulpice on arrive à Saint-Germain, l'un des noms les plus trompeurs de la toponymie française. En effet, il ne faut pas confondre l'église Saint-Germain avec le boulevard Saint-Germain, artère longeant l'église, ni avec le quartier Saint-Germain, région s'étendant de part et d'autre du boulevard, ni avec le faubourg Saint-Germain, terme désignant non pas un lieu mais l'ensemble des vieilles demeures du quartier où habitaient les familles aristocratiques aux XVIIIème et XIXème siècles et qui, souvent, leur appartiennent encore.

L'église Saint-Germain-des-Prés est l'une des plus anciennes de Paris. Il est piquant de songer que c'est autour d'elle qu'ont fleuri les cafés littéraires où est né l'existentialisme, doctrine révolutionnaire et athée, dont les premiers adeptes se signalaient à l'attention du public (vingt ans avant les *hippies*) par des cheveux longs et des vêtements crasseux. Les cafés littéraires sont une institution française qui date du XVIIIème siècle. Actuellement, les trois les plus connus sont le Flore, séjour habituel de plusieurs écrivains ; les Deux Magots, que hantent nombre de personnages pittoresques ; la brasserie Lipp, où les hommes politiques se donnent rendez-vous. Ici également est venu s'installer le second drugstore parisien (le premier étant aux Champs-Elysées). Aucun rapport entre les honnêtes drugstores américains et leurs imitations françaises, où la prétention le dispute à la vulgarité.

Les plus grands éditeurs (Hachette, Julliard, Flammarion, Plon, Laffont, le Seuil, Grasset, Gallimard) ne sont pas loin ; ce sont eux qui donnet au Saint-Germain diurne son aspect sérieux et compassé, tandis que les « cabarets rive gauche » et les « cafés-théâtres », dont la plupart se blottissent dans d'anciennes caves aux voûtes séculaires, représentent « l'esprit d'avant-garde » qui y règne la nuit.

Saint-Germain est en vérité le quartier le plus varié, le plus coloré, de Paris. De la mystérieuse cour de Rohan à la romantique place Furstenberg, du marché de Buci où l'on vend encore fruits et légumes à la criée jusqu'aux

Ville de la causerie avec tous ses cafés, littéraires et autres...

Ville du passé toujours présent avec les vieilles maisons de la cour de Rohan...

Ville de tous les commerces, depuis les magasins les plus luxueux jusqu'à l'étal de cette marchande des quatre saisons...

Il n'est bon bec que de Paris.

VILLON

étals des bouquinistes disposés au bord de la Seine, des antiquaires et des marchands d'instruments de musique anciens aux restaurateurs à la page qui cuisinent au feu de bois dans des décors 1900, des vieilles maisons datant de Louis XIII aux luxueux appartements modernes qu'y installent de riches étrangers, des ruelles obscures aux noms pittoresques (rue du Dragon, rue Gît-le-Cœur) à l'élégant hôtel de Biron où a été logé le musée Rodin, tout Saint-Germain respire la continuité historique, la perpétuelle richesse d'invention d'une population où, selon la vieille habitude française, se mêlent les races et les origines sociales.

Invalides   En sortant de Saint-Germain, on aboutit aux Invalides et au Champ-de-Mars. C'est la région la plus « rive droite » de la rive gauche. Les avenues y sont spacieuses, les appartements cossus bien que surannés. L'École militaire, Saint-Louis des Invalides, le tombeau de Napoléon, donnent une allure militaire à cette partie de la ville où les rues portent des noms d'amiraux et de généraux.

La Tour Eiffel, vieille fille bientôt septuagénaire, se dresse à l'extrême limite du quartier et semble fasciner les touristes, alors que la plupart des Parisiens ne lui ont jamais accordé un coup d'œil. Des hauteurs de la rive droite, le Palais de Chaillot, ce fer à cheval de pierre blanche, lui fait face; et ces deux monuments se regardent comme des chiens de faïence par-dessus le fleuve.

Grenelle, Vaugirard   Vers l'ouest s'étendent Grenelle et Vaugirard, naguère populaires mais qui commencent à s'embourgeoiser. Le métro aérien surgit de terre et prête le charme de son architecture métallique début de siècle à un paysage urbain aux tons pauvres, gris sales à peine teintés de rose pour les murs et de bleu pour les toits.

Alésia, Gobelins, Denfert-Rochereau   Si l'on revient vers l'est en suivant un itinéraire plus méridional, on traverse toute une région (XIVème et XIIIème arrondissements) où les touristes ne s'aventurent guère, parce que les monuments n'y abondent pas et que, si tout y semble vieux, rien n'y est véritablement ancien. C'est pourtant là que l'on peut retrouver les traces vivantes du Paris du XIXème siècle, celui d'Eugène Sue et d'Émile Zola. On y parle un français plus dru, plus gouailleur et plus bon enfant. Au détour d'une rue, on débouche dans une ancienne ferme qui a conservé son potager ; entre deux supermarchés, on trouve une librairie spécialisée dans les sciences occultes. Les bouchers, les forgerons, les rempailleurs de chaise, s'y considèrent encore comme des artisans, passés maîtres dans un métier qui leur paraît le plus beau du monde.

Je l'aime tendrement jusqu'à ses verrues et à ses taches ; je ne suis Français que par cette grande cité.

MONTAIGNE

Les clochards Ici, les clochards sont rois. Ronflant sur les grilles du métro qui répandent une chaleur bienfaisante, s'offrant un « kil de rouge » sous les ponts de la Seine, s'abritant dans des cours intérieures dont personne qu'eux ne soupçonne l'existence, jouant à la belote comme des enragés chez le bougnat du coin, ils mènent une vie en quelque sorte exemplaire, sans domicile, sans famille, sans revenu, ne se préoccupant que du pinard,[1] du bricheton[2] et du calandos.[3] A leur façon, ils sont les derniers témoins d'une civilisation moins perfectionnée et plus humaine où l'individu savait se passer de la société.

Le Paris insolite Ils appartiennent à ce Paris insolite qui a hanté tant d'imaginations et qui englobe, pêle-mêle, les Catacombes, anciennes carrières transformées en dépotoirs de squelettes ; les Égoûts de la ville ; la Bièvre, rivière que les hommes ont forcée à rentrer sous terre ; l'ancien musée de la torture transformé en salle pour concerts de jazz ; les abattoirs de Vaugirard ; certains locaux tendus de noir où se célèbrent des anti-messes en l'honneur de Belzébuth ; et des clubs plus ou moins privés où se pratiquent des cultes et des orgies pour tous les goûts.

Montparnasse Montparnasse, qui fut l'un des centres de la vie artistique au début du siècle, a perdu toute sa séduction. La Coupole, le Dôme, la Rotunde, vieux cafés où traînèrent Picasso, Modigliani et plus tard Simone de Beauvoir, se sont modernisés. Le genre débraillé est tout ce qui reste du genre artiste, et les demoiselles de petite vertu qui se font remarquer aux bars et aux terrasses n'ont plus même l'excuse de servir de modèles à des peintres de génie.

L'Estrapade, la Mouffe Le quartier de l'Estrapade et de la Mouffe (du nom de la rue Mouffetard) est un des carrefours sociaux de Paris. Dans ces rues, dangereuses de nuit, on rencontre non seulement des intellectuels et des clochards mais aussi des poètes, des chanteurs, des artisans, des marchands de tout ce qu'on voudra. Dans de petites salles crasseuses, des troupes étrangères viennent donner des spectacles ; de vieux messieurs jouent au billard dans des cafés obscurs, en sirotant des boissons dont la plupart des Parisiens ont oublié le nom ; une nombreuse population d'origine arabe a été attirée ici par la proximité de la Mosquée.

[1] vin rouge
[2] pain
[3] fromage de Camembert

Ville où la vie est dans la rue, même en hiver, grâce aux marchands de marrons chauds...

Le Jardin des Plantes La Mosquée elle-même est le centre d'un quartier mystérieux qui entoure le Jardin des plantes. Les cafés-théâtres y fleurissent. De vieux professeurs à bésicles s'y passionnent pour l'entomologie ou la botanique. Les Arènes de Lutèce et le voisinage du musée de Cluny avec ses thermes — derniers vestiges de l'occupation romaine — donnent une sorte de profondeur temporelle à cet ensemble disparate qui débouchait, naguère encore, sur les Halles aux vins. Maintenant ces pittoresques halles où s'entreposaient des milliers de fûts faisant régner alentour une odeur de vinaigre ont disparu. A leur place s'élève la nouvelle Faculté des sciences, qui honore l'Université mais déshonore le paysage, comme la nouvelle Faculté de médecine en plein quartier Saint-Germain.

LA RIVE DROITE

L'usage français voulait que les fortunés et les humbles habitassent les mêmes quartiers et les mêmes maisons, tout en se partageant les étages à la verticale en fonction de leurs moyens respectifs : plus on était pauvre, plus on habitait près du ciel. Cependant, sur la rive droite, beaucoup plus étendue que la gauche, l'usage anglais a prévalu au XIXème siècle et la société s'y répartit horizontalement.

Le XVIème Le XVIème arrondissement est presque entièrement résidentiel. Dans les quartiers d'Auteuil et de Passy, écrasés par la masse de la Maison de la Radio, serpentent encore quelques rues anciennes ombragées d'arbres, se dressent toujours quelques maisons qui furent construites à la campagne il y a cent ou deux cents ans et qui, insensiblement, se sont trouvées en pleine ville — elles en gardent une bonhomie du meilleur aloi — mais la plupart des rues, avec leurs maisons identiques de six étages plus la mansarde, leurs balcons de fer forgé et leurs concierges professionnellement de mauvaise humeur, respirent l'ennui, l'aisance et la respectabilité.

Plus près de l'Étoile, les hôtels du XIXème siècle ont été rachetés par diverses compagnies ; le cliquetis des machines à écrire et l'éclairage au néon des salons Napoléon III donnent une impression d'activités commerciales, ce qui repousse les Parisiens exigeants plus à l'ouest, vers les réserves d'oxygène et de calme du Bois de Boulogne.

Ville de la promenade solitaire par de vieux quartiers comme celui de la rue Berthon...

Place de l'Étoile   La place de l'Étoile elle-même, au centre de quoi se dresse l'Arc de Triomphe, est un monument napoléonien qui manque de grâce mais non pas de grandeur. Sous l'Arc palpite la flamme éternelle allumée sur le tombeau du Soldat inconnu. Diverses délégations se partagent le soin de la ranimer presque tous les soirs. Les gouvernants étrangers y viennent déposer des fleurs.

Par l'Arc de triomphe passe la ligne de mire de l'une des plus belles perspectives du monde. Vers l'ouest-nord-ouest, elle descend l'avenue de la Grande Armée, traverse Neuilly et finit par aboutir au rond-point de la Défense. Vers l'est-sud-est, elle suit les Champs-Elysées, franchit le rond-point Franklin Roosevelt, laisse de part et d'autre les Jardins de Paris, traverse la place de la Concorde, saute par-dessus l'obélisque, pénètre aux Tuileries, file sous l'Arc du Carrousel et va se ficher en plein milieu du Palais du Louvre.

Champs-Elysées   A la différence de ce que croient beaucoup d'étrangers, les Champs-Elysées ne sont nullement une avenue élégante, même pas une avenue riche. Ils le furent, il y a cinquante ans. Actuellement, ils ne sont plus qu'une artère commerciale. Seuls le Drugstore (qui n'a rien du drugstore) et le Pub Renault (qui n'a rien d'un pub) ont la prétention d'être à la mode.

Faubourg   Les magasins élégants se trouvent non loin de là, rue du Faubourg Saint-Honoré et avenue Matignon. C'est dans ce quartier que siègent les augures de la haute couture, les ambassadeurs de plusieurs pays, les fabricants de produits de beauté, le Président de la République en son Palais de l'Élysée, des coiffeurs au renom international — bref, tout ce qui concourt aux aspects les plus brillants de la vie parisienne.

En descendant les Champs-Elysées, on trouve sur la droite le Grand Palais et le Petit Palais, monuments élevés par le XIXème siècle à sa propre nullité architecturale. Ne sachant qu'en faire, on y a organisé des banquets et exposé des automobiles, des tableaux, des articles ménagers ; on y enseigne maintenant des étudiants de lettres.

Plus loin coule la Seine, sillonnée par les péniches et les bateaux-mouches.

Place de la Concorde   La place de la Concorde, construite par Louis XV, est dominée par les édifices du Ministère de la Marine et de l'hôtel Crillon.

Ville d'art où les jardins publics sont des musées en plein air...

Elle a été conçue toute en lignes horizontales avec, pour rythmer la perspective, des balustrades, des fontaines et des statues représentant les principales villes de France sous forme allégorique. A l'époque où l'Alsace avait été arrachée au territoire national par les Allemands, la statue de Strasbourg était voilée de crêpe noir. L'idée d'installer un obélisque dérobé en Égypte au centre de la place, et celle de la hérisser de mâts de drapeaux comme on vient de le faire, en abîment un peu le coup d'œil. Néanmoins la noblesse des proportions demeure inchangée. L'église de la Madeleine qu'on aperçoit à un bout, et la Chambre des députés qui lui fait face de l'autre côté du fleuve, font ressortir, par la lourdeur de leurs formes, la grâce et la distinction de la place elle-même.

Elle s'appelait place Louis XV sous l'Ancien Régime. La Terreur y guillotina Louis XVI et la baptisa place de la Révolution. L'appellation actuelle est censée symboliser les passions apaisées du siècle dernier.

Tuileries Les Tuileries forment un jardin d'une grande élégance. Parmi les statues de pierre blanche, des enfants lancent des voiliers sur l'eau des bassins. Un théâtre de marionnettes se cache dans un bosquet. Des jardiniers rognent les bordures de buis et plantent des massifs de bégonias au dessin compliqué. Un flot interminable de voitures cherchant vainement une place

La Seine est une amante,
Et Paris dort dans son lit.
CHANSON

pour se garer — il n'y a guère de stationnements payants à Paris — passent sous les énormes arches de maçonnerie qui donnent accès d'un côté aux quais de la Seine, de l'autre à la rue de Rivoli.

Louvre   La masse gigantesque du Louvre — ce monument inégal commencé sous la Renaissance et terminé sous Napoléon III, sans parler de ses parties médiévales complètement détruites — sert de toile de fond au décor. Le plus beau morceau en est, sans conteste, la cour carrée, éblouissant exemple d'architecture Louis XIV ; où la scansion des colonnes et des ornements est adoucie par la sensualité des pierres, d'un jaune crayeux et chaud.

Palais-Royal   A deux pas s'étend le Palais-Royal. Moins pompeux, plus souriant, il fut le centre des quartiers à la mode vers la fin de l'ancien régime. Des conspirations libérales se tramaient alors dans ses jardins où l'on ne rencontre plus que des promeneurs attirés par le charme des lieux.

Vendôme, Opéra   La rue de Rivoli, qui longe les Tuileries, est connue pour ses arcades, sous lesquels s'alignent des magasins. Elle communique avec la place Vendôme, autre exemple d'architecture Louis XIV, tout aussi remarquable malgré son austérité et la fausse colonne romaine, qui commémore les victoires de Napoléon Ier et à vrai dire dépare l'ensemble. Plus loin on s'engage dans la rue de la Paix, célèbre pour ses joailliers et ses fourreurs. Plus loin encore on débouche sur l'Opéra, tarte à la crème de l'architecture post-romantique, qui annonce les quartiers des journaux, des banques, des compagnies d'assurance et des gares.

Châtelet, Halles, Temple   Si l'on ne s'égare point par là, mais que l'on continue à suivre la rue de Rivoli, on arrive dans des régions d'où la beauté est absente mais où les surprises se trouvent à chaque pas : quartier du Châtelet, où stationnent toute la nuit des dames entreprenantes défendant âprement chacune son bout de trottoir ; quartier des Halles, où tout Paris s'approvisionnait naguère en fruits, en légumes, en laitages, et où l'on allait manger une soupe à l'oignon vers quatre heures du matin après avoir dansé le reste de la nuit (ce quartier est, hélas, en démolition : les Halles ont été expulsées a l'éxtérieur de la capitale et de charmants restaurants appelés Le Chien qui fume ou Le Pied de Cochon en mourront sans doute) ; quartier des grands magasins débordant sur les trottoirs par des étals disparates et des comptoirs d'exhibitions ; quartier du Temple, véritable ghetto où toutes les viandes sont kacher, où des graveurs à barbes de Mathusalem cisèlent minutieusement des chevalières pour les Gentils, où les touristes ne se hasardent jamais et où les Français eux-mêmes passent pour des touristes.

Marais   Plus loin tout se transforme, et l'on arrive de nouveau dans un district noble : le Marais. Ce fut le quartier à la mode au début du XVII^(ème) siècle, et les vieux hôtels y portent la marque d'une époque toute de vigueur, où la grandeur n'avait encore rien de redondant. Depuis quelques années, des efforts considérables sont faits pour redonner au Marais envahi par les taudis un peu de son lustre passé. L'été, pendant le festival, des pièces et des concerts sont joués dans les cours, les jardins et les salons des vieilles demeures qui renaissent peu à peu. La place des Vosges, vaste carré de brique aux coins de pierre, donne une idée exacte et romanesque à la fois de tous les mérites architecturaux du style qui fut commun aux règnes d'Henri IV et de Louis XIII.

Bastille, République   Toujours plus à l'est s'étendent les quartiers de la Bastille et de la République, résolument populaires. C'est là que viennent s'installer les fêtes foraines, avec leurs manèges, leurs tirs et leurs loteries. Les rugissements de leurs haut-parleurs couvrent le bruit des voitures. Des voleurs à la tire circulent entre les baraques. Aux coins des rues, des recéleurs vendent des piles de draps et de torchons volés dans les magasins. Une atmosphère de boulevard du Crime flotte dans l'air.

Dans les temps passés, Paris fut une ville forte. Il est ceinturé d'une triple série de boulevards concentriques qui ont pris la place des anciennes fortifications.

Ville de la debrouillardise *avec les camelots et leur* baratin...

Grands boulevards   Si l'on se dirige vers le nord, on rencontre d'abord les grands boulevards, où l'animation ne cesse jamais. Ils ont été tracés sous le Second Empire par un urbaniste, le baron Haussmann, qui, dit-on, les a voulus très larges pour que d'éventuels révolutionnaires n'y pussent construire de barricades et pour que la cavalerie y chargeât à l'aise. Entre deux rangées de grands cinémas et de restaurants de troisième ordre s'écoule une population apparemment oisive. Des camelots viennent vendre les marchandises les plus variées sur de petits étals démontables. D'autres disposent la leur — bretelles, cravates, pierres à briquet — dans des parapluies renversés sur le trottoir.

Pigalle   Plus au nord s'étend le quartier du boulevard Pigalle, qui fait partie de la deuxième ceinture. Ici on ne vit que la nuit. Des boîtes démodées affichent des spectacles de strip-tease. Des Levantins en complets trop clairs circulent, l'œil aux aguets. Le métro aérien et les enseignes lumineuses multicolores achèvent de donner un aspect fantasmagorique à ce coin de Paris, tout luisant de fard, de crasse et de néon.

Goutte d'or   Ce quartier communique avec un autre, où la police elle-même se risque le moins qu'elle peut : une population nord-africaine aux revenus indéterminés s'y est installée et demeure en contact permanent avec ce que l'on appelle « le milieu », c'est-à-dire les associations de souteneurs et de bandits professionnels.

Boulevards extérieurs   Encore plus au nord, entre les abattoirs de la Villette, le sinistre canal de l'Ourcq, le Marché aux puces et les garages de Levallois-Perret, où l'on vend des voitures plus ou moins volées, on débouche

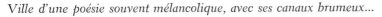

Ville d'une poésie souvent mélancolique, avec ses canaux brumeux...

enfin dans un paysage d'entrepôts, d'usines et de chantiers, qui s'étend de part et d'autre des boulevards extérieurs. Qu'on les prenne à droite ou à gauche, on finira par revenir à son point de départ, car ils encerclent Paris de leur monotonie. Des autobus les parcourent, qu'on reconnaît aux deux lettres PC inscrites sur leurs panneaux et signifiant « petite ceinture ».

Montmartre   Tout le nord de Paris est dominé par la butte Montmartre, qui fut le séjour d'artistes comme Utrillo et qui garde encore un charme 1900 abondamment exploité par les restaurateurs, les peintres et les chansonniers de second ordre. Certaines rues ont conservé leur aspect début de siècle ; des jardins secrets se nichent entre deux maisons ; des ateliers de sculpteur se cachent dans des bâtisses étranges, d'un pseudo-gothique délirant. Sur la place du Tertre, on dîne en plein air, aux lampions. Des vendeuses ambulantes viennent proposer des violettes ; des dessinateurs faméliques croquent des portraits éclairs. Plus haut se dresse — énorme gâteau de mariage — la basilique du Sacré-Cœur, élevée en tribut expiatoire, pour les atrocités de la Commune de Paris, par des vainqueurs qui en avaient commis davantage.

LE GRAND PARIS

Paris vu d'en-haut   On peut grimper jusqu'au sommet de ses tours disgracieuses et contempler tout Paris déroulé au pied de la butte. Le coup

Ville de la sentimentalité, avec le Sacré-Cœur; du bonheur vénal avec Montmartre...

Ville avant tout urbaine : on va au Bois pour retrouver un peu de verdure.

d'œil vaut celui qu'on a de la Tour Eiffel, de la colonne de Juillet ou de l'Arc de Triomphe. Seules les tours presque millénaires de Notre-Dame, hérissées de gargouilles, taraudées d'escaliers en colimaçon, offrent une perspective plus délicieuse. Elle permet en effet d'admirer de plus près des monuments qui, noirs de poussière et de suie depuis des siècles, viennent d'être nettoyés par jet de sable et sont redevenus blancs, ou ivoire, ou à peine jaunes, ou à peine orangés, selon la teinte propre de leur pierre originelle. La grisaille des immeubles d'appartements ne fait que mieux ressortir la splendeur retrouvée de l'Institut, du Luxembourg, et du Palais Conti.

Vu de haut, on constate que Paris manque beaucoup de verdure : le bois de Boulogne (dit le Bois tout court) à l'ouest, le bois de Vincennes à l'est, quelques jardins publics, quelques squares, des avenues plantées d'arbres, et voilà tous les espaces verts d'une ville qui en compte proportionnellement dix fois moins que Londres ou que New York. Mais les Parisiens ne s'en plaignent guère. Pourquoi voudraient-ils des parcs alors qu'ils se trouvent bien dans les rues, dans les cafés et dans le métro ? Ils l'aiment tant, cet immense réseau souterrain et aérien, d'une logique cartésienne mais d'un confort

Paris, c'est une blonde.

CHANSON

relatif, qui dessert commodément les quartiers les plus reculés comme les plus centraux de la capitale !

Banlieue   Autour de Paris, sur des dizaines de kilomètres, s'étale la banlieue. Les maisons ouvrières y alternent avec de petits pavillons à toit de tuiles rouges, devant lesquels croissent quelques roses et quelques poireaux. On habite les unes tant qu'on travaille et on rêve des autres pour quand l'on sera retraité. De toute manière, on finit dans de vastes cimetières décorés de croix, d'urnes, de colonnes brisées et de petites chapelles familiales.

Des « grands ensembles », sortes de ruches humaines, avec parcs, terrains de jeux, piscines, supermarchés, écoles et dispensaires, bornent depuis peu l'horizon. On y enregistre un record de suicides, et l'on commence à se demander si le genre de vie qu'ils assurent n'est pas en contradiction formelle avec le tempérament français.

Projets   Au demeurant, Paris ne cesse pas de croître et de se congestionner en même temps. Il est déjà question de bâtir un nouveau Paris, soit résidentiel, soit administratif et commercial, à cinquante kilomètres à l'ouest de l'actuel. Il est question aussi de raser la plus grande partie des vieux quartiers et de les remplacer par des constructions modernes : on gagnerait ainsi en confort ce que l'on perdrait en poésie... Les urbanistes hésitent encore entre les deux solutions et appliquent des plans de fortune, qui inquiètent périodiquement les amoureux de la beauté de Paris. C'est qu'ils sous-estiment peut-être les capacités d'absorption de la capitale : ayant survécu à tant de mutilations au cours des siècles (incendies divers, canonnades de la Fronde, démolitions révolutionnaires, embellissements du Second Empire, bombardements de 1870, de 1916 et de 1942–1943), il serait bien étrange qu'elle ne résistât pas aux transformations bien intentionnées que lui infligeront les architectes contemporains.

LA FRANCE 15
A TRAVERS
LES AGES

IDÉE GÉNÉRALE

Sans avoir pour son passé la tendresse attentive que la Grande-Bretagne a longtemps eu pour le sien, sans vivre pour ainsi dire à l'ombre de son passé comme l'a longtemps fait l'Espagne, la France est constamment consciente de ce qu'elle fut, mesure toujours ce qu'elle est à ce qu'elle a été et n'envisage jamais les siècles à venir que par rapport aux siècles écoulés.

Les campagnes et les villes françaises sont pleines de chapelles et de châteaux qui chuchotent à l'oreille du passant : « Je suis le roman... Je suis le gothique... Je suis la Renaissance... ». Les salons français sont pleins de causeuses et de consoles qui murmurent en grinçant tout bas : « Le Louis XV, c'est moi... Le Louis XVI, c'est moi... Et moi, c'est le Directoire... ». Les livres, les articles de journaux, abondent en références au passé : un journaliste ne saurait préconiser des réformes sociales sans rappeler le souvenir des « grands ancêtres » ; pour dénoncer le régime autoritaire du général de Gaulle, les pamphlétaires le comparaient à Louis XIV, ou, projetant le passé dans l'avenir, le baptisaient tout simplement « Charles XI ».

La France est un pays à quatre dimensions, la temporelle étant peut-être plus importante que les trois autres.

Non que les Français soient amateurs de dates, ni qu'ils aient des idées très précises sur le déroulement de leur histoire. Mais ils savent qu'ils représentent le stade actuel d'une certaine évolution, d'une certaine continuité, et ils portent en eux-mêmes l'image des stades précédents. Ces images, moins exactes que colorées, moins documentées que symboliques, se lèvent spontanément dans l'esprit des Français, pour peu qu'on prononce devant eux des mots comme *Moyen Age* ou *XVII*ème *siècle* : c'est sur elles que l'on veut terminer cet aperçu de la civilisation française.

LE MOYEN AGE

La perspective temporelle fait que le Moyen Age, qui a pourtant duré mille ans — de 410, prise de Rome par les Barbares, à 1453, prise de Constantinople par les Turcs — ne constitue qu'une seule étape dans cette évolution, telle que se la figure non pas le spécialiste mais l'honnête homme contemporain. C'est que le Moyen Age, avec son alternance de périodes obscurantistes et de renaissances partielles, avec cette longue maturation que furent ses six premiers siècles, avec cette magnifique explosion culturelle qui dura du XIème au XIIIème et la décadence relative qui suivit, a milité de bout en bout pour les mêmes valeurs, et a finalement fondé un héritage homogène.

Longtemps on a parlé de « la longue nuit du Moyen Age ». C'est qu'en effet la science et l'humanisme tels que nous les entendons en étaient absents ; Charlemagne lui-même ne savait pas lire ; l'Église demeurait toute-puissante sur les esprits ; la société vivait dans un système d'assujetissement mutuel dit féodal, qui ignorait jusqu'aux notions mêmes de liberté et d'égalité. Aujourd'hui, des historiens plus ouverts aux valeurs spirituelles que leurs aînés du XIXème siècle ont tendance au contraire à évoquer « la grande lumière du Moyen Age », ce qui est contradictoire mais pas autant peut-être qu'on le croit : à l'honnête homme, le Moyen Age apparaît en effet comme une nuit, mais comme une nuit merveilleusement étoilée, et dont l'esprit persiste encore en nous, dans la mesure où nous restons ouverts aux valeurs mystérieuses du sacré.

Le droit divin   C'est la notion de sacré qui, pour le moderne, caractérise l'héritage médiéval dans tous les domaines où le souvenir nous en est parvenu. Sacré était alors le droit divin des princes : l'imagerie populaire qui veut que Saint-Louis ait eu l'habitude d'aller s'asseoir sous un chêne de Vincennes pour y rendre justice à noble et à vilain, de même que l'iconographie qui nous montre ce souverain tenant la Main de justice, sceptre des rois de France appelés aussi Rois très chrétiens, indiquent une profonde assimilation du roi-juge au Christ-roi. Ne l'oublions pas : le roi de France, du fait de l'huile sacrée

La sainteté de Louis IX symbolise le caractère sacral de la royauté française.

qui oignait son front, ses paumes, ses pieds, était censé devenir thaumaturge[1] et, détenant ainsi des pouvoirs proprement surnaturels, apparaissait à la fois comme le symbole et le délégué de Dieu sur terre.

La chevalerie   Sacrée aussi — du moins dans son inspiration sinon toujours dans les faits — était la vocation des hommes qui décidaient de porter les armes pour défendre des causes considérées comme saintes et dont la hiérarchie tient dans la devise tardive mais révélatrice « Mon Dieu, mon roi, ma dame ».

La courtoisie   Pour Dieu, les chevaliers combattaient les Infidèles et, au cours des croisades, dont l'initiative fut française et qui durèrent deux siècles, tentaient de libérer la Terre-Sainte de l'emprise musulmane. Pour le roi, ils luttaient à armes inégales contre les vassaux en révolte. Pour leur dame, ils faisaient plus encore : par les épreuves qu'ils s'imposaient pour prouver qu'ils étaient dignes d'elles, ils modifiaient tout simplement une structure sociale qui n'avait guère varié depuis l'Antiquité. Les hétaïres de Grecs n'avaient été, après tout, que des courtisanes ; les matrones des Romains, que des pondeuses ; et les premiers siècles chrétiens avaient fait de la femme, fille d'Ève, l'agent secret du diable, l'instrument par excellence de la damnation. Les chevaliers changèrent tout cela : voyant dans chaque femme un reflet

[1] faiseur de miracles

Cette Ève romane, tortueuse, insinuante, sensuelle, c'est la femme-damnation.

Cette Vierge-Mère
gothique, c'est la
femme-pureté, la
femme-médiation, la
femme-salut.

sacré de la Vierge Marie, ils les invoquèrent toutes comme des médiatrices de leur salut, en créant ce mouvement spirituel dont nous subissons, si affaiblis qu'ils soient, les derniers effets : la courtoisie.

Arts et lettres   Si, du Moyen Age tout entier, nous ne devions garder qu'une seule image, sans doute retiendrions-nous celle du futur chevalier qui, après une nuit passée en prières dans une chappelle obscure, tombe à genoux en public, prononce son serment et, du plat de la main ou de l'épée, reçoit d'un autre chevalier cet adoubement qui ressemble à l'imposition des mains conférant le sacerdoce. En fait, les châteaux-forts en ruine qui surplombent les campagnes de France et les églises qui en dominent les villes, aussi bien que les statues dans leur statisme roman ou dans leur chorégraphie gothique, les vitraux aux flamboiements mystiques, les tapisseries, les enluminures, les tableaux de Fouquet, les mystères et les drames religieux, les fabliaux, les chansons de geste et les romans bretons, les ballades de Villon, le chant grégorien et les motets polyphoniques de Pérotin, sont autant de représentations diverses mais convergentes d'un monde où, sous le nom de sacré, le spirituel prétendait — à tort ou à raison — à une autorité absolue sur les êtres et les choses.

La sensibilité française n'est pas que frivole : la sculpture funèbre du Moyen Age dégage bien son autre face : le mysticisme.

L'un des derniers rois à être armé chevalier fut François Ier. Son parrain était Bayard, surnommé « sans peur et sans reproche ». Quelques années plus tard, Bayard tomba, mortellement blessé d'un coup d'arquebuse. C'est là un événement dont on retiendra la portée symbolique : François Ier, sa vie durant, se soucia peu de respecter le code chevaleresque de défense du faible et de l'opprimé. Quoi d'étonnant ? Il vivait dans un monde en métamorphose ; il n'avait plus à compter avec les valeurs spirituelles appliquées que représentaient la féodalité et la chrétienté : il avait à compter avec la poudre à canon. Le coup d'arquebuse qui tua Bayard tua aussi le Moyen Age et son idéal.

LA RENAISSANCE

Le seul mot de Renaissance est un jugement porté sur la période correspondante (en France, les XVème et XVIème siècles). Qu'est-ce donc qui avait été mort et qui renaissait ? La culture antique, a-t-on dit : la culture païenne serait une expression plus exacte, car, après tout, le Moyen Age avait été imprégné d'Aristote et de Platon, les moins païens des philosophes antiques. En revanche, la Renaissance apporta, avec la mythologie retrouvée et de nouveau florissante, avec l'exaltation poétique d'une sensualité libérée des

La Renaissance fait découvrir simultanément aux artistes français (à Goujon en particulier) la splendeur du corps féminin et de l'art pour l'art, dégagé de tout préoccupation religieuse.

interdits chrétiens, une véritable résurrection des dieux les plus féconds de l'Antiquité : Apollon, Dionysos et Pan.

Le nu Symboliquement, la Renaissance découvrit le nu féminin ; non que les sculpteurs du Moyen Age l'eussent ignoré, mais ils se croyaient obligés de toujours flanquer leurs femmes nues d'un diable armé d'une fourche. Au contraire, le spiritualisme chrétien ayant régressé et l'épicurisme amoral de la Méditerranée devenant prépondérant sous l'influence italienne, Jean Goujon n'hésita plus à représenter sans le moindre voile — et sans le moindre diable — Diane de Poitiers, maîtresse du roi. C'est que, sans s'en douter, les artistes français qui n'avaient été jusque-là que des artisans de génie occupés à décorer des églises ou à portraiturer de généreux donateurs, venaient de déterrer l'idée païenne de l'art pour l'art.

Arts et lettres Alors une merveilleuse griserie s'empara d'eux. Si les peintres, tel Clouet, n'abandonnaient pas encore le portrait, avec quelle fougue les architectes faisaient sortir de terre des châteaux inspirés, avec quelle passion les musiciens se précipitaient dans la polyphonie profane, avec quelle rage de créer les écrivains s'attaquaient, dans le sillage de Rabelais, à une œuvre titanesque : la création d'une langue française suffisamment riche, souple et rigoureuse pour véhiculer une littérature renouvelée de l'Antiquité. On ne saurait trop admirer la logique amoureuse avec laquelle Ronsard, du Bellay et leurs compagnons, voulant doter la France d'une littérature classique, appliquèrent tous leurs efforts à forger d'abord le premier instrument indispensable à son expression : ce vocabulaire français que, après qu'il ait été épuré et doublé d'une syntaxe rigide par leurs successeurs du XVIIème, les Vaugelas et les Chapelain, nous utilisons encore aujourd'hui.

La Place des Vosges : ordre, élégance, bonhomie — la France à l'aube du classicisme.

Le même vertige créateur s'était emparé des philosophes : vertige du scepticisme pour Montaigne, de la Réforme pour Calvin. La pensée, soudain libérée de la double servitude aristotélicienne et catholique, allait enfanter l'humanisme moderne.

Guerres de religion Cet enfantement ne se fit pas sans mal. Pendant près de cent ans, « papistes » et « parpaillots » s'entre-massacrèrent au nom d'une foi chrétienne qui devenait d'autant plus exacerbée qu'elle produisait moins de penseurs et moins de saints. L'humanisme un peu cynique — déjà complètement étranger au spiritualisme du Moyen Age — sur lequel allait se fonder le classicisme est partiellement le fruit de ces guerres au cours desquelles la fréquence des trahisons et des conversions de part et d'autre ne pouvait manquer de faire apparaître la relativité des valeurs humaines, fût-ce les plus hautes.

Cela ne signifie nullement que la Renaissance ait été une période de détachement : au contraire, c'est avec l'impétuosité d'une civilisation encore toute jeune que les Français du XVIème embrassaient les diverses causes qu'ils voulaient servir. Tout leur paraissait possible ; la grandeur dont ils rêvaient pour leur pays, leur art ou leur religion, ils la situaient dans un avenir qu'ils construiraient de leurs mains. A l'homme cultivé moderne, la Renaissance, avec son énergie bouillonnante et ses virtualités infinies, apparaît comme un matin clair, frais, tonifiant : le matin de la France.

LE XVIIÈME SIÈCLE

Le XVIIème, c'est déjà midi, l'heure où les ombres disparaissent, où la lumière de la Raison, de la royauté, du classicisme, parvient à son zénith, où tous les mythes solaires s'organisent autour de la personnalité appollinienne de Louis XIV, et où la France, sortant des démêlés intérieurs dans lesquels elle avait été absorbée jusqu'alors, prend sa place au premier rang des grandes nations européennes.

Arts et lettres   Une étonnante floraison artistique et littéraire accompagne la conquête de l'ordre intérieur et des frontières naturelles. Les mères françaises semblaient s'être donné le mot pour faire naître en l'espace de cent ans les Français les plus doués, et cela dans presque tous les domaines.

En architecture, il y eut Mansart et Le Nôtre ; en peinture, Philippe de Champaigne, Georges de La Tour et les frères Le Nain ; en musique, Delalande, Charpentier, et le Florentin Lully qu'on adopta ; en philosophie, Pascal et Descartes. En littérature, tous les genres furent illustrés : la poésie par Malherbe ; la critique par Boileau ; la fable par La Fontaine ; l'essai psychologique par La Bruyère ; la prédication par Bossuet ; la maxime par La Rochefoucauld ; le roman par Mme de La Fayette ; la correspondance par Mme de Sévigné ; le théâtre enfin par Corneille, Molière et Racine.

A noter que cette production, à quelques exceptions près, est essentiellement grave et pondérée, quelquefois solennelle, toujours — même pour les comédies les plus drôlatiques — placée sous le signe olympien de la Raison. Le petit Français badin qui courtise les femmes et ne prend rien au sérieux n'était pas encore né : le haut du pavé était tenu par « l'honnête homme ».

L'honnête homme   L'honnête homme est aussi caractéristique de la France du XVIIème que le gentleman de l'Angleterre du XVIIIème, et, comme celui du gentleman, son type s'est conservé jusqu'à aujourd'hui : il figure encore — avec quelques modifications historiques — le parangon du Français bien élevé.

La devise de l'honnête homme du XVIIème est le « rien de trop » de l'Antiquité. Le bon sens cher à Descartes, c'est-à-dire le don de reconnaître l'évidence, est sa qualité principale. Croyant et pratiquant, mais ni dévot ni bigot (Dieu l'en garde !), fidèle au prince et à l'ordre établi, frotté de latin et peut-être même de grec mais ne s'en vantant jamais, dilettante éclairé pour tout ce qui touche à la littérature mais prenant soin de ne pas s'y spécialiser, soucieux de décence plus que de morale et d'honneur plus que de vertu, craignant par-dessus tout de paraître expert en quelque chose, se piquant de ne se piquer de rien, fuyant les superstitions comme les idées avancées qu'il qualifie de libertinage, noble ou bourgeois, militaire ou civil, l'honnête homme s'astreint, en contenant ses passions, à appliquer à sa propre vie un idéal de clarté, de modération et d'équilibre. La Rochefoucauld dans l'histoire, le Philinte de Molière dans la fiction, sont les modèles les plus accomplis de l'honnête homme. A la différence des chevaliers du Moyen Age ou des révolutionnaires du XVIIIème, les honnêtes gens proclament par la voix de Philinte dans *Le Misanthrope* :

> Il faut parmi le monde une vertu traitable ;
> A force de sagesse on peut être blâmable.

Profonde leçon, et qui devait être bien méconnue plus tard !

Fin du XVIIème   Le XVIIème, qui dans la représentation moderne va de 1610 (avènement de Louis XIII) à 1715 (mort de Louis XIV), et qu'on appelle aussi le siècle de Louis XIV, apparaît maintenant comme la création presque personnelle de ce prestigieux monarque. Sans doute y a-t-il là bien de l'exagération. Il n'en est pas moins vrai que, au temps où Louis le Grand volait de victoire en victoire et papillonnait de maîtresse en maîtresse, la France dictait ses volontés à l'Europe. Lorsque, sous l'influence conjuguée de l'âge, de la dévotion, et de son épouse morganatique (Mme de Maintenon), le souve-

---

J'ai toutes les passions assez douces et assez réglées : on ne m'a presque jamais vu en colère, et je n'ai jamais eu de haine pour personne. Je ne suis pas pourtant incapable de me venger, si l'on m'avait offensé, et qu'il y allât de mon honneur à me ressentir de l'injure qu'on m'aurait faite. Au contraire, je suis assuré que le devoir ferait si bien en moi l'office de la haine, que je poursuivrais ma vengeance avec encore plus de vigueur qu'un autre... Je suis extrêmement régulier à ma parole : je n'y manque jamais, de quelque conséquence que puisse être ce que j'ai promis, et je m'en suis fait toute ma vie une obligation indispensable. J'ai une civilité fort exacte parmi les femmes, et je ne crois pas avoir jamais rien dit devant elles qui leur ait pu faire de la peine. Quand elles ont l'esprit bien fait, j'aime mieux leur conversation que celle des hommes : on y trouve une certaine douceur qui ne se rencontre point parmi nous ; et il me semble outre cela qu'elles s'expliquent avec plus de netteté, et qu'elles donnent un tour plus agréable aux choses qu'elles disent. Pour galant, je l'ai été un peu autrefois ; présentement je ne le suis plus, quelque jeune que je sois. J'ai renoncé aux fleurettes, et je m'étonne seulement de ce qu'il y a encore tant d'honnêtes gens qui s'occupent à en débiter. J'approuve extrêmement les belles passions ; elles marquent la grandeur de l'âme, et quoique dans les inquiétudes qu'elles donnent il y ait quelque chose de contraire à la sévère sagesse, elles s'accommodent si bien d'ailleurs avec la plus austère vertu, que je crois qu'on ne les saurait condamner avec justice.

LA ROCHEFOUCAULD

A Vaux-le-Vicomte, *les jardins sont géométriques, classiques,* français.

Au Parc Monceau, *le « naturel artificiel »* anglais *a triomphé.*

rain décida de se ranger, la fortune les abandonna, son peuple et lui. Louis XIV survécut à ses enfants, à ses petits-enfants, et à tous les grands hommes de son siècle, même à l'essayiste Bayle qui, premier esprit destructeur à annoncer les philosophes du XVIIIème, avait déjà apporté quelques accents discordants au concert de certitude du classicisme ; la France, elle, partagée entre une frivolité décadente et un afflux d'idées nouvelles, s'empressait de perdre en prestige national ce qu'elle devait bientôt regagner en influence intellectuelle. Le testament de Louis XIV fut cassé par le Parlement : c'est par cet acte de révolte (1715) que s'ouvre le XVIIIème siècle.

LE XVIIIÈME SIÈCLE

La science Le XVIIIème est le premier siècle où la science française entre en scène. Non seulement l'intérêt pour les phénomènes naturels y fut général, non seulement les salons mondains s'y doublèrent de laboratoires (tel celui de Mme du Châtelet, où Voltaire s'amusa à des expériences de chimie et de physique), mais encore de véritables savants y firent des découvertes considérables : ce fut le cas des mathématiciens astronomes Lagrange et Laplace, du naturaliste Lamarck, du zoologiste Buffon et des frères Montgolfier, créateurs des premiers aérostats.

Les lumières Cet éveil scientifique participait du mouvement dit « des lumières » ou « des philosophes », lesquels, prenant la succession de Descartes, allaient passer au crible de la Raison les vérités révélées de la foi pour aboutir au déisme, à l'agnosticisme ou à l'athéisme pur et simple, et celles de l'ordre social pour aboutir, selon le cas, à un idéal despotique, constitutionnel

---

Ce temps profane est tout fait pour mes mœurs.
J'aime le luxe, et même la mollesse,
Tous les plaisirs, les arts de toute espèce,
La propreté, le goût, les ornements :
Tout honnête homme a de tels sentiments.
Il est bien doux pour mon cœur très immonde
De voir ici l'abondance à la ronde,
Mère des arts et des heureux travaux,
Nous apporter, de sa source féconde,
Et des besoins et des plaisirs nouveaux.
L'or de la terre et les trésors de l'onde,
Leurs habitants et les peuples de l'air,
Tout sert au luxe, aux plaisirs de ce monde.
Oh ! le bon temps que ce siècle de fer !

                                        VOLTAIRE

Dans le Nid, *Boucher fait éclater une sensualité tout amorale, très Ancien* Régime.

Dans la Malédiction Paternelle, *Greuze prêche la vertu : la Révolution n'est plus* loin.

ou démocratique, sans rapport aucun avec des fondations sacrales de la royauté française. Ce mouvement fut marqué par des luttes constantes entre les esprits forts (Montesquieu, Voltaire) et les cœurs sensibles (Rousseau, Diderot). Le principal monument qui en reste est l'*Encyclopédie* de d'Alembert, véritable arsenal des philosophes français et européens dans leur guerre contre les valeurs traditionnelles.

L'élégance   Plus encore peut-être que le siècle de la philosophie, le XVIIIème fut celui de l'élégance et de l'art de vivre. Les principaux interdits de la religion ayant perdu ce qu'ils avaient d'imprescriptible, on s'organisa pour vivre le plus agréablement que l'on pouvait. La distinction des costumes, la subtilité de la décoration, l'utilisation des talents, la préférence systéma-

Watteau ou le sommet de l'élégance. Ses Fêtes Vénitiennes *représentent peut-être l'apogée d'une certaine France — qui n'est pas la seule France.*

La Place de la Concorde : clarté, grâce, harmonie — la France à la fin du classicisme.

tiquement accordée à la grâce sur la grandeur, tout concordait à raffiner de mille façons le simple plaisir d'être. Des architectes tels Gabriel, des sculpteurs comme Falconet et Houdon, des peintres tels Chardin, Watteau, Fragonard ou Boucher, des musiciens comme Couperin et Rameau, contribuaient autant et plus que les hommes de lettres à donner toute sa saveur à cet âge de scepticisme, de plaisir et de bon goût que fut « le siècle de Louis XV ».

La Révolution   La finesse même de ce goût qui devenait de plus en plus délicat, de plus en plus énervé, annonçait le déclin, sinon de la France, du moins d'une certaine France. Cette douce après-midi que fut le XVIIIème siècle, tiède et lumineux, allait s'achever sur un coucher de soleil sanglant : la Révolution française.

La révolution industrielle d'une part, l'apparition de milieux intellectuels d'autre part, faisaient de la bourgeoisie une classe montante, qui pesait de plus en plus lourd dans la balance de la nation et s'impatientait de n'y être pas reconnue pour ce qu'elle valait. La noblesse, elle, avait fait son temps : ces grandes dames qui, sous l'ancien régime finissant, se déguisaient en ouvrières pour aller s'amuser aux foires du peuple, ces gentilshommes qui, au cours de la nuit du 4 août 1789 votèrent la suppression de leurs propres privilèges, témoignaient assez que la noblesse ne pouvait plus être en fait ce qu'elle était encore en droit : une aristocratie.

Heureux celui qui a reçu de nature une âme sensible et mobile ! Il porte en lui la source d'une multitude d'instants délicieux que les autres ignorent. Tous les hommes s'affligent, mais c'est lui seul qui sait se plaindre et pleurer... C'est son cœur qui lie ses idées. Celui qui n'a que de l'esprit, que du génie ne l'entend pas. Il est un organe qui leur manque. La langue du cœur est mille fois plus variée que celle de l'esprit, et il est impossible de donner les règles de sa dialectique. Cela tient du délire et ce n'est pas le délire ; cela tient du rêve et ce n'est pas le rêve. Mais comme dans le rêve ou le délire, ce sont les fils du réseau qui commandent à leur origine, le maître se résout à la condition d'interprète.

DIDEROT

Sous l'action des Mirabeau fluctuants, des Danton rapaces, des Robespierre incorruptibles, l'ancien régime croula, bientôt suivi dans la ruine par le rêve messianique d'une république « pure et dure » qui aurait dû apporter un nouvel âge d'or à l'humanité. Les Français ne datèrent jamais leurs lettres que de l'an I ou de l'an II de la République. Bientôt, ils reprirent la chaîne des 94, 95, 96, cessèrent de planter des arbres de la liberté sur la place des villages, et, quand ils souffraient d'un trop plein d'énergie, allèrent le dépenser sur tous les champs de bataille d'Europe, au nom de la gloire nationale et non plus des droits de l'homme. Saignée par la Terreur révolutionnaire (1793), saignée

Puisque l'âme de la République est la vertu, l'égalité, et que votre but est de fonder, de consolider la République, il s'ensuit que la première règle de votre conduite politique doit être de rapporter toutes vos opérations au maintien de l'égalité et au développement de la vertu ; car le premier soin du législateur doit être de fortifier le principe du gouvernement. Ainsi tout ce qui tend à exciter l'amour de la patrie, à purifier les mœurs, à élever les âmes, à diriger les passions du cœur humain vers l'intérêt public, doit être adopté ou établi par vous ; tout ce qui tend à les concentrer dans l'abjection du moi personnel, à réveiller l'engouement pour les petites choses, et le mépris des grandes, doit être rejeté ou réprimé par vous. Dans le système de la révolution française, ce qui est immoral est impolitique, ce qui est corrupteur est contre-révolutionnaire. La faiblesse, les vices, les préjugés sont le chemin de la royauté.

ROBESPIERRE

par les guerres de Napoléon (1795–1815), la France allait bientôt sortir de ce qui fut un cauchemar de sang pour les uns, un rêve de grandeur et d'affranchissement pour les autres, et se réveiller au service de nouveaux maîtres : les bourgeois. Le monde entier cependant demeurait bouleversé par deux mots français : *liberté* et *égalité*.

LE XIXÈME SIÈCLE

« Le XIXème, ce siècle bête », disait le pamphlétaire Léon Daudet, qui n'avait pas l'habitude de mâcher ses mots. Le paradoxe est de taille.

La science N'est-ce pas du XIXème que date cet épanouissement de la science française qu'illustrèrent le mathématicien Monge, l'astronome Le Verrier, découvreur de la planète Neptune. l'électricien Ampère, l'opticien Arago, Gay-Lussac, spécialiste des gaz, Berthelot, créateur de la thermochimie, Cuvier, paléontologue, et les trois ancêtres de la médecine moderne : Claude Bernard, père de la méthode expérimentale, Laennec, inventeur de l'auscultation au stéthoscope, et Pasteur, grand maître des vaccins ?

Arts et lettres Le XIXème ne connut-il pas aussi une pléthore de poètes romantiques (Lamartine, Vigny, Musset, Hugo), parnassiens (Gautier, Le-

A la France latine, classique, de l'Ancien Régime, s'oppose la France gauloise, idéaliste, de la Révolution : celle qu'exalta le sculpteur Rude dans sa Marseillaise (XIXème).

conte de Lisle, Hérédia), symbolistes (Mallarmé) ou défiant toute classification (Nerval, Baudelaire, Verlaine, Rimbaud) ? Les romans ne déferlèrent-ils pas sur ce siècle comme un raz-de-marée — romantiques avec Chateaubriand, Balzac et Stendhal, réalistes avec Flaubert et Maupassant, naturalistes avec Zola, artistes avec les Goncourt ? Les essais critiques n'y furent-ils pas nombreux et pertinents avec Sainte-Beuve et Taine ? L'histoire n'y devint-elle pas une science nouvelle avec Michelet et Fustel de Coulanges ? Comte, Renan et surtout Bergson n'en firent-ils pas, aussi, un siècle philosophique ? Les arts n'abondaient pas moins en talents : ni la musique, avec Berlioz, Debussy, Ravel ; ni la peinture, avec les traditionnels Ingres, Delacroix, Courbet, Corot, les impressionnistes Manet, Monet, Degas, Renoir, les post-impressionnistes Gauguin, Cézanne et Toulouse-Lautrec ; ni certes la sculpture avec le géant Rodin. — Alors, qu'entendait donc Léon Daudet par sa boutade mémorable ?

Le romantisme   D'abord, il entendait sans doute reprocher au XIXème le romantisme militant sous les auspices duquel ce siècle débuta vers 1815. Toutes ces promenades au clair de lune, tous ces orages déchaînés, tous ces échevelés professionnels, bref cet égotisme aussi complaisant que larmoyant, il est bien clair que l'intelligence y avait peu de part : ce n'est pas pour rien qu'un admirateur moderne de Victor Hugo s'est exclamé, « Il est bête comme l'Himalaya ! »

Le positivisme   La réaction qui suivit et qui fut, comme l'on sait, positiviste, malgré tous ses efforts pour renier le romantisme, malgré le culte

---

L'aplatissement, l'effacement de nos mœurs va croissant. Il y a dix ans, l'auteur de ce livre écrivait qu'il n'y avait plus que des nuances ; mais aujourd'hui, les nuances disparaissent... Il n'y a plus d'énergie que dans les êtres séparés de la société. La littérature actuelle manque de contrastes, et il n'y a pas de contrastes possibles sans distances. Les distances se suppriment de jour en jour. Aujourd'hui, la voiture tend à se mettre au-dessous du piéton, et c'est le fantassin qui bientôt éclaboussera le riche dans la petite voiture basse. L'habit noir triomphe. Ce qui est dans les habits et dans les roues anime également les esprits, vit dans les manières et dans les mœurs. Un ministre va très bien en demi-fortune chez le roi ; nous avons vu des fiacres dans la cour des Tuileries. Les habits brodés du ministre, du général, du membre de l'Institut, le costume en un mot est honteux de se montrer, et a l'air d'une mascarade. Nous avons trop raison contre notre époque, et, comme le vice auquel nous nous attaquons est une effroyable hypocrisie, il va sans dire que nous devenons immoraux.

BALZAC

Le Déjeuner sur l'herbe, *de Manet, occasionna l'un des scandales du XIXème siècle : n'est-ce pas parce que l'Artifice en faux-col y voisine avec la Vérité toute nue ?*

qu'elle voua à l'intelligence, n'en sombra pas moins dans une étrange naïveté : croire que la science résoudrait peu à peu tous les problèmes humains, c'était sans doute exiger d'elle plus qu'elle ne pouvait donner. Cependant Daudet avait peut-être des raisons plus profondes encore pour dénoncer la « bêtise » du XIXème siècle, raisons que l'on groupe d'ordinaire sous l'appellation générique de « bovarisme ».

La méthode expérimentale est la méthode scientifique qui proclame la liberté de l'esprit et de la pensée. Elle secoue non seulement le joug philosophique et théologique, mais elle n'admet pas non plus d'autorité scientifique personnelle.

CLAUDE BERNARD

La conservation, la propagation de la langue française importent à l'ordre général de la civilisation. Quelque chose d'essentiel manquerait au monde le jour où ce grand flambeau, clair et pétillant, cesserait de briller. L'humanité serait amoindrie, si ce merveilleux instrument de civilisation venait à disparaître ou à s'amoindrir... Le français peut vraiment être appelé une langue classique, un instrument de culture et de civilisation pour tous. Cette langue améliore ; elle est une école ; elle a le naturel, la bonhomie, elle sait rire, elle porte avec elle un aimable scepticisme mêlé de bonté (sans bonté, le scepticisme est une très mauvaise chose). Le fanatisme est impossible en français... Le français réjouit ; ses locutions favorites impliquent un sentiment gai de la vie, l'idée qu'au fond rien n'est bien sérieux et qu'on entre dans les intentions de l'Eternel par un peu d'ironie. La grande infériorité du barbare, de l'Oriental surtout, c'est qu'il ne sait pas rire. Apprenez à toutes les nations à rire en français. C'est la chose du monde la plus philosophique et la plus saine... Qui donc a dit que Dieu prenait plus de plaisir aux jurons du soldat français qu'aux prières d'un ministre de telle ou telle secte puritaine ?... Tenez, Messieurs, il y a surtout un jour où l'usage du français sera bien nécessaire ; c'est le jour de la vallée de Josaphat. Prolongez la vie du français jusqu'au jugement dernier. Je vous assure que, si on parle allemand ce jour-là, il y aura des confusions, des erreurs sans nombre... Messieurs, je vous en prie, faites qu'on ne parle pas allemand dans la vallée de Josaphat.

ERNEST RENAN

Le bovarisme, ou le refus d'être ce que l'on est   On demandait à Flaubert si *Madame Bovary* était un roman à clef, et quel était le modèle dont il s'était inspiré pour le rôle titre. « Madame Bovary, répondit-il, c'est moi. » Ce disant, il fournissait en effet à l'historien une des clefs du XIXème siècle.

Mme Bovary avait la nostalgie d'un milieu dans lequel elle n'était pas née : c'est le cas des romantiques rêvant d'Italie ou d'Écosse, de Moyen Age ou de XVIIIème de fantaisie. Mme Bovary se résignait mal à la vie quotidienne : c'est le cas de Flaubert lui-même, préférant écrire des *Salammbô* alors qu'il réussissait mieux des *Bouvard et Pécuchet*, ou de Baudelaire, qui exprime éloquemment dans *L'Albatros* l'incapacité du poète à s'adapter à la vie réelle. Mme Bovary n'hésitait pas à tarabuster[2] ses servantes quand l'envie lui en venait : ce fut le cas de la plupart des chefs d'État du XIXème, qui n'hésitèrent

[2] traiter avec dureté et inconséquence

<blockquote>
Pasteur ou roi, qu'aurais-je fait de mon sceptre ou de ma houlette ? Je me serais également fatigué de la gloire et du génie, du travail et du loisir, de la prospérité et de l'infortune. Tout me lasse : je remorque avec peine mon ennui avec mes jours, et je vais partout bâillant ma vie.

CHATEAUBRIAND
</blockquote>

pas à réprimer, au nom de l'ordre bourgeois, les divers mouvements populaires qui les dérangeaient. Et ainsi de suite. Or, le complexe bovariste n'est pas précisément le propre des gens intelligents.

La grisaille   Plus digne encore de l'épithète irrévérencieuse de Léon Daudet fut sans doute cette grisaille dans laquelle commencèrent à se fondre, au XIXème siècle, les classes sociales, les origines ethniques, les grades, les fonctions et les professions. Symboliquement, les hommes renoncèrent à

L'Angélus de Millet : *ce qui reste après un millénaire et demi de christianisme.*

porter des couleurs et se noyèrent dans une bouillie mélancolique, noire et grise, dont la vue aurait consterné les joyeux compagnons de Jeanne d'Arc, d'Henri V et même de Napoléon Ier. Or, l'intelligence française exige, d'abord, de distinguer : tout ce qui est indistinct lui paraît stupide *a priori*.

Considéré dans cette perspective, pour tous ceux des modernes qui voient, dans le XVIIème siècle, l'apogée de la France, le XIXème, malgré sa richesse extrême dans bien des domaines, ne peut faire figure que de crépuscule de la civilisation française.

LE XXÈME SIÈCLE

Alors qu'est-ce que le XXème ? Une nuit, de nouveau, comme celle du Moyen Age ? Si c'est une nuit, il faut reconnaître qu'elle est, comme l'autre, généreusement étoilée.

Sciences, arts et lettres Les Curie, puis les Joliot-Curie, pour la radioactivité et la physique nucléaire, Louis de Broglie pour la mécanique ondulatoire et la théorie des quanta, Poincaré pour les mathématiques et plusieurs tenants du prix Nobel de médecine prouvent que la science française est toujours florissante. Quant à la technologie, elle a reçu une brillante consécration lorsque le système français de télévision en couleurs a été adopté par la plupart des pays d'Europe. Avec des peintres comme Braque, Matisse, Rouault, Bonnard, un sculpteur comme Maillol, un musicien comme Messiaen, la France artistique semble soutenir la comparaison avec ses voisins européens ; la France littéraire, avec ses Proust, ses Saint-John Perse, ses Claudel, ne leur paraît pas inférieure non plus ; quant à la France philosophique de Teilhard de Chardin, de Sartre, de Camus et de Simone Weil, elle paraît être à la tête de la pensée contemporaine.

Seulement, il est bien trop tôt encore pour porter un jugement absolu sur les grands hommes de la France moderne. Certains qui nous paraissent des géants deviendront peut-être des nains aux yeux de la postérité, et *vice versa* ; aussi s'abstiendra-t-on ici d'aucune conclusion précipitée. En revanche, il peut n'être pas prématuré de dégager plusieurs points majeurs de l'évolution de ce siècle.

Groupes nouveaux Trois groupes nouveaux semblent acquérir une importance toujours croissante : les jeunes, qu'un renouveau de natalité rend essentiels par le nombre et qui, de plus en plus souvent, poursuivent leurs études et prétendent agir sur les destinées de la nation ; les femmes, maintenant complètement affranchies de la tutelle masculine ; les intellectuels, de plus en plus écoutés, soit qu'ils militent dans l'opposition, soit qu'ils se rallient à l'État.

Conflits dépassés   Au contraire, certains groupes qui ont été déterminants pendant la première moitié d'un siècle qu'on a l'habitude de faire commencer en 1914, avec la Première Guerre mondiale, passent maintenant au second plan : ainsi des syndicats, qui ont su imposer à la France une législation sociale très avancée ; ainsi des partis politiques, aspirés et dévorés par la Cinquième République ; ainsi des écrivains engagés à titre personnel, dont l'influence ne cesse de décroître au profit des intellectuels organisés en équipes.

Une évolution caractéristique   En résumé, on ne saurait mieux faire, pour retracer l'évolution du XXème siècle, que de donner les grands traits de la biographie, à bien des titres exemplaire, d'un de ces intellectuels : André Malraux.

Né pratiquement avec le siècle, Malraux part tout jeune pour une mission au Cambodge où il s'approprie, dit-on, quelques statues khmères. Rebelle de tempérament, communiste d'occasion, il est mêlé ensuite à la révolution chinoise. Retour d'Asie, il publie quelques romans et se précipite en Espagne où la guerre civile fait rage (1936) ; il y commande l'aviation des volontaires républicains, expérience d'où il retire la matière d'un roman et d'un film. Officier de chars pendant la Deuxième Guerre mondiale, il est fait prisonnier, s'évade, se rallie à la France libre, et commande l'un des maquis de la Résistance. A la Libération, il devient Ministre de l'Information du gouvernement provisoire, puis, lorsque le général de Gaulle fonde le Rassemblement du peuple français (dissous depuis lors), secrétaire général de ce parti. Il se consacre ensuite à des méditations esthétiques et publie une série d'ouvrages révolutionnaires sur l'art, groupés sous le titre *Les Voix du silence*. Lui, dont l'action a été toute la vie, il se voue entièrement au culte de la beauté plastique.

Il faudra le retour au pouvoir du général de Gaulle (1958) pour que Malraux, communiste de la première heure, accepte à soixante ans un portefeuille dans un gouvernement nationaliste et, sous certains rapports, réactionnaire.

Cet aboutissement d'une quête qui dura toute une vie est typique du XXème siècle, jetant sa gourme, enregistrant la faillite des reniements absolus, acceptant la nécessité de composer avec la réalité, bref concédant, fût-ce à regret, un « oui » empirique à la *condition humaine*. Ce « oui » peut être interprété comme celui de la France entière résignée — après les doutes et les abandons du début du siècle — à assumer une fois de plus son destin.

L'AVENIR

La France continuera-t-elle à jouer son rôle de grande nation, comme le voudraient les hommes de la Cinquième République ? Se mettra-t-elle à la traîne d'une autre puissance, en s'intégrant au bloc américain, au bloc soviétique, ou à un bloc européen à prépondérance allemande, comme le réclament les partisans des puissances correspondantes ? Deviendra-t-elle, comme le souhaitent certains, une sorte de Suisse universaliste, vouée à la conservation des valeurs intellectuelles ? Et qu'arrivera-t-il, dans tout cela, à la civilisation française proprement dite ?

On ne se donnera pas le ridicule d'essayer de répondre ici à ce genre de question. Il suffira de montrer que la France, telle qu'elle est, peut encore jouer dans le monde, tel qu'il est, un rôle de premier plan — si elle le veut. Elle le peut par son poids propre, par le rayonnement de sa civilisation millénaire, par l'importance universelle de sa langue, par les positions politiques intermédiaires qu'il dépend d'elle de maintenir.

Près de cinquante millions de Français ; une des natalités les plus fortes du monde ; un territoire ramené à ses limites naturelles ; une population paraissant lasse des factions et qui donne, malgré des troubles nombreux, des preuves d'une certaine unité d'esprit : voilà ce que pèse la France d'aujour-

Les artistes français ont toujours été à la recherche d'Idées platoniciennes universelles : cette quête classique, le romantique Viollet-le-Duc y a contribué en dessinant la Cathédrale idéale.

d'hui. Soixante-dix pour cent des Français se considèrent comme croyants en Dieu ; la majorité absolue du people se déclare régulièrement dans le même sens que la majorité absolue du Parlement ; pour la première fois dans l'histoire, c'est le citoyen qui élit le chef de l'État ; une éducation nationale en pleine réforme tend à niveler de plus en plus les classes de la société ; les différences provinciales s'estompent ; de plus en plus la France — il ne nous appartient pas de déterminer si c'est un progrès ou un déclin — se présente comme un bloc, sinon homogène, du moins plus homogène que par le passé.

Le français est la langue maternelle de soixante-dix millions d'hommes, la langue écrite de presque toute l'Afrique noire, la première langue commune de l'ensemble eurafricain, l'une des deux langues officielles de la diplomatie en général et des Nations unies en particulier, la seule langue vivante officielle du Vatican. Deux mille journaux et périodiques n'appartenant pas à la France sont rédigés en Français.

Pays de la raison déductive, constructive et critique (Descartes) mais aussi d'un mysticisme austère et exigeant (Pascal), pays des valeurs évolutives et libérales (la Révolution, le romantisme) mais aussi d'une continuité tenace, sacrale, imprescriptible (les cathédrales, Louis XIV, le général de Gaulle), la France semble arrivée à un âge où, renonçant aux excès et aux abus de la jeunesse, elle pourra suivre spontanément la voie à laquelle sa position géographique et ethnique la prédisposait de tout temps, et qui demeure sans doute la plus favorable à toute civilisation : la voie moyenne.

When I was a child, owing to my misapprehension of a picture in a history book, I got it into my head that France was a real person, a woman with a crown which she doffed at certain times to wear a Phrygian cap, and one of my main sources of worry was that, sooner or later, this person with whom I was in love would grow old and eventually die. Hence the strange questions I used to ask my mother: "How old is France? Is she twenty, or thirty? Do you think she will live a long time?" So deeply embedded in my mind was this idea that, even as a full grown man, I could never quite get rid of it, neither did I really want to get rid of it, because it seemed to me that somehow it contained more truth, more hidden truth, than I was able to realize as a child.

What is going to happen to her, we cannot tell. We know that she will not die, because a spirit does not die and she is, essentially, a spirit, but her physical life is threatened and her physical life is as precious to many of us as the life of a mother. We need her presence. Her place cannot be filled by other nations. It is impossible that she will disappear, but if she did, a great many reasons for being attached to this life would disappear with her. She has given

---

us more than we know, she has made this world richer and more beautiful for millions of men and women; if she ever went, we might not cease to live, but we should be poorer and something in us would die.

JULIAN GREEN
Memories of happy days
(Harper)

SUJETS DE RÉFLEXION

CHAPITRE 1

1. La France est-elle seulement le pays de la mesure, de l'équilibre, de l'harmonie, ou bien aussi celui de la démesure, des oppositions, des dissonances ? Donnez des exemples.
2. (a) Comparez la situation géographique de la France à celle d'autres pays États-Unis, Grande-Bretagne, etc.). (b) Montrez comment la situation géographique d'un pays influence son histoire.
3. Relations entre la situation géographique des principales provinces françaises et leur histoire : faites les recherches nécessaires.
4. Essayez de mesurer l'apport relatif des diverses provinces à la civilisation française, en particulier à la littérature, en recherchant les lieux d'origine des plus grands artistes et écrivains.
5. Quelle province française aimeriez-vous visiter plus particulièrement ? Donnez voz raisons (géographiques, ethnologiques, historiques, etc.).

CHAPITRE 2

1. La France a connu plusieurs régimes : la royauté de droit divin, l'empire, la royauté bourgeoise, la république révolutionnaire, la république bourgeoise, la république présidentielle du général de Gaulle. (a) Quels étaient leurs buts respectifs ? (b) Lequel de ces régimes vous paraît avoir le mieux mérité de la France ? Pourquoi ? Répondez de façon documentée en vous efforçant de faire taire vos préjugés personnels.

2. L'auteur explique l'évolution de l'État français par une centralisation croissante. Donnez-en une explication plus dialectique en montrant que cette évolution a progressé par à-coups, grâce à des oppositions brutales. Si vous connaissez la dialectique hégélienne (thèse, antithèse synthèse), appliquez-la.
3. Le schéma marxiste de la lutte des classes s'applique-t-il à l'évolution de l'État français ? Comment ?
4. Quel est, selon vous, le plus grand homme d'État français ? Pourquoi ? Quel est celui pour lequel vous éprouvez le plus de sympathie ? Est-ce le même ? Pourquoi ?
5. Y a-t-il des grands hommes d'État français dont vous ayez entendu parler et que l'auteur ait négligés ? Pourquoi pensez-vous qu'il l'ait fait ? A-t-il eu raison ?

CHAPITRE 3

1. Quels vous paraissent être les traits distinctifs de la pensée française ? Si vous n'êtes pas d'accord avec l'auteur, donnez vos raisons. Quel est l'apport français à la pensée mondiale ?
2. Les Français se veulent *cartésiens*. Qu'est-ce que cela signifie ? Est-ce vrai ? Dans quelle mesure ?
3. Qu'est-ce que la méthode expérimentale de Claude Bernard ? En quoi se distingue-t-elle de la méthode de Descartes ? Que veut-on dire lorsqu'on considère celui-ci comme un rationaliste, celui-là comme un empiriste ? Pourquoi les appelle-t-on quelquefois rationalistes l'un et l'autre ?
4. L'existentialisme se place-t-il dans la ligne de l'évolution séculaire de la pensée française ? Pourquoi ?
5. La France a donné Calvin à Genève au XVIème siècle ; au XVIIIème, Genève lui a rendu Rousseau. Quel symbolisme pourrait-on trouver dans cette coïncidence ?
6. Montrez l'influence exercée dans le monde entier par les idées des révolutionnaires français (a) en Europe, (b) aux États-Unis, (c) actuellement, dans les pays sous-développés.
7. Le « siècle des lumières » vous paraît-il présenter un bilan positif ou négatif ? Pourquoi ?
8. Comment la France a-t-elle pu concilier le culte de la liberté et de l'égalité avec sa politique de conquête coloniale au XIXème siècle ?

CHAPITRE 4

1. On peut dire que Victor Hugo est un romantique à tendance baroque ; Lamartine, un romantique à tendance classique ; Théophile Gautier, un romantique à tendance précieuse. Montrez-le. Si vous n'êtes pas d'accord, défendez vos idées.
2. Appliquez la boussole des styles à des écrivains français ou américains que vous connaissez bien.
3. L'auteur a-t-il raison de penser que, *du point de vue du style*, le réalisme est un développement du romantisme ? Pourquoi ?

4. Commentez l'aphorisme de Buffon : « Le style, c'est l'homme même. »
5. Avec quel style vous sentez-vous le plus d'affinités comme lecteur ? Pourquoi ? Et comme auteur, quand vous écrivez ? Est-ce le même ? Pourquoi ?

CHAPITRE 5

1. Dessinez en perspective une église romane et une église gothique. Indiquez les différences.
2. Tracez un jardin à la française et un jardin anglais. Indiquez les différences.
3. Faites le plan d'une grande place. Dessinez-la en perspective. Quelles seront ses qualités principales (esthétiques, utilitaires, etc.) ?
4. Commentez le rôle de l'architecture française dans le monde. Influences subies. Influences exercées.
5. Qu'est-ce qui détermine un style d'architecture ? Le matériau ? La technique ? La fonction de l'édifice ? Le goût de l'architecte ? Défendez votre point de vue par des exemples.

CHAPITRE 6

1. Quelle période de la peinture française vous attire surtout ? Pourquoi ?
2. Quel est votre peintre français préféré ? Comparez-le à un peintre étanger. Montrez les ressemblances et les différences.
3. La peinture française vous paraît-elle bien traduire le génie propre de la France ? Pourquoi ?
4. Comment expliquez-vous que la grande révolution picturale de la fin du XIXème siècle et du début du XXème siècle ait eu lieu précisément à Paris ? (Donnez des raisons tenant à la géographie, au climat, à la culture, à la civilisation, à l'histoire, à l'histoire de la peinture, à la structure de la société, etc.)

CHAPITRE 7

1. Écoutez des passages de Rameau et de Berlioz et comparez leurs styles : classique et romantique.
2. Écoutez des passages de Debussy et de Ravel. Dégagez les oppositions (impressionniste contre néo-classique) et les ressemblances (impressionnisme).
3. Comparez le récitatif de Rameau avec celui de Debussy.
4. Comparez les musiciens classiques français à leurs contemporains baroques allemands et italiens.
5. La France vous paraît-elle aussi douée en musique qu'en littérature, en peinture, en sculpture ? Pourquoi ?
6. Discutez la dette musicale de la France envers l'Allemagne, l'Italie et la Russie ; la dette musicale des autres pays à l'égard de la France.
7. Cherchez des correspondances entre (a) les musiciens, les écrivains et les peintres classiques ; (b) les musiciens, les écrivains et les peintres romantiques.

CHAPITRE 8

1. Comparez les styles d'ameublement Louis-Philippe et Napoléon III (a) au Victorien, (b) au Chippendale.
2. A quels moments de leur histoire les décorateurs français ont-ils voulu revenir à la simplicité ? Qu'en est-il résulté ?
3. Évoquez l'atmosphère d'un appartement meublé (a) en Louis XIII, (b) en Louis XV, (c) en Louis XVI, (d) en Modern style.
4. Le costume exprime-t-il l'âme d'une époque ? Pourquoi ?
5. A juger d'eux d'après leur costume, que faut-il penser de nos contemporains ?

CHAPITRE 9

1. Jugez (a) les ambitions, (b) les réalisations, de la Cinquième République. Justifiez votre jugement.
2. Comparez la démocratie française à l'américaine aux niveaux municipal, intermédiaire, gouvernemental.
3. L'exécutif français a évolué dernièrement dans un sens américain. Comment ? Pourquoi ?
4. Quelle est la portée de la réforme selon laquelle le Président de la République est maintenant élu au suffrage universel ?
5. Discutez les avantages et les défauts du système des partis multiples.
6. Comparez l'homme de droite français à l'homme de droite américain. Même chose pour les hommes de gauche.
7. France et États-Unis : recherchez l'histoire de leurs relations.
8. Recherchez les raisons qui ont conduit le général de Gaulle à abandonner la barre de l'État.
9. Comparez le président Pompidou à son illustre prédécesseur.
10. Que pensez-vous de la dévaluation du franc ? L'auteur a-t-il raison d'en minimiser l'importance ?

CHAPITRE 10

1. La radio et la télévision françaises appartiennent à l'État. Avantages ? Inconvénients ? Réfléchissez.
2. Pourquoi les intellectuels français se méfient-ils de la télévision ? Ont-ils raison ? Leurs raisons seraient-elles valables dans un autre pays ?
3. Les journaux français sont tous politisés. Avantages ? Inconvénients ?
4. Les journaux s'efforcent de satisfaire leur public. Que pensez-vous du public français ?
5. Pourquoi les journaux de province français sont-ils des « parents pauvres » ?
6. La distinction introduite par l'auteur entre « presse du rêve » et « presse de l'idée » vous paraît-elle justifiée ? Pourquoi ? Serait-elle applicable ailleurs qu'en France ?

CHAPITRE 11

1. Que savez-vous, que pensez-vous, de l'anti-théâtre en France et ailleurs ?
2. Quelles différences trouvez-vous entre l'attitude des publics français et américain à l'égard du cinéma ?
3. Vous dirigez une troupe d'étudiants montant des pièces françaises. Lesquelles choisissez-vous ? Pourquoi ?
4. Quelle place octroyez-vous aux spectacles légers dan une civilisation idéale ? Quelle place tiennent-ils dans la civilisation française réelle ? Comparez.
5. Racontez un spectacle français que vous avez vu.

CHAPITRE 12

1. Discutez la notion d'art de vivre. Vivre peut-il, doit-il, être une art ? A quelles conditions ? A quel prix ? Avez-vous un art de vivre ?
2. Comment les Français entendent-ils l'épicurisme ?
3. Est-il vrai que l'épicurisme soit le fruit d'une société aristocratique ?
4. Discutez les qualités et les défauts d'une société aristocratique.

CHAPITRE 13

1. A quoi attribuez-vous la place que tient dans le monde la haute couture française ? Même question pour les parfums.
2. Comparez le savoir-vivre français au savoir-vivre américain.
3. Comparez la structure de la société américaine à celle de la société française (bases historiques, relations entre les diverses classes, rôle sociologique du snobisme, etc.).
4. Pour les Français, la cuisine est un art. Ont-ils raison ? Ont-ils tort ? Pourquoi ?

CHAPITRE 14

1. Si vous avez visité Paris, racontez vos impressions. Sinon, dites quel quartier vous aimeriez visiter plus particulièrement.
2. Pourquoi peut-on dire que « Paris est la grosse tête de la France » ? Est-ce une situation saine ?
3. Comparez Paris à une autre grande ville que vous connaissez bien (répartition géographique, rôle historique, monuments, population, etc.).
4. Recherchez (a) quelques grands hommes nés à Paris, (b) quelques grands hommes morts à Paris, (c) ceux sur lesquels Paris a eu le plus d'influence.

CHAPITRE 15

1. Expliquer les raisons de « l'universalité de la langue française ».
2. Commentez la politique française à l'égard (a) du Canada, (b) de l'Amérique du Sud, (c) de l'U. R. S. S., (d) des États-Unis.

3. Le poète Charles Péguy, parlant des vertus fondamentales des Français, a écrit : « L'espérance, il n'y en a que pour eux. » Expliquez.
4. Les Français ont longtemps passé pour un peuple léger. Pourquoi ? Cette réputation est-elle justifiée ?
5. Imaginez un monde dans lequel il n'y aurait plus de France. Comment serait-il différent du monde actuel ?
6. Imaginez un monde dans lequel il n'y aurait jamais eu de France. Comment serait-il différent du monde actuel ?
7. Pourquoi avez-vous commencé à apprendre le français ? Votre conception du monde, de la vie, de la civilisation, a-t-elle changé depuis que votre esprit s'est ouvert aux valeurs françaises ? Comment ?

PICTURE CREDITS

2 Yan—Rapho-Guillumette
5 Dorka Raynor—Nancy Palmer Agency
7 (top) Pierre Berger—Photo Researchers
   (bottom) French Government Tourist Office
8 Louis Courteville—Photo Researchers
9 E. Boubat—Photo Researchers
10 Janine Niepce—Rapho-Guillumette
11 Dorka Raynor—Nancy Palmer Agency
12 Courtesy Bordeaux Wine Information Bureau
16 pfi
17 Wes Kemp
20 French Cultural Services
26 (top) Alinari-Giraudon
   (bottom) Photo Yvon—Permission SPADEM 1969 by French Reproduction Rights, Inc.
45 Gravure 1823, Collection of Dr. Payen (Bibliothèque Nationale, Paris)
47 Musée d'Arts et Métiers, Paris —Photo Giraudon
48 Musée du Louvre—Photo Bulloz
51 New York Public Library
53 New York Public Library
55 French Embassy Press and Information Division
66 (top) Musée du Louvre—Photo Bulloz
   (bottom) Museum of Modern Art, New York
67 (top) Photo Bulloz
   (bottom) Auguste Rodin: Gates of Hell 1880. Rodin Museum, Philadelphia
74 (top) Collection of Dr. S. H. Jurmand, Paris
   (bottom) Museum of Art, Carnegie Institute. Pittsburgh, Pennsylvania
75 (top) French Cultural Services
   (bottom) Collection of Mr. and Mrs. Morton G. Neumann, Chicago
82 Jean Roubier, Paris
84 Jean Roubier, Paris
85 (all) Jean Roubier, Paris
86 Jean Roubier, Paris
87 Jean Roubier, Paris
90 Elliot Erwitt—Magnum
91 H. Roger-Viollet, Paris
95 (top) H. Roger-Viollet, Paris
   (bottom) Photo Yvon—Permission SPADEM 1969 by French Reproduction Rights, Inc.
97 Photo Yvon—Permission SPADEM 1970 by French Reproduction Rights, Inc.
98 Eileen Michels—University of Minnesota
99 Photo Yvon—Permission SPADEM 1969 by French Reproduction Rights, Inc.
104 Musée des Monuments Français—Photo Giraudon
106 Jean Roubier, Paris
107 Musée du Louvre—Photo Giraudon
108 Jean Clouet: Charles de Cossé, Metropolitan Museum of Art, Fletcher Fund, 1935
110 Musée du Louvre—Photo Giraudon
111 © The Frick Collection, New York
113 Musée du Louvre—Photo Giraudon
115 Musée du Louvre—Photo Bulloz
116 Musée du Louvre—Cliché des Musées Nationaux
117 Musée du Louvre—Cliché des Musées Nationaux
118 Musée Fabre, Montpellier— Photo Giraudon

A 0
B 1
C 2
D 3
E 4
F 5
G 6
H 7
I 8
J 9

	800	IX	900	X	1000	XI	1100	XII	1200	XIII	130

FONDATION DE
LA MONARCHIE
CAPÉTIENNE

APOGÉE DU
MOYEN AGE

CROISADES

Charlemagne   Hugues Capet   Saint Louis

Abélard   Saint Thomas d

PHILOSOPHIE

LITTÉRATURE

CHANSONS DE GESTE

ROMANS COURTOIS

FABLIAUX

ARCHITECTURE

ROMAN   GOTHIQUE   RAY

VITRAIL HAUTE ÉPOQUE

PEINTURE

MINIATURE ENLUMINURE

FRESC

SCULPTURE

GO

ROMANE

MUSIQUE

MUSIQU

Pérotin

SCIENCES

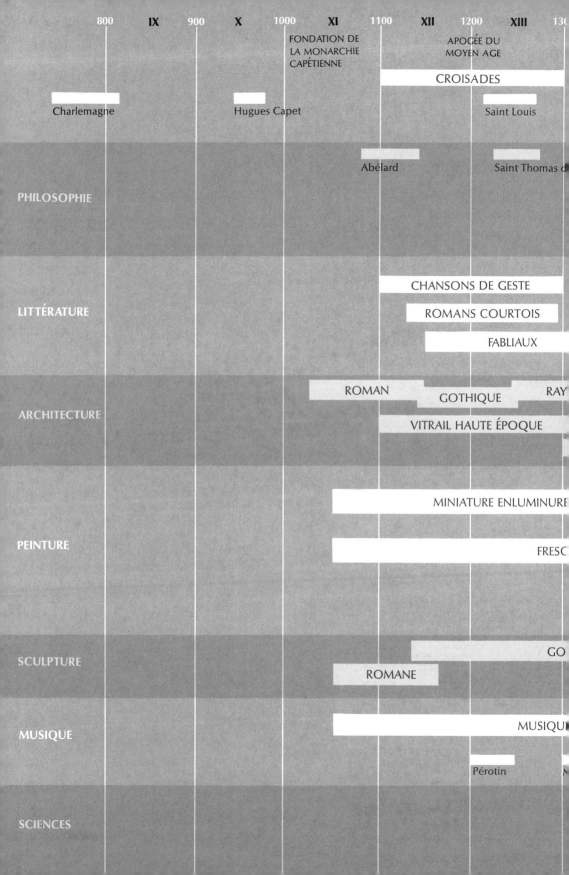